From the Pages of
The Wings of the Dove

"Even now it's not a question of anything I should ask you in a way to 'do.' It's simply a question of your not turning me away—taking yourself out of my life. It's simply a question of your saying: 'Yes then, since you will, we'll stand together. We won't worry in advance about how or where; we'll have a faith and find a way.' That's all—*that* would be the good you'd do me. I should *have* you, and it would be for my benefit."   (page 36)

"She fixed upon me herself, settled on me with her wonderful gilded claws."   (page 71)

The lady in question, at all events, with her slightly Michael-angelesque squareness, her eyes of other days, her full lips, her long neck, her recorded jewels, her brocaded and wasted reds, was a very great personage—only unaccompanied by a joy. And she was dead, dead, dead. Milly recognised her exactly in words that had nothing to do with her. "I shall never be better than this."   (page 169)

"As I told you before, I'm American. Not that I mean that makes me worse. However, you'll probably know what it makes me."
                    (page 183)

"That's the way people are. What they think of their enemies, goodness knows, is bad enough; but I'm still more struck with what they think of their friends."   (page 265)

"*I* lie well, thank God."   (page 302)

"Since she's to die I'm to marry her?"   (page 375)

Venice glowed and plashed and called and chimed again; the air was like a clap of hands, and the scattered pinks, yellows, blues, sea-greens, were like a hanging-out of vivid stuffs, a laying-down of fine carpets. (page 420)

"She won't have loved you for nothing." (page 445)

"I used to call her, in my stupidity—for want of anything better—a dove. Well she stretched out her wings, and it was to *that* they reached. They cover us." (page 491)

THE WINGS OF THE DOVE

Henry James

With an Introduction and Notes
by Bruce R. L. Smith

George Stade
Consulting Editorial Director

BARNES & NOBLE CLASSICS
NEW YORK

BARNES & NOBLE CLASSICS

NEW YORK

Published by Barnes & Noble Books
122 Fifth Avenue
New York, NY 10011

www.barnesandnoble.com/classics

The Wings of the Dove was first published in 1902. The present text
follows James's revised "New York Edition" of 1907.

Published in 2005 by Barnes & Noble Classics with new Introduction, Notes,
Biography, Chronology, Comments & Questions, and For Further Reading.

The Wings of the Dove
ISBN 1-59308-296-7
LC Control Number 2004111990

Produced and published in conjunction with:
Fine Creative Media, Inc.
322 Eighth Avenue
New York, NY 10001

Michael J. Fine, President and Publisher

Printed in the United States of America
QM
1 3 5 7 9 10 8 6 4 2
FIRST PRINTING

Henry James

The writer Henry James was born into a wealthy family in New York City in 1843. His father, Henry, Sr., was a religious free-thinker and follower of the philosopher Swedenborg, and associated with many of the literary men of his day, including Nathaniel Hawthorne and Ralph Waldo Emerson. Young Henry was educated privately in New York, Geneva, Paris, and London; the family lived alternately in Europe and the United States for much of his childhood.

He began his literary career writing for magazines. Having dropped out of Harvard Law School to pursue writing, he associated with the literary set in Cambridge, Massachusetts, and was a good friend of budding novelist and critic William Dean Howells. In 1864 James's first published piece of fiction, the story "A Tragedy of Error," appeared in the *Continental Monthly*. He also wrote reviews and articles for the *Atlantic Monthly* and the *Nation*. He frequently traveled to Europe and in 1876 settled permanently in London.

James is often cited as one of literature's great stylists; it has been said that his writing surrounds a subject and illuminates it with a flickering light, rather than pinning it down; according to Virginia Woolf in her diaries, he spoke in the same way. His style became more and more indirect as he moved from his early period, when he produced novels that considered the differences between American and European culture and character—*Roderick Hudson* (1876), *The American* (1877), *The Europeans* (1878), *Daisy Miller* (1879), *Washington Square* (1881), and *The Portrait of a Lady* (1881)—to his middle period, when he wrote two novels about social reformers and revolutionaries, *The Bostonians* and *The Princess Casamassima*, both in 1886, as well as the novellas *The Aspern Papers* (1888) and *The Turn of the Screw* (1898).

In 1898 James retreated to Lamb House, a mansion he had purchased in Rye, England. There he produced the great works of his final period, in which in complex prose he subtly portrayed his characters' inner lives: *The Wings of the Dove* (1902), *The Ambassadors* (1903), and *The Golden Bowl* (1904). He returned to the United States for the last time to supervise production of a twenty-six-volume edition of his most important fictional works that was published between 1907 and 1917. *The American Scene* (1907), an account of his last journey to America, is highly critical of his native land. He became a British citizen in 1915. Shortly after receiving the Order of Merit, Henry James died, on February 28, 1916, leaving behind a prodigious body of work: twenty completed novels, 112 stories, and twelve plays, as well as voluminous travel writing and literary journalism and criticism.

Table of Contents

The World of Henry James and
The Wings of the Dove

1789 William James, Henry's grandfather, emigrates to the United States from Ireland.

1811 Henry James, Sr., the author's father, is born.

1826 Washington Square is dedicated as a public place and military parade ground. Originally a marsh, then a graveyard, it served as a spot for duels and executions prior to this transformation.

1828 Construction begins on the first house on the north side of Washington Square; over the next thirty years Washington Square North will become the most expensive and fashionable street bordering Washington Square.

1832 William James dies, leaving a $3 million estate to his twelve children.

1835 Henry James's maternal grandmother, Elizabeth Walsh, moves into a townhouse at 18 Washington Square North (now part of 2 Fifth Avenue), occupying it until 1847. James visits her often as an infant and toddler.

1836 Ralph Waldo Emerson publishes his essay "Nature," setting forth the main principles of Transcendentalism.

1837 William Dean Howells is born; he will be James's colleague, an important editor, and a founder of American "realism."

1842 Henry's brother William is born.

1843 On April 15, Henry James, Jr., is born at 21 Washington Place, in New York City, around the corner from his grandmother. In October the James family relocates to Europe.

1844 The family returns to New York City.

1849 Henry, Sr.'s social circle comprises philosophers and writers, including Nathaniel Hawthorne and Ralph Waldo Emerson. Henry, Jr., is educated privately in the United

States and Europe. His exposure to the Old World during his formative years establishes in him a lifelong preference for Europe over America.

1853 The New York City Commission pays $5,000,000 for land that will become Central Park, a vast public recreation space in the European style. The first portion of the park will open in 1858; it will be complete some sixteen years hence.

1857 The *Atlantic Monthly* is founded by Moses Dresser Phillips and Francis H. Underwood. Early contributors include Ralph Waldo Emerson, Henry Wadsworth Longfellow, James Russell Lowell (the magazine's first editor), and Oliver Wendell Holmes. In coming years James will be a frequent contributor.

1859 In October Henry, Sr., takes his family to Geneva.

1860 The family returns to America in September and settles in Newport, Rhode Island.

1861 The American Civil War begins.

1862 James enrolls at Harvard Law School but drops out after a year to pursue a writing career. He becomes friendly with William Dean Howells.

1864 In February James publishes his first piece of fiction, the story "A Tragedy of Error," in the *Continental Monthly*. Nathaniel Hawthorne dies.

1865 James begins to write reviews for the *Nation*, a new liberal weekly. The American Civil War ends.

1866 The first permanent transatlantic telegraph cable links Europe and America, vastly increasing the speed of information transmittal.

1869 In England James meets George Eliot and writes reviews of her works, including *Romola, Middlemarch,* and *Daniel Deronda*, which are published in the *Atlantic Monthly* and the *Galaxy*, a literary journal. Mark Twain publishes the best-selling travel book *The Innocents Abroad,* based on letters he had written while journeying by steamship to Europe and the Holy Land; it treats hallowed Old World landmarks with irreverence and parodies the manners and mores of Europeans and Americans.

1870   James's cousin Mary ("Minny") Temple dies in March, and the author, devastated, moves back to New York. His social opportunities are abundant; he spends time at Emerson's house in Concord, Massachusetts, and meets Henry Adams, who has just been appointed editor of the *North American Review*. The Metropolitan Museum opens in New York City.

1871   James publishes his first novel, *Watch and Ward*, in installments in the *Atlantic*; it introduces what will be a prominent Jamesian theme: the development of a young girl into womanhood.

1872   Assigned to write a travel series for the *Nation*, James sails to Liverpool and spends time in Europe. Susan B. Anthony casts a vote in the presidential election in Rochester, New York, and is arrested.

1873   Financial panic grips New York with the failure of Jay Cooke and Company, the nation's preeminent investment bank. After a ten-year economic boom, the United States enters its worst depression to date, although New York continues its prodigious growth.

1875   James publishes in the *Atlantic Monthly* the novel *Roderick Hudson*, about an American sculptor in Rome and his struggle to reconcile art and passion. During his early period (also called his international period), he compares the people and cultures of the United States and Europe, focusing especially on the differences. While living in Paris, James associates with the writers Gustave Flaubert and Émile Zola, as well as Russian expatriate authors, including the novelist Ivan Turgenev. He works on his novel *The American*, about a self-made American millionaire who tries to marry the daughter of French aristocrats.

1876   *Roderick Hudson* is published in book form. Impatient with America's foreign policy and disaffected with the United States in general, James joins other expatriates in London and settles permanently there. Throughout the rest of the 1870s, he associates with many leading English writers and thinkers and becomes an important presence on the Anglo-American literary scene.

1877   *The American* is published in book form. James is friendly with Alfred Tennyson, William Gladstone, and Robert Browning. While in Rome, James hears about an American "child of nature and of freedom" who consorted with a "good-looking Roman, of vague identity." James is immediately inspired to turn this story into a novel, *Daisy Miller*.

1878   James publishes the short novel *The Europeans*. The Macmillan Publishing Company of London asks him to write a biography of either Washington Irving or Nathaniel Hawthorne.

1879   James publishes *Daisy Miller*, about a young American woman in Rome, in book form. He signs a contract for the British copyright on *Hawthorne*, which is published in the English Men of Letters series in London.

1880–   The focus of James's writing shifts to social and psychologi-
1881   cal drama. *Washington Square* is serialized in *Cornhill Magazine* and *Harper's* (1880) and released in book form (1881); the novel concerns a young American woman whose father rejects the man she wants to marry. *The Portrait of a Lady* is serialized in *Macmillan's Magazine* and the *Atlantic Monthly* (1880–1881), and in book form (1881); this brilliant novel depicts a young American woman who out of a kind of generosity marries the wrong man. James vows "never again to return" to New York, in a fit of disdain over the way the city's "oppressive" economic growth has lowered the quality of life.

1882   James travels to Washington, D.C., where he briefly meets Oscar Wilde.

1886   James publishes the first novels of his middle period: *The Bostonians*, the story of a struggle between a southern conservative and an embittered suffragist, and *The Princess Casamassima*, an exploration of the personal dangers involved in taking up anarchism and revolution.

1888   James publishes the short novel *The Aspern Papers*, about a man who woos the custodian of letters by a poet he idolizes.

1889   Psychologically and financially depressed by the failure of *The Bostonians*, James shifts his focus to playwriting for the next six years.

1890   He publishes *The Tragic Muse*, about art and theater in London and Paris. His brother William publishes his groundbreaking and influential *Principles of Psychology*, in which pragmatism and "radical empiricism" are key elements.

1891   James's dramatization of *The American* fares moderately well.

1895   James's first dramatic work written as such, *Guy Domville*, is booed by the opening-night audience and receives mostly negative reviews, though George Bernard Shaw praises it. After little success with playwriting, James returns to writing fiction. The United States increases its involvement in a conflict between Spain and Cuba, which wants independence from Spanish rule. James opposes this involvement, calling it "none of our business."

1897   He publishes *What Maisie Knew*, the story of a preadolescent girl who must chose between her parents and a governess.

1898   James publishes the ghost story *The Turn of the Screw*. He purchases Lamb House, in Rye, England, where he will write his last novels and letters. The Spanish-American War takes place.

1900   During the final stage of his writing career, James's style becomes increasingly complex and convoluted. Over the next few years, he produces what are often considered his greatest works.

1902   He publishes *The Wings of the Dove*, about a group of people who scheme to inherit a dying woman's fortune.

1903   *The Ambassadors*, about an American suspicious of European ways who is won over by life in Paris, is published, as is "The Beast in the Jungle," a story of a man who believes he is intended for something remarkable. In London, James meets Edith Wharton.

1904   His novel of adultery *The Golden Bowl* is published. He travels to the United States to oversee the production of a revised collection of his most important works of fiction.

1907   James publishes *The American Scene*, his observations on what America has become. Publication of the twenty-six volumes of the revised fiction collection, *The Novels and Tales of Henry James*, begins; it will continue until 1917.

1908   James publishes the story "The Jolly Corner," an oblique commentary on the America he has left behind.

1910   In January James becomes very ill. He is nursed by his siblings Alice and William, with whom he returns to Cambridge. He visits New York, where he receives psychiatric care.

1911   In August he returns to England.

1914   James begins work on two novels, *The Ivory Tower* and *The Sense of the Past*, which he will not complete before his death.

1915   James's health deteriorates. He becomes a British subject.

1916   On New Year's Day he receives the Order of Merit. On February 28 Henry James dies. His ashes are taken to Cambridge, Massachusetts, to be buried in American soil, near his brother William.

1917   *Ivory Tower* and *The Sense of the Past* are published in their unfinished state.

Introduction

The Wings of the Dove, published in 1902 in New York and London, ranks as one of the three masterpieces of Henry James's "major period"[1] (along with *The Ambassadors* [1903] and *The Golden Bowl* [1904]). Of all of Henry James's prodigious literary output—he wrote twenty-two novels (two unfinished); 112 shorter tales or stories; autobiographical works; twelve plays; a vast array of travel essays; scores of critical essays, commentaries, and reviews of all kinds; and an astonishing number of letters to family and friends—the three late novels seem to have won the most enduring critical acclaim. They were written, roughly one a year, in a burst of creative energy from 1901 to 1904 as James approached his sixtieth birthday. The original idea for *Wings* was formed about 1894 when James wrote in his notebooks, at the top of a list of a dozen potential stories: "*La Mourante*: the girl who is dying, the young man, and the girl he is engaged to." The popular appeal of the three late novels has never quite matched their critical plaudits. For some, the reason is that the three works are not as accessible as much of James's other work. The novels are stylistically complex, written in an allusive and poetic prose, and they depart from the "realism" of such earlier works as *The Portrait of a Lady* (1881), *The American* (1877), *The Bostonians* (1886), and *Washington Square* (1881), and from the allegorical structure of *Roderick Hudson* (1875–1876).

While the reader cruises along smoothly in the realistic works, easily engrossed in the narrative as the action unfolds in a leisurely fashion, to be caught up in the "action" of the late novels is a different experience. Much more effort and close attention is demanded of the reader. The main action, indeed, is often in the minds of the characters, in their nuances of consciousness, and in the interplay of their moral sentiments. The individuals furthermore act within a framework of complex social forces and circumstances. The moral sensibilities of the characters precipitate agonizing choices for them, and yet the social context constrains the choices. The modern reader, on tackling *Wings* or one of the other major novels, may be inclined to echo the exasperated sentiments that William James once addressed to his brother apropos the late prose style:

> You can't skip a word if you are to get the effect, and 19 out of 20 worthy readers grow intolerant. 'Say it *out*, for God's sake,' they cry, 'and have done with it.' . . . For gleams and innuendos and felicitous verbal insinuations you are unapproachable, but the *core* of literature is solid. Give it to us once again.[2]

Some friends have expressed to me the fear that the language of the late James works is so far removed from modern usage that the novels may come to be regarded as in a category with, say, a Shakespearean comedy whose allusions are hopelessly beyond the ken of today's readers. I believe that this view is mistaken. In rereading *Wings* in preparing this essay I was struck once again by the novel's richness and vitality, the humanness of the characters, and the moral relevance of their struggles. The rewards are great for the reader who perseveres. Once you are caught up in the story, you will be swept along and you will very likely join the ranks of the James enthusiasts.

William James, in the same letter in which he complained to his brother about the dense prose in the late novels, referred to Henry's 1907 travel book, *The American Scene*, as "in its peculiar way . . . *supremely* great." To struggle with the moral dilemmas of the characters in the late James novels is to be transformed along with them, to experience the ambiguities and complexities that are very much a part of our modern lives. William James was right—there is something supremely great in his brother's work. Whether one reads Henry James's late novels primarily for aesthetic reasons, for social awareness, or to explore the clash of European and American sensibilities, the effort will be repaid manyfold. The richness, subtlety, and depth of characterization, the relevance of the moral issues, and the unforgettable portrayal of human dilemmas secure a place for James's late novels among the treasures of world literature.

Fans of Henry James have long debated the respective virtues of the three major novels. *The Wings of the Dove* has risen in critical esteem in recent years, though it still has detractors among the critics. A familiar complaint is that *Wings* lacks the symmetry that James achieved in *The Ambassadors* and *The Golden Bowl*. Some have found the ending unconvincing. James himself feared that the early sections in *Wings* might be too drawn out and that other sections may have thus become too crowded. At the time he completed *The Ambassadors*, James was convinced that it was his greatest achievement. James ultimately considered *The Golden Bowl* his best work but ranked *Wings* as one of his "advanced" works. The arguments over which of the late novels is the most accessible, or has the most followers among the *cognoscenti* or the general public, or best represents the true genius of Henry James are lively and diverting. But much of this disputation, I think, misses the mark. The three major novels can be better understood and more deeply appreciated in reference to each other. Each deserves a wider readership; each has been to some degree a neglected classic. There are, however, favorable signs. There has been a steady growth in the number of James devotees in recent years, if one can judge by the number of Web sites and "hits" on them, the college courses featuring James, the number of journal articles, and the like. In publishing *The Wings of the Dove* in this Barnes & Noble Classics edition, our intent is not only to bring this classic to a broad audience but to increase the readership for and interest in all of the James works.

A few words are in order about the circumstances of the publication of *The Wings of the Dove*. James was in the habit of working on more than one project at a time, and he had originally contracted to finish *Wings* by September 1, 1901. *The Ambassadors* was to be prepared for serialization in the *North American Review* but was not finished until the summer of 1901, and only then could James concentrate his energies fully on *Wings*. He had determined that *Wings* should not be bound by the formalities and rules of serial publication in a magazine, which usually dictated twelve installments of roughly equal length. He was committed therefore to submit a complete manuscript of *Wings* to Constable in England and Scribner's in America. Seeing that the initial deadline for *Wings* would be impossible to meet, he asked for an extension to August 1902, with publication to be deferred to the fall of 1902. The proposal was unacceptable to his publishers, who argued that their fall schedule was already too crowded and that James's usual readers would want to read the book on their summer holidays. A compromise was worked out: The manuscript would be submitted in April 1902 with publication a few months later in June. James worked furiously in late 1901 and submitted a large installment of the manuscript of *Wings* to the publishers in December. But in January 1902 he became ill and his production slowed. (As with *The Ambassadors* and subsequently with *The Golden Bowl,* he dictated *Wings* to his typist Mary Weld.) Despite his best efforts, he could not meet the April deadline. He did dispatch some 400 pages of typescript, however, and promised his publishers the finished manuscript by May 15. He estimated that it would take an additional 100 pages to finish the novel. Winding up the story actually required more than twice that number of pages. He sent in the final 220 pages on May 20, 1902.

Delays in typesetting, the pressures of correcting proofs, the vagaries of transatlantic mail, and the task of trying to coordinate the dates of publication in New York and London, as well as continuing problems with *The Ambassadors,* brought further delays. *The Wings of the Dove* finally appeared on August 20, 1902 (ahead, as it turned out, of *The Ambassadors,* which was serialized in the *North American Review* from January to December 1903). The print run for *Wings* was 3,000 copies in America and 4,000 in England. Initial sales of *Wings* were disappointing. In addition, there were numerous typos, misspellings, misprints, and other errors in both editions. Worse yet, differences appeared between the British and American editions, evidence that James corrected the respective proofs at different times and did not correlate the versions sent to the different publishers.

The errors were largely corrected in the New York Edition, the series in which James painstakingly revised and reissued an authoritative text for a large part of his entire literary output. James finished his revisions of *Wings* in 1909; it was the eleventh novel issued in the New York Edition. It is a tribute to his artistic conscience that he persevered, for by the time he set to work on *Wings* it was clear that sales of the whole New York series were well below what he had hoped for. He could expect no profits on *Wings*, and the publisher reduced the print run to only 1,000 copies. Unknown to James, his friend Edith Wharton colluded with his publisher to subsidize in part the New York Edition and make it possible for the series to appear.

James made no substantive textual changes in the New York Edition of *Wings* comparable, for example, to what he did with *The Portrait of a Lady*, in which he made significant alterations, including most notably changes in the novel's ending, or with some of the other works that he drastically revised. In *Wings*, in addition to correcting mistakes, he sharpened the language of the text, by substituting more active and concrete images, and made his symbols more truly poetic.

This Barnes & Noble Classics edition is based on the 1909 New York Edition and incorporates a small number of additional editorial changes made by subsequent scholars. The aim is to present a text that is authoritative without burdening the general reader with an elaborate scholarly apparatus. Brief explanatory notes appear at the bottom of the page where necessary for clarity, and endnotes and a list of suggested references for further study are also included. But, as with all great works of literature, the reader will gain his or her greatest satisfaction by engaging the text directly, without being constrained by a critic's interpretative framework.

As with much else in the Jamesian oeuvre, however, we can gain important clues to *The Wings of the Dove* by noting James's own views on what he was trying to accomplish. James was an astute critic of his own work, and in his preface to the New York Edition (included in this edition), he gives us an illuminating statement of his aims. "The idea [of *Wings*]," he says, "reduced to its essence, is that of a young person conscious of a great capacity for life but early stricken and doomed, condemned to die under short respite, while also enamored of the world . . . and passionately desiring to 'put in' before extinction as many of the finer vibrations as possible, and so achieve however briefly and brokenly, the sense of having lived" (p. 3). The story, however, was not to be "the record predominantly of a collapse" (p. 5). Quite the contrary, James intended that his victim be seen as "contesting every

inch of the road, as catching at every object the grasp of which
might make for delay" (p. 5). She expresses in her fight the nobility of the human spirit. The novel therefore consists in working
out an elaboration of the nuances and the twists and turns along
the path, and the memorable human encounters that occur in a
noble, but untimely, doomed struggle against her fate. The struggles of James's heroine are nothing but the "soul of drama—which
is the portrayal, as we know, of a catastrophe determined in spite
of oppositions" (p. 5).

James's heroine is Milly Theale, a twenty-four-year-old New
Yorker who embodies all the finest virtues of the American
woman: freshness, spontaneity, innocence, a thirst for life. Milly is
fabulously wealthy and is the sole survivor of a large upper-class
New York family. The rest of family died off in the period since her
tenth birthday. We learn that they died from "different causes," lest
we infer that Milly is the victim of some strange hereditary illness.
Milly's illness is never specified, except that we learn in book sixth
that it is "not lungs," when Kate Croy and Merton Densher, the
other two protagonists of the novel, are discussing Milly's health
(p. 260).

James's beloved cousin, Mary ("Minny") Temple, who did die
of tuberculosis some twenty years before, was the model for Milly,
as she was for Isabel Archer of *The Portrait of a Lady* and Maggie
Verver of *The Golden Bowl*. Milly Theale is a more fully realized
creation than Isabel Archer and probably outshines Maggie Verver
as well. Milly dominates the events of *Wings* even when she is not
physically present. Milly is "there" when she is not there, whereas
Maggie Verver, a more passive figure, does not always seem to be
there when she is there. Milly's disease in *Wings*, though certainly
real since it will ultimately claim her life, has almost a spiritual
quality. Milly's will to live can keep the disease at bay, for a time at
least, and the loss of her will to live can cause its progress to ac-
celerate.

Milly's initial consultation with the famous London physician
Sir Luke Strett in book fifth is surely the most unphysical of all
medical examinations in literature. It consists mainly of the two of
them conversing amiably for a time. Gently interjecting a question
now and then, the benignant Sir Luke encourages Milly to talk

about herself, her family, and her hopes. Presumably from this he gleans a kind of medical history, but James gives no clear indication of the fact and does not dwell on this kind of realistic detail. Sir Luke is in every respect unlike another famous physician of nineteenth-century English literature, the young Dr. Lydgate of George Eliot's *Middlemarch* (1871–1872). While Lydgate is ardent, impetuous, and scientifically inclined, the avuncular Sir Luke is worldly, urbane, and, in modern jargon, laid back. He is so confident of his skills that he scarcely bothers with pills, powders, and the usual armamentaria of medical practice. Sir Luke, through a process of divination or intuition, does, however, diagnose Milly's condition precisely. He understands what is required. He is enamored (in a fatherly way) with Milly; her kindness, courage, and nobility of spirit make her irresistible to him. He promises to help her, and he gives the message that she wants to hear: She must live to the fullest, and not be bound or limited in any way by her condition.

It is part of the novel's design that we know more of Milly's state of mind than of her physical appearance. But we do have clues to her appearance. Milly apparently is not beautiful. Her nose and mouth are too big, and her pale skin makes her appear almost white, which in turn accentuates the redness of her hair. She generally wears black clothes that give her a slightly eccentric appearance. When we last see her at the rented *palazzo* in Venice, she is wearing a dazzling white gown and white pearls. This contrasts strikingly with her past costume and makes her inner beauty come radiantly to life. What counts is her inner beauty, her qualities of goodness and kindness that endear her to others. Of course her enormous wealth is part of her aura. Milly herself is completely unselfconscious about her wealth. She no more thinks of money than of the air she breathes. She will simply spend what she has to even if she is occasionally taken to the cleaners by those who serve her.

Henry James clearly worshiped Milly as much as he did his dead cousin Minny Temple. The memory of his cousin never left James. To Susan Shepherd Stringham, the Boston writer and Milly's traveling companion in the novel, Milly seems almost "a princess" or "an heir of all the ages." This latter characterization is how James wishes us to see Milly (see the preface, p. 6), and the phrase is a useful shorthand for everything she represents.

To some observers, Milly is so unreal in her goodness as to belong in a fairy tale. There are certainly fairy-tale qualities to *The Wings of the Dove*: The good princess encounters evil forces and a kind of magical tale unfolds. Indeed, Milly herself feels as if she were "on a carpet" as she whirls through the hubbub and bustle of London life. James's less-noble female characters may appear more "real" to some readers. Certainly, Kate Croy is a memorable literary creation of this type. Other critics, some of a feminist bent, counter that Milly is a much more forceful figure than merely the long-suffering victim. In their view Milly is by no means a mere patsy; rather, she is someone who flexes her muscles in a quiet way and who makes full use of all the power that her great wealth confers.

The other major characters, whose relations with Milly form the heart of the novel, are two very different people. Kate Croy and Merton Densher have little in common beyond their mutual sexual attraction and their poverty. Kate is pure action, a handsome, strong, willful, dark-haired young woman who knows her mind exactly. Kate has a talent for living and habitually devises practical plans of action to cope with any problems she encounters. James had sketched Kate in his notebook as a willful, unsympathetic figure. But she turns out to be more fully rounded, a complex and compelling figure with a mixture of attractive and unattractive qualities. Whatever James's original intentions, Kate Croy becomes through his artistry a sympathetic character even though she is the instigator of an unsavory, not to say immoral scheme to exploit her sick friend. She is also the one figure in the book who is brutally honest. She is in a tough game, and it is hardly surprising that she plays to win. Self-deception is not something she can afford.

Densher, in contrast, is pure thought, a man who delights in his own cerebrations. He is happiest when he is thinking and pondering about events, examining other people's motives (or his own), or when he is studying historical events or uncovering a scandal to put in his newspaper. He is passive where Kate is active. He is a loner, while she recognizes (if she does not always like) the necessity and inevitability of seeking one's goals by manipulating others in a web of social interactions. Their opposite personalities and qualities of mind attract and apparently are complementary, even though we may well wonder how long such an attachment will last. If they were forced to survive on Densher's meager pay as a journalist, their relationship would probably soon fizzle out. Densher has a conviction deep down that "he will never be rich." Unless pushed by Kate, he would be content to drift through life reading, writing the occasional piece for his newspaper, and contemplating the state of affairs from the margins of society. He is not wholly without ambition. He does want to get ahead in his chosen profession of journalism, as is evidenced by his willingness to visit America (where he first makes the acquaintance of Milly). But he doesn't have the relentless drive to advance his career with real vigor, just as he doesn't have the will to resist Kate when she propels him into the scheme to entrap Milly. Kate is willing to roll the dice, whereas Densher on his own could hardly imagine doing so. He admires her precisely for her uncanny knack of knowing what she wants and for her boldness in trying to achieve her goals. How, why, and to what degree he modifies his feelings toward Kate are critical turning points in the novel.

Rounding out the cast of characters is a host of lesser figures who play their parts in the drama. They are background figures, providing a kind of color, tint, scenery, and atmosphere. I use visual images advisedly, for James's text is like a canvas on which he has painted an intricate scene. The eye is drawn to the characters in the foreground, but the others are necessary for the complete portrait. James's metaphors and allusions are predominantly visual. His bent, his artistic taste is to painting, in contrast to that of Proust or Mann, whose novels are filled with musical references and allusions. That the visual arts seize the imaginations of James's characters further reinforces the whole effect of portraiture.

Kate's aunt, Maud Lowder, is the rich, iron-willed, and domineering matriarch with whom Kate lives. Aunt Maud is determined to use her niece to advance her own ends. Maud Lowder acquired her money through marriage, and she lacks the aristocratic pedigree that is necessary to function at the top of London's disintegrating, but still snobbish, social order. As a social climber and would-be aristocrat, Maud seeks to use her beautiful niece to advance her own social standing by marrying Kate off to a member of the nobility. The immediate candidate for this end is Lord Mark, who has a beautiful estate but is otherwise essentially broke. He needs money to keep up his lifestyle and is unabashedly in the hunt for a bride so that he can barter his social position for a fortune. He is none too finicky, requiring only that the woman's fortune be large enough. Lord Mark, a somewhat shadowy figure, turns out to be the closest thing to a purely evil force in the novel. His visit to Milly in Venice, in which he reveals to her the true state of the relationship between Kate and Densher, is as an act of malevolence and vengeance.

Aunt Maud's social control extends also to Kate's unfortunate and widowed sister Marian, who lives in lower-class penury with three children to care for. Marian has fallen out of favor with Aunt Maud because she married a man of whom Aunt Maud disapproved, and is now, after her husband's early death, reduced to living in conditions close to squalor. Her only hope in the short run is for occasional acts of minor benevolence from her aunt. Both Marian and Lionel Croy, Kate and Marian's disgraced father, harbor the idea that Kate one day will be able to care for them handsomely if she only submits entirely to Aunt Maud's wishes. Lionel Croy has besmirched the family through unspecified criminal acts; he has been ostracized by Aunt Maud but from time to time extracts small sums of money from her.

Though Milly is the center of the novel's action, she is not present in the first two books, and after one brief episode in book eighth, she disappears in the last two books of the novel. The novel's first two books are given over entirely to Kate, to her relationship with Densher and to her family background. The initial chapters set the stage for Milly's arrival in London and her debut in the London social scene. James had his doubts about this device of leaving Milly to a later appearance, fearing that he may be too long-winded in setting the stage. The novel then could end up having "too big a head for its body."[3] He feared that, by having to cram too much into the middle sections, he might cause sudden shifts of focus and make the narrative hard for the reader to follow. While *Wings* does lack the structural symmetry of *The Ambassadors* and

The Golden Bowl, the technique of deferring Milly's appearance heightens the drama and brilliantly succeeds in the final analysis.

Milly arrives on the scene in book third, and we learn all that we need to know of her New York background and her family circumstances. In demonstrating the force of her character by showing how she affects the others, James dramatizes her the more, just as he does with the figure of Mrs. Newsome in *The Ambassadors* (who never actually appears in the novel). Milly's presence is powerfully felt even in her absence. She animates the other characters; they are at first preoccupied with trying to figure her out and then they scheme to use her for their own purposes. Her seeming victimhood is demonstrated by the way the others constantly plot behind her back. The tawdriness of their intrigues contrasts with Milly's own lonely struggle to live.

Milly's character is initially presented through the eyes of Susan Stringham, who is accompanying her to Europe. Susan's role in *Wings* is similar to that of Maria Gostrey in *The Ambassadors* or to Colonel Bob Assingham's role in the narrative structure of *The Golden Bowl.* James refers to this literary device as the *ficelle* (literally, a little piece of string), by which he means the use of a lesser character to facilitate the flow of events and to link the major scenes.[4] One day in Switzerland, while looking for Milly, Susan Stringham sees the book Milly was reading left by the side of the trail and follows the path that leads to the edge of a precipice. She sees Milly sitting in a precarious position on a rock slab, gazing down at the valley stretched out below her. For a moment Susan is frightened, thinking that her friend might be contemplating suicide. She is afraid to call out for fear that a sudden disturbance might startle Milly and send her over the edge. Then, as Susan contemplates her friend, she slowly realizes that as Milly "was looking down at the kingdoms of the earth . . . it wouldn't be with a view of renouncing them. Was she choosing among them or did she want them all?" (p. 106). She understands that her friend is not running from life but hungers for life. Shortly, Milly announces to her friend that she wants to go directly to London. She has evidently had enough of Switzerland's bucolic charms, and wants to be at the center of activity in the world's most bustling metropolis.

Susan Stringham happens to have an old friend in London from the days before the marriage to her late husband. This friend of her youth, now also widowed, is Maud Manningham Lowder, who is Kate Croy's aunt. Susan writes to her friend Maud, and upon their arrival in London renews the friendship. Milly, with her "heir of all the ages" qualities, quickly captivates Maud, and is introduced into Maud's London circle. Milly's wealth, though she carries it gracefully, inevitably attracts attention. In the London scene of the day, wealth makes one "a great personage." Maud and her friends treat Milly as such, although they also regard her as eccentric. Milly is sensitive enough to see that she is being patronized, and wishes she could escape from the stereotype. She especially wants to be respected by her new friend Kate and by Merton Densher (whom she had met in New York when he visited the city as a journalist). Milly sees that the Londoners she meets seem preoccupied with money, but she does not yet understand the deeper currents and plots being hatched around her. For the moment she is happy to be caught up in the excitement of London, in broadening her knowledge of the world (and her knowledge of herself). She is living more fully through her new friends.

Milly is a symbol of the innocent but thoughtful American guided by an innate idealism and an intuitive sense of what is right. Milly, like her country, is without a significant past to shape her identity, and is also without culture but is hungry to learn. In Kate, equally a creature of her circumstances, opposing qualities are represented: She is shrewd, knowing, a survivor by temperament and by necessity. She is driven by values forged within a framework of practical reality. Her values are purely exigent, and she is on the make because she has no other choice. In the general condition of *fin-de-siècle* England, Kate suffers both from too much history and from a radical uncertainty about the future. Kate's family fortunes are on the wane (as England's commercial fortunes, too, are under siege). Kate, living by her wits like other Londoners, faces a crumbling social order, still beset with vestiges of privilege, and a crass, cash-driven morality where money and competition reign. Although *Wings* is framed almost in mythic terms—the fair princess versus the Dark Lady, innocence against guile, America's innate goodness against England's expediential morality—James's genius lies in his making the characters alive and concrete, palpably real as they interact and make their ways within the London scene, and never mere caricatures.

Milly is caught up almost immediately in a plan of Aunt Maud's to detach Kate once and for all from the impoverished Densher. Maud finds out that Milly has met Densher in New York and quickly decides to try to link Milly with Densher—to her it is self-evident that any sensible man would be attracted to a woman of Milly's wealth, along with the added bonus of Milly's apparent pliability. Once attached to Milly, Densher would be moved to the periphery and Maud would be free to advance her plan to marry Kate to Lord Mark. As subterfuge, Maud advances the notion that Merton Densher is a "family friend." Kate, who is in love with Densher, at first resents this move by her aunt, but soon enough realizes its potential uses for her own purposes. Gradually, with the twists and turns of real life, Kate's own plot takes shape as a way to thwart her aunt. She will outsmart her aunt by adopting her aunt's very plan.

Kate's plan begins to take shape when she discovers that Milly may be seriously ill. The idea is that Kate will encourage Densher to be nice to Milly—she senses at once that Milly is attracted to him—and she will thus persuade Milly that there is nothing between Densher and herself. Milly will in due course fall in love with Densher, Kate believes, and want to marry him, which will result in Densher inheriting her fortune. By exploiting the dying girl's desperate wish to find love, Kate will escape her aunt's and Lord Mark's clutches. She will have it all: the man she loves as her husband, Milly's money, and her own freedom of action. Kate's approach to life is epitomized by her comment to Densher in book second that "I *shan't* sacrifice you. Don't cry out till you're hurt. I shall sacrifice nobody and nothing, and that's just my situation, that I want and that I shall try for everything. That . . . is how I see myself" (p. 70).

The burden of actually implementing the scheme, however, falls on Merton Densher. Once having set things in motion, Kate steps into the background, and it will be Densher's job to deceive Milly, to become her lover and/or husband, and thus to inherit her money. His emotions, and his awakening moral sensibilities as he proceeds, and the impact of all this on his relations with Kate provide the main dramatic tension for the novel. Densher, who becomes something of an exemplar for the anti-hero figure so prominent in twentieth-century fiction, is passive, a spectator type of person, someone to whom things happen. His moral struggles grow out of his reaction to the circumstances he finds himself in — his dilemma has come about, seemingly, only because he wanted to be kind. He is meant, as Henry James originally envisaged the character's development, to undergo a spiritual transformation as he comes to see the horror of his role in exploiting the dying girl's quest to hang on to life. Whether the reader will be convinced that Densher's conversion is genuine remains an open question. James, in the actual writing of the novel as opposed to his notebook projections, made Densher's spiritual development a more nuanced affair, and left us to judge Densher's motives. Is Densher's ostensible renunciation of Milly's fortune merely a self-righteous gesture, an effort to conceal the extent of his own moral responsibility? Some readers may find Densher's late actions priggish and bizarre — far removed, indeed, from any true signs of respect for Milly's memory.

Kate stays in character to the end. She is not squeamish; she is resolute and matter-of-fact. She holds to her rationale that the deception brought Milly a degree of solace in her fight for life. After all, Kate remarks on an earlier occasion, "Who does Milly have but us?" Kate wonders, in the final scene with Densher after Milly has died and after Densher has received notice from Milly's New York attorneys of the bequest of her fortune, why he hadn't simply denied to Milly the truth of Lord Mark's vengeful revelation. Susan Stringham at the time had also urged Densher to deny Lord Mark's accusation, which had devastated Milly and caused her to "turn her face to the wall." Densher is shocked by the suggestion. This is the one thing he could not do. He could only seek Milly's forgiveness in his final interview with her. Kate presses him to tell her what actually happened — did Milly, in fact, forgive him? Densher is vague — all he can recall is that the encounter lasted about twenty minutes and ended when she grew tired and asked him to leave her. Densher assumes that he was forgiven, but he assumed all along that his moral responsibility was mitigated by the fact that his role was passive and because he was motivated by kindliness. He has, in fact, deceived himself repeatedly. The meeting with Sir Luke Strett in Venice, for example, shows Densher at his self-righteous worst. Sir Luke tells him that Milly would like to see him, and Densher grandly imagines that Sir Luke thinks highly of him and sees him as someone seeking only to comfort Milly. This manifest self-deception makes us wonder about Densher's state of mind.

Densher presents Kate with a choice between having Milly's money without him or him without the money. But she cannot have both. Kate has failed the tests that Densher has devised for her, and apparently she now finds herself back where she started: having to choose between love and money. But will Densher be able to carry out his grand gesture? Will he be able to resist Kate's stronger will and her greater capacity for life? Densher is the quintessential loser thrust into circumstances he does not fully understand. James still has sympathy for Densher even if this troubled soul's spiritual transformation falls short. Densher, in his moral confusions and hesitations, is truer to life and more credible without the full moral awakening. Though polarities of good and evil are often implied in the novel, James endows his characters with a mixture of motives and with nuanced qualities that prevent us from making easy moral judgments. James's characters are vividly alive, struggling in their imperfect ways to realize their destinies in a world that lacks moral clarity. For James, there is a sense of foreboding in the air. The cash nexus is the spirit of the new post-Victorian age. Everywhere in *The Wings of the Dove*, from the thrusting commercialism of London to the dilapidation and fading glory of Venice, there is the sense that the old order is passing and the higher values of Western civilization are under assault.

Kate, with her quick perception, recognizes in the novel's final scene that something fundamental has happened. Densher has changed; he is no longer a reliable ally. She believes that Densher has fallen in love with a ghost; he has become enamored of Milly's memory. Just when Kate's scheme has apparently brilliantly succeeded, the whole effort has in fact fallen apart. Densher's equivocal attempt to absolve himself from blame and his quixotic attitude toward Milly's money have doomed Kate's best-laid plans.

Densher assures her that he is still ready to marry her "in an hour." Kate asks, "As we were?" The "as we were" means what exactly — as they were in the old days before Milly came on the scene? As they were before Densher's renounces Milly's money? "As we were," he replies. Kate, ever clear-headed and decisive, gives a firm shake of the head and turns to the door, declaring, "We shall never be again as we were!" (p. 492).

There are in *Wings* few of the "big scenes" that one finds in many nineteenth-century novels. James's method of indirection means that we as readers, as well as the characters, learn of critical developments as they are refracted through another character's consciousness, or in what somebody says offhandedly, or by means of a poetic image or symbol that brings a sudden burst of understanding. In James's late fiction, meanings are conveyed, as John Auchard has shown, through the "silences."[5] Effects are communicated via a glance; a mood is captured in a momentary intrusion of a shaft of light. The emotional aftereffects of a chance encounter linger and the characters ponder the meaning of gestures fraught with wider significance. As in life, great moral issues seem to dissolve into myriad small choices, and the continuous flow of little encounters sweeps the characters along toward ends that they cannot foresee.

Yet in *Wings* circumstances do not control events to the exclusion of human will. The Jamesian world is not like the naturalist order of a Zola or Dreiser novel, where the individual is subject to the iron determinism of circumstance. Individual moral choices do matter. Important corners are turned in *Wings*, and decisions are made at every turn that carry a string of consequences. For Kate, deciding to live with her aunt brings her under the sway of her aunt's values. In choosing money, and in postponing marriage to Densher, she turns her life onto the path of the London "scene." This scene is marked by crassness and grasping ambition. Densher's decision that he will be kind to Milly as the gentlemanly thing to do is a pious rationalization. Once he takes the first steps, he is implicated deeply in Kate's venture. He places himself on a slippery moral slope. Once in the action, he cannot get out. Milly encounters critical turning points, too, and in those moments she makes decisions that will shape her life. How long she can fight off her fate is in some measure a reflection of her own will and of whether she is fully engaged in life. She chooses to ignore Kate's warning to "drop us while you can." The scene in which Milly stands with Lord Mark in front of the Bronzino portrait that resembles her sticks in our minds as a decisive moment. She has the first symptoms of her illness on that occasion, and perhaps she surrenders to her fate and loses some of her will to live. Milly thereupon makes a series of important decisions. She decides to consult with Sir Luke Strett. She invites Kate to accompany her on the first visit to the doctor but not on the second visit, and she does not confide in Kate what the doctor tells her. Milly's pride thus assures that she will face her fate essentially alone.

Why does James—one of the most secular of authors, whose only religious inclination seems to have been a nodding interest in his brother William's ideas about consciousness and the afterlife[6]— choose the religious symbol of the dove for his heroine? At one level the answer seems obvious enough. Kate calls Milly a "dove" early in the novel when the two of them are alone in a drawing room, and just after Milly has had the thought that Kate is "like a panther" pacing before her. Milly's dove-like qualities and Kate's fierceness are nicely juxtaposed here for the reader. The dove image next appears in book seventh at Milly's grand party in Venice. Kate and Densher are watching Milly from across the room as Kate lays out her instructions to him concerning how he should maneuver to be assured of getting Milly's money. Milly is dressed in white at the party and wears white pearls, and the image of the dove pops into Kate's mind. But when Kate refers to Milly as a dove the word does not seem apt to Densher; he does not think of Milly as a passive, demure creature. However, a dove has large wings, and it strikes him that at the very moment they all are nestled under Milly's wings. Indeed, they have all lived for some time under Milly's patronage and protection. Psalm 55, it may be recalled, is actually a prayer for the release from suffering and persecution:

> My heart is in anguish within me, the terrors of death have fallen upon me. Fear and trembling come upon me, and horror overwhelms me. And I say, "O that I had wings like a dove! I would fly

away and be at rest; yea, I would wander afar, I would lodge in the wilderness, I would haste to find me a shelter from the raging wind and tempest" (verses 4–8).[7]

Is it a final irony of *The Wings of the Dove* that Milly escapes from—not to say, triumphs over—her tormentors? In giving away her fortune to Densher despite his deception, she has shown both the softness and the strength of her wings. She has demonstrated her generosity and forgiving spirit, and at the same time has exacted a certain vengeance. Kate and Densher apparently have become permanently estranged as a result of the bequest. Kate has learned that she cannot have everything. For Densher's part, his grand gesture of renunciation would leave him with nothing. Like all of Henry James's endings, the end of *Wings* is more of a beginning than a resolution: Will Densher be redeemed and will he find a new life without Kate? Will Kate free herself from her aunt and from the London "scene," or will she, after all, fall into a marriage with Lord Mark? Like Lambert Strether in *The Ambassadors*, who realizes that money has poisoned his relationship with his patroness Mrs. Newsome, and like Maggie Verver in *The Golden Bowl*, who must at last confront her husband without the presence and emotional support of her father, Kate and Densher must build their lives anew with only a heightened moral awareness to guide them. For Henry James, there is a darkness and a sense of doom hovering over the scene. His characters, and the civilization they represent, may be incapable of redemption, and may instead spiral toward moral decay and social disintegration.

Bruce L. R. Smith is a fellow at the Heyman Center of the Humanities of Columbia University. He previously was a professor of government at Columbia University (1966–1979), a deputy assistant secretary in the U. S. Department of State (1979–1980), and a senior fellow at the Brookings Institution in Washington, D.C. (1980–1996). He is the author or editor of sixteen scholarly books, and he continues to lecture widely in the United States and abroad.

Notes to the Introduction

1. F. O. Matthiessen, *Henry James: The Major Period*, London and New York, Oxford University Press, 1945.
2. William James to Henry James, letter dated May 4, 1907, in *The Letters of William James*, edited by Henry James, Boston, Atlantic Monthly Press, 1920, vol. 2, p. 278.
3. James made this comment in a letter to Mrs. Cadwalader Jones, dated October 23, 1902; reprinted in *The Wings of the Dove*, Norton Critical Edition, second edition, edited by J. Donald Crowley and Richard A. Hocks, New York, W. W. Norton, 2003, p. 468.
4. The idea of the *ficelle* is discussed most extensively by James in the preface to *The Ambassadors* (see Henry James, *The Art of the Novel: Critical Prefaces*, with an introduction by Richard P. Blackmur, New York, Charles Scribner's Sons, 1937, pp. 307–327). The discussion in James's preface to *Wings* is also of interest in this connexion (see *The Art of the Novel*, pp. 46–47).
5. John Auchard, *Silence in Henry James: The Heritage of Symbolism and Decadence*, University Park, Pennsylvania State University Press, 1986; especially chapter 5 on *The Wings of the Dove*.
6. Henry James, "Is There a Life After Death," in *In After Days: Thoughts on the Future Life*, New York and London, Harper and Brothers, 1910, pp. 201–233.
7. *The New Oxford Annotated Bible*, Revised Standard Version, New York, Oxford University Press, 1977, pp. 696–697.

THE WINGS OF
THE DOVE

Preface

The Wings of the Dove," published in 1902, represents to my memory a very old—if I shouldn't perhaps rather say a very young—motive; I can scarce remember the time when the situation on which this long-drawn fiction mainly rests was not vividly present to me. The idea, reduced to its essence, is that of a young person conscious of a great capacity for life, but early stricken and doomed, condemned to die under short respite, while also enamoured of the world; aware moreover of the condemnation and passionately desiring to "put in" before extinction as many of the finer vibrations as possible, and so achieve, however briefly and brokenly, the sense of having lived. Long had I turned it over, standing off from it, yet coming back to it; convinced of what might be done with it, yet seeing the theme as formidable.[1] The image so figured would be, at best, but half the matter; the rest would be all the picture of the struggle involved, the adventure brought about, the gain recorded or the loss incurred, the precious experience somehow compassed. These things, I had from the first felt, would require much working-out; that indeed was the case with most things worth working at all; yet there are subjects and subjects, and this one seemed particularly to bristle. It was formed, I judged, to make the wary adventurer walk round and round it—it had in fact a charm that invited and mystified alike that attention; not being somehow what one thought of as a "frank" subject, after the fashion of some, with its elements well in view and its whole character in its face. It stood there with secrets and compartments, with possible treacheries and traps; it might have a great deal to give, but would probably ask for equal services in return, and would collect this debt to the last shilling. It involved, to begin with, the placing in the strongest light a person infirm and ill—a case sure to prove difficult and to require much handling; though giving perhaps, with other matters, one of those chances for good taste, possibly even for the play of the very best

3

in the world, that are not only always to be invoked and cultivated, but that are absolutely to be jumped at from the moment they make a sign.

Yes then, the case prescribed for its central figure a sick young woman, at the whole course of whose disintegration and the whole ordeal of whose consciousness one would have quite honestly to assist. The expression of her state and that of one's intimate relation to it might therefore well need to be discreet and ingenious; a reflexion that fortunately grew and grew, however, in proportion as I focussed my image—roundabout which, as it persisted, I repeat, the interesting possibilities and the attaching wonderments, not to say the insoluble mysteries, thickened apace. Why had one to look so straight in the face and so closely to cross-question that idea of making one's protagonist "sick"?—as if to be menaced with death or danger hadn't been from time immemorial, for heroine or hero, the very shortest of all cuts to the interesting state. Why should a figure be disqualified for a central position by the particular circumstance that might most quicken, that might crown with a fine intensity, its liability to many accidents, its consciousness of all relations? This circumstance, true enough, might disqualify it for many activities—even though we should have imputed to it the unsurpassable activity of passionate, of inspired resistance. This last fact was the real issue, for the way grew straight from the moment one recognised that the poet essentially *can't* be concerned with the act of dying. Let him deal with the sickest of the sick, it is still by the act of living that they appeal to him, and appeal the more as the conditions plot against them and prescribe the battle.[2] The process of life gives way fighting, and often may so shine out on the lost ground as in no other connexion. One had had moreover, as a various chronicler, one's secondary physical weaklings and failures, one's accessory invalids—introduced with a complacency that made light of criticism. To Ralph Touchett in "The Portrait of a Lady," for instance, his deplorable state of health was not only no drawback; I had clearly been right in counting it, for any happy effect he should produce, a positive good mark, a direct aid to pleasantness and vividness. The reason of this moreover could never in the world have been his fact of sex; since men, among the mortally afflicted, suffer on the whole more overtly and more grossly than women, and resist with a ruder, an inferior strategy. I had thus to take *that* anomaly for what it was worth, and I give it here but as one of the ambiguities amid which my subject ended by making itself at home and seating itself quite in confidence.

With the clearness I have just noted, accordingly, the last thing in the world it proposed to itself was to be the record predominantly of a collapse. I don't mean to say that my offered victim was not present to my imagination, constantly, as dragged by a greater force than any she herself could exert; she had been given me from far back as contesting every inch of the road, as catching at every object the grasp of which might make for delay, as clutching these things to the last moment of her strength. Such an attitude and such movements, the passion they expressed and the success they in fact represented, what were they in truth but the soul of drama?—which is the portrayal, as we know, of a catastrophe determined in spite of oppositions. My young woman would *herself* be the opposition—to the catastrophe announced by the associated Fates, powers conspiring to a sinister end and, with their command of means, finally achieving it, yet in such straits really to *stifle* the sacred spark that, obviously, a creature so animated, an adversary so subtle, couldn't but be felt worthy, under whatever weaknesses, of the foreground and the limelight. She would meanwhile wish, moreover, all along, to live for particular things, she would found her struggle on particular human interests, which would inevitably determine, in respect to her, the attitude of other persons, persons affected in such a manner as to make them part of the action. If her impulse to wrest from her shrinking hour still as much of the fruit of life as possible, if this longing can take effect only by the aid of others, their participation (appealed to, entangled and coerced as they find themselves) becomes their drama too—that of their promoting her illusion, under her importunity, for reasons, for interests and advantages, from motives and points of view, of their own. Some of these promptings, evidently, would be of the highest order—others doubtless mightn't; but they would make up together, for her, contributively, her sum of experience, represent to her somehow, in good faith or in bad, what she should have *known*. Somehow, too, at such a rate, one would see the persons subject to them drawn in as by some pool of a Lorelei*—see them terrified and tempted and charmed; bribed away, it may even be, from more prescribed and natural orbits, inheriting from their connexion with her strange difficulties and still stranger opportunities, confronted with rare questions and called upon for new discriminations. Thus the scheme of her situation would, in a comprehensive way, see itself constituted; the rest of the interest would be in the number and nature of the particulars. Strong among these, naturally, the need that life should, apart from her infirmity, present itself to our young woman as quite dazzlingly liveable, and that if the great pang for her is in what she must give up we shall appreciate it the more from the sight of all she has.

One would see her then as possessed of all things, all but the single most precious assurance; freedom and money and a mobile mind and personal charm, the power to interest and attach; attributes, each one, enhancing the value of a future. From the moment his imagination began to deal with her at close quarters, in fact, nothing could more engage her designer than to work out the detail of her perfect rightness for her part; nothing above all more solicit him than to recognise fifty reasons for her national and social status. She should be the last fine flower—blooming alone, for the fullest attestation of her freedom—of an "old" New York stem; the happy congruities thus preserved for her being matters, however, that I may not now go into, and this even though the fine association that shall yet elsewhere await me is of a sort, at the best, rather to defy than to encourage exact expression. There goes with it, for the heroine of "The Wings of the Dove," a strong and special implication of liberty, liberty of action, of choice, of appreciation, of contact—proceeding from sources that provide better for large independence, I think, than any other conditions in the world—and this would be in particular what we should feel ourselves deeply concerned with. I had from far back mentally projected a certain sort of young American as more the "heir of all the ages" than any other young person whatever (and precisely on those grounds I

---

*Rock on the Rhine River associated with a number of legendary tales; in the commonest form, the Lorelei is the spirit of a maiden who drowned herself in despair over a faithless lover and who now acts as a siren luring fishermen to their deaths.

have just glanced at but to pass them by for the moment); so that here was a chance to confer on some such figure a supremely touching value. To be the heir of all the ages only to know yourself, as that consciousness should deepen, balked of your inheritance, would be to play the part, it struck me, or at least to arrive at the type, in the light on the whole the most becoming. Otherwise, truly, what a perilous part to play *out*—what a suspicion of "swagger" in positively attempting it! So at least I could reason—so I even think I *had* to—to keep my subject to a decent compactness. For already, from an early stage, it had begun richly to people itself: the difficulty was to see whom the situation I had primarily projected might, by this, that or the other turn, *not* draw in. My business was to watch its turns as the fond parent watches a child perched, for its first riding-lesson, in the saddle; yet its interest, I had all the while to recall, was just in its making, on such a scale, for developments.

What one had discerned, at all events, from an early stage, was that a young person so devoted and exposed, a creature with her security hanging so by a hair, couldn't but fall somehow into some abysmal trap—this being, dramatically speaking, what such a situation most naturally implied and imposed. Didn't the truth and a great part of the interest also reside in the appearance that she would constitute for others (given her passionate yearning to live while she might) a complication as great as any they might constitute for herself?—which is what I mean when I speak of such matters as "natural." They would be as natural, these tragic, pathetic, ironic, these indeed for the most part sinister, liabilities, to her living associates, as they could be to herself as prime subject. If her story was to consist, as it could so little help doing, of her being let in, as we say, for this, that and the other irreducible anxiety, how could she not have put a premium on the acquisition, by any close sharer of her life, of a consciousness similarly embarrassed? I have named the Rhine-maiden, but our young friend's existence would create rather, all round her, very much that whirlpool movement of the waters produced by the sinking of a big vessel or the failure of a great business; when we figure to ourselves the strong narrowing eddies, the immense force of suction, the general engulfment that, for any neighbouring object, makes immersion inevitable. I need scarce say, however, that in spite of these communities of doom I saw the main dramatic complication much more prepared *for* my vessel of sensibility than by her—the work of other hands (though with her own imbrued too, after all, in the measure of their never not being, in some direction, generous and extravagant, and thereby provoking).

The great point was, at all events, that if in a predicament she was to be, accordingly, it would be of the essence to create the predicament promptly and build it up solidly, so that it should have for us as much as possible its ominous air of awaiting her. That reflexion I found, betimes, not less inspiring than urgent; one begins so, in such a business, by looking about for one's compositional key, unable as one can only be to move till one has found it. To start without it is to pretend to enter the train and, still more, to remain in one's seat, without a ticket. Well—in the steady light and for the continued charm of these verifications—I had secured my ticket over the tolerably long line laid down for "The Wings of the Dove" from the moment I had noted that there could be no full presentation of Milly Theale as *engaged* with elements amid which she was to draw her breath in such pain, should not the elements have been, with all solicitude, duly prefigured. If one had seen that her stricken state was but half her case, the correlative half being the state of others as affected by her (they too should have a "case," bless them, quite as much as she!) then I was free to choose, as it were, the half with which I should begin. If, as I had fondly noted, the little world determined for her was to "bristle"— I delighted in the term!—with meanings, so, by the same token, could I but make my medal hang free, its obverse and its reverse, its face and its back, would beautifully become optional for the spectator. I somehow wanted them correspondingly embossed, wanted them inscribed and figured with an equal salience; yet it was none the less visibly my "key," as I have said, that though my regenerate young New Yorker, and what might depend on her, should form my centre, my circumference was every whit as treatable. Therefore I must trust myself to know when to proceed from the one and when from the other. Preparatively and, as it were, yearningly—given the whole ground—one began, in the event, with the outer ring, approaching the centre thus by narrowing circumvallations. There, full-blown, accordingly, from one hour to the other, rose one's process—for which there remained all the while so many amusing formulae.

The medal *did* hang free—I felt this perfectly, I remember, from the moment I had comfortably laid the ground provided in my first Book, ground from which Milly is superficially so absent. I scarce remember perhaps a case—I like even with this public grossness to insist on it—in which the curiosity of "beginning far back," as far back as possible, and even of going, to the same tune, far "behind," that is behind the face of the subject, was to assert itself with less scruple. The free hand, in this connexion, was above all agreeable—the hand the freedom of which I owed to the fact that the work had ignominiously failed, in advance, of all power to see itself "serialized." This failure had repeatedly waited, for me, upon shorter fictions; but the considerable production we here discuss was (as "The Golden Bowl" was to be, two or three years later) born, not otherwise than a little bewilderedly, into a world of periodicals and editors, of roaring "successes" in fine, amid which it was well-nigh unnotedly to lose itself. There is fortunately something bracing, ever, in the alpine chill, that of some high icy *arête*,* shed by the cold editorial shoulder; sour grapes may at moments fairly intoxicate and the story-teller worth his salt rejoice to feel again how many accommodations he can practise. Those addressed to "conditions of publication" have in a degree their interesting, or at least their provoking, side; but their charm is qualified by the fact that the prescriptions here spring from a soil often wholly alien to the ground of the work itself. They are almost always the fruit of another air altogether and conceived in a light liable to represent *within* the circle of the work itself little else than darkness. Still, when not too blighting, they often operate as a tax on ingenuity—that ingenuity of the expert craftsman which likes to be taxed very much to the same tune to which a well-bred horse likes to be saddled. The best and finest ingenuities, nevertheless, with all respect to that truth, are apt to be, not one's compromises, but one's fullest conformities, and I well remember, in the case be-

---

*Mountain ridge (French).

fore us, the pleasure of feeling my divisions, my proportions and general rhythm, rest all on permanent rather than in any degree on momentary proprieties. It was enough for my alternations, thus, that they were good in themselves; it was in fact so much for them that I really think any further account of the constitution of the book reduces itself to a just notation of the law they followed.

There was the "fun," to begin with, of establishing one's successive centres—of fixing them so exactly that the portions of the subject commanded by them as by happy points of view, and accordingly treated from them, would constitute, so to speak, sufficiently solid *blocks* of wrought material, squared to the sharp edge, as to have weight and mass and carrying power; to make for construction, that is, to conduce to effect and to provide for beauty. Such a block, obviously, is the whole preliminary presentation of Kate Croy, which, from the first, I recall, absolutely declined to enact itself save in terms of amplitude. Terms of amplitude, terms of atmosphere, those terms, and those terms only, in which images assert their fulness and roundness, their power to revolve, so that they have sides and backs, parts in the shade as true as parts in the sun—these were plainly to be my conditions, right and left, and I was so far from overrating the amount of expression the whole thing, as I saw and felt it, would require, that to retrace the way at present is, alas, more than anything else, but to mark the gaps and the lapses, to miss, one by one, the intentions that, with the best will in the world, were not to fructify. I have just said that the process of the general attempt is described from the moment the "blocks" are numbered, and that would be a true enough picture of my plan. Yet one's plan, alas, is one thing and one's result another; so that I am perhaps nearer the point in saying that this last strikes me at present as most characterised by the happy features that *were*, under my first and most blest illusion, to have contributed to it. I meet them all, as I renew acquaintance, I mourn for them all as I remount the stream, the absent values, the palpable voids, the missing links, the mocking shadows, that reflect, taken together, the early bloom of one's good faith. Such cases are of course far from abnormal—so far from it that some acute mind ought surely to have worked out by this time the "law" of the degree in which the artist's energy fairly depends on his fallibility.

How much and how often, and in what connexions and with what almost infinite variety, must he be a dupe, that of his prime object, to be at all measurably a master, that of his actual substitute for it—or in other words at all appreciably to exist? He places, after an earnest survey, the piers of his bridge—he has at least sounded deep enough, heaven knows, for their brave position; yet the bridge spans the stream, after the fact, in apparently complete independence of these properties, the principal grace of the original design. *They* were an illusion, for their necessary hour; but the span itself, whether of a single arch or of many, seems by the oddest chance in the world to be a reality; since, actually, the rueful builder, passing under it, sees figures and hears sounds above: he makes out, with his heart in his throat, that it bears and is positively being "used."

The building-up of Kate Croy's consciousness to the capacity for the load little by little to be laid on it was, by way of example, to have been a matter of as many hundred close-packed bricks as there are actually poor dozens. The image of her so compromised and compromising father was all effectively to have pervaded her life, was in a certain particular way to have tampered with her spring; by which I mean that the shame and the irritation and the depression, the general poisonous influence of him, were to have been *shown*, with a truth beyond the compass even of one's most emphasised "word of honour" for it, to do these things. But where do we find him, at this time of day, save in a beggarly scene or two which scarce arrives at the dignity of functional reference? He but "looks in," poor beautiful dazzling, damning apparition that he was to have been; he sees his place so taken, his company so little missed, that, cocking again that fine form of hat which has yielded him for so long his one effective cover, he turns away with a whistle of indifference that nobly misrepresents the deepest disappointment of his life. One's poor word of honour has *had* to pass muster for the show. Every one, in short, was to have enjoyed so much better a chance that, like stars of the theatre condescending to oblige, they have had to take small parts, to content themselves with minor identities, in order to come on at all. I haven't the heart now, I confess, to adduce the detail of so many lapsed importances; the explanation of most of which, after all, I take to

have been in the crudity of a truth beating full upon me through
these reconsiderations, the odd inveteracy with which picture, at
almost any turn, is jealous of drama, and drama (though on the
whole with a greater patience, I think) suspicious of picture. Between them, no doubt, they do much for the theme; yet each baf-
fles insidiously the other's ideal and eats round the edges of its
position; each is too ready to say "I can take the thing for 'done'
only when done in *my* way." The residuum of comfort for the witness of these broils is of course meanwhile in the convenient reflexion, invented for him in the twilight of time and the infancy of
art by the Angel, not to say by the Demon, of Compromise, that
nothing is so easy to "do" as not to be thankful for almost any stray
help in its getting done. It wasn't, after this fashion, by making
good one's dream of Lionel Croy that my structure was to stand on
its feet—any more than it was by letting him go that I was to be left
irretrievably lamenting. The who and the what, the how and the
why, the whence and the whither of Merton Densher, these, no
less, were quantities and attributes that should have danced about
him with the antique grace of nymphs and fauns circling round a
bland Hermes* and crowning him with flowers. One's main anxiety, for each one's agents, is that the air of each shall be *given*; but
what does the whole thing become, after all, as one goes, but a
series of sad places at which the hand of generosity has been
cautioned and stayed? The young man's situation, personal, professional, social, was to have been so decanted for us that we
should get all the taste; we were to have been penetrated with Mrs.
Lowder, by the same token, saturated with her presence, her "personality," and felt all her weight in the scale. We were to have rev-
elled in Mrs. Stringham, my heroine's attendant friend, her fairly
choral Bostonian, a subject for innumerable touches, and in an extended and above all an *animated* reflexion of Milly Theale's experience of English society; just as the strength and sense of the
situation in Venice, for our gathered friends, was to have come to
us in a deeper draught out of a larger cup, and just as the pattern
of Densher's final position and fullest consciousness there was to

---

*Greek god, protector of cattle, sheep, and travelers, who was a messenger of the
gods and guided the dead to the underworld; son of Zeus.

have been marked in fine stitches, all silk and gold, all pink and silver, that have had to remain, alas, but entwined upon the reel.

It isn't, no doubt, however—to recover, after all, our critical balance—that the pattern didn't, for each compartment, get itself somehow wrought, and that we mightn't thus, piece by piece, opportunity offering, trace it over and study it. The thing has doubtless, as a whole, the advantage that each piece is true to its pattern, and that while it pretends to make no simple statement it yet never lets go its scheme of clearness. Applications of this scheme are continuous and exemplary enough, though I scarce leave myself room to glance at them. The clearness is obtained in Book First—or otherwise, as I have said, in the first "piece," each Book having its subordinate and contributive pattern—through the associated consciousness of my two prime young persons, for whom I early recognised that I should have to consent, under stress, to a practical *fusion* of consciousness. It is into the young woman's "ken" that Merton Densher is represented as swimming; but her mind is not here, rigorously, the one reflector. There are occasions when it plays this part, just as there are others when his plays it, and an intelligible plan consists naturally not a little in fixing such occasions and making them, on one side and the other, sufficient to themselves. Do I sometimes in fact forfeit the advantage of that distinctness? Do I ever abandon one centre for another after the former has been postulated? From the moment we proceed by "centres"—and I have never, I confess, embraced the logic of any superior process—they must *be*, each, as a basis, selected and fixed; after which it is that, in the high interest of economy of treatment, they determine and rule. There is no economy of treatment without an adopted, a related point of view,[3] and though I understand, under certain degrees of pressure, a represented community of vision between several parties to the action when it makes for concentration, I understand no breaking-up of the register, no sacrifice of the recording consistency, that doesn't rather scatter and weaken. In this truth resides the secret of the discriminated occasion—that aspect of the subject which we have our noted choice of treating either as picture or scenically, but which is apt, I think, to show its fullest worth in the Scene. Beautiful exceedingly, for that matter, those occasions or parts of an occasion when the boundary line between picture and scene bears a little the weight of the double pressure.

Such would be the case, I can't but surmise, for the long passage that forms here before us the opening of Book Fourth, where all the offered life centres, to intensity, in the disclosure of Milly's single throbbing consciousness, but where, for a due rendering, everything has to be brought to a head. This passage, the view of her introduction to Mrs. Lowder's circle, has its mate, for illustration, later on in the book and at a crisis for which the occasion submits to another rule. My registers or "reflectors," as I so conveniently name them (burnished indeed as they generally are by the intelligence, the curiosity, the passion, the force of the moment, whatever it be directing them), work, as we have seen, in arranged alternation; so that in the second connexion I here glance at it is Kate Croy who is; "for all she is worth," turned on. She is turned on largely at Venice, where the appearances, rich and obscure and portentous (another word I rejoice in) as they have by that time become and altogether exquisite as they remain, are treated almost wholly through her vision of them and Densher's (as to the lucid interplay of which conspiring and conflicting agents there would be a great deal to say). It is in Kate's consciousness that at the stage in question the drama is brought to a head, and the occasion on which, in the splendid saloon of poor Milly's hired palace, she takes the measure of her friend's festal evening, squares itself to the same synthetic firmness as the compact constructional block inserted by the scene at Lancaster Gate. Milly's situation ceases at a given moment to be "renderable" in terms closer than those supplied by Kate's intelligence, or, in a richer degree, by Densher's, or, for one fond hour, by poor Mrs. Stringham's (since to that sole brief futility is this last participant, crowned by my original plan with the quaintest functions, in fact reduced); just as Kate's relation with Densher and Densher's with Kate have ceased previously, and are then to cease again, to be projected for us, so far as Milly is concerned with them, on any more responsible plate than that of the latter's admirable anxiety. It is as if, for these aspects, the impersonal plate—in other words the poor author's comparatively cold affirmation or thin guarantee—had felt itself a figure of attestation at once too gross and too bloodless, likely to affect us as an abuse of privilege when not as an abuse of knowledge.

Heaven forbid, we say to ourselves during almost the whole Venetian climax, heaven forbid we should "know" anything more of our ravaged sister than what Densher darkly pieces together, or than what Kate Croy pays, heroically, it must be owned, at the hour of her visit alone to Densher's lodging, for her superior handling and her dire profanation of. For we have time, while this passage lasts, to turn round critically; we have time to recognise intentions and proprieties; we have time to catch glimpses of an economy of composition, as I put it, interesting in itself: all in spite of the author's scarce more than half-dissimulated despair at the inveterate displacement of his general centre. "The Wings of the Dove" happens to offer perhaps the most striking example I may cite (though with public penance for it already performed) of my regular failure to keep the appointed halves of my whole equal. Here the makeshift middle—for which the best I can say is that it's always rueful and never impudent—reigns with even more than its customary contrition, though passing itself off perhaps too with more than its usual craft. Nowhere, I seem to recall, had the need of dissimulation been felt so as anguish; nowhere had I condemned a luckless theme to complete its revolution, burdened with the accumulation of its difficulties, the difficulties that grow with a theme's development, in quarters so cramped. Of course, as every novelist knows, it is difficulty that inspires; only, for that perfection of charm, it must have been difficulty inherent and congenital, and not difficulty "caught" by the wrong frequentations. The latter half, that is the false and deformed half, of "The Wings" would verily, I think, form a signal object-lesson for a literary critic bent on improving his occasion to the profit of the budding artist. This whole corner of the picture bristles with "dodges"—such as he should feel himself all committed to recognise and denounce—for disguising the reduced scale of the exhibition, for foreshortening at any cost, for imparting to patches the value of presences, for dressing objects in an *air* as of the dimensions they can't possibly have. Thus he would have his free hand for pointing out what a tangled web we weave when—well, when, through our mislaying or otherwise trifling with our blest pair of compasses, we have to produce the illusion of mass without the illusion of extent. *There* is a job quite to the measure of most of our monitors—and with the interest for them well enhanced by the preliminary cunning quest for the spot where deformity has begun.

I recognise meanwhile, throughout the long earlier reach of the book, not only no deformities but, I think, a positively close and felicitous application of method, the preserved consistencies of which, often illusive, but never really lapsing, it would be of a certain diversion, and might be of some profit, to follow. The author's accepted task at the outset has been to suggest with force the nature of the tie formed between the two young persons first introduced—to give the full impression of its peculiar worried and baffled, yet clinging and confident, ardour. The picture constituted, so far as may be, is that of a pair of natures well-nigh consumed by a sense of their intimate affinity and congruity, the reciprocity of their desire, and thus passionately impatient of barriers and delays, yet with qualities of intelligence and character that they are meanwhile extraordinarily able to draw upon for the enrichment of their relation, the extension of their prospect and the support of their "game." They are far from a common couple, Merton Densher and Kate Croy, as befits the remarkable fashion in which fortune was to waylay and opportunity was to distinguish them—the whole strange truth of their response to which opening involves also, in its order, no vulgar art of exhibition; but what they have most to tell us is that, all unconsciously and with the best faith in the world, all by mere force of the terms of their superior passion combined with their superior diplomacy, they are laying a trap for the great innocence to come. If I like, as I have confessed, the "portentous" look, I was perhaps never to set so high a value on it as for all this prompt provision of forces unwittingly waiting to close round my eager heroine (to the eventual deep chill of her eagerness) as the result of her mere lifting of a latch. Infinitely interesting to have built up the relation of the others to the point at which its aching restlessness, its need to affirm itself otherwise than by an exasperated patience, meets as with instinctive relief and recognition the possibilities shining out of Milly Theale. Infinitely interesting to have prepared and organised, correspondingly, that young woman's precipitations and liabilities, to have con-

structed, for Drama essentially to take possession, the whole bright
house of her exposure.

These references, however, reflect too little of the detail of the
treatment imposed; such a detail as I for instance get hold of in the
fact of Densher's interview with Mrs. Lowder before he goes to
America. It forms, in this preliminary picture, the one patch not
strictly seen over Kate Croy's shoulder; though it's notable that immediately after, at the first possible moment, we surrender again to
our major convenience, as it happens to be at the time, that of our
drawing breath through the young woman's lungs. Once more, in
other words, before we know it, Densher's direct vision of the
scene at Lancaster Gate is replaced by her apprehension, her contributive assimilation, of his experience: it melts back into that accumulation, which we have been, as it were, saving up. Does my
apparent deviation here count accordingly as a muddle?—one of
the muddles ever blooming so thick in any soil that fails to grow
reasons and determinants. No, distinctly not; for I had definitely
opened the door, as attention of perusal of the first two Books will
show, to the subjective community of my young pair. (Attention of
perusal, I thus confess by the way, is what I at every point, as well
as here, absolutely invoke and take for granted; a truth I avail myself of this occasion to note once for all—in the interest of that variety of ideal reigning, I gather, in the connexion. The enjoyment
of a work of art, the acceptance of an irresistible illusion, constituting, to my sense, our highest experience of "luxury," the luxury
is not greatest, by my consequent measure, when the work asks for
as little attention as possible. It is greatest, it is delightfully, divinely
great, when we feel the surface, like the thick ice of the skater's
pond, bear without cracking the strongest pressure we throw on it.
The sound of the crack one may recognise, but never surely to call
it a luxury.) That I had scarce availed myself of the privilege of seeing with Densher's eyes is another matter; the point is that I had
intelligently marked my possible, my occasional need of it. So, at
all events, the constructional "block" of the first two Books com-
pactly forms itself. A new block, all of the squarest and not a little
of the smoothest, begins with the Third—by which I mean of
course a new mass of interest governed from a new centre. Here
again I make prudent *provision*—to be sure to keep my centre

strong. It dwells mainly, we at once see, in the depths of Milly Theale's "case," where, close beside it, however, we meet a supplementary reflector, that of the lucid even though so quivering spirit of her dedicated friend.

The more or less associated consciousness of the two women deals thus, unequally, with the next presented face of the subject—deals with it to the exclusion of the dealing of others; and if, for a highly particular moment, I allot to Mrs. Stringham the responsibility of the direct appeal to us, it is again, charming to relate, on behalf of that play of the portentous which I cherish so as a "value" and am accordingly for ever setting in motion. There is an hour of evening, on the alpine height, at which it becomes of the last importance that our young woman should testify eminently in this direction. But as I was to find it long since of a blest wisdom that no expense should be incurred or met, in any corner of picture of mine, without some concrete image of the account kept of it, that is of its being organically re-economised, so under that dispensation Mrs. Stringham has to register the transaction. Book Fifth is a new block mainly in its provision of a new set of occasions, which readopt, for their order, the previous centre, Milly's now almost full-blown consciousness. At my game, with renewed zest, of driving portents home, I have by this time all the choice of those that are to brush that surface with a dark wing. They are used, to our profit, on an elastic but a definite system; by which I mean that having to sound here and there a little deep, as a test, for my basis of method, I find it everywhere obstinately present. It draws the "occasion" into tune and keeps it so, to repeat my tiresome term; my nearest approach to muddlement is to have sometimes—but not too often—to break my occasions small. Some of them succeed in remaining ample and in really aspiring then to the higher, the sustained lucidity. The whole actual centre of the work, resting on a misplaced pivot and lodged in Book Fifth, pretends to a long reach, or at any rate to the larger foreshortening— though bringing home to me, on reperusal, what I find striking, charming and curious, the author's instinct everywhere for the *indirect* presentation of his main image. I note how, again and again, I go but a little way with the direct—that is with the straight exhibition of Milly; it resorts for relief, this process, whenever it can, to some kinder, some merciful indirection: all as if to approach her circuitously, deal with her at second hand, as an unspotted princess is ever dealt with; the pressure all round her kept easy for her, the sounds, the movements regulated, the forms and ambiguities made charming. All of which proceeds, obviously, from her painter's tenderness of imagination about her, which reduces him to watching her, as it were, through the successive windows of other people's interest in her. So, if we talk of princesses, do the balconies opposite the palace gates, do the coigns of vantage and respect enjoyed for a fee, rake from afar the mystic figure in the gilded coach as it comes forth into the great *place*. But my use of windows and balconies is doubtless at best an extravagance by itself, and as to what there may be to note, of this and other super-subtleties, other arch-refinements, of tact and taste, of design and instinct, in "The Wings of the Dove," I become conscious of over-stepping my space without having brought the full quantity to light. The failure leaves me with a burden of residuary comment of which I yet boldly hope elsewhere to discharge myself.

HENRY JAMES

VOLUME I

BOOK FIRST

— I —

She waited, Kate Croy, for her father to come in, but he kept her unconscionably, and there were moments at which she showed herself, in the glass over the mantel, a face positively pale with the irritation that had brought her to the point of going away without sight of him. It was at this point, however, that she remained; changing her place, moving from the shabby sofa to the armchair upholstered in a glazed cloth that gave at once—she had tried it—the sense of the slippery and of the sticky. She had looked at the sallow prints on the walls and at the lonely magazine, a year old, that combined, with a small lamp in coloured glass and a knitted white centre-piece wanting in freshness, to enhance the effect of the purplish cloth on the principal table; she had above all from time to time taken a brief stand on the small balcony to which the pair of long windows gave access. The vulgar little street, in this view, offered scant relief from the vulgar little room; its main office was to suggest to her that the narrow black house-fronts, adjusted to a standard that would have been low even for backs, constituted quite the publicity implied by such privacies. One felt them in the room exactly as one felt the room—the hundred like it or worse—in the street. Each time she turned in again, each time, in her impatience, she gave him up, it was to sound to a deeper depth, while she tasted the faint flat emanation of things, the failure of fortune and of honour. If she continued to wait it was really in a manner that she mightn't add the shame of fear, of individual, of personal collapse, to all the other shames. To feel the street, to feel the room, to feel the table-cloth and the centre-piece and the lamp, gave her a small salutary sense at least of neither shirking nor lying. This whole vision was the worse thing yet—as including in particular the interview to which she had braced herself; and for what had she come but for the worst? She tried to be sad so as not to be angry, but it made her angry that she couldn't be sad. And yet where was misery, misery too beaten for blame and chalk-marked by fate like a "lot" at a common auction, if not in these merciless signs of mere mean stale feelings?

Her father's life, her sister's, her own, that of her two lost brothers—the whole history of their house had the effect of some fine florid voluminous phrase, say even a musical, that dropped first into words and notes without sense and then, hanging unfinished, into no words or any notes at all. Why should a set of people have been put in motion, on such a scale and with such an air of being equipped for a profitable journey, only to break down without an accident, to stretch themselves in the wayside dust without a reason? The answer to these questions was not in Chirk Street, but the questions themselves bristled there, and the girl's repeated pause before the mirror and the chimney-place might have represented her nearest approach to an escape from them. Wasn't it in fact the partial escape from this "worst" in which she was steeped to be able to make herself out again as agreeable to see? She stared into the tarnished glass too hard indeed to be staring at her beauty alone. She readjusted the poise of her black closely-feathered hat; retouched, beneath it, the thick fall of her dusky hair; kept her eyes aslant no less on her beautiful averted than on her beautiful presented oval. She was dressed altogether in black, which gave an even tone, by contrast, to her clear face and made her hair more harmoniously dark. Outside, on the balcony, her eyes showed as blue; within, at the mirror, they showed almost as black. She was handsome, but the degree of it was not sustained by items and aids; a circumstance moreover playing its part at almost any time in the impression she produced. The impression was one that remained, but as regards the sources of it no sum in addition would have made up the total. She had stature without height, grace without motion, presence without mass. Slender and simple, frequently soundless, she was somehow always in the line of the eye—she counted singularly for its pleasure. More "dressed," often, with fewer accessories, than other women, or less dressed, should occasion require, with more, she probably couldn't have given the key to these felicities. They were mysteries of which her friends were conscious—those friends whose general explanation was to say that she was clever, whether or not it were taken by the world as the cause or as the effect of her charm. If she saw more things than her fine face in the dull glass of her father's lodgings she might have seen that after all she was not herself a fact in the collapse. She didn't hold herself cheap, she didn't make for misery. Personally, no, she wasn't chalk-marked for auction. She hadn't given up yet, and the broken sentence, if she was the last word, *would* end with a sort of meaning. There was a minute during which, though her eyes were fixed, she quite visibly lost herself in the thought of the way she might still pull things round had she only been a man. It was the name, above all, she would take in hand—the precious name she so liked and that, in spite of the harm her wretched father had done it, wasn't yet past praying for. She loved it in fact the more tenderly for that bleeding wound. But what could a penniless girl do with it but let it go?

When her father at last appeared she became, as usual, instantly aware of the futility of any effort to hold him to anything. He had written her he was ill, too ill to leave his room, and that he must see her without delay; and if this had been, as was probable, the sketch of a design he was indifferent even to the moderate finish required for deception. He had clearly wanted, for the perversities he called his reasons, to see her, just as she herself had sharpened for a talk; but she now again felt, in the inevitability of the freedom he used with her, all the old ache, her poor mother's very own, that he couldn't touch you ever so lightly without setting up. No relation with him could be so short or so superficial as not to be somehow to your hurt; and this, in the strangest way in the world, not because he desired it to be—feeling often, as he surely must, the profit for him of its not being—but because there was never a mistake for you that he could leave unmade, nor a conviction of his impossibility in you that he could approach you without strengthening. He might have awaited her on the sofa in his sitting-room, or might have stayed in bed and received her in that situation. She was glad to be spared the sight of such penetralia, but it would have reminded her a little less that there was no truth in him. This was the weariness of every fresh meeting; he dealt out lies as he might the cards from the greasy old pack for the game of diplomacy to which you were to sit down with him. The inconvenience—as always happens in such cases—was not that you minded what was false, but that you missed what was true.

He might be ill and it might suit you to know it, but no contact
with him, for this, could ever be straight enough. Just so he even
might die, but Kate fairly wondered on what evidence of his own
she would some day have to believe it.

He had not at present come down from his room, which she
knew to be above the one they were in: he had already been out of
the house, though he would either, should she challenge him,
deny it or present it as a proof of his extremity. She had, however,
by this time, quite ceased to challenge him; not only, face to face
with him, vain irritation dropped, but he breathed upon the tragic
consciousness in such a way that after a moment nothing of it was
left. The difficulty was not less that he breathed in the same way
upon the comic: she almost believed that with this latter she might
still have found a foothold for clinging to him. He had ceased to
be amusing—he was really too inhuman. His perfect look, which
had floated him so long, was practically perfect still; but one had
long since for every occasion taken it for granted. Nothing could
have better shown than the actual how right one had been. He
looked exactly as much as usual—all pink and silver as to skin and
hair, all straightness and starch as to figure and dress; the man in
the world least connected with anything unpleasant. He was so
particularly the English gentleman and the fortunate settled normal person. Seen at a foreign table d'hôte he suggested but one
thing: "In what perfection England produces them!" He had kind
safe eyes, and a voice which, for all its clean fulness, told the quiet
tale of its having never had once to raise itself. Life had met him
so, halfway, and had turned round so to walk with him, placing a
hand in his arm and fondly leaving him to choose the pace. Those
who knew him a little said "How he does dress!"—those who knew
him better said "How *does* he?" The one stray gleam of comedy
just now in his daughter's eyes was the absurd feeling he momentarily made her have of being herself "looked up" by him in sordid
lodgings. For a minute after he came in it was as if the place were
her own and he the visitor with susceptibilities. He gave you absurd feelings, he had indescribable arts, that quite turned the tables: this had been always how he came to see her mother so long
as her mother would see him. He came from places they had often
not known about, but he patronised Lexham Gardens. Kate's only

actual expression of impatience, however, was "I'm glad you're so much better!"

"I'm not so much better, my dear—I'm exceedingly unwell; the proof of which is precisely that I've been out to the chemist's—that beastly fellow at the corner." So Mr. Croy showed he could qualify the humble hand that assuaged him. "I'm taking something he has made up for me. It's just why I've sent for you—that you may see me as I really am."

"Oh papa, it's long since I've ceased to see you otherwise than as you really are! I think we've all arrived by this time at the right word for that: 'You're beautiful—*n'en parlons plus*.'* You're as beautiful as ever—you look lovely." He judged meanwhile her own appearance, as she knew she could always trust him to do; recognising, estimating, sometimes disapproving, what she wore, showing her the interest he continued to take in her. He might really take none at all, yet she virtually knew herself the creature in the world to whom he was least indifferent. She had often enough wondered what on earth, at the pass he had reached, could give him pleasure, and had come back on these occasions to that. It gave him pleasure that she was handsome, that she was in her way a tangible value. It was at least as marked, nevertheless, that he derived none from similar conditions, so far as they *were* similar, in his other child. Poor Marian might be handsome, but he certainly didn't care. The hitch here of course was that, with whatever beauty, her sister, widowed and almost in want, with four bouncing children, had no such measure. She asked him the next thing how long he had been in his actual quarters, though aware of how little it mattered, how little any answer he might make would probably have in common with the truth. She failed in fact to notice his answer, truthful or not, already occupied as she was with what she had on her own side to say to him. This was really what had made her wait—what superseded the small remainder of her resentment at his constant practical impertinence; the result of all of which was that within a minute she had brought it out. "Yes—even now I'm willing to go with you. I don't know what you

---

*Let's not speak of it further (French).

may have wished to say to me, and even if you hadn't written you would within a day or two have heard from me. Things have happened, and I've only waited, for seeing you, till I should be quite sure. I *am* quite sure. I'll go with you."

It produced an effect. "Go with me where?"

"Anywhere. I'll stay with you. Even here." She had taken off her gloves and, as if she had arrived with her plan, she sat down.

Lionel Croy hung about in his disengaged way—hovered there as if looking, in consequence of her words, for a pretext to back out easily: on which she immediately saw she had discounted, as it might be called, what he had himself been preparing. He wished her not to come to him, still less to settle with him, and had sent for her to give her up with some style and state; a part of the beauty of which, however, was to have been his sacrifice to her own detachment. There was no style, no state, unless she wished to forsake him. His idea had accordingly been to surrender her to her wish with all nobleness; it had by no means been to have positively to keep her off. She cared, however, not a straw for his embarrassment—feeling how little, on her own part, she was moved by charity. She had seen him, first and last, in so many attitudes that she could now deprive him quite without compunction of the luxury of a new one. Yet she felt the disconcerted gasp in his tone as he said: "Oh my child, I can never consent to that!"

"What then are you going to do?"

"I'm turning it over," said Lionel Croy. "You may imagine if I'm not thinking."

"Haven't you thought then," his daughter asked, "of what I speak of? I mean of my being ready."

Standing before her with his hands behind him and his legs a little apart, he swayed slightly to and fro, inclined toward her as if rising on his toes. It had an effect of conscientious deliberation. "No—I haven't. I couldn't. I wouldn't." It was so respectable a show that she felt afresh, and with the memory of their old despair, the despair at home, how little, his appearance ever by any chance told about him. His plausibility had been the heaviest of her mother's crosses; inevitably so much more present to the world than whatever it was that was horrid—thank God they didn't really know!—that he had done. He had positively been, in his way, by the force of his particular type, a terrible husband not to live with; this type reflecting so invidiously on the woman who had found him distasteful. Had this thereby not kept directly present to Kate herself that it might, on some sides, prove no light thing for her to leave uncompanion'd a parent with such a face and such a manner? Yet if there was much she neither knew nor dreamed of it passed between them at this very moment that he was quite familiar with himself as the subject of such quandaries. If he recognised his younger daughter's happy aspect as a tangible value, he had from the first still more exactly appraised every point of his own. The great wonder was not that in spite of everything these points had helped him; the great wonder was that they hadn't helped him more. However, it was, to its eternal recurrent tune, helping him all the while; her drop into patience with him showed how it was helping him at this moment. She saw the next instant precisely the line he would take. "Do you really ask me to believe you've been making up your mind to that?"

She had to consider her own line. "I don't think I care, papa, what you believe. I never, for that matter, think of you as believing anything; hardly more," she permitted herself to add, "than I ever think of you as yourself believed. I don't know you, father, you see."

"And it's your idea that you may make that up?"

"Oh dear, no; not at all. That's no part of the question. If I haven't understood you by this time I never shall, and it doesn't matter. It has seemed to me you may be lived with, but not that you may be understood. Of course I've not the least idea how you get on."

"I don't get on," Mr. Croy almost gaily replied.

His daughter took the place in again, and it might well have seemed odd that with so little to meet the eye there should be so much to show. What showed was the ugliness—so positive and palpable that it was somehow sustaining. It was a medium, a setting, and to that extent, after all, a dreadful sign of life; so that it fairly gave point to her answer. "Oh I beg your pardon. You flourish."

"Do you throw it up at me again," he pleasantly put to her, "that I've not made away with myself?"

She treated the question as needing no reply; she sat there for real things. "You know how all our anxieties, under mamma's will, have come out. She had still less to leave than she feared. We don't know how we lived. It all makes up about two hundred a year for Marian, and two for me, but I give up a hundred to Marian."

"Oh you weak thing!" her father sighed as from depths of enlightened experience.

"For you and me together," she went on, "the other hundred would do something."

"And what would do the rest?"

"Can you yourself do nothing?"

He gave her a look; then, slipping his hands into his pockets and turning away, stood for a little at the window she had left open. She said nothing more—she had placed him there with that question, and the silence lasted a minute, broken by the call of an appealing costermonger, which came in with the mild March air, with the shabby sunshine, fearfully unbecoming to the room, and with the small homely hum of Chirk Street. Presently he moved nearer, but as if her question had quite dropped. "I don't see what has so suddenly wound you up."

"I should have thought you might perhaps guess. Let me at any rate tell you. Aunt Maud has made me a proposal. But she has also made me a condition. She wants to keep me."

"And what in the world else *could* she possibly want?"

"Oh I don't know—many things. I'm not so precious a capture," the girl a little dryly explained. "No one has ever wanted to keep me before."

Looking always what was proper, her father looked now still more surprised than interested. "You've not had proposals?" He spoke as if that were incredible of Lionel Croy's daughter; as if indeed such an admission scarce consorted, even in filial intimacy, with her high spirit and general form.

"Not from rich relations. She's extremely kind to me, but it's time, she says, that we should understand each other."

Mr. Croy fully assented. "Of course it is—high time; and I can quite imagine what she means by it."

"Are you very sure?"

"Oh perfectly. She means that she'll 'do' for you handsomely if you'll break off all relations with me. You speak of her condition. Her condition's of course that."

"Well then," said Kate, "it's what has wound me up. Here I am."

He showed with a gesture how thoroughly he had taken it in; after which, within a few seconds, he had quite congruously turned the situation about. "Do you really suppose me in a position to justify your throwing yourself upon me?"

She waited a little, but when she spoke it was clear. "Yes."

"Well then, you're of feebler intelligence than I should have ventured to suppose you."

"Why so? You live. You flourish. You bloom."

"Ah how you've all always hated me!" he murmured with a pensive gaze again at the window.

"No one could be less of a mere cherished memory," she declared as if she had not heard him. "You're an actual person, if there ever was one. We agreed just now that you're beautiful. You strike me, you know, as—in your own way—much more firm on your feet than I. Don't put it to me therefore as monstrous that the fact that we're after all parent and child should at present in some manner count for us. My idea has been that it should have some effect for each of us. I don't at all, as I told you just now," she pursued, "make out your life; but whatever it is I hereby offer to accept it. And, on my side, I'll do everything I can for you."

"I see," said Lionel Croy. Then with the sound of extreme relevance: "And what *can* you?" She only, at this, hesitated, and he took up her silence. "You can describe yourself—*to* yourself—as, in a fine flight, giving up your aunt for me; but what good, I should like to know, would your fine flight do me?" As she still said nothing he developed a little. "We're not possessed of so much, at this charming pass, please to remember, as that we can afford not to take hold of any perch held out to us. I like the way you talk, my dear, about "giving up"! One doesn't give up the use of a spoon because one's reduced to living on broth. And your spoon, that is your aunt, please consider, is partly mine as well." She rose now, as if in sight of the term of her effort, in sight of the futility and the weariness of many things, and moved back to the poor little glass with which she had communed before. She retouched here again the poise of her hat, and this brought to her father's lips another remark—in which impatience, however, had already been re-placed by a free flare of appreciation. "Oh you're all right! Don't muddle yourself up with *me!*"

His daughter turned round to him. "The condition Aunt Maud makes is that I shall have absolutely nothing to do with you; never see you, nor speak nor write to you, never go near you nor make you a sign, nor hold any sort of communication with you. What she requires is that you shall simply cease to exist for me."

He had always seemed—it was one of the marks of what they called the "unspeakable" in him—to walk a little more on his toes, as if for jauntiness, under the touch of offence. Nothing, however, was more wonderful than what he sometimes would take for of-fence, unless it might be what he sometimes wouldn't. He walked at any rate on his toes now. "A very proper requirement of your Aunt Maud, my dear—I don't hesitate to say it!" Yet as this, much as she had seen, left her silent at first from what might have been a sense of sickness, he had time to go on: "That's her condition then. But what are her promises? Just what does she engage to do? You must work it, you know."

"You mean make her feel," Kate asked after a moment, "how much I'm attached to you?"

"Well, what a cruel invidious treaty it is for you to sign. I'm a poor ruin of an old dad to make a stand about giving up—I quite agree. But I'm not, after all, quite the old ruin not to get something *for* giving up."

"Oh I think her idea," said Kate almost gaily now, "is that I shall get a great deal."

He met her with his inimitable amenity. "But does she give you the items?"

The girl went through the show. "More or less, I think. But many of them are things I dare say I may take for granted—things women can do for each other and that you wouldn't understand."

"There's nothing I understand so well, always, as the things I needn't! But what I want to do, you see," he went on, "is to put it to your conscience that you've an admirable opportunity; and that it's moreover one for which, after all, damn you, you've really to thank *me.*"

"I confess I don't see," Kate observed, "what my 'conscience' has to do with it."

"Then, my dear girl, you ought simply to be ashamed of yourself. Do you know what you're a proof of, all you hard hollow people together?" He put the question with a charming air of sudden spiritual heat. "Of the deplorably superficial morality of the age. The family sentiment, in our vulgarised brutalised life, has gone utterly to pot. There was a day when a man like me—by which I mean a parent like me—would have been for a daughter like you quite a distinct value; what's called in the business world, I believe, an 'asset.'"[4] He continued sociably to make it out. "I'm not talking only of what you might, with the right feeling, do *for* me, but of what you might—it's what I call your opportunity—do *with* me. Unless indeed," he the next moment imperturbably threw off, "they come a good deal to the same thing. Your duty as well as your chance, if you're capable of seeing it, is to use me. Show family feeling by seeing what I'm good for. If you had it as *I* have it you'd see I'm still good—well, for a lot of things. There's in fact, my dear," Mr. Croy wound up, "a coach-and-four* to be got out of me." His lapse, or rather his climax, failed a little of effect indeed through an undue precipitation of memory. Something his daughter had said came back to him. "You've settled to give away half your little inheritance?"

Her hesitation broke into laughter. "No—I haven't 'settled' anything."

"But you mean practically to let Marian collar it?" They stood there face to face, but she so denied herself to his challenge that he could only go on. "You've a view of three hundred a year for her in addition to what her husband left her with? Is *that*," the remote progenitor of such wantonness audibly wondered, "your morality?"

Kate found her answer without trouble. "Is it your idea that I should give you everything?"

The "everything" clearly struck him—to the point even of determining the tone of his reply. "Far from it. How can you ask that when I refuse what you tell me you came to offer? Make of my idea what you can; I think I've sufficiently expressed it, and it's at any rate to take or to leave. It's the only one, I may nevertheless add; it's the basket with all my eggs. It's my conception, in short, of your duty."

The girl's tired smile watched the word as if it had taken on a small grotesque visibility. "You're wonderful on such subjects! I think I should leave you in no doubt," she pursued, "that if I were to sign my aunt's agreement I should carry it out, in honour, to the letter."

"Rather, my own love! It's just your honour that I appeal to. The only way to play the game *is* to play it. There's no limit to what your aunt can do for you."

"Do you mean in the way of marrying me?"

"What else should I mean? Marry properly—"

"And then?" Kate asked as he hung fire.

"And then—well, I *will* talk with you. I'll resume relations."

She looked about her and picked up her parasol. "Because you're not so afraid of any one else in the world as you are of *her*? My husband, if I should marry, would be at the worst less of a terror? If that's what you mean there may be something in it. But doesn't it depend a little also on what you mean by my getting a proper one? However," Kate added as she picked out the frill of her little umbrella, "I don't suppose your idea of him is *quite* that he should persuade you to live with us."

"Dear no—not a bit." He spoke as not resenting either the fear or the hope she imputed; met both imputations in fact with a sort of intellectual relief. "I place the case for you wholly in your aunt's hands. I take her view with my eyes shut; I accept in all confidence any man she selects. If he's good enough for *her*—elephantine snob as she is—he's good enough for me; and quite in spite of the fact that she'll be sure to select one who can be trusted to be nasty to me. My only interest is in your doing what she wants. You shan't be so beastly poor, my darling," Mr. Croy declared, "if I can help it."

"Well then good-bye, papa," the girl said after a reflexion on this that had perceptibly ended for her in a renunciation of further debate. "Of course you understand that it may be for long."

Her companion had hereupon one of his finest inspirations. "Why not frankly for ever? You must do me the justice to see that I don't do things, that I've never done them, by halves—that if I offer you to efface myself it's for the final fatal sponge I ask, well saturated and well applied."

She turned her handsome quiet face upon him at such length that it might indeed have been for the last time. "I don't know what you're like."

"No more do I, my dear. I've spent my life in trying in vain to discover. Like nothing—more's the pity. If there had been many of us and we could have found each other out there's no knowing what we mightn't have done. But it doesn't matter now. Good-bye, love." He looked even not sure of what she would wish him to suppose on the subject of a kiss, yet also not embarrassed by his uncertainty.

She forbore in fact for a moment longer to clear it up. "I wish there were some one here who might serve—for any contingency—as a witness that I *have* put it to you that I'm ready to come."

"Would you like me," her father asked, "to call the landlady?"

"You may not believe me," she pursued, "but I came really hoping you might have found some way. I'm very sorry at all events to leave you unwell." He turned away from her on this and, as he had done before, took refuge, by the window, in a stare at the street. "Let me put it—unfortunately without a witness," she added after a moment, "that there's only one word you really need speak."

When he took these words up it was still with his back to her. "If I don't strike you as having already spoken it our time has been singularly wasted."

"I'll engage with you in respect to my aunt exactly to what she wants of me in respect to you. She wants me to choose. Very well, I *will* choose. I'll wash my hands of her for you to just that tune."

He at last brought himself round. "Do you know, dear, you make me sick? I've tried to be clear, and it isn't fair."

But she passed this over; she was too visibly sincere. "Father!"

"I don't quite see what's the matter with you," he said, "and if you can't pull yourself together I'll—upon my honour—take you in hand. Put you into a cab and deliver you again safe at Lancaster Gate."*

She was really absent, distant. "Father."

It was too much, and he met it sharply. "Well?"

"Strange as it may be to you to hear me say it, there's a good you can do me and a help you can render."

"Isn't it then exactly what I've been trying to make you feel?"

"Yes," she answered patiently, "but so in the wrong way. I'm perfectly honest in what I say, and I know what I'm talking about. It isn't that I'll pretend I could have believed a month ago in anything to call aid or support from you. The case is changed—that's what has happened; my difficulty is a new one. But even now it's not a question of anything I should ask you in a way to 'do.' It's simply a question of your not turning me away—taking yourself out of my life. It's simply a question of your saying: 'Yes then, since you will, we'll stand together. We won't worry in advance about how or where; we'll have a faith and find a way.' That's all—*that* would be the good you'd do me. I should *have* you, and it would be for my benefit. Do you see?"

If he didn't it wasn't for want of looking at her hard. "The matter with you is that you're in love, and that your aunt knows and—for reasons, I'm sure, perfect—hates and opposes it. Well she may! It's a matter in which I trust her with my eyes shut. Go, please." Though he spoke not in anger—rather in infinite sadness—he fairly turned her out. Before she took it up he had, as the fullest expression of what he felt, opened the door of the room. He had fairly, in his deep disapproval, a generous compassion to spare. "I'm sorry for her; deluded woman, if she builds on you."

Kate stood a moment in the draught. "She's not the person *I* pity most, for, deluded in many ways though she may be, she's not the person who's most so. I mean," she explained, "if it's a question of what you call building on me."

He took it as if what she meant might be other than her description of it. "You're deceiving *two* persons then, Mrs. Lowder and somebody else?"

---

*Aunt Maud Lowder's elegant house, a mansion on Hyde Park and Kensington Gardens, in an upper-crust section of London.

She shook her head with detachment. "I've no intention of that sort with respect to any one now—to Mrs. Lowder least of all. If you fail me"—she seemed to make it out for herself—"that has the merit at least that it simplifies. I shall go my way—as I see my way."

"Your way, you mean then, will be to marry some blackguard without a penny?"

"You demand a great deal of satisfaction," she observed, "for the little you give."

It brought him up again before her as with a sense that she was not to be hustled, and though he glared at her a little this had long been the practical limit to his general power of objection. "If you're base enough to incur your aunt's reprobation you're base enough for my argument. What, if you're not thinking of an utterly improper person, do your speeches to me signify? Who *is* the beggarly sneak?" he went on as her response failed.

Her response, when it came, was cold but distinct. "He has every disposition to make the best of you. He only wants in fact to be kind to you."

"Then he *must* be an ass! And how in the world can you consider it to improve him for me," her father pursued, "that he's also destitute and impossible? There are boobies and boobies even—the right and the wrong—and you appear to have carefully picked out one of the wrong. Your aunt knows *them*, by good fortune; I perfectly trust, as I tell you, her judgement for them; and you may take it from me once for all that I won't hear of any one of whom *she* won't." Which led up to his last word. "If you should really defy us both—!"

"Well, papa?"

"Well, my sweet child, I think that—reduced to insignificance as you may fondly believe me—I should still not be quite without some way of making you regret it."

She had a pause, a grave one, but not, as appeared, that she might measure this danger. "If I shouldn't do it, you know, it wouldn't be because I'm afraid of you."

"Oh if you don't do it," he retorted, "you may be as bold as you like!"

"Then you can do nothing at all for me?"

He showed her, this time unmistakeably—it was before her

there on the landing, at the top of the tortuous stairs and in the midst of the strange smell that seemed to cling to them—how vain her appeal remained. "I've never pretended to do more than my duty; I've given you the best and the clearest advice." And then came up the spring that moved him. "If it only displeases you, you can go to Marian to be consoled." What he couldn't forgive was her dividing with Marian her scant share of the provision their mother had been able to leave them. She should have divided it with *him*.

— II —

She had gone to Mrs. Lowder on her mother's death—gone with an effort the strain and pain of which made her at present, as she recalled them, reflect on the long way she had travelled since then. There had been nothing else to do—not a penny in the other house, nothing but unpaid bills that had gathered thick while its mistress lay mortally ill, and the admonition that there was nothing she must attempt to raise money on, since everything belonged to the "estate." How the estate would turn out at best presented itself as a mystery altogether gruesome; it had proved in fact since then a residuum a trifle less scant than, with her sister, she had for some weeks feared; but the girl had had at the beginning rather a wounded sense of its being watched on behalf of Marian and her children. What on earth was it supposed that *she* wanted to do to it? She wanted in truth only to give up— to abandon her own interest, which she doubtless would already have done hadn't the point been subject to Aunt Maud's sharp intervention. Aunt Maud's intervention was all sharp now, and the other point, the great one, was that it was to be, in this light, either all put up with or all declined. Yet at the winter's end, nevertheless, she could scarce have said what stand she conceived she had taken. It wouldn't be the first time she had seen herself obliged to accept with smothered irony other people's interpretation of her conduct. She often ended by giving up to them—it seemed really the way to live—the version that met their convenience.

The tall rich heavy house at Lancaster Gate, on the other side of the Park and the long South Kensington stretches, had figured to her, through childhood, through girlhood, as the remotest limit of her vague young world. It was further off and more occasional than anything else in the comparatively compact circle in which she revolved, and seemed, by a rigour early marked, to be reached through long, straight, discouraging vistas, perfect telescopes of streets, and which kept lengthening and straightening, whereas almost everything else in life was either at the worst roundabout Cromwell Road or at the furthest in the nearer parts of Kensington Gardens. Mrs. Lowder was her only "real" aunt, not the wife of an uncle, and had been thereby, both in ancient days and when the greater trouble came, the person, of all persons, properly to make some sign; in accord with which our young woman's feeling was founded on the impression, quite cherished for years, that the signs made across the interval just mentioned had never been really in the note of the situation. The main office of this relative for the young Croys—apart from giving them their fixed measure of social greatness—had struck them as being to form them to a conception of what they were not to expect. When Kate came to think matters over with wider knowledge, she failed quite to see how Aunt Maud could have been different—she had rather perceived by this time how many other things might have been; yet she also made out that if they had all consciously lived under a liability to the chill breath of *ultima Thule** they couldn't, either, on the facts, very well have done less. What in the event appeared established was that if Mrs. Lowder had disliked them she yet hadn't disliked them so much as they supposed. It had at any rate been for the purpose of showing how she struggled with her aversion that she sometimes came to see them, that she at regular periods invited them to her house and in short, as it now looked, kept them along on the terms that would best give her sister the perennial luxury of a grievance. This sister, poor Mrs. Croy, the girl knew, had always judged her resentfully, and had brought them up, Marian, the boys and herself, to the idea of a particular attitude, for

---

*Latin name for the outermost limit of the inhabited world; hence, barren and cold.

signs of the practice of which they watched each other with awe. The attitude was to make plain to Aunt Maud, with the same regularity as her invitations, that they sufficed—thanks awfully—to themselves. But the ground of it, Kate lived to discern, was that this was only because *she* didn't suffice to them. The little she offered was to be accepted under protest, yet not really because it was excessive. It wounded them—there was the rub!—because it fell short.

The number of new things our young lady looked out on from the high south window that hung over the Park—this number was so great (though some of the things were only old ones altered and, as the phrase was of other matters, done up) that life at present turned to her view from week to week more and more the face of a striking and distinguished stranger. She had reached a great age—for it quite seemed to her that at twenty-five it was late to reconsider, and her most general sense was a shade of regret that she hadn't known earlier. The world was different—whether for worse or for better—from her rudimentary readings, and it gave her the feeling of a wasted past. If she had only known sooner she might have arranged herself more to meet it. She made at all events discoveries every day, some of which were about herself and others about other persons. Two of these—one under each head—more particularly engaged, in alternation, her anxiety. She saw as she had never seen before how material things spoke to her. She saw, and she blushed to see, that if in contrast with some of its old aspects life now affected her as a dress successfully "done up," this was exactly by reason of the trimmings and lace, was a matter of ribbons and silk and velvet. She had a dire accessibility to pleasure from such sources. She liked the charming quarters her aunt had assigned her—liked them literally more than she had in all her other days liked anything; and nothing could have been more uneasy than her suspicion of her relative's view of this truth. Her relative was prodigious—she had never done her relative justice. These larger conditions all tasted of her, from morning till night; but she was a person in respect to whom the growth of acquaintance could only—strange as it might seem—keep your heart in your mouth.

The girl's second great discovery was that, so far from having

been for Mrs. Lowder a subject of superficial consideration, the
blighted home in Lexham Gardens had haunted her nights and
her days. Kate had spent, all winter, hours of observation that were
not less pointed for being spent alone; recent events, which her
mourning explained, assured her a measure of isolation, and it was
in the isolation above all that her neighbour's influence worked.
Sitting far downstairs Aunt Maud was yet a presence from which a
sensitive niece could feel herself extremely under pressure. She
knew herself now, the sensitive niece, as having been marked from
far back. She knew more than she could have told you, by the upstairs fire, in a whole dark December afternoon. She knew so
much that her knowledge was what fairly kept her there, making
her at times circulate more endlessly between the small silk-
covered sofa that stood for her in the firelight and the great grey
map of Middlesex spread beneath her lookout. To go down, to forsake her refuge, was to meet some of her discoveries halfway, to
have to face them or fly before them; whereas they were at such a
height only like the rumble of a far-off siege heard in the provisioned citadel. She had almost liked, in these weeks, what had created her suspense and her stress: the loss of her mother, the
submersion of her father, the discomfort of her sister, and confirmation of their shrunken prospects, the certainty, in especial, of
her having to recognise that should she behave, as she called it, decently—that is still do something for others—she would be herself
wholly without supplies. She held that she had a right to sadness
and stillness; she nursed them for their postponing power. What
they mainly postponed was the question of a surrender, though she
couldn't yet have said exactly of what: a general surrender of everything—that was at moments the way it presented itself—to Aunt
Maud's looming "personality." It was by her personality that Aunt
Maud was prodigious, and the great mass of it loomed because, in
the thick, the foglike air of her arranged existence, there were parts
doubtless magnified and parts certainly vague. They represented
at all events alike, the dim and the distinct, a strong will and a high
hand. It was perfectly present to Kate that she might be devoured,
and she compared herself to a trembling kid, kept apart a day or
two till her turn should come, but sure sooner or later to be introduced into the cage of the lioness.

The cage was Aunt Maud's own room, her office, her counting-house, her battlefield, her especial scene, in fine, of action, situated on the ground-floor, opening from the main hall and figuring rather to our young woman on exit and entrance as a guard-house or a toll-gate. The lioness waited—the kid had at least that consciousness; was aware of the neighbourhood of a morsel she had reason to suppose tender. She would have been meanwhile a wonderful lioness for a show, an extraordinary figure in a cage or anywhere; majestic, magnificent, high-coloured, all brilliant gloss, perpetual satin, twinkling bugles and flashing gems, with a lustre of agate eyes, a sheen of raven hair, a polish of complexion that was like that of well-kept china and that—as if the skin were too tight—told especially at curves and corners. Her niece had a quiet name for her—she kept it quiet: thinking of her, with a free fancy, as somehow typically insular, she talked to herself of Britannia of the Market Place—Britannia unmistakeable but with a pen on her ear—and felt she should not be happy till she might on some occasion add to the rest of the panoply a helmet, a shield, a trident and a ledger. It wasn't in truth, however, that the forces with which, as Kate felt, she would have to deal were those most suggested by an image simple and broad; she was learning after all each day to know her companion, and what she had already most perceived was the mistake of trusting to easy analogies. There was a whole side of Britannia, the side of her florid philistinism, her plumes and her train, her fantastic furniture and heaving bosom, the false gods of her taste and false notes of her talk, the sole contemplation of which would be dangerously misleading. She was a complex and subtle Britannia, as passionate as she was practical, with a reticule for her prejudices as deep as that other pocket, the pocket full of coins stamped in her image, that the world best knew her by. She carried on in short, behind her aggressive and defensive front, operations determined by her wisdom. It was in fact as a besieger, we have hinted, that our young lady, in the provisioned citadel, had for the present most to think of her, and what made her formidable in this character was that she was unscrupulous and immoral. So at all events in silent sessions and a youthful off-hand way Kate conveniently pictured her: what this sufficiently represented being that her weight was in the scale of certain dangers—those dangers that, by our showing, made the younger woman linger and lurk above, while the elder, below, both militant and diplomatic, covered as much of the ground as possible. Yet what were the dangers, after all, but just the dangers of life and of London? Mrs. Lowder *was* London, *was* life—the roar of the siege and the thick of the fray. There were some things, after all, of which Britannia was afraid; but Aunt Maud was afraid of nothing—not even, it would appear, of arduous thought.

These impressions, none the less, Kate kept so much to herself that she scarce shared them with poor Marian, the ostensible purpose of her frequent visits to whom yet continued to be to talk over everything. One of her reasons for holding off from the last concession to Aunt Maud was that she might be the more free to commit herself to this so much nearer and so much less fortunate relative, with whom Aunt Maud would have almost nothing direct to do. The sharpest pinch of her state, meanwhile, was exactly that all intercourse with her sister had the effect of casting down her courage and tying her hands, adding daily to her sense of the part, not always either uplifting or sweetening, that the bond of blood might play in one's life. She was face to face with it now, with the bond of blood; the consciousness of it was what she seemed most clearly to have "come into" by the death of her mother, much of that consciousness as her mother had absorbed and carried away. Her haunting harassing father, her menacing uncompromising aunt, her portionless little nephews and nieces, were figures that caused the chord of natural piety superabundantly to vibrate. Her manner of putting it to herself—but more especially in respect to Marian—was that she saw what you might be brought to by the cultivation of consanguinity. She had taken, in the old days, as she supposed, the measure of this liability; those being the days when, as the second-born, she had thought no one in the world so pretty as Marian, no one so charming, so clever, so assured in advance of happiness and success. The view was different now, but her attitude had been obliged, for many reasons, to show as the same. The subject of this estimate was no longer pretty, as the reason for thinking her clever was no longer plain; yet, bereaved, disappointed, demoralised, querulous, she was all the more sharply and insistently Kate's elder and Kate's own. Kate's most constant feeling about her was that she would make her, Kate, do things; and always, in comfortless Chelsea, at the door of the small house the small rent of which she couldn't help having on her mind, she fatalistically asked herself, before going in, which thing it would probably be this time. She noticed with profundity that disappointment made people selfish; she marvelled at the serenity—it was the poor woman's only one—of what Marian took for granted: her own state of abasement as the second-born, her life reduced to mere inexhaustible sisterhood. She existed in that view wholly for the small house in Chelsea; the moral of which moreover, of course, was that the more you gave yourself the less of you was left. There were always people to snatch at you, and it would never occur to *them* that they were eating you up. They did that without tasting.

There was no such misfortune, or at any rate no such discomfort, she further reasoned, as to be formed at once for being and for seeing. You always saw, in this case something else than what you were, and you got in consequence none of the peace of your condition. However, as she never really let Marian see what she was Marian might well not have been aware that she herself saw. Kate was accordingly to her own vision not a hypocrite of virtue, for she gave herself up; but she was a hypocrite of stupidity, for she kept to herself everything that was not herself. What she most kept was the particular sentiment with which she watched her sister instinctively neglect nothing that would make for her submission to their aunt; a state of the spirit that perhaps marked most sharply how poor you might become when you minded so much the absence of wealth. It was through Kate that Aunt Maud should be worked, and nothing mattered less than what might become of Kate in the process. Kate was to burn her ships in short, so that Marian should profit; and Marian's desire to profit was quite oblivious of a dignity that had after all its reasons—if it had only understood them—for keeping itself a little stiff. Kate, to be properly stiff for both of them, would therefore have had to be selfish, have had to prefer an ideal of behaviour—than which nothing ever was more selfish—to the possibility of stray crumbs for the four small creatures. The tale of Mrs. Lowder's disgust at her elder niece's marriage to Mr. Condrip had lost little of its point; the incredibly fatuous behaviour of Mr. Condrip, the parson of a dull suburban parish, with a saintly profile which was always in evidence, being so distinctly on record to keep criticism consistent. He had presented his profile on system, having, goodness knew, nothing else to present—nothing at all to full-face the world with, no imagination of the propriety of living and minding his business. Criticism had remained on Aunt Maud's part consistent enough; she was not a person to regard such proceedings as less of a mistake for having acquired more of the privilege of pathos. She hadn't been forgiving, and the only approach she made to overlooking them was by overlooking—with the surviving delinquent—the solid little phalanx that now represented them. Of the two sinister ceremonies that she lumped together, the marriage and the interment, she had been present at the former, just as she had sent Marian before it a liberal cheque; but this had not been for her more than the shadow of an admitted link with Mrs. Condrip's course. She disapproved of clamorous children for whom there was no prospect; she disapproved of weeping widows who couldn't make their errors good; and she had thus put within Marian's reach one of the few luxuries left when so much else had gone, an easy pretext for a constant grievance. Kate Croy remembered well what their mother, in a different quarter, had made of it; and it was Marian's marked failure to pluck the fruit of resentment that committed them as sisters to an almost equal fellowship in abjection. If the theory was that, yes, alas, one of the pair had ceased to be noticed, but that the other was noticed enough to make up for it, who would fail to see that Kate couldn't separate herself without a cruel pride? That lesson became sharp for our young lady the day after her interview with her father.

"I can't imagine," Marian on this occasion said to her, "how you can think of anything else in the world but the horrid way we're situated."

"And, pray, how do you know," Kate enquired in reply, "anything about my thoughts? It seems to me I give you sufficient proof of how much I think of *you*. I don't really, my dear, know what else you've to do with!"

Marian's retort on this was a stroke as to which she had supplied herself with several kinds of preparation, but there was none the less something of an unexpected note in its promptitude. She had foreseen her sister's general fear; but here, ominously, was the special one. "Well, your own business is of course your own business, and you may say there's no one less in a position than I to preach to you. But, all the same, if you wash your hands of me for ever in consequence, I won't, for this once, keep back that I don't consider you've a right, as we all stand, to throw yourself away."

It was after the children's dinner, which was also their mother's, but which their aunt mostly contrived to keep from ever becoming her own luncheon; and the two young women were still in the presence of the crumbled table-cloth, the dispersed pinafores, the scraped dishes, the lingering odour of boiled food. Kate had asked with ceremony if she might put up a window a little, and Mrs. Condrip had replied without it that she might do as she liked. She often received such enquiries as if they reflected in a manner on the pure essence of her little ones. The four had retired, with much movement and noise, under imperfect control of the small Irish governess whom their aunt had hunted up for them and whose brooding resolve not to prolong so uncrowned a martyrdom she already more than suspected. Their mother had become for Kate—who took it just for the effect of being their mother—quite a different thing from the mild Marian of the past: Mr. Condrip's widow expansively obscured that image. She was little more than a ragged relic, a plain prosaic result of him—as if she had somehow been pulled through him as through an obstinate funnel, only to be left crumpled and useless and with nothing in her but what he accounted for. She had grown red and almost fat, which were not happy signs of mourning; less and less like any Croy, particularly a Croy in trouble, and sensibly like her husband's two unmarried sisters, who came to see her, in Kate's view, much too often and stayed too long, with the consequence of inroads upon the tea and bread-and-butter—matters as to which Kate, not unconcerned with the tradesmen's books, had feelings. About them moreover Marian *was* touchy, and her nearer relative, who observed and weighed things, noted as an oddity that she would have taken any reflexion on them as a reflexion on herself. If that was what marriage necessarily did to you Kate Croy would have questioned marriage. It was at any rate a grave example of what a

man—and such a man!—might make of a woman. She could see
how the Condrip pair pressed their brother's widow on the subject
of Aunt Maud—who wasn't, after all, *their* aunt; made her, over
their interminable cups, chatter and even swagger about Lancaster
Gate, made her more vulgar than it had seemed written that any
Croy could possibly become on such a subject. They laid it down,
they rubbed it in, that Lancaster Gate was to be kept in sight, and
that she, Kate, was to keep it; so that, curiously, or at all events
sadly, our young woman was sure of being in her own person more
permitted to them as an object of comment than they would in
turn ever be permitted to herself. The beauty of which too was that
Marian didn't love them. But they were Condrips—they had
grown near the rose; they were almost like Bertie and Maudie, like
Kitty and Guy. They talked of the dead to her, which Kate never
did; it being a relation in which Kate could but mutely listen. She
couldn't indeed too often say to herself that if that was what marriage did to you—! It may easily be guessed therefore that the
ironic light of such reserves fell straight across the field of Marian's
warning. "I don't quite see," she answered, "where in particular it
strikes you that my danger lies. I'm not conscious, I assure you, of
the least disposition to 'throw' myself anywhere. I feel that for the
present I've been quite sufficiently thrown."

"You don't feel"—Marian brought it all out—"that you'd like to
marry Merton Densher?"

Kate took a moment to meet this enquiry. "Is it your idea that if
I should feel so I would be bound to give you notice, so that you
might step in and head me off? Is that your idea?" the girl asked.
Then as her sister also had a pause, "I don't know what makes you
talk of Mr. Densher," she observed.

"I talk of him just because you don't. That you never do, in
spite of what I know—that's what makes me think of him. Or
rather perhaps it's what makes me think of *you*. If you don't know
by this time what I hope for you, what I dream of—my attachment
being what it is—it's no use my attempting to tell you." But Marian had in fact warmed to her work, and Kate was sure she had discussed Mr. Densher with the Miss Condrips. "If I name that
person I suppose it's because I'm so afraid of him. If you want

really to know, he fills me with terror. If you want really to know, in fact, I dislike him as much as I dread him."

"And yet don't think it dangerous to abuse him to me?"

"Yes," Mrs. Condrip confessed, "I do think it dangerous; but how can I speak of him otherwise? I dare say, I admit, that I shouldn't speak of him at all. Only I do want you for once, as I said just now, to know."

"To know what, my dear?"

"That I should regard it," Marian promptly returned, "as far and away the worst thing that has happened to us yet."

"Do you mean because he hasn't money?"

"Yes, for one thing. And because I don't believe in him."

Kate was civil but mechanical. "What do you mean by not believing in him?"

"Well, being sure he'll never get it. And you *must* have it. You *shall* have it."

"To give it to you?"

Marian met her with a readiness that was practically pert. "To *have* it, first. Not at any rate to go on not having it. Then we should see."

"We should indeed!" said Kate Croy. It was talk of a kind she loathed, but if Marian chose to be vulgar what was one to do? It made her think of the Miss Condrips with renewed aversion. "I like the way you arrange things—I like what you take for granted. If it's so easy for us to marry men who want us to scatter gold, I wonder we any of us do anything else. I don't see so many of them about, nor what interest I might ever have for them. You live, my dear," she presently added, "in a world of vain thoughts."

"Not so much as you, Kate; for I see what I see and you can't turn it off that way." The elder sister paused long enough for the younger's face to show, in spite of superiority, an apprehension. "I'm not talking of any man but Aunt Maud's man, nor of any money even, if you like, but Aunt Maud's money. I'm not talking of anything but your doing what *she* wants. You're wrong if you speak of anything that I want of you; I want nothing but what she does. That's good enough for me!"—and Marian's tone struck her companion as of the lowest. "If I don't believe in Merton Densher I do at least in Mrs. Lowder."

"Your ideas are the more striking," Kate returned, "that they're the same as papa's. I had them from him, you'll be interested to know—and with all the brilliancy you may imagine—yesterday."

Marian clearly was interested to know. "He has been to see you?"

"No, I went to him."

"Really?" Marian wondered. "For what purpose?"

"To tell him I'm ready to go to him."

Marian stared. "To leave Aunt Maud—?"

"For my father, yes."

She had fairly flushed, poor Mrs. Condrip, with horror. "You're ready—?"

"So I told him. I couldn't tell him less."

"And pray could you tell him more?" Marian gasped in her distress. "What in the world is he *to* us? You bring out such a thing as that this way?"

They faced each other—the tears were in Marian's eyes. Kate watched them there a moment and then said: "I had thought it well over—over and over. But you needn't feel injured. I'm not going. He won't have me."

Her companion still panted—it took time to subside. "Well, *I* wouldn't have you—wouldn't receive you at all, I can assure you—if he had made you any other answer. I do feel injured—at your having been willing. If you were to go to papa, my dear, you'd have to stop coming to me." Marian put it thus, indefinably, as a picture of privation from which her companion might shrink. Such were the threats she could complacently make, could think herself masterful for making. "But if he won't take you," she continued, "he shows at least his sharpness."

Marian had always her views of sharpness; she was, as her sister privately commented, great on that resource. But Kate had her refuge from irritation. "He won't take me," she simply repeated. "But he believes, like you, in Aunt Maud. He threatens me with his curse if I leave her."

"So you *won't?*" As the girl at first said nothing her companion caught at it. "You won't, of course? I see you won't. But I don't see why, conveniently, I shouldn't insist to you once for all on the plain truth of the whole matter. The truth, my dear, of your duty. Do you ever think about *that?* It's the greatest duty of all."

"There you are again," Kate laughed. "Papa's also immense on my duty."

"Oh I don't pretend to be immense, but I pretend to know more than you do of life; more even perhaps than papa." Marian seemed to see that personage at this moment, nevertheless, in the light of a kinder irony. "Poor old papa!"

She sighed it with as many condonations as her sister's ear had more than once caught in her "Dear old Aunt Maud!" These were things that made Kate turn for the time sharply away, and she gathered herself now to go. They were the note again of the abject; it was hard to say which of the persons in question had most shown how little they liked her. The younger woman proposed at any rate to let discussion rest, and she believed that, for herself, she had done so during the ten minutes elapsing, thanks to her wish not to break off short, before she could gracefully withdraw. It then appeared, however, that Marian had been discussing still, and there was something that at the last Kate had to take up. "Whom do you mean by Aunt Maud's young man?"

"Whom should I mean but Lord Mark?"

"And where do you pick up such vulgar twaddle?" Kate demanded with her clear face. "How does such stuff, in this hole, get to you?"

She had no sooner spoken than she asked herself what had become of the grace to which she had sacrificed. Marian certainly did little to save it, and nothing indeed was so inconsequent as her ground of complaint. She desired her to "work" Lancaster Gate as she believed that scene of abundance could be worked; but she now didn't see why advantage should be taken of the bloated connexion to put an affront on her own poor home. She appeared in fact for the moment to take the position that Kate kept her in her "hole" and then heartlessly reflected on her being in it. Yet she didn't explain how she had picked up the report on which her sister had challenged her—so that it was thus left to her sister to see in it once more a sign of the creeping curiosity of the Miss Condrips. They lived in a deeper hole than Marian, but they kept their ear to the ground, they spent their days in prowling, whereas Marian, in garments and shoes that seemed steadily to grow looser and larger, never prowled. There were times when Kate wondered if the Miss Condrips were offered her by fate as a warning for her own future—to be taken as showing her what she herself might become at forty if she let things too recklessly go. What was expected of her by others—and by so many of them—could, all the same, on occasion, present itself as beyond a joke; and this was just now the aspect it particularly wore. She was not only to quarrel with Merton Densher for the pleasure of her five spectators—with the Miss Condrips there were five; she was to set forth in pursuit of Lord Mark on some preposterous theory of the premium attached to success. Mrs. Lowder's hand had hung out the premium, and it figured at the end of the course as a bell that would ring, break out into public clamour, as soon as touched. Kate reflected sharply enough on the weak points of this fond fiction, with the result at last of a certain chill for her sister's confidence; though Mrs. Condrip still took refuge in the plea—which was after all the great point—that their aunt would be munificent when their aunt should be content. The exact identity of her candidate was a detail; what was of the essence was her conception of the kind of match it was open to her niece to make with her aid. Marian always spoke of marriages as "matches," but that was again a detail. Mrs. Lowder's "aid" meanwhile awaited them—if not to light the way to Lord Mark, then to somebody better. Marian would put up, in fine, with somebody better; she only wouldn't put up with somebody so much worse. Kate had once more to go through all this before a graceful issue was reached. It was reached by her paying with the sacrifice of Mr. Densher for her reduction of Lord Mark to the absurd. So they separated softly enough. She was to be let off hearing about Lord Mark so long as she made it good that she wasn't underhand about any one else. She had denied everything and every one, she reflected as she went away—and that was a relief; but it also made rather a clean sweep of the future. The prospect put on a bareness that already gave her something in common with the Miss Condrips.

BOOK SECOND

– I –

Merton Densher, who passed the best hours of each night at the office of his newspaper, had at times, during the day, to make up for it, a sense, or at least an appearance, of leisure, in accordance with which he was not infrequently to be met in different parts of the town at moments when men of business are hidden from the public eye. More than once during the present winter's end[5] he had deviated toward three o'clock, or toward four, into Kensington Gardens, where he might for a while, on each occasion, have been observed to demean himself as a person with nothing to do. He made his way indeed, for the most part, with a certain directness over to the north side; but once that ground was reached his behaviour was noticeably wanting in point. He moved, seemingly at random, from alley to alley; he stopped for no reason and remained idly agaze; he sat down in a chair and then changed to a bench; after which he walked about again, only again to repeat both the vagueness and the vivacity. Distinctly he was a man either with nothing at all to do or with ever so much to think about; and it was not to be denied that the impression he might often thus easily make had the effect of causing the burden of proof in certain directions to rest on him. It was a little the fault of his aspect, his personal marks, which made it almost impossible to name his profession.

He was a longish, leanish, fairish young Englishman, not unamenable, on certain sides, to classification—as for instance by being a gentleman, by being rather specifically one of the educated, one of the generally sound and generally civil; yet, though to that degree neither extraordinary nor abnormal, he would have failed to play straight into an observer's hands. He was young for the House of Commons, he was loose for the Army. He was refined, as might have been said, for the City and, quite apart from the cut of his cloth, sceptical, it might have been felt, for the Church. On the other hand he was credulous for diplomacy, or perhaps even for science, while he was perhaps at the same time too much in his mere senses for poetry and yet too little in them for art. You would have got fairly near him by making out in his eyes the potential recognition of ideas; but you would have quite fallen away again on the question of the ideas themselves. The difficulty with Densher was that he looked vague without looking weak—idle without looking empty. It was the accident, possibly, of his long legs, which were apt to stretch themselves; of his straight hair and his well-shaped head, never, the latter, neatly smooth, and apt into the bargain, at the time of quite other calls upon it, to throw itself suddenly back and, supported behind by his uplifted arms and interlocked hands, place him for unconscionable periods in communion with the ceiling, the tree-tops, the sky. He was in short visibly absentminded, irregularly clever, liable to drop what was near and to take up what was far; he was more a prompt critic than a prompt follower of custom. He suggested above all, however, that wondrous state of youth in which the elements, the metals more or less precious, are so in fusion and fermentation that the question of the final stamp, the pressure that fixes the value, must wait for comparative coolness. And it was a mark of his interesting mixture that if he was irritable it was by a law of considerable subtlety—a law that in intercourse with him it might be of profit, though not easy, to master. One of the effects of it was that he had for you surprises of tolerance as well as of temper.

He loitered, on the best of the relenting days, the several occasions we speak of, along the part of the Gardens nearest to Lancaster Gate, and when, always, in due time, Kate Croy came out of her aunt's house, crossed the road and arrived by the nearest entrance, there was a general publicity in the proceeding which made it slightly anomalous. If their meeting was to be bold and free it might have taken place within-doors; if it was to be shy or secret it might have taken place almost anywhere better than under Mrs. Lowder's windows. They failed indeed to remain attached to that spot; they wandered and strolled, taking in the course of more than one of these interviews a considerable walk, or else picked out a couple of chairs under one of the great trees and sat as much apart—apart from every one else—as possible. But Kate had each time, at first, the air of wishing to expose herself to pursuit and capture if those things were in question. She made the point that she wasn't underhand, any more than she was vulgar; that the Gardens were charming in themselves and this use of them a matter of taste; and that, if her aunt chose to glare at her from the drawing-room or to cause her to be tracked and over-taken, she could at least make it convenient that this should be easily done. The fact was that the relation between these young persons abounded in such oddities as were not inaptly symbolised by assignations that had a good deal more appearance than mo-tive. Of the strength of the tie that held them we shall sufficiently take the measure; but it was meanwhile almost obvious that if the great possibility had come up for them it had done so, to an ex-ceptional degree, under the protection of the famous law of con-traries. Any deep harmony that might eventually govern them would not be the result of their having much in common — having anything in fact but their affection; and would really find its ex-planation in some sense, on the part of each, of being poor where the other was rich. It is nothing new indeed that generous young persons often admire most what nature hasn't given them — from which it would appear, after all, that our friends were both gener-ous.

Merton Densher had repeatedly said to himself — and from far back — that he should be a fool not to marry a woman whose value would be in her differences; and Kate Croy, though without hav-ing quite so philosophised, had quickly recognised in the young man a precious unlikeness. He represented what her life had never given her and certainly, without some such aid as his, never would give her; all the high dim things she lumped together as of the mind.[6] It was on the side of the mind that Densher was rich for her and mysterious and strong; and he had rendered her in especial the sovereign service of making that element real. She had had all her days to take it terribly on trust, no creature she had ever en-countered having been able to testify for it directly. Vague rumours of its existence had made their precarious way to her; but nothing had, on the whole, struck her as more likely than that she should live and die without the chance to verify them. The chance had come — it was an extraordinary one — on the day she first met Den-sher; and it was to the girl's lasting honour that she knew on the spot what she was in presence of. That occasion indeed, for everything that straightway flowered in it, would be worthy of high commemoration; Densher's perception went out to meet the young woman's and quite kept pace with her own recognition. Having so often concluded on the fact of his weakness, as he called it, for life—his strength merely for thought—life, he logically opined, was what he must somehow arrange to annex and possess. This was so much a necessity that thought by itself only went on in the void; it was from the immediate air of life that it must draw its breath. So the young man, ingenious but large, critical but ardent too, made out both his case and Kate Croy's. They had originally met before her mother's death—an occasion marked for her as the last pleasure permitted by the approach of that event; after which the dark months had interposed a screen and, for all Kate knew, made the end one with the beginning.

The beginning—to which she often went back—had been a scene, for our young woman, of supreme brilliancy; a party given at a "gallery" hired by a hostess who fished with big nets. A Spanish dancer, understood to be at that moment the delight of the town, an American reciter, the joy of a kindred people, an Hungarian fiddler, the wonder of the world at large—in the name of these and other attractions the company in which Kate, by a rare privilege, found herself had been freely convoked. She lived under her mother's roof, as she considered, obscurely, and was acquainted with few persons who entertained on that scale; but she had had dealings with two or three connected, as appeared, with such—two or three through whom the stream of hospitality, filtered or diffused, could thus now and then spread to outlying receptacles. A good-natured lady in fine, a friend of her mother and a relative of the lady of the gallery, had offered to take her to the party in question and had there fortified her, further, with two or three of those introductions that, at large parties, lead to other things—that had at any rate on this occasion culminated for her in conversation with a tall fair, a slightly unbrushed and rather awkward, but on the whole a not dreary, young man. The young man had affected her as detached, as—it was indeed what he called himself—awfully at sea, as much more distinct from what surrounded them than any one else appeared to be, and even as probably qui&e disposed to be making his escape when pulled up to be placed in relation with her. He gave her his word for it indeed, this same evening, that only their meeting had prevented his flight, but that now he saw how sorry he should have been to miss it. This point they had reached by midnight, and though for the value of such remarks everything was in the tone, by midnight the tone was there too. She had had originally her full apprehension of his co-erced, certainly of his vague, condition—full apprehensions often being with her immediate; then she had had her equal conscious-ness that within five minutes something between them had—well, she couldn't call it anything but *come*. It was nothing to look at or to handle, but was somehow everything to feel and to know; it was that something for each of them had happened.

They had found themselves regarding each other straight, and for a longer time on end than was usual even at parties in galleries; but that in itself after all would have been a small affair for two such handsome persons. It wasn't, in a word, simply that their eyes had met; other conscious organs, faculties, feelers had met as well, and when Kate afterwards imaged to herself the sharp deep fact she saw it, in the oddest way, as a particular performance. She had observed a ladder against a garden-wall and had trusted herself so to climb it as to be able to see over into the probable garden on the other side. On reaching the top she had found herself face to face with a gentleman engaged in a like calculation at the same mo-ment, and the two enquirers had remained confronted on their ladders. The great point was that for the rest of that evening they had been perched—they had not climbed down; and indeed dur-ing the time that followed Kate at least had had the perched feel-ing—it was as if she were there aloft without a retreat. A simpler expression of all this is doubtless but that they had taken each other in with interest; and without a happy hazard six months later the incident would have closed in that account of it. The accident meanwhile had been as natural as anything in London ever is: Kate had one afternoon found herself opposite Mr. Densher on the Underground Railway. She had entered the train at Sloane Square to go to Queen's Road, and the carriage in which she took her place was all but full. Densher was already in it—on the other bench and at the furthest angle; she was sure of him before they had again started. The day and the hour were darkness, there were six other persons and she had been busy seating herself; but her consciousness had gone to him as straight as if they had come together in some bright stretch of a desert. They had on neither part a second's hesitation; they looked across the choked compartment exactly as if she had known he would be there and he had expected her to come in; so that, though in the conditions they could only exchange the greeting of movements, smiles, abstentions, it would have been quite in the key of these passages that they should have alighted for ease at the very next station. Kate was in fact sure the very next station was the young man's true goal—which made it clear he was going on only from the wish to speak to her. He had to go on, for this purpose, to High Street Kensington, as it was not till then that the exit of a passenger gave him his chance.

His chance put him however in quick possession of the seat facing her, the alertness of his capture of which seemed to show her his impatience. It helped them moreover, with strangers on either side, little to talk; though this very restriction perhaps made such a mark for them as nothing else could have done. If the fact that their opportunity had again come round for them could be so intensely expressed without a word, they might very well feel on the spot that it had not come round for nothing. The extraordinary part of the matter was that they were not in the least meeting where they had left off, but ever so much further on, and that these added links added still another between High Street and Notting Hill Gate, and then worked between the latter station and Queen's Road an extension really inordinate. At Notting Hill Gate Kate's right-hand neighbour descended, whereupon Densher popped straight into that seat; only there was not much gained when a lady the next instant popped into Densher's. He could say almost nothing—Kate scarce knew, at least, what he said; she was so occupied with a certainty that one of the persons opposite, a youngish man with a single eye-glass which he kept constantly in position, had made her out from the first as visibly, as strangely affected. If such a person made her out what then did Densher do?—a question in truth sufficiently answered when, on their reaching her station, he instantly followed her out of the train. That had been the real beginning—the beginning of everything else; the other time, the time at the party, had been but the beginning of *that*. Never in life before had she so let herself go; for always before—so far as small adventures could have been in question for her—there had been, by the vulgar measure, more to go upon. He had walked with her to Lancaster Gate, and then she had walked with him away from it—for all the world, she said to herself, like the housemaid giggling to the baker.

This appearance, she was afterwards to feel, had been all in order for a relation that might precisely best be described in the terms of the baker and the housemaid. She could say to herself that from that hour they had kept company: that had come to represent, technically speaking, alike the range and the limit of their tie. He had on the spot, naturally, asked leave to call upon her—which, as a young person who wasn't really young, who didn't pretend to be a sheltered flower, she as rationally gave. That—she was promptly clear about it—was now her only possible basis; she was just the contemporary London female, highly modern, inevitably battered, honourably free. She had of course taken her aunt straight into her confidence—had gone through the form of asking her leave; and she subsequently remembered that though on this occasion she had left the history of her new alliance as scant as the facts themselves, Mrs. Lowder had struck her at the time as surprisingly mild. The occasion had been in every way full of the reminder that her hostess was deep: it was definitely then that she had begun to ask herself what Aunt Maud was, in vulgar parlance, "up to." "You may receive, my dear, whom you like"—that was what Aunt Maud, who in general objected to people's doing as they liked, had replied; and it bore, this unexpectedness, a good deal of looking into. There were many explanations, and they were all amusing—amusing, that is, in the line of the sombre and brooding amusement cultivated by Kate in her actual high retreat. Merton Densher came the very next Sunday; but Mrs. Lowder was so consistently magnanimous as to make it possible to her niece to see him alone. She saw him, however, on the Sunday following, in order to invite him to dinner; and when, after dining, he came again—which he did three times, she found means to treat his visit as preponderantly to herself. Kate's conviction that she didn't like him made that remarkable; it added to the evidence, by this time voluminous, that she was remarkable all round. If she had been, in the way of energy, merely usual she would have kept her dislike direct; whereas it was now as if she were seeking to know him in order to see best where to "have" him. That was one of the reflexions made in our young woman's high retreat; she smiled from her lookout, in the silence that was only the fact of hearing irrelevant sounds, as she caught the truth that you could easily accept people when you wanted them so to be delivered to you. When Aunt Maud wished them dispatched it was not to be done by deputy; it was clearly always a matter reserved for her own hand.

But what made the girl wonder most was the implication of so much diplomacy in respect to her own value. What view might she take of her position in the light of this appearance that her companion feared so as yet to upset her? It was as if Densher were accepted partly under the dread that if he hadn't been she would act in resentment. Hadn't her aunt considered the danger that she would in that case have broken off, have seceded? The danger was exaggerated—she would have done nothing so gross; but that, it would seem, was the way Mrs. Lowder saw her and believed her to be reckoned with. What importance therefore did she really attach to her, what strange interest could she take in their keeping on terms? Her father and her sister had their answer to this—even without knowing how the question struck her: they saw the lady of Lancaster Gate as panting to make her fortune, and the explanation of that appetite was that, on the accident of a nearer view than she had before enjoyed, she had been charmed, been dazzled. They approved, they admired in her one of the belated fancies of rich capricious violent old women—the more marked moreover because the result of no plot; and they piled up the possible fruits for the person concerned. Kate knew what to think of her own power thus to carry by storm; she saw herself as handsome, no doubt, but as hard, and felt herself as clever but as cold; and as so much too imperfectly ambitious, furthermore, that it was a pity, for a quiet life, she couldn't decide to be either finely or stupidly indifferent. Her intelligence sometimes kept her still—too still—but her want of it was restless; so that she got the good, it seemed to her, of neither extreme. She saw herself at present, none the less, in a situation, and even her sad disillusioned mother, dying, but with Aunt Maud interviewing the nurse on the stairs, had not failed to remind her that it was of the essence of situations to be, under Providence, worked. The dear woman had died in the belief that she was actually working the one then recognised.

Kate took one of her walks with Densher just after her visit to Mr. Croy; but most of it went, as usual, to their sitting in talk. They had under the trees by the lake the air of old friends—particular phases of apparent earnestness in which they might have been settling every question in their vast young world; and periods of silence, side by side, perhaps even more, when "A long engagement!" would have been the final reading of the signs on the part of a passer struck with them, as it was so easy to be. They would have presented themselves thus as very old friends rather than as young persons who had met for the first time but a year before and had spent most of the interval without contact. It was indeed for each, already, as if they were older friends; and though the succession of their meetings might, between them, have been straightened out, they only had a confused sense of a good many, very much alike, and a confused intention of a good many more, as little different as possible. The desire to keep them just as they were had perhaps to do with the fact that in spite of the presumed diagnosis of the stranger there had been for them as yet no formal, no final understanding. Densher had at the very first pressed the question, but that, it had been easy to reply, was too soon; so that a singular thing had afterwards happened. They had accepted their acquaintance as too short for an engagement, but they had treated it as long enough for almost anything else, and marriage was somehow before them like a temple without an avenue. They belonged to the temple and they met in the grounds; they were in the stage at which grounds in general offered much scattered refreshment. But Kate had meanwhile had so few confidants that she wondered at the source of her father's suspicions. The diffusion of rumour was of course always remarkable in London, and for Marian not less—as Aunt Maud touched neither directly—the mystery had worked. No doubt she had been seen. Of course she had been seen. She had taken no trouble not to be seen, and it was a thing she was clearly incapable of taking. But she had been seen

how?—and what *was* there to see? She was in love—she knew that:
but it was wholly her own business, and she had the sense of having conducted herself, of still so doing, with almost violent con-
formity.

"I've an idea—in fact I feel sure—that Aunt Maud means to
write to you; and I think you had better know it." So much as this
she said to him as soon as they met, but immediately adding to it:
"So as to make up your mind how to take her. I know pretty well
what she'll say to you."

"Then will you kindly tell me?"

She thought a little. "I can't do that. I should spoil it. She'll do
the best for her own idea."

"Her idea, you mean, that I'm a sort of a scoundrel; or, at the
best, not good enough for you?"

They were side by side again in their penny chairs, and Kate
had another pause. "Not good enough for *her*."

"Oh I see. And that's necessary."

He put it as a truth rather more than as a question; but there
had been plenty of truths between them that each had contradicted. Kate, however, let this one sufficiently pass, only saying the
next moment: "She has behaved extraordinarily."

"And so have we," Densher declared. "I think, you know, we've
been awfully decent."

"For ourselves, for each other, for people in general, yes. But
not for *her*. For her," said Kate, "we've been monstrous. She has
been giving us rope. So if she does send for you," the girl repeated,
"you must know where you are."

"That I always know. It's where *you* are that concerns me."

"Well," said Kate after an instant, "her idea of that is what you'll
have from her." He gave her a long look, and whatever else people
who wouldn't let her alone might have wished, for her advance-
ment, his long looks were the thing in the world she could never
have enough of. What she felt was that, whatever might happen,
she must keep them, must make them most completely her possession; and it was already strange enough that she reasoned, or at
all events began to act, as if she might work them in with other and
alien things, privately cherish them and yet, as regards the rigour
of it, pay no price. She looked it well in the face, she took it in-

tensely home, that they were lovers; she rejoiced to herself and, frankly, to him, in their wearing of the name; but, distinguished creature that, in her way, she was, she took a view of this character that scarce squared with the conventional. The character itself she insisted on as their right, taking that so for granted that it didn't seem even bold; but Densher, though he agreed with her, found himself moved to wonder at her simplifications, her values. Life might prove difficult—was evidently going to; but meanwhile they had each other, and that was everything. This was her reasoning, but meanwhile, for *him*, each other was what they didn't have, and it was just the point. Repeatedly, however, it was a point that, in the face of strange and special things, he judged it rather awkwardly gross to urge. It was impossible to keep Mrs. Lowder out of their scheme. She stood there too close to it and too solidly; it had to open a gate, at a given point, do what they would, to take her in. And she came in, always, while they sat together rather helplessly watching her, as in a coach-and-four; she drove round their prospect as the principal lady at the circus drives round the ring, and she stopped the coach in the middle to alight with majesty. It was our young man's sense that she was magnificently vulgar, but yet quite that this wasn't all. It wasn't with her vulgarity that she felt his want of means, though that might have helped her richly to embroider it; nor was it with the same infirmity that she was strong original dangerous.

His want of means—of means sufficient for any one but himself—was really the great ugliness, and was moreover at no time more ugly for him than when it rose there, as it did seem to rise, all shameless, face to face with the elements in Kate's life colloquially and conveniently classed by both of them as funny. He sometimes indeed, for that matter, asked himself if these elements were as funny as the innermost fact, so often vivid to him, of his own consciousness—his private inability to believe he should ever be rich. His conviction on this head was in truth quite positive and a thing by itself; he failed, after analysis, to understand it, though he had naturally more lights on it than any one else. He knew how it subsisted in spite of an equal consciousness of his being neither mentally nor physically quite helpless, neither a dunce nor a cripple; he knew it to be absolute, though secret, and also, strange to say, about common undertakings, not discouraging, not prohibitive. Only now was he having to think if it were prohibitive in respect to marriage; only now, for the first time, had he to weigh his case in scales. The scales, as he sat with Kate, often dangled in the line of his vision; he saw them, large and black, while he talked or listened, take, in the bright air, singular positions. Sometimes the right was down and sometimes the left; never a happy equipoise — one or the other always kicking the beam. Thus was kept before him the question of whether it were more ignoble to ask a woman to take her chance with you, or to accept it from your conscience that her chance could be at the best but one of the degrees of privation; whether too, otherwise, marrying for money mightn't after all be a smaller cause of shame than the mere dread of marrying without. Through these variations of mood and view, nevertheless, the mark on his forehead stood clear; he saw himself remain without whether he married or not. It was a line on which his fancy could be admirably active; the innumerable ways of making money were beautifully present to him; he could have handled them for his newspaper as easily as he handled everything. He was quite aware how he handled everything; it was another mark on his forehead: the pair of smudges from the thumb of fortune, the brand on the passive fleece, dated from the primal hour and kept each other company. He wrote, as for print, with deplorable ease; since there had been nothing to stop him even at the age of ten, so there was as little at twenty; it was part of his fate in the first place and part of the wretched public's in the second. The innumerable ways of making money were, no doubt, at all events, what his imagination often was busy with after he had tilted his chair and thrown back his head with his hands clasped behind it. What would most have prolonged that attitude, moreover, was the reflexion that the ways were ways only for others. Within the minute now — however this might be — he was aware of a nearer view than he had yet quite had of those circumstances on his companion's part that made least for simplicity of relation. He saw above all how she saw them herself, for she spoke of them at present with the last frankness, telling him of her visit to her father and giving him, in an account of her subsequent scene with her sister, an instance of how she was perpetually reduced to patching-up, in one way or another, that unfortunate woman's hopes.

"The tune," she exclaimed, "to which we're a failure as a family!" With which he had it all again from her—and this time, as it seemed to him, more than all: the dishonour her father had brought them, his folly and cruelty and wickedness; the wounded state of her mother, abandoned despoiled and helpless, yet, for the management of such a home as remained to them, dreadfully unreasonable too; the extinction of her two young brothers—one, at nineteen, the eldest of the house, by typhoid fever contracted at a poisonous little place, as they had afterwards found out, that they had taken for a summer; the other, the flower of the flock, a middy on the *Britannia*, dreadfully drowned, and not even by an accident at sea, but by cramp, unrescued, while bathing, too late in the autumn, in a wretched little river during a holiday visit to the home of a shipmate. Then Marian's unnatural marriage, in itself a kind of spiritless turning of the other cheek to fortune: her actual wretchedness and plaintiveness, her greasy children, her impossible claims, her odious visitors—these things completed the proof of the heaviness, for them all, of the hand of fate. Kate confessedly described them with an excess of impatience; it was much of her charm for Densher that she gave in general that turn to her descriptions, partly as if to amuse him by free and humourous colour, partly—and that charm was the greatest—as if to work off, for her own relief, her constant perception of the incongruity of things. She had seen the general show too early and too sharply, and was so intelligent that she knew it and allowed for that misfortune; therefore when, in talk with him, she was violent and almost unfeminine, it was quite as if they had settled, for intercourse, on the short cut of the fantastic and the happy language of exaggeration. It had come to be definite between them at a primary stage that, if they could have no other straight way, the realm of thought at least was open to them. They could think whatever they liked about whatever they would—in other words they could say it. Saying it for each other, for each other alone, only of course added to the taste. The implication was thereby constant that what they said when not together had no taste for them at all, and nothing could have served more to launch them, at special hours, on their small floating island than such an assumption that they were only making believe everywhere else. Our young man, it must be added, was conscious enough that it was Kate who profited most by this particular play of the fact of intimacy. It always struck him she had more life than he to react from, and when she recounted the dark disasters of her house and glanced at the hard odd offset of her present exaltation—since as exaltation it was apparently to be considered—he felt his own grey domestic annals make little show. It was naturally, in all such reference, the question of her father's character that engaged him most, but her picture of her adventure in Chirk Street* gave him a sense of how little as yet that character was clear to him. What was it, to speak plainly, that Mr. Croy had originally done?

"I don't know—and I don't want to. I only know that years and years ago—when I was about fifteen—something or other happened that made him impossible. I mean impossible for the world at large first, and then, little by little, for mother. We of course didn't know it at the time," Kate explained, "but we knew it later; and it was, oddly enough, my sister who first made out that he had done something. I can hear her now—the way, one cold black Sunday morning when, on account of an extraordinary fog, we hadn't gone to church, she broke it to me by the school-room fire. I was reading a history-book by the lamp—when we didn't go to church we had to read history-books—and I suddenly heard her say, out of the fog, which was in the room, and apropos of nothing: 'Papa has done something wicked.' And the curious thing was that I believed it on the spot and have believed it ever since, though she could tell me nothing more—neither what was the wickedness, nor how she knew, nor what would happen to him, nor anything else about it. We had our sense always that all sorts of things *had* happened, were all the while happening, to him; so that when Marian only said she was sure, tremendously sure, that she had made it out for herself, but that that was enough, I took her word for it—it seemed somehow so natural. We were not, however, to ask mother—which made it more natural still, and I said never a

---

*Densher is thinking of Kate's visit to her father in the novel's opening scene.

word. But mother, strangely enough, spoke of it to me, in time, of her own accord—this was very much later on. He hadn't been with us for ever so long, but we were used to that. She must have had some fear, some conviction that I had an idea, some idea of her own that it was the best thing to do. She came out as abruptly as Marian had done: 'If you hear anything against your father—anything I mean except that he's odious and vile—remember it's perfectly false.' That was the way I knew it was true, though I recall my saying to her then that I of course knew it wasn't. She might have told me it was true, and yet have trusted me to contradict fiercely enough any accusation of him that I should meet—to contradict it much more fiercely and effectively, I think, than she would have done herself. As it happens, however," the girl went on, "I've never had occasion, and I've been conscious of it with a sort of surprise. It has made the world seem at times more decent. No one has so much as breathed to me. That has been a part of the silence, the silence that surrounds him, the silence that, for the world, has washed him out. He doesn't exist for people. And yet I'm as sure as ever. In fact, though I know no more than I did then, I'm more sure. And that," she wound up, "is what I sit here and tell you about my own father. If you don't call it a proof of confidence I don't know what will satisfy you."

"It satisfies me beautifully," Densher returned, "but it doesn't, my dear child, very greatly enlighten me. You don't, you know, really tell me anything. It's so vague that what am I to think but that you may very well be mistaken? What has he done, if no one can name it?"

"He has done everything."

"Oh—everything! Everything's nothing."

"Well then," said Kate, "he has done some particular thing. It's known—only, thank God, not to us. But it has been the end of him. *You* could doubtless find out with a little trouble. You can ask about."

Densher for a moment said nothing; but the next moment he made it up. "I wouldn't find out for the world, and I'd rather lose my tongue than put a question."

"And yet it's a part of me," said Kate.

"A part of you?"

"My father's dishonour." Then she sounded for him, but more deeply than ever yet, her note of proud still pessimism. "How can such a thing as that not be the great thing in one's life?"

She had to take from him again, on this, one of his long looks, and she took it to its deepest, its headiest dregs. "I shall ask you, for the great thing in your life," he said, "to depend on *me* a little more." After which, just debating, "Doesn't he belong to some club?" he asked.

She had a grave headshake. "He used to—to many."

"But he has dropped them?"

"They've dropped *him*. Of that I'm sure. It ought to do for you. I offered him," the girl immediately continued—"and it was for that I went to him—to come and be with him, make a home for him so far as is possible. But he won't hear of it."

Densher took this in with marked but generous wonder. "You offered him—'impossible' as you describe him to me—to live with him and share his disadvantages?" The young man saw for the moment only the high beauty of it. "You *are* gallant!"

"Because it strikes you as being brave for him?" She wouldn't in the least have this. "It wasn't courage—it was the opposite. I did it to save myself—to escape."

He had his air, so constant at this stage, as of her giving him finer things than any one to think about. "Escape from what?"

"From everything."

"Do you by any chance mean from me?"

"No; I spoke to him of you, told him—or what amounted to it—that I would bring you, if he would allow it, with me."

"But he won't allow it," said Densher.

"Won't hear of it on any terms. He won't help me, won't save me, won't hold out a finger to me," Kate went on. "He simply wriggles away, in his inimitable manner, and throws me back."

"Back then, after all, thank goodness," Densher concurred, "on me."

But she spoke again as with the sole vision of the whole scene she had evoked. "It's a pity, because you'd like him. He's wonderful—he's charming." Her companion gave one of the laughs that showed again how inveterately he felt in her tone something that banished the talk of other women, so far as he knew other women,

to the dull desert of the conventional, and she had already continued. "He would make himself delightful to you."

"Even while objecting to me?"

"Well, he likes to please," the girl explained—"personally. I've
seen it make him wonderful. He would appreciate you and be
clever with you. It's to *me* he objects—that is as to my liking you."

"Heaven be praised then," cried Densher, "that you like me
enough for the objection!"

But she met it after an instant with some inconsequence. "I
don't. I offered to give you up, if necessary, to go to him. But it
made no difference, and that's what I mean," she pursued, "by his
declining me on any terms. The point is, you see, that I don't escape."

Densher wondered. "But if you didn't wish to escape *me?*"

"I wished to escape Aunt Maud. But he insists that it's through
her and through her only that I may help him; just as Marian insists that it's through her, and through her only, that I can help *her*.
That's what I mean," she again explained, "by their turning me
back."

The young man thought. "Your sister turns you back too?"

"Oh with a push!"

"But have you offered to live with your sister?"

"I would in a moment if she'd have me. That's all my virtue—
a narrow little family feeling. I've a small stupid piety—I don't
know what to call it." Kate bravely stuck to that; she made it out.
"Sometimes, alone, I've to smother my shrieks when I think of my
poor mother. She went through things—they pulled her down; I
know what they were now—I didn't then, for I was a pig; and my
position, compared with hers, is an insolence of success. That's
what Marian keeps before me; that's what papa himself, as I say, so
inimitably does. My position's a value, a great value, for them
both"—she followed and followed. Lucid and ironic, she knew no
merciful muddle. "It's *the* value—the only one they have."

Everything between our young couple moved today, in spite of
their pauses, their margin, to a quicker measure—the quickness of
anxiety playing lightning-like in the sultriness. Densher watched,
decidedly, as he had never done before. "And the fact you speak of
holds you!"

"Of course it holds me. It's a perpetual sound in my ears. It makes me ask myself if I've any right to personal happiness, any right to anything but to be as rich and overflowing, as smart and shining, as I can be made."

Densher had a pause. "Oh you might by good luck have the personal happiness too."

Her immediate answer to this was a silence like his own; after which she gave him straight in the face, but quite simply and quietly: "Darling!"

It took him another moment; then he was also quiet and simple. "Will you settle it by our being married tomorrow—as we can, with perfect ease, civilly?"

"Let us wait to arrange it," Kate presently replied, "till after you've seen her."

"Do you call that adoring me?" Densher demanded.

They were talking, for the time, with the strangest mixture of deliberation and directness, and nothing could have been more in the tone of it than the way she at last said: "You're afraid of her yourself."

He gave rather a glazed smile. "For young persons of a great distinction and a very high spirit we're a caution!"

"Yes," she took it straight up; "we're hideously intelligent. But there's fun in it too. We must get our fun where we can. I think," she added, and for that matter not without courage, "our relation's quite beautiful. It's not a bit vulgar. I cling to some saving romance in things."

It made him break into a laugh that had more freedom than his smile. "How you must be afraid you'll chuck me!"

"No, no, *that* would be vulgar. But of course," she admitted, "I do see my danger of doing something base."

"Then what can be so base as sacrificing me?"

"I *shan't* sacrifice you. Don't cry out till you're hurt. I shall sacrifice nobody and nothing, and that's just my situation, that I want and that I shall try for everything. That," she wound up "is how I see myself (and how I see you quite as much) acting for them."

"For 'them'?"—and the young man extravagantly marked his coldness. "Thank you!"

"Don't you care for them?"

"Why should I? What are they to me but a serious nuisance?" As soon as he had permitted himself this qualification of the unfortunate persons she so perversely cherished he repented of his roughness—and partly because he expected a flash from her. But it was one of her finest sides that she sometimes flashed with a mere mild glow. "I don't see why you don't make out a little more that if we avoid stupidity we may do *all*. We may keep her."

He stared. "Make her pension us?"

"Well, wait at least till we've seen."

He thought. "Seen what can be got out of her?"

Kate for a moment said nothing. "After all I never asked her; never, when our troubles were at the worst, appealed to her nor went near her. She fixed upon me herself, settled on me with her wonderful gilded claws."

"You speak," Densher observed, "as if she were a vulture."

"Call it an eagle—with a gilded beak as well, and with wings for great flights. If she's a thing of the air, in short—say at once a great seamed silk balloon—I never myself got into her car. I was her choice."

It had really, her sketch of the affair, a high colour and a great style; at all of which he gazed a minute as at a picture by a master. "What she must see in you!"

"Wonders!" And, speaking it loud, she stood straight up. "Everything. There it is."

Yes, there it was, and as she remained before him he continued to face it. "So that what you mean is that I'm to do my part in somehow squaring her?"

"See her, see her," Kate said with impatience.

"And grovel to her?"

"Ah do what you like!" And she walked in her impatience away.

— II —

His eyes had followed her at this time quite long enough, before he overtook her, to make out more than ever in the poise of her head, the pride of her step—he didn't know

what best to call it—a part at least of Mrs. Lowder's reasons. He
consciously winced while he figured his presenting himself as a
reason opposed to these; though at the same moment, with the
source of Aunt Maud's inspiration thus before him, he was prepared to conform, by almost any abject attitude or profitable compromise, to his companion's easy injunction. He would do as *she*
liked—his own liking might come off as it would. He would help
her to the utmost of his power; for, all the rest of this day and the
next, her easy injunction, tossed off that way as she turned her
beautiful back, was like the crack of a great whip in the blue air,
the high element in which Mrs. Lowder hung. He wouldn't grovel
perhaps—he wasn't quite ready for that; but he would be patient,
ridiculous, reasonable, unreasonable, and above all deeply diplomatic. He would be clever with all his cleverness—which he now
shook hard, as he sometimes shook his poor dear shabby old
watch, to start it up again. It wasn't, thank goodness, as if there
weren't plenty of that "factor" (to use one of his great newspaper-
words), and with what they could muster between them it would
be little to the credit of their star, however pale, that defeat and surrender—surrender so early, so immediate—should have to ensue.
It was not indeed that he thought of that disaster as at the worst a
direct sacrifice of their possibilities: he imaged it—which was
enough—as some proved vanity, some exposed fatuity in the idea
of bringing Mrs. Lowder round. When shortly afterwards, in this
lady's vast drawing-room—the apartments at Lancaster Gate had
struck him from the first as of prodigious extent—he awaited her,
at her request, conveyed in a "reply-paid" telegram, his theory was
that of their still clinging to their idea, though with a sense of the
difficulty of it really enlarged to the scale of the place.

　　He had the place for a long time—it seemed to him a quarter
of an hour—to himself; and while Aunt Maud kept him and kept
him, while observation and reflexion crowded on him, he asked
himself what was to be expected of a person who could treat one
like that.[7] The visit, the hour were of her own proposing, so that
her delay, no doubt, was but part of a general plan of putting him
to inconvenience. As he walked to and fro, however, taking in the
message of her massive florid furniture, the immense expression of
her signs and symbols, he had as little doubt of the inconvenience

he was prepared to suffer. He found himself even facing the thought that he had nothing to fall back on, and that that was as great an humiliation in a good cause as a proud man could desire. It hadn't yet been so distinct to him that he made no show—literally not the smallest; so complete a show seemed made there all about him; so almost abnormally affirmative, so aggressively erect, were the huge heavy objects that syllabled his hostess's story. "When all's said and done, you know, she's colossally vulgar"—he had once all but noted that of her to her niece; only just keeping it back at the last, keeping it to himself with all its danger about it. It mattered because it bore so directly, and he at all events quite felt it a thing that Kate herself would some day bring out to him. It bore directly at present, and really all the more that somehow, strangely, it didn't in the least characterise the poor woman as dull or stale. She was vulgar with freshness, almost with beauty, since there was beauty, to a degree, in the play of so big and bold a temperament. She was in fine quite the largest possible quantity to deal with; and he was in the cage of the lioness without his whip— the whip, in a word, of a supply of proper retorts. He had no retort but that he loved the girl—which in such a house as that was painfully cheap. Kate had mentioned to him more than once that her aunt was Passionate, speaking of it as a kind of offset and uttering it as with a capital P, marking it as something that he might, that he in fact ought to, turn about in some way to their advantage. He wondered at this hour to what advantage he could turn it; but the case grew less simple the longer he waited. Decidedly there was something he hadn't enough of.

His slow march to and fro seemed to give him the very measure; as he paced and paced the distance it became the desert of his poverty; at the sight of which expanse moreover he could pretend to himself as little as before that the desert looked redeemable. Lancaster Gate looked rich—that was all the effect; which it was unthinkable that any state of his own should ever remotely resemble. He read more vividly, more critically, as has been hinted, the appearances about him; and they did nothing so much as make him wonder at his aesthetic reaction. He hadn't known—and in spite of Kate's repeated reference to her own rebellions of taste— that he should "mind" so much how an independent lady might decorate her house. It was the language of the house itself that spoke to him, writing out for him with surpassing breadth and freedom the associations and conceptions, the ideals and possibilities of the mistress. Never, he felt sure, had he seen so many things so unanimously ugly—operatively, ominously so cruel. He was glad to have found this last name for the whole character; "cruel" somehow played into the subject for an article—an article that his impression put straight into his mind. He would write about the heavy horrors that could still flourish, that lifted their undiminished heads, in an age so proud of its short way with false gods; and it would be funny if what he should have got from Mrs. Lowder were to prove after all but a small amount of copy. Yet the great thing, really the dark thing, was that, even while he thought of the quick column he might add up, he felt it less easy to laugh at the heavy horrors than to quail before them. He couldn't describe and dismiss them collectively, call them either Mid-Victorian or Early—not being certain they were rangeable under one rubric. It was only manifest they were splendid and were furthermore conclusively British. They constituted an order and abounded in rare material—precious woods, metals, stuffs, stones. He had never dreamed of anything so fringed and scalloped, so buttoned and corded, drawn everywhere so tight and curled everywhere so thick. He had never dreamed of so much gilt and glass, so much satin and plush, so much rosewood and marble and malachite. But it was above all the solid forms, the wasted finish, the misguided cost, the general attestation of morality and money, a good conscience and a big balance. These things finally represented for him a portentous negation of his own world of thought—of which, for that matter, in presence of them, he became as for the first time hopelessly aware. They revealed it to him by their merciless difference.

His interview with Aunt Maud, none the less, took by no means the turn he had expected. Passionate though her nature, no doubt, Mrs. Lowder on this occasion neither threatened nor appealed. Her arms of aggression, her weapons of defence, were presumably close at hand, but she left them untouched and unmentioned, and was in fact so bland that he properly perceived only afterwards how adroit she had been. He properly perceived something else as well, which complicated his case; he shouldn't have known what to call it if he hadn't called it her really imprudent good nature. Her blandness, in other words, wasn't mere policy—he wasn't dangerous enough for policy: it was the result, he could see, of her fairly liking him a little. From the moment she did that she herself became more interesting, and who knew what might happen should he take to liking *her?* Well, it was a risk he naturally must face. She fought him at any rate but with one hand, with a few loose grains of stray powder. He recognised at the end of ten minutes, and even without her explaining it, that if she had made him wait it hadn't been to wound him; they had by that time almost directly met on the fact of her intention. She had wanted him to think for himself of what she proposed to say to him—not having otherwise announced it; wanted to let it come home to him on the spot, as she had shrewdly believed it would. Her first question, on appearing, had practically been as to whether he hadn't taken her hint, and this enquiry assumed so many things that it immediately made discussion frank and large. He knew, with the question put, that the hint was just what he *had* taken; knew that she had made him quickly forgive her the display of her power; knew that if he didn't take care he should understand her, and the strength of her purpose, to say nothing of that of her imagination, nothing of the length of her purse, only too well. Yet he pulled himself up with the thought too that he wasn't going to be afraid of understanding her; he was just going to understand and understand without detriment to the feeblest, even, of his passions. The play of one's mind gave one away, at the best, dreadfully, in action, in the need for action, where simplicity was all; but when one couldn't prevent it the thing was to make it complete. There would never be mistakes but for the original fun of mistakes. What he must *use* his fatal intelligence for was to resist. Mrs. Lowder meanwhile might use it for whatever she liked.

It was after she had begun her statement of her own idea about Kate that he began on his side to reflect that—with her manner of offering it as really sufficient if he would take the trouble to embrace it—she couldn't half hate him. That was all, positively, she seemed to show herself for the time as attempting; clearly, if she did her intention justice she would have nothing more disagreeable to do. "If I hadn't been ready to go very much further, you understand, I wouldn't have gone so far. I don't care what you repeat to her—the more you repeat to her perhaps the better; and at any rate there's nothing she doesn't already know. I don't say it for her; I say it for you—when I want to reach my niece I know how to do it straight." So Aunt Maud delivered herself—as with homely benevolence, in the simplest but the clearest terms; virtually conveying that, though a word to the wise was doubtless, in spite of the adage, *not* always enough, a word to the good could never fail to be. The sense our young man read into her words was that she liked him because he was good—was really by her measure good enough: good enough that is to give up her niece for her and go his way in peace. But *was* he good enough—by his own measure? He fairly wondered, while she more fully expressed herself, if it might be his doom to prove so. "She's the finest possible creature—of course you flatter yourself you know it. But I know it quite as well as you possibly can—by which I mean a good deal better yet; and the tune to which I'm ready to prove my faith compares favourably enough, I think, with anything you can do. I don't say it because she's my niece—that's nothing to me: I might have had fifty nieces, and I wouldn't have brought one of them to this place if I hadn't found her to my taste. I don't say I wouldn't have done something else, but I wouldn't have put up with her presence. Kate's presence, by good fortune, I marked early. Kate's presence—unluckily for *you*—is everything I could possibly wish. Kate's presence is, in short, as fine as you know, and I've been keeping it for the comfort of my declining years. I've watched it long; I've been saving it up and letting it, as you say of investments, appreciate; and you may judge whether, now it has begun to pay so, I'm likely to consent to treat for it with any but a high bidder. I can do the best with her, and I've my idea of the best."

"Oh I quite conceive," said Densher, "that your idea of the best isn't me."

It was an oddity of Mrs. Lowder's that her face in speech was like a lighted window at night, but that silence immediately drew the curtain. The occasion for reply allowed by her silence was never easy to take, yet she was still less easy to interrupt. The great glaze of her surface, at all events, gave her visitor no present help.

"I didn't ask you to come to hear what it isn't—I asked you to come to hear what it *is*."

"Of course," Densher laughed, "that's very great indeed."

His hostess went on as if his contribution to the subject were barely relevant. "I want to see her high, high up—high up and in the light."

"Ah you naturally want to marry her to a duke and are eager to smooth away any hitch."

She gave him so, on this, the mere effect of the drawn blind that it quite forced him at first into the sense, possibly just, of his having shown for flippant, perhaps even for low. He had been looked at so, in blighted moments of presumptuous youth, by big cold public men, but never, so far as he could recall, by any private lady. More than anything yet it gave him the measure of his companion's subtlety, and thereby of Kate's possible career. "Don't be *too* impossible!"—he feared from his friend, for a moment, some such answer as that; and then felt, as she spoke otherwise, as if she were letting him off easily. "I want her to marry a great man." That was all; but, more and more, it was enough; and if it hadn't been her next words would have made it so. "And I think of her what I think. There you are."

They sat for a little face to face upon it, and he was conscious of something deeper still, of something she wished him to understand if he only would. To that extent she did appeal—appealed to the intelligence she desired to show she believed him to possess. He was meanwhile, at all events, not the man wholly to fail of comprehension. "Of course I'm aware how little I can answer to any fond proud dream. You've a view—a grand one; into which I perfectly enter. I thoroughly understand what I'm not, and I'm much obliged to you for not reminding me of it in any rougher way." She said nothing—she kept that up; it might even have been to let him go further, if he was capable of it, in the way of poorness of spirit. It was one of those cases in which a man couldn't show, if he showed at all, save for poor; unless indeed he preferred to show for asinine. It was the plain truth: he *was*—on Mrs. Lowder's basis, the only one in question—a very small quantity, and he did know, damnably, what made quantities large. He desired to be perfectly simple, yet in the midst of that effort a deeper apprehension throbbed. Aunt Maud clearly conveyed it, though he couldn't later on have said how. "You don't really matter, I believe, so much as you think, and I'm not going to make you a martyr by banishing you. Your performances with Kate in the Park are ridiculous so far as they're meant as consideration for me; and I had much rather see you myself—since you're, in your way, my dear young man, delightful—and arrange with you, count with you, as I easily, as I perfectly should. Do you suppose me so stupid as to quarrel with you if it's not really necessary? It won't—it would be too absurd!— *be* necessary. I can bite your head off any day, any day I really open my mouth; and I'm dealing with you now, see—and successfully judge—without opening it. I do things handsomely all round—I place you in the presence of the plan with which, from the moment it's a case of taking you seriously, you're incompatible. Come then as near as you like, walk all round it—don't be afraid you'll hurt it!—and live on with it before you."

He afterwards felt that if she hadn't absolutely phrased all this it was because she so soon made him out as going with her far enough. He was so pleasantly affected by her asking no promise of him, her not proposing he should pay for her indulgence by his word of honour not to interfere, that he gave her a kind of general assurance of esteem. Immediately afterwards then he was to speak of these things to Kate, and what by that time came back to him first of all was the way he had said to her—he mentioned it to the girl—very much as one of a pair of lovers says in a rupture by mutual consent: "I hope immensely of course that you'll always regard me as a friend." This had perhaps been going far—he submitted it all to Kate; but really there had been so much in it that it was to be looked at, as they might say, wholly in its own light. Other things than those we have presented had come up before the close of his scene with Aunt Maud, but this matter of her not treating him as a peril of the first order easily predominated. There was moreover plenty to talk about on the occasion of his subsequent passage with our young woman, it having been put to him abruptly, the night before, that he might give himself a lift and do his newspaper a service—so flatteringly was the case expressed—by going for fifteen or twenty weeks to America. The idea of a series of letters from the United States from the strictly so-

cial point of view had for some time been nursed in the inner sanc-
tuary at whose door he sat, and the moment was now deemed
happy for letting it loose. The imprisoned thought had, in a word,
on the opening of the door, flown straight out into Densher's face,
or perched at least on his shoulder, making him look up in surprise from his mere inky office-table. His account of the matter to
Kate was that he couldn't refuse—not being in a position as yet to
refuse anything; but that his being chosen for such an errand con-
founded his sense of proportion. He was definite as to his scarce
knowing how to measure the honour, which struck him as equivocal; he hadn't quite supposed himself the man for the class of job.
This confused consciousness, he intimated, he had promptly
enough betrayed to his manager; with the effect, however, of seeing the question surprisingly clear up. What it came to was that the
sort of twaddle that wasn't in his chords was, unexpectedly, just
what they happened this time not to want. They wanted his letters,
for queer reasons, about as good as he could let them come; he was
to play his own little tune and not be afraid; that was the whole
point.

It would have been the whole, that is, had there not been a
sharper one still in the circumstance that he was to start at once.
His mission, as they called it at the office, would probably be over
by the end of June, which was desirable; but to bring that about he
must now not lose a week; his enquiries, he understood, were to
cover the whole ground, and there were reasons of state—reasons
operating at the seat of empire in Fleet Street—why the nail
should be struck on the head. Densher made no secret to Kate of
his having asked for a day to decide; and his account of that matter was that he felt he owed it to her to speak to her first. She assured him on this that nothing so much as that scruple had yet
shown her how they were bound together: she was clearly proud of
his letting a thing of such importance depend on her, but she was
clearer still as to his instant duty. She rejoiced in his prospect and
urged him to his task; she should miss him too dreadfully—of
course she should miss him; but she made so little of it that she
spoke with jubilation of what he would see and would do. She
made so much of this last quantity that he laughed at her innocence, though also with scarce the heart to give her the real size of

his drop in the daily bucket. He was struck at the same time with her happy grasp of what had really occurred in Fleet Street—all the more that it was his own final reading. He was to pull the subject up—that was just what they wanted; and it would take more than all the United States together, visit them each as he might, to let *him* down. It was just because he didn't nose about and babble, because he wasn't the usual gossip-monger, that they had picked him out. It was a branch of their correspondence with which they evidently wished a new tone associated, such a tone as, from now on, it would have always to take from his example.

"How you ought indeed, when you understand so well, to be a journalist's wife!" Densher exclaimed in admiration even while she struck him as fairly hurrying him off.

But she was almost impatient of the praise. "What do you expect one *not* to understand when one cares for you?"

"Ah then I'll put it otherwise and say 'How much you care for me!'"

"Yes," she assented; "it fairly redeems my stupidity. I *shall*, with a chance to show it," she added, "have some imagination for you."

She spoke of the future this time as so little contingent that he felt a queerness of conscience in making her the report that he presently arrived at on what had passed for him with the real arbiter of their destiny. The way for that had been blocked a little by his news from Fleet Street; but in the crucible of their happy discussion this element soon melted into the other, and in the mixture that ensued the parts were not to be distinguished. The young man moreover, before taking his leave, was to see why Kate had spoken with a wisdom indifferent to that, and was to come to the vision by a devious way that deepened the final cheer. Their faces were turned to the illumined quarter as soon as he had answered her question on the score of their being to appearance able to play patience, a prodigious game of patience, with success. It was for the possibility of the appearance that she had a few days before so earnestly pressed him to see her aunt; and if after his hour with that lady it had not struck Densher that he had seen her to the happiest purpose the poor facts flushed with a better meaning as Kate, one by one, took them up.

"If she consents to your coming why isn't that everything?"

"It *is* everything; everything *she* thinks it. It's the probability—I mean as Mrs. Lowder measures probability—that I may be prevented from becoming a complication for her by some arrangement, *any* arrangement, through which you shall see me often and easily. She's sure of my want of money, and that gives her time. She believes in my having a certain amount of delicacy, in my wishing to better my state before I put the pistol to your head in respect to sharing it. The time this will take figures for her as the time that will help her if she doesn't spoil her chance by treating me badly. She doesn't at all wish moreover," Densher went on, "to treat me badly, for I believe, upon my honour, odd as it may sound to you, that she personally rather likes me and that if you weren't in question I might almost become her pet young man. She doesn't disparage intellect and culture—quite the contrary; she wants them to adorn her board and be associated with her name; and I'm sure it has sometimes cost her a real pang that I should be so desirable, at once, and so impossible." He paused a moment, and his companion then saw how strange a smile was in his face—a smile as strange even as the adjunct in her own of this informing vision. "I quite suspect her of believing that, if the truth were known, she likes me literally better than—deep down—you yourself do: wherefore she does me the honour to think I may be safely left to kill my own cause. There, as I say, comes in her margin. I'm not the sort of stuff of romance that wears, that washes, that survives use, that resists familiarity. Once in any degree admit that, and your pride and prejudice will take care of the rest!—the pride fed full, meanwhile, by the system she means to practise with you, and the prejudice excited by the comparisons she'll enable you to make, from which I shall come off badly. She likes me, but she'll never like me so much as when she has succeeded a little better in making me look wretched. For then *you'll* like me less."

Kate showed for this evocation a due interest, but no alarm; and it was a little as if to pay his tender cynicism back in kind that she after an instant replied: "I see, I see—what an immense affair she must think me! One was aware, but you deepen the impression."

"I think you'll make no mistake," said Densher, "in letting it go as deep as it will."

He had given her indeed, she made no scruple of showing,

plenty to amuse herself with. "Her facing the music, her making you boldly as welcome as you say—that's an awfully big theory, you know, and worthy of all the other big things that in one's acquaintance with people give her a place so apart."

"Oh she's grand," the young man allowed; "she's on the scale altogether of the car of Juggernaut*—which was a kind of image that came to me yesterday while I waited for her at Lancaster Gate. The things in your drawing-room there were like the forms of the strange idols, the mystic excrescences, with which one may suppose the front of the car to bristle."

"Yes, aren't they?" the girl returned; and they had, over all that aspect of their wonderful lady, one of those deep and free interchanges that made everything but confidence a false note for them. There were complications, there were questions; but they were so much more together than they were anything else. Kate uttered for a while no word of refutation of Aunt Maud's "big" diplomacy, and they left it there, as they would have left any other fine product, for a monument to her powers. But, Densher related further, he had had in other respects too the car of Juggernaut to face; he omitted nothing from his account of his visit; least of all the way Aunt Maud had frankly at last—though indeed only under artful pressure—fallen foul of his very type, his want of the right marks, his foreign accidents, his queer antecedents. She had told him he was but half a Briton, which, he granted Kate, would have been dreadful if he hadn't so let himself in for it.

"I was really curious, you see," he explained, "to find out from her what sort of queer creature, what sort of social anomaly, in the light of such conventions as hers, such an education as mine makes one pass for."

---

*Corruption of the Sanskrit word *Jagannatha*, the manifestation of the Hindu god Krishna. The deity was honoured at a festival in which wooden images of the god were placed in an extremely heavy, highly carved chariot (car) that was pulled forward by hundreds of followers. Contemporary Europeans erroneously believed that devotees threw themselves under the wheels of the chariot to be crushed; hence, the colloquial usage of "Juggernaut" as a relentless, overpowering, and irrational force.

Kate said nothing for a little; but then, "Why should you care?" she asked.

"Oh," he laughed, "I like her so much; and then, for a man of my trade, her views, her spirit, are essentially a thing to get hold of: they belong to the great public mind that we meet at every turn and that we must keep setting up 'codes' with. Besides," he added, "I want to please her personally."

"Ah yes, we must please her personally!" his companion echoed; and the words may represent all their definite recognition, at the time, of Densher's politic gain. They had in fact between this and his start for New York many matters to handle, and the question he now touched upon came up for Kate above all. She looked at him as if he had really told her aunt more of his imme-diate personal story than he had ever told herself. This, if it had been so, was an accident, and it perched him there with her for half an hour, like a cicerone* and his victim on a tower-top, before as much of the bird's-eye view of his early years abroad, his migra-tory parents, his Swiss schools, his German university, as she had easy attention for. A man, he intimated, a man of their world, would have spotted him straight as to many of these points; a man of their world, so far as they had a world, would have been through the English mill. But it was none the less charming to make his confession to a woman; women had in fact for such differences blessedly more imagination and blessedly more sympathy. Kate showed at present as much of both as his case could require; when she had had it from beginning to end she declared that she now made out more than ever yet what she loved him for. She had her-self, as a child, lived with some continuity in the world across the Channel, coming home again still a child; and had participated after that, in her teens, in her mother's brief but repeated retreats to Dresden, to Florence, to Biarritz, weak and expensive attempts at economy from which there stuck to her—though in general coldly expressed, through the instinctive avoidance of cheap rap-tures—the religion of foreign things. When it was revealed to her how many more foreign things were in Merton Densher than he

---

*Tourist guide.

had hitherto taken the trouble to catalogue, she almost faced him as if he were a map of the continent or a handsome present of a delightful new "Murray."* He hadn't meant to swagger, he had rather meant to plead, though with Mrs. Lowder he had meant also a little to explain. His father had been, in strange countries, in twenty settlements of the English, British chaplain, resident or occasional, and had had for years the unusual luck of never wanting a billet. His career abroad had therefore been unbroken, and as his stipend had never been great he had educated his children, at the smallest cost, in the schools nearest; which was also a saving of railway-fares. Densher's mother, it further appeared, had practised on her side a distinguished industry, to the success of which—so far as success ever crowned it—this period of exile had much contributed: she copied, patient lady, famous pictures in great museums, having begun with a happy natural gift and taking in betimes the scale of her opportunity. Copyists abroad of course swarmed, but Mrs. Densher had had a sense and a hand of her own, had arrived at a perfection that persuaded, that even deceived, and that made the "placing" of her work blissfully usual. Her son, who had lost her, held her image sacred, and the effect of his telling Kate all about her, as well as about other matters until then mixed and dim, was to render his history rich, his sources full, his outline anything but common. He had come round, he had come back, he insisted abundantly, to being a Briton: his Cambridge years, his happy connexion, as it had proved, with his father's college, amply certified to that, to say nothing of his subsequent plunge into London, which filled up the measure. But brave enough though his descent to English earth, he had passed, by the way, through zones of air that had left their ruffle on his wings—he had been exposed to initiations indelible. Something had happened to him that could never be undone.

When Kate Croy said to him as much he besought her not to insist, declaring that this indeed was what was gravely the matter with him, that he had been but too probably spoiled for native, for insular use. On which, not unnaturally, she insisted the more, as-

---

*The London firm of John Murray published tourist handbooks.

suring him, without mitigation, that if he was various and complicated, complicated by wit and taste, she wouldn't for the world
have had him more helpless; so that he was driven in the end to
accuse her of putting the dreadful truth to him in the hollow guise
of flattery. She was making him out as all abnormal in order that
she might eventually find him impossible, and since she could
make it out but with his aid she had to bribe him by feigned delight to help her. If her last word for him in the connexion was that
the way he saw himself was just a precious proof the more of his
having tasted of the tree and being thereby prepared to assist her
to eat, this gives the happy tone of their whole talk; the measure of
the flight of time in the near presence of his settled departure.
Kate showed, however, that she was to be more literally taken
when she spoke of the relief Aunt Maud would draw from the
prospect of his absence.

"Yet one can scarcely see why," he replied, "when she fears me
so little."

His friend weighed his objection. "Your idea is that she likes
you so much that she'll even go so far as to regret losing you?"

Well, he saw it in their constant comprehensive way. "Since
what she builds on is the gradual process of your alienation, she
may take the view that the process constantly requires me. Mustn't
I be there to keep it going? It's in my exile that it may languish."

He went on with that fantasy, but at this point Kate ceased to attend. He saw after a little that she had been following some
thought of her own, and he had been feeling the growth of something determinant even through the extravagance of much of the
pleasantry, the warm transparent irony, into which their livelier intimacy kept plunging like a confident swimmer. Suddenly she said
to him with extraordinary beauty: "I engage myself to you for ever."

The beauty was in everything, and he could have separated
nothing—couldn't have thought of her face as distinct from the
whole joy. Yet her face had a new light. "And I pledge you—I call
God to witness!—every spark of my faith; I give you every drop of
my life." That was all, for the moment, but it was enough, and it
was almost as quiet as if it were nothing. They were in the open
air, in an alley of the Gardens; the great space, which seemed to
arch just then higher and spread wider for them, threw them back

into deep concentration. They moved by a common instinct to a spot, within sight, that struck them as fairly sequestered, and there, before their time together was spent, they had extorted from concentration every advance it could make them. They had exchanged vows and tokens, sealed their rich compact, solemnised, so far as breathed words and murmured sounds and lighted eyes and clasped hands could do it, their agreement to belong only, and to belong tremendously, to each other. They were to leave the place accordingly an affianced couple, but before they left it other things still had passed. Densher had declared his horror of bringing to a premature end her happy relation with her aunt; and they had worked round together to a high level of discretion. Kate's free profession was that she wished not to deprive *him* of Mrs. Lowder's countenance, which in the long run she was convinced he would continue to enjoy; and as by a blest turn Aunt Maud had demanded of him no promise that would tie his hands they should be able to propitiate their star in their own way and yet remain loyal. One difficulty alone stood out, which Densher named.

"Of course it will never do—we must remember that—from the moment you allow her to found hopes of you for any one else in particular. So long as her view is content to remain as general as at present appears I don't see that we deceive her. At a given hour, you see, she must be undeceived: the only thing therefore is to be ready for the hour and to face it. Only, after all, in that case," the young man observed, "one doesn't quite make out what we shall have got from her."

"What she'll have got from *us?*" Kate put it with a smile. "What she'll have got from us," the girl went on, "is her own affair—it's for *her* to measure. I asked her for nothing," she added; "I never put myself upon her. She must take her risks, and she surely understands them. What we shall have got from her is what we've already spoken of," Kate further explained; "it's that we shall have gained time. And so, for that matter, will she."

Densher gazed a little at all this clearness; his gaze was not at the present hour into romantic obscurity. "Yes; no doubt, in our particular situation, time's everything. And then there's the joy of it."

She hesitated. "Of our secret?"

"Not so much perhaps of our secret in itself, but of what's represented and, as we must somehow feel, secured to us and made deeper and closer by it." And his fine face, relaxed into happiness, covered her with all his meaning. "Our being as we are."

It was as if for a moment she let the meaning sink into her. "So gone?"

"So gone. So extremely gone. However," he smiled, "we shall go a good deal further." Her answer to which was only the softness of her silence—a silence that looked out for them both at the far reach of their prospect. This was immense, and they thus took final possession of it. They were practically united and splendidly strong; but there were other things—things they were precisely strong enough to be able successfully to count with and safely to allow for; in consequence of which they would for the present, subject to some better reason, keep their understanding to themselves. It was not indeed however till after one more observation of Densher's that they felt the question completely straightened out. "The only thing of course is that she may any day absolutely put it to you."

Kate considered. "Ask me where, on my honour, we are? She may, naturally; but I doubt if in fact she will. While you're away she'll make the most of that drop of the tension. She'll leave me alone."

"But there'll be my letters."

The girl faced his letters. "Very, very many?"

"Very, very, very many—more than ever; and you know what that is! And then," Densher added, "there'll be yours."

"Oh I shan't leave mine on the hall-table. I shall post them myself."

He looked at her a moment. "Do you think then I had best address you elsewhere?" After which, before she could quite answer, he added with some emphasis: "I'd rather not, you know. It's straighter."

She might again have just waited. "Of course it's straighter. Don't be afraid I shan't be straight. Address me," she continued, "where you like. I shall be proud enough of its being known you write to me."

He turned it over for the last clearness. "Even at the risk of its really bringing down the inquisition?"

Well, the last clearness now filled her. "I'm not afraid of the inquisition. If she asks if there's anything definite between us I know perfectly what I shall say."

"That I *am* of course 'gone' for you?"

"That I love you as I shall never in my life love any one else, and that she can make what she likes of that." She said it out so splendidly that it was like a new profession of faith, the fulness of a tide breaking through; and the effect of that in turn was to make her companion meet her with such eyes that she had time again before he could otherwise speak. "Besides, she's just as likely to ask *you.*"

"Not while I'm away."

"Then when you come back."

"Well then," said Densher, "we shall have had our particular joy. But what I feel is," he candidly added, "that, by an idea of her own, her superior policy, she *won't* ask me. She'll let me off. I shan't have to lie to her."

"It will be left all to me?" asked Kate.

"All to you!" he tenderly laughed.

But it was oddly, the very next moment, as if he had perhaps been a shade too candid. His discrimination seemed to mark a possible, a natural reality, a reality not wholly disallowed by the account the girl had just given of her own intention. There *was* a difference in the air—even if none other than the supposedly usual difference in truth between man and woman; and it was almost as if the sense of this provoked her. She seemed to cast about an instant, and then she went back a little resentfully to something she had suffered to pass a minute before. She appeared to take up rather more seriously than she need the joke about her freedom to deceive. Yet she did this too in a beautiful way. "Men are too stupid—even you. You didn't understand just now why, if I post my letters myself, it won't be for anything so vulgar as to hide them."

"Oh you named it—for the pleasure."

"Yes; but you didn't, you don't, understand what the pleasure may be. There are refinements—!" she more patiently dropped. "I mean of consciousness, of sensation, of appreciation," she went on. "No," she sadly insisted—"men *don't* know. They know in such matters almost nothing but what women show them."

This was one of the speeches, frequent in her, that, liberally, joyfully, intensely adopted and, in itself, as might be, embraced, drew him again as close to her, and held him as long, as their conditions permitted. "Then that's exactly why we've such an abysmal need of you!"

BOOK THIRD

— I —

The two ladies who, in advance of the Swiss season, had been warned that their design was unconsidered, that the passes wouldn't be clear, nor the air mild, nor the inns open—the two ladies who, characteristically, had braved a good deal of possibly interested remonstrance were finding themselves, as their adventure turned out, wonderfully sustained. It was the judgement of the head-waiters and other functionaries on the Italian lakes that approved itself now as interested; they themselves had been conscious of impatiences, of bolder dreams—at least the younger had; so that one of the things they made out together—making out as they did in endless variety—was that in those operatic palaces of the Villa d'Este, of Cadenabbia, of Pallanza and Stresa, lone women, however re-enforced by a travelling-library of instructive volumes, were apt to be beguiled and undone. Their flights of fancy moreover had been modest; they had for instance risked nothing vital in hoping to make their way by the Brünig. They were making it in fact happily enough as we meet them, and were only wishing that, for the wondrous beauty of the early high-climbing spring, it might have been longer and the places to pause and rest more numerous.

Such at least had been the intimated attitude of Mrs. Stringham, the elder of the companions, who had her own view of the impatiences of the younger, to which, however, she offered an opposition but of the most circuitous. She moved, the admirable Mrs. Stringham, in a fine cloud of observation and suspicion; she was in the position, as she believed, of knowing much more about Milly Theale than Milly herself knew, and yet of having to darken her knowledge as well as make it active. The woman in the world least formed by nature, as she was quite aware, for duplicities and labyrinths, she found herself dedicated to personal subtlety by a new set of circumstances, above all by a new personal relation; had now in fact to recognise that an education in the occult—she

could scarce say what to call it—had begun for her the day she left
New York with Mildred. She had come on from Boston for that
purpose; had seen little of the girl—or rather had seen her but
briefly, for Mrs. Stringham, when she saw anything at all, saw
much, saw everything—before accepting her proposal; and had accordingly placed herself, by her act, in a boat that she more and
more estimated as, humanly speaking, of the biggest, though likewise, no doubt, in many ways, by reason of its size, of the safest. In
Boston, the winter before, the young lady in whom we are interested had, on the spot, deeply, yet almost tacitly, appealed to her,
dropped into her mind the shy conceit of some assistance, some
devotion to render. Mrs. Stringham's little life had often been visited by shy conceits—secret dreams that had fluttered their hour
between its narrow walls without, for any great part, so much as
mustering courage to look out of its rather dim windows. But this
imagination—the fancy of a possible link with the remarkable
young thing from New York—*had* mustered courage: had
perched, on the instant, at the clearest lookout it could find, and
might be said to have remained there till, only a few months later,
it* had caught, in surprise and joy, the unmistakeable flash of a
signal.

Milly Theale had Boston friends, such as they were, and of recent making; and it was understood that her visit to them—a visit
that was not to be meagre—had been undertaken, after a series of
bereavements, in the interest of the particular peace that New York
couldn't give. It was recognised, liberally enough, that there were
many things—perhaps even too many—New York *could* give; but
this was felt to make no difference in the important truth that what
you had most to do, under the discipline of life, or of death, was
really to feel your situation as grave. Boston could help you to that
as nothing else could, and it had extended to Milly, by every presumption, some such measure of assistance. Mrs. Stringham was
never to forget—for the moment had not faded, nor the infinitely
fine vibration it set up in any degree ceased—her own first sight of
the striking apparition, then unheralded and unexplained: the

---

*The "it" refers to Mrs. Stringham's imagination.

slim, constantly pale, delicately haggard, anomalously, agreeably
angular young person, of not more than two-and-twenty summers,
in spite of her marks, whose hair was somehow exceptionally red
even for the real thing, which it innocently confessed to being,
and whose clothes were remarkably black even for robes of mourning, which was the meaning they expressed. It was New York
mourning, it was New York hair, it was a New York history, confused as yet, but multitudinous, of the loss of parents, brothers, sisters, almost every human appendage, all on a scale and with a
sweep that had required the greater stage; it was a New York legend of affecting, of romantic isolation, and, beyond everything, it
was by most accounts, in respect to the mass of money so piled on
the girl's back, a set of New York possibilities. She was alone, she
was stricken, she was rich, and in particular was strange—a combination in itself of a nature to engage Mrs. Stringham's attention.
But it was the strangeness that most determined our good lady's
sympathy, convinced as she had to be that it was greater than any
one else—any one but the sole Susan Stringham—supposed.
Susan privately settled it that Boston was not in the least seeing
her, was only occupied with her seeing Boston, and that any assumed affinity between the two characters was delusive and vain.
She was seeing her, and she had quite the finest moment of her
life in now obeying the instinct to conceal the vision. She
couldn't explain it—no one would understand. They would say
clever Boston things—Mrs. Stringham was from Burlington Vermont, which, she boldly upheld as the real heart of New England, Boston being "too far south"—but they would only darken
counsel.

There could be no better proof (than this quick intellectual
split) of the impression made on our friend, who shone herself, she
was well aware, with but the reflected light of the admirable city.
She too had had her discipline, but it had not made her striking;
it had been prosaically usual, though doubtless a decent dose; and
had only made her usual to match it—usual, that is, as Boston
went. She had lost first her husband and then her mother, with
whom, on her husband's death, she had lived again; so that now,
childless, she was but more sharply single than before. Yet she sat
rather coldly light, having, as she called it, enough to live on—so

far, that is, as she lived by bread alone: how little indeed she was regularly content with that diet appeared from the name she had made—Susan Shepherd Stringham—as a contributor to the best magazines. She wrote short stories, and she fondly believed she had her "note," the art of showing New England without showing it wholly in the kitchen. She had not herself been brought up in the kitchen; she knew others who had not; and to speak for them had thus become with her a literary mission. To be in truth literary had ever been her dearest thought, the thought that kept her bright little nippers* perpetually in position. There were masters, models, celebrities, mainly foreign, whom she finally accounted so and in whose light she ingeniously laboured; there were others whom, however chattered about, she ranked with the inane, for she bristled with discriminations; but all categories failed her— they ceased at least to signify—as soon as she found herself in presence of the real thing, the romantic life itself. That was what she saw in Mildred—what positively made her hand a while tremble too much for the pen. She had had, it seemed to her, a revelation—such as even New England refined and grammatical couldn't give; and, all made up as she was of small neat memories and ingenuities, little industries and ambitions, mixed with something moral, personal, that was still more intensely responsive, she felt her new friend would have done her an ill turn if their friendship shouldn't develop, and yet that nothing would be left of anything else if it should. It was for the surrender of everything else that she was, however, quite prepared, and while she went about her usual Boston business with her usual Boston probity she was really all the while holding herself. She wore her "handsome" felt hat, so Tyrolese, yet somehow, though feathered from the eagle's wing, so truly domestic, with the same straightness and security; she attached her fur boa with the same honest precautions; she preserved her balance on the ice-slopes with the same practised skill; she opened, each evening, her *Transcript*† with the same in-

---

*Colloquial term for tools or implements; in this context a reference to Mrs. String-ham's literary skills being honed and ready. Elsewhere, James uses "nippers" to mean the nosepiece of a pair of eyeglasses.
†Boston newspaper of the period.

terfusion of suspense and resignation; she attended her almost daily concert with the same expenditure of patience and the same economy of passion; she flitted in and out of the Public Library with the air of conscientiously returning or bravely carrying off in her pocket the key of knowledge itself; and finally—it was what she most did—she watched the thin trickle of a fictive "love-interest" through that somewhat serpentine channel, in the magazines, which she mainly managed to keep clear for it. But the real thing all the while was elsewhere; the real thing had gone back to New York, leaving behind it the two unsolved questions, quite distinct, of why it *was* real, and whether she should ever be so near it again.

For the figure to which these questions attached themselves she had found a convenient description—she thought of it for herself always as that of a girl with a background. The great reality was in the fact that, very soon, after but two or three meetings, the girl with the background, the girl with the crown of old gold and the mourning that was not as the mourning of Boston, but at once more rebellious in its gloom and more frivolous in its frills, had told her she had never seen any one like her. They had met thus as opposed curiosities, and that simple remark of Milly's—if simple it was—became the most important thing that had ever happened to her; it deprived the love-interest, for the time, of actuality and even of pertinence; it moved her first, in short, in a high degree, to gratitude, and then to no small compassion. Yet in respect to this relation at least it was what did prove the key of knowledge; it lighted up as nothing else could do the poor young woman's history. That the potential heiress of all the ages should never have seen any one like a mere typical subscriber, after all, to the *Transcript* was a truth that—in especial as announced with modesty, with humility, with regret—described a situation. It laid upon the elder woman, as to the void to be filled, a weight of responsibility; but in particular it led her to ask whom poor Mildred *had* then seen, and what range of contacts it had taken to produce such queer surprises. That was really the enquiry that had ended by clearing the air: the key of knowledge was felt to click in the lock from the moment it flashed upon Mrs. Stringham that her friend had been starved for culture. Culture was what she herself represented for her, and it was living up to that principle that would surely prove the great business. She knew, the clever lady, what the principle itself represented, and the limits of her own store; and a certain alarm would have grown upon her if something else hadn't grown faster. This was, fortunately for her—and we give it in her own words—the sense of a harrowing pathos. That, primarily, was what appealed to her, what seemed to open the door of romance for her still wider than any, than a still more reckless, connexion with the "picture-papers." For such was essentially the point: it was rich, romantic, abysmal, to have, as was evident, thousands and thousands a year, to have youth and intelligence and, if not beauty, at least in equal measure a high dim charming ambiguous oddity, which was even better, and then on top of all to enjoy boundless freedom, the freedom of the wind in the desert—it was unspeakably touching to be so equipped and yet to have been reduced by fortune to little humble-minded mistakes.

It brought our friend's imagination back again to New York, where aberrations were so possible in the intellectual sphere, and it in fact caused a visit she presently paid there to overflow with interest. As Milly had beautifully invited her, so she would hold out if she could against the strain of so much confidence in her mind; and the remarkable thing was that even at the end of three weeks she *had* held out. But by this time her mind had grown comparatively bold and free; it was dealing with new quantities, a different proportion altogether—and that had made for refreshment: she had accordingly gone home in convenient possession of her subject. New York was vast, New York was startling, with strange histories, with wild cosmopolite backward generations that accounted for anything; and to have got nearer the luxuriant tribe of which the rare creature was the final flower, the immense extravagant unregulated cluster, with free-living ancestors, handsome dead cousins, lurid uncles, beautiful vanished aunts, persons all busts and curls, preserved, though so exposed, in the marble of famous French chisels—all this, to say nothing of the effect of closer growths of the stem, was to have had one's small world-space both crowded and enlarged. Our couple had at all events effected an exchange; the elder friend had been as consciously intellectual as possible, and the younger, abounding in personal revelation, had been as distinguished. This was poetry—it was also history—

Mrs. Stringham thought, to a finer tune even than Maeterlinck and Pater, than Marbot and Gregorovius.* She appointed occasions for the reading of these authors with her hostess, rather perhaps than actually achieved great spans; but what they managed and what they missed speedily sank for her into the dim depths of the merely relative, so quickly, so strongly had she clutched her central clue. All her scruples and hesitations, all her anxious enthusiasms, had reduced themselves to a single alarm—the fear that she really might act on her companion clumsily and coarsely. She was positively afraid of what she might do to her, and to avoid that, to avoid it with piety and passion, to do, rather, nothing at all, to leave her untouched because no touch one could apply, however light, however just, however earnest and anxious, would be half good enough, would be anything but an ugly smutch upon perfection—this now imposed itself as a consistent, an inspiring thought.

Less than a month after the event that had so determined Mrs. Stringham's attitude—close upon the heels, that is, of her return from New York—she was reached by a proposal that brought up for her the kind of question her delicacy might have to contend with. Would she start for Europe with her young friend at the earliest possible date, and should she be willing to do so without making conditions? The enquiry was launched by wire; explanations, in sufficiency, were promised; extreme urgency was suggested and a general surrender invited. It was to the honour of her sincerity that she made the surrender on the spot, though it was not perhaps altogether to that of her logic. She had wanted, very consciously, from the first, to give something up for her new acquaintance, but she had now no doubt that she was practically giving up all. What settled this was the fulness of a particular impression, the impression that had throughout more and more supported her and which she would have uttered so far as she might by saying that the charm of the creature was positively in the creature's greatness.

---

*Literary figures of the nineteenth century: Belgian dramatist and poet Maurice Maeterlinck; British critic Walter Pater; French nobleman and memoirist Jean-Baptiste Antoine Marcellin Marbot; and German historian Ferdinand Adolf Gregorovius.

She would have been content so to leave it; unless indeed she had said, more familiarly, that Mildred was the biggest impression of her life. That was at all events the biggest account of her, and none but a big clearly would do. Her situation, as such things were called, was on the grand scale; but it still was not that. It was her nature, once for all—a nature that reminded Mrs. Stringham of the term always used in the newspapers about the great new steamers, the inordinate number of "feet of water" they drew; so that if, in your little boat, you had chosen to hover and approach, you had but yourself to thank, when once motion was started, for the way the draught pulled you. Milly drew the feet of water, and odd though it might seem that a lonely girl, who was not robust and who hated sound and show, should stir the stream like a leviathan, her companion floated off with the sense of rocking violently at her side. More than prepared, however, for that excitement, Mrs. Stringham mainly failed of ease in respect to her own consistency. To attach herself for an indefinite time seemed a roundabout way of holding her hands off. If she wished to be sure of neither touching nor smutching, the straighter plan would doubtless have been not to keep her friend within reach. This in fact she fully recognised, and with it the degree to which she desired that the girl should lead her life, a life certain to be so much finer than that of anybody else. The difficulty, however, by good fortune, cleared away as soon as she had further recognised, as she was speedily able to do, that she Susan Shepherd—the name with which Milly for the most part amused herself—was *not* anybody else. She had renounced that character; she had now no life to lead; and she honestly believed that she was thus supremely equipped for leading Milly's own. No other person whatever, she was sure, had to an equal degree this qualification, and it was really to assert it that she fondly embarked.

Many things, though not in many weeks, had come and gone since then, and one of the best of them doubtless had been the voyage itself, by the happy southern course, to the succession of Mediterranean ports, with the dazzled wind-up at Naples. Two or three others had preceded this; incidents, indeed rather lively marks, of their last fortnight at home, and one of which had determined on Mrs. Stringham's part a rush to New York, forty-eight breathless hours there, previous to her final rally. But the great sustained sea-light had drunk up the rest of the picture, so that for many days other questions and other possibilities sounded with as little effect as a trio of penny whistles might sound in a Wagner overture. It was the Wagner overture that practically prevailed, up through Italy, where Milly had already been, still further up and across the Alps, which were also partly known to Mrs. Stringham; only perhaps "taken" to a time not wholly congruous, hurried in fact on account of the girl's high restlessness. She had been expected, she had frankly promised, to be restless—that was partly why she was "great"—or was a consequence, at any rate, if not a cause; yet she had not perhaps altogether announced herself as straining so hard at the cord. It was familiar, it was beautiful to Mrs. Stringham that she had arrears to make up, the chances that had lapsed for her through the wanton ways of forefathers fond of Paris, but not of its higher sides, and fond almost of nothing else; but the vagueness, the openness, the eagerness without point and the interest without pause—all a part of the charm of her oddity as at first presented—had become more striking in proportion as they triumphed over movement and change. She had arts and idiosyncrasies of which no great account could have been given, but which were a daily grace if you lived with them; such as the art of being almost tragically impatient and yet making it as light as air; of being inexplicably sad and yet making it as clear as noon; of being unmistakeably gay and yet making it as soft as dusk. Mrs. Stringham by this time understood everything, was more than ever confirmed in wonder and admiration, in her view that it was life enough simply to feel her companion's feelings; but there were special keys she had not yet added to her bunch, impressions that of a sudden were apt to affect her as new.

This particular day on the great Swiss road had been, for some reason, full of them, and they referred themselves, provisionally, to some deeper depth than she had touched—though into two or three such depths, it must be added, she had peeped long enough to find herself suddenly draw back. It was not Milly's unpacified state, in short, that now troubled her—though certainly, as Europe was the great American sedative, the failure was to some extent to be noted: it was the suspected presence of something behind the state—which, however, could scarcely have taken its place there since their departure. What a fresh motive of unrest could suddenly have sprung from was in short not to be divined. It was but half an explanation to say that excitement, for each of them, had naturally dropped, and that what they had left behind, or tried to—the great serious facts of life, as Mrs. Stringham liked to call them—was once more coming into sight as objects loom through smoke when smoke begins to clear; for these were general appearances from which the girl's own aspect, her really larger vagueness, seemed rather to disconnect itself. The nearest approach to a personal anxiety indulged in as yet by the elder lady was on her taking occasion to wonder if what she had more than anything else got hold of mightn't be one of the finer, one of the finest, one of the rarest—as she called it so that she might call it nothing worse—cases of American intensity. She had just had a moment of alarm—asked herself if her young friend were merely going to treat her to some complicated drama of nerves. At the end of a week, however, with their further progress, her young friend had effectively answered the question and given her the impression, indistinct indeed as yet, of something that had a reality compared with which the nervous explanation would have been coarse. Mrs. Stringham found herself from that hour, in other words, in presence of an explanation that remained a muffled and intangible form, but that assuredly, should it take on sharpness, would explain everything and more than everything, would become instantly the light in which Milly was to be read.

Such a matter as this may at all events speak of the style in which our young woman could affect those who were near her, may testify to the sort of interest she could inspire. She worked—and seemingly quite without design—upon the sympathy, the curiosity, the fancy of her associates, and we shall really ourselves scarce otherwise come closer to her than by feeling their impression and sharing, if need be, their confusion.[8] She reduced them, Mrs. Stringham would have said, to a consenting bewilderment; which was precisely, for that good lady, on a last analysis, what was most in harmony with her greatness. She exceeded, escaped measure, was surprising only because *they* were so far from great. Thus it was that on this wondrous day by the Brünig the spell of watching her had grown more than ever irresistible; a proof of what—or of a part of what—Mrs. Stringham had, with all the rest, been reduced to. She had almost the sense of tracking her young friend as if at a given moment to pounce. She knew she shouldn't pounce, she hadn't come out to pounce; yet she felt her attention secretive, all the same, and her observation scientific. She struck herself as hovering like a spy, applying tests, laying traps, concealing signs. This would last, however, only till she should fairly know what was the matter; and to watch was after all, meanwhile, a way of clinging to the girl, not less than an occupation, a satisfaction in itself. The pleasure of watching moreover, if a reason were needed, came from a sense of her beauty. Her beauty hadn't at all originally seemed a part of the situation, and Mrs. Stringham had even in the first flush of friendship not named it grossly to any one; having seen early that for stupid people—and who, she sometimes secretly asked herself, wasn't stupid?—it would take a great deal of explaining. She had learned not to mention it till it was mentioned first—which occasionally happened, but not too often; and then she was there in force. Then she both warmed to the perception that met her own perception, and disputed it, suspiciously, as to special items; while, in general, she had learned to refine even to the point of herself employing the word that most people employed. She employed it to pretend she was also stupid and so have done with the matter; spoke of her friend as plain, as ugly even, in a case of especially dense insistence; but as, in appearance, so "awfully full of things." This was her own way of describing a face that, thanks doubtless to rather too much forehead, too much nose and too much mouth, together with too little mere conventional colour and conventional line, was expressive, irregular, exquisite, both for speech and for silence. When Milly smiled it was a public event—when she didn't it was a chapter of history. They had stopped on the Brünig for luncheon, and there had come up for them under the charm of the place the question of a longer stay.

Mrs. Stringham was now on the ground of thrilled recognitions, small sharp echoes of a past which she kept in a well-thumbed case, but which, on pressure of a spring and exposure to the air, still showed itself ticking as hard as an honest old watch. The embalmed "Europe" of her younger time had partly stood for three

years of Switzerland, a term of continuous school at Vevey, with rewards of merit in the form of silver medals tied by blue ribbons
and mild mountain-passes attacked with alpenstocks. It was the
good girls who, in the holidays, were taken highest, and our friend
could now judge, from what she supposed her familiarity with the
minor peaks, that she had been one of the best. These reminis-
cences, sacred to-day because prepared in the hushed chambers of
the past, had been part of the general train laid for the pair of sisters, daughters early fatherless, by their brave Vermont mother,
who struck her at present as having apparently, almost like
Columbus, worked out, all unassisted, a conception of the other
side of the globe. She had focussed Vevey, by the light of nature
and with extraordinary completeness, at Burlington; after which
she had embarked, sailed, landed, explored and, above all, made
good her presence. She had given her daughters the five years in
Switzerland and Germany that were to leave them ever afterwards
a standard of comparison for all cycles of Cathay,* and to stamp
the younger in especial—Susan was the younger—with a character, that, as Mrs. Stringham had often had occasion, through life,
to say to herself, made all the difference. It made all the difference
for Mrs. Stringham, over and over again and in the most remote
connexions, that, thanks to her parent's lonely thrifty hardy faith,
she was a woman of the world. There were plenty of women who
were all sorts of things that she wasn't, but who, on the other hand,
were not that, and who didn't know *she* was (which she liked—it
relegated them still further) and didn't know either how it enabled
her to judge them. She had never seen herself so much in this
light as during the actual phase of her associated, if slightly undi-
rected, pilgrimage; and the consciousness gave perhaps to her plea
for a pause more intensity than she knew. The irrecoverable days
had come back to her from far off; they were part of the sense of
the cool upper air and of everything else that hung like an indestructible scent to the torn garment of youth—the taste of honey
and the luxury of milk, the sound of cattle-bells and the rush of

---

*Allusion to Alfred Tennyson's poem "Locksley Hall" (1842), in which European
cosmopolitanism is ironically contrasted with English provincialism.

streams, the fragrance of trodden balms and the dizziness of deep gorges.

Milly clearly felt these things too, but they affected her companion at moments—that was quite the way Mrs. Stringham would have expressed it—as the princess in a conventional tragedy might have affected the confidant if a personal emotion had ever been permitted to the latter. That a princess could only be a princess was a truth with which, essentially, a confidant, however responsive, had to live. Mrs. Stringham was a woman of the world, but Milly Theale was a princess, the only one she had yet had to deal with, and this, in its way too, made all the difference. It was a perfectly definite doom for the wearer—it was for every one else an office nobly filled. It might have represented possibly, with its involved loneliness and other mysteries, the weight under which she fancied her companion's admirable head occasionally, and ever so submissively, bowed. Milly had quite assented at luncheon to their staying over, and had left her to look at rooms, settle questions, arrange about their keeping on their carriage and horses; cares that had now moreover fallen to Mrs. Stringham as a matter of course and that yet for some reason, on this occasion particularly, brought home to her—all agreeably, richly, almost grandly— what it was to live with the great. Her young friend had in a sublime degree a sense closed to the general question of difficulty, which she got rid of furthermore not in the least as one had seen many charming persons do, by merely passing it on to others. She kept it completely at a distance: it never entered the circle; the most plaintive confidant couldn't have dragged it in; and to tread the path of a confidant was accordingly to live exempt. Service was in other words so easy to render that the whole thing was like court life without the hardships. It came back of course to the question of money, and our observant lady had by this time repeatedly reflected that if one were talking of the "difference," it was just this, this incomparably and nothing else, that when all was said and done most made it. A less vulgarly, a less obviously purchasing or parading person she couldn't have imagined; but it prevailed even as the truth of truths that the girl couldn't get away from her wealth. She might leave her conscientious companion as freely alone with it as possible and never ask a question, scarce even tol-

erate a reference; but it was in the fine folds of the helplessly expensive little black frock that she drew over the grass as she now
strolled vaguely off; it was in the curious and splendid coils of hair,
"done" with no eye whatever to the *mode du jour*,* that peeped
from under the corresponding indifference of her hat, the merely
personal tradition that suggested a sort of noble inelegance; it
lurked between the leaves of the uncut but antiquated Tauchnitz[†]
volume of which, before going out, she had mechanically possessed herself. She couldn't dress it away, nor walk it away, nor
read it away, nor think it away; she could neither smile it away in
any dreamy absence nor blow it away in any softened sigh. She
couldn't have lost it if she had tried—that was what it was to be
really rich. It had to be *the* thing you were. When at the end of an
hour she hadn't returned to the house Mrs. Stringham, though the
bright afternoon was yet young, took, with precautions, the same
direction, went to join her in case of her caring for a walk. But the
purpose of joining her was in truth less distinct than that of a due
regard for a possibly preferred detachment: so that, once more, the
good lady proceeded with a quietness that made her slightly "underhand" even in her own eyes. She couldn't help that, however,
and she didn't care, sure as she was that what she really wanted
wasn't to overstep but to stop in time. It was to be able to stop in
time that she went softly, but she had on this occasion further to
go than ever yet, for she followed in vain, and at last with some
anxiety, the footpath she believed Milly to have taken. It wound
up a hillside and into the higher Alpine meadows in which, all
these last days, they had so often wanted, as they passed above or
below, to stray; and then it obscured itself in a wood, but always
going up, up, and with a small cluster of brown old high-perched
châlets evidently for its goal. Mrs. Stringham reached in due
course the châlets, and there received from a bewildered old
woman, a very fearful person to behold, an indication that sufficiently guided her. The young lady had been seen not long before
passing further on, over a crest and to a place where the way would

---

*Fashion of the day (French).
†German publishing house that specialized in reprinting British and American
works.

drop again, as our unappeased enquirer found it in fact, a quarter
of an hour later, markedly and almost alarmingly to do. It led
somewhere, yet apparently quite into space, for the great side of
the mountain appeared, from where she pulled up, to fall away altogether, though probably but to some issue below and out of
sight. Her uncertainty moreover was brief, for she next became
aware of the presence on a fragment of rock, twenty yards off, of
the Tauchnitz volume the girl had brought out and that therefore
pointed to her shortly previous passage. She had rid herself of the
book, which was an encumbrance, and meant of course to pick it
up on her return; but as she hadn't yet picked it up what on earth
had become of her? Mrs. Stringham, I hasten to add,[9] was within
a few moments to see; but it was quite an accident that she hadn't,
before they were over, betrayed by her deeper agitation the fact of
her own nearness.

The whole place, with the descent of the path and as a sequel
to a sharp turn that was masked by rocks and shrubs, appeared to
fall precipitously and to become a "view" pure and simple, a view
of great extent and beauty, but thrown forward and vertiginous.
Milly, with the promise of it from just above, had gone straight
down to it, not stopping till it was all before her; and here, on what
struck her friend as the dizzy edge of it, she was seated at her ease.
The path somehow took care of itself and its final business, but the
girl's seat was a slab of rock at the end of a short promontory or ex-
crescence that merely pointed off to the right at gulfs of air and
that was so placed by good fortune, if not by the worst, as to be at
last completely visible. For Mrs. Stringham stifled a cry on taking
in what she believed to be the danger of such a perch for a mere
maiden; her liability to slip, to slide, to leap, to be precipitated by
a single false movement, by a turn of the head—how could one
tell?—into whatever was beneath. A thousand thoughts, for the
minute, roared in the poor lady's ears, but without reaching, as
happened, Milly's. It was a commotion that left our observer intensely still and holding her breath. What had first been offered
her was the possibility of a latent intention—however wild the
idea—in such a posture; of some betrayed accordance of Milly's
caprice with a horrible hidden obsession. But since Mrs. Stringham stood as motionless as if a sound, a syllable, must have pro-

duced the start that would be fatal, so even the lapse of a few seconds had partly a reassuring effect. It gave her time to receive the
impression which, when she some minutes later softly retraced her
steps, was to be the sharpest she carried away. This was the impression that if the girl was deeply and recklessly meditating there
she wasn't meditating a jump; she was on the contrary, as she sat,
much more in a state of uplifted and unlimited possession that had
nothing to gain from violence. She was looking down on the kingdoms of the earth, and though indeed that of itself might well go
to the brain, it wouldn't be with a view of renouncing them. Was
she choosing among them or did she want them all? This question, before Mrs. Stringham had decided what to do, made others
vain; in accordance with which she saw, or believed she did, that
if it might be dangerous to call out, to sound in any way a surprise,
it would probably be safe enough to withdraw as she had come.
She watched a while longer, she held her breath, and she never
knew afterwards what time had elapsed.

Not many minutes probably, yet they hadn't seemed few, and
they had given her so much to think of, not only while creeping
home, but while waiting afterwards at the inn, that she was still
busy with them when, late in the afternoon, Milly reappeared. She
had stopped at the point of the path where the Tauchnitz lay, had
taken it up and, with the pencil attached to her watch-guard, had
scrawled a word—*à bientôt!** —across the cover; after which, even
under the girl's continued delay, she had measured time without a
return of alarm. For she now saw that the great thing she had
brought away was precisely a conviction that the future wasn't to
exist for her princess in the form of any sharp or simple release
from the human predicament. It wouldn't be for her a question of
a flying leap and thereby of a quick escape. It would be a question
of taking full in the face the whole assault of life, to the general
muster of which indeed her face might have been directly presented as she sat there on her rock. Mrs. Stringham was thus able
to say to herself during still another wait of some length that if her
young friend still continued absent it wouldn't be because—what-

---

* "Till then!" or "Soon!" (French).

ever the opportunity—she had cut short the thread. She wouldn't have committed suicide; she knew herself unmistakeably reserved for some more complicated passage; this was the very vision in which she had, with no little awe, been discovered. The image that thus remained with the elder lady kept the character of a revelation. During the breathless minutes of her watch she had seen her companion afresh; the latter's type, aspect, marks, her history, her state, her beauty, her mystery, all unconsciously betrayed themselves to the Alpine air, and all had been gathered in again to feed Mrs. Stringham's flame. They are things that will more distinctly appear for us, and they are meanwhile briefly represented by the enthusiasm that was stronger on our friend's part than any doubt. It was a consciousness she was scarce yet used to carrying, but she had as beneath her feet a mine of something precious. She seemed to herself to stand near the mouth, not yet quite cleared. The mine but needed working and would certainly yield a treasure. She wasn't thinking, either, of Milly's gold.

— II —

The girl said nothing, when they met, about the words scrawled on the Tauchnitz, and Mrs. Stringham then noticed that she hadn't the book with her. She had left it lying and probably would never remember it at all. Her comrade's decision was therefore quickly made not to speak of having followed her; and within five minutes of her return, wonderfully enough, the preoccupation denoted by her forgetfulness further declared itself. "Should you think me quite abominable if I were to say that after all—?"

Mrs. Stringham had already thought, with the first sound of the question, everything she was capable of thinking, and had immediately made such a sign that Milly's words gave place to visible relief at her assent. "You don't care for our stop here—you'd rather go straight on? We'll start then with the peep of tomorrow's dawn—or as early as you like; it's only rather late now to take the road again." And she smiled to show how she meant it for a joke that an instant onward rush was what the girl would have wished. "I bullied you into stopping," she added; "so it serves me right."

Milly made in general the most of her good friend's jokes; but she humoured this one a little absently. "Oh yes, you do bully me." And it was thus arranged between them, with no discussion at all, that they would resume their journey in the morning. The younger tourist's interest in the detail of the matter—in spite of a declaration from the elder that she would consent to be dragged anywhere—appeared almost immediately afterwards quite to lose itself; she promised, however, to think till supper of where, with the world all before them, they might go—supper having been ordered for such time as permitted of lighted candles. It had been agreed between them that lighted candles at wayside inns, in strange countries, amid mountain scenery, gave the evening meal a peculiar poetry—such being the mild adventures, the refinements of impression, that they, as they would have said, went in for. It was now as if, before this repast, Milly had designed to "lie down"; but at the end of three minutes more she wasn't lying down, she was saying instead, abruptly, with a transition that was like a jump of four thousand miles: "What was it that, in New York, on the ninth, when you saw him alone, Doctor Finch said to you?"

It was not till later that Mrs. Stringham fully knew why the question had startled her still more than its suddenness explained; though the effect of it even at the moment was almost to frighten her into a false answer. She had to think, to remember the occasion, the "ninth," in New York, the time she had seen Doctor Finch alone, and to recall the words he had then uttered; and when everything had come back it was quite, at first, for a moment, as if he had said something that immensely mattered. He hadn't, however, in fact; it was only as if he might perhaps after all have been going to. It was on the sixth—within ten days of their sailing—that she had hurried from Boston under the alarm, a small but a sufficient shock, of hearing that Mildred had suddenly been taken ill, had had, from some obscure cause, such an upset as threatened to stay their journey. The bearing of the accident had happily soon presented itself as slight, and there had been in the event but a few hours of anxiety; the journey had been pronounced again not only possible, but, as representing "change," highly advisable; and if the zealous guest had had five minutes by herself with the Doctor this was clearly no more at his insistence than at her own. Almost nothing had passed between them but an easy exchange of enthusiasms in respect to the remedial properties of "Europe"; and due assurance, as the facts came back to her, she was now able to give. "Nothing whatever, on my word of honour, that you mayn't know or mightn't then have known. I've no secret with him about you. What makes you suspect it? I don't quite make out how you know I did see him alone."

"No—you never told me," said Milly. "And I don't mean," she went on, "during the twenty-four hours while I was bad, when your putting your heads together was natural enough. I mean after I was better—the last thing before you went home."

Mrs. Stringham continued to wonder. "Who told you I saw him then?"

"*He* didn't himself—nor did you write me it afterwards. We speak of it now for the first time. That's exactly why!" Milly declared—with something in her face and voice that, the next moment, betrayed for her companion that she had really known nothing, had only conjectured and, chancing her charge, made a hit. Yet why had her mind been busy with the question? "But if you're not, as you now assure me, in his confidence," she smiled, "it's no matter."

"I'm not in his confidence—he had nothing to confide. But are you feeling unwell?"

The elder woman was earnest for the truth, though the possibility she named was not at all the one that seemed to fit—witness the long climb Milly had just indulged in. The girl showed her constant white face, but this her friends had all learned to discount, and it was often brightest when superficially not bravest. She continued for a little mysteriously to smile. "I don't know—haven't really the least idea. But it might be well to find out."

Mrs. Stringham at this flared into sympathy. "Are you in trouble—in pain?"

"Not the least little bit. But I sometimes wonder—!"

"Yes"—she pressed: "wonder what?"

"Well, if I shall have much of it."

Mrs. Stringham stared. "Much of what? Not of pain?"

"Of everything. Of everything I have."

Anxiously again, tenderly, our friend cast about. "You 'have' everything; so that when you say 'much' of it—"

"I only mean," the girl broke in, "shall I have it for long? That is if I *have* got it."

She had at present the effect, a little, of confounding, or at least of perplexing her comrade, who was touched, who was always touched, by something helpless in her grace and abrupt in her turns, and yet actually half made out in her a sort of mocking light. "If you've got an ailment?"

"If I've got everything," Milly laughed.

"Ah *that*—like almost nobody else."

"Then for how long?"

Mrs. Stringham's eyes entreated her; she had gone close to her, half-enclosed her with urgent arms. "Do you want to see some one?" And then as the girl only met it with a slow headshake, though looking perhaps a shade more conscious: "We'll go straight to the best near doctor." This too, however, produced but a gaze of qualified assent and a silence, sweet and vague, that left everything open. Our friend decidedly lost herself. "Tell me, for God's sake, if you're in distress."

"I don't think I've really *everything*," Milly said as if to explain— and as if also to put it pleasantly.

"But what on earth can I do for you?"

The girl debated, then seemed on the point of being able to say; but suddenly changed and expressed herself otherwise. "Dear, dear thing—I'm only too happy!"

It brought them closer, but it rather confirmed Mrs. Stringham's doubt. "Then what's the matter?"

"That's the matter—that I can scarcely bear it."

"But what is it you think you haven't got?"

Milly waited another moment; then she found it, and found for it a dim show of joy. "The power to resist the bliss of what I *have!*"

Mrs. Stringham took it in—her sense of being "put off" with it, the possible, probable irony of it—and her tenderness renewed it- self in the positive grimness of a long murmur. "Whom will you see?"—for it was as if they looked down from their height at a continent of doctors. "Where will you first go?"

Milly had for the third time her air of consideration; but she came back with it to her plea of some minutes before. "I'll tell you at supper—good-bye till then." And she left the room with a lightness that testified for her companion to something that again particularly pleased her in the renewed promise of motion. The odd passage just concluded, Mrs. Stringham mused as she once more sat alone with a hooked needle and a ball of silk, the "fine" work with which she was always provided—this mystifying mood had simply been precipitated, no doubt, by their prolonged halt, with which the girl hadn't really been in sympathy. One had only to admit that her complaint was in fact but the excess of the joy of life, and everything *did* then fit. She couldn't stop for the joy, but she could go on for it, and with the pulse of her going on she floated again, was restored to her great spaces. There was no evasion of any truth—so at least Susan Shepherd hoped—in one's sitting there while the twilight deepened and feeling still more finely that the position of this young lady was magnificent. The evening at that height had naturally turned to cold, and the travellers had bespoken a fire with their meal; the great Alpine road asserted its brave presence through the small panes of the low clean windows, with incidents at the inn-door, the yellow diligence,* the great waggons, the hurrying hooded private conveyances, reminders, for our fanciful friend, of old stories, old pictures, historic flights, escapes, pursuits, things that had happened, things indeed that by a sort of strange congruity helped her to read the meanings of the greatest interest into the relation in which she was now so deeply involved. It was natural that this record of the magnificence of her companion's position should strike her as after all the best meaning she could extract; for she herself was seated in the magnificence as in a court-carriage—she came back to that, and such a method of progression, such a view from crimson cushions, would evidently have a great deal more to give. By the time the candles were lighted for supper and the short white curtains drawn Milly

---

*Stagecoach.

had reappeared, and the little scenic room had then all its romance. That charm moreover was far from broken by the words in
which she, without further loss of time, satisfied her patient mate.
"I want to go straight to London."

It was unexpected, corresponding with no view positively taken
at their departure; when England had appeared, on the contrary,
rather relegated and postponed—seen for the moment, as who
should say, at the end of an avenue of preparations and introductions. London, in short, might have been supposed to be the
crown, and to be achieved, like a siege, by gradual approaches.
Milly's actual fine stride was therefore the more exciting, as any
simplification almost always was to Mrs. Stringham; who, besides,
was afterwards to recall as a piece of that very "exposition" dear to
the dramatist the terms in which, between their smoky candles,
the girl had put her preference and in which still other things had
come up, come while the clank of waggon-chains in the sharp air
reached their ears, with the stamp of hoofs, the rattle of buckets
and the foreign questions, foreign answers, that were all alike a
part of the cheery converse of the road. The girl brought it out in
truth as she might have brought a huge confession, something she
admitted herself shy about and that would seem to show her as frivolous; it had rolled over her that what she wanted of Europe was
"people," so far as they were to be had, and that, if her friend really
wished to know, the vision of this same equivocal quantity was
what had haunted her during their previous days, in museums and
churches, and what was again spoiling for her the pure taste of
scenery. She was all for scenery—yes; but she wanted it human
and personal, and all she could say was that there would be in
London—wouldn't there?—more of that kind than anywhere else.
She came back to her idea that if it wasn't for long—if nothing
should happen to be so for *her*—why the particular thing she
spoke of would probably have most to give her in the time, would
probably be less than anything else a waste of her remainder. She
produced this last consideration indeed with such gaiety that Mrs.
Stringham was not again disconcerted by it, was in fact quite
ready—if talk of early dying was in order—to match it from her
own future. Good, then; they would eat and drink because of what
might happen to-morrow; and they would direct their course from

that moment with a view to such eating and drinking. They ate and drank that night, in truth, as in the spirit of this decision; whereby the air, before they separated, felt itself the clearer.

It had cleared perhaps to a view only too extensive—extensive, that is, in proportion to the signs of life presented. The idea of "people" was not so entertained on Milly's part as to connect itself with particular persons, and the fact remained for each of the ladies that they would, completely unknown, disembark at Dover amid the completely unknowing. They had no relation already formed; this plea Mrs. Stringham put forward to see what it would produce. It produced nothing at first but the observation on the girl's side that what she had in mind was no thought of society nor of scraping acquaintance; nothing was further from her than to desire the opportunities represented for the compatriot in general by a trunkful of "letters." It wasn't a question, in short, of the people the compatriot was after; it was the human, the English picture itself, as they might see it in their own way—the concrete world inferred so fondly, from what one had read and dreamed. Mrs. Stringham did every justice to this concrete world, but when later on an occasion chanced to present itself she made a point of not omitting to remark that it might be a comfort to know in advance one or two of the human particles of its concretion. This still, however, failed, in vulgar parlance, to "fetch" Milly, so that she had presently to go all the way. "Haven't I understood from you, for that matter, that you gave Mr. Densher something of a promise?"

There was a moment, on this, when Milly's look had to be taken as representing one of two things—either that she was completely vague about the promise or that Mr. Densher's name itself started no train. But she really couldn't be so vague about the promise, the partner of these hours quickly saw, without attaching it to something; it had to be a promise to somebody in particular to be so repudiated. In the event, accordingly, she acknowledged Mr. Merton Densher, the so unusually "bright" young Englishman who had made his appearance in New York on some special literary business—wasn't it?—shortly before their departure, and who had been three or four times in her house during the brief period between her visit to Boston and her companion's subsequent stay with her; but she required much reminding before it came

back to her that she had mentioned to this companion just afterwards the confidence expressed by the personage in question in
her never doing so dire a thing as to come to London without, as
the phrase was, looking a fellow up. She had left him the enjoyment of his confidence, the form of which might have appeared a
trifle free—this she now reasserted; she had done nothing either to
impair or to enhance it; but she had also left Mrs. Stringham, in
the connexion and at the time, rather sorry to have missed Mr.
Densher. She had thought of him again after that, the elder
woman; she had likewise gone so far as to notice that Milly appeared not to have done so—which the girl might easily have betrayed; and, interested as she was in everything that concerned
her, she had made out for herself, for herself only and rather idly,
that, but for interruptions, the young Englishman might have become a better acquaintance. His being an acquaintance at all was
one of the signs that in the first days had helped to place Milly, as
a young person with the world before her, for sympathy and wonder. Isolated, unmothered, unguarded, but with her other strong
marks, her big house, her big fortune, her big freedom, she had
lately begun to "receive," for all her few years, as an older woman
might have done—as was done, precisely, by princesses who had
public considerations to observe and who came of age very early.
If it was thus distinct to Mrs. Stringham then that Mr. Densher
had gone off somewhere else in connexion with his errand before
her visit to New York, it had been also not undiscoverable that he
had come back for a day or two later on, that is after her own second excursion—that he had in fine reappeared on a single occasion on his way to the West: his way from Washington as she
believed, though he was out of sight at the time of her joining her
friend for their departure. It hadn't occurred to her before to exaggerate—it had not occurred to her that she could; but she
seemed to become aware to-night that there had been just enough
in this relation to meet, to provoke, the free conception of a little
more.

   She presently put it that, at any rate, promise or no promise,
Milly would at a pinch be able, in London, to act on his permission to make him a sign; to which Milly replied with readiness that
her ability, though evident, would be none the less quite wasted,

inasmuch as the gentleman would to a certainty be still in America. He had a great deal to do there—which he would scarce have begun; and in fact she might very well not have thought of London at all if she hadn't been sure he wasn't yet near coming back. It was perceptible to her companion that the moment our young woman had so far committed herself she had a sense of having overstepped; which was not quite patched up by her saying the next minute, possibly with a certain failure of presence of mind, that the last thing she desired was the air of running after him. Mrs. Stringham wondered privately what question there could be of any such appearance—the danger of which thus suddenly came up; but she said for the time nothing of it—she only said other things: one of which was, for instance, that if Mr. Densher was away he was away, and this the end of it: also that of course they must be discreet at any price. But what was the measure of discretion, and how was one to be sure? So it was that, as they sat there, she produced her own case: *she* had a possible tie with London, which she desired as little to disown as she might wish to risk presuming on it. She treated her companion, in short, for their evening's end, to the story of Maud Manningham, the odd but interesting English girl who had formed her special affinity in the old days at the Vevey school; whom she had written to, after their separation, with a regularity that had at first faltered and then altogether failed, yet that had been for the time quite a fine case of crude constancy; so that it had in fact flickered up again of itself on the occasion of the marriage of each. They had then once more fondly, scrupulously written—Mrs. Lowder first; and even another letter or two had afterwards passed. This, however, had been the end—though with no rupture, only a gentle drop: Maud Manningham had made, she believed, a great marriage, while she herself had made a small; on top of which, moreover, distance, difference, diminished community and impossible reunion had done the rest of the work. It was but after all these years that reunion had begun to show as possible—if the other party to it, that is, should be still in existence. That was exactly what it now appeared to our friend interesting to ascertain, as, with one aid and another, she believed she might. It was an experiment she would at all events now make if Milly didn't object.

Milly in general objected to nothing, and though she asked a question or two she raised no present plea. Her questions—or at least her own answers to them—kindled on Mrs. Stringham's part a backward train: she hadn't known till to-night how much she re-membered, or how fine it might be to see what had become of large high-coloured Maud, florid, alien, exotic—which had been just the spell—even to the perceptions of youth. There was the danger—she frankly touched it—that such a temperament mightn't have matured, with the years, all in the sense of fineness: it was the sort of danger that, in renewing relations after long breaks, one had always to look in the face. To gather in strayed threads was to take a risk—for which, however, she was prepared if Milly was. The possible "fun," she confessed, was by itself rather tempting; and she fairly sounded, with this—wound up a little as she was—the note of fun as the harmless final right of fifty years of mere New England virtue. Among the things she was afterwards to recall was the indescribable look dropped on her, at that, by her companion; she was still seated there between the candles and before the fin-ished supper, while Milly moved about, and the look was long to figure for her as an inscrutable comment on her notion of free-dom. Challenged, at any rate, as for the last wise word, Milly showed perhaps, musingly, charmingly, that, though her attention had been mainly soundless, her friend's story—produced as a re-source unsuspected, a card from up the sleeve—half-surprised, half-beguiled her. Since the matter, such as it was, depended on that, she brought out before she went to bed an easy, a light "Risk everything!"

This quality in it seemed possibly a little to deny weight to Maud Lowder's evoked presence—as Susan Stringham, still sitting up, became, in excited reflexion, a trifle more conscious. Some-thing determinant, when the girl had left her, took place in her—nameless but, as soon as she had given way, coercive. It was as if she knew again, in this fulness of time, that she had been, after Maud's marriage, just sensibly outlived or, as people nowadays said, shunted. Mrs. Lowder had left her behind, and on the occa-sion, subsequently, of the corresponding date in her own life—not the second, the sad one, with its dignity of sadness, but the first, with the meagreness of its supposed felicity—she had been, in the same spirit, almost patronisingly pitied. If that suspicion, even when it had ceased to matter, had never quite died out for her, there was doubtless some oddity in its now offering itself as a link, rather than as another break, in the chain; and indeed there might well have been for her a mood in which the notion of the development of patronage in her quondam* schoolmate would have settled her question in another sense. It was actually settled—if the case be worth our analysis—by the happy consummation, the poetic justice, the generous revenge, of her having at last something to show. Maud, on their parting company, had appeared to have so much, and would now—for wasn't it also in general quite the rich law of English life?—have, with accretions, promotions, expansions, ever so much more. Very good; such things might be; she rose to the sense of being ready for them. Whatever Mrs. Lowder might have to show—and one hoped one did the presumptions all justice—she would have nothing like Milly Theale, who constituted the trophy producible by poor Susan. Poor Susan lingered late—till the candles were low, and as soon as the table was cleared she opened her neat portfolio. She hadn't lost the old clue; there were connexions she remembered, addresses she could try; so the thing was to begin. She wrote on the spot.

---

*Former (Latin).

BOOK FOURTH

– I –

It had all gone so fast after this that Milly uttered but the truth nearest to hand in saying to the gentleman on her right—who was, by the same token, the gentleman on her hostess's left— that she scarce even then knew where she was: the words marking her first full sense of a situation really romantic. They were already dining, she and her friend, at Lancaster Gate, and surrounded, as it seemed to her, with every English accessory; though her consciousness of Mrs. Lowder's existence, and still more of her remarkable identity, had been of so recent and so sudden a birth. Susie, as she was apt to call her companion for a lighter change, had only had to wave a neat little wand for the fairy-tale to begin at once; in consequence of which Susie now glittered—for, with Mrs. Stringham's new sense of success, it came to that—in the character of a fairy godmother. Milly had almost insisted on dressing her, for the present occasion, as one; and it was no fault of the girl's if the good lady hadn't now appeared in a peaked hat, a short petticoat and diamond shoe-buckles, brandishing the magic crutch. The good lady bore herself in truth not less contentedly than if these insignia had marked her work; and Milly's observation to Lord Mark had doubtless just been the result of such a light exchange of looks with her as even the great length of the table couldn't baffle. There were twenty persons between them, but this sustained passage was the sharpest sequel yet to that other comparison of views during the pause on the Swiss pass. It almost appeared to Milly that their fortune had been unduly precipitated— as if properly they were in the position of having ventured on a small joke and found the answer out of proportion grave. She couldn't at this moment for instance have said whether, with her quickened perceptions, she were more enlivened or oppressed; and the case might in fact have been serious hadn't she, by good fortune, from the moment the picture loomed, quickly made up her mind that what finally most concerned her was neither to seek

119

nor to shirk, wasn't even to wonder too much, but was to let things come as they would, since there was little enough doubt of how they would go.

Lord Mark had been brought to her before dinner—not by Mrs. Lowder, but by the handsome girl, that lady's niece, who was now at the other end and on the same side as Susie; he had taken her in, and she meant presently to ask him about Miss Croy, the handsome girl, actually offered to her sight—though now in a splendid way—but for the second time. The first time had been the occasion—only three days before—of her calling at their hotel with her aunt and then making, for our other two heroines, a great impression of beauty and eminence. This impression had remained so with Milly that at present, and although her attention was aware at the same time of everything else, her eyes were mainly engaged with Kate Croy when not engaged with Susie. That wonderful creature's eyes moreover readily met them—she ranked now as a wonderful creature; and it seemed part of the swift prosperity of the American visitors that, so little in the original reckoning, she should yet appear conscious, charmingly, frankly conscious, of possibilities of friendship for them. Milly had easily and, as a guest, gracefully generalised: English girls had a special strong beauty which particularly showed in evening dress—above all when, as was strikingly the case with this one, the dress itself was what it should be. That observation she had all ready for Lord Mark when they should, after a little, get round to it. She seemed even now to see that there might be a good deal they would get round to; the indication being that, taken up once for all with her other neighbour, their hostess would leave them much to themselves. Mrs. Lowder's other neighbour was the Bishop of Murrum—a real bishop, such as Milly had never seen, with a complicated costume, a voice like an old-fashioned wind instrument, and a face all the portrait of a prelate; while the gentleman on our young lady's left, a gentleman thick-necked, large and literal, who looked straight before him and as if he were not to be diverted by vain words from that pursuit, clearly counted as an offset to the possession of Lord Mark. As Milly made out these things—with a shade of exhilaration at the way she already fell in—she saw how she was justified of her plea for people and her love of life. It wasn't then, as the prospect seemed to show, so difficult to get into the current, or to stand at any rate on the bank. It was easy to get near—if they *were* near; and yet the elements were different enough from any of her old elements, and positively rich and strange.

She asked herself if her right-hand neighbour would understand what she meant by such a description of them should she throw it off; but another of the things to which precisely her sense was awakened was that no, decidedly, he wouldn't. It was nevertheless by this time open to her that his line would be to be clever; and indeed, evidently, no little of the interest was going to be in the fresh reference and fresh effect both of people's cleverness and of their simplicity. She thrilled, she consciously flushed, and all to turn pale again, with the certitude—it had never been so present—that she should find herself completely involved: the very air of the place, the pitch of the occasion, had for her both so sharp a ring and so deep an undertone. The smallest things, the faces, the hands, the jewels of the women, the sound of words, especially of names, across the table, the shape of the forks, the arrangement of the flowers, the attitude of the servants, the walls of the room, were all touches in a picture and denotements in a play; and they marked for her moreover her alertness of vision. She had never, she might well believe, been in such a state of vibration; her sensibility was almost too sharp for her comfort: there were for example more indications than she could reduce to order in the manner of the friendly niece, who struck her as distinguished and interesting, as in fact surprisingly genial. This young woman's type had, visibly, other possibilities; yet here, of its own free movement, it had already sketched a relation. Were they, Miss Croy and she, to take up the tale where their two elders had left it off so many years before?—were they to find they liked each other and to try for themselves whether a scheme of constancy on more modern lines could be worked? She had doubted, as they came to England, of Maud Manningham, had believed her a broken reed and a vague resource, had seen their dependence on her as a state of mind that would have been shamefully silly—so far as it *was* dependence—had they wished to do anything so inane as "get into society." To have made their pilgrimage all for the sake of such society as Mrs. Lowder might have in reserve for them—that didn't bear thinking of at all, and she herself had quite chosen her course for curiosity about other matters. She would have described this curiosity as a desire to see the places she had read about, and *that* description of her motive she was prepared to give her neighbour—even though, as a consequence of it, he should find how little she had read. It was almost at present as if her poor prevision had been rebuked by the majesty—she could scarcely call it less—of the event, or at all events by the commanding character of the two figures (she could scarcely call *that* less either) mainly presented. Mrs. Lowder and her niece, however dissimilar, had at least in common that each was a great reality. That was true, primarily, of the aunt—so true that Milly wondered how her own companion had arrived in other years at so odd an alliance; yet she none the less felt Mrs. Lowder as a person of whom the mind might in two or three days roughly make the circuit. She would sit there massive at least while one attempted it; whereas Miss Croy, the handsome girl, would indulge in incalculable movements that might interfere with one's tour. She was the amusing resisting ominous fact, none the less, and each other person and thing was just such a fact; and it served them right, no doubt, the pair of them, for having rushed into their adventure.

Lord Mark's intelligence meanwhile, however, had met her own quite sufficiently to enable him to tell her how little he could clear up her situation. He explained, for that matter—or at least he hinted—that there was no such thing to-day in London as saying where any one was. Every one was everywhere—nobody was anywhere. He should be put to it—yes, frankly—to give a name of any sort or kind to their hostess's "set." *Was* it a set at all, or wasn't it, and were there not really no such things as sets in the place any more?—was there anything but the groping and pawing, that of the vague billows of some great greasy sea in mid-Channel, of masses of bewildered people trying to "get" they didn't know what or where? He threw out the question, which seemed large; Milly felt that at the end of five minutes he had thrown out a great many, though he followed none more than a step or two; perhaps he would prove suggestive, but he helped her as yet to no discriminations: he spoke as if he had given them up from too much knowledge. He was thus at the opposite extreme from herself, but, as a consequence of it, also wandering and lost; and he was furthermore, for all his temporary incoherence, to which she guessed there would be some key, as packed a concretion as either Mrs. Lowder or Kate. The only light in which he placed the former of these ladies was that of an extraordinary woman—a most extraordinary woman, and "the more extraordinary the more one knows her," while of the latter he said nothing for the moment but that she was tremendously, yes, quite tremendously, good-looking. It was some time, she thought, before his talk showed his cleverness, and yet each minute she believed in that mystery more, quite apart from what her hostess had told her on first naming him. Perhaps he was one of the cases she had heard of at home—those characteristic cases of people in England who concealed their play of mind so much more than they advertised it. Even Mr. Densher a little did that. And what made Lord Mark, at any rate, so real either, when this was a trick he had apparently so mastered? His type somehow, as by a life, a need, an intention of its own, took all care for vividness off his hands; that was enough. It was difficult to guess his age—whether he were a young man who looked old or an old man who looked young; it seemed to prove nothing, as against other things, that he was bald and, as might have been said, slightly stale, or, more delicately perhaps, dry: there was such a fine little fidget of preoccupied life in him, and his eyes, at moments—though it was an appearance they could suddenly lose— were as candid and clear as those of a pleasant boy. Very neat, very light, and so fair that there was little other indication of his moustache than his constantly feeling it—which was again boyish—he would have affected her as the most intellectual person present if he had not affected her as the most frivolous. The latter quality was rather in his look than in anything else, though he constantly wore his double eye-glass, which was, much more, Bostonian and thoughtful.

The idea of his frivolity had, no doubt, to do with his personal designation, which represented—as yet, for our young woman, a

little confusedly—a connexion with an historic patriciate, a class
that in turn, also confusedly, represented an affinity with a social
element she had never heard otherwise described than as "fashion." The supreme social element in New York had never known
itself but as reduced to that category, and though Milly was aware
that, as applied to a territorial and political aristocracy, the label
was probably too simple, she had for the time none other at hand.
She presently, it is true, enriched her idea with the perception
that her interlocutor was indifferent; yet this, indifferent as aris-
tocracies notoriously were, saw her but little further, inasmuch as
she felt that, in the first place, he would much rather get on with
her than not, and in the second was only thinking of too many
matters of his own. If he kept her in view on the one hand and
kept so much else on the other—the way he crumbed up his
bread was a proof—why did he hover before her as a potentially
insolent noble? She couldn't have answered the question, and it
was precisely one of those that swarmed. They were complicated,
she might fairly have said, by his visibly knowing, having known
from afar off, that she was a stranger and an American, and by his
none the less making no more of it than if she and her like were
the chief of his diet. He took her, kindly enough, but imperturbably, irreclaimably, for granted, and it wouldn't in the least
help that she herself knew him, as quickly, for having been in her
country and threshed it out. There would be nothing for her to
explain or attenuate or brag about; she could neither escape nor
prevail by her strangeness; he would have, for that matter, on
such a subject, more to tell her than to learn from her. She might
learn from *him* why she was so different from the handsome
girl—which she didn't know, being merely able to feel it; or at any
rate might learn from him why the handsome girl was so different
from her.

On these lines, however, they would move later; the lines immediately laid down were, in spite of his vagueness for his own
convenience, definite enough. She was already, he observed to
her, thinking what she should say on her other side—which was
what Americans were always doing. She needn't in conscience
say anything at all; but Americans never knew that, nor ever,
poor creatures, yes (*she* had interposed the "poor creatures!")

what not to do. The burdens they took on—the things, positively, they made an affair of! This easy and after all friendly jibe at her race was really for her, on her new friend's part, the note of personal recognition so far as she required it; and she gave him a prompt and conscious example of morbid anxiety by insisting that her desire to be, herself, "lovely" all round was justly founded on the lovely way Mrs. Lowder had met her. He was directly interested in that, and it was not till afterwards she fully knew how much more information about their friend he had taken than given. Here again for instance was a characteristic note: she had, on the spot, with her first plunge into the obscure depths of a society constituted from far back, encountered the interesting phenomenon of complicated, of possibly sinister motive. However, Maud Manningham (her name, even in her presence, somehow still fed the fancy) *had*, all the same, been lovely, and one was going to meet her now quite as far on as one had one's self been met. She had been with them at their hotel— they were a pair—before even they had supposed she could have got their letter. Of course indeed they had written in advance, but they had followed that up very fast. She had thus engaged them to dine but two days later, and on the morrow again, without waiting for a return visit, without waiting for anything, she had called with her niece. It was as if she really cared for them, and it was magnificent fidelity—fidelity to Mrs. Stringham, her own companion and Mrs. Lowder's former school-mate, the lady with the charming face and the rather high dress down there at the end.

Lord Mark took in through his nippers these balanced attributes of Susie. "But isn't Mrs. Stringham's fidelity then equally magnificent?"

"Well, it's a beautiful sentiment; but it isn't as if she had anything to *give*."

"Hasn't she got you?" Lord Mark asked without excessive delay.

"Me—to give Mrs. Lowder?" Milly had clearly not yet seen herself in the light of such an offering. "Oh I'm rather a poor present; and I don't feel as if, even at that, I had as yet quite been given."

"You've been shown, and if our friend has jumped at you it comes to the same thing." He made his jokes, Lord Mark, without amusement for himself; yet it wasn't that he was grim. "To be seen, you must recognise, *is*, for you, to be jumped at; and, if it's a question of being shown, here you are again. Only it has now been taken out of your friend's hands; it's Mrs. Lowder already who's getting the benefit. Look round the table, and you'll make out, I think, that you're being, from top to bottom, jumped at."

"Well then," said Milly, "I seem also to feel that I like it better than being made fun of."

It was one of the things she afterwards saw—Milly was for ever seeing things afterwards—that her companion had here had some way of his own, quite unlike any one's else, of assuring her of his consideration. She wondered how he had done it, for he had neither apologised nor protested. She said to herself at any rate that he had led her on; and what was most odd was the question by which he had done so.

"Does she know much about you?"

"No, she just likes us."

Even for this his travelled lordship, seasoned and saturated, had no laugh. "I mean *you* particularly. Has that lady with the charming face, which *is* charming, told her?"

Milly cast about. "Told her what?"

"Everything."

This, with the way he dropped it, again considerably moved her—made her feel for a moment that as a matter of course she was a subject for disclosures. But she quickly found her answer. "Oh as for that you must ask *her*."

"Your clever companion?"

"Mrs. Lowder."

He replied to this that their hostess was a person with whom there were certain liberties one never took, but that he was none the less fairly upheld, inasmuch as she was for the most part kind to him and as, should he be very good for a while, she would probably herself tell him. "And I shall have at any rate in the meantime the interest of seeing what she does with you. That will teach me more or less, you see, how much she knows."

Milly followed this—it was lucid, but it suggested something apart. "How much does she know about *you?*"

"Nothing," said Lord Mark serenely. "But that doesn't matter—for what she does with me." And then as to anticipate Milly's question about the nature of such doing: "This for instance—turning me straight on for *you.*"

The girl thought. "And you mean she wouldn't if she did know—?"

He met it as if it were really a point. "No. I believe, to do her justice, she still would. So you can be easy."

Milly had the next instant then acted on the permission. "Because you're even at the worst the best thing she has?"

With this he was at last amused. "I was till you came. You're the best now."

It was strange his words should have given her the sense of his knowing, but it was positive that they did so, and to the extent of making her believe them, though still with wonder. That really from this first of their meetings was what was most to abide with her: she accepted almost helplessly—she surrendered so to the inevitable in it—being the sort of thing, as he might have said, that he at least thoroughly believed he had, in going about, seen enough of for all practical purposes. Her submission was naturally moreover not to be impaired by her learning later on that he had paid at short intervals, though at a time apparently just previous to her own emergence from the obscurity of extreme youth, three separate visits to New York, where his nameable friends and his contrasted contacts had been numerous. His impression, his recollection of the whole mixed quantity, was still visibly rich. It had helped him to place her, and she was more and more sharply conscious of having—as with the door sharply slammed upon her and the guard's hand raised in signal to the train—been popped into the compartment in which she was to travel for him. It was a use of her that many a girl would have been doubtless quick to resent; and the kind of mind that thus, in our young lady, made all for mere seeing and taking is precisely one of the charms of our subject. Milly had practically just learned from him, had made out, as it were, from her rumbling compartment, that he gave her the highest place among their friend's actual properties. She was a success, that was what it came to, he presently assured her, and this was what it was to be a success; it always happened before one could know it. One's ignorance was in fact often the greatest part of it. "You haven't had time yet," he said; "this is nothing. But you'll see. You'll see everything. You *can*, you know—everything you dream of."

He made her more and more wonder; she almost felt as if he were showing her visions while he spoke; and strangely enough, though it was visions that had drawn her on, she hadn't had them in connexion—that is in such preliminary and necessary connexion—with such a face as Lord Mark's, such eyes and such a voice, such a tone and such a manner. He had for an instant the effect of making her ask herself if she were after all going to be afraid; so distinct was it for fifty seconds that a fear passed over her. There they were again—yes, certainly: Susie's overture to Mrs. Lowder had been their joke, but they had pressed in that gaiety an electric bell that continued to sound. Positively while she sat there she had the loud rattle in her ears, and she wondered during these moments why the others didn't hear it. They didn't stare, they didn't smile, and the fear in her that I speak of was but her own desire to stop it. That dropped, however, as if the alarm itself had ceased; she seemed to have seen in a quick though tempered glare that there were two courses for her, one to leave London again the first thing in the morning, the other to do nothing at all. Well, she would do nothing at all; she was already doing it; more than that, she had already done it, and her chance was gone. She gave herself up—she had the strangest sense, on the spot, of so deciding; for she had turned a corner before she went on again with Lord Mark. Inexpressive but intensely significant, he met as no one else could have done the very question she had suddenly put to Mrs. Stringham on the Brünig. Should she have it, whatever she did have, that question had been, for long? "Ah so possibly not," her neighbour appeared to reply; "therefore, don't you see? *I'm* the way." It was vivid that he might be, in spite of his absence of flourish; the way being doubtless just *in* that absence. The handsome girl, whom she didn't lose sight of and who, she felt, kept her also in view—Mrs. Lowder's striking niece would perhaps be the way as well, for in her too was the absence of flourish,

though she had little else, so far as one could tell, in common
with Lord Mark. Yet how indeed *could* one tell, what did one understand, and of what was one, for that matter, provisionally conscious but of their being somehow together in what they
represented? Kate Croy, fine but friendly, looked over at her as
really with a guess at Lord Mark's effect on her. If she could guess
this effect what then did she know about it and in what degree
had she felt it herself? Did that represent, as between them, anything particular, and should she have to count with them as du-
plicating, as intensifying by a mutual intelligence, the relation
into which she was sinking? Nothing was so odd as that she
should have to recognise so quickly in each of these glimpses of
an instant the various signs of a relation; and this anomaly itself,
had she had more time to give to it, might well, might almost terribly have suggested to her that her doom was to live fast. It was
queerly a question of the short run and the consciousness propor-
tionately crowded.

These were immense excursions for the spirit of a young person
at Mrs. Lowder's mere dinner-party; but what was so significant
and so admonitory as the fact of their being possible? What could
they have been just a part, already, of the crowded consciousness?
And it was just a part likewise that while plates were changed and
dishes presented and periods in the banquet marked; while appearances insisted and phenomena multiplied and words reached
her from here and there like plashes of a slow thick tide; while
Mrs. Lowder grew somehow more stout and more instituted and
Susie, at her distance and in comparison, more thinly improvised
and more different—different, that is, from every one and every
thing: it was just a part that while this process went forward our
young lady alighted, came back, taking up her destiny again as if
she had been able by a wave or two of her wings to place herself
briefly in sight of an alternative to it. Whatever it was it had
showed in this brief interval as better than the alternative; and it
now presented itself altogether in the image and in the place in
which she had left it. The image was that of her being, as Lord
Mark had declared, a success. This depended more or less of
course on his idea of the thing—into which at present, however,
she wouldn't go. But, renewing soon, she had asked him what he

meant then that Mrs. Lowder would do with her, and he had replied that this might safely be left. "She'll get back," he pleasantly said, "her money." He could say it too—which was singular—without affecting her either as vulgar or as "nasty"; and he had soon explained himself by adding: "Nobody here, you know, does anything for nothing."

"Ah if you mean that we shall reward her as hard as ever we can, nothing is more certain. But she's an idealist," Milly continued, "and idealists, in the long run, I think, *don't* feel that they lose."

Lord Mark seemed, within the limits of his enthusiasm, to find this charming. "Ah she strikes you as an idealist?"

"She idealises *us*, my friend and me, absolutely. She sees us in a light," said Milly. "That's all I've got to hold on by. So don't deprive me of it."

"I wouldn't think of such a thing for the world. But do you suppose," he continued as if it were suddenly important for him—"do you suppose she sees *me* in a light?"

She neglected his question for a little, partly because her attention attached itself more and more to the handsome girl, partly because, placed so near their hostess, she wished not to show as discussing her too freely. Mrs. Lowder, it was true, steering in the other quarter a course in which she called at subjects as if they were islets in an archipelago, continued to allow them their ease, and Kate Croy at the same time steadily revealed herself as interesting. Milly in fact found of a sudden her ease—found it all as she bethought herself that what Mrs. Lowder was really arranging for was a report on her quality and, as perhaps might be said her value, from Lord Mark. She wished him, the wonderful lady, to have no pretext for not knowing what he thought of Miss Theale. Why his judgement so mattered remained to be seen; but it was this divination that in any case now determined Milly's rejoinder. "No. She knows you. She has probably reason to. And you all here know each other—I see that—so far as you know anything. You know what you're used to, and it's your being used to it—that, and that only—that makes you. But there are things you don't know."

He took it in as if it might fairly, to do him justice, be a point.

"Things that *I* don't—with all the pains I take and the way I've run about the world to leave nothing unlearned?"

Milly thought, and it was perhaps the very truth of his claim—its not being negligible—that sharpened her impatience and thereby her wit. "You're *blasé*, but you're not enlightened. You're familiar with everything, but conscious really of nothing. What I mean is that you've no imagination."

Lord Mark at this threw back his head, ranging with his eyes the opposite side of the room and showing himself at last so much more flagrantly diverted that it fairly attracted their hostess's notice. Mrs. Lowder, however, only smiled on Milly for a sign that something racy was what she had expected, and resumed, with a splash of her screw, her cruise among the islands. "Oh I've heard that," the young man replied, "beforc!"

"There it is then. You've heard everything before. You've heard *me* of course before, in my country, often enough."

"Oh never too often," he protested. "I'm sure I hope I shall still hear you again and again."

"But what good then has it done you?" the girl went on as if now frankly to amuse him.

"Oh you'll see when you know me."

"But most assuredly I shall never know you."

"Then that will be exactly," he laughed, "the good!"

If it established thus that they couldn't or wouldn't mix, why did Milly none the less feel through it a perverse quickening of the relation to which she had been in spite of herself appointed? What queerer consequence of their not mixing than their talking—for it was what they had arrived at—almost intimately? She wished to get away from him, or indeed, much rather, away from herself so far as she was present to him. She saw already—wonderful creature, after all, herself too—that there would be a good deal more of him to come for her, and that the special sign of their intercourse would be to keep herself out of the question. Everything else might come in—only never that; and with such an arrangement they would perhaps even go far. This in fact might quite have begun, on the spot, with her returning again to the topic of the handsome girl. If she was to keep herself out she could naturally best do so by putting in somebody else. She accordingly put in Kate Croy, being ready to that extent—as she was not at all afraid for her—to sacrifice her if necessary. Lord Mark himself, for that matter, had made it easy by saying a little while before that no one among them did anything for nothing. "What then"—she was aware of being abrupt—"does Miss Croy, if she's so interested, do it for? What has she to gain by *her* lovely welcome? Look at her *now!*" Milly broke out with characteristic freedom of praise, though pulling herself up also with a compunctious "Oh!" as the direction thus given to their eyes happened to coincide with a turn of Kate's face to them. All she had meant to do was to insist that this face was fine; but what she had in fact done was to renew again her effect of showing herself to its possessor as conjoined with Lord Mark for some interested view of it. He had, however, promptly met her question.

"To gain? Why your acquaintance."

"Well, what's my acquaintance to *her?* She can care for me—she must feel that—only by being sorry for me; and that's why she's lovely: to be already willing to take the trouble to be. It's the height of the disinterested."

There were more things in this than one that Lord Mark might have taken up; but in a minute he had made his choice. "Ah then I'm nowhere, for I'm afraid *I'm* not sorry for you in the least. What do you make then," he asked, "of your success?"

"Why just the great reason of all. It's just because our friend there sees it that she pities me. She understands," Milly said; "she's better than any of you. She's beautiful."

He appeared struck with this at last—with the point the girl made of it; to which she came back even after a diversion created by a dish presented between them. "Beautiful in character, I see. *Is* she so? You must tell me about her."

Milly wondered. "But haven't you known her longer than I? Haven't you seen her for yourself?"

"No—I've failed with her. It's no use. I don't make her out. And I assure you I really should like to." His assurance had in fact for his companion a positive suggestion of sincerity; he affected her as now saying something he did feel; and she was the more struck with it as she was still conscious of the failure even of curiosity he had just shown in respect to herself. She had meant something—

though indeed for herself almost only—in speaking of their friend's natural pity; it had doubtless been a note of questionable taste, but it had quavered out in spite of her and he hadn't so much as cared to enquire "Why 'natural'?" Not that it wasn't really much better for her that he shouldn't: explanations would in truth have taken her much too far. Only she now perceived that, in comparison, her word about this other person really "drew" him; and there were things in that probably, many things, as to which she would learn more and which glimmered there already as part and parcel of that larger "real" with which, in her new situation, she was to be beguiled. It was in fact at the very moment, this element, not absent from what Lord Mark was further saying. "So you're wrong, you see, as to our knowing all about each other. There are cases where we break down. I at any rate give *her* up—up, that is, to you. You must do her for me—tell me, I mean, when you know more. You'll notice," he pleasantly wound up, "that I've confidence in you."

"Why shouldn't you have?" Milly asked, observing in this, as she thought, a fine, though for such a man a surprisingly artless, fatuity. It was as if there might have been a question of her falsifying for the sake of her own show—that is of the failure of her honesty to be proof against her desire to keep well with him herself. She didn't, none the less, otherwise protest against his remark; there was something else she was occupied in seeing. It was the handsome girl alone, one of his own species and his own society, who had made him feel uncertain; of his certainties about a mere little American, a cheap exotic, imported almost wholesale and whose habitat, with its conditions of climate, growth and cultivation, its immense profusion but its few varieties and thin development, he was perfectly satisfied. The marvel was too that Milly understood his satisfaction—feeling she expressed the truth in presently saying: "Of course; I make out that she must be difficult; just as I see that I myself must be easy." And that was what, for all the rest of this occasion, remained with her—as the most interesting thing that *could* remain. She was more and more content herself to be easy; she would have been resigned, even had it been brought straighter home to her, to passing for a cheap exotic. Provisionally, at any rate, that protected her wish to keep herself, with Lord Mark, in abeyance. They *had* all affected her as inevitably knowing each other, and if the handsome girl's place among them was something even their initiation couldn't deal with—why then she would indeed be a quantity.

— II —

That sense of quantities, separate or mixed, was really, no doubt, what most prevailed at first for our slightly gasping American pair; it found utterance for them in their frequent remark to each other that they had no one but themselves to thank. It dropped from Milly more than once that if she had ever known it was so easy—! though her exclamation mostly ended without completing her idea. This, however, was a trifle to Mrs. Stringham, who cared little whether she meant that in this case she would have come sooner. She couldn't have come sooner, and she perhaps on the contrary meant—for it would have been like her—that she wouldn't have come at all; why it was so easy being at any rate a matter as to which her companion had begun quickly to pick up views. Susie kept some of these lights for the present to herself, since, freely communicated, they might have been a little disturbing; with which, moreover, the quantities that we speak of as surrounding the two ladies were in many cases quantities of things—and of other things—to talk about. Their immediate lesson accordingly was that they just had been caught up by the incalculable strength of a wave that was actually holding them aloft and that would naturally dash them wherever it liked. They meanwhile, we hasten to add, made the best of their precarious position, and if Milly had had no other help for it she would have found not a little in the sight of Susan Shepherd's state. The girl had had nothing to say to her, for three days, about the "success" announced by Lord Mark—which they saw, besides, otherwise established; she was too taken up, too touched, by Susie's own exaltation. Susie glowed in the light of her justified faith; everything had happened that she had been acute enough to think least probable; she had appealed to a possible delicacy in Maud Manningham—a delicacy, mind you, but *barely* possible—and her appeal had been met in a way that was an honour to human nature. This proved sensibility of the lady of Lancaster Gate performed verily for both our friends during these first days the office of a fine floating gold-dust, something that threw over the prospect a harmonising blur. The forms, the colours behind it were strong and deep—we have seen how they already stood out for Milly; but nothing, comparatively, had had so much of the dignity of truth as the fact of Maud's fidelity to a sentiment. That was what Susie was proud of, much more than of her great place in the world, which she was moreover conscious of not as yet wholly measuring. That was what was more vivid even than her being—in senses more worldly and in fact almost in the degree of a revelation—English and distinct and positive, with almost no inward but with the finest outward resonance.

Susan Shepherd's word for her, again and again, was that she was "large"; yet it was not exactly a case, as to the soul, of echoing chambers: she might have been likened rather to a capacious receptacle, originally perhaps loose, but now drawn as tightly as possible over its accumulated contents—a packed mass, for her American admirer, of curious detail. When the latter good lady, at home, had handsomely figured her friends as not small—which was the way she mostly figured them—there was a certain implication that they were spacious because they were empty. Mrs. Lowder, by a different law, was spacious because she was full, because she had something in common, even in repose, with a projectile, of great size, loaded and ready for use. That indeed, to Susie's romantic mind, announced itself as half the charm of their renewal—a charm as of sitting in springtime, during a long peace, on the daisied grassy bank of some great slumbering fortress. True to her psychological instincts, certainly, Mrs. Stringham had noted that the "sentiment" she rejoiced in on her old schoolmate's part was all a matter of action and movement, was not, save for the interweaving of a more frequent plump "dearest" than she would herself perhaps have used, a matter of much other embroidery. She brooded with interest on this further mark of race, feeling in her own spirit a different economy. The joy, for her, was to know *why* she acted—the reason was half the business; whereas with Mrs. Lowder there might have been no reason: "why" was the trivial seasoning-substance, the vanilla or the nutmeg, omittable from the nutritive pudding without spoiling it. Mrs. Lowder's desire was clearly sharp that their young companions should also prosper together; and Mrs. Stringham's account of it all to Milly, during the first days, was that when, at Lancaster Gate, she was not occupied in telling, as it were, about her, she was occupied in hearing much of the history of her hostess's brilliant niece.

They had plenty, on these lines, the two elder women, to give and to take, and it was even not quite clear to the pilgrim from Boston that what she should mainly have arranged for in London was not a series of thrills for herself. She had a bad conscience, indeed almost a sense of immorality, in having to recognise that she was, as she said, carried away. She laughed to Milly when she also said that she didn't know where it would end; and the principle of her uneasiness was that Mrs. Lowder's life bristled for her with elements that she was really having to look at for the first time. They represented, she believed, the world, the world that, as a consequence of the cold shoulder turned to it by the Pilgrim Fathers, had never yet boldly crossed to Boston—it would surely have sunk the stoutest Cunarder—and she couldn't pretend that she faced the prospect simply because Milly had had a caprice. She was in the act herself of having one, directed precisely to their present spectacle. She could but seek strength in the thought that she had never had one—or had never yielded to one, which came to the same thing—before. The sustaining sense of it all moreover as literary material—that quite dropped from her. She must wait, at any rate, she should see: it struck her, so far as she had got, as vast, obscure, lurid. She reflected in the watches of the night that she was probably just going to love it for itself—that is for itself and Milly. The odd thing was that she could think of Milly's loving it without dread—or with dread at least not on the score of conscience, only on the score of peace. It was a mercy at all events, for the hour, that their two spirits jumped together.

While, for this first week that followed their dinner, she drank deep at Lancaster Gate, her companion was no less happily, appeared to be indeed on the whole quite as romantically, provided for. The handsome English girl from the heavy English house had been as a figure in a picture stepping by magic out of its frame: it was a case in truth for which Mrs. Stringham presently found the perfect image. She had lost none of her grasp, but quite the contrary, of that other conceit in virtue of which Milly was the wandering princess: so what could be more in harmony now than to see the princess waited upon at the city gate by the worthiest maiden, the chosen daughter of the burgesses? It was the real again, evidently, the amusement of the meeting for the princess too; princesses living for the most part, in such an appeased way, on the plane of mere elegant representation. That was why they pounced, at city gates, on deputed flower-strewing damsels; that was why, after effigies, processions and other stately games, frank human company was pleasant to them. Kate Croy really presented herself to Milly—the latter abounded for Mrs. Stringham in accounts of it—as the wondrous London girl in person (by what she had conceived, from far back, of the London girl; conceived from the tales of travellers and the anecdotes of New York, from old porings over *Punch* and a liberal acquaintance with the fiction of the day). The only thing was that she was nicer, since the creature in question had rather been, to our young woman, an image of dread. She had thought of her, at her best, as handsome just as Kate was, with turns of head and tones of voice, felicities of stature and attitude, things "put on" and, for that matter, put off, all the marks of the product of a packed society who should be at the same time the heroine of a strong story. She placed this striking young person from the first in a story, saw her, by a necessity of the imagination, for a heroine, felt it the only character in which she wouldn't be wasted; and this in spite of the heroine's pleasant abruptness, her forbearance from gush, her umbrellas and jackets and shoes—as these things sketched themselves to Milly—and something rather of a breezy boy in the carriage of her arms and the occasional freedom of her slang.

When Milly had settled that the extent of her good will itself made her shy, she had found for the moment quite a sufficient key, and they were by that time thoroughly afloat together. This might well have been the happiest hour they were to know, attacking in friendly independence their great London—the London of shops

and streets and suburbs oddly interesting to Milly, as well as of museums, monuments, "sights" oddly unfamiliar to Kate, while their
elders pursued a separate course; these two rejoicing not less in
their intimacy and each thinking the other's young woman a great
acquisition for her own. Milly expressed to Susan Shepherd more
than once that Kate had some secret, some smothered trouble, besides all the rest of her history; and that if she had so good-
naturedly helped Mrs. Lowder to meet them this was exactly to
create a diversion, to give herself something else to think about.
But on the case thus postulated our young American had as yet
had no light: she only felt that when the light should come it
would greatly deepen the colour; and she liked to think she was
prepared for anything. What she already knew moreover was
full, to her vision, of English, of eccentric, of Thackerayan character[10]—Kate Croy having gradually become not a little explicit
on the subject of her situation, her past, her present, her general
predicament, her small success, up to the present hour, in con-
tenting at the same time her father, her sister, her aunt and herself. It was Milly's subtle guess, imparted to her Susie, that the girl
had somebody else as well, as yet unnamed, to content—it being
manifest that such a creature couldn't help having; a creature not
perhaps, if one would, exactly formed to inspire passions, since
that always implied a certain silliness, but essentially seen, by the
admiring eye of friendship, under the clear shadow of some probably eminent male interest. The clear shadow, from whatever
source projected, hung at any rate over Milly's companion the
whole week, and Kate Croy's handsome face smiled out of it,
under bland skylights, in the presence alike of old masters passive
in their glory and of thoroughly new ones, the newest, who bristled
restlessly with pins and brandished snipping shears.

It was meanwhile a pretty part of the intercourse of these
young ladies that each thought the other more remarkable than
herself—that each thought herself, or assured the other she did, a
comparatively dusty object and the other a favourite of nature and
of fortune and covered thereby with the freshness of the morning.
Kate was amused, amazed, at the way her friend insisted on "taking" her, and Milly wondered if Kate were sincere in finding her
the most extraordinary—quite apart from her being the most

charming—person she had come across. They had talked, in long
drives, and quantities of history had not been wanting—in the
light of which Mrs. Lowder's niece might superficially seem to
have had the best of the argument. Her visitor's American references, with their bewildering immensities, their confounding
moneyed New York, their excitements of high pressure, their opportunities of wild freedom, their record of used-up relatives, parents, clever eager fair slim brothers—these the most loved—all
engaged, as well as successive superseded guardians, in a high extravagance of speculation and dissipation that had left this exquisite being her black dress, her white face and her vivid hair as
the mere last broken link: such a picture quite threw into the
shade the brief biography, however sketchily amplified, of a mere
middle-class nobody in Bayswater. And though that indeed might
be but a Bayswater way of putting it, in addition to which Milly
was in the stage of interest in Bayswater ways, this critic so far prevailed that, like Mrs. Stringham herself, she fairly got her companion to accept from her that she was quite the nearest approach
to a practical princess Bayswater could hope ever to know. It was
a fact—it became one at the end of three days—that Milly actually began to borrow from the handsome girl a sort of view of her
state; the handsome girl's impression of it was clearly so sincere.
This impression was a tribute, a tribute positively to power, power
the source of which was the last thing Kate treated as a mystery.
There were passages, under all their skylights, the succession of
their shops being large, in which the latter's easy yet the least bit
dry manner sufficiently gave out that if *she* had had so deep a
pocket—!

It was not moreover by any means with not having the imagination of expenditure that she appeared to charge her friend, but
with not having the imagination of terror, of thrift, the imagination or in any degree the habit of a conscious dependence on others. Such moments, when all Wigmore Street, for instance,
seemed to rustle about and the pale girl herself to be facing the different rustlers, usually so undiscriminated, as individual Britons
too, Britons personal, parties to a relation and perhaps even in-
trinsically remarkable—such moments in especial determined for
Kate a perception of the high happiness of her companion's lib-

erty. Milly's range was thus immense; she had to ask nobody for anything, to refer nothing to any one; her freedom, her fortune and her fancy were her law; an obsequious world surrounded her, she could sniff up at every step its fumes. And Kate, these days, was altogether in the phase of forgiving her so much bliss; in the phase moreover of believing that, should they continue to go on together, she would abide in that generosity. She had at such a point as this no suspicion of a rift within the lute—by which we mean not only none of anything's coming between them, but none of any definite flaw in so much clearness of quality. Yet, all the same, if Milly, at Mrs. Lowder's banquet, had described herself to Lord Mark as kindly used by the young woman on the other side because of some faintly-felt special propriety in it, so there really did match with this, privately, on the young woman's part, a feeling not analysed but divided, a latent impression that Mildred Theale was not, after all, a person to change places, to change even chances with. Kate, verily, would perhaps not quite have known what she meant by this discrimination, and she came near naming it only when she said to herself that, rich as Milly was, one probably wouldn't—which was singular—ever hate her for it. The handsome girl had, with herself, these felicities and crudities: it wasn't obscure to her that, without some very particular reason to help, it might have proved a test of one's philosophy not to be irritated by a mistress of millions, or whatever they were, who, as a girl, so easily might have been, like herself, only vague and cruelly female. She was by no means sure of liking Aunt Maud as much as *she* deserved, and Aunt Maud's command of funds was obviously inferior to Milly's. There was thus clearly, as pleading for the latter, some influence that would later on become distinct; and meanwhile, decidedly, it was enough that she was as charming as she was queer and as queer as she was charming—all of which was a rare amusement; as well, for that matter, as further sufficient that there were objects of value she had already pressed on Kate's acceptance. A week of her society in these conditions—conditions that Milly chose to sum up as ministering immensely, for a blind vague pilgrim, to aid and comfort—announced itself from an early hour as likely to become a week of presents, acknowledgements, mementoes, pledges of gratitude and admiration, that were all on one side. Kate as promptly embraced the propriety of making it clear that she must forswear shops till she should receive some guarantee that the contents of each one she entered as a humble companion shouldn't be placed at her feet; yet that was in truth not before she had found herself in possession, under whatever protests, of several precious ornaments and other minor conveniences.

Great was the absurdity too that there should have come a day, by the end of the week, when it appeared that all Milly would have asked in definite "return," as might be said, was to be told a little about Lord Mark and to be promised the privilege of a visit to Mrs. Condrip. Far other amusements had been offered her, but her eagerness was shamelessly human, and she seemed really to count more on the revelation of the anxious lady at Chelsea than on the best nights of the opera. Kate admired, and showed it, such an absence of fear: to the fear of being bored in such a connexion she would have been so obviously entitled. Milly's answer to this was the plea of her curiosities—which left her friend wondering as to their odd direction. Some among them, no doubt, were rather more intelligible, and Kate had heard without wonder that she was blank about Lord Mark. This young lady's account of him, at the same time, professed itself frankly imperfect; for what they best knew him by at Lancaster Gate was a thing difficult to explain. One knew people in general by something they had to show, something that, either for them or against, could be touched or named or proved; and she could think of no other case of a value taken as so great and yet flourishing untested. His value was his future, which had somehow got itself as accepted by Aunt Maud as if it had been his good cook or his steam-launch. She, Kate, didn't mean she thought him a humbug; he might do great things—but they were as yet, so to speak, all he had done. On the other hand it was of course something of an achievement, and not open to every one, to have got one's self taken so seriously by Aunt Maud. The best thing about him doubtless, on the whole, was that Aunt Maud believed in him. She was often fantastic, but she knew a humbug, and—no, Lord Mark wasn't that. He had been a short time in the House, on the Tory side, but had lost his seat on the first opportunity, and this was all he had to point to. However, he pointed to nothing; which was very possibly just a sign of his real cleverness, one of those that the really clever had in common with the really void. Even Aunt Maud frequently admitted that there was a good deal, for her view of him, to bring up the rear. And he wasn't meanwhile himself indifferent—indifferent to himself—for he was working Lancaster Gate for all it was worth: just as it was, no doubt, working *him*, and just as the working and the worked were in London, as one might explain, the parties to every relation.

Kate did explain, for her listening friend; every one who had anything to give—it was true they were the fewest—made the sharpest possible bargain for it, got at least its value in return. The strangest thing furthermore was that this might be in cases a happy understanding. The worker in one connexion was the worked in another; it was as broad as it was long—with the wheels of the system, as might be seen, wonderfully oiled. People could quite like each other in the midst of it, as Aunt Maud, by every appearance, quite liked Lord Mark, and as Lord Mark, it was to be hoped, liked Mrs. Lowder, since if he didn't he was a greater brute than one could believe. She, Kate, hadn't yet, it was true, made out what he was doing for her—besides which the dear woman needed him, even at the most he could do, much less than she imagined; so far as all of which went, moreover, there were plenty of things on every side she hadn't yet made out. She believed, on the whole, in any one Aunt Maud took up; and she gave it to Milly as worth thinking of that, whatever wonderful people this young lady might meet in the land, she would meet no more extraordinary woman. There were greater celebrities by the million, and of course greater swells, but a bigger *person*, by Kate's view, and a larger natural handful every way, would really be far to seek. When Milly enquired with interest if Kate's belief in *her* was primarily on the lines of what Mrs. Lowder "took up," her interlocutress could handsomely say yes, since by the same principle she believed in herself. Whom but Aunt Maud's niece, pre-eminently, had Aunt Maud taken up, and who was thus more in the current, with her, of working and of being worked? "You may ask," Kate said, "what in the world *I* have to give; and that indeed is just what I'm trying to learn. There must be something, for her to think she can get it out of me. She *will* get it—trust her; and then I shall see what it is; which I beg you to believe I should never have found out for myself." She declined to treat any question of Milly's own "paying" power as discussable; that Milly would pay a hundred per cent—and even to the end, doubtless, through the nose—was just the beautiful basis on which they found themselves.

These were fine facilities, pleasantries, ironies, all these luxuries of gossip and philosophies of London and of life, and they became quickly, between the pair, the common form of talk, Milly professing herself delighted to know that something was to be done with her. If the most remarkable woman in England was to do it, so much the better, and if the most remarkable woman in England had them both in hand together why what could be jollier for each? When she reflected indeed a little on the oddity of her wanting two at once Kate had the natural reply that it was exactly what showed her sincerity. She invariably gave way to feeling, and feeling had distinctly popped up in her on the advent of her girlhood's friend. The way the cat would jump was always, in presence of anything that moved her, interesting to see; visibly enough, moreover, it hadn't for a long time jumped anything like so far. This in fact, as we already know, remained the marvel for Milly Theale, who, on sight of Mrs. Lowder, had found fifty links in respect to Susie absent from the chain of association. She knew so herself what she thought of Susie, that she would have expected the lady of Lancaster Gate to think something quite different; the failure of which endlessly mystified her. But her mystification was the cause for her of another fine impression, inasmuch as when she went so far as to observe to Kate that Susan Shepherd—and especially Susan Shepherd emerging so uninvited from an irrelevant past—ought by all the proprieties simply to have bored Aunt Maud, her confidant agreed to this without a protest and abounded in the sense of her wonder. Susan Shepherd at least bored the niece—that was plain; this young woman saw nothing in her—nothing to account for anything, not even for Milly's own indulgence: which little fact became in turn to the latter's mind a fact of significance. It was a light on the handsome girl—representing more than merely showed—that poor Susie was simply as nought to her. This was in a manner too a general admonition to poor Susie's companion, who seemed to see marked by it the direction in which she had best most look out. It just faintly rankled in her that a person who was good enough and to spare for Milly Theale shouldn't be good enough for another girl; though, oddly enough, she could easily have forgiven Mrs. Lowder herself the impatience. Mrs. Lowder didn't feel it, and Kate Croy felt it with ease; yet in the end, be it added, she grasped the reason, and the reason enriched her mind. Wasn't it sufficiently the reason that the handsome girl was, with twenty other splendid qualities, the least bit brutal too, and didn't she suggest, as no one yet had ever done for her new friend, that there might be a wild beauty in that, and even a strange grace? Kate wasn't brutally brutal—which Milly had hitherto benightedly supposed the only way; she wasn't even aggressively so, but rather indifferently, defensively and, as might be said, by the habit of anticipation. She simplified in advance, was beforehand with her doubts, and knew with singular quickness what she wasn't, as they said in New York, going to like. In that way at least people were clearly quicker in England than at home; and Milly could quite see after a little how such instincts might become usual in a world in which dangers abounded. There were clearly more dangers roundabout Lancaster Gate than one suspected in New York or could dream of in Boston. At all events, with more sense of them, there were more precautions, and it was a remarkable world altogether in which there could be precautions, on whatever ground, against Susie.

— III —

She certainly made up with Susie directly, however, for any allowance she might have had privately to extend to tepid appreciation; since the late and long talks of these two embraced not only everything offered and suggested by the hours they spent apart, but a good deal more besides. She might be as detached as the occasion required at four o'clock in the afternoon, but she used no such freedom to any one about anything as she habitually used about everything to Susan Shepherd at midnight. All the same, it should with much less delay than this have been mentioned, she hadn't yet—hadn't, that is, at the end of six days—produced any news for her comrade to compare with an announcement made her by the latter as a result of a drive with Mrs. Lowder, for a change, in the remarkable Battersea Park. The elder friends had sociably revolved there while the younger ones followed bolder fancies in the admirable equipage appointed to Milly at the hotel—a heavier, more emblazoned, more amusing chariot than she had ever, with "stables" notoriously mismanaged, known at home; whereby, in the course of the circuit, more than once repeated, it had "come out," as Mrs. Stringham said, that the couple at Lancaster Gate were, of all people, acquainted with Mildred's other English friend, the gentleman, the one connected with the English newspaper (Susie hung fire a little over his name) who had been with her in New York so shortly previous to present adventures. He had been named of course in Battersea Park—else he couldn't have been identified; and Susie had naturally, before she could produce her own share in the matter as a kind of confession, to make it plain that her allusion was to Mr. Merton Densher. This was because Milly had at first a little air of not knowing whom she meant; and the girl really kept, as well, a certain control of herself while she remarked that the case was surprising, the chance one in a thousand. They knew him, both Maud and Miss Croy knew him, she gathered too, rather well, though indeed it wasn't on any show of intimacy that he had happened to be mentioned. It hadn't been—Susie made the point—she herself who brought him in; he had in fact not been brought in at all, but only referred to as a young journalist known to Mrs. Lowder and who had lately gone to their wonderful country—Mrs. Lowder always said "your wonderful country"—on behalf of his journal. But Mrs. Stringham had taken it up—with the tips of her fingers indeed; and that was the confession: she had, without meaning any harm, recognised Mr. Densher as an acquaintance of Milly's, though she had also pulled herself up before getting in too far. Mrs. Lowder had been struck, clearly—it wasn't too much to say; then she also, it had rather seemed, had pulled herself up; and there had been a little moment during which each might have been keeping something from the other. "Only," said Milly's informant, "I luckily remembered in time that I had nothing whatever to keep—which was much simpler and nicer. I don't know what Maud has, but there it is. She was interested, distinctly, in your knowing him—in his having met you over there with so little loss of time. But I ventured to tell her it hadn't been so long as to make you as yet great friends. I don't know if I was right."

Whatever time this explanation might have taken, there had been moments enough in the matter now—before the elder woman's conscience had done itself justice—to enable Milly to reply that although the fact in question doubtless had its importance she imagined they wouldn't find the importance overwhelming. It *was* odd that their one Englishman should so instantly fit; it wasn't, however, miraculous—they surely all had often seen how extraordinarily "small," as every one said, was the world. Undoubtedly also Susie had done just the plain thing in not letting his name pass. Why in the world should there be a mystery?—and what an immense one they would appear to have made if he should come back and find they had concealed their knowledge of him! "I don't know, Susie dear," the girl observed, "what you think I have to conceal."

"It doesn't matter, at a given moment," Mrs. Stringham returned, "what you know or don't know as to what I think; for you always find out the very next minute, and when you do find out, dearest, you never *really* care. Only," she presently asked, "have you heard of him from Miss Croy?"

"Heard of Mr. Densher? Never a word. We haven't mentioned him. Why should we?"

"That *you* haven't I understand; but that your friend hasn't," Susie opined, "may mean something."

"May mean what?"

"Well," Mrs. Stringham presently brought out, "I tell you all when I tell you that Maud asks me to suggest to you that it may perhaps be better for the present not to speak of him: not to speak of him to her niece, that is, unless she herself speaks to you first. But Maud thinks she won't."

Milly was ready to engage for anything; but in respect to the facts—as they so far possessed them—it all sounded a little complicated. "Is it because there's anything between them?"

"No—I gather not; but Maud's state of mind is precautionary. She's afraid of something. Or perhaps it would be more correct to say she's afraid of everything."

"She's afraid, you mean," Milly asked, "of their—a—liking each other?"

Susie had an intense thought and then an effusion. "My dear child, we move in a labyrinth."

"Of course we do. That's just the fun of it!" said Milly with a strange gaiety. Then she added: "Don't tell me that—in this for instance—there are not abysses. I want abysses."

Her friend looked at her—it was not unfrequently the case—a little harder than the surface of the occasion seemed to require; and another person present at such times might have wondered to what inner thought of her own the good lady was trying to fit the speech. It was too much her disposition, no doubt, to treat her young companion's words as symptoms of an imputed malady. It was none the less, however, her highest law to be light when the girl was light. She knew how to be quaint with the new quaintness—the great Boston gift; it had been happily her note in the magazines; and Maud Lowder, to whom it was new indeed and who had never heard anything remotely like it, quite cherished her, as a social resource, by reason of it. It shouldn't therefore fail her now; with it in fact one might face most things. "Ah then let us hope we shall sound the depths—I'm prepared for the worst—of sorrow and sin! But she would like her niece—we're not ignorant of that, are we?—to marry Lord Mark. Hasn't she told you so?"

"Hasn't Mrs. Lowder told me?"

"No; hasn't Kate? It isn't, you know, that she doesn't know it."

Milly had, under her comrade's eyes, a minute of mute detachment. She had lived with Kate Croy for several days in a state of intimacy as deep as it had been sudden, and they had clearly, in talk, in many directions, proceeded to various extremities. Yet it now came over her as in a clear cold wave that there was a possible account of their relations in which the quantity her new friend had told her might have figured as small, as smallest, beside the quantity she hadn't. She couldn't say at any rate whether or no Kate had made the point that her aunt designed her for Lord

Mark: it had only sufficiently come out—which had been, moreover, eminently guessable—that she was involved in her aunt's designs. Somehow, for Milly, brush it over nervously as she might
and with whatever simplifying hand, this abrupt extrusion of Mr.
Densher altered all proportions, had an effect on all values. It was
fantastic of her to let it make a difference that she couldn't in the
least have defined—and she was at least, even during these instants, rather proud of being able to hide, on the spot, the difference it did make. Yet all the same the effect for her was, almost
violently, of that gentleman's having been there—having been
where she had stood till now in her simplicity—before her. It
would have taken but another free moment to make her see
abysses—since abysses were what she wanted—in the mere circumstance of his own silence, in New York, about his English
friends. There had really been in New York little time for anything; but, had she liked, Milly could have made it out for herself
that he had avoided the subject of Miss Croy and that Miss Croy
was yet a subject it could never be natural to avoid, it was to be
added at the same time that even if his silence had been a
labyrinth—which was absurd in view of all the other things too he
couldn't possibly have spoken of—this was exactly what must suit
her, since it fell under the head of the plea she had just uttered to
Susie. These things, however, came and went, and it set itself up
between the companions, for the occasion, in the oddest way, both
that their happening all to know Mr. Densher—except indeed that
Susie didn't, but probably would—was a fact attached, in a world
of rushing about, to one of the common orders of chance; and yet
further that it was amusing—oh awfully amusing!—to be able
fondly to hope that there was "something *in*" its having been left
to crop up with such suddenness. There seemed somehow a possibility that the ground or, as it were, the air might in a manner
have undergone some pleasing preparation; though the question
of this possibility would probably, after all, have taken some
threshing out. The truth, moreover—and there they were, already,
our pair, talking about it, the "truth"!—hadn't in fact quite
cropped out. This, obviously, in view of Mrs. Lowder's request to
her old friend.

It was accordingly on Mrs. Lowder's recommendation that

nothing should be said to Kate—it was on all this might cover in
Aunt Maud that the idea of an interesting complication could best
hope to perch; and when in fact, after the colloquy we have re-
ported, Milly saw Kate again without mentioning any name, her
silence succeeded in passing muster with her as the beginning of
a new sort of fun. The sort was all the newer by its containing
measurably a small element of anxiety: when she had gone in for
fun before it had been with her hands a little more free. Yet it was,
none the less, rather exciting to be conscious of a still sharper reason for interest in the handsome girl, as Kate continued even now
pre-eminently to remain for her; and a reason—this was the great
point—of which the young woman herself could have no suspicion. Twice over thus, for two or three hours together, Milly found
herself seeing Kate, quite fixing her, in the light of the knowledge
that it was a face on which Mr. Densher's eyes had more or less familiarly rested and which, by the same token, had looked, rather
more beautifully than less, into his own. She pulled herself up indeed with the thought that it had inevitably looked, as beautifully
as one would, into thousands of faces in which one might one's
self never trace it; but just the odd result of the thought was to intensify for the girl that side of her friend which she had doubtless
already been more prepared than she quite knew to think of as the
"other," the not wholly calculable. It was fantastic, and Milly was
aware of this; but the other side was what had, of a sudden, been
turned straight toward her by the show of Mr. Densher's propinquity. She hadn't the excuse of knowing it for Kate's own, since
nothing whatever as yet proved it particularly to be such. Never
mind; it was with this other side now fully presented that Kate
came and went, kissed her for greeting and for parting, talked, as
usual, of everything but—as it had so abruptly become for Milly—
the thing. Our young woman, it is true, would doubtless not have
tasted so sharply a difference in this pair of occasions hadn't she
been tasting so peculiarly her own possible betrayals. What happened was that afterwards, on separation, she wondered if the matter hadn't mainly been that she herself was so "other," so taken up
with the unspoken; the strangest thing of all being, still subsequently, that when she asked herself how Kate could have failed to
feel it she became conscious of being here on the edge of a great

darkness. She should never know how Kate truly felt about anything such a one as Milly Theale should give her to feel. Kate
would never—and not from ill will nor from duplicity, but from a
sort of failure of common terms—reduce it to such a one's comprehension or put it within her convenience.

It was as such a one, therefore, that, for three or four days more,
Milly watched Kate as just such another; and it was presently as
such a one that she threw herself into their promised visit, at last
achieved, to Chelsea, the quarter of the famous Carlyle,* the field
of exercise of his ghost, his votaries, and the residence of "poor
Marian," so often referred to and actually a somewhat incongruous
spirit there. With our young woman's first view of poor Marian
everything gave way but the sense of how in England, apparently,
the social situation of sisters could be opposed, how common
ground for a place in the world could quite fail them: a state of
things sagely perceived to be involved in an hierarchical, an aristocratic order. Just whereabouts in the order Mrs. Lowder had established her niece was a question not wholly void as yet, no
doubt, of ambiguity—though Milly was withal sure Lord Mark
could exactly have fixed the point if he would, fixing it at the same
time for Aunt Maud herself; but it was clear Mrs. Condrip was, as
might have been said, in quite another geography.[11] She wouldn't
have been to be found on the same social map, and it was as if her
visitors had turned over page after page together before the final
relief of their benevolent "Here!" The interval was bridged of
course, but the bridge verily was needed, and the impression left
Milly to wonder if, in the general connexion, it were of bridges or
of intervals that the spirit not locally disciplined would find itself
most conscious. It was as if at home, by contrast, there were neither—neither the difference itself, from position to position, nor,
on either side, and particularly on one, the awfully good manner,
the conscious sinking of a consciousness, that made up for it. The
conscious sinking, at all events, and the awfully good manner, the
difference, the bridge, the interval, the skipped leaves of the social
atlas—these, it was to be confessed, had a little, for our young lady,

---

*Thomas Carlyle (1795–1881), eminent Scottish-born essayist, philosopher, and
man of letters.

in default of stouter stuff, to work themselves into the light literary legend—a mixed wandering echo of Trollope, of Thackeray, perhaps mostly of Dickens—under favour of which her pilgrimage had so much appealed. She could relate to Susie later on, late the same evening, that the legend, before she had done with it, had run clear, that the adored author of "The Newcomes,"* in fine, had been on the whole the note: the picture lacking thus more than she had hoped, or rather perhaps showing less than she had feared, a certain possibility of Pickwickian outline. She explained how she meant by this that Mrs. Condrip hadn't altogether proved another Mrs. Nickleby, nor even—for she might have proved almost anything, from the way poor worried Kate had spoken—a widowed and aggravated Mrs. Micawber.

Mrs. Stringham, in the midnight conference, intimated rather yearningly, that, however the event might have turned, the side of English life such experiences opened to Milly were just those she herself seemed "booked"—as they were all, roundabout her now, always saying—to miss: she had begun to have a little, for her fellow observer, these moments of fanciful reaction (reaction in which she was once more all Susan Shepherd) against the high sphere of colder conventions into which her overwhelming connexion with Maud Manningham had rapt her. Milly never lost sight for long of the Susan Shepherd side of her, and was always there to meet it when it came up and vaguely, tenderly, impatiently to pat it, abounding in the assurance that they would still provide for it. They had, however, to-night another matter in hand; which proved to be presently, on the girl's part, in respect to her hour of Chelsea, the revelation that Mrs. Condrip, taking a few minutes when Kate was away with one of the children, in bed upstairs for some small complaint, had suddenly (without its being in the least "led up to") broken ground on the subject of Mr. Densher, mentioned him with impatience as a person in love with her sister. "She wished me, if I cared for Kate, to know," Milly said— "for it would be quite too dreadful, and one might do something."

---

*Novel by William Makepeace Thackeray, published in 1855.

Susie wondered. "Prevent anything coming of it? That's easily said. Do what?"

Milly had a dim smile. "I think that what she would like is that I should come a good deal to see *her* about it."

"And doesn't she suppose you've anything else to do?"

The girl had by this time clearly made it out. "Nothing but to admire and make much of her sister—whom she doesn't, however, herself in the least understand—and give up one's time, and everything else, to it." It struck the elder friend that she spoke with an almost unprecedented approach to sharpness; as if Mrs. Condrip had been rather indescribably disconcerting. Never yet so much as just of late had Mrs. Stringham seen her companion exalted, and by the very play of something within, into a vague golden air that left irritation below. That was the great thing with Milly—it was her characteristic poetry, or at least it was Susan Shepherd's. "But she made a point," the former continued, "of my keeping what she says from Kate. I'm not to mention that she has spoken."

"And why," Mrs. Stringham presently asked, "is Mr. Densher so dreadful?"

Milly had, she thought, a delay to answer—something that suggested a fuller talk with Mrs. Condrip than she inclined perhaps to report. "It isn't so much he himself." Then the girl spoke a little as for the romance of it; one could never tell, with her, where romance would come in. "It's the state of his fortunes."

"And is that very bad?"

"He has no 'private means,' and no prospect of any. He has no income, and no ability, according to Mrs. Condrip, to make one. He's as poor, she calls it, as 'poverty,' and she says she knows what that is."

Again Mrs. Stringham considered, and it presently produced something. "But isn't he brilliantly clever?"

Milly had also then an instant that was not quite fruitless. "I haven't the least idea."

To which, for the time, Susie only replied "Oh!"—though by the end of a minute she had followed it with a slightly musing "I see"; and that in turn with: "It's quite what Maud Lowder thinks."

"That he'll never do anything?"

"No—quite the contrary: that he's exceptionally able."

"Oh yes; I know"—Milly had again, in reference to what her friend had already told her of this, her little tone of a moment before. "But Mrs. Condrip's own great point is that Aunt Maud herself won't hear of any such person. Mr. Densher, she holds—that's the way, at any rate, it was explained to me—won't ever be either a public man or a rich man. If he were public she'd be willing, as I understand, to help him; if he were rich—without being anything else—she'd do her best to swallow him. As it is she taboos him."

"In short," said Mrs. Stringham as with a private purpose, "she told you, the sister, all about it. But Mrs. Lowder likes him," she added.

"Mrs. Condrip didn't tell me that."

"Well, she does, all the same, my dear, extremely."

"Then there it is!" On which, with a drop and one of those sudden slightly sighing surrenders to a vague reflux and a general fatigue that had recently more than once marked themselves for her companion, Milly turned away. Yet the matter wasn't left so, that night, between them, albeit neither perhaps could afterwards have said which had first come back to it. Milly's own nearest approach at least, for a little, to doing so, was to remark that they appeared all—every one they saw—to think tremendously of money. This prompted in Susie a laugh, not untender, the innocent meaning of which was that it came, as a subject for indifference, money did, easier to some people than to others: she made the point in fairness, however, that you couldn't have told, by any too crude transparency of air, what place it held for Maud Manningham. She did her worldliness with grand proper silences—if it mightn't better be put perhaps that she did her detachment with grand occasional pushes. However Susie put it, in truth, she was really, in justice to herself, thinking of the difference, as favourites of fortune, between her old friend and her new. Aunt Maud sat somehow in the midst of her money, founded on it and surrounded by it, even if with a masterful high manner about it, her manner of looking, hard and bright, as if it weren't there. Milly, about hers, had no manner at all—which was possibly, from a point of view, a fault: she was at any rate far away on the edge of it, and you hadn't, as might be said, in order to get at her nature, to traverse, by whatever avenue, any piece of her property. It was clear, on the other hand, that Mrs. Lowder was keeping her wealth as for purposes, imaginations, ambitions, that would figure as large, as honourably unselfish, on the day they should take effect. She would impose her will, but her will would be only that a person or two shouldn't lose a benefit by not submitting if they could be made to submit. To Milly, as so much younger, such far views couldn't be imputed: there was nobody she was supposable as interested for. It was too soon, since she wasn't interested for herself. Even the richest woman, at her age, lacked motive, and Milly's motive doubtless had plenty of time to arrive. She was meanwhile beautiful, simple, sublime without it—whether missing it and vaguely reaching out for it or not; and with it, for that matter, in the event, would really be these things just as much. Only then she might very well have, like Aunt Maud, a manner. Such were the connexions, at all events, in which the colloquy of our two ladies freshly flickered up—in which it came round that the elder asked the younger if she had herself, in the afternoon, named Mr. Densher as an acquaintance.

"Oh no—I said nothing of having seen him. I remembered," the girl explained, "Mrs. Lowder's wish."

"But that," her friend observed after a moment, "was for silence to Kate."

"Yes—but Mrs. Condrip would immediately have told Kate."

"Why so?—since she must dislike to talk about him."

"Mrs. Condrip must?" Milly thought. "What she would like most is that her sister should be brought to think ill of him; and if anything she can tell her will help that—" But the girl dropped suddenly here, as if her companion would see.

Her companion's interest, however, was all for what she herself saw. "You mean she'll immediately speak?" Mrs. Stringham gathered that this was what Milly meant, but it left still a question. "How will it be against him that you know him?"

"Oh how can I say? It won't be so much one's knowing him as one's having kept it out of sight."

"Ah," said Mrs. Stringham as for comfort, "*you* haven't kept it out of sight. Isn't it much rather Miss Croy herself who has?"

"It isn't my acquaintance with him," Milly smiled, "that she has dissimulated."

"She has dissimulated only her own? Well then the responsibility's hers."

"Ah but," said the girl, not perhaps with marked consequence, "she has a right to do as she likes."

"Then so, my dear, have you!" smiled Susan Shepherd.

Milly looked at her as if she were almost venerably simple, but also as if this were what one loved her for. "We're not quarrelling about it, Kate and I, *yet*."

"I only meant," Mrs. Stringham explained, "that I don't see what Mrs. Condrip would gain."

"By her being able to tell Kate?" Milly thought. "I only meant that I don't see what I myself should gain."

"But it will have to come out—that he knows you both—some time."

Milly scarce assented. "Do you mean when he comes back?"

"He'll find you both here, and he can hardly be looked to, I take it, to 'cut' either of you for the sake of the other."

This placed the question at last on a basis more distinctly cheerful. "I might get at him somehow beforehand," the girl suggested; "I might give him what they call here the 'tip'—that he's not to know me when we meet. Or, better still, I mightn't be here at all."

"Do you want to run away from him?"

It was, oddly enough, an idea Milly seemed half to accept. "I don't know *what* I want to run away from!"

It dispelled, on the spot—something, to the elder woman's ear, in the sad, sweet sound of it—any ghost of any need of explaining. The sense was constant for her that their relation might have been afloat, like some island of the south, in a great warm sea that represented, for every conceivable chance, a margin, an outer sphere, of general emotion; and the effect of the occurrence of anything in particular was to make the sea submerge the island, the margin flood the text. The great wave now for a moment swept over. "I'll go anywhere else in the world you like."

But Milly came up through it. "Dear old Susie—how I do work you!"

"Oh this is nothing yet."

"No indeed—to what it will be."

"You're not—and it's vain to pretend," said dear old Susie, who had been taking her in, "as sound and strong as I insist on having you."

"Insist, insist—the more the better. But the day I *look* as sound and strong as that, you know," Milly went on—"on that day I shall be just sound and strong enough to take leave of you sweetly for ever. That's where one is," she continued thus agreeably to embroider, "when even one's *most* 'beaux moments'* aren't such as to qualify, so far as appearance goes, for anything gayer than a handsome cemetery. Since I've lived all these years as if I were dead, I shall die, no doubt, as if I were alive—which will happen to be as you want me. So, you see," she wound up, "you'll never really know where I am. Except indeed when I'm gone; and then you'll only know where I'm not."

"I'd die *for* you," said Susan Shepherd after a moment.

"'Thanks awfully'! Then stay here for me."

"But we can't be in London for August, nor for many of all these next weeks."

"Then we'll go back."

Susie blenched. "Back to America?"

"No, abroad—to Switzerland, Italy, anywhere. I mean by your staying 'here' for me," Milly pursued, "your staying with me wherever I may be, even though we may neither of us know at the time where it is. No," she insisted, "I *don't* know where I am, and you never will, and it doesn't matter—and I dare say it's quite true," she broke off, "that everything will have to come out." Her friend would have felt of her that she joked about it now, hadn't her scale from grave to gay been a thing of such unnameable shades that her contrasts were never sharp. She made up for failures of gravity by failures of mirth; if she hadn't, that is, been at times as earnest as might have been liked, so she was certain not to be at other times as easy as she would like herself. "I must face the music. It isn't at

---

*Beautiful (memorable) moments; perhaps akin to the "spots in time" of poet William Wordsworth (1770–1850). Milly's speech here comes close to revealing her true condition to Susie for the first time; it is the closest thing to a religious conviction or belief in the afterlife that we hear from Milly.

any rate its 'coming out,'" she added; "it's that Mrs. Condrip
would put the fact before her to his injury."

Her companion wondered. "But how to *his?*"

"Why if he pretends to love her—!"

"And does he only 'pretend'?"

"I mean if, trusted by her in strange countries, he forgets her so
far as to make up to other people."

The amendment, however, brought Susie in, as with gaiety, for
a comfortable end. "Did he make up, the false creature, to *you?*"

"No—but the question isn't of that. It's of what Kate might be
made to believe."

"That, given the fact of his having evidently more or less followed up his acquaintance with you, to say nothing of your obvious weird charm, he must have been all ready if you had a little bit
led him on?"

Milly neither accepted nor qualified this; she only said after a
moment and as with a conscious excess of the pensive: "No, I don't
think she'd quite wish to suggest that I made up to *him*; for that I
should have had to do so would only bring out his constancy. All
I mean is," she added—and now at last as with a supreme impatience—"that her being able to make him out a little a person who
could give cause for jealousy would evidently help her, since she's
afraid of him, to do him in her sister's mind a useful ill turn."

Susan Shepherd perceived in this explanation such signs of an
appetite for motive as would have sat gracefully even on one of her
own New England heroines. It was seeing round several corners;
but that was what New England heroines did, and it was moreover
interesting for the moment to make out how many her young
friend had actually undertaken to see round. Finally, too, weren't
they braving the deeps? They got their amusement where they
could. "Isn't it only," she asked, "rather probable she'd see that
Kate's knowing him as (what's the pretty old word?) *volage*—?"*

"Well?" She hadn't filled out her idea, but neither, it seemed,
could Milly.

"Well, might but do what that often does—by all *our* blessed lit-

---

*Fickle; flighty (French).

tle laws and arrangements at least: excite Kate's own sentiment instead of depressing it."

The idea was bright, yet the girl but beautifully stared. "Kate's
own sentiment? Oh she didn't speak of that. I don't think," she
added as if she had been unconsciously giving a wrong impression,
"I don't think Mrs. Condrip imagines *she's* in love."

It made Mrs. Stringham stare in turn. "Then what's her fear?"

"Well, only the fact of Mr. Densher's possibly himself keeping
it up—the fear of some final result from *that*."

"Oh," said Susie, intellectually a little disconcerted—"she looks
far ahead!"

At this, however, Milly threw off another of her sudden vague
"sports." "No—it's only we who do."

"Well, don't let us be more interested for them than they are for
themselves!"

"Certainly not"—the girl promptly assented. A certain interest
nevertheless remained; she appeared to wish to be clear. "It wasn't
of anything on Kate's own part she spoke."

"You mean she thinks her sister distinctly doesn't care for him?"

It was still as if, for an instant, Milly had to be sure of what she
meant; but there it presently was. "If she did care Mrs. Condrip
would have told me."

What Susan Shepherd seemed hereupon for a little to wonder
was why then they had been talking so. "But did you ask her?"

"Ah no!"

"Oh!" said Susan Shepherd.

Milly, however, easily explained that she wouldn't have asked
her for the world.

BOOK FIFTH

— I —

Lord Mark looked at her to-day in particular as if to wring from her a confession that she had originally done him injustice; and he was entitled to whatever there might be in it of advantage or merit that his intention really in a manner took effect: he cared about something, after all, sufficiently to make her feel absurdly as if she *were* confessing—all the while it was quite the case that neither justice nor injustice was what had been in question between them. He had presented himself at the hotel, had found her and had found Susan Shepherd at home, had been "civil" to Susan—it was just that shade, and Susan's fancy had fondly caught it; and then had come again and missed them, and then had come and found them once more: besides letting them easily see that if it hadn't by this time been the end of everything— which they could feel in the exhausted air, that of the season at its last gasp—the places they might have liked to go to were such as they would have had only to mention. Their feeling was—or at any rate their modest general plea—that there was no place they would have liked to go to; there was only the sense of finding they liked, wherever they were, the place to which they had been brought. Such was highly the case as to their current consciousness—which could be indeed, in an equally eminent degree, but a matter of course; impressions this afternoon having by a happy turn of their wheel been gathered for them into a splendid cluster, an offering like an armful of the rarest flowers. They were in presence of the offering—they had been led up to it; and if it had been still their habit to look at each other across distances for increase of unanimity his hand would have been silently named between them as the hand applied to the wheel. He had administered the touch that, under light analysis, made the difference—the difference of their not having lost, as Susie on the spot and at the hour phrased it again and again, both for herself and for such others as the question might concern, so beautiful and interesting an expe-

rience; the difference also, in fact, of Mrs. Lowder's not having lost
it either, though it was superficially with Mrs. Lowder they had
come, and though it was further with that lady that our young
woman was directly engaged during the half-hour or so of her most
agreeably inward response to the scene.

The great historic house* had, for Milly, beyond terrace and
garden, as the centre of an almost extravagantly grand Watteau-
composition, a tone as of old gold kept "down" by the quality of
the air, summer full-flushed but attuned to the general perfect
taste. Much, by her measure, for the previous hour, appeared, in
connexion with this revelation of it, to have happened to her—a
quantity expressed in introductions of charming new people, in
walks through halls of armour, of pictures, of cabinets, of tapestry,
of tea-tables, in an assault of reminders that this largeness of style
was the sign of *appointed* felicity. The largeness of style was the
great containing vessel, while everything else, the pleasant personal affluence, the easy murmurous welcome, the honoured age
of illustrious host and hostess, all at once so distinguished and so
plain, so public and so shy, became but this or that element of the
infusion. The elements melted together and seasoned the draught,
the essence of which might have struck the girl as distilled into the
small cup of iced coffee she had vaguely accepted from somebody,
while a fuller flood somehow kept bearing her up—all the freshness of response of her young life, the freshness of the first and
only prime. What had perhaps brought on just now a kind of climax was the fact of her appearing to make out, through Aunt
Maud, what was really the matter. It couldn't be less than a climax
for a poor shaky maiden to find it put to her of a sudden that she
herself was the matter—for that was positively what, on Mrs. Lowder's part, it came to. Everything was great, of course, in great pictures, and it was doubtless precisely a part of the brilliant
life—since the brilliant life, as one had faintly figured it, just *was*
humanly led—that all impressions within its area partook of its
brilliancy; still, letting that pass, it fairly stamped an hour as with
the official seal for one to be able to take in so comfortably one's

*Milly and Susan are now visiting Lord Mark's county estate; the scene is a garden
party.

companion's broad blandness. "You must stay among us—you must stay; anything else is impossible and ridiculous; you don't know yet, no doubt—you can't; but you will soon enough: you can stay in *any* position." It had been as the murmurous consecration to follow the murmurous welcome; and even if it were but part of Aunt Maud's own spiritual ebriety—for the dear woman, one could see, was spiritually "keeping" the day—it served to Milly, then and afterwards, as a high-water mark of the imagination.

It was to be the end of the short parenthesis which had begun but the other day at Lancaster Gate with Lord Mark's informing her that she was a "success"—the key thus again struck; and though no distinct, no numbered revelations had crowded in, there had, as we have seen, been plenty of incident for the space and the time. There had been thrice as much, and all gratuitous and genial—if, in portions, not exactly hitherto *the* revelation—as three unprepared weeks could have been expected to produce. Mrs. Lowder had improvised a "rush" for them, but out of elements, as Milly was now a little more freely aware, somewhat roughly combined. Therefore if at this very instant she had her reasons for thinking of the parenthesis as about to close—reasons completely personal—she had on behalf of her companion a divination almost as deep. The parenthesis would close with this admirable picture, but the admirable picture still would show Aunt Maud as not absolutely sure either if she herself were destined to remain in it. What she was doing, Milly might even not have escaped seeming to see, was to talk herself into a sublimer serenity while she ostensibly talked Milly. It was fine, the girl fully felt, the way she did talk *her*, little as, at bottom, our young woman needed it or found other persuasions at fault. It was in particular during the minutes of her grateful absorption of iced coffee— qualified by a sharp doubt of her wisdom—that she most had in view Lord Mark's relation to her being there, or at least to the question of her being amused at it. It wouldn't have taken much by the end of five minutes quite to make her feel that this relation was charming. It might, once more, simply have been that everything, anything, was charming when one was so justly and completely charmed; but, frankly, she hadn't supposed anything so serenely sociable could settle itself between them as the friendly understanding that was at present somehow in the air. They were, many of them together, near the marquee that had been erected on a stretch of sward as a temple of refreshment and that happened to have the property—which was all to the good—of making Milly think of a "durbar";* her iced coffee had been a consequence of this connexion, through which, further, the bright company scattered about fell thoroughly into place. Certain of its members might have represented the contingent of "native princes"—familiar, but scarce the less grandly gregarious term!—and Lord Mark would have done for one of these even though for choice he but presented himself as a supervisory friend of the family. The Lancaster Gate family, he clearly intended, in which he included its American recruits, and included above all Kate Croy—a young person blessedly easy to take care of. She knew people, and people knew her, and she was the handsomest thing there—this last a declaration made by Milly, in a sort of soft midsummer madness, a straight skylark-flight of charity, to Aunt Maud.

Kate had for her new friend's eyes the extraordinary and attaching property of appearing at a given moment to show as a beautiful stranger, to cut her connexions and lose her identity, letting the imagination for the time make what it would of them—make her merely a person striking from afar, more and more pleasing as one watched, but who was above all a subject for curiosity. Nothing could have given her, as a party to a relation, a greater freshness than this sense, which sprang up at its own hours, of one's being as curious about her as if one hadn't known her. It had sprung up, we have gathered, as soon as Milly had seen her after hearing from Mrs. Stringham of her knowledge of Merton Densher; she had *looked* then other and, as Milly knew the real critical mind would call it, more objective; and our young woman had foreseen it of her on the spot that she would often look so again. It was exactly what she was doing this afternoon; and Milly, who had amusements of thought that were like the secrecies of a little girl playing with dolls when conventionally "too

---

*Diplomatic reception held by an Indian prince.

big," could almost settle to the game of what one would suppose her, how one would place her, if one didn't know her. She became thus, intermittently, a figure conditioned only by the great facts of aspect, a figure to be waited for, named and fitted. This was doubtless but a way of feeling that it was of her essence to be peculiarly what the occasion, whatever it might be, demanded when its demand was highest. There were probably ways enough, on these lines, for such a consciousness; another of them would be for instance to say that she was made for great social uses. Milly wasn't wholly sure she herself knew what great social uses might be—unless, as a good example, to exert just that sort of glamour in just that sort of frame were one of them: she would have fallen back on knowing sufficiently that they existed at all events for her friend. It imputed a primness, all round, to be reduced but to saying, by way of a translation of one's amusement, that she was always so *right*—since that, too often, was what the *insupportables** themselves were; yet it was, in overflow to Aunt Maud, what she had to content herself withal—save for the lame enhancement of saying she was lovely, it served, despite everything, the purpose, strengthened the bond that for the time held the two ladies together, distilled in short its drop of rose-colour for Mrs. Lowder's own view. That was really the view Milly had, for most of the rest of the occasion, to give herself to immediately taking in; but it didn't prevent the continued play of those swift crosslights, odd beguilements of the mind, at which we have already glanced.

Mrs. Lowder herself found it enough simply to reply, in respect to Kate, that she was indeed a luxury to take about the world: she expressed no more surprise than that at her "rightness" today. Didn't it by this time sufficiently shine out that it was precisely as the very luxury she was proving that she had, from far back, been appraised and waited for? Crude elation, however, might be kept at bay, and the circumstance none the less made clear that they were all swimming together in the blue. It came back to Lord Mark again, as he seemed slowly to pass and repass and conve-

*Boorish people (French).

niently to linger before them; he was personally the note of the
blue—like a suspended skein of silk within reach of the broiderer's
hand. Aunt Maud's free-moving shuttle took a length of him at
rhythmic intervals; and one of the accessory truths that flickered
across to Milly was that he ever so consentingly knew he was being
worked in. This was almost like an understanding with her at Mrs.
Lowder's expense, which she would have none of; she wouldn't for
the world have had him make any such point as that he wouldn't
have launched them at Matcham—or whatever it was he *had*
done—only for Aunt Maud's *beaux yeux*.* What he had done, it
would have been guessable, was something he had for some time
been desired in vain to do; and what they were all now profiting by
was a change comparatively sudden, the cessation of hope delayed. What had caused the cessation easily showed itself as none
of Milly's business; and she was luckily, for that matter, in no real
danger of hearing from him directly that her individual weight had
been felt in the scale. Why then indeed was it an effect of his diffused but subdued participation that he might absolutely have
been saying to her "Yes, let the dear woman take her own tone"?
"Since she's here she may stay," he might have been adding—"for
whatever she can make of it. But you and I are different." Milly
knew *she* was different in truth—his own difference was his own
affair; but also she knew that after all, even at their distinctest, Lord
Mark's "tips" in this line would be tacit. He practically placed
her—it came round again to that—under no obligation whatever.
It was a matter of equal ease, moreover, her letting Mrs. Lowder
take a tone. She might have taken twenty—they would have
spoiled nothing.

"You must stay on with us; you *can*, you know, in any position
you like; any, any, *any*, my dear child"—and her emphasis went
deep. "You must make your home with us; and it's really open to
you to make the most beautiful one in the world. You mustn't be
under a mistake—under any of any sort; and you must let us all
think for you a little, take care of you and watch over you. Above
all you must help me with Kate, and you must stay a little *for* her;

---

*Beautiful eyes (French).

nothing for a long time has happened to me so good as that you and she should have become friends. It's beautiful; it's great; it's everything. What makes it perfect is that it should have come about through our dear delightful Susie, restored to me, after so many years, by such a miracle. No—that's more charming to me than even your hitting it off with Kate. God has been good to one—positively; for I couldn't, at my age, have made a new friend—undertaken, I mean, out of whole cloth, the real thing. It's like changing one's bankers—after fifty: one doesn't do that. That's why Susie has been kept for me, as you seem to keep people in your wonderful country, in lavender and pink paper—coming back at last as straight as out of a fairy-tale and with you as an attendant fairy." Milly hereupon replied appreciatively that such a description of herself made her feel as if pink paper were her dress and lavender its trimming; but Aunt Maud wasn't to be deterred by a weak joke from keeping it up. The young person under her protection could feel besides that she kept it up in perfect sincerity. She was somehow at this hour a very happy woman, and a part of her happiness might precisely have been that her affections and her views were moving as never before in concert. Unquestionably she loved Susie; but she also loved Kate and loved Lord Mark, loved their funny old host and hostess, loved every one within range, down to the very servant who came to receive Milly's empty ice-plate—down, for that matter, to Milly herself, who was, while she talked, really conscious of the enveloping flap of a protective mantle, a shelter with the weight of an Eastern carpet. An Eastern carpet, for wishing-purposes of one's own, was a thing to be on rather than under; still, however, if the girl should fail of breath it wouldn't be, she could feel, by Mrs. Lowder's fault. One of the last things she was afterwards to recall of this was Aunt Maud's going on to say that she and Kate must stand together because together they could do anything. It was for Kate of course she was essentially planning; but the plan, enlarged and uplifted now, somehow required Milly's prosperity too for its full operation, just as Milly's prosperity at the same time involved Kate's. It was nebulous yet, it was slightly confused, but it was comprehensive and genial, and it made our young woman understand things Kate had said of her aunt's possibilities, as well as

characterisations that had fallen from Susan Shepherd. One of
the most frequent on the lips of the latter had been that dear
Maud was a grand natural force.

— II —

A prime reason, we must add, why sundry impressions were
not to be fully present to the girl till later on was that they
yielded at this stage, with an effect of sharp supersession, to
a detached quarter of an hour—her only one—with Lord Mark.
"Have you seen the picture in the house, the beautiful one that's
so like you?"—he was asking that as he stood before her; having
come up at last with his smooth intimation that any wire he had
pulled and yet wanted not to remind her of wasn't quite a reason
for his having no joy at all.

"I've been through rooms and I've seen pictures. But if I'm 'like'
anything so beautiful as most of them seemed to me—!" It needed
in short for Milly some evidence which he only wanted to supply.
She was the image of the wonderful Bronzino,* which she must
have a look at on every ground. He had thus called her off and led
her away; the more easily that the house within was above all what
had already drawn round her its mystic circle. Their progress
meanwhile was not of the straightest; it was an advance, without
haste, through innumerable natural pauses and soft concussions,
determined for the most part by the appearance before them of
ladies and gentlemen, singly, in couples, in clusters, who brought
them to a stand with an inveterate "I say, Mark." What they said
she never quite made out; it was their all so domestically knowing
him, and his knowing them, that mainly struck her, while her impression, for the rest, was but of fellow strollers more vaguely afloat
than themselves, supernumeraries mostly a little battered, whether
as jaunty males or as ostensibly elegant women. They might have
been moving a good deal by a momentum that had begun far

---

*Agnolo Bronzino (1503–1572), a well-known Venetian portraitist.

back, but they were still brave and personable, still warranted for
continuance as long again, and they gave her, in especial collectively, a sense of pleasant voices, pleasanter than those of actors, of
friendly empty words and kind lingering eyes that took somehow
pardonable liberties. The lingering eyes looked her over, the lingering eyes were what went, in almost confessed simplicity, with
the pointless "I say, Mark"; and what was really most flagrant of all
was that, as a pleasant matter of course, if she didn't mind, he
seemed to suggest their letting people, poor dear things, have the
benefit of her.

The odd part was that he made her herself believe, for amusement, in the benefit, measured by him in mere manner—for wonderful, of a truth, was, as a means of expression, his slightness of
emphasis—that her present good nature conferred. It was, as she
could easily see, a mild common carnival of good nature—a mass
of London people together, of sorts and sorts, but who mainly
knew each other and who, in their way, did, no doubt, confess to
curiosity. It had gone round that she was there; questions about
her would be passing; the easiest thing was to run the gauntlet with
him—just as the easiest thing was in fact to trust him generally.
Couldn't she know for herself, passively, how little harm they
meant her?—to that extent that it made no difference whether or
not he introduced them. The strangest thing of all for Milly was
perhaps the uplifted assurance and indifference with which she
could simply give back the particular bland stare that appeared in
such cases to mark civilisation at its highest. It was so little her
fault, this oddity of what had "gone round" about her, that to accept it without question might be as good a way as another of feeling life. It was inevitable to supply the probable description—that
of the awfully rich young American who was so queer to behold,
but nice, by all accounts, to know; and she had really but one instant of speculation as to fables or fantasies perchance originally
launched. She asked herself once only if Susie could, inconceiv-
ably, have been blatant about her; for the question, on the spot,
was really blown away for ever. She knew in fact on the spot and
with sharpness just why she had "elected" Susan Shepherd: she
had had from the first hour the conviction of her being precisely
the person in the world least possibly a trumpeter. So it wasn't

their fault, it wasn't their fault, and anything might happen that would, and everything now again melted together, and kind eyes were always kind eyes—if it were never to be worse than that! She got with her companion into the house; they brushed, beneficently, past all their accidents. The Bronzino was, it appeared, deep within, and the long afternoon light lingered for them on patches of old colour and waylaid them, as they went, in nooks and opening vistas.

It was all the while for Milly as if Lord Mark had really had something other than this spoken pretext in view; as if there were something he wanted to say to her and were only—consciously yet not awkwardly, just delicately—hanging fire. At the same time it was as if the thing had practically been said by the moment they came in sight of the picture; since what it appeared to amount to was "Do let a fellow who isn't a fool take care of you a little." The thing somehow, with the aid of the Bronzino, was done; it hadn't seemed to matter to her before if he were a fool or no; but now, just where they were, she liked his not being; and it was all moreover none the worse for coming back to something of the same sound as Mrs. Lowder's so recent reminder. She too wished to take care of her—and wasn't it, *à peu près,** what all the people with the kind eyes were wishing? Once more things melted together—the beauty and the history and the facility and the splendid midsummer glow: it was a sort of magnificent maximum, the pink dawn of an apotheosis coming so curiously soon. What in fact befell was that, as she afterwards made out, it was Lord Mark who said nothing in particular—it was she herself who said all. She couldn't help that—it came; and the reason it came was that she found herself, for the first moment, looking at the mysterious portrait through tears. Perhaps it was her tears that made it just then so strange and fair—as wonderful as he had said: the face of a young woman, all splendidly drawn, down to the hands, and splendidly dressed; a face almost livid in hue, yet handsome in sadness and crowned with a mass of hair, rolled back and high, that must, before fading with time, have had a family resemblance

*More or less (French).

to her own.* The lady in question, at all events, with her slightly
Michael-angelesque squareness, her eyes of other days, her full
lips, her long neck, her recorded jewels, her brocaded and wasted
reds, was a very great personage—only unaccompanied by a joy.
And she was dead, dead, dead. Milly recognised her exactly in
words that had nothing to do with her. "I shall never be better
than this."

He smiled for her at the portrait. "Than she? You'd scarce need
to be better, for surely that's well enough. But you *are*, one feels,
as it happens, better; because, splendid as she is, one doubts if she
was good."

He hadn't understood. She was before the picture, but she had
turned to him, and she didn't care if for the minute he noticed her
tears. It was probably as good a moment as she should ever have
with him. It was perhaps as good a moment as she should have
with any one, or have in any connexion whatever. "I mean that
everything this afternoon has been too beautiful, and that perhaps
everything together will never be so right again. I'm very glad
therefore you've been a part of it."

Though he still didn't understand her he was as nice as if he
had; he didn't ask for insistence, and that was just a part of his
looking after her. He simply protected her now from herself, and
there was a world of practice in it. "Oh we must talk about these
things!"

Ah they had already done that, she knew, as much as she ever
would; and she was shaking her head at her pale sister the next
moment with a world, on her side, of slowness. "I wish I could see
the resemblance. Of course her complexion's green," she laughed;
"but mine's several shades greener."[12]

"It's down to the very hands," said Lord Mark.

"Her hands are large," Milly went on, "but mine are larger.
Mine are huge."

"Oh you go her, all round, 'one better'—which is just what I
said. But you're a pair. You must surely catch it," he added as if it

---

*The portrait is of Lucrezia Panciatichi (c.1540); it is in the Uffizi museum in Flo-
rence. Lord Mark's estate is a product of Henry James's imagination.

were important to his character as a serious man not to appear to have invented his plea.

"I don't know—one never knows one's self. It's a funny fancy, and I don't imagine it would have occurred—"

"I see it *has* occurred"—he had already taken her up. She had her back, as she faced the picture, to one of the doors of the room, which was open, and on her turning as he spoke she saw that they were in the presence of three other persons, also, as appeared, interested enquirers. Kate Croy was one of these; Lord Mark had just become aware of her, and she, all arrested, had immediately seen, and made the best of it, that she was far from being first in the field. She had brought a lady and a gentleman to whom she wished to show what Lord Mark was showing Milly, and he took her straightway as a re-enforcement. Kate herself had spoken, however, before he had had time to tell her so.

"*You* had noticed too?"—she smiled at him without looking at Milly. "Then I'm not original—which one always hopes one has been. But the likeness is so great." And now she looked at Milly—for whom again it was, all round indeed, kind, kind eyes. "Yes, there you are, my dear, if you want to know. And you're superb." She took now but a glance at the picture, though it was enough to make her question to her friends not too straight. "Isn't she superb?"

"I brought Miss Theale," Lord Mark explained to the latter, "quite off my own bat."

"I wanted Lady Aldershaw," Kate continued to Milly, "to see for herself."

"*Les grands esprits se rencontrent!*"* laughed her attendant gentleman, a high but slightly stooping, shambling and wavering person who represented urbanity by the liberal aid of certain prominent front teeth and whom Milly vaguely took for some sort of great man.

Lady Aldershaw meanwhile looked at Milly quite as if Milly had been the Bronzino and the Bronzino only Milly. "Superb, superb. Of course I had noticed you. It *is* wonderful," she went

*Great minds think alike! (French).

on with her back to the picture, but with some other eagerness
which Milly felt gathering, felt directing her motions now. It
was enough—they were introduced, and she was saying "I wonder if you could give us the pleasure of coming—" She wasn't
fresh, for she wasn't young, even though she denied at every
pore that she was old; but she was vivid and much bejewelled for
the midsummer daylight; and she was all in the palest pinks and
blues. She didn't think, at this pass, that she could "come" anywhere—Milly didn't; and she already knew that somehow Lord
Mark was saving her from the question. He had interposed, taking the words out of the lady's mouth and not caring at all if the
lady minded. That was clearly the right way to treat her—at least
for him; as she had only dropped, smiling, and then turned away
with him. She had been dealt with—it would have done an
enemy good. The gentleman still stood, a little helpless, addressing himself to the intention of urbanity as if it were a large
loud whistle; he had been sighing sympathy, in his way, while
the lady made her overture; and Milly had in this light soon arrived at their identity. They were Lord and Lady Aldershaw, and
the wife was the clever one. A minute or two later the situation
had changed, and she knew it afterwards to have been by the
subtle operation of Kate. She was herself saying that she was
afraid she must go now if Susie could be found; but she was sitting down on the nearest seat to say it. The prospect, through
opened doors, stretched before her into other rooms, down the
vista of which Lord Mark was strolling with Lady Aldershaw,
who, close to him and much intent, seemed to show from behind as peculiarly expert. Lord Aldershaw, for his part, had been
left in the middle of the room, while Kate, with her back to him,
was standing before her with much sweetness of manner. The
sweetness was all for *her*; she had the sense of the poor gentleman's having somehow been handled as Lord Mark had handled his wife. He dangled there, he shambled a little; then he
bethought himself of the Bronzino, before which, with his eye-
glass, he hovered. It drew from him an odd vague sound, not
wholly distinct from a grunt, and a "Humph—most remarkable!" which lighted Kate's face with amusement. The next moment he had creaked away over polished floors after the others

and Milly was feeling as if *she* had been rude. But Lord Aldershaw was in every way a detail and Kate was saying to her that
she hoped she wasn't ill.

Thus it was that, aloft there in the great gilded historic chamber and the presence of the pale personage on the wall, whose
eyes all the while seemed engaged with her own, she found herself suddenly sunk in something quite intimate and humble and
to which these grandeurs were strange enough witnesses. It had
come up, in the form in which she had had to accept it, all suddenly, and nothing about it, at the same time, was more marked
than that she had in a manner plunged into it to escape from
something else. Something else, from her first vision of her
friend's appearance three minutes before, had been present to
her even through the call made by the others on her attention;
something that was perversely *there*, she was more and more un-
comfortably finding, at least for the first moments and by some
spring of its own, with every renewal of their meeting. "Is it the
way she looks to *him*?" she asked herself—the perversity being
how she kept in remembrance that Kate was known to him. It
wasn't a fault in Kate—nor in him assuredly; and she had a horror, being generous and tender, of treating either of them as if it
had been. To Densher himself she couldn't make it up—he was
too far away; but her secondary impulse was to make it up to
Kate. She did so now with a strange soft energy—the impulse immediately acting. "Will you render me to-morrow a great service?"

"Any service, dear child, in the world."

"But it's a secret one—nobody must know. I must be wicked
and false about it."

"Then I'm your woman," Kate smiled, "for that's the kind of
thing I love. *Do* let us do something bad. You're impossibly without sin, you know."

Milly's eyes, on this, remained a little with their companion's.
"Ah I shan't perhaps come up to your idea. It's only to deceive
Susan Shepherd."

"Oh!" said Kate as if this were indeed mild.

"But thoroughly—as thoroughly as I can."

"And for cheating," Kate asked, "my powers will contribute?

Well, I'll do my best for you." In accordance with which it was presently settled between them that Milly should have the aid and comfort of her presence for a visit to Sir Luke Strett. Kate had needed a minute for enlightenment, and it was quite grand for her comrade that this name should have said nothing to her. To Milly herself it had for some days been secretly saying much. The personage in question was, as she explained, the greatest of medical lights—if she had got hold, as she believed (and she had used to this end the wisdom of the serpent) of the right, the special man. She had written to him three days before, and he had named her an hour, eleven-twenty; only it had come to her on the eve that she couldn't go alone. Her maid on the other hand wasn't good enough, and Susie was too good. Kate had listened above all with high indulgence. "And I'm betwixt and between, happy thought! Too good for what?"

Milly thought. "Why to be worried if it's nothing. And to be still more worried—I mean before she need be—if it isn't."

Kate fixed her with deep eyes. "What in the world is the matter with you?" It had inevitably a sound of impatience, as if it had been a challenge really to produce something; so that Milly felt her for the moment only as a much older person, standing above her a little, doubting the imagined ailments, suspecting the easy complaints, of ignorant youth. It somewhat checked her, further, that the matter with her was what exactly as yet she wanted knowledge about; and she immediately declared, for conciliation, that if she were merely fanciful Kate would see her put to shame. Kate vividly uttered, in return, the hope that, since she could come out and be so charming, could so universally dazzle and interest, she wasn't all the while in distress or in anxiety— didn't believe herself to be in any degree seriously menaced. "Well, I want to make out—to make out!" was all that this consistently produced. To which Kate made clear answer: "Ah then let us by all means!"

"I thought," Milly said, "you'd like to help me. But I must ask you, please, for the promise of absolute silence."

"And how, if you *are* ill, can your friends remain in ignorance?"

"Well, if I am it must of course finally come out. But I can go for a long time." Milly spoke with her, eyes again on her painted

sister's—almost as if under their suggestion. She still sat there before Kate, yet not without a light in her face. "That will be one of
my advantages. I think I could die without its being noticed."

"You're an extraordinary young woman," her friend, visibly held
by her, declared at last. "What a remarkable time to talk of such
things!"

"Well, we won't talk, precisely"—Milly got herself together
again. "I only wanted to make sure of you."

"Here in the midst of—!" But Kate could only sigh for wonder—almost visibly too for pity.

It made a moment during which her companion waited on her
word; partly as if from a yearning, shy but deep, to have her case
put to her just as Kate was struck by it; partly as if the hint of pity
were already giving a sense to her whimsical "shot," with Lord
Mark, at Mrs. Lowder's first dinner. Exactly this—the handsome
girl's compassionate manner, her friendly descent from her own
strength—was what she had then foretold. She took Kate up as if
positively for the deeper taste of it. "Here in the midst of what?"

"Of everything. There's nothing you can't have. There's nothing you can't do."

"So Mrs. Lowder tells me."

It just kept Kate's eyes fixed as possibly for more of that; then,
however, without waiting, she went on. "We all adore you."

"You're wonderful—you dear things!" Milly laughed.

"No, it's *you*." And Kate seemed struck with the real interest of
it. "In three weeks!"

Milly kept it up. "Never were people on such terms! All the
more reason," she added, "that I shouldn't needlessly torment you."

"But me? what becomes of *me*?" said Kate.

"Well, you"—Milly thought—"if there's anything to bear you'll
bear it."

"But I *won't* bear it!" said Kate Croy.

"Oh yes you will: all the same! You'll pity me awfully, but you'll
help me very much. And I absolutely trust you. So there we are."
There they were then, since Kate had so to take it; but there, Milly
felt, she herself in particular was; for it was just the point at which
she had wished to arrive. She had wanted to prove to herself that
she didn't horribly blame her friend for any reserve; and what bet-

ter proof could there be than this quite special confidence? If she
desired to show Kate that she really believed Kate liked her, could
she show it more than by asking her help?

— III —

W hat it really came to, on the morrow, this first time—the
time Kate went with her—was that the great man had, a
little, to excuse himself; had, by a rare accident—for he
kept his consulting-hours in general rigorously free—but ten minutes to give her; ten mere minutes which he yet placed at her service in a manner that she admired still more than she could meet
it: so crystal-clean the great empty cup of attention that he set between them on the table. He was presently to jump into his carriage, but he promptly made the point that he must see her again,
see her within a day or two; and he named for her at once another
hour—easing her off beautifully too even then in respect to her
possibly failing of justice to her errand. The minutes affected her
in fact as ebbing more swiftly than her little army of items could
muster, and they would probably have gone without her doing
much more than secure another hearing, hadn't it been for her
sense, at the last, that she had gained above all an impression. The
impression—all the sharp growth of the final few moments—was
neither more nor less than that she might make, of a sudden, in
quite another world, another straight friend, and a friend who
would moreover be, wonderfully, the most appointed, the most
thoroughly adjusted of the whole collection, inasmuch as he
would somehow wear the character scientifically, ponderably,
proveably—not just loosely and sociably. Literally, furthermore, it
wouldn't really depend on herself, Sir Luke Strett's friendship, in
the least: perhaps what made her most stammer and pant was its
thus queerly coming over her that she might find she had interested him even beyond her intention, find she was in fact
launched in some current that would lose itself in the sea of science. At the same time that she struggled, however, she also surrendered; there was a moment at which she almost dropped the

form of stating, of explaining, and threw herself, without violence, only with a supreme pointless quaver that had turned the next instant to an intensity of interrogative stillness, upon his general good will. His large settled face, though firm, was not, as she had thought at first, hard; he looked, in the oddest manner, to her fancy, half like a general and half like a bishop, and she was soon sure that, within some such handsome range, what it would show her would be what was good, what was best for her. She had established, in other words, in this time-saving way, a relation with it; and the relation was the special trophy that, for the hour, she bore off. It was like an absolute possession, a new resource altogether, something done up in the softest silk and tucked away under the arm of memory. She hadn't had it when she went in, and she had it when she came out, she had it there under her cloak, but dissimulated, invisibly carried, when smiling, smiling, she again faced Kate Croy. That young lady had of course awaited her in another room, where, as the great man was to absent himself, no one else was in attendance; and she rose for her with such a face of sympathy as might have graced the vestibule of a dentist. "Is it out?" she seemed to ask as if it had been a question of a tooth; and Milly indeed kept her in no suspense at all.

"He's a dear. I'm to come again."

"But what does he say?"

Milly was almost gay. "That I'm not to worry about anything in the world, and that if I'll be a good girl and do exactly what he tells me he'll take care of me for ever and ever."

Kate wondered as if things scarce fitted. "But does he allow then that you're ill?"

"I don't know what he allows, and I don't care. I *shall* know, and whatever it is it will be enough. He knows all about me, and I like it. I don't hate it a bit."

Still, however, Kate stared. "But could he, in so few minutes, ask you enough—?"

"He asked me scarcely anything—he doesn't need to do anything so stupid," Milly said. "He can tell. He knows," she repeated; "and when I go back—for he'll have thought me over a little—it will be all right."

Kate after a moment made the best of this. "Then when are we to come?"

It just pulled her friend up, for even while they talked—at least it was one of the reasons—she stood there suddenly, irrelevantly, in the light of her *other* identity, the identity she would have for Mr. Densher. This was always, from one instant to another, an incalculable light, which, though it might go off faster than it came on, necessarily disturbed. It sprang, with a perversity all its own, from the fact that, with the lapse of hours and days, the chances themselves that made for his being named continued so oddly to fail. There were twenty, there were fifty, but none of them turned up. This in particular was of course not a juncture at which the least of them would naturally be present; but it would make, none the less, Milly saw, another day practically all stamped with avoidance. She saw in a quick glimmer, and with it all Kate's unconsciousness; and then she shook off the obsession. But it had lasted long enough to qualify her response. No, she had shown Kate how she trusted her; and that, for loyalty, would somehow do. "Oh, dear thing, now that the ice is broken I shan't trouble *you* again."[13]

"You'll come alone?"

"Without a scruple. Only I shall ask you, please, for your absolute discretion still."

Outside, at a distance from the door, on the wide pavement of the great contiguous square, they had to wait again while their carriage, which Milly had kept, completed a further turn of exercise, engaged in by the coachman for reasons of his own. The footman was there and had indicated that he was making the circuit; so Kate went on while they stood. "But don't you ask a good deal, darling, in proportion to what you give?"

This pulled Milly up still shorter—so short in fact that she yielded as soon as she had taken it in. But she continued to smile. "I see. Then you *can* tell."

"I don't want to 'tell,'" said Kate. "I'll be as silent as the tomb if I can only have the truth from you. All I want is that you shouldn't keep from me how you find out that you really are."

"Well then I won't ever. But you see for yourself," Milly went on, "how I really am. I'm satisfied. I'm happy."

Kate looked at her long. "I believe you like it. The way things turn out for you—!"

Milly met her look now without a thought of anything but the spoken. She had ceased to be Mr. Densher's image; she stood for nothing but herself, and she was none the less fine. Still, still, what had passed was a fair bargain and it would do. "Of course I like it. I feel—I can't otherwise describe it—as if I had been on my knees to the priest. I've confessed and I've been absolved. It has been lifted off."

Kate's eyes never quitted her. "He must have liked *you*."

"Oh—doctors!" Milly said. "But I hope," she added, "he didn't like me too much." Then as if to escape a little from her friend's deeper sounding, or as impatient for the carriage, not yet in sight, her eyes, turning away, took in the great stale square. As its staleness, however, was but that of London fairly fatigued, the late hot London with its dance all danced and its story all told, the air seemed a thing of blurred pictures and mixed echoes, and an impression met the sense—an impression that broke the next moment through the girl's tightened lips. "Oh it's a beautiful big world, and every one, yes, every one—!" it presently brought her back to Kate, and she hoped she didn't actually look as much as if she were crying as she must have looked to Lord Mark among the portraits at Matcham.*

Kate at all events understood. "Every one wants to be so nice?"

"So nice," said the grateful Milly.

"Oh," Kate laughed, "we'll pull you through! And won't you now bring Mrs. Stringham?"

But Milly after an instant was again clear about that. "Not till I've seen him once more."

She was to have found this preference, two days later, abundantly justified; and yet when, in prompt accordance with what had passed between them, she reappeared before her distinguished friend—that character having for him in the interval built itself up still higher—the first thing he asked her was whether she had been accompanied. She told him, on this, straightway, every-

---

*Lord Mark's estate.

thing; completely free at present from her first embarrassment, disposed even—as she felt she might become—to undue volubility, and conscious moreover of no alarm from his thus perhaps wishing she had not come alone. It was exactly as if, in the forty-eight hours that had passed, her acquaintance with him had somehow increased and his own knowledge in particular received mysterious additions. They had been together, before, scarce ten minutes; but the relation, the one the ten minutes had so beautifully created, was there to take straight up: and this not, on his own part, from mere professional heartiness, mere bedside manner, which she would have disliked—much rather from a quiet pleasant air in him of having positively asked about her, asked here and asked there and found out. Of course he couldn't in the least have asked, or have wanted to; there was no source of information to his hand, and he had really needed none: he had found out simply by his genius—and found out, she meant, literally everything. Now she knew not only that she didn't dislike this—the state of being found out about; but that on the contrary it was truly what she had come for, and that for the time at least it would give her something firm to stand on. She struck herself as aware, aware as she had never been, of really not having had from the beginning anything firm. It would be strange for the firmness to come, after all, from her learning in these agreeable conditions that she was in some way doomed; but above all it would prove how little she had hitherto had to hold her up. If she was now to be held up by the mere process—since that was perhaps on the cards—of being let down, this would only testify in turn to her queer little history. *That* sense of loosely rattling had been no process at all; and it was ridiculously true that her thus sitting there to see her life put into the scales represented her first approach to the taste of orderly living. Such was Milly's romantic version—that her life, especially by the fact of this second interview, was put into the scales; and just the best part of the relation established might have been, for that matter, that the great grave charming man knew, had known at once, that it was romantic, and in that measure allowed for it. Her only doubt, her only fear, was whether he perhaps wouldn't even take advantage of her being a little romantic to treat her as romantic altogether. This doubtless was her danger with him; but she should see, and dangers in general meanwhile dropped and dropped.

The very place, at the end of a few minutes, the commodious "handsome" room, far back in the fine old house, soundless from position, somewhat sallow with years of celebrity, somewhat sombre even at midsummer—the very place put on for her a look of custom and use, squared itself solidly round her as with promises and certainties. She had come forth to see the world, and this then was to be the world's light, the rich dusk of a London "back," these the world's walls, those the world's curtains and carpet. She should be intimate with the great bronze clock and mantel-ornaments, conspicuously presented in gratitude and long ago; she should be as one of the circle of eminent contemporaries, photographed, engraved, signatured, and in particular framed and glazed, who made up the rest of the decoration, and made up as well so much of the human comfort; and while she thought of all the clean truths, unfringed, unfingered, that the listening stillness, strained into pauses and waits, would again and again, for years, have kept distinct, she also wondered what *she* would eventually decide upon to present in gratitude. She would give something better at least than the brawny Victorian bronzes. This was precisely an instance of what she felt he knew of her before he had done with her: that she was secretly romancing at that rate, in the midst of so much else that was more urgent, all over the place. So much for her secrets with him, none of which really required to be phrased. It would have been thoroughly a secret for her from any one else that without a dear lady she had picked up just before coming over she wouldn't have a decently near connexion of any sort, for such an appeal as she was making, to put forward: no one in the least, as it were, to produce for respectability. But *his* seeing it she didn't mind a scrap, and not a scrap either his knowing how she had left the dear lady in the dark. She had come alone, putting her friend off with a fraud: giving a pretext of shops, of a whim, of she didn't know what—the amusement of being for once in the streets by herself. The streets by herself were new to her—she had always had in them a companion or a maid; and he was never to believe moreover that she couldn't take full in the face anything he might have to say. He was softly amused at her account of her courage; though he yet showed it somehow without soothing her too grossly. Still, he did want to know whom she had. Hadn't there been a lady with her on Wednesday?

"Yes—a different one. Not the one who's travelling with me. I've told *her*."

Distinctly he was amused, and it added to his air—the greatest charm of all—of giving her lots of time. "You've told her what?"

"Well," said Milly, "that I visit you in secret."

"And how many persons will she tell?"

"Oh she's devoted. Not one."

"Well, if she's devoted doesn't that make another friend for you?"

It didn't take much computation, but she nevertheless had to think a moment, conscious as she was that he distinctly *would* want to fill out his notion of her—even a little, as it were, to warm the air for her. That however—and better early than late—he must accept as of no use; and she herself felt for an instant quite a competent certainty on the subject of any such warming. The air, for Milly Theale, was, from the very nature of the case, destined never to rid itself of a considerable chill. This she could tell him with authority, if she could tell him nothing else; and she seemed to see now, in short, that it would importantly simplify. "Yes, it makes another; but they all together wouldn't make—well, I don't know what to call it but the difference. I mean when one *is*—really alone. I've never seen anything like the kindness." She pulled up a minute while he waited—and waited again as if with his reasons for letting her, for almost making her, talk. What she herself wanted was not, for the third time, to cry, as it were, in public. She *had* never seen anything like the kindness, and she wished to do it justice; but she knew what she was about, and justice was not wronged by her being able presently to stick to her point. "Only one's situation is what it is. It's *me* it concerns. The rest is delightful and useless. Nobody can really help. That's why I'm by myself to-day. I *want* to be—in spite of Miss Croy, who came with me last. If you can help, so much the better—and also of course if one can a little one's self. Except for that—you and me doing our best—I like you to see me just as I am. Yes, I like it—and I don't exaggerate. Shouldn't one, at the start, show the worst—so that anything after that may be better? It wouldn't make any real difference—it *won't* make any, anything that may happen won't—to any one. Therefore I feel myself, this way, with you, just as I am; and—if you do in the least care to know—it quite positively bears me up."

She put it as to his caring to know, because his manner seemed to give her all her chance, and the impression was there for her to take. It was strange and deep for her, this impression, and she did accordingly take it straight home. It showed him—showed him in spite of himself—as allowing, somewhere far within, things comparatively remote, things in fact quite, as she would have said, outside, delicately to weigh with him; showed him as interested on her behalf in other questions beside the question of what was the matter with her. She accepted such an interest as regular in the highest type of scientific mind—his own *being* the highest, magnificently—because otherwise obviously it wouldn't be there; but she could at the same time take it as a direct source of light upon herself, even though that might present her a little as pretending to equal him. Wanting to know more about a patient than how a patient was constructed or deranged couldn't be, even on the part of the greatest doctors, anything, but some form or other of the desire to let the patient down easily. When that was the case the reason, in turn, could only be, too manifestly, pity; and when pity held up its telltale face like a head on a pike, in a French revolution, bobbing before a window, what was that inference but that the patient was bad? He might say what he would now—she would always have seen the head at the window; and in fact from this moment she only wanted him to say what he would. He might say it too with the greater ease to himself as there wasn't one of her divinations that—*as* her own—he would in any way put himself out for. Finally, if he was making her talk she *was* talking, and what it could at any rate come to for him was that she wasn't afraid. If he wanted to do the dearest thing in the world for her he would show her he believed she wasn't; which undertaking of hers—not to have misled him—was what she counted at the moment as her presumptuous little hint to him that she was as good as himself. It put forward the bold idea that he could really *be* misled; and there actually passed between them for some seconds a sign, a sign of the eyes only, that they knew together where they were. This made, in their brown old temple of truth, its momentary flicker; then what followed it was that he had her, all the same, in his pocket; and the whole thing wound up for that consummation with his kind dim smile. Such kindness was wonderful with such dimness; but brightness—that even of sharp steel—was of course for the other side of the business, and it would all come in for her to one tune or another. "Do you mean," he asked, "that you've no relations at all?—not a parent, not a sister, not even a cousin nor an aunt?"

She shook her head as with the easy habit of an interviewed heroine or a freak of nature at a show. "Nobody whatever"—but the last thing she had come for was to be dreary about it. "I'm a survivor—a survivor of a general wreck. You see," she added, "how that's to be taken into account—that every one else *has* gone. When I was ten years old there were, with my father and my mother, six of us. I'm all that's left. But they died," she went on, to be fair all round, "of different things. Still, there it is. And, as I told you before, I'm American. Not that I mean that makes me worse. However, you'll probably know what it makes me."

"Yes"—he even showed amusement for it. "I know perfectly what it makes you. It makes you, to begin with, a capital case."

She sighed, though gratefully, as if again before the social scene. "Ah there you are!"

"Oh no; there 'we' aren't at all! There I am only—but as much as you like. I've no end of American friends: there *they* are, if you please, and it's a fact that you couldn't very well be in a better place than in their company. It puts you with plenty of others— and that isn't pure solitude." Then he pursued: "I'm sure you've an excellent spirit; but don't try to bear more things than you need." Which after an instant he further explained. "Hard things have come to you in youth, but you mustn't think life will be for you all hard things. You've the right to be happy. You must make up your mind to it. You must accept any form in which happiness may come."

"Oh I'll accept any whatever!" she almost gaily returned. "And it seems to me, for that matter, that I'm accepting a new one every day. Now *this!*" she smiled.

"This is very well so far as it goes. You can depend on me," the great man said, "for unlimited interest. But I'm only, after all, one element in fifty. We must gather in plenty of others. Don't mind who knows. Knows, I mean, that you and I are friends."

"Ah you do want to see some one!" she broke out. "You want to get at some one who cares for me." With which, however, as he simply met this spontaneity in a manner to show that he had often had it from young persons of her race, and that he was familiar even with the possibilities of *their* familiarity, she felt her freedom rendered vain by his silence, and she immediately tried to think of the most reasonable thing she could say. This would be, precisely, on the subject of that freedom, which she now quickly spoke of as complete. "That's of course by itself a great boon; so please don't think I don't know it. I can do exactly what I like—anything in all the wide world. I haven't a creature to ask—there's not a finger to stop me. I can shake about till I'm black and blue. That perhaps isn't *all* joy; but lots of people, I know, would like to try it." He had appeared about to put a question, but then had let her go on, which she promptly did, for she understood him the next moment as having thus taken it from her that her means were as great as might be. She had simply given it to him so, and this was all that would ever pass between them on the odious head. Yet she couldn't help also knowing that an important effect, for his judgement, or at least for his amusement—which was his feeling, since, marvellously, he did have feeling—was produced by it. All her little pieces had now then fallen together for him like the morsels of coloured glass that used to make combinations, under the hand, in the depths of one of the polygonal peepshows* of childhood. "So that if it's a question of my doing anything under the sun that will help—!"

"You'll *do* anything under the sun? Good." He took that beautifully, ever so pleasantly, for what it was worth; but time was needed—the minutes or so were needed on the spot—to deal even provisionally with the substantive question. It was convenient, in its degree, that there was nothing she wouldn't do; but it seemed also highly and agreeably vague that she should have to do any-

---

*Literally, a series of miniature scenes viewed through a pinhole in a special box; in this case, the designs seen in a kaleidoscope.

thing. They thus appeared to be taking her, together, for the moment, and almost for sociability, as prepared to proceed to gratuitous extremities; the upshot of which was in turn that after much interrogation, auscultation, exploration, much noting of his own sequences and neglecting of hers, had duly kept up the vagueness, they might have struck themselves, or may at least strike us, as coming back from an undeterred but useless voyage to the North Pole. Milly was ready, under orders, for the North Pole; which fact was doubtless what made a blinding anticlimax of her friend's actual abstention from orders. "No," she heard him again distinctly repeat it, "I don't want you for the present to do anything at all; anything, that is, but obey a small prescription or two that will be made clear to you, and let me within a few days come to see you at home."

It was at first heavenly. "Then you'll see Mrs. Stringham." But she didn't mind a bit now.

"Well, I shan't be afraid of Mrs. Stringham." And he said it once more as she asked once more: "Absolutely not; I 'send' you nowhere. England's all right—anywhere that's pleasant, convenient, decent, will be all right. You say you can do exactly as you like. Oblige me therefore by being so good as to do it. There's only one thing: you ought of course, now, as soon as I've seen you again, to get out of London."[14]

Milly thought. "May I then go back to the Continent?"

"By all means back to the Continent. Do go back to the Continent."

"Then how will you keep seeing me? But perhaps," she quickly added, "you won't want to keep seeing me."

He had it all ready; he had really everything all ready. "I shall follow you up; though if you mean that I don't want you to keep seeing *me*—"

"Well?" she asked.

It was only just here that he struck her the least bit as stumbling. "Well, see all you can. That's what it comes to. Worry about nothing. You *have* at least no worries. It's a great rare chance."

She had got up, for she had had from him both that he would send her something and would advise her promptly of the date of his coming to her, by which she was virtually dismissed. Yet for herself one or two things kept her. "May I come back to England too?"

"Rather! Whenever you like. But always, when you do come, immediately let me know."

"Ah," said Milly, "it won't be a great going to and fro."

"Then if you'll stay with us so much the better."

It touched her, the way he controlled his impatience of her; and the fact itself affected her as so precious that she yielded to the wish to get more from it. "So you don't think I'm out of my mind?"

"Perhaps that *is*," he smiled, "all that's the matter."

She looked at him longer. "No, that's too good. Shall I at any rate suffer?"

"Not a bit."

"And yet then live?"

"My dear young lady," said her distinguished friend, "isn't to 'live' exactly what I'm trying to persuade you to take the trouble to do?"

— IV —

S he had gone out with these last words so in her ears that when once she was well away—back this time in the great square alone—it was as if some instant application of them had opened out there before her. It was positively, that effect, an excitement that carried her on; she went forward into space under the sense of an impulse received—an impulse simple and direct, easy above all to act upon. She was borne up for the hour, and now she knew why she had wanted to come by herself. No one in the world could have sufficiently entered into her state; no tie would have been close enough to enable a companion to walk beside her without some disparity. She literally felt, in this first flush, that her only company must be the human race at large, present all round her, but inspiringly impersonal, and that her only field must be, then and there, the grey immensity of London. Grey immensity had somehow of a sudden become her element; grey immensity was what her distinguished friend had, for the moment, furnished her world with and what the question of "living," as he put it to her, living by option, by volition, inevitably took on for its immediate face. She went straight before her, without weakness, altogether with strength; and still as she went she was more glad to be alone, for nobody—not Kate Croy, not Susan Shepherd either— would have wished to rush with her as she rushed. She had asked him at the last whether, being on foot, she might go home so, or elsewhere, and he had replied as if almost amused again at her extravagance: "You're active, luckily, by nature—it's beautiful: therefore rejoice in it. *Be* active, without folly—for you're not foolish: be as active as you can and as you like." That had been in fact the final push, as well as the touch that most made a mixture of her consciousness—a strange mixture that tasted at one and the same time of what she had lost and what had been given her. It was wonderful to her, while she took her random course, that these quantities felt so equal; she had been treated—hadn't she?—as if it were in her power to live; and yet one wasn't treated so—was one?—unless it had come up, quite as much, that one might die. The beauty of the bloom had gone from the small old sense of safety—that was distinct: she had left it behind her there for ever. But the beauty of the idea of a great adventure, a big dim experiment or struggle in which she might more responsibly than ever before take a hand, had been offered her instead. It was as if she had had to pluck off her breast, to throw away, some friendly ornament, a familiar flower, a little old jewel, that was part of her daily dress; and to take up and shoulder as a substitute some queer defensive weapon, a musket, a spear, a battle-axe—conducive possibly in a higher degree to a striking appearance, but demanding all the effort of the military posture.

She felt this instrument, for that matter, already on her back, so that she proceeded now in very truth after the fashion of a soldier on a march—proceeded as if, for her initiation, the first charge had been sounded. She passed along unknown streets, over dusty littery ways, between long rows of fronts not enhanced by the August light; she felt good for miles and only wanted to get lost; there were moments at corners, where she stopped and chose her direction, in which she quite lived up to his injunction to rejoice that she was active. It was like a new pleasure to have so new a reason;

she would affirm without delay her option, her volition; taking this personal possession of what surrounded her was a fair affirmation to start with; and she really didn't care if she made it at the cost of alarms for Susie. Susie would wonder in due course "whatever," as she said at the hotel, had become of her; yet this would be nothing either, probably, to wonderments still in store. Wonderments in truth, Milly felt, even now attended her steps: it was quite as if she saw in people's eyes the reflexion of her appearance and pace. She found herself moving at times in regions visibly not haunted by odd-looking girls from New York, duskily draped, sable-plumed, all but incongruously shod and gazing about them with extravagance; she might, from the curiosity she clearly excited in by-ways, in side-streets peopled with grimy children and costermongers' carts,* which she hoped were slums, literally have had her musket on her shoulder, have announced herself as freshly on the warpath. But for the fear of overdoing the character she would here and there have begun conversation, have asked her way; in spite of the fact that, as this would help the requirements of adventure, her way was exactly what she wanted not to know. The difficulty was that she at last accidentally found it; she had come out, she presently saw, at the Regent's Park, round which on two or three occasions with Kate Croy her public chariot had solemnly rolled. But she went into it further now; this was the real thing; the real thing was to be quite away from the pompous roads, well within the centre and on the stretches of shabby grass. Here were benches and smutty sheep; here were idle lads at games of ball, with their cries mild in the thick air; here were wanderers anxious and tired like herself; here doubtless were hundreds of others just in the same box. Their box, their great common anxiety, what was it, in this grim breathing-space, but the practical question of life? They could live if they would; that is, like herself, they had been told so: she saw them all about her, on seats, digesting the information, recognising it again as something in a slightly different shape familiar enough, the blessed old truth that they would live if they could. All she thus shared with them made her wish to sit in their

---

*Peddlers' carts.

company; which she so far did that she looked for a bench that was empty, eschewing a still emptier chair that she saw hard by and for which she would have paid, with superiority, a fee.

The last scrap of superiority had soon enough left her, if only because she before long knew herself far more tired than she had proposed. This and the charm, after a fashion, of the situation in itself made her linger and rest; there was an accepted spell in the sense that nobody in the world knew where she was. It was the first time in her life that this had happened; somebody, everybody appeared to have known before, at every instant of it, where she was; so that she was now suddenly able to put it to herself that that hadn't been a life. This present kind of thing therefore might be — which was where precisely her distinguished friend seemed to be wishing her to come out. He wished her also, it was true, not to make, as she was perhaps doing now, too much of her isolation; at the same time, however, as he clearly desired to deny her no decent source of interest. He was interested — she arrived at that — in her appealing to as many sources as possible; and it fairly filtered into her, as she sat and sat, that he was essentially propping her up. Had she been doing it herself she would have called it bolstering — the bolstering that was simply for the weak; and she thought and thought as she put together the proofs that it was as one of the weak he was treating her. It was of course as one of the weak that she had gone to him — but oh with how sneaking a hope that he might pronounce her, as to all indispensables, a veritable young lioness! What indeed she was really confronted with was the consciousness that he hadn't after all pronounced her anything: she nursed herself into the sense that he had beautifully got out of it. Did he think, however, she wondered, that he could keep out of it to the end? — though as she weighed the question she yet felt it a little unjust. Milly weighed, in this extraordinary hour, questions numerous and strange; but she had happily, before she moved, worked round to a simplification. Stranger than anything for instance was the effect of its rolling over her that, when one considered it, he might perhaps have "got out" by one door but to come in with a beautiful beneficent dishonesty by another. It kept her more intensely motionless there that what he might fundamentally be "up to" was some disguised intention of standing by her as a friend. Wasn't that what women always said they wanted to do when they deprecated the addresses of gentlemen they couldn't more intimately go on with? It was what they, no doubt, sincerely fancied they could make of men of whom they couldn't make husbands. And she didn't even reason that it was by a similar law the expedient of doctors in general for the invalids of whom they couldn't make patients: she was somehow so sufficiently aware that *her* doctor was—however fatuous it might sound—exceptionally moved. This was the damning little fact—if she could talk of damnation: that she could believe herself to have caught him in the act of irrelevantly liking her. She hadn't gone to him to be liked, she had gone to him to be judged; and he was quite a great enough man to be in the habit, as a rule, of observing the difference. She could like *him*, as she distinctly did—that was another matter; all the more that her doing so was now, so obviously for herself, compatible with judgement. Yet it would have been all portentously mixed had not, as we say, a final and merciful wave, chilling rather, but washing clear, come to her assistance.

It came of a sudden when all other thought was spent. She had been asking herself why, if her case was grave—and she knew what she meant by that—he should have talked to her at all about what she might with futility "do"; or why on the other hand, if it were light, he should attach an importance to the office of friendship. She had him, with her little lonely acuteness—as acuteness went during the dog-days in the Regent's Park—in a cleft stick: she either mattered, and then she was ill; or she didn't matter, and then she was well enough. Now he was "acting," as they said at home, as if she did matter—until he should prove the contrary. It was too evident that a person at his high pressure must keep his inconsistencies, which were probably his highest amusements, only for the very greatest occasions. Her prevision, in fine, of just where she should catch him furnished the light of that judgement in which we describe her as daring to indulge. And the judgement it was that made her sensation simple. He *had* distinguished her—that was the chill. He hadn't known—how could he?—that she was devilishly subtle, subtle exactly in the manner of the suspected, the suspicious, the condemned. He in fact confessed to it, in his way, as to an interest in her combinations, her funny race, her

funny losses, her funny gains, her funny freedom, and, no doubt,
above all, her funny manners—funny, like those of Americans at
their best, without being vulgar, legitimating amiability and helping to pass it off. In his appreciation of these redundancies he
dressed out for her the compassion he so signally permitted himself to waste; but its operation for herself was as directly divesting,
denuding, exposing. It reduced her to her ultimate state, which
was that of a poor girl—with her rent to pay for example—staring
before her in a great city. Milly had her rent to pay, her rent for her
future; everything else but how to meet it fell away from her in
pieces, in tatters. This was the sensation the great man had doubtless not purposed. Well, she must go home, like the poor girl, and
see. There might after all be ways; the poor girl too would be
thinking. It came back for that matter perhaps to views already presented. She looked about her again, on her feet, at her scattered
melancholy comrades—some of them so melancholy as to be
down on their stomachs in the grass, turned away, ignoring, bur-
rowing; she saw once more, with them, those two faces of the question between which there was so little to choose for inspiration. It
was perhaps superficially more striking that one could live if one
would; but it was more appealing, insinuating, irresistible in short,
that one would live if one could.

   She found after this, for the day or two, more amusement than
she had ventured to count on in the fact, if it were not a mere
fancy, of deceiving Susie; and she presently felt that what made
the difference was the mere fancy—as this *was* one—of a coun-
termove to her great man. His taking on himself—should he do
so—to get at her companion made her suddenly, she held, irre-
sponsible, made any notion of her own all right for her; though
indeed at the very moment she invited herself to enjoy this impunity she became aware of new matter for surprise, or at least for
speculation. Her idea would rather have been that Mrs. Stringham would have looked at her hard—her sketch of the grounds of
her independent long excursion showing, she could feel, as almost cynically superficial. Yet the dear woman so failed, in the
event, to avail herself of any right of criticism that it was sensibly
tempting to wonder for an hour if Kate Croy had been playing
perfectly fair. Hadn't she possibly, from motives of the highest

benevolence, promptings of the finest anxiety, just given poor Susie what she would have called the straight tip? It must immediately be mentioned, however, that, quite apart from a remembrance of the distinctness of Kate's promise, Milly, the next thing, found her explanation in a truth that had the merit of being general. If Susie at this crisis suspiciously spared her, it was really that Susie was always suspiciously sparing her—yet occasionally too with portentous and exceptional mercies. The girl was conscious of how she dropped at times into inscrutable impenetrable deferences—attitudes that, thought without at all intending it, made a difference for familiarity, for the ease of intimacy. It was as if she recalled herself to manners, to the law of court-etiquette—which last note above all helped our young woman to a just appreciation. It was definite for her, even if not quite solid, that to treat her as a princess was a positive need of her companion's mind; wherefore she couldn't help it if this lady had her transcendent view of the way the class in question were treated. Susan had read history, had read Gibbon and Froude and Saint-Simon;[15] she had high lights as to the special allowances made for the class, and, since she saw them, when young, as effete and overtutored, inevitably ironic and infinitely refined, one must take it for amusing if she inclined to an indulgence verily Byzantine.* If one *could* only be Byzantine!—wasn't *that* what she insidiously led one on to sigh? Milly tried to oblige her—for it really placed Susan herself so handsomely to be Byzantine now. The great ladies of that race—it would be somewhere in Gibbon—were apparently not questioned about their mysteries. But oh poor Milly and hers! Susan at all events proved scarce more inquisitive than if she had been a mosaic at Ravenna. Susan was a porcelain monument to the odd moral that consideration might, like cynicism, have abysses. Besides, the Puritan finally disencumbered—! What starved generations wasn't Mrs. Stringham, in fancy, going to make up for?

Kate Croy came straight to the hotel—came that evening shortly before dinner; specifically and publicly moreover, in a han-

---

*The term refers to the Eastern Roman Empire prior to the Turkish conquest in the fifteenth century.

som that, driven apparently very fast, pulled up beneath their windows almost with the clatter of an accident, a "smash." Milly, alone, as happened, in the great garnished void of their sitting-room, where, a little, really, like a caged Byzantine, she had been pacing through the queer long-drawn almost sinister delay of night, an effect she yet liked—Milly, at the sound, one of the French windows standing open, passed out to the balcony that overhung, with pretensions, the general entrance, and so was in time for the look that Kate, alighting, paying her cabman, happened to send up to the front. The visitor moreover had a shilling back to wait for, during which Milly, from the balcony, looked down at her, and a mute exchange, but with smiles and nods, took place between them on what had occurred in the morning. It was what Kate had called for, and the tone was thus almost by accident determined for Milly before her friend came up. What was also, however, determined for her was, again, yet irrepressibly again, that the image presented to her, the splendid young woman who looked so particularly handsome in impatience, with the fine freedom of her signal, was the peculiar property of somebody else's vision, that this fine freedom in short was the fine freedom she showed Mr. Densher. Just so was how she looked to him, and just so was how Milly was held by her—held as by the strange sense of seeing through that distant person's eyes. It lasted, as usual, the strange sense, but fifty seconds; yet in so lasting it produced an effect. It produced in fact more than one, and we take them in their order. The first was that it struck our young woman as absurd to say that a girl's looking so to a man could possibly be without connexions; and the second was that by the time Kate had got into the room Milly was in mental possession of the main connexion it must have for herself.

She produced this commodity on the spot—produced it in straight response to Kate's frank "Well, what?" The enquiry bore of course, with Kate's eagerness, on the issue of the morning's scene, the great man's latest wisdom, and it doubtless affected Milly a little as the cheerful demand for news is apt to affect troubled spirits when news is not, in one of the neater forms, prepared for delivery. She couldn't have said what it was exactly that on the instant determined her; the nearest description of it would perhaps have been as the more vivid impression of all her friend took for granted. The contrast between this free quantity and the maze of possibilities through which, for hours, she had herself been picking her way, put on, in short, for the moment, a grossness that even friendly forms scarce lightened: it helped forward in fact the revelation to herself that she absolutely had nothing to tell. Besides which, certainly, there was something else—an influence at the particular juncture still more obscure. Kate had lost, on the way upstairs, the look—*the* look—that made her young hostess so subtly think and one of the signs of which was that she never kept it for many moments at once; yet she stood there, none the less, so in her bloom and in her strength, so completely again the "handsome girl" beyond all others, the "handsome girl" for whom Milly had at first gratefully taken her, that to meet her now with the note of the plaintive would amount somehow to a surrender, to a confession. *She* would never in her life be ill; the greatest doctor would keep her, at the worst, the fewest minutes; and it was as if she had asked just *with* all this practical impeccability for all that was most mortal in her friend. These things, for Milly, inwardly danced their dance; but the vibration produced and the dust kicked up had lasted less than our account of them. Almost before she knew it she was answering, and answering beautifully, with no consciousness of fraud, only as with a sudden flare of the famous "will-power" she had heard about, read about, and which was what her medical adviser had mainly thrown her back on. "Oh it's all right. He's lovely."

Kate was splendid, and it would have been clear for Milly now, had the further presumption been needed, that she had said no word to Mrs. Stringham. "You mean you've been absurd?"

"Absurd." It was a simple word to say, but the consequence of it, for our young woman, was that she felt it, as soon as spoken, to have done something for her safety.

And Kate really hung on her lips. "There's nothing at all the matter?"

"Nothing to worry about. I shall need a little watching, but I shan't have to do anything dreadful, or even in the least inconvenient. I can do in fact as I like." It was wonderful for Milly how just to put it so made all its pieces fall at present quite properly into their places.

Yet even before the full effect came Kate had seized, kissed, blessed her. "My love, you're too sweet! It's too dear! But it's as I was sure." Then she grasped the full beauty. "You can do as you like?"

"Quite. Isn't it charming?"

"Ah but catch you," Kate triumphed with gaiety, "*not* doing— And what *shall* you do?"

"For the moment simply enjoy it. Enjoy"—Milly was completely luminous—"having got out of my scrape."

"Learning, you mean, so easily, that you *are* well?"

It was as if Kate had but too conveniently put the words into her mouth. "Learning, I mean, so easily, that I *am* well."

"Only no one's of course well enough to stay in London now. He can't," Kate went on, "want this of you."

"Mercy no—I'm to knock about. I'm to go to places."

"But not beastly 'climates'—Engadines, Rivieras, boredoms?"

"No; just, as I say, where I prefer. I'm to go in for pleasure."

"Oh the duck!"—Kate, with her own shades of familiarity, abounded. "But what kind of pleasure?"

"The highest," Milly smiled.

Her friend met it as nobly. "Which *is* the highest?"

"Well, it's just our chance to find out. You must help me."

"What have I wanted to do but help you," Kate asked, "from the moment I first laid eyes on you?" Yet with this too Kate had her wonder. "I like your talking, though, about that. What help, with your luck all round, do you need?"

— V —

Milly indeed at last couldn't say; so that she had really for the time brought it along to the point so oddly marked for her by her visitor's arrival, the truth that she was enviably strong. She carried this out, from that evening, for each hour still left her, and the more easily perhaps that the

hours were now narrowly numbered. All she actually waited for
was Sir Luke Strett's promised visit; as to her proceeding on
which, however, her mind was quite made up. Since he wanted
to get at Susie he should have the freest access, and then perhaps he would see how he liked it. What was between *them* they
might settle as between them, and any pressure it should lift
from her own spirit they were at liberty to convert to their use.
If the dear man wished to fire Susan Shepherd with a still higher
ideal, he would only after all, at the worst, have Susan on his
hands. If devotion, in a word, was what it would come up for the
interested pair to organise, she was herself ready to consume it
as the dressed and served dish. He had talked to her of her "appetite," her account of which, she felt, must have been vague.
But for devotion, she could now see, this appetite would be of
the best. Gross, greedy, ravenous—these were doubtless the
proper names for her: she was at all events resigned in advance
to the machinations of sympathy. The day that followed her
lonely excursion was to be the last but two or three of their stay
in London; and the evening of that day practically ranked for
them as, in the matter of outside relations, the last of all. People
were by this time quite scattered, and many of those who had so
liberally manifested in calls, in cards, in evident sincerity about
visits, later on, over the land, had positively passed in music out
of sight; whether as members, these latter, more especially, of
Mrs. Lowder's immediate circle or as members of Lord Mark's—
our friends being by this time able to make the distinction. The
general pitch had thus decidedly dropped, and the occasions
still to be dealt with were special and few. One of these, for
Milly, announced itself as the doctor's call already mentioned,
as to which she had now had a note from him: the single other,
of importance, was their appointed leave-taking—for the shortest separation—in respect to Mrs. Lowder and Kate. The aunt
and the niece were to dine with them alone, intimately and easily—as easily as should be consistent with the question of their
afterwards going on together to some absurdly belated party, at
which they had had it from Aunt Maud that they would do well
to show. Sir Luke was to make his appearance on the morrow of

this, and in respect to that complication Milly had already her plan.

The night was at all events hot and stale, and it was late enough by the time the four ladies had been gathered in, for their small session, at the hotel, where the windows were still open to the high balconies and the flames of the candles, behind the pink shades—disposed as for the vigil of watchers—were motionless in the air in which the season lay dead. What was presently settled among them was that Milly, who betrayed on this occasion a preference more marked than usual, shouldn't hold herself obliged to climb that evening the social stair, however it might stretch to meet her, and that, Mrs. Lowder and Mrs. Stringham facing the ordeal together, Kate Croy should remain with her and await their return. It was a pleasure to Milly, ever, to send Susan Shepherd forth; she saw her go with complacency, liked, as it were, to put people off with her, and noted with satisfaction, when she so moved to the carriage, the further denudation—a markedly ebbing tide—of her little benevolent back. If it wasn't quite Aunt Maud's ideal, moreover, to take out the new American girl's funny friend instead of the new American girl herself, nothing could better indicate the range of that lady's merit than the spirit in which—as at the present hour for instance—she made the best of the minor advantage. And she did this with a broad cheerful absence of illusion; she did it—confessing even as much to poor Susie—because, frankly, she *was* good-natured. When Mrs. Stringham observed that her own light was too abjectly borrowed and that it was as a link alone, fortunately not missing, that she was valued, Aunt Maud concurred to the extent of the remark: "Well, my dear, you're better than nothing." To-night furthermore it came up for Milly that Aunt Maud had something particular in mind. Mrs. Stringham, before adjourning with her, had gone off for some shawl or other accessory, and Kate, as if a little impatient for their withdrawal, had wandered out to the balcony, where she hovered for the time unseen, though with scarce more to look at than the dim London stars and the cruder glow, up the street, on a corner, of a small public-house in front of which a fagged cab-horse was thrown into relief. Mrs. Lowder made use of the moment: Milly felt as soon as she had spoken that what she was doing was somehow for use.

"Dear Susan tells me that you saw in America Mr. Densher— whom I've never till now, as you may have noticed, asked you about. But do you mind at last, in connexion with him, doing something for me?" She had lowered her fine voice to a depth, though speaking with all her rich glibness; and Milly, after a small sharpness of surprise, was already guessing the sense of her appeal. "Will you name him, in any way you like, to *her*"—and Aunt Maud gave a nod at the window; "so that you may perhaps find out whether he's back?"

Ever so many things, for Milly, fell into line at this; it was a wonder, she afterwards thought, that she could be conscious of so many at once. She smiled hard, however, for them all. "But I don't know that it's important to me to 'find out.'" The array of things was further swollen, however, even as she said this, by its striking her as too much to say. She therefore tried as quickly to say less. "Except you mean of course that it's important to *you*." She fancied Aunt Maud was looking at her almost as hard as she was herself smiling, and that gave her another impulse. "You know I never *have* yet named him to her; so that if I should break out now—"

"Well?"—Mrs. Lowder waited.

"Why she may wonder what I've been making a mystery of. She hasn't mentioned him, you know," Milly went on, "herself."

"No"—her friend a little heavily weighed it—"she wouldn't. So it's she, you see then, who has made the mystery."

Yes, Milly but wanted to see; only there was so much. "There has been of course no particular reason." Yet that indeed was neither here nor there. "Do you think," she asked, "he *is* back?"

"It will be about his time, I gather, and rather a comfort to me definitely to know."

"Then can't you ask her yourself?"

"Ah we never speak of him!"

It helped Milly for the moment to the convenience of a puzzled pause. "Do you mean he's an acquaintance of whom you disapprove for her?"

Aunt Maud, as well, just hung fire. "I disapprove of *her* for the poor young man. She doesn't care for him."

"And *he* cares so much—?"

"Too much, too much. And my fear is," said Mrs. Lowder, "that he privately besets her. She keeps it to herself, but I don't want her worried. Neither, in truth," she both generously and confidentially concluded, "do I want *him*."

Milly showed all her own effort to meet the case. "But what can *I* do?"

"You can find out where they are. If I myself try," Mrs. Lowder explained, "I shall appear to treat them as if I supposed them deceiving me."

"And you don't. You don't," Milly mused for her, "suppose them deceiving you."

"Well," said Aunt Maud, whose fine onyx eyes failed to blink even though Milly's questions might have been taken as drawing her rather further than she had originally meant to go—"well, Kate's thoroughly aware of my views for her, and that I take her being with me at present, in the way she *is* with me, if you know what I mean, for a loyal assent to them. Therefore as my views don't happen to provide a place at all for Mr. Densher, much, in a manner, as I like him"—therefore in short she had been prompted to this step, though she completed her sense, but sketchily, with the rattle of her large fan.

It assisted them for the moment perhaps, however, that Milly was able to pick out of her sense what might serve as the clearest part of it. "You do like him then?"

"Oh dear yes. Don't you?"

Milly waited, for the question was somehow as the sudden point of something sharp on a nerve that winced. She just caught her breath, but she had ground for joy afterwards, she felt, in not really having failed to choose with quickness sufficient, out of fifteen possible answers, the one that would best serve her. She was then almost proud, as well, that she had cheerfully smiled. "I did— three times—in New York." So came and went, in these simple words, the speech that was to figure for her later on, that night, as the one she had ever uttered that cost her most. She was to lie

awake for the gladness of not having taken any line so really inferior as the denial of a happy impression.

For Mrs. Lowder also moreover her simple words were the right
ones; they were at any rate, that lady's laugh showed, in the natural note of the racy. "You dear American thing! But people may be
very good and yet not good for what one wants."

"Yes," the girl assented, "even I suppose when what one wants
is something very good."

"Oh my child, it would take too long just now to tell you all *I*
want! I want everything at once and together—and ever so much
for you too, you know. But you've seen us," Aunt Maud continued;
"you'll have made out."

"Ah," said Milly, "I *don't* make out;" for again—it came that way
in rushes—she felt an obscurity in things. "Why, if our friend here
doesn't like him—"

"Should I conceive her interested in keeping things from me?"
Mrs. Lowder did justice to the question. "My dear, how can you
ask? Put yourself in her place. She meets me, but on *her* terms.
Proud young women are proud young women. And proud old
ones are—well, what *I* am. Fond of you as we both are, you can
help us."

Milly tried to be inspired. "Does it come back then to my asking her straight?"

At this, however, finally, Aunt Maud threw her up. "Oh if
you've so many reasons not—!"

"I've not so many," Milly smiled—"but I've one. If I break out
so suddenly on my knowing him, what will she make of my not
having spoken before?"

Mrs. Lowder looked blank at it. "Why should you care what she
makes? You may have only been decently discreet."

"Ah I *have* been," the girl made haste to say.

"Besides," her friend went on, "I suggested to you, through
Susan, your line."

"Yes, that reason's a reason for *me*."

"And for *me*," Mrs. Lowder insisted. "She's not therefore so stupid as not to do justice to grounds so marked. You can tell her perfectly that I had asked you to say nothing."

"And may I tell her that you've asked me now to speak?"

Mrs. Lowder might well have thought, yet, oddly, this pulled her up. "You can't do it without—?"

Milly was almost ashamed to be raising so many difficulties. "I'll do what I can if you'll kindly tell me one thing more." She faltered a little—it was so prying; but she brought it out. "Will he have been writing to her?"

"It's exactly, my dear, what I should like to know!" Mrs. Lowder was at last impatient. "Push in for yourself and I dare say she'll tell you."

Even now, all the same, Milly had not quite fallen back. "It will be pushing in," she continued to smile, "for *you*." She allowed her companion, however, no time to take this up. "The point will be that if he *has* been writing she may have answered."

"But what point, you subtle thing, is that?"

"It isn't subtle, it seems to me, but quite simple," Milly said, "that if she has answered she has very possibly spoken of me."

"Very certainly indeed. But what difference will it make?"

The girl had a moment, at this, of thinking it natural Mrs. Lowder herself should so fail of subtlety. "It will make the difference that he'll have written her in reply that he knows me. And that, in turn," our young woman explained, "will give an oddity to my own silence."

"How so, if she's perfectly aware of having given you no opening? The only oddity," Aunt Maud lucidly professed, "is for yourself. It's in *her* not having spoken."

"Ah there we are!" said Milly.

And she had uttered it, evidently, in a tone that struck her friend. "Then it *has* troubled you?"

But the enquiry had only to be made to bring the rare colour with fine inconsequence to her face. "Not really the least little bit!" And, quickly feeling the need to abound in this sense, she was on the point, to cut short, of declaring that she cared, after all, no scrap how much she obliged. Only she felt at this instant too the intervention of still other things. Mrs. Lowder was in the first place already beforehand, already affected as by the sudden vision of her having herself pushed too far. Milly could never judge from her face of her uppermost motive—it was so little, in its hard smooth sheen, that kind of human countenance. She looked hard when she spoke fair; the only thing was that when she spoke hard she didn't likewise look soft. Something, none the less, had arisen in her now—a full appreciable tide, entering by the rupture of some bar. She announced that if what she had asked was to prove in the least a bore her young friend was not to dream of it; making her young friend at the same time, by the change in her tone, dream on the spot more profusely. She spoke, with a belated light, Milly could apprehend—she could always apprehend—from pity; and the result of that perception, for the girl, was singular: it proved to her as quickly that Kate, keeping her secret, had been straight with her. From Kate distinctly then, as to why she was to be pitied, Aunt Maud knew nothing, and was thereby simply putting in evidence the fine side of her own character. This fine side was that she could almost at any hour, by a kindled preference or a diverted energy, glow for another interest than her own. She exclaimed as well, at this moment, that Milly must have been thinking round the case much more than she had supposed; and this remark could affect the girl as quickly and as sharply as any other form of the charge of weakness. It was what every one, if she didn't look out, would soon be saying—"There's something the matter with you!" What one was therefore one's self concerned immediately to establish was that there was nothing at all. "I shall like to help you; I shall like, so far as that goes, to help Kate herself," she made such haste as she could to declare; her eyes wandering meanwhile across the width of the room to that dusk of the balcony in which their companion perhaps a little unaccountably lingered. She suggested hereby her impatience to begin; she almost overtly wondered at the length of the opportunity this friend was giving them—referring it, however, so far as words went, to the other friend and breaking off with an amused: "How tremendously Susie must be beautifying!"

It only marked Aunt Maud, none the less, as too preoccupied for her allusion. The onyx eyes were fixed upon her with a polished pressure that must signify some enriched benevolence. "Let it go, my dear. We shall after all soon enough see."

"If he *has* come back we shall certainly see," Milly after a moment replied; "for he'll probably feel that he can't quite civilly not come to see me. Then *there*," she remarked, "we shall be. It wouldn't then, you see, come through Kate at all — it would come through him. Except," she wound up with a smile, "that he won't find me."

She had the most extraordinary sense of interesting her guest, in spite of herself, more than she wanted; it was as if her doom so floated her on that she couldn't stop — by very much the same trick it had played her with her doctor. "Shall you run away from him?"

She neglected the question, wanting only now to get off. "Then," she went on, "you'll deal with Kate directly."

"Shall you run away from *her*?" Mrs. Lowder profoundly enquired, while they became aware of Susie's return through the room, opening out behind them, in which they had dined.

This affected Milly as giving her but an instant; and suddenly, with it, everything she felt in the connexion rose to her lips for a question that even as she put it, she knew she was failing to keep colourless. "Is it your own belief that he *is* with her?"

Aunt Maud took it in — took in, that is, everything of the tone that she just wanted her not to; and the result for some seconds was but to make their eyes meet in silence. Mrs. Stringham had rejoined them and was asking if Kate had gone — an enquiry at once answered by this young lady's reappearance. They saw her again in the open window, where, looking at them, she had paused — producing thus on Aunt Maud's part almost too impressive a "Hush!" Mrs. Lowder indeed without loss of time smothered any danger in a sweeping retreat with Susie; but Milly's words to her, just uttered, about dealing with her niece directly, struck our young woman as already recoiling on herself. Directness, however evaded, would be, fully, for *her*; nothing in fact would ever have been for her so direct as the evasion. Kate had remained in the window, very handsome and upright, the outer dark framing in a highly favourable way her summery simplicities and lightnesses of dress. Milly had, given the relation of space, no real fear she had heard their talk; only she hovered there as with conscious eyes and some added advantage. Then indeed, with small delay, her friend sufficiently saw. The conscious eyes, the added advantage were but those she had now always at command — those proper to the person Milly knew as known to Mer-

ton Densher. It was for several seconds again as if the *total* of her
identity had been that of the person known to him—a determination having for result another sharpness of its own. Kate had
positively but to be there just as she was to tell her he had come
back. It seemed to pass between them in fine without a word that
he was in London, that he was perhaps only round the corner;
and surely therefore no dealing of Milly's with her would yet have
been so direct.

— VI —

I t was doubtless because this queer form of directness had in itself, for the hour, seemed so sufficient that Milly was afterwards
aware of having really, all the while—during the strange indescribable session before the return of their companions—done
nothing to intensify it. If she was most aware only afterwards,
under the long and discurtained ordeal of the morrow's dawn, that
was because she had really, till their evening's end came, ceased
after a little to miss anything from their ostensible comfort. What
was behind showed but in gleams and glimpses; what was in front
never at all confessed to not holding the stage. Three minutes
hadn't passed before Milly quite knew she should have done nothing Aunt Maud had just asked her. She knew it moreover by much
the same light that had acted for her with that lady and with Sir
Luke Strett. It pressed upon her then and there that she was still
in a current determined, through her indifference, timidity, bravery, generosity—she scarce could say which—by others; that not
she but the current acted, and that somebody else always was the
keeper of the lock or the dam. Kate for example had but to open
the flood-gate: the current moved in its mass—the current, as it
had been, of her doing as Kate wanted. What, somehow, in the
most extraordinary way in the world, *had* Kate wanted but to be, of
a sudden, more interesting than she had ever been? Milly, for their
evening then, quite held her breath with the appreciation of it. If
she hadn't been sure her companion would have had nothing,
from her moments with Mrs. Lowder, to go by, she would almost

have seen the admirable creature "cutting in" to anticipate a danger. This fantasy indeed, while they sat together, dropped after a little; even if only because other fantasies multiplied and clustered, making fairly, for our young woman, the buoyant medium in which her friend talked and moved. They sat together, I say, but Kate moved as much as she talked; she figured there, restless and charming, just perhaps a shade perfunctory, repeatedly quitting her place, taking slowly, to and fro, in the trailing folds of her light dress, the length of the room—almost avowedly performing for the pleasure of her hostess.

Mrs. Lowder had said to Milly at Matcham that she and her niece, as allies, could practically conquer the world; but though it was a speech about which there had even then been a vague grand glamour the girl read into it at present more of an approach to a meaning. Kate, for that matter, by herself, could conquer anything, and *she*, Milly Theale, was probably concerned with the "world" only as the small scrap of it that most impinged on her and that was therefore first to be dealt with. On this basis of being dealt with she would doubtless herself do her share of the conquering: she would have something to supply, Kate something to take—each of them thus, to that tune, something for squaring with Aunt Maud's ideal. This in short was what it came to now— that the occasion, in the quiet late lamplight, had the quality of a rough rehearsal of the possible big drama. Milly knew herself dealt with—handsomely, completely: she surrendered to the knowledge, for so it was, she felt, that she supplied her helpful force. And what Kate had to take Kate took as freely and to all appearance as gratefully; accepting afresh, with each of her long, slow walks, the relation between them so established and consecrating her companion's surrender simply by the interest she gave it. The interest to Milly herself we naturally mean; the interest to Kate Milly felt as probably inferior. It easily and largely came for their present talk, for the quick flight of the hour before the breach of the spell—it all came, when considered, from the circumstance, not in the least abnormal, that the handsome girl was in extraordinary "form." Milly remembered her having said that she was at her best late at night; remembered it by its having, with its fine assurance, made her wonder when *she* was at her best and

how happy people must be who had such a fixed time. She had
no time at all; she was never at her best—unless indeed it were exactly, as now, in listening, watching, admiring, collapsing. If Kate
moreover, quite mercilessly, had never been so good, the beauty
and the marvel of it was that she had never really been so frank:
being a person of such a calibre, as Milly would have said, that,
even while "dealing" with you and thereby, as it were, picking her
steps, she could let herself go, could, in irony, in confidence, in
extravagance, tell you things she had never told before. That was
the impression—that she was telling things, and quite conceivably for her own relief as well; almost as if the errors of vision, the
mistakes of proportion, the residuary innocence of spirit still to be
remedied on the part of her auditor, had their moments of proving too much for her nerves. She went at them just now, these
sources of irritation, with an amused energy that it would have
been open to Milly to regard as cynical and that was nevertheless
called for—as to this the other was distinct—by the way that in
certain connexions the American mind broke down. It seemed at
least—the American mind as sitting there thrilled and dazzled in
Milly—not to understand English society without a separate con-
frontation with *all* the cases. It couldn't proceed by—there was
some technical term she lacked until Milly suggested both anal-
ogy and induction, and then, differently, instinct, none of which
were right: it had to be led up and introduced to each aspect of
the monster, enabled to walk all round it, whether for the consequent exaggerated ecstasy or for the still more (as appeared to this
critic) disproportionate shock. It might, the monster, Kate con-
ceded, loom large for those born amid forms less developed and
therefore no doubt less amusing; it might on some sides be a
strange and dreadful monster, calculated to devour the unwary, to
abase the proud, to scandalise the good; but if one had to live with
it one must, not to be for ever sitting up, learn how: which was virtually in short to-night what the handsome girl showed herself as
teaching.

      She gave away publicly, in this process, Lancaster Gate and
everything it contained; she gave away, hand over hand, Milly's
thrill continued to note, Aunt Maud and Aunt Maud's glories
and Aunt Maud's complacencies; she gave herself away most of

all, and it was naturally what most contributed to her candour. She didn't speak to her friend once more, in Aunt Maud's strain, of how they could scale the skies; she spoke, by her bright perverse preference on this occasion, of the need, in the first place, of being neither stupid nor vulgar. It might have been a lesson, for our young American, in the art of seeing things as they were—a lesson so various and so sustained that the pupil had, as we have shown, but receptively to gape. The odd thing furthermore was that it could serve its purpose while explicitly disavowing every personal bias. It wasn't that she disliked Aunt Maud, who was everything she had on other occasions declared; but the dear woman, ineffaceably stamped by inscrutable nature and a dreadful art, wasn't—how *could* she be?—what she wasn't. She wasn't any one. She wasn't anything. She wasn't anywhere. Milly mustn't think it—one couldn't, as a good friend, let her. Those hours at Matcham were *inespérées,** were pure manna from heaven; or if not wholly that perhaps, with humbugging old Lord Mark as a backer, were vain as a ground for hopes and calculations. Lord Mark was very well, but he wasn't *the* cleverest creature in England, and even if he had been he still wouldn't have been the most obliging. He weighed it out in ounces, and indeed each of the pair was really waiting for what the other would put down.

"She has put down *you*," said Milly, attached to the subject still; "and I think what you mean is that, on the counter, she still keeps hold of you."

"Lest"—Kate took it up—"he should suddenly grab me and run? Oh as he isn't ready to run he's much less ready, naturally, to grab. I *am*—you're so far right as that—on the counter, when I'm not in the shop-window; in and out of which I'm thus conveniently, commercially whisked: the essence, all of it, of my position, and the price, as properly of my aunt's protection." Lord Mark was substantially what she had begun with as soon as they were alone; the impression was even yet with Milly of her having sounded his name, having imposed it, as a topic, in direct opposi-

---

*Unhoped for; unexpected (French).

tion to the other name that Mrs. Lowder had left in the air and that all her own look, as we have seen, kept there at first for her companion. The immediate strange effect had been that of her consciously needing, as it were, an *alibi*—which, successfully, she so found. She had worked it to the end, ridden it to and fro across the course marked for Milly by Aunt Maud, and now she had quite, so to speak, broken it in. "The bore is that if she wants him so much—wants him, heaven forgive her! for *me*—he has put us all out, since your arrival, by wanting somebody else. I don't mean somebody else than you."

Milly threw off the charm sufficiently to shake her head. "Then I haven't made out who it is. If I'm any part of his alternative he had better stop where he is."

"Truly, truly?—always, always?"

Milly tried to insist with an equal gaiety. "Would you like me to swear?"

Kate appeared for a moment—though that was doubtless but gaiety too—to think. "Haven't we been swearing enough?"

"You have perhaps, but I haven't, and I ought to give you the equivalent. At any rate there it is. 'Truly, truly' as you say—'always, always.' So I'm not in the way."

"Thanks," said Kate—"but that doesn't help me."

"Oh it's as simplifying for *him* that I speak of it."

The difficulty really is that he's a person with so many ideas that it's particularly hard to simplify for him. That's exactly of course what Aunt Maud has been trying. He won't," Kate firmly continued, "make up his mind about me."

"Well," Milly smiled, "give him time."

Her friend met it in perfection. "One's *doing* that—one *is*. But one remains all the same but one of his ideas."

"There's no harm in that," Milly returned, "if you come out in the end as the best of them. What's a man," she pursued, "especially an ambitious one, without a variety of ideas?"

"No doubt. The more the merrier." And Kate looked at her grandly. "One can but hope to come out, and do nothing to prevent it."

All of which made for the impression, fantastic or not, of the *alibi*. The splendour, the grandeur were for Milly the bold ironic spirit behind it, so interesting too in itself. What, further, was not less interesting was the fact, as our young woman noted it, that Kate confined her point to the difficulties, so far as *she* was concerned, raised only by Lord Mark. She referred now to none that her own taste might present; which circumstance again played its little part. She was doing what she liked in respect to another person, but she was in no way committed to the other person, and her moreover talking of Lord Mark as not young and not true were only the signs of her clear self-consciousness, were all in the line of her slightly hard but scarce the less graceful extravagance. She didn't wish to show too much her consent to be arranged for, but that was a different thing from not wishing sufficiently to give it. There was something on it all, as well, that Milly still found occasion to say. "If your aunt has been, as you tell me, put out by me, I feel she has remained remarkably kind."

"Oh but she has—whatever might have happened in that respect—plenty of use for you! You put her in, my dear, more than you put her out. You don't half see it, but she has clutched your petticoat. You can do anything—you can do, I mean, lots that *we* can't. You're an outsider, independent and standing by yourself; you're not hideously relative to tiers and tiers of others." And Kate, facing in that direction, went further and further; wound up, while Milly gaped, with extraordinary words. "We're of no use to you—it's decent to tell you. You'd be of use to us, but that's a different matter. My honest advice to you would be—" she went indeed all lengths—"to drop us while you can. It would be funny if you didn't soon see how awfully better you can do. We've not really done for you the least thing worth speaking of—nothing you mightn't easily have had in some other way. Therefore you're under no obligation. You won't want us next year; we shall only continue to want *you*. But that's no reason for you, and you mustn't pay too dreadfully for poor Mrs. Stringham's having let you in. She has the best conscience in the world; she's enchanted with what she has done; but you shouldn't take your people from *her*. It has been quite awful to see you do it."

Milly tried to be amused, so as not—it was too absurd—to be fairly frightened. Strange enough indeed—if not natural enough—that, late at night thus, in a mere mercenary house, with Susie away, a want of confidence should possess her. She recalled, with all the rest of it, the next day, piecing things together in the dawn, that she had felt herself alone with a creature who paced like a panther. That was a violent image, but it made her a little less ashamed of having been scared. For all her scare, none the less, she had now the sense to find words. "And yet without Susie I shouldn't have had *you*."

It had been at this point, however, that Kate flickered highest. "Oh you may very well loathe me yet!"[16]

Really at last, thus, it had been too much; as, with her own least feeble flare, after a wondering watch, Milly had shown. She hadn't cared; she had too much wanted to know; and, though a small solemnity of remonstrance, a sombre strain, had broken into her tone, it was to figure as her nearest approach to serving Mrs. Lowder. "Why do you say such things to me?"

This unexpectedly had acted, by a sudden turn of Kate's attitude, as a happy speech. She had risen as she spoke, and Kate had stopped before her, shining at her instantly with a softer brightness. Poor Milly hereby enjoyed one of her views of how people, wincing oddly, were often touched by her. "Because you're a dove." With which she felt herself ever so delicately, so considerately, embraced; not with familiarity or as a liberty taken, but almost ceremonially and in the manner of an *accolade*; partly as if, though a dove who could perch on a finger, one were also a princess with whom forms were to be observed. It even came to her, through the touch of her companion's lips, that this form, this cool pressure, fairly sealed the sense of what Kate had just said. It was moreover, for the girl, like an inspiration: she found herself accepting as the right one, while she caught her breath with relief, the name so given her. She met it on the instant as she would have met revealed truth; it lighted up the strange dusk in which she lately had walked. *That* was what was the matter with her. She was a dove. Oh *wasn't* she?—it echoed within her as she became aware of the sound, outside, of the return of their friends. There was, the next thing, little enough doubt about it after Aunt Maud had been two minutes in the room. She had come up, Mrs. Lowder, with Susan—which she needn't have done, at that hour, instead of letting Kate come down to her; so that Milly could be quite sure it was to catch hold, in some way, of the loose end they had left. Well, the way she did catch was simply to make the point that it didn't now in the least matter. She had mounted the stairs for this, and she had her moment again with her younger hostess while Kate, on the spot, as the latter at the time noted, gave Susan Shepherd unwonted opportunities. Kate was in other words, as Aunt Maud engaged her friend, listening with the handsomest response to Mrs. Stringham's impression of the scene they had just quitted. It was in the tone of the fondest indulgence—almost, really, that of dove cooing to dove—that Mrs. Lowder expressed to Milly the hope that it had all gone beautifully. Her "all" had an ample benevolence; it soothed and simplified; she spoke as if it were the two young women, not she and her comrade, who had been facing the town together. But Milly's answer had prepared itself while Aunt Maud was on the stair; she had felt in a rush all the reasons that would make it the most dovelike; and she gave it, while she was about it, as earnest, as candid. "I don't *think*, dear lady, he's here."

It gave her straightway the measure of the success she could have as a dove: that was recorded in the long look of deep criticism, a look without a word, that Mrs. Lowder poured forth. And the word, presently, bettered it still. "Oh you exquisite thing!" The luscious innuendo of it, almost startling, lingered in the room, after the visitors had gone, like an oversweet fragrance. But left alone with Mrs. Stringham Milly continued to breathe it: she studied again the dovelike and so set her companion to mere rich reporting that she averted all enquiry into her own case.

That, with the new day, was once more her law—though she saw before her, of course, as something of a complication, her need, each time, to decide. She should have to be clear as to how a dove *would* act. She settled it, she thought, well enough this morning by quite readopting her plan in respect to Sir Luke Strett. That, she was pleased to reflect, had originally been pitched in the key of a merely iridescent drab; and although Mrs. Stringham, after breakfast, began by staring at it as if it had been

a priceless Persian carpet suddenly unrolled at her feet, she had
no scruple, at the end of five minutes, in leaving her to make the
best of it. "Sir Luke Strett comes, by appointment, to see me at
eleven, but I'm going out on purpose. He's to be told, please, de-
ceptively, that I'm at home, and you, as my representative, when
he comes up, are to see him instead. He'll like that, this time, better. So do be nice to him." It had taken, naturally, more explanation, and the mention, above all, of the fact that the visitor was the
greatest of doctors; yet when once the key had been offered Susie
slipped it on her bunch, and her young friend could again feel
her lovely imagination operate. It operated in truth very much as
Mrs. Lowder's, at the last, had done the night before: it made the
air heavy once more with the extravagance of assent. It might,
afresh, almost have frightened our young woman to see how people rushed to meet her: *had* she then so little time to live that the
road must always be spared her? It was as if they were helping her
to take it out on the spot. Susie—she couldn't deny, and didn't
pretend to—might, of a truth, on *her* side, have treated such news
as a flash merely lurid; as to which, to do Susie justice, the pain
of it was all there. But, none the less, the margin always allowed
her young friend was all there as well; and the proposal now made
her—what was it in short but Byzantine? The vision of Milly's
perception of the propriety of the matter had, at any rate, quickly
engulfed, so far as her attitude was concerned, any surprise and
any shock; so that she only desired, the next thing, perfectly to
possess the facts. Milly could easily speak, on this, as if there were
only one: she made nothing of such another as that she had felt
herself menaced. The great fact, in fine, was that she *knew* him to
desire just now, more than anything else, to meet, quite apart,
some one interested in her. Who therefore so interested as her
faithful Susan? The only other circumstance that, by the time she
had quitted her friend, she had treated as worth mentioning was
the circumstance of her having at first intended to keep quiet.
She had originally best seen herself as sweetly secretive. As to that
she had changed, and her present request was the result. She
didn't say why she had changed, but she trusted her faithful
Susan. Their visitor would trust her not less, and she herself
would adore their visitor. Moreover he wouldn't—the girl felt

sure—tell her anything dreadful. The worst would be that he was in love and that he needed a confidant to work it. And now she was going to the National Gallery.

— VII —

The idea of the National Gallery had been with her from the moment of her hearing from Sir Luke Strett about his hour of coming. It had been in her mind as a place so meagrely visited, as one of the places that had seemed at home one of the attractions of Europe and one of its highest aids to culture, but that—the old story—the typical frivolous always ended by sacrificing to vulgar pleasures. She had had perfectly, at those whimsical moments on the Brünig, the half-shamed sense of turning her back on such opportunities for real improvement as had figured to her, from of old, in connexion with the continental tour, under the general head of "pictures and things"; and at last she knew for what she had done so. The plea had been explicit—she had done so for life as opposed to learning; the upshot of which had been that life was now beautifully provided for. In spite of those few dips and dashes into the many-coloured stream of history for which of late Kate Croy had helped her to find time, there were possible great chances she had neglected, possible great moments she should, save for to-day, have all but missed. She might still, she had felt, overtake one or two of them among the Titians and the Turners; she had been honestly nursing the hour, and, once she was in the benignant halls, her faith knew itself justified. It was the air she wanted and the world she would now exclusively choose; the quiet chambers, nobly overwhelming, rich but slightly veiled, opened out round her and made her presently say "If I could lose myself *here!*" There were people, people in plenty, but, admirably, no personal question. It was immense, outside, the personal question; but she had blissfully left it outside, and the nearest it came, for a quarter of an hour, to glimmering again into view was when she watched for a little one of the more earnest of the lady-copyists. Two or three in particular, spectacled, aproned, absorbed, engaged her sympathy to an absurd extent, seemed to show her for the time the right way to live. She should have been a lady-copyist—it met so the case. The case was the case of escape, of living under water, of being at once impersonal and firm. There it was before one—one had only to stick and stick.

Milly yielded to this charm till she was almost ashamed; she watched the lady-copyists till she found herself wondering what would be thought by others of a young woman, of adequate aspect, who should appear to regard them as the pride of the place. She would have liked to talk to them, to get, as it figured to her, into their lives, and was deterred but by the fact that she didn't quite see herself as purchasing imitations and yet feared she might excite the expectation of purchase. She really knew before long that what held her was the mere refuge, that something within her was after all too weak for the Turners and Titians. They joined hands about her in a circle too vast, though a circle that a year before she would only have desired to trace. They were truly for the larger, not for the smaller life, the life of which the actual pitch, for example, was an interest, the interest of compassion, in misguided efforts. She marked absurdly her little stations, blinking, in her shrinkage of curiosity, at the glorious walls, yet keeping an eye on vistas and approaches, so that she shouldn't be flagrantly caught. The vistas and approaches drew her in this way from room to room, and she had been through many parts of the show, as she supposed, when she sat down to rest. There were chairs in scant clusters, places from which one could gaze. Milly indeed at present fixed her eyes more than elsewhere on the appearance, first, that she couldn't quite, after all, have accounted to an examiner for the order of her "schools," and then on that of her being more tired than she had meant, in spite of her having been so much less intelligent. They found, her eyes, it should be added, other occupation as well, which she let them freely follow: they rested largely, in her vagueness, on the vagueness of her visitors; they attached themselves in especial, with mixed results, to the surprising stream of her compatriots. She was struck with the circumstance that the great museum, early in August, was haunted with these pilgrims, as also with that of her knowing them from afar, marking them easily, each and all, and recognising not less promptly that they had ever new lights for her—new lights on their own darkness. She gave herself up at last, and it was a consummation like another: what she should have come to the National Gallery for today would be to watch the copyists and reckon the Baedekers. That perhaps was the moral of a menaced state of health—that one would sit in public places and count the Americans. It passed the time in a manner; but it seemed already the second line of defence, and this notwithstanding the pattern, so unmistakeable, of her countryfolk. They were cut out as by scissors, coloured, labelled, mounted; but their relation to her failed to act—they somehow did nothing for her. Partly, no doubt, they didn't so much as notice or know her, didn't even recognise their community of collapse with her, the sign on her, as she sat there, that for her too Europe was "tough." It came to her idly thus—for her humour could still play—that she didn't seem then the same success with them as with the inhabitants of London, who had taken her up on scarce more of an acquaintance. She could wonder if they would be different should she go back with this glamour attached; and she could also wonder, if it came to that, whether she should ever go back. Her friends straggled past, at any rate, in all the vividness of their absent criticism, and she had even at last the sense of taking a mean advantage.

There was a finer instant, however, at which three ladies, clearly a mother and daughters, had paused before her under compulsion of a comment apparently just uttered by one of them and referring to some object on the other side of the room. Milly had her back to the object, but her face very much to her young compatriot, the one who had spoken and in whose look she perceived a certain gloom of recognition. Recognition, for that matter, sat confessedly in her own eyes: she *knew* the three, generically, as easily as a school-boy with a crib in his lap would know the answer in class; she felt, like the school-boy, guilty enough—questioned, as honour went, as to her right so to possess, to dispossess, people who hadn't consciously provoked her. She would have been able to say where they lived, and also how, had the place and the way been but amenable to the positive; she bent tenderly, in imagination, over marital, paternal Mr. Whatever-he-was, at home, eternally named, with all the honours and placidities, but eternally unseen and existing only as some one who could be financially heard from. The mother, the puffed and composed whiteness of whose hair had no relation to her apparent age, showed a countenance almost chemically clean and dry; her companions wore an air of vague resentment humanised by fatigue; and the three were equally adorned with short cloaks of coloured cloth surmounted by little tartan hoods. The tartans were doubtless conceivable as different, but the cloaks, curiously, only thinkable as one. "Handsome? Well, if you choose to say so." It was the mother who had spoken, who herself added, after a pause during which Milly took the reference as to a picture: "In the English style." The three, pair of eyes had converged, and their possessors had for an instant rested, with the effect of a drop of the subject, on this last characterisation—with that, too, of a gloom not less mute in one of the daughters than murmured in the other. Milly's heart went out to them while they turned their backs; she said to herself that they ought to have known her, that there was something between them they might have beautifully put together. But she had lost *them* also—they were cold; they left her in her weak wonder as to what they had been looking at. The "handsome" disposed her to turn— all the more that the "English style" would be the English school, which she liked; only she saw, before moving, by the array on the side facing her, that she was in fact among small Dutch pictures. The action of this was again appreciable—the dim surmise that it wouldn't then be by a picture that the spring in the three ladies had been pressed. It was at all events time she should go, and she turned as she got on her feet. She had had behind her one of the entrances and various visitors who had come in while she sat, visitors single and in pairs—by one of the former of whom she felt her eyes suddenly held.

This was a gentleman in the middle of the place, a gentleman who had removed his hat and was for a moment, while he glanced, absently, as she could see, at the top tier of the collection, tapping his forehead with his pocket-handkerchief. The occupation held him long enough to give Milly time to take for granted— and a few seconds sufficed—that his face was the object just observed by her friends. This could only have been because she concurred in their tribute, even qualified; and indeed "the English

style" of the gentleman—perhaps by instant contrast to the American—was what had had the arresting power. This arresting power,
at the same time—and that was the marvel—had already sharpened almost to pain, for in the very act of judging the bared head
with detachment she felt herself shaken by a knowledge of it. It
was Merton Densher's own, and he was standing there, standing
long enough unconscious for her to fix him and then hesitate.
These successions were swift, so that she could still ask herself in
freedom if she had best let him see her. She could still reply to this
that she shouldn't like him to catch her in the effort to prevent it;
and she might further have decided that he was too preoccupied
to see anything had not a perception intervened that surpassed the
first in violence. She was unable to think afterwards how long she
had looked at him before knowing herself as otherwise looked at;
all she was coherently to put together was that she had had a second recognition without his having noticed her. The source of this
latter shock was nobody less than Kate Croy—Kate Croy who was
suddenly also in the line of vision and whose eyes met her eyes at
their next movement. Kate was but two yards off—Mr. Densher
wasn't alone. Kate's face specifically said so, for after a stare as
blank at first as Milly's it broke into a far smile. That was what,
wonderfully—in addition to the marvel of their meeting—passed
from her for Milly; the instant reduction to easy terms of the fact
of their being there, the two young women, together. It was perhaps only afterwards that the girl fully felt the connexion between
this touch and her already established conviction that Kate was a
prodigious person; yet on the spot she none the less, in a degree,
knew herself handled and again, as she had been the night before,
dealt with—absolutely even dealt with for her greater pleasure. A
minute in fine hadn't elapsed before Kate had somehow made her
provisionally take everything as natural. The provisional was just
the charm—acquiring that character from one moment to the
other; it represented happily so much that Kate would explain on
the very first chance. This left moreover—and that was the greatest wonder—all due margin for amusement at the way things happened, the monstrous oddity of their turning up in such a place on
the very heels of their having separated without allusion to it. The
handsome girl was thus literally in control of the scene by the time

Merton Densher was ready to exclaim with a high flush or a vivid
blush—one didn't distinguish the embarrassment from the joy—
"Why Miss Theale: fancy!" and "Why Miss Theale: what luck!"

Miss Theale had meanwhile the sense that for him too, on
Kate's part, something wonderful and unspoken was determinant;
and this although, distinctly, his companion had no more looked
at him with a hint than he had looked at her with a question. He
had looked and was looking only at Milly herself, ever so pleasantly and considerately—she scarce knew what to call it; but without prejudice to her consciousness, all the same, that women got
out of predicaments better than men. The predicament of course
wasn't definite nor phraseable—and the way they let all phrasing
pass was presently to recur to our young woman as a characteristic
triumph of the civilised state; but she took it for granted, insistently, with a small private flare of passion, because the one thing
she could think of to do for him was to show him how she eased
him off. She would really, tired and nervous, have been much disconcerted if the opportunity in question hadn't saved her. It was
what had saved her most, what had made her, after the first few
seconds, almost as brave for Kate as Kate was for her, had made
her only ask herself what their friend would like of her. That he
was at the end of three minutes, without the least complicated reference, so smoothly "their" friend was just the effect of their all
being sublimely civilised. The flash in which he saw this was, for
Milly, fairly inspiring—to that degree in fact that she was even
now, on such a plane, yearning to be supreme. It took, no doubt,
a big dose of inspiration to treat as not funny—or at least as not unpleasant—the anomaly, for Kate, that *she* knew their gentleman,
and for herself, that Kate was spending the morning with him; but
everything continued to make for this after Milly had tasted of her
draught. She was to wonder in subsequent reflexion what in the
world they had actually said, since they had made such a success
of what they didn't say; the sweetness of the draught for the time,
at any rate, was to feel success assured. What depended on this for
Mr. Densher was all obscurity to her, and she perhaps but invented the image of his need as a short cut to accommodation.
Whatever the facts, their perfect manners, all round, saw them
through. The finest part of Milly's own inspiration, it may further

be mentioned, was the quick perception that what would be of most service was, so to speak, her own native wood-note. She had long been conscious with shame for her thin blood, or at least for her poor economy, of her unused margin as an American girl—closely indeed as in English air the text might appear to cover the page. She still had reserves of spontaneity, if not of comicality; so that all this cash in hand could now find employment. She became as spontaneous as possible and as American as it might conveniently appeal to Mr. Densher, after his travels, to find her. She said things in the air, and yet flattered herself that she struck him as saying them not in the tone of agitation but in the tone of New York. In the tone of New York agitation was beautifully discounted, and she had now a sufficient view of how much it might accordingly help her.

The help was fairly rendered before they left the place; when her friends presently accepted her invitation to adjourn with her to luncheon at her hotel it was in Fifth Avenue that the meal might have waited. Kate had never been there so straight, but Milly was at present taking her; and if Mr. Densher had been he had at least never had to come so fast. She proposed it as the natural thing—proposed it as the American girl; and she saw herself quickly justified by the pace at which she was followed. The beauty of the case was that to do it all she had only to appear to take Kate's hint. This had said in its fine first smile "Oh yes, our look's queer—but give me time"; and the American girl could give time as nobody else could. What Milly thus gave she therefore made them take—even if, as they might surmise, it was rather more than they wanted. In the porch of the museum she expressed her preference for a four-wheeler; they would take their course in that guise precisely to multiply the minutes. She was more than ever justified by the positive charm that her spirit imparted even to their use of this conveyance; and she touched·her highest point—that is certainly for herself—as she ushered her companions into the presence of Susie. Susie was there with luncheon as well as with her return in prospect; and nothing could now have filled her own consciousness more to the brim than to see this good friend take in how little she was abjectly anxious. The cup itself actually offered to this good friend might in truth well be startling, for it was com-

posed beyond question of ingredients oddly mixed. She caught
Susie fairly looking at her as if to know whether she had brought
in guests to hear Sir Luke Strett's report. Well, it was better her
companion should have too much than too little to wonder about;
she had come out "anyway," as they said at home, for the interest
of the thing; and interest truly sat in her eyes. Milly was none the
less, at the sharpest crisis, a little sorry for her; she could of necessity extract from the odd scene so comparatively little of a soothing
secret. She saw Mr. Densher suddenly popping up, but she saw
nothing else that had happened. She saw in the same way her
young friend indifferent to her young friend's doom, and she
lacked what would explain it. The only thing to keep her in patience was the way, after luncheon, Kate almost, as might be said,
made up to her. This was actually perhaps as well what most kept
Milly herself in patience. It had in fact for our young woman a
positive beauty—was so marked as a deviation from the handsome
girl's previous courses. Susie had been a bore to the handsome
girl, and the change was now suggestive. The two sat together,
after they had risen from table, in the apartment in which they had
lunched, making it thus easy for the other guest and his entertainer to sit in the room adjacent. This, for the latter personage,
was the beauty; it was almost, on Kate's part, like a prayer to be relieved. If she honestly liked better to be "thrown with" Susan
Shepherd than with their other friend, why that said practically
everything. It didn't perhaps altogether say why she had gone out
with him for the morning, but it said, as one thought, about as
much as she could say to his face.

Little by little indeed, under the vividness of Kate's behaviour,
the probabilities fell back into their order. Merton Densher was in
love and Kate couldn't help it—could only be sorry and kind:
wouldn't that, without wild flurries, cover everything? Milly at all
events tried it as a cover, tried it hard, for the time; pulled it over
her, in the front, the larger room, drew it up to her chin with energy. If it didn't, so treated, do everything for her, it did so much
that she could herself supply the rest. She made that up by the interest of her great question, the question of whether, seeing him
once more, with all that, as she called it to herself, had come and
gone, her impression of him would be different from the impres-

sion received in New York. That had held her from the moment of
their leaving the museum; it kept her company through their drive
and during luncheon; and now that she was a quarter of an hour
alone with him it became acute. She was to feel at this crisis that
no clear, no common answer, no direct satisfaction on this point,
was to reach her; she was to see her question itself simply go to
pieces. She couldn't tell if he were different or not, and she didn't
know nor care if *she* were: these things had ceased to matter in the
light of the only thing she did know. This was that she liked him,
as she put it to herself, as much as ever; and if that were to amount
to liking a new person the amusement would be but the greater.
She had thought him at first very quiet, in spite of his recovery
from his original confusion; though even the shade of bewilderment, she yet perceived, had not been due to such vagueness on
the subject of her reintensified identity as the probable sight, over
there, of many thousands of her kind would sufficiently have justified. No, he was quiet, inevitably, for the first half of the time, because Milly's own lively line—the line of spontaneity—made
everything else relative; and because too, so far as Kate was spontaneous, it was ever so finely in the air among them that the normal pitch must be kept. Afterwards, when they had got a little
more used, as it were, to each other's separate felicity, he had
begun to talk more, clearly bethinking himself at a given moment
of what *his* natural lively line would be. It would be to take for
granted she must wish to hear of the States, and to give her in its
order everything he had seen and done there. He abounded, of a
sudden—he almost insisted; he returned, after breaks, to the
charge; and the effect was perhaps the more odd as he gave no
clue whatever to what he had admired, as he went, or to what he
hadn't. He simply drenched her with his sociable story—especially
during the time they were away from the others. She had stopped
then being American—all to let him be English; a permission of
which he took, she could feel, both immense and unconscious advantage. She had really never cared less for the States than at this
moment; but that had nothing to do with the matter. It would have
been the occasion of her life to learn about them, for nothing
could put him off, and he ventured on no reference to what had
happened for herself. It might have been almost as if he had

known that the greatest of all these adventures was her doing just
what she did then.

It was at this point that she saw the smash of her great question
complete, saw that all she had to do with was the sense of being
there with him. And there was no chill for this in what she also
presently saw—that, however he had begun, he was now acting
from a particular desire, determined either by new facts or new
fancies, to be like every one else, simplifyingly "kind" to her. He
had caught on already as to manner—fallen into line with every
one else; and if his spirits verily *had* gone up it might well be that
he had thus felt himself lighting on the remedy for all awkwardness. Whatever he did or he didn't Milly knew she should still like
him—there was no alternative to that; but her heart could none
the less sink a little on feeling how much his view of her was destined to have in common with—as she now sighed over it—*the*
view. She could have dreamed of his not having *the* view, of his
having something or other, if need be quite viewless, of his own;
but he might have what he could with least trouble, and *the* view
wouldn't be after all a positive bar to her seeing him. The defect
of it in general—if she might so ungraciously criticise—was that,
by its sweet universality, it made relations rather prosaically a matter of course. It anticipated and superseded the—likewise sweet—
operation of real affinities. It was this that was doubtless marked in
her power to keep him now—this and her glassy lustre of attention
to his pleasantness about the scenery in the Rockies. She was in
truth a little measuring her success in detaining him by Kate's success in "standing" Susan. It wouldn't be, if she could help it, Mr.
Densher who should first break down. Such at least was one of the
forms of the girl's inward tension; but beneath even this deep reason was a motive still finer. What she had left at home on going
out to give it a chance was meanwhile still, was more sharply and
actively, there. What had been at the top of her mind about it and
then been violently pushed down—this quantity was again working up. As soon as their friends should go Susie would break out,
and what she would breakout upon wouldn't be—interested in
that gentleman as she had more than once shown herself—the
personal fact of Mr. Densher. Milly had found in her face at
luncheon a feverish glitter, and it told what she was full of. She

didn't care now for Mr. Densher's personal fact. Mr. Densher had risen before her only to find his proper place in her imagination already of a sudden occupied. His personal fact failed, so far as she was concerned, to *be* personal, and her companion noticed the failure. This could only mean that she was full to the brim of Sir Luke Strett and of what she had had from him. What *had* she had from him? It was indeed now working upward again that Milly would do well to know, though knowledge looked stiff in the light of Susie's glitter. It was therefore on the whole because Densher's young hostess was divided from it by so thin a partition that she continued to cling to the Rockies.

END OF VOLUME I

VOLUME II

BOOK SIXTH

– I –

"I say, you know, Kate—you *did* stay!" had been Merton Densher's punctual remark on their adventure after they had, as it were, got out of it; an observation which she not less promptly, on her side, let him see that she forgave in him only because he was a man. She had to recognise, with whatever disappointment, that it was doubtless the most helpful he could make in this character. The fact of the adventure was flagrant between them; they had looked at each other, on gaining the street, as people look who have just rounded together a dangerous corner, and there was therefore already enough unanimity sketched out to have lighted, for her companion, anything equivocal in her action. But the amount of light men *did* need!—Kate could have been eloquent at this moment about that. What, however, on his seeing more, struck him as most distinct in her was her sense that, reunited after his absence and having been now half the morning together, it behooved them to face without delay the question of handling their immediate future. That it would require some handling, that they should still have to deal, deal in a crafty manner, with difficulties and delays, was the great matter he had come back to, greater than any but the refreshed consciousness of their personal need of each other. This need had had twenty minutes, the afternoon before, to find out where it stood, and the time was fully accounted for by the charm of the demonstration. He had arrived at Euston at five, having wired her from Liverpool the moment he landed, and she had quickly decided to meet him at the station, whatever publicity might attend such an act. When he had praised her for it on alighting from his train she had answered frankly enough that such things should be taken at a jump. She didn't care to-day who saw her, and she profited by it for her joy. To-morrow, inevitably, she should have time to think and then, as inevitably, would become a baser creature, a creature of alarms and precautions. It was none the less for to-morrow at an early hour

227

that she had appointed their next meeting, keeping in mind for the
present a particular obligation to show at Lancaster Gate by six
o'clock. She had given, with imprecations, her reason—people to
tea, eternally, and a promise to Aunt Maud; but she had been liberal enough on the spot and had suggested the National Gallery
for the morning quite as with an idea that had ripened in ex-
pectancy. They might be seen there too, but nobody would know
them; just as, for that matter, now, in the refreshment-room to
which they had adjourned, they would incur the notice but, at the
worst, of the unacquainted. They would "have something" there
for the facility it would give. Thus had it already come up for them
again that they had no place of convenience.

He found himself on English soil with all sorts of feelings, but
he hadn't quite faced having to reckon with a certain ruefulness in
regard to that subject as one of the strongest. He was aware later on
that there were questions his impatience had shirked; whereby it
actually rather smote him, for want of preparation and assurance,
that he had nowhere to "take" his love. He had taken it thus, at
Euston—and on Kate's own suggestion—into the place where
people had beer and buns, and had ordered tea at a small table in
the corner; which, no doubt, as they were lost in the crowd, did
well enough for a stop-gap. It perhaps did as well as her simply
driving with him to the door of his lodging, which had had to figure as the sole device of his own wit. That wit, the truth was, had
broken down a little at the sharp prevision that once at his door
they would have to hang back. She would have to stop there,
wouldn't come in with him, couldn't possibly; and he shouldn't be
able to ask her, would feel he couldn't without betraying a deficiency of what would be called, even at their advanced stage, respect for her: that again was all that was clear except the further
fact that it was maddening. Compressed and concentrated, confined to a single sharp pang or two, but none the less in wait for
him there on the Euston platform and lifting its head as that of a
snake in the garden, was the disconcerting sense that "respect," in
their game, seemed somehow—he scarce knew what to call it—a
fifth wheel to the coach. It was properly an inside thing, not an
outside, a thing to make love greater, not to make happiness less.
They had met again for happiness, and he distinctly felt, during

his most lucid moment or two, how he must keep watch on anything that really menaced that boon. If Kate had consented to
drive away with him and alight at his house there would probably
enough have occurred for them, at the foot of his steps, one of
those strange instants between man and woman that blow upon
the red spark, the spark of conflict, ever latent in the depths of passion. She would have shaken her head—oh sadly, divinely—on
the question of coming in; and he, though doing all justice to her
refusal, would have yet felt his eyes reach further into her own
than a possible word at such a time could reach. This would have
meant the suspicion, the dread of the shadow, of an adverse will.
Lucky therefore in the actual case that the scant minutes took another turn and that by the half-hour she did in spite of everything
contrive to spend with him Kate showed so well how she could
deal with things that maddened. She seemed to ask him, to be-
seech him, and all for his better comfort, to leave her, now and
henceforth, to treat them in her own way.

She had still met it in naming so promptly, for their early convenience, one of the great museums; and indeed with such happy
art that his fully seeing where she had placed him hadn't been till
after he left her. His absence from her for so many weeks had had
such an effect upon him that his demands, his desires had grown;
and only the night before, as his ship steamed, beneath summer
stars, in sight of the Irish coast, he had felt all the force of his particular necessity. He hadn't in other words at any point doubted he
was on his way to say to her that really their mistake must end.
Their mistake was to have believed that they *could* hold out—hold
out, that is, not against Aunt Maud, but against an impatience
that, prolonged and exasperated, made a man ill. He had known
more than ever, on their separating in the court of the station, how
ill a man, and even a woman, could feel from such a cause; but he
struck himself as also knowing that he had already suffered Kate to
begin finely to apply antidotes and remedies and subtle sedatives.
It had a vulgar sound—as throughout, in love, the names of things,
the verbal terms of intercourse, were, compared with love itself,
horribly vulgar; but it was as if, after all, he might have come back
to find himself "put off," though it would take him of course a day
or two to see. His letters from the States had pleased whom it con-

cerned, though not so much as he had meant they should; and he should be paid according to agreement and would now take up his money. It wasn't in truth very much to take up, so that he hadn't in the least come back flourishing a cheque-book; that new motive for bringing his mistress to terms he couldn't therefore pretend to produce. The ideal certainty would have been to be able to present a change of prospect as a warrant for the change of philosophy, and without it he should have to make shift but with the pretext of the lapse of time. The lapse of time—not so many weeks, after all, she might always of course say—couldn't at any rate have failed to do something for him; and that consideration it was that had just now tided him over, all the more that he had his vision of what it had done personally for Kate. This had come out for him with a splendour that almost scared him even in their small corner of the room at Euston—almost scared him because it just seemed to blaze at him that waiting was the game of dupes. Not yet had she been so the creature he had originally seen; not yet had he felt so soundly safely sure. It was all there for him, playing on his pride of possession as a hidden master in a great dim church might play on the grandest organ. His final sense was that a woman couldn't be like that and then ask of one the impossible.

She had been like that afresh on the morrow; and so for the hour they had been able to float in the mere joy of contact—such contact as their situation in pictured public halls permitted. This poor makeshift for closeness confessed itself in truth, by twenty small signs of unrest even on Kate's part, inadequate; so little could a decent interest in the interesting place presume to remind them of its claims. They had met there in order not to meet in the streets and not again, with an equal want of invention and of style, at a railway-station; not again, either, in Kensington Gardens, which, they could easily and tacitly agree, would have had too much of the taste of their old frustrations. The present taste, the taste that morning in the pictured halls, had been a variation; yet Densher had at the end of a quarter of an hour fully known what to conclude from it. This fairly consoled him for their awkwardness, as if he had been watching it affect her. She might be as nobly charming as she liked, and he had seen nothing to touch her in the States; she couldn't pretend that in such conditions as those she herself *believed* it enough to appease him. She couldn't pretend she believed he would believe it enough to render her a like service. It wasn't enough for that purpose—she as good as showed him it wasn't. That was what he could be glad, by demonstration, to have brought her to. He would have said to her had he put it crudely and on the spot: "*Now* am I to understand you that you consider this sort of thing can go on?" It would have been open to her, no doubt, to reply that to have him with her again, to have him all kept and treasured, so still, under her grasping hand, as she had held him in their yearning interval, was a sort of thing that he must allow her to have no quarrel about; but that would be a mere gesture of her grace, a mere sport of her subtlety. She knew as well as he what they wanted; in spite of which indeed he scarce could have said how beautifully he mightn't once more have named it and urged it if she hadn't, at a given moment, blurred, as it were, the accord. They had soon seated themselves for better talk, and so they had remained a while, intimate and superficial. The immediate things to say had been many, for they hadn't exhausted them at Euston. They drew upon them freely now, and Kate appeared quite to forget—which was prodigiously becoming to her—to look about for surprises. He was to try afterwards, and try in vain, to remember what speech or what silence of his own, what natural sign of the eyes or accidental touch of the hand, had precipitated for her, in the midst of this, a sudden different impulse. She had got up, with inconsequence, as if to break the charm, though he wasn't aware of what he had done at the moment to make the charm a danger. She had patched it up agreeably enough the next minute by some odd remark about some picture, to which he hadn't so much as replied; it being quite independently of this that he had himself exclaimed on the dreadful closeness of the rooms. He had observed that they must go out again to breathe; and it was as if their common consciousness, while they passed into another part, was that of persons who, infinitely engaged together, had been startled and were trying to look natural. It was probably while they were so occupied—as the young man subsequently reconceived—that they had stumbled upon his little New York friend. He thought of her for some reason as little, though she was of

about Kate's height, to which, any more than to any other felicity
in his mistress, he had never applied the diminutive.

What was to be in the retrospect more distinct to him was the
process by which he had become aware that Kate's acquaintance
with her was greater than he had gathered. She had written of it in
due course as a new and amusing one, and he had written back
that he had met over there, and that he much liked, the young person; whereupon she had answered that he must find out about her
at home. Kate, in the event, however, had not returned to that, and
he had of course, with so many things to find out about, been otherwise taken up. Little Miss Theale's individual history was not
stuff for his newspaper; besides which, moreover, he was seeing
but too many little Miss Theales. They even went so far as to impose themselves as one of the groups of social phenomena that fell
into the scheme of his public letters. For this group in especial
perhaps—the irrepressible, the supereminent young persons—his
best pen was ready. Thus it was that there could come back to him
in London, an hour or two after their luncheon with the American
pair, the sense of a situation for which Kate hadn't wholly prepared him. Possibly indeed as marked as this was his recovered
perception that preparations, of more than one kind, had been exactly what, both yesterday and to-day, he felt her as having in hand.
That appearance in fact, if he dwelt on it, so ministered to apprehension as to require some brushing away. He shook off the suspicion to some.extent, on their separating first from their hostesses
and then from each other, by the aid of a long and rather aimless
walk. He was to go to the office later, but he had the next two or
three hours, and he gave himself as a pretext that he had eaten
much too much. After Kate had asked him to put her into a cab—
which, as an announced, a resumed policy on her part, he found
himself deprecating—he stood a while by a corner and looked
vaguely forth at his London. There was always doubtless a moment for the absentee recaptured—*the* moment, that of the reflux
of the first emotion—at which it was beyond disproof that one was
back. His full parenthesis was closed, and he was once more but a
sentence, of a sort, in the general text, the text that, from his momentary street-corner, showed as a great grey page of print that
somehow managed to be crowded without being "fine." The grey,

however, was more or less the blur of a point of view not yet quite seized again; and there would be colour enough to come out. He was back, flatly enough, but back to possibilities and prospects, and the ground he now somewhat sightlessly covered was the act of renewed possession.

He walked northward without a plan, without suspicion, quite in the direction his little New York friend, in her restless ramble, had taken a day or two before. He reached, like Milly, the Regent's Park; and though he moved further and faster he finally sat down, like Milly, from the force of thought. For him too in this position, be it added—and he might positively have occupied the same bench—various troubled fancies folded their wings. He had no more yet said what he really wanted than Kate herself had found time. She should hear enough of that in a couple of days. He had practically not pressed her as to what most concerned them; it had seemed so to concern them during these first hours but to hold each other, spiritually speaking, close. This at any rate was palpable, that there were at present more things rather than fewer between them. The explanation about the two ladies would be part of the lot, yet could wait with all the rest. They were not meanwhile certainly what most made him roam—the missing explanations weren't. That was what she had so often said before, and always with the effect of suddenly breaking off: "Now please call me a good cab." Their previous encounters, the times when they had reached in their stroll the south side of the park, had had a way of winding up with this special irrelevance. It was effectively what most divided them, for he would generally, but for her reasons, have been able to jump in with her. What did she think he wished to do to her?—it was a question he had had occasion to put. A small matter, however, doubtless—since, when it came to that, they didn't depend on cabs good or bad for the sense of union: its importance was less from the particular loss than as a kind of irritating mark of her expertness. This expertness, under providence, had been great from the first, so far as joining him was concerned; and he was critical only because it had been still greater, even from the first too, in respect to leaving him. He had put the question to her again that afternoon, on the repetition of her appeal—had asked her once more what she supposed he wished to do. He recalled, on his bench in the Regent's Park, the freedom of fancy, funny and pretty, with which she had answered; recalled the moment itself, while the usual hansom charged them, during which he felt himself, disappointed as he was, grimacing back at the superiority of her very "humour," in its added grace of gaiety, to the celebrated solemn American. Their fresh appointment had been at all events by that time made, and he should see what her choice in respect to it—a surprise as well as a relief—would do toward really simplifying. It meant either new help or new hindrance, though it took them at least out of the streets. And her naming this privilege had naturally made him ask if Mrs. Lowder knew of his return.

"Not from me," Kate had replied. "But I shall speak to her now." And she had argued, as with rather a quick fresh view, that it would now be quite easy. "We've behaved for months so properly that I've margin surely for my mention of you. You'll come to see *her*, and she'll leave you with me; she'll show her good nature, and her lack of betrayed fear, in that. With her, you know, you've never broken, quite the contrary, and she likes you as much as ever. We're leaving town; it will be the end; just now therefore it's nothing to ask. I'll ask to-night," Kate had wound up, "and if you'll leave it to me—my cleverness, I assure you, has grown infernal—I'll make it all right."

He had of course thus left it to her and he was wondering more about it now than he had wondered there in Brook Street. He repeated to himself that if it wasn't in the line of triumph it was in the line of muddle. This indeed, no doubt, was as a part of his wonder for still other questions. Kate had really got off without meeting his little challenge about the terms of their intercourse with her dear Milly. Her dear Milly, it was sensible, *was* somehow in the picture. Her dear Milly, popping up in his absence, occupied—he couldn't have said quite why he felt it—more of the foreground than one would have expected her in advance to find clear. She took up room, and it was almost as if room had been made for her. Kate had appeared to take for granted he would know why it had been made; but that was just the point. It was a foreground in which he himself, in which his connexion with Kate, scarce enjoyed a space to turn round. But Miss Theale was perhaps at the present juncture a possibility of the same sort as the softened, if not the squared, Aunt Maud. It might be true of her also that if she weren't a bore she'd be a convenience. It rolled over him of a sudden, after he had resumed his walk, that this might easily be what Kate had meant. The charming girl adored her—Densher had for himself made out that—and would protect, would lend a hand, to their interviews. These might take place, in other words, on her premises, which would remove them still better from the streets. *That* was an explanation which did hang together. It was impaired a little, of a truth, by this fact that their next encounter was rather markedly not to depend upon her. Yet this fact in turn would be accounted for by the need of more preliminaries. One of the things he conceivably should gain on Thursday at Lancaster Gate would be a further view of that propriety.

— II —

It was extraordinary enough that he should actually be finding himself, when Thursday arrived, none so wide of the mark. Kate hadn't come all the way to this for him, but she had come to a good deal by the end of a quarter of an hour. What she had begun with was her surprise at her appearing to have left him on Tuesday anything more to understand. The parts, as he now saw, under her hand, did fall more or less together, and it wasn't even as if she had spent the interval in twisting and fitting them. She was bright and handsome, not fagged and worn, with the general clearness; for it certainly stuck out enough that if the American ladies themselves weren't to be squared, which was absurd, they fairly imposed the necessity of trying Aunt Maud again. One couldn't say to them, kind as she had been to them: "We'll meet, please, whenever you'll let us, at your house; but we count on you to help us to keep it secret." They must in other terms inevitably speak to Aunt Maud—it would be of the last awkwardness to ask them not to: Kate had embraced all this in her choice of speaking first. What Kate embraced altogether was indeed wonderful today for Densher, though he perhaps struck himself rather as getting it out of her piece by piece than as receiving it in a steady light. He had always felt, however, that the more he asked of her the more he found her prepared, as he imaged it, to hand out. He had said to her more than once even before his absence: "You keep the key of the cupboard, and I foresee that when we're married you'll dole me out my sugar by lumps." She had replied that she rejoiced in his assumption that sugar would be his diet, and the domestic arrangement so prefigured might have seemed already to prevail. The supply from the cupboard at this hour was doubtless, of a truth, not altogether cloyingly sweet; but it met in a manner his immediate requirements. If her explanations at any rate prompted questions the questions no more exhausted them than they exhausted her patience. And they were naturally, of the series, the simpler; as for instance in his taking it from her that Miss Theale then could do nothing for them. He frankly brought out what he had ventured to think possible. "If we can't meet here and we've really exhausted the charms of the open air and the crowd, some such little raft in the wreck, some occasional opportunity like that of Tuesday, has been present to me these two days as better than nothing. But if our friends are so accountable to this house of course there's no more to be said. And it's one more nail, thank God, in the coffin of our odious delay." He was but too glad without more ado to point the moral. "Now I hope you see we can't work it anyhow."

If she laughed for this—and her spirits seemed really high—it was because of the opportunity that, at the hotel, he had most shown himself as enjoying. "Your idea's beautiful when one remembers that you hadn't a word except for Milly." But she was as beautifully good-humoured. "You might of course get used to her—you *will*. You're quite right—so long as they're with us or near us." And she put it, lucidly, that the dear things couldn't *help*, simply as charming friends, giving them a lift. "They'll speak to Aunt Maud, but they won't shut their doors to us: that would be another matter. A friend always helps—and she's a friend." She had left Mrs. Stringham by this time out of the question; she had reduced it to Milly. "Besides, she particularly likes us. She particularly likes *you*. I say, old boy, make something of that." He felt her dodging the ultimatum he had just made sharp, his definite re-

minder of how little, at the best, they could work it; but there were
certain of his remarks—those mostly of the sharper penetration—
that it had been quite her practice from the first not formally, not
reverently to notice. She showed the effect of them in ways less
trite. This was what happened now: he didn't think in truth that
she wasn't really minding. She took him up, none the less, on a
minor question. "You say we can't meet here, but you see it's just
what we do. What could be more lovely than this?"

It wasn't to torment him—that again he didn't believe; but he
had to come to the house in some discomfort, so that he frowned
a little at her calling it thus a luxury. Wasn't there an element in it
of coming back into bondage? The bondage might be veiled and
varnished, but he knew in his bones how little the very highest
privileges of Lancaster Gate could ever be a sign of their freedom.
They were upstairs, in one of the smaller apartments of state, a
room arranged as a boudoir, but visibly unused—it defied familiarity—and furnished in the ugliest of blues. He had immediately
looked with interest at the closed doors, and Kate had met his interest with the assurance that it was all right, that Aunt Maud did
them justice—so far, that was, as this particular time was concerned; that they should be alone and have nothing to fear. But
the fresh allusion to this that he had drawn from her acted on him
now more directly, brought him closer still to the question. They
were alone—it *was* all right: he took in anew the shut doors and the
permitted privacy, the solid stillness of the great house. They connected themselves on the spot with something made doubly vivid
in him by the whole present play of her charming strong will.
What it amounted to was that he couldn't have her—hanged if he
could!—evasive. He couldn't and he wouldn't—wouldn't have
her inconvenient and elusive. He didn't want her deeper than
himself, fine as it might be as wit or as character; he wanted to
keep her where their communications would be straight and easy
and their intercourse independent. The effect of this was to make
him say in a moment: "Will you take me just as I am?"

She turned a little pale for the tone of truth in it—which qualified to his sense delightfully the strength of her will; and the
pleasure he found in this was not the less for her breaking out after
an instant into a strain that stirred him more than any she had ever

used with him. "Ah do let me try myself! I assure you I see my
way—so don't spoil it: wait for me and give me time. Dear man,"
Kate said, "only believe in me, and it will be beautiful."

He hadn't come back to hear her talk of his believing in her as
if he didn't; but he had come back—and it all was upon him
now—to seize her with a sudden intensity that her manner of
pleading with him had made, as happily, appeared, irresistible.
He laid strong hands upon her to say, almost in anger, "Do you
love me, love me, love me?" and she closed her eyes as with the
sense that he might strike her but that she could gratefully take it.
Her surrender was her response, her response her surrender; and,
though scarce hearing what she said, he so profited by these
things that it could for the time be ever so intimately appreciable
to him that he was keeping her. The long embrace in which they
held each other was the rout of evasion, and he took from it the
certitude that what she had from him was real to her. It was
stronger than an uttered vow, and the name he was to give it in af-
terthought was that she had been sublimely sincere. *That* was all
he asked—sincerity making a basis that would bear almost anything. This settled so much, and settled it so thoroughly, that
there was nothing left to ask her to swear to. Oaths and vows apart,
now they could talk. It seemed in fact only now that their questions were put on the table. He had taken up more expressly at
the end of five minutes her plea for her own plan, and it was
marked that the difference made by the passage just enacted was
a difference in favour of her choice of means. Means had somehow suddenly become a detail—her province and her care; it had
grown more consistently vivid that her intelligence was one with
her passion. "I certainly don't want," he said—and he could say it
with a smile of indulgence—"to be all the while bringing it up
that I don't trust you."

"I should hope not! What do you think I want to do?"

He had really at this to make out a little what he thought, and
the first thing that put itself in evidence was of course the oddity,
after all, of their game, to which he could but frankly allude.
"We're doing, at the best, in trying to temporise in so special a way,
a thing most people would call us fools for." But his visit passed,
all the same, without his again attempting to make "just as he was"

serve. He had no more money just as he was than he had had just as he had been, or than he should have, probably, when it came to that, just as he always would be; whereas she, on her side, in comparison with her state of some months before, had measureably more to relinquish. He easily saw how their meeting at Lancaster Gate gave more of an accent to that quantity than their meeting at stations or in parks; and yet on the other hand he couldn't urge this against it. If Mrs. Lowder was indifferent her indifference added in a manner to what Kate's taking him as he was would call on her to sacrifice. Such in fine was her art with him that she seemed to put the question of their still waiting into quite other terms than the terms of ugly blue, of florid Sèvres,* of complicated brass, in which their boudoir expressed it. She said almost all in fact by saying, on this article of Aunt Maud, after he had once more pressed her, that when he should see her, as must inevitably soon happen, he would understand. "Do you mean," he asked at this, "that there's any *definite* sign of her coming round? I'm not talking," he explained, "of mere hypocrisies in her, or mere brave duplicities. Remember, after all, that supremely clever as we are, and as strong a team, I admit, as there is going—remember that she can play with us quite as much as we play with her."

"She doesn't want to play with *me*, my dear," Kate lucidly replied; "she doesn't want to make me suffer a bit more than she need. She cares for me too much, and everything she does or doesn't do has a value. *This* has a value—her being as she has been about us to-day. I believe she's in her room, where she's keeping strictly to herself while you're here with me. But that isn't 'playing'—not a bit."

"What is it then," the young man returned—"from the moment it isn't her blessing and a cheque?"

Kate was complete. "It's simply her absence of smallness. There is something in her above trifles. She *generally* trusts us; she doesn't propose to hunt us into corners; and if we frankly ask for a thing—why," said Kate, "she shrugs, but she lets it go. She has really but one fault—she's indifferent, on such ground as she has

*Allusion to Aunt Maud's expensive porcelain from Sèvres, France.

taken about us, to details. However," the girl cheerfully went on, "it isn't in detail we fight her."

"It seems to me," Densher brought out after a moment's thought of this, "that it's in detail we deceive her"—a speech that, as soon as he had uttered it, applied itself for him, as also visibly for his companion, to the afterglow of their recent embrace.

Any confusion attaching to this adventure, however, dropped from Kate, whom, as he could see with sacred joy, it must take more than that to make compunctious. "I don't say we can do it again. I mean," she explained, "meet here."

Densher indeed had been wondering where they could do it again. If Lancaster Gate was so limited that issue reappeared. "I mayn't come back at all?"

"Certainly—to see her. It's she, really," his companion smiled, "who's in love with you."

But it made him—a trifle more grave—look at her a moment. "Don't make out, you know, that every one's in love with me."

She hesitated. "I don't say every one."

"You said just now Miss Theale."

"I said she liked you—yes."

"Well, it comes to the same thing." With which, however, he pursued: "Of course I ought to thank Mrs. Lowder in person. I mean for *this*—as from myself."

"Ah but, you know, not too much!" She had an ironic gaiety for the implications of his "this," besides wishing to insist on a general prudence. "She'll wonder what you're thanking her for!"

Densher did justice to both considerations. "Yes, I can't very well tell her all."

It was perhaps because he said it so gravely that Kate was again in a manner amused. Yet she gave out light. "You can't very well 'tell' her anything, and that doesn't matter. Only be nice to her. Please her; make her see how clever you are—only without letting her see that you're trying. If you're charming to her you've nothing else to do."

But she oversimplified too. "I can be 'charming' to her, so far as I see, only by letting her suppose I give you up—which I'll be hanged if I do! It *is*," he said with feeling, "a game."

"Of course it's a game. But she'll never suppose you give me up—or I give *you*—if you keep reminding her how you enjoy our interviews."

"Then if she has to see us as obstinate and constant," Densher asked, "what good does it do?"

Kate was for a moment checked. "What good does what—?"

"Does my pleasing her—does anything. I *can't*," he impatiently declared, "please her."

Kate looked at him hard again, disappointed at his want of consistency; but it appeared to determine in her something better than a mere complaint. "Then *I* can! Leave it to me." With which she came to him under the compulsion, again, that had united them shortly before, and took hold of him in her urgency to the same tender purpose. It was her form of entreaty renewed and repeated, which made after all, as he met it, their great fact clear. And it somehow clarified *all* things so to possess each other. The effect of it was that, once more, on these terms, he could only be generous. He had so on the spot then left everything to her that she reverted in the course of a few moments to one of her previous—and as positively seemed—her most precious ideas. "You accused me just now of saying that Milly's in love with you. Well, if you come to that, I do say it. So there you are. That's the good she'll do us. It makes a basis for her seeing you—so that she'll help us to go on."

Densher stared—she was wondrous all round. "And what sort of a basis does it make for my seeing *her?*"

"Oh I don't mind!" Kate smiled.

"Don't mind my leading her on?"

She put it differently. "Don't mind her leading *you*."

"Well, she won't—so it's nothing not to mind. But how can that 'help,'" he pursued, "with what she knows?"

"What she knows? That needn't prevent."

He wondered. "Prevent her loving us?"

"Prevent her helping you. She's *like* that," Kate Croy explained.

It took indeed some understanding. "Making nothing of the fact that I love another?"

"Making everything," said Kate. "To console you."

"But for what?"

"For not getting your other."

He continued to stare. "But how does she know—?"

"That you *won't* get her? She doesn't; but on the other hand she doesn't know you will. Meanwhile she sees you baffled, for she knows of Aunt Maud's stand. *That*"—Kate was lucid—"gives her the chance to be nice to you."

"And what does it give *me*," the young man none the less rationally asked, "the chance to be? A brute of a humbug to her?"

Kate so possessed her facts, as it were, that she smiled at his violence. "You'll extraordinarily like her. She's exquisite. And there are reasons. I mean others."

"What others?"

"Well, I'll tell you another time.[17] Those I give you," the girl added, "are enough to go on with."

"To go on to what?"

"Why, to seeing her again—say as soon as you can: which, moreover, on all grounds, is no more than decent of you."

He of course took in her reference, and he had fully in mind what had passed between them in New York. It had been no great quantity, but it had made distinctly at the time for his pleasure; so that anything in the nature of an appeal in the name of it could have a slight kindling consequence. "Oh I shall naturally call again without delay. Yes," said Densher, "her being in love with me is nonsense; but I must, quite independently of that, make every acknowledgement of favours received."

It appeared practically all Kate asked. "Then you see. I shall meet you there."

"I don't quite see," he presently returned, "why she should wish to receive *you* for it."

"She receives me for myself—that is for *her* self. She thinks no end of me. That I should have to drum it into you!"

Yet still he didn't take it. "Then I confess she's beyond me."

Well, Kate could but leave it as she saw it. "She regards me as already—in these few weeks—her dearest friend. It's quite separate. We're in, she and I, ever so deep." And it was to confirm this that, as if it had flashed upon her that he was somewhere at sea, she threw out at last her own real light. "She doesn't of course know I care for *you*. She thinks I care so little that it's not worth speaking of." That he *had* been somewhere at sea these remarks made quickly clear, and Kate hailed the effect with surprise. "Have you been supposing that she does know—?"

"About our situation? Certainly, if you're such friends as you show me—and if you haven't otherwise represented it to her." She uttered at this such a sound of impatience that he stood artlessly vague. "You *have* denied it to her?"

She threw up her arms at his being so backward. "'Denied it'? My dear man, we've never spoken of you."

"Never, never?"

"Strange as it may appear to your glory—never."

He couldn't piece it together. "But won't Mrs. Lowder have spoken?"

"Very probably. But of *you*. Not of me."

This struck him as obscure. "How does she know me but as part and parcel of you?"

"How?" Kate triumphantly asked. "Why exactly to make nothing of it, to have nothing to do with it, to stick consistently to her line about it. Aunt Maud's line is to keep all reality out of our relation—that is out of my being in danger from you—by not having so much as suspected or heard of it. She'll get rid of it, as she believes, by ignoring it and sinking it—if she only does so hard enough. Therefore *she*, in her manner, 'denies' it if you will. That's how she knows you otherwise than as part and parcel of me. She won't for a moment have allowed either to Mrs. Stringham or to Milly that I've in any way, as they say, distinguished you."

"And you don't suppose," said Densher, "that, they must have made it out for themselves?"

"No, my dear, I don't; not even," Kate declared, "after Milly's so funnily bumping against us on Tuesday."

"She doesn't see from *that*—?"

"That you're, so to speak, mad about me. Yes, she sees, no doubt, that you regard me with a complacent eye—for you show it, I think, always too much and too crudely. But nothing beyond that. *I* don't show it too much; I don't perhaps—to please you completely where others are concerned—show it enough."

"Can you show it or not as you like?" Densher demanded.

It pulled her up a little, but she came out resplendent. "Not where *you* are concerned. Beyond seeing that you're rather gone," she went on, "Milly only sees that I'm decently good to you."

"Very good indeed she must think it!"

"Very good indeed then. She easily sees me," Kate smiled, "as very good indeed."

The young man brooded. "But in a sense to take some explaining."

"Then I explain." She was really fine; it came back to her essential plea for her freedom of action and his beauty of trust. "I mean," she added, "I *will* explain."

"And what will *I* do?"

"Recognise the difference it must make if she thinks." But here in truth Kate faltered. It was his silence alone that, for the moment, took up her apparent meaning; and before he again spoke she had returned to remembrance and prudence. They were now not to forget that, Aunt Maud's liberality having put them on their honour, they mustn't spoil their case by abusing it. He must leave her in time; they should probably find it would help them. But she came back to Milly too. "Mind you go to see her."

Densher still, however, took up nothing of this. "Then I may come again?"

"For Aunt Maud—as much as you like. But we can't again," said Kate, "play her *this* trick. I can't see you here alone."

"Then where?"

"Go to see Milly," she for all satisfaction repeated.

"And what good will that do me?"

"Try it and you'll see."

"You mean you'll manage to be there?" Densher asked. "Say you are, how will that give us privacy?"

"Try it—you'll see," the girl once more returned. "We must manage as we can."

"That's precisely what *I* feel. It strikes me we might manage better." His idea of this was a thing that made him an instant hesitate; yet he brought it out with conviction. "Why won't you come to *me?*"

It was a question her troubled eyes seemed to tell him he was scarce generous in expecting her definitely to answer, and by looking to him to wait at least she appealed to something that she presently made him feel as his pity. It was on that special shade of tenderness that he thus found himself thrown back; and while he asked of his spirit and of his flesh just what concession they could arrange she pressed him yet again on the subject of her singular remedy for their embarrassment. It might have been irritating had she ever struck him as having in her mind a stupid corner. "You'll see," she said, "the difference it will make."

Well, since she wasn't stupid she was intelligent; it was he who was stupid—the proof of which was that he would do what she liked. But he made a last effort to understand, her allusion to the "difference" bringing him round to it. He indeed caught at something subtle but strong even as he spoke. "Is what you meant a moment ago that the difference will be in her being made to believe you hate me?"

Kate, however, had simply, for this gross way of putting it, one of her more marked shows of impatience; with which in fact she sharply closed their discussion. He opened the door on a sign from her, and she accompanied him to the top of the stairs with an air of having so put their possibilities before him that questions were idle and doubts peryerse. "I verily believe I *shall* hate you if you spoil for me the beauty of what I see!"

— III —

He was really, notwithstanding, to hear more from her of what she saw; and the very next occasion had for him still other surprises than that. He received from Mrs. Lowder on the morning after his visit to Kate the telegraphic expression of a hope that he might be free to dine with them that evening; and his freedom affected him as fortunate even though in some degree qualified by her missive. "Expecting American friends whom I'm so glad to find you know!" His knowledge of American friends was clearly an accident of which he was to taste the fruit to the last bitterness. This apprehension, however, we hasten to add, enjoyed for him, in the immediate event, a certain merciful shrinkage; the immediate event being that, at Lancaster Gate, five minutes after his due arrival, prescribed him for eight-thirty, Mrs. Stringham came in alone. The long daylight, the postponed lamps, the habit of the hour, made dinners late and guests still later; so that, punctual as he was, he had found Mrs. Lowder alone, with Kate herself not yet in the field. He had thus had with her several bewildering moments—bewildering by reason, fairly, of their tacit invitation to him to be supernaturally simple. This was exactly, goodness knew, what he wanted to be; but he had never had it so largely and freely—*so* supernaturally simply, for that matter—imputed to him as of easy achievement. It was a particular in which Aunt Maud appeared to offer herself as an example, appeared to say quite agreeably: "What I want of you, don't you see? is to be just exactly as *I* am." The quantity of the article required was what might especially have caused him to stagger—he liked so, in general, the quantities in which Mrs. Lowder dealt. He would have liked as well to ask her how feasible she supposed it for a poor young man to resemble her at any point; but he had after all soon enough perceived that he was doing as she wished by letting his wonder show just a little as silly. He was conscious moreover of a small strange dread of the results of discussion with her—strange, truly, because it was her good nature, not her asperity, that he feared. Asperity might have made him angry—in which there was always a comfort; good nature, in his conditions, had a tendency to make him ashamed—which Aunt Maud indeed, wonderfully, liking him for himself, quite struck him as having guessed. To spare him therefore she also avoided discussion; she kept him down by refusing to quarrel with him. This was what she now proposed to him to enjoy, and his secret discomfort was his sense that on the whole it was what would best suit him. Being kept down was a bore, but his great dread, verily, was of being ashamed, which was a thing distinct; and it mattered but little that he was ashamed of that too.

It was of the essence of his position that in such a house as this the tables could always be turned on him. "What do you offer, what do you offer?"—the place, however muffled in convenience and decorum, constantly hummed for him with that thick irony. The irony was a renewed reference to obvious bribes, and he had already seen how little aid came to him from denouncing the bribes as ugly in form. That was what the precious metals—they alone—could afford to be; it was vain enough for him accordingly to try to impart a gloss to his own comparative brummagem.* The humiliation of this impotence was precisely what Aunt Maud sought to mitigate for him by keeping him down; and as her effort to that end had doubtless never yet been so visible he had probably never felt so definitely placed in the world as while he waited with her for her half-dozen other guests. She welcomed him genially back from the States, as to his view of which her few questions, though not coherent, were comprehensive, and he had the amusement of seeing in her, as through a clear glass, the outbreak of a plan and the sudden consciousness of a curiosity. She became aware of America, under his eyes, as a possible scene for social operations; the idea of a visit to the wonderful country had clearly but just occurred to her, yet she was talking of it, at the end of a minute, as her favourite dream. He didn't believe in it, but he pretended to; this helped her as well as anything else to treat him as harmless and blameless. She was so engaged, with the further aid of a complete absence of allusions, when the highest effect was given her method by the beautiful entrance of Kate. The method therefore received support all round, for no young man could have been less formidably than the person to the relief of whose shyness her niece ostensibly came. The ostensible, in Kate, struck him altogether, on this occasion, as prodigious; while scarcely less prodigious, for that matter, was his own reading, on the spot, of the relation between his companions—a relation lighted for him by the straight look, not exactly loving nor lingering, yet searching and soft, that, on the part of their hostess, the girl had to reckon with as she advanced. It took her in from head to foot, and in doing so it told a story that made poor Densher again the least bit sick: it marked so something with which Kate habitually and consummately reckoned.

That was the story—that she was always, for her beneficent dragon, under arms; living up, every hour, but especially at festal hours, to the "value" Mrs. Lowder had attached to her. High and fixed, this estimate ruled on each occasion at Lancaster Gate the

---

*Tawdry beginnings.

social scene; so that he now recognised in it something like the
artistic idea, the plastic substance, imposed by tradition, by genius,
by criticism, in respect to a given character, on a distinguished actress. As such a person was to dress the part, to walk, to look, to
speak, in every way to express, the part, so all this was what Kate
was to do for the character she had undertaken, under her aunt's
roof, to represent. It was made up, the character, of definite elements and touches—things all perfectly ponderable to criticism;
and the way for her to meet criticism was evidently at the start to
be sure her make-up had had the last touch and that she looked at
least no worse than usual. Aunt Maud's appreciation of that to-
night was indeed managerial, and the performer's own contribution fairly that of the faultless soldier on parade. Densher saw
himself for the moment as in his purchased stall at the play; the
watchful manager was in the depths of a box and the poor actress
in the glare of the footlights. But she *passed*, the poor performer—
he could see how she always passed; her wig, her paint, her jewels,
every mark of her expression impeccable, and her entrance accordingly greeted with the proper round of applause. Such impressions as we thus note for Densher come and go, it must be
granted, in very much less time than notation demands; but we
may none the less make the point that there was, still further, time
among them for him to feel almost too scared to take part in the
ovation. He struck himself as having lost, for the minute, his presence of mind—so that in any case he only stared in silence at the
older woman's technical challenge and at the younger one's disciplined face. It was as if the drama—it thus came to him, for the
fact of a drama there was no blinking—was between *them*, them
quite preponderantly; with Merton Densher relegated to mere
spectatorship, a paying place in front, and one of the most expensive. This was why his appreciation had turned for the instant to
fear—had just turned, as we have said, to sickness; and in spite of
the fact that the disciplined face did offer him over the footlights,
as he believed, the small gleam, fine faint but exquisite, of a special intelligence. So might a practised performer, even when raked
by double-barrelled glasses, seem to be all in her part and yet con-
vey a sign to the person in the house she loved best.

The drama, at all events, as Densher saw it, meanwhile went

on—amplified soon enough by the advent of two other guests,
stray gentlemen both, stragglers in the rout of the season, who visibly presented themselves to Kate during the next moments as subjects for a like impersonal treatment and sharers in a like usual
mercy. At opposite ends of the social course, they displayed, in respect to the "figure" that each, in his way, made, one the expansive, the other the contractile effect of the perfect white waistcoat.
A scratch company of two innocuous youths and a pacified veteran
was therefore what now offered itself to Mrs. Stringham, who rus-
tled in a little breathless and full of the compunction of having
had to come alone. Her companion, at the last moment, had been
indisposed—positively not well enough, and so had packed her
off, insistently, with excuses, with wild regrets. This circumstance
of their charming friend's illness was the first thing Kate took up
with Densher on their being able after dinner, without bravado, to
have ten minutes "naturally," as she called it—which wasn't what
he did—together; but it was already as if the young man had, by an
odd impression, throughout the meal, not been wholly deprived of
Miss Theale's participation. Mrs. Lowder had made dear Milly the
topic, and it proved, on the spot, a topic as familiar to the enthu-
siastic younger as to the sagacious older man. Any knowledge they
might lack Mrs. Lowder's niece was moreover alert to supply,
while Densher himself was freely appealed to as the most privi-
leged, after all, of the group. Wasn't it he who had in a manner invented the wonderful creature—through having seen her first,
caught her in her native jungle? Hadn't he more or less paved the
way for her by his prompt recognition of her rarity, by preceding
her, in a friendly spirit—as he had the "ear" of society—with a
sharp flashlight or two?

He met, poor Densher, these enquiries as he could, listening
with interest, yet with discomfort; wincing in particular, dry journalist as he was, to find it seemingly supposed of him that he had
put his pen—oh his "pen!"—at the service of private distinction.
The ear of society?—they were talking, or almost, as if he had publicly paragraphed a modest young lady. They dreamt dreams, in
truth, he appeared to perceive, that fairly waked *him* up, and he
settled himself in his place both to resist his embarrassment and to
catch the full revelation. His embarrassment came naturally from

the fact that if he could claim no credit for Miss Theale's success, so neither could he gracefully insist on his not having been concerned with her. What touched him most nearly was that the occasion took on somehow the air of a commemorative banquet, a feast to celebrate a brilliant if brief career. There was of course more said about the heroine than if she hadn't been absent, and he found himself rather stupefied at the range of Milly's triumph. Mrs. Lowder had wonders to tell of it; the two wearers of the waistcoat, either with sincerity or with hypocrisy, professed in the matter an equal expertness; and Densher at last seemed to know himself in presence of a social "case." It was Mrs. Stringham, obviously, whose testimony would have been most invoked hadn't she been, as her friend's representative, rather confined to the function of inhaling the incense; so that Kate, who treated her beautifully, smiling at her, cheering and consoling her across the table, appeared benevolently both to speak and to interpret for her. Kate spoke as if she wouldn't perhaps understand *their* way of appreciating Milly, but would let them none the less, in justice to their good will, express it in their coarser fashion. Densher himself wasn't unconscious in respect to this of a certain broad brotherhood with Mrs. Stringham; wondering indeed, while he followed the talk, how it might move American nerves. He had only heard of them before, but in his recent tour he had caught them in the remarkable fact, and there was now a moment or two when it came to him that he had perhaps—and not in the way of an escape—taken a lesson from them.

They quivered, clearly, they hummed and drummed, they leaped and bounded in Mrs. Stringham's typical organism—this lady striking him as before all things excited, as, in the native phrase, keyed-up, to a perception of more elements in the occasion than he was himself able to count. She was accessible to sides of it, he imagined, that were as yet obscure to him; for, though she unmistakeably rejoiced and soared, he none the less saw her at moments as even more agitated than pleasure required. It was a state of emotion in her that could scarce represent simply an impatience to report at home. Her little dry New England brightness—he had "sampled" all the shades of the American complexity, if complexity it were—had its actual reasons for finding relief most in silence; so that before the subject was changed he perceived (with surprise at the others) that they had given her enough of it. He had quite had enough of it himself by the time he was asked if it were true that their friend had really not made in her own country the mark she had chalked so large in London. It was Mrs. Lowder herself who addressed him that enquiry; while he scarce knew if he were the more impressed with her launching it under Mrs. Stringham's nose or with her hope that he would allow to London the honour of discovery. The less expansive of the white waistcoats propounded the theory that they saw in London—for all that was said—much further than in the States: it wouldn't be the first time, he urged, that they had taught the Americans to appreciate (especially when it was funny) some native product. He didn't mean that Miss Theale was funny—though she was weird, and this was precisely her magic; but it might very well be that New York, in having her to show, hadn't been aware of its luck. There *were* plenty of people who were nothing over there and yet were awfully taken up in England; just as—to make the balance right, thank goodness—they sometimes sent out beauties and celebrities who left the Briton cold. The Briton's temperature in truth wasn't to be calculated—a formulation of the matter that was not reached, however, without producing in Mrs. Stringham a final feverish sally. She announced that if the point of view for a proper admiration of her young friend *had* seemed to fail a little in New York, there was no manner of doubt of her having carried Boston by storm. It pointed the moral that Boston, for the finer taste, left New York nowhere; and the good lady, as the exponent of this doctrine—which she set forth at a certain length—made, obviously, to Densher's mind, her nearest approach to supplying the weirdness in which Milly's absence had left them deficient. She made it indeed effective for him by suddenly addressing him. "You know nothing, sir—but not the least little bit—about my friend."

He hadn't pretended he did, but there was a purity of reproach in Mrs. Stringham's face and tone, a purity charged apparently with solemn meanings; so that for a little, small as had been his claim, he couldn't but feel that she exaggerated. He wondered what she did mean, but while doing so he defended himself. "I certainly don't know enormously much—beyond her having been most kind to me, in New York, as a poor bewildered and newly landed alien, and my having tremendously appreciated it." To which he added, he scarce knew why, what had an immediate success. "Remember, Mrs. Stringham, that you weren't then present."

"Ah there you are!" said Kate with much gay expression, though what it expressed he failed at the time to make out.

"You weren't present *then*, dearest," Mrs. Lowder richly concurred. "You don't know," she continued with mellow gaiety, "how far things may have gone."

It made the little woman, he could see, really lose her head. She had more things in that head than any of them in any other; unless perhaps it were Kate, whom he felt as indirectly watching him during this foolish passage, though it pleased him—and because of the foolishness—not to meet her eyes. He met Mrs. Stringham's, which affected him: with her he could on occasion clear it up—a sense produced by the mute communion between them and really the beginning, as the event was to show, of something extraordinary. It was even already a little the effect of this communion that Mrs. Stringham perceptibly faltered in her retort to Mrs. Lowder's joke. "Oh it's precisely my point that Mr. Densher *can't* have had vast opportunities." And then she smiled at him. "I wasn't away, you know, long."

It made everything, in the oddest way in the world, immediately right for him. "And I wasn't *there* long, either." He positively saw with it that nothing for him, so far as she was concerned, would again be wrong. "She's beautiful, but I don't say she's easy to know."

"Ah she's a thousand and one things!" replied the good lady, as if now to keep well with him.

He asked nothing better. "She was off with you to these parts before I knew it. I myself was off too—away off to wonderful parts, where I had endlessly more to see."

"But you didn't forget her!" Aunt Maud interposed with almost menacing archness.

"No, of course I didn't forget her. One doesn't forget such

charming impressions. But I never," he lucidly maintained, "chattered to others about her."

"She'll thank you for that, sir," said Mrs. Stringham with a flushed firmness.

"Yet doesn't silence in such a case," Aunt Maud blandly enquired, "very often quite prove the depth of the impression?"

He would have been amused, hadn't he been slightly displeased, at all they seemed desirous to fasten on him. "Well, the impression was as deep as you like. But I really want Miss Theale to know," he pursued for Mrs. Stringham, "that I don't figure by any consent of my own as an authority about her."

Kate came to his assistance—if assistance it was—before their friend had had time to meet this charge. "You're right about her not being easy to know. One *sees* her with intensity—sees her more than one sees almost any one; but then one discovers that that isn't knowing her and that one may know better a person whom one doesn't 'see,' as I say, half so much."

The discrimination was interesting, but it brought them back to the fact of her success; and it was at that comparatively gross circumstance, now so fully placed before them, that Milly's anxious companion sat and looked—looked very much as some spectator in an old-time circus might have watched the oddity of a Christian maiden, in the arena, mildly, caressingly, martyred. It was the nosing and fumbling not of lions and tigers but of domestic animals let loose as for the joke. Even the joke made Mrs. Stringham uneasy, and her mute communion with Densher, to which we have alluded, was more and more determined by it. He wondered afterwards if Kate had made this out; though it was not indeed till much later on that he found himself, in thought, dividing the things she might have been conscious of from the things she must have missed. If she actually missed, at any rate, Mrs. Stringham's discomfort, that but showed how her own idea held her. Her own idea was, by insisting on the fact of the girl's prominence as a feature of the season's end, to keep Densher in relation, for the rest of them, both to present and to past. "It's everything that has happened *since* that makes you naturally a little shy about her. You don't know what has happened since, but we do; we've seen it and followed it; we've a little been *of* it." The

great thing for him, at this, as Kate gave it, *was* in fact quite irresistibly that the case was a real one—the kind of thing that, when
one's patience was shorter than one's curiosity, one had vaguely
taken for possible in London, but in which one had never been
even to this small extent concerned. The little American's sudden
social adventure, her happy and, no doubt, harmless flourish, had
probably been favoured by several accidents, but it had been
favoured above all by the simple spring-board of the scene, by one
of those common caprices of the numberless foolish flock, gregarious movements as inscrutable as ocean-currents. The huddled herd had drifted to her blindly—it might as blindly have
drifted away. There had been of course a signal, but the great reason was probably the absence at the moment of a larger lion. The
bigger beast would come and the smaller would then inconti-
nently vanish. It was at all events characteristic, and what was of
the essence of it was grist to his scribbling mill, matter for his jour-
nalising hand. That hand already, in intention, played over it, the
"motive," as a sign of the season, a feature of the time, of the
purely expeditious and rough-and-tumble nature of the social
boom. The boom as in *itself* required—that would be the note;
the subject of the process a comparatively minor question. Anything was boomable enough when nothing else was more so: the
author of the "rotten" book, the beauty who was no beauty, the
heiress who was only that, the stranger who was for the most part
saved from being inconveniently strange but by being inconveniently familiar, the American whose Americanism had been
long desperately discounted, the creature in fine as to whom
spangles or spots of any sufficiently marked and exhibited sort
could be loudly enough predicated.

So he judged at least, within his limits, and the idea that what
he had thus caught in the fact was the trick of fashion and the
tone of society went so far as to make him take up again his sense
of independence. He had supposed himself civilised; but if this
was civilisation—! One could smoke one's pipe outside when
twaddle was within. He had rather avoided, as we have remarked,
Kate's eyes, but there came a moment when he would fairly have
liked to put it, across the table, to her: "I say, light of my life, is
this the great world?" There came another, it must be added—

and doubtless as a result of something that, over the cloth, did hang between them—when she struck him as having quite answered: "Dear no—for what do you take me? Not the least little bit: only a poor silly, though quite harmless, imitation." What she might have passed for saying, however, was practically merged in what she did say, for she came overtly to his aid, very much as if guessing some of his thoughts. She enunciated, to relieve his bewilderment, the obvious truth that you couldn't leave London for three months at that time of the year and come back to find your friends just where they were. As they had *of course* been jigging away they might well be so red in the face that you wouldn't know them. She reconciled in fine his disclaimer about Milly with that honour of having discovered her which it was vain for him modestly to shirk. He *had* unearthed her, but it was they, all of them together, who had developed her. She was always a charmer, one of the greatest ever seen, but she wasn't the person he had "backed."

Densher was to feel sure afterwards that Kate had had in these pleasantries no conscious, above all no insolent purpose of making light of poor Susan Shepherd's property in their young friend—which property, by such remarks, was very much pushed to the wall; but he was also to know that Mrs. Stringham had secretly resented them, Mrs. Stringham holding the opinion, of which he was ultimately to have a glimpse, that all the Kate Croys in Christendom were but dust for the feet of her Milly. That, it was true, would be what she must reveal only when driven to her last entrenchments and well cornered in her passion—the rare passion of friendship, the sole passion of her little life save the one other, more imperturbably cerebral, that she entertained for the art of Guy de Maupassant.* She slipped in the observation that her Milly was incapable of change, was just exactly, on the contrary, the same Milly; but this made little difference in the drift of Kate's contention. She was perfectly kind to Susie: it was as if she positively knew her as handicapped for any disagreement by feeling that she, Kate, had "type," and by being

_____

*French short-story writer and novelist (1850–1893) of the "naturalist" school.

committed to admiration of type. Kate had occasion subsequently—she found it somehow—to mention to our young man
Milly's having spoken to her of this view on the good lady's part.
She would like—Milly had had it from her—to put Kate Croy in
a book and see what she could so do with her. "Chop me up fine
or serve me whole"—it was a way of being got at that Kate professed she dreaded. It would be Mrs. Stringham's, however, she
understood, because Mrs. Stringham, oddly, felt that with such
stuff as the strange English girl was made of, stuff that (in spite
of Maud Manningham, who was full of sentiment) she had never
known, there was none other to be employed. These things were
of later evidence, yet Densher might even then have felt them in
the air. They were practically in it already when Kate, waiving
the question of her friend's chemical change, wound up with the
comparatively unobjectionable proposition that he must now,
having missed so much, take them all up, on trust, further on. He
met it peacefully, a little perhaps as an example to Mrs. Stringham—"Oh as far on as you like!" This even had its effect: Mrs.
Stringham appropriated as much of it as might be meant for herself. The nice thing about her was that she could measure how
much; so that by the time dinner was over they had really covered ground.

— IV —

T he younger of the other men, it afterwards appeared, was
most in his element at the piano; so that they had coffee
and comic songs upstairs—the gentlemen, temporarily re-
linquished, submitting easily in this interest to Mrs. Lowder's
parting injunction not to sit too tight. Our especial young man sat
tighter when restored to the drawing-room; he made it out perfectly with Kate that they might, off and on, foregather without of-
fence. He had perhaps stronger needs in this general respect than
she; but she had better names for the scant risks to which she consented. It was the blessing of a big house that intervals were large
and, of an August night, that windows were open; whereby, at a

given moment, on the wide balcony, with the songs sufficiently sung, Aunt Maud could hold her little court more freshly. Densher and Kate, during these moments, occupied side by side a small sofa—a luxury formulated by the latter as the proof, under criticism, of their remarkably good conscience. "To seem not to know each other—once you're here—would be," the girl said, "to overdo it"; and she arranged it charmingly that they *must* have some passage to put Aunt Maud off the scent. She would be wondering otherwise what in the world they found their account in. For Densher, none the less, the profit of snatched moments, snatched contacts, was partial and poor; there were in particular at present more things in his mind than he could bring out while watching the windows. It was true, on the other hand, that she suddenly met most of them—and more than he could see on the spot—by coming out for him with a reference to Milly that was not in the key of those made at dinner. "She's not a bit right, you know. I mean in health. Just see her to-night. I mean it looks grave. For you she would have come, you know, if it had been at all possible."

He took this in such patience as he could muster. "What in the world's the matter with her?"

But Kate continued without saying. "Unless indeed your being here has been just a reason for her funking it."

"What in the world's the matter with her?" Densher asked again.

"Why just what I've told you—that she likes you so much."

"Then why should she deny herself the joy of meeting me?"

Kate cast about—it would take so long to explain. "And perhaps it's true that she *is* bad. She easily may be."

"Quite easily, I should say, judging by Mrs. Stringham, who's visibly preoccupied and worried."

"Visibly enough. Yet it mayn't," said Kate, "be only for that."

"For what then?"

But this question too, on thinking, she neglected. "Why, if it's anything real, doesn't that poor lady go home? She'd be anxious, and she has done all she need to be civil."

"I think," Densher remarked, "she has been quite beautifully civil."

It made Kate, he fancied, look at him the least bit harder; but she was already, in a manner, explaining. "Her preoccupation is probably on two different heads. One of them would make her hurry back, but the other makes her stay. She's commissioned to tell Milly all about you."

"Well then," said the young man between a laugh and a sigh, "I'm glad I felt, downstairs, a kind of 'drawing' to her. Wasn't I rather decent to her?"

"Awfully nice. You've instincts, you fiend. It's all," Kate declared, "as it should be."

"Except perhaps," he after a moment cynically suggested, "that she isn't getting much good of me now. Will she report to Milly on *this*?" And then as Kate seemed to wonder what "this" might be: "On our present disregard for appearances."

"Ah leave appearances to me!" She spoke in her high way. "I'll make them all right. Aunt Maud, moreover," she added, "has her so engaged that she won't notice." Densher felt, with this, that his companion had indeed perceptive flights he couldn't hope to match—had for instance another when she still subjoined: "And Mrs. Stringham's appearing to respond just in order to make that impression."

"Well," Densher dropped with some humour, "life's very interesting! I hope it's really as much so for you as you make it for others; I mean judging by what you make it for me. You seem to me to represent it as thrilling for *ces dames*,* and in a different way for each: Aunt Maud, Susan Shepherd, Milly. But what *is*," he wound up, "the matter? Do you mean she's as ill as she looks?"

Kate's face struck him as replying at first that his derisive speech deserved no satisfaction; then she appeared to yield to a need of her own—the need to make the point that "as ill as she looked" was what Milly scarce could be. If she had been as ill as she looked she could scarce be a question with them, for her end would in that case be near. She believed herself nevertheless— and Kate couldn't help believing her too—seriously menaced. There was always the fact that they had been on the point of leav-

---

*These ladies (French).

ing town, the two ladies, and had suddenly been pulled up. "We bade them good-bye—or all but—Aunt Maud and I, the night before Milly, popping so very oddly into the National Gallery for a farewell look, found you and me together. They were then to get off a day or two later. But they've not got off—they're not getting off. When I see them—and I saw them this morning—they have showy reasons. They do mean to go, but they've postponed it." With which the girl brought out: "They've postponed it for *you*." He protested so far as a man might without fatuity, since a protest was itself credulous; but Kate, as ever, understood herself. "You've made Milly change her mind. She wants not to miss you—though she wants also not to show she wants you; which is why, as I hinted a moment ago, she may consciously have hung back to-night. She doesn't know when she may see you again— she doesn't know she ever may. She doesn't see the future. It has opened out before her in these last weeks as a dark confused thing."

Densher wondered. "After the tremendous time you've all been telling me she has had?"

"That's it. There's a shadow across it."

"The shadow, you consider, of some physical break-up?"

"Some physical break-down. Nothing less. She's scared. She has so much to lose. And she wants more."

"Ah well," said Densher with a sudden strange sense of discomfort, "couldn't one say to her that she can't have everything?"

"No—for one wouldn't want to. She really," Kate went on, "has been somebody here. Ask Aunt Maud—you may think me prejudiced," the girl oddly smiled. "Aunt Maud will tell you— the world's before her. It has all come since you saw her, and it's a pity you've missed it, for it certainly would have amused you. She has really been a perfect success—I mean of course so far as possible in the scrap of time—and she has taken it like a perfect angel. If you can imagine an angel with a thumping bank-account you'll have the simplest expression of the kind of thing. Her fortune's absolutely huge; Aunt Maud has had all the facts, or enough of them, in the last confidence, from 'Susie,' and Susie speaks by book. Take them then, in the last confidence, from *me*. There she is." Kate expressed above all what it most came to. "It's open to her to make, you see, the very greatest marriage. I assure you we're not vulgar about her. Her possibilities are quite plain."

Densher showed he neither disbelieved nor grudged them. "But what good then on earth can I do her?"

Well, she had it ready. "You can console her."

"And for what?"

"For all that, if she's stricken, she must see swept away. I shouldn't care for her if she hadn't so much," Kate very simply said. And then as it made him laugh not quite happily: "I shouldn't trouble about her if there were one thing she did have." The girl spoke indeed with a noble compassion. "She has nothing."

"Not all the young dukes?"

"Well we must see—see if anything can come of them. She at any rate does love life. To have met a person like you," Kate further explained, "is to have felt you become, with all the other fine things, a part of life. Oh she has you arranged!"   .

"*You* have, it strikes me, my dear"—and he looked both detached and rueful. "Pray what am I to do with the dukes?"

"Oh the dukes will be disappointed!"

"Then why shan't I be?"

"You'll have expected less," Kate wonderfully smiled. "Besides, you *will* be. You'll have expected enough for that."

"Yet it's what you want to let me in for?"

"I want," said the girl, "to make things pleasant for her. I use, for the purpose, what I have. You're what I have of most precious, and you're therefore what I use most."

He looked at her long. "I wish I could use *you* a little more." After which, as she continued to smile at him, "Is it a bad case of lungs?" he asked.

Kate showed for a little as if she wished it might be. "Not lungs, I think. Isn't consumption, taken in time, now curable?"

"People are, no doubt, patched up." But he wondered. "Do you mean she has something that's past patching?" And before she could answer: "It's really as if her appearance put her outside of such things—being, in spite of her youth, that of a person who has been through all it's conceivable she should be exposed to. She affects one, I should say, as a creature saved from a shipwreck. Such a creature may surely, in these days, on the doctrine of chances, go to sea again with confidence. She has *had* her wreck—she has met her adventure."

"Oh I grant you her wreck!"—Kate was all response so far. "But do let her have still her adventure. There are wrecks that are not adventures."

"Well—if there be also adventures that are not wrecks!" Densher in short was willing, but he came back to his point. "What I mean is that she has none of the effect—on one's nerves or whatever—of an invalid."

Kate on her side did this justice. "No—that's the beauty of her."

"The beauty—?"

"Yes, she's so wonderful. She won't show for that, any more than your watch, when it's about to stop for want of being wound up, gives you convenient notice or shows as different from usual. She won't die, she won't live, by inches. She won't smell, as it were, of drugs. She won't taste, as it were, of medicine. No one will know."

"Then what," he demanded, frankly mystified now, "are we talking about? In what extraordinary state *is* she?"

Kate went on as if, at this, making it out in a fashion for herself. "I believe that if she's ill at all she's very ill. I believe that if she's bad she's not a *little* bad. I can't tell you why, but that's how I see her. She'll really live or she'll really not. She'll have it all or she'll miss it all. Now I don't think she'll have it all."

Densher had followed this with his eyes upon her, her own having thoughtfully wandered, and as if it were more impressive than lucid. "You 'think' and you 'don't think,' and yet you remain all the while without an inkling of her complaint?"

"No, not without an inkling; but it's a matter in which I don't want knowledge. She moreover herself doesn't want one to want it: she has, as to what may be preying upon her, a kind of ferocity of modesty, a kind of—I don't know what to call it—intensity of pride. And then and then—" But with this she faltered.

"And then what?"

"I'm a brute about illness. I hate it. It's well for you, my dear," Kate continued, "that you're as sound as a bell."

"Thank you!" Densher laughed. "It's rather good then for yourself too that you're as strong as the sea."

She looked at him now a moment as for the selfish gladness of their young immunities. It was all they had together, but they had it at least without a flaw—each had the beauty, the physical felicity, the personal virtue, love and desire of the other. Yet it was as if that very consciousness threw them back the next moment into pity for the poor girl who had everything else in the world, the great genial good they, alas, didn't have, but failed on the other hand of this. "How we're talking about her!" Kate compunctiously sighed. But there were the facts. "From illness I keep away."

"But you don't—since here you are, in spite of all you say, in the midst of it."

"Ah I'm only watching—!"

"And putting me forward in your place? Thank you!"

"Oh," said Kate, "I'm breaking you in. Let it give you the measure of what I shall expect of you. One can't begin too soon."

She drew away, as from the impression of a stir on the balcony, the hand of which he had a minute before possessed himself; and the warning brought him back to attention. "You haven't even an idea if it's a case for surgery?"

"I dare say it may be; that is that if it comes to anything it may come to that. Of course she's in the highest hands."

"The doctors are after her then?"

"She's after *them*—it's the same thing. I think I'm free to say it now—she sees Sir Luke Strett."

It made him quickly wince. "Ah fifty thousand knives!" Then after an instant: "One seems to guess."

Yes, but she waved it away. "Don't guess. Only do as I tell you."

For a moment now, in silence, he took it all in, might have had it before him. "What you want of me then is to make up to a sick girl."

"Ah but you admit yourself that she doesn't affect you as sick. You understand moreover just how much—and just how little."

"It's amazing," he presently answered, "what you think I understand."

"Well, if you've brought me to it, my dear," she returned, "that has been your way of breaking *me* in. Besides which, so far as making up to her goes, plenty of others will."

Densher for a little, under this suggestion, might have been seeing their young friend on a pile of cushions and in a perpetual tea-gown, amid flowers and with drawn blinds, surrounded by the higher nobility. "Others can follow their tastes. Besides, others are free."

"But so are you, my dear!"

She had spoken with impatience, and her suddenly quitting him had sharpened it; in spite of which he kept his place, only looking up at her. "You're prodigious!"

"Of course I'm prodigious!"—and, as immediately happened, she gave a further sign of it that he fairly sat watching. The door from the lobby had, as she spoke, been thrown open for a gentleman who, immediately finding her within his view, advanced to greet her before the announcement of his name could reach her companion. Densher none the less felt himself brought quickly into relation; Kate's welcome to the visitor became almost precipitately an appeal to her friend, who slowly rose to meet it. "I don't know whether you know Lord Mark." And then for the other party: "Mr. Merton Densher—who has just come back from America."

"Oh!" said the other party while Densher said nothing—occupied as he mainly was on the spot with weighing the sound in question. He recognised it in a moment as less imponderable than it might have appeared, as having indeed positive claims. It wasn't, that is, he knew, the "Oh!" of the idiot, however great the superficial resemblance: it was that of the clever, the accomplished man; it was the very specialty of the speaker, and a deal of expensive training and experience had gone to producing it. Densher felt somehow that, as a thing of value accidentally picked up, it would retain an interest of curiosity. The three stood for a little together in an awkwardness to which he was conscious of contributing his share; Kate failing to ask Lord Mark to be seated, but letting him know that he would find Mrs. Lowder, with some others, on the balcony.

"Oh and Miss Theale I suppose?—as I seemed to hear outside, from below, Mrs. Stringham's unmistakeable voice."

"Yes, but Mrs. Stringham's alone. Milly's unwell," the girl explained, "and was compelled to disappoint us."

"Ah 'disappoint'—rather!" And, lingering a little, he kept his eyes on Densher. "She isn't really bad, I trust?"

Densher, after all he had heard, easily supposed him interested in Milly; but he could imagine him also interested in the young man with whom he had found Kate engaged and whom he yet considered without visible intelligence. That young man concluded in a moment that he was doing what he wanted, satisfying himself as to each. To this he was aided by Kate, who produced a prompt: "Oh dear no; I think not. I've just been reassuring Mr. Densher," she added—"who's as concerned as the rest of us. I've been calming his fears."

"Oh!" said Lord Mark again—and again it was just as good. That was for Densher, the latter could see, or think he saw. And then for the others: "*My* fears would want calming. We must take great care of her. This way?"

She went with him a few steps, and while Densher, hanging about, gave them frank attention, presently paused again for some further colloquy. What passed between them their observer lost, but she was presently with him again, Lord Mark joining the rest. Densher was by this time quite ready for her. "It's *he* who's your aunt's man?"

"Oh immensely."

"I mean for *you*."

"That's what I mean too," Kate smiled. "There he is. Now you can judge."

"Judge of what?"

"Judge of him."

"Why should I judge of him?" Densher asked. "I've nothing to do with him."

"Then why do you ask about him?"

"To judge of you—which is different."

Kate seemed for a little to look at the difference. "To take the measure, do you mean, of my danger?"

He hesitated; then he said: "I'm thinking, I dare say, of Miss Theale's. How does your aunt reconcile his interest in her—?"

"With his interest in me?"

"With her own interest in you," Densher said while she reflected. "If that interest—Mrs. Lowder's—takes the form of Lord Mark, hasn't he rather to look out for the forms *he* takes?"

Kate seemed interested in the question, but "Oh he takes them easily," she answered. "The beauty is that she doesn't trust him."

"That Milly doesn't?"

"Yes—Milly either. But I mean Aunt Maud. Not really."

Densher gave it his wonder. "Takes him to her heart and yet thinks he cheats?"

"Yes," said Kate—"that's the way people are. What they think of their enemies, goodness knows, is bad enough; but I'm still more struck with what they think of their friends. Milly's own state of mind, however," she went on, "is lucky. That's Aunt Maud's security, though she doesn't yet fully recognise it—besides being Milly's own."

"You conceive it a real escape then not to care for him?"

She shook her head in beautiful grave deprecation. "You oughtn't to make me say too much. But I'm glad I don't."

"Don't say too much?"

"Don't care for Lord Mark."

"Oh!" Densher answered with a sound like his lordship's own. To which he added: "You absolutely hold that that poor girl doesn't?"

"Ah you know what I hold about that poor girl!" It had made her again impatient.

Yet he stuck a minute to the subject. "You scarcely call him, I suppose, one of the dukes."

"Mercy, no—far from it. He's not, compared with other possibilities, 'in' it. Milly, it's true," she said, to be exact, "has no natural sense of social values, doesn't in the least understand our differences or know who's who or what's what."

"I see. That," Densher laughed, "is her reason for liking *me*."

"Precisely. She doesn't resemble me," said Kate, "who at least know what I lose."

Well, it had all risen for Densher to a considerable interest. "And Aunt Maud—why shouldn't *she* know? I mean that your friend there isn't really anything. Does she suppose him of ducal value?"

"Scarcely; save in the sense of being uncle to a duke. That's undeniably something. He's the best moreover we can get."

"Oh, oh!" said Densher; and his doubt was not all derisive.

"It isn't Lord Mark's grandeur," she went on without heeding this; "because perhaps in the line of that alone—as he has no money—more could be done. But she's not a bit sordid; she only counts with the sordidness of others. Besides, he's grand enough, with a duke in his family and at the other end of the string. *The* thing's his genius."

"And do you believe in that?"

"In Lord Mark's genius?" Kate, as if for a more final opinion than had yet been asked of her, took a moment to think. She balanced indeed so that one would scarce have known what to expect; but she came out in time with a very sufficient "Yes!"

"Political?"

"Universal. I don't know at least," she said, "what else to call it when a man's able to make himself without effort, without violence, without machinery of any sort, so intensely felt. He has somehow an effect without his being in any traceable way a cause."

"Ah but if the effect," said Densher with conscious superficiality, "isn't agreeable—?"

"Oh but it is!"

"Not surely for every one."

"If you mean not for you," Kate returned, "you may have reasons—and men don't count. Women don't know if it's agreeable or not."

"Then there you are!"

"Yes, precisely—that takes, on his part, genius."

Densher stood before her as if he wondered what everything she thus promptly, easily and above all amusingly met him with, would have been found, should it have come to an analysis, to "take." Something suddenly, as if under a last determinant touch, welled up in him and overflowed—the sense of his good fortune and her variety, of the future she promised, the interest she supplied. "All women but you are stupid. How can I look at another?

You're different and different—and then you're different again. No
marvel Aunt Maud builds on you—except that you're so much too
good for what she builds *for*. Even 'society' won't know how good
for it you are; it's too stupid, and you're beyond it. You'd have to
pull it uphill—it's you yourself who are at the top. The women one
meets—what are they but books one has already read? You're a
whole library of the unknown, the uncut." He almost moaned, he
ached, from the depth of his content. "Upon my word I've a sub-
scription!"

She took it from him with her face again giving out all it had in
answer, and they remained once more confronted and united
in their essential wealth of life. "It's you who draw me out. I exist
in you. Not in others."

It had been, however, as if the thrill of their association itself
pressed in him, as great felicities do, the sharp spring of fear. "See
here, you know: don't, *don't*—"

"Don't what?"

"Don't fail me. It would kill me."

She looked at him a minute with no response but her eyes. "So
you think you'll kill *me* in time to prevent it?" She smiled, but he
saw her the next instant as smiling through tears; and the instant
after this she had got, in respect to the particular point, quite off.
She had come back to another, which was one of her own; her
own were so closely connected that Densher's were at best but parenthetic. Still she had a distance to go. "You do then see your
way?" She put it to him before they joined—as was high time—
the others. And she made him understand she meant his way with
Milly.

He had dropped a little in presence of the explanation; then she
had brought him up to a sort of recognition. He could make out
by this light something of what he saw, but a dimness also there
was, undispelled since his return. "There's something you must
definitely tell me. If our friend knows that all the while—?"

She came straight to his aid, formulating for him his anxiety,
though quite to smooth it down. "All the while she and I here were
growing intimate, you and I were in unmentioned relation? If she
knows that, yes, she knows our relation must have involved your
writing to me."

"Then how could she suppose you weren't answering?"

"She doesn't suppose it."

"How then can she imagine you never named her?"

"She doesn't. She knows now I did name her. I've told her everything. She's in possession of reasons that will perfectly do."

Still he just brooded. "She takes things from you exactly as I take them?"

"Exactly as you take them."

"She's just such another victim?"

"Just such another. You're a pair."

"Then if anything happens," said Densher, "we can console each other?"

"Ah something *may* indeed happen," she returned, "if you'll only go straight!"

He watched the others an instant through the window. "What do you mean by going straight?"

"Not worrying. Doing as you like. Try, as I've told you before, and you'll see. You'll have me perfectly, always, to refer to."

"Oh rather, I hope! But if she's going away?"

It pulled Kate up but a moment. "I'll bring her back. There you are. You won't be able to say I haven't made it smooth for you."

He faced it all, and certainly it was queer. But it wasn't the queerness that after another minute was uppermost. He was in a wondrous silken web, and it was amusing. "You spoil me!"

He wasn't sure if Mrs. Lowder, who at this juncture reappeared, had caught his word as it dropped from him; probably not, he thought, her attention being given to Mrs. Stringham, with whom she came through and who was now, none too soon, taking leave of her. They were followed by Lord Mark and by the other men, but two or three things happened before any dispersal of the company began. One of these was that Kate found time to say to him with furtive emphasis: "You must go now!" Another was that she next addressed herself in all frankness to Lord Mark, drew near to him with an almost reproachful "Come and talk to *me!*"—a challenge resulting after a minute for Densher in a consciousness of their installation together in an out-of-the-way corner, though not the same he himself had just occupied with her. Still another was that Mrs. Stringham, in the random intensity of her farewells, af-

fected him as looking at him with a small grave intimation, something into which he afterwards read the meaning that if he had
happened to desire a few words with her after dinner he would
have found her ready. This impression was naturally light, but it
just left him with the sense of something by his own act over-
looked, unappreciated. It gathered perhaps a slightly sharper shade
from the mild formality of her "Good-night, sir!" as she passed
him; a matter as to which there was now nothing more to be done,
thanks to the alertness of the young man he by this time had appraised as even more harmless than himself. This personage had
forestalled him in opening the door for her and was evidently—
with a view, Densher might have judged, to ulterior designs on
Milly—proposing to attend her to her carriage. What further occurred was that Aunt Maud, having released her, immediately had
a word for himself. It was an imperative "Wait a minute," by which
she both detained and dismissed him; she was particular about her
minute, but he hadn't yet given her, as happened, a sign of withdrawal.

"Return to our little friend. You'll find her really interesting."

"If you mean Miss Theale," he said, "I shall certainly not forget
her. But you must remember that, so far as her 'interest' is concerned, I myself discovered, I—as was said at dinner—invented
her."

"Well, one seemed rather to gather that you hadn't taken out
the patent. Don't, I only mean, in the press of other things, too
much neglect her."

Affected, surprised by the coincidence of her appeal with
Kate's, he asked himself quickly if it mightn't help him with her.
He at any rate could but try. "You're all looking after my manners. That's exactly, you know, what Miss Croy has been saying
to me. *She* keeps me up—she has had so much to say about
them."

He found pleasure in being able to give his hostess an account
of his passage with Kate that, while quite veracious, might be reassuring to herself. But Aunt Maud, wonderfully and facing him
straight, took it as if her confidence were supplied with other
props. If she saw his intention in it she yet blinked neither with
doubt nor with acceptance; she only said imperturbably: "Yes,

she'll herself do anything for her friend; so that she but preaches what she practises."

Densher really quite wondered if Aunt Maud knew how far Kate's devotion went. He was moreover a little puzzled by this special harmony; in face of which he quickly asked himself if Mrs. Lowder had bethought herself of the American girl as a distraction for him, and if Kate's mastery of the subject were therefore but an appearance addressed to her aunt. What might really *become* in all this of the American girl was therefore a question that, on the latter contingency, would lose none of its sharpness. However, questions could wait, and it was easy, so far as he understood, to meet Mrs. Lowder. "It isn't a bit, all the same, you know, that I resist. I find Miss Theale charming."

Well, it was all she wanted. "Then don't miss a chance."

"The only thing is," he went on, "that she's—naturally now—leaving town and, as I take it, going abroad."

Aunt Maud looked indeed an instant as if she herself had been dealing with this difficulty. "She won't go," she smiled in spite of it, "till she has seen you. Moreover, when she does go—" She paused, leaving him uncertain. But the next minute he was still more at sea. "We shall go too."

He gave a smile that he himself took for slightly strange. "And what good will that do *me*?"

"We shall be near them somewhere, and you'll come out to us."

"Oh!" he said a little awkwardly.

"I'll see that you do. I mean I'll write to you."

"Ah thank you, thank you!" Merton Densher laughed. She was indeed putting him on his honour, and his honour winced a little at the use he rather helplessly saw himself suffering her to believe she could make of it. "There are all sorts of things," he vaguely remarked, "to consider."

"No doubt. But there's above all the great thing."

"And pray what's that?"

"Why the importance of your not losing the occasion of your life. I'm treating you handsomely, I'm looking after it for you. I *can*—I can smooth your path. She's charming, she's clever and she's good. And her fortune's a real fortune."

Ah there she was, Aunt Maud! The pieces fell together for him as he felt her thus buying him off, and buying him—it would have been funny if it hadn't been so grave—with Miss Theale's money. He ventured, derisive, fairly to treat it as extravagant. "I'm much obliged to you for the handsome offer—"

"Of what doesn't belong to me?" She wasn't abashed. "I don't say it does—but there's no reason it shouldn't to *you*. Mind you, moreover"—she kept it up—"I'm not one who talks in the air. And you owe me something—if you want to know why."

Distinct he felt her pressure; he felt, given her basis, her consistency; he even felt, to a degree that was immediately to receive an odd confirmation, her truth. Her truth, for that matter, was that she believed him bribeable: a belief that for his own mind as well, while they stood there, lighted up the impossible. What then in this light did Kate believe him? But that wasn't what he asked aloud. "Of course I know I owe you thanks for a deal of kind treatment. Your inviting me for instance to-night—!"

"Yes, my inviting you to-night's a part of it. But you don't know," she added, "how far I've gone for you."

He felt himself red and as if his honour were colouring up; but he laughed again as he could. "I see how far you're going."

"I'm the most honest woman in the world, but I've nevertheless done for you what was necessary." And then as her now quite sombre gravity only made him stare: "To start you it *was* necessary. From *me* it has the weight." He but continued to stare, and she met his blankness with surprise. "Don't you understand me? I've told the proper lie for you." Still he only showed her his flushed strained smile; in spite of which, speaking with force and as if he must with a minute's reflexion see what she meant, she turned away from him. "I depend upon you now to make me right!"

The minute's reflexion he was of course more free to take after he had left the house. He walked up the Bayswater Road, but he stopped short, under the murky stars, before the modern church, in the middle of the square that, going eastward, opened out on his left. He had had his brief stupidity, but now he understood. She had guaranteed to Milly Theale through Mrs. Stringham that Kate didn't care for him. She had affirmed through the same source that the attachment was only his. He made it out, he made it out, and he could see what she meant by its starting him. She had described Kate as merely compassionate, so that Milly might be compassionate too. "Proper" indeed it was, her lie—the very properest possible and the most deeply, richly diplomatic. So Milly was successfully deceived.

— V —

To see her alone, the poor girl, he none the less promptly felt, was to see her after all very much on the old basis, the basis of his three visits in New York; the new element, when once he was again face to face with her, not really amounting to much more than a recognition, with a little surprise, of the positive extent of the old basis. Everything but that, everything embarrassing fell way after he had been present five minutes: it was in fact wonderful that their excellent, their pleasant, their permitted and proper and harmless American relation—the legitimacy of which he could thus scarce express in names enough—should seem so unperturbed by other matters. They had both since then had great adventures—such an adventure for him was his mental annexation of her country; and it was now, for the moment, as if the greatest of them all were this acquired consciousness of reasons other than those that had already served. Densher had asked for her, at her hotel, the day after Aunt Maud's dinner, with a rich, that is with a highly troubled, preconception of the part likely to be played for him at present, in any contact with her, by Kate's and Mrs. Lowder's so oddly conjoined and so really superfluous attempts to make her interesting. She had been interesting enough without them—that appeared to-day to come back to him; and, admirable and beautiful as was the charitable zeal of the two ladies, it might easily have nipped in the bud the germs of a friendship inevitably limited but still perfectly open to him. What had happily averted the need of his breaking off, what would as happily continue to avert it, was his own good sense and good humour, a certain spring of mind in him which ministered, imagination aiding, to understandings and allowances and which he had positively never felt such ground as just now to rejoice in the possession of. Many men—he practically made the reflexion—wouldn't have taken the matter that way, would have lost patience, finding the appeal in question irrational, exorbitant; and, thereby making short work with it, would have let it render any further acquaintance with Miss Theale impossible. He had talked with Kate of this young woman's being "sacrificed," and that would have been one way, so far as he was concerned, to sacrifice her. Such, however, had not been the tune to which his at first bewildered view had, since the night before, cleared itself up. It wasn't so much that he failed of being the kind of man who "chucked," for he knew himself as the kind of man wise enough to mark the case in which chucking might be the minor evil and the least cruelty. It was that he liked too much every one concerned willingly to show himself merely impracticable. He liked Kate, goodness knew, and he also clearly enough liked Mrs. Lowder. He liked in particular Milly herself; and hadn't it come up for him the evening before that he quite liked even Susan Shepherd? He had never known himself so generally merciful. It was a footing, at all events, whatever accounted for it, on which he should surely be rather a muff not to manage by one turn or another to escape disobliging. Should he find he couldn't work it there would still be time enough. The idea of working it crystallized before him in such guise as not only to promise much interest—fairly, in case of success, much enthusiasm; but positively to impart to failure an appearance of barbarity.

Arriving thus in Brook Street both with the best intentions and with a margin consciously left for some primary awkwardness, he found his burden, to his great relief, unexpectedly light. The awkwardness involved in the responsibility so newly and so ingeniously traced for him turned round on the spot to present him another face. This was simply the face of his old impression, which he now fully recovered—the impression that American girls, when, rare case, they had the attraction of Milly, were clearly the easiest people in the world. Had what had happened been that this specimen of the class was from the first so committed to ease that nothing subsequent *could* ever make her difficult? That affected him now as still more probable than on the occasion of the hour or two lately passed with her in Kate's society. Milly Theale had recognized no complication, to Densher's view, while bringing him, with his companion, from the National Gallery and entertaining them at luncheon; it was therefore scarce supposable that complications had become so soon too much for her. His pretext for presenting himself was fortunately of the best and simplest; the least he could decently do, given their happy acquaintance, was to call with an enquiry after learning that she had been prevented by illness from meeting him at dinner. And then there was the beautiful accident of her other demonstration; he must at any rate have given a sign as a sequel to the hospitality he had shared with Kate. Well, he was giving one now—such as it was; he was finding her, to begin with, accessible, and very naturally and prettily glad to see him. He had come, after luncheon, early, though not so early but that she might already be out if she were well enough; and she was well enough and yet was still at home. He had an inner glimpse, with this, of the comment Kate would have made on it; it wasn't absent from his thought that Milly would have been at home by *her* account because expecting, after a talk with Mrs. Stringham, that a certain person might turn up. He even—so pleasantly did things go—enjoyed freedom of mind to welcome, on that supposition, a fresh sign of the beautiful hypocrisy of women. He went so far as to enjoy believing the girl *might* have stayed in for him; it helped him to enjoy her behaving as if she hadn't. She expressed, that is, exactly the right degree of surprise; she didn't a bit overdo it: the lesson of which was, perceptibly, that, so far as his late lights had opened the door to any want of the natural in their meetings, he might trust her to take care of it for him as well as for herself.

She had begun this, admirably, on his entrance, with her turning away from the table at which she had apparently been engaged in letter-writing; it was the very possibility of his betraying a concern for her as one of the afflicted that she had within the first minute conjured way. She was never, never—did he understand?—to be one of the afflicted for him; and the manner in which he understood it, something of the answering pleasure that he couldn't help knowing he showed, constituted, he was very soon after to acknowledge, something like a start for intimacy.

When things like that could pass people had in truth to be equally conscious of a relation. It soon made one, at all events, when it didn't find one made. She had let him ask—there had been time for that, his allusion to her friend's explanatory arrival at Lancaster Gate without her being inevitable; but she had blown away, and quite as much with the look in her eyes as with the smile on her lips, every ground for anxiety and every chance for insistence. How was she?—why she was as he thus saw her and as she had reasons of her own, nobody else's business, for desiring to appear. Kate's account of her as too proud for pity, as fiercely shy about so personal a secret, came back to him; so that he rejoiced he could take a hint, especially when he wanted to. The question the girl had quickly disposed of—"Oh it was nothing: I'm all right, thank you!"—was one he was glad enough to be able to banish. It wasn't at all, in spite of the appeal Kate had made to him on it, his affair; for his interest had been invoked in the name of compassion, and the name of compassion was exactly what he felt himself at the end of two minutes forbidden so much as to whisper. He had been sent to see her in order to be sorry for her, and how sorry he might be, quite privately, he was yet to make out. Didn't that signify, however, almost not at all?—inasmuch as, whatever his upshot, he was never to give her a glimpse of it. Thus the ground was unexpectedly cleared; though it was not till a slightly longer time had passed that he read clear, at first with amusement and then with a strange shade of respect, what had most operated. Extraordinarily, quite amazingly, he began to see that if his pity hadn't had to yield to still other things it would have had to yield quite definitely to her own. That was the way the case had turned round: he had made his visit to be sorry for her, but he would repeat it—if he did repeat it—in order that she might be sorry for him. His situation made him, she judged—when once one liked him—a subject for that degree of tenderness: he felt this judgement in her, and felt it as something he should really, in decency, in dignity, in common honesty, have very soon to reckon with.

Odd enough was it certainly that the question originally before him, the question placed there by Kate, should so of a sudden find itself quite dislodged by another. This other, it was easy to see, came straight up with the fact of her beautiful delusion and her

wasted charity; the whole thing preparing for him as pretty a case
of conscience as he could have desired, and one at the prospect of
which he was already wincing. If he was interesting it was because
he was unhappy; and if he was unhappy it was because his passion
for Kate had spent itself in vain; and if Kate was indifferent, inex-
orable, it was because she had left Milly in no doubt of it. That
above all was what came up for him—how clear an impression of
this attitude, how definite an account of his own failure, Kate must
have given her friend. His immediate quarter of an hour there with
the girl lighted up for him almost luridly such an inference; it was
almost as if the other party to their remarkable understanding had
been with them as they talked, had been hovering about, had
dropped in to look after her work. The value of the work affected
him as different from the moment he saw it so expressed in poor
Milly. Since it was false that he wasn't loved, so his right was quite
quenched to figure on that ground as important; and if he didn't
look out he should find himself appreciating in a way quite at odds
with straightness the good faith of Milly's benevolence. *There* was
the place for scruples; there the need absolutely to mind what he
was about. If it wasn't proper for him to enjoy consideration on a
perfectly false footing, where was the guarantee that, if he kept on,
he mightn't soon himself pretend to the grievance in order not to
miss the sweet? Consideration—from a charming girl—was soothing on whatever theory; and it didn't take him far to remember
that he had himself as yet done nothing deceptive. It was Kate's description of him, his defeated state, it was none of his own; his responsibility would begin, as he might say, only with acting it out.
The sharp point was, however, in the difference between acting
and not acting: this difference in fact it was that made the case of
conscience. He saw it with a certain alarm rise before him that
everything was acting that was not speaking the particular word. "If
you like me because you think *she* doesn't, it isn't a bit true: she
does like me awfully!"—that would have been the particular word;
which there were at the same time but too palpably such difficulties about his uttering. Wouldn't it be virtually as indelicate to
challenge her as to leave her deluded?—and this quite apart from
the exposure, so to speak, of Kate, as to whom it would constitute
a kind of betrayal. Kate's design was something so extraordinarily

special to Kate that he felt himself shrink from the complications involved in judging it. Not to give away the woman one loved, but to back her up in her mistakes—once they had gone a certain length—that was perhaps chief among the inevitabilities of the abjection of love. Loyalty was of course supremely prescribed in presence of any design on her part, however roundabout, to do one nothing but good.

Densher had quite to steady himself not to be awestruck at the immensity of the good his own friend must on all this evidence have wanted to do him. Of one thing indeed meanwhile he was sure: Milly Theale wouldn't herself precipitate his necessity of intervention. She would absolutely never say to him: "*Is* it so impossible she shall ever care for you seriously?"—without which nothing could well be less delicate than for him aggressively to set her right. Kate would be free to do that if Kate, in some prudence, some contrition, for some better reason in fine, should revise her plan; but he asked himself what, failing this, *he* could do that wouldn't be after all more gross than dong nothing. This brought him round again to the acceptance of the fact that the poor girl liked him. She put it, for reasons of her own, on a simple, a beautiful ground, a ground that already supplied her with the pretext she required. The ground was there, that is, in the impression she had received, retained, cherished; the pretext, over and above it, was the pretext for acting on it. That she now believed as she did made her sure at last that she might act; so that what Densher therefore would have struck at would be the root, in her soul, of a pure pleasure. It positively lifted its head and flowered, this pure pleasure, while the young man now sat with her, and there were things she seemed to say that took the words out of his mouth. These were not all the things she did say; they were rather what such things meant in the light of what he knew. Her warning him for instance off the question of how she was, the quick brave little art with which she did that, represented to his fancy a truth she didn't utter. "I'm well for *you*—that's all you have to do with or need trouble about: I shall never be anything so horrid as ill for you. So there you are; worry about me, spare me, please, as little as you can. Don't be afraid, in short, to ignore my 'interesting' side. It isn't, you see, even now while you sit here, that there aren't

lots of others. Only do *them* justice and we shall get on beautifully." This was what was folded finely up in her talk—all quite ostensibly about her impressions and her intentions. She tried to put
Densher again on his American doings, but he wouldn't have that
today. As he thought of the way in which, the other afternoon, before Kate, he had sat complacently "jawing," he accused himself of
excess, of having overdone it, having made—at least apparently—
more of a "set" at their entertainer than he was at all events than
intending. He turned the tables, drawing her out about London,
about her vision of life there, and only too glad to treat her as a person with whom he could easily have other topics than her aches
and pains. He spoke to her above all the evidence offered him at
Lancaster Gate that she had come but to conquer; and when she
had met this with full and gay assent—"How could I help being
the feature of the season, the what-do-you-call-it, the theme of
every tongue?"—they fraternized freely over all that had come and
gone for each since their interrupted encounter in New York.

At the same time, while many things in quick succession came
up for them, came up in particular for Densher, nothing perhaps
was just so sharp as the odd influence of their present conditions
on their view of their past ones. It was as if they hadn't known how
"thick" they had originally become, as if, in a manner, they had
really fallen to remembrance of more passages of intimacy than
there had in fact at the time quite been room for. They were in a
relation now so complicated, whether by what they said or by what
they didn't say, that it might have been seeking to justify its speedy
growth by reaching back to one of those fabulous periods in which
prosperous states place their beginnings. He recalled what had
been said at Mrs. Lowder's about the steps and stages, in people's
careers, that absence caused one to miss, and about the resulting
frequent sense of meeting them further on; which, with some
other matters also recalled, he took occasion to communicate to
Milly. The matters he couldn't mention mingled themselves with
those he did; so that it would doubtless have been hard to say
which of the two groups now played most of a part. He was kept
face to face with this young lady by a force absolutely resident in
their situation and operating, for his nerves, with the swiftness of
the forces commonly regarded by sensitive persons as beyond their

control. The current thus determined had positively become for him, by the time he had been ten minutes in the room, something that, but for the absurdity of comparing the very small with the very great, he would freely have likened to the rapids of Niagara. An uncriticized acquaintance between a clever young man and a responsive young woman could do nothing more, at the most, than go, and his actual experiment went and went and went. Nothing probably so conduced to make it go as the marked circumstance that they had spoken all the while not a word about Kate; and this in spite of the fact that, if it were a question for them of what had occurred in the past weeks, nothing had occurred comparable to Kate's predominance. Densher had but the night before appealed to her for instruction as to what he must do about her, but he fairly winced to find how little this came to. She had foretold him of course how little; but it was a truth that looked different when shown him by Milly. It proved to him that the latter had in fact been dealt with, but it produced in him the thought that Kate might perhaps again conveniently be questioned. He would have liked to speak to her before going further—to make sure she really meant him to succeed quite so much. With all the difference that, as we say, came up for him, it came up afresh, naturally, that he might make his visit brief and never renew it; yet the strangest thing of all was that the argument against that issue would have sprung precisely from the beautiful little eloquence involved in Milly's avoidances.

Precipitate these well might be, since they emphasized the fact that she was proceeding in the sense of the assurances she had taken. Over the latter she had visibly not hesitated, for hadn't they had the merit of giving her a chance? Densher quite saw her, felt her take it; the chance, neither more nor less, of help rendered him according to her freedom. It was what Kate had left her with: "Listen to him, *I*? Never! So do as you like." What Milly "liked" was to do, it thus appeared, as she was doing: our young man's glimpse of which was just what would have been for him not less a glimpse of the peculiar brutality of shaking her off. The choice exhaled its shy fragrance of heroism, for it was not aided by any question of parting with Kate. She would be charming to Kate as well as to Kate's adorer; she would incur whatever pain could dwell for her in the sight—should she continue to be exposed to the sight—of the adorer thrown with the adored. It wouldn't really have taken much more to make him wonder if he hadn't before him one of those rare case of exaltation—food for fiction, food for poetry—in which a man's fortune with the woman who doesn't care for him is positively promoted by the woman who does. It was as if Milly had said to herself: "Well, he can at least meet her in my society, if that's anything to him; so that my line can only be to make my society attractive." She certainly couldn't have made a different impression if she *had* so reasoned. All of which, none the less, didn't prevent his soon enough saying to her, quite as if she were to be whirled into space: "And now, then, what becomes of you? Do you begin to rush about on visits to country-houses?"

She disowned the idea with a headshake that, put on what face she would, couldn't help betraying to him something of her suppressed view of the possibility—ever, ever perhaps—of any such proceedings. They weren't at any rate for her now. "Dear no. We go abroad for a few weeks somewhere of high air. That has been before us for many days; we've only been kept on by last necessities here. However, everything's done and the wind's in our sails."

"May you scud then happily before it! But when," he asked, "do you come back?"

She looked ever so vague; then as if to correct it: "Oh when the wind turns. And what do you do with your summer?"

"Ah I spend it in sordid toil. I drench it with mercenary ink. My work in your country counts for play as well. You see what's thought of the pleasure your country can give. My holiday's over."

"I'm sorry you had to take it," said Milly, "at such a different time from ours. If you could but have worked while we've been working—"

"I might be playing while you play? Oh the distinction isn't so great with me. There's a little of each for me, of work and of play, in either. But you and Mrs. Stringham, with Miss Croy and Mrs. Lowder—you all," he went on, "have been given up, like navvies or niggers, to real physical toil. Your rest is something you've earned and you need. My labour's comparatively light."

"Very true," she smiled; "but all the same I like mine."

"It doesn't leave you 'done'?"

"Not a bit. I don't get tired when I'm interested. Oh I could go far."

He bethought himself. "Then why don't you?—since you've got here, as I learn, the whole place in your pocket."

"Well, it's a kind of economy—I'm saving things up. I've enjoyed so what you speak of—though your account of it's fantastic—that I'm watching over its future, that I can't help being anxious and careful. I want—in the interest itself of what I've had and may still have—not to make stupid mistakes. The way not to make them is to get off again to a distance and see the situation from there. I shall keep it fresh," she wound up as if herself rather pleased with the ingenuity of her statement—"I shall keep it fresh, by that prudence, for my return."

"Ah then you *will* return? Can you promise one that?"

Her face fairly lighted at his asking for a promise; but she made as if bargaining a little. "Isn't London rather awful in winter?"

He had been going to ask her if she meant for the invalid; but he checked the infelicity of this and took the enquiry as referring to social life. "No—I like it, with one thing and another; it's less of a mob than later on; and it would have for *us* the merit—should you come here then—that we should probably see more of you. So do reappear for us—if it isn't a question of climate."

She looked at that a little graver. "If what isn't a question—?"

"Why the determination of your movements. You spoke just now of going somewhere for that."

"For better air?"—she remembered. "Oh yes, one certainly wants to get out of London in August."

"Rather, of course!"—he fully understood. "Though I'm glad you've hung on long enough for me to catch you. Try us at any rate," he continued, "once more."

"Whom do you mean by 'us'?" she presently asked.

It pulled him up an instant—representing, as he saw it might have seemed, an allusion to himself as conjoined with Kate, whom he was proposing not to mention any more than his hostess did. But the issue was easy. "I mean all of us together, every one you'll find ready to surround you with sympathy."

It made her, none the less, in her odd charming way, challenge him afresh. "Why do you say sympathy?"

"Well, it's doubtless a pale word. What we *shall* feel for you will be much nearer worship."

"As near then as you like!" With which at last Kate's name was sounded. "The people I'd most come back for are the people you know. I'd do it for Mrs. Lowder, who has been beautifully kind to me."

"So she has to *me*," said Densher. "I feel," he added as she at first answered nothing, "that, quite contrary to anything I originally expected, I've made a good friend of her."

"*I* didn't expect it either—its turning out as it has. But I did," said Milly, "with Kate. I shall come back for her too. I'd do anything—she kept it up—"for Kate."

Looking at him as with conscious clearness while she spoke, she might for the moment have effectively laid a trap for whatever remains of the ideal straightness in him were still able to pull themselves together and operate. He was afterwards to say to himself that something had at that moment hung for him by a hair. "Oh I know what one would do for Kate!"—it had hung for him by a hair to break out with that, which he felt he had really been kept from by an element in his consciousness stronger still. The proof of the truth in question was precisely in his silence; resisting the impulse to break out was what he *was* doing for Kate. This at the time moreover came and went quickly enough; he was trying the next minute but to make Milly's allusion easy for herself. "Of course I know what friends you are—and of course I understand," he permitted himself to add, "any amount of devotion to a person so charming. That's the good turn then she'll do us all—I mean her working for your return."

"Oh you don't know," said Milly, "how much I'm really on her hands."

He could but accept the appearance of wondering how much he might show he knew. "Ah she's very masterful."

"She's great. Yet I don't say she bullies me."

"No—that's not the way. At any rate it isn't hers," he smiled. He remembered, however, then that an undue acquaintance with Kate's ways was just what he mustn't show; and he pursued the subject no further than to remark with a good intention that had the further merit of representing a truth: "I don't feel as if I knew her—really to call know."

"Well, if you come to that, I don't either!" she laughed. The words gave him, as soon as they were uttered, a sense of responsibility for his own; though during a silence that ensued for a minute he had time to recognize that his own contained after all no element of falsity. Strange enough therefore was it that he could go too far—if it *was* too far—without being false. His observation was one he would perfectly have made to Kate herself. And before he again spoke, and before Milly did, he took time for more still—for feeling how just here it was that he must break short off if his mind was really made up not to go further. It was as if he had been at a corner—and fairly put there by his last speech; so that it depended on him whether or no to turn it. The silence, if prolonged but an instant, might even have given him a sense of her waiting to see what he would do. It was filled for them the next thing by the sound, rather voluminous for the August afternoon, of the approach, in the street below them, of heavy carriage-wheels and of horses trained to "step." A rumble, a great shake, a considerable effective clatter, had been apparently succeeded by a pause at the door of the hotel, which was in turn accompanied by a due display of diminished prancing and stamping. "You've a visitor," Densher laughed, "and it must be at least an ambassador."

"It's only my own carriage; it does that—isn't it wonderful?—every day. But we find it, Mrs. Stringham and I, in the innocence of our hearts, very amusing." She had got up, as she spoke, to assure herself of what she said; and at the end of a few steps they were together on the balcony and looking down at her waiting chariot, which made indeed a brave show. "Is it very awful?"

It was to Densher's eyes—save for its absurd heaviness—only pleasantly pompous. "It seems to me delightfully rococo. But how do I know? You're mistress of these things, in contact with the highest wisdom. You occupy a position, moreover, thanks to which your carriage—well, by this time, in the eye of London, also occupies one." But she was going out, and he mustn't stand in her way. What had happened the next minutes was first that she had denied she was going out, so that he might prolong his stay; and second that she had said she would go out with pleasure if he would like to drive—that in fact there were always things to do, that there had been a question for her to-day of several in particular, and that this in short was why the carriage had been ordered so early. They perceived, as she said these things, that an enquirer had presented himself, and, coming back, they found Milly's servant announcing the carriage and prepared to accompany her. This appeared to have for her the effect of settling the matter—on the basis, that is, of Densher's happy response. Densher's happy response, however, had as yet hung fire, the process we have described in him operating by this time with extreme intensity. The system of not pulling up, not breaking off, had already brought him headlong, he seemed to feel, to where they actually stood; and just now it was, with a vengeance, that he must do either one thing or the other. He had been waiting for some moments, which probably seemed to him longer than they were; this was because he was anxiously watching himself wait. He couldn't keep that up for ever; and since one thing or the other was what he must do, it was for the other that he presently became conscious of having decided. If he had been drifting it settled itself in the manner of a bump, of considerable violence, against a firm object in the stream. "Oh yes; I'll go with you with pleasure. It's a charming idea."

She gave no look to thank him—she rather looked away; she only said at once to her servant, "In ten minutes"; and then to her visitor, as the man went out, "We'll go somewhere—I shall like that. But I must ask of you time—as little as possible—to get ready." She looked over the room to provide for him, keep him there. "There are books and things—plenty; and I dress very quickly." He caught her eyes only as she went, on which he thought them pretty and touching.

Why especially touching at that instant he could certainly scarce have said; it was involved, it was lost in the sense of her wishing to oblige him. Clearly what had occurred was her having wished it so that she had made him simply wish, in civil acknowledgement, to oblige *her*; which he had now fully done by turning his corner. He was quite round it, his corner, by the time the door had closed upon her and he stood there alone. Alone he remained for three minutes more—remained with several very living little matters to think about. One of these was the phenomenon—typical, highly American, he would have said—of Milly's extreme spontaneity. It was perhaps rather as if he had sought refuge—refuge from another question—in the almost exclusive contemplation of this. Yet this, in its way, led him nowhere; not even to a sound generalization about American girls. It was spontaneous for his young friend to have asked him to drive with her alone—since she hadn't mentioned her companion; but she struck him after all as no more advanced in doing it than Kate, for instance, who wasn't an American girl, might have struck him in not doing it. Besides, Kate *would* have done it, though Kate wasn't at all, in the same sense as Milly, spontaneous. And then in addition Kate *had* done it—or things very like it. Furthermore he was engaged to Kate—even if his ostensibly not being put her public freedom on other grounds. On all grounds, at any rate, the relation between Kate and freedom, between freedom and Kate, was a different one from any he could associate or cultivate, as to anything, with the girl who had just left him to prepare to give herself up to him. It had never struck him before, and he moved about the room while he thought of it, touching none of the books placed at his disposal. Milly was forward, as might be said, but not advanced; whereas Kate was backward—backward still, comparatively, as an English girl—and yet advanced in a high degree. However—though this didn't straighten it out—Kate was of course two or three years older; which at their time of life considerably counted.

Thus ingeniously discriminating, Densher continued slowly to wander; yet without keeping at bay for long the sense of having rounded his corner. He had so rounded it that he felt himself lose even the option of taking advantage of Milly's absence to retrace his steps. If he might have turned tail, vulgarly speaking, five minutes before, he couldn't turn tail now; he must simply wait there with his consciousness charged to the brim. Quickly enough moreover that issue was closed from without; in the course of three minutes more Miss Theale's servant had returned. He preceded a visitor whom he had met, obviously, at the foot of the stairs and whom, throwing open the door, he loudly announced as Miss Croy. Kate, on following him in, stopped short at sight of Densher—only, after an instant, as the young man saw with free amusement, not from surprise and still less from discomfiture. Densher immediately gave his explanation—Miss Theale had gone to prepare to drive—on receipt of which the servant effaced himself.

"And you're going with her?" Kate asked.

"Yes—with your approval; which I've taken, as you see, for granted."

"Oh," she laughed, "my approval's complete!" She was thoroughly consistent and handsome about it.

"What I mean is of course," he went on—for he was sensibly affected by her gaiety—"at your so lively instigation."

She had looked about the room—she might have been vaguely looking for signs of the duration, of the character of his visit, a momentary aid in taking a decision. "Well, instigation then, as much as you like." She treated it as pleasant, the success of her plea with him; she made a fresh joke of this direct impression of it. "So much so as that? Do you know I think I won't wait?"

"Not to see her—after coming?"

"Well, with you in the field—! I came for news of her, but she must be all right. If she *is*—"

But he took her straight up. "Ah how do I know?" He was moved to say more. "It's not *I* who am responsible for her, my dear. It seems to me it's you." She struck him as making light of a matter that had been costing him sundry qualms; so that they couldn't both be quite just. Either she was too easy or he had been too anxious. He didn't want at all events to feel a fool for that. "I'm doing nothing—and shall not, I assure you, do anything but what I'm told."

Their eyes met with some intensity over the emphasis he had given his words; and he had taken it from her the next moment that he really needn't get into a state. What in the world was the matter? She asked it, with interest, for all answer. "Isn't she better—if she's able to see you?"

"She assures me she's in perfect health."

Kate's interest grew. "I knew she would." On which she added:

"It won't have been really for illness that she stayed away last night."

"For what then?"

"Well—for nervousness."

"Nervousness about what?"

"Oh you know!" She spoke with a hint of impatience, smiling however the next moment. "I've told you that."

He looked at her to recover in her face what she had told him; then it was as if what he saw there prompted him to say: "What have you told *her?*"

She gave him her controlled smile, and it was all as if they remembered where they were, liable to surprise, talking with softened voices, even stretching their opportunity, by such talk, beyond a quite right feeling. Milly's room would be close at hand, and yet they were saying things—! For a moment, none the less, they kept it up. "Ask *her*, if you like; you're free—she'll tell you. Act as you think best; don't trouble about what you think I may or mayn't have told. I'm all right with her," said Kate. "So there you are."

"If you mean *here* I am," he answered, "it's unmistakable. If you also mean that her believing in you is all I have to do with you're so far right as that she certainly does believe in you."

"Well then take example by her."

"She's really doing it for you," Densher continued. "She's driving me out for you."

"In that case," said Kate with her soft tranquillity, "you can do it a little for *her*. I'm not afraid," she smiled.

He stood before her a moment, taking in again the face she put on it and affected again, as he had already so often been, by more things in this face and in her whole person and presence than he was, to his relief, obliged to find words for. It wasn't, under such impressions, a question of words. "I do nothing for any one in the world but you. But for you I'll do anything."

"Good, good," said Kate. "That's how I like you."

He waited again an instant. "Then you swear to it?"

"To 'it'? To what?"

"Why that you do 'like' me. Since it's all for that, you know, that I'm letting you do—well, God knows what with me."

She gave at this, with a stare, a disheartened gesture—the sense of which she immediately further expressed. "If you don't believe in me then, after all, hadn't you better break off before you've gone further?"

"Break off with you?"

"Break off with Milly. You might go now," she said, "and I'll stay and explain to her why it is."

He wondered—as if it struck him. "What would you say?"

"Why that you find you can't stand her, and that there's nothing for me but to bear with you as I best may."

He considered of this. "How much do you abuse me to her?"

"Exactly enough. As much as you see by her attitude."

Again he thought. "It doesn't seem to me I ought to mind her attitude."

"Well then, just as you like. I'll stay and do my best for you."

He saw she was sincere, was really giving him a chance; and that of itself made things clearer. The feeling of how far he had gone came back to him not in repentance, but in this very vision of an escape; and it was not of what he had done, but of what Kate offered, that he now weighed the consequence. "Won't it make her—her not finding me here—be rather more sure there's something between us?"

Kate thought. "Oh I don't know. It will of course greatly upset her. But you needn't trouble about that. She won't die of it."

"Do you mean she *will?*" Densher presently asked.

"Don't put me questions when you don't believe what I say. You make too many conditions."

She spoke now with a shade of rational weariness that made the want of pliancy, the failure to oblige her, look poor and ugly; so that what it suddenly came back to for him was his deficiency in the things a man of any taste, so engaged, so enlisted, would have liked to make sure of being able to show—imagination, tact, positively even humour. The circumstance is doubtless odd, but the truth is none the less that the speculation uppermost with him at this juncture was: "What if I should begin to bore this creature?" And that, within a few seconds, had translated itself. "If you'll swear again you love me—!"

She looked about, at door and window, as if he were asking for more than he said. "Here? There's nothing between us here," Kate smiled.

"Oh *isn't* there?" Her smile itself, with this, had so settled something for him that he had come to her pleadingly and holding out his hands, which she immediately seized with her own as if both to check him and to keep him. It was by keeping him thus for a minute that she did check him; she held him long enough, while, with their eyes deeply meeting, they waited in silence for him to recover himself and renew his discretion. He coloured as with a return of the sense of where they were, and that gave her precisely one of her usual victories, which immediately took further form. By the time he had dropped her hands he had again taken hold, as it were, of Milly's. It was not at any rate with Milly he had broken. "I'll do all you wish," he declared as if to acknowledge the acceptance of his condition that he had practically, after all, drawn from her—a declaration on which she then, recurring to her first idea, promptly acted.

"If you *are* as good as that I go. You'll tell her that, finding you with her, I wouldn't wait. Say that, you know, from yourself. She'll understand."

She had reached the door with it—she was full of decision; but he had before she left him one more doubt. "I don't see how she can understand enough, you know, without understanding too much."

"You don't need to see."[18]

He required then a last injunction. "I must simply go it blind?"

"You must simply be kind to her."

"And leave the rest to you?"

"Leave the rest to *her*," said Kate disappearing. It came back then afresh to that, as it had come before. Milly, three minutes after Kate had gone, returned in her array—her big black hat, so little superstitiously in the fashion, her fine black garments throughout, the swathing of her throat, which Densher vaguely took for an infinite number of yards of priceless lace, and which, its folded fabric kept in place by heavy rows of pearls, hung down to her feet like the stole of a priestess. He spoke to her at once of their friend's visit and flight. "She hadn't known she'd find me," he said—and said at present without difficulty. He had so rounded his corner that it wasn't a question of a word more or less.

She took this account of the matter as quite sufficient; she glossed over whatever might be awkward. "I'm sorry—but I of course often see *her*." He felt the discrimination in his favor and how it justified Kate. This was Milly's tone when the matter was left to her. Well, it should now be wholly left.

BOOK SEVENTH

— I —

When Kate and Densher abandoned her to Mrs. Stringham on the day of her meeting them together and bringing them to luncheon, Milly, face to face with that
companion, had had one of those moments in which the warned,
the anxious fighter of the battle of life, as if once again feeling for
the sword at his side, carries his hand straight to the quarter of his
courage. She laid hers firmly on her heart, and the two women
stood there showing each other a strange front. Susan Shepherd
had received their great doctor's visit, which had been clearly no
small affair for her; but Milly had since then, with insistence, kept
in place, against communication and betrayal, as she now practically confessed, the barrier of their invited guests. "You've been too
dear. With what I see you're full of you treated them beautifully.
Isn't Kate charming when she wants to be?"

Poor Susie's expression, contending at first, as in a high fine
spasm, with different dangers, had now quite let itself go. She had
to make an effort to reach a point in space already so remote. "Miss
Croy? Oh she was pleasant and clever. She knew," Mrs. Stringham
added. "She knew."

Milly braced herself—but conscious above all, at the moment,
of a high compassion for her mate. She made her out as struggling—struggling in all her nature against the betrayal of pity,
which in itself, given her nature, could only be a torment. Milly
gathered from the struggle how much there was of the pity, and
how therefore it was both in her tenderness and in her conscience
that Mrs. Stringham suffered. Wonderful and beautiful it was that
this impression instantly steadied the girl. Ruefully asking herself
on what basis of ease, with the drop of their barrier, they were to
find themselves together, she felt the question met with a relief
that was almost joy. The basis, the inevitable basis, was that she
was going to be sorry for Susie, who, to all appearance, had been
condemned in so much more uncomfortable a manner to be sorry

291

for *her.* Mrs. Stringham's sorrow would hurt Mrs. Stringham, but how could her own ever hurt? She had, the poor girl, at all events, on the spot, five minutes of exaltation in which she turned the tables on her friend with a pass of the hand, a gesture of an energy that made a wind in the air. "Kate knew," she asked, "that you were full of Sir Luke Strett?"

"She spoke of nothing, but she was gentle and nice; she seemed to want to help me through." Which the good lady had no sooner said, however, than she almost tragically gasped at herself. She glared at Milly with a pretended pluck. "What I mean is that she saw one had been taken up with something. When I say she knows I should say she's a person who guesses." And her grimace was also, on its side, heroic. "But *she* doesn't matter, Milly."

The girl felt she by this time could face anything. "Nobody matters, Susie. Nobody." Which her next words, however, rather contradicted. "Did he take it ill that I wasn't here to see him? Wasn't it really just what he wanted—to have it out, so much more simply, with *you?*"

"We didn't have anything 'out,' Milly," Mrs. Stringham delicately quavered.

"Didn't he awfully like you," Milly went on, "and didn't he think you the most charming person I could possibly have referred him to for an account of me? Didn't you hit it off tremendously together and in fact fall quite in love, so that it will really be a great advantage for you to have me as a common ground? You're going to make, I can see, no end of a good thing of me."

"My own child, my own child!" Mrs. Stringham pleadingly murmured; yet showing as she did so that she feared the effect even of deprecation.

"Isn't he beautiful and good too himself?—altogether, whatever he may say, a lovely acquaintance to have made? You're just the right people for me—I see it now; and do you know what, between you, you must do?" Then as Susie still but stared, wonderstruck and holding herself: "You must simply see me through. Any way you choose. Make it out together. I, on my side, will be beautiful too, and we'll be—the three of us, with whatever others, oh as many as the case requires, any one you like!—a sight for the gods. I'll be as easy for you as carrying a feather." Susie took it for a moment in such silence that her young friend almost saw her—and scarcely withheld the observation—as taking it for "a part of the disease." This accordingly helped Milly to be, as she judged, definite and wise. "He's at any rate awfully interesting, isn't he?— which is so much to the good. We haven't at least—as we might have, with the way we tumbled into it—got hold of one of the dreary."

"Interesting, dearest?"—Mrs. Stringham felt her feet firmer. "I don't know if he's interesting or not; but I do know, my own," she continued to quaver, "that he's just as much interested as you could possibly desire."

"Certainly—that's it. Like all the world."

"No, my precious, not like all the world. Very much more deeply and intelligently."

"Ah there you are!" Milly laughed. "That's the way, Susie, I want you. So 'buck' up, my dear. We'll have beautiful times with him. Don't worry."

"I'm not worrying, Milly." And poor Susie's face registered the sublimity of her lie.

It was at this that, too sharply penetrated, her companion went to her, met by her with an embrace in which things were said that exceeded speech. Each held and clasped the other as if to console her for this unnamed woe, the woe for Mrs. Stringham of learning the torment of helplessness, the woe for Milly of having *her*, at such a time, to think of. Milly's assumption was immense, and the difficulty for her friend was that of not being able to gainsay it without bringing it more to the proof than tenderness and vagueness could permit. Nothing in fact came to the proof between them but that they could thus cling together—except indeed that, as we have indicated, the pledge of protection and support was all the younger woman's own. "I don't ask you," she presently said, "what he told you for yourself, nor what he told you to tell me, nor how he took it, really, that I had left him to you, nor what passed between you about me in any way. It wasn't to get that out of you that I took my means to make sure of your meeting freely—for there are things I don't want to know. I shall see him again and again and shall know more than enough. All I do want is that you shall see me through on *his* basis, whatever it is; which it's enough—for

the purpose—that you yourself should know: that is with him to
show you how. I'll make it charming for you—that's what I mean;
I'll keep you up to it in such a way that half the time you won't
know you're doing it. And for that you're to rest upon me. There.
It's understood. We keep each other going, and you may absolutely
feel of me that I shan't break down. So, with the way you haven't
so much as a dig of the elbow to fear, how could you be safer?"

"He told me I *can* help you—of course he told me that," Susie,
on her side, eagerly contended. "Why shouldn't he, and for what
else have I come out with you? But he told me nothing dreadful—
nothing, nothing, nothing," the poor lady passionately protested.
"Only that you must do as you like and as he tells you—which *is*
just simply to do as you like."

"I must keep in sight of him. I must from time to time go to
him. But that's of course doing as I like. It's lucky," Milly smiled,
"that I like going to him."

Mrs. Stringham was here in agreement; she gave a clutch at the
account of their situation that most showed it was workable.
"That's what *will* be charming for me, and what I'm sure he really
wants of me—to help you do as you like."

"And also a little, won't it be," Milly laughed, "to save me from
the consequences? Of course," she added, "there must first *be*
things I like."

"Oh I think you'll find some," Mrs. Stringham more bravely
said. "I think there *are* some—as for instance just this one. I
mean," she explained, "really having us so."

Milly thought. "Just as if I wanted you comfortable about *him*,
and him the same about you? Yes—I shall get the good of it."

Susan Shepherd appeared to wander from this into a slight confusion. "Which of them are you talking of?"

Milly wondered an instant—then had a light. "I'm not talking
of Mr. Densher." With which moreover she showed amusement.
"Though if you can be comfortable about Mr. Densher too so
much the better."

"Oh you meant Sir Luke Strett? Certainly he's a fine type. Do
you know," Susie continued, "whom he reminds me of? Of *our*
great man—Dr. Buttrick of Boston."

Milly recognized Dr. Buttrick of Boston, but she dropped him after a tributary pause. "What do you think, now that you've seen him, of Mr. Densher?"

It was not till after consideration, with her eyes fixed on her friend's, that Susie produced her answer. "I think he's very handsome."

Milly remained smiling at her, though putting on a little the manner of a teacher with a pupil. "Well, that will do for the first time. I *have* done," she went on, "what I wanted."

"Then that's all *we* want. You see there are plenty of things."

Milly shook her head for the "plenty." "The best is not to know—that includes them all. I don't—I don't know. Nothing about anything—except that you're *with* me. Remember that, please. There won't be anything that, on my side, for you, I shall forget. So it's all right."

The effect of it by this time was fairly, as intended, to sustain Susie, who dropped in spite of herself into the reassuring. "Most certainly it's all right. I think you ought to understand that he sees no reason—"

"Why I shouldn't have a grand long life?" Milly had taken it straight up, as to understand it and for a moment consider it. But she disposed of it otherwise. "Oh of course I know *that*." She spoke as if her friend's point were small.

Mrs. Stringham tried to enlarge it. "Well, what I mean is that he didn't say to me anything that he hasn't said to yourself."

"Really?—I would in his place!" She might have been disappointed, but she had her good humour. "He tells me to *live*"—and she oddly limited the word.

It left Susie a little at sea. "Then what do you want more?"

"My dear," the girl presently said, "I don't 'want,' as I assure you, anything. Still," she added, "I *am* living. Oh yes, I'm living."

It put them again face to face, but it had wound Mrs. Stringham up. "So am I then, you'll see!"—she spoke with the note of her recovery. Yet it was her wisdom now—meaning by it as much as she did—not to say more than that. She had risen by Milly's aid to a certain command of what was before them; the ten minutes of their talk had in fact made her more distinctly aware of the presence in her mind of a new idea. It was really perhaps an old idea with a new value; it had at all events begun during the last hour,

though at first but feebly, to shine with a special light. That was because in the morning darkness had so suddenly descended—a sufficient shade of night to bring out the power of a star. The dusk
might be thick yet, but the sky had comparatively cleared; and
Susan Shepherd's star from this time on continued to twinkle for
her. It was for the moment, after her passage with Milly, the one
spark left in the heavens. She recognized, as she continued to
watch it, that it had really been set there by Sir Luke Strett's visit
and that the impressions immediately following had done no more
than fix it. Milly's reappearance with Mr. Densher at her heels—
or, so oddly perhaps, at Miss Croy's heels, Miss Croy being at
Milly's—had contributed to this effect, though it was only with the
lapse of the greater obscurity that Susie made that out. The obscurity had reigned during the hour of their friends' visit, faintly
clearing indeed while, in one of the rooms, Kate Croy's remarkable advance to her intensified the fact that Milly and the young
man were conjoined in the other. If it hadn't acquired on the spot
all the intensity of which it was capable, this was because the poor
lady still sat in her primary gloom, the gloom the great benignant
doctor had practically left behind him.

The intensity the circumstance in question *might* wear to the informed imagination would have been sufficiently revealed for us,
no doubt—and with other things to our purpose—in two or three
of those confidential passages with Mrs. Lowder that she now permitted herself. She hadn't yet been so glad that she believed in her
old friend; for if she hadn't had, at such a pass, somebody or other
to believe in she should certainly have stumbled by the way. Discretion had ceased to consist of silence; silence was gross and thick,
whereas wisdom should taper, however tremulously, to a point. She
betook herself to Lancaster Gate the morning after the colloquy
just noted; and there, in Maud Manningham's own sanctum, she
gradually found relief in giving an account of herself. An account
of herself was one of the things that she had long been in the habit
of expecting herself regularly to give—the regularity depending of
course much on such tests of merit as might, by laws beyond her
control, rise in her path. She never spared herself in short a proper
sharpness of conception of how she had behaved, and it was a statement that she for the most part found herself able to make. What

had happened at present was that nothing, as she felt, was left of her to report to; she was all too sunk in the inevitable and the abysmal. To give an account of herself she must give it to somebody else, and her first installment of it to her hostess was that she must please let her cry. She couldn't cry, with Milly in observation, at the hotel, which she had accordingly left for that purpose; and the power happily came to her with the good opportunity. She cried and cried at first—she confined herself to that; it was for the time the best statement of her business. Mrs. Lowder moreover intelligently took it as such, though knocking off a note or two more, as she said, while Susie sat near her table. She could resist the contagion of tears, but her patience did justice to her visitor's most vivid plea for it. "I shall never be able, you know, to cry again—at least not ever with *her*; so I must take it out when I can. Even if she does herself it won't be for me to give away; for what would that be but a confession of despair? I'm not with her for that—I'm with her to be regularly sublime. Besides, Milly won't cry herself."

"I'm sure I hope," said Mrs. Lowder, "that she won't have occasion to."

"She won't even if she does have occasion. She won't shed a tear. There's something that will prevent her."

"Oh!" said Mrs. Lowder.

"Yes, her pride," Mrs. Stringham explained in spite of her friend's doubt, and it was with this that her communication took consistent form. It had never been pride, Maud Manningham had hinted, that kept *her* from crying when other things made for it; it had only been that these same things, at such times, made still more for business, arrangements, correspondence, the ringing of bells, the marshalling of servants, the taking of decisions. "I might be crying now," she said, "if I weren't writing letters"—and this quite without harshness for her anxious companion, to whom she allowed just the administrative margin for difference. She had interrupted her no more than she would have interrupted the piano-tuner. It gave poor Susie time; and when Mrs. Lowder, to save appearances and catch the post, had, with her addressed and stamped notes, met at the door of the room the footman summoned by the pressure of a knob, the facts of the case were sufficiently ready for her. It took but two or three, however, given their importance, to lay the ground for the great one—Mrs. Stringham's interview of the day before with Sir Luke, who had wished to see her about Milly.

"He had wished it himself?"

"I think he was glad of it. Clearly indeed he was. He stayed a quarter of an hour. I could see that for *him* it was long. He's interested," said Mrs. Stringham.

"Do you mean in her case?"

"He says it *isn't* a case."

"What then is it?"

"It isn't, at least," Mrs. Stringham explained, "the case she believed it to be—though it at any rate *might* be—when, without my knowledge, she went to see him. She went because there was something she was afraid of, and he examined her thoroughly—he has made sure. She's wrong—she hasn't what she thought."

"And what did she think?" Mrs. Lowder demanded.

"He didn't tell me."

"And you didn't ask?"

"I asked nothing," said poor Susie—"I only took what he gave me. He gave me no more than he had to—he was beautiful," she went on. "He *is*, thank God, interested."

"He must have been interested in *you*, dear," Maud Manningham observed with kindness.

Her visitor met it with candor. "Yes, love, I think he *is*. I mean that he sees what he can do with me."

Mrs. Lowder took it rightly. "For *her*."

"For her. Anything in the world he will or he must. He can use me to the last bone, and he likes at least that. He says the great thing for her is to be happy."

"It's surely the great thing for every one. Why, therefore," Mrs. Lowder handsomely asked, "should we cry so hard about it?"

"Only," poor Susie wailed, "that it's so strange, so beyond us. I mean if she can't be."

"She must be." Mrs. Lowder knew no impossibles. "She *shall* be."

"Well—if you'll help. He thinks, you know, we *can* help."

Mrs. Lowder faced a moment, in her massive way, what Sir Luke Strett thought. She sat back there, her knees apart, not unlike a picturesque ear-ringed matron at a market-stall; while her friend, before her, dropped their items, tossed the separate truths of the matter one by one, into her capacious apron. "But is that all he came to you for—to tell you she must be happy?"

"That she must be *made* so—that's the point. It seemed enough, as he told me," Mrs. Stringham went on; "he makes it somehow such a grand possible affair."

"Ah well, if he makes it possible!"

"I mean especially he makes it grand. He gave it to me, that is, as *my* part. The rest's his own."

"And what's the rest?" Mrs. Lowder asked.

"I don't know. *His* business. He means to keep hold of her."

"Then why do you say it isn't a 'case'? It must be very much of one."

Everything in Mrs. Stringham confessed to the extent of it. "It's only that it isn't *the* case she herself supposed."

"It's another?"

"It's another."

"Examining her for what she supposed he finds something else?"

"Something else."

"And what does he find?"

"Ah," Mrs. Stringham cried, "God keep me from knowing!"

"He didn't tell you that?"

But poor Susie had recovered herself. "What I mean is that if it's there I shall know in time. He's considering, but I can trust him for it—because he does, I feel, trust me. He's considering," she repeated.

"He's in other words not sure?"

"Well, he's watching. I think that's what he means. She's to get away now, but to come back to him in three months."

"Then I think," said Maud Lowder, "that he oughtn't meanwhile to scare us."

It roused Susie a little, Susie, being already enrolled in the great doctor's cause. This came out at least in her glimmer of reproach. "Does it scare us to enlist us for her happiness?"

Mrs. Lowder was rather stiff for it. "Yes; it scares *me*. I'm always scared—I may call it so—till I understand. What happiness is he talking about?"

Mrs. Stringham at this came straight. "Oh you know!"

She had really said it so that her friend had to take it; which the latter in fact after a moment showed herself as having done. A strange light humour in the matter even perhaps suddenly aiding, she met it with a certain accommodation. "Well, say one seems to see. The point is—!" But, fairly too full now of her question, she dropped.

"The point is will it *cure?*"

"Precisely. Is it absolutely a remedy—*the* specific?"

"Well, I should think we might know!" Mrs. Stringham delicately declared.

"Ah but we haven't the complaint."

"Have you never, dearest, been in love?" Susan Shepherd inquired.

"Yes, my child; but not by the doctor's direction."

Maud Manningham had spoken perforce with a break into momentary mirth, which operated—and happily too—as a challenge to her visitor's spirit. "Oh of course we don't ask his leave to fall. But it's something to know he thinks it good for us."

"My dear woman," Mrs. Lowder cried, "it strikes me we know it without him. So that when *that's* all he has to tell us—!"

"Ah," Mrs. Stringham interposed, "it isn't 'all.' I feel Sir Luke will have more; he won't have put me off with anything inadequate. I'm to see him again; he as good as told me that he'll wish it. So it won't be for nothing."

"Then what will it be for? Do you mean he has somebody of his own to propose? Do you mean you told him nothing?"

Mrs. Stringham dealt with these questions. "I showed him I understood him. That was all I could do. I didn't feel at liberty to be explicit; but I felt, even though his visit so upset me, the comfort of what I had from you night before last."

"What I spoke to you of in the carriage when we had left her with Kate?"

"You had *seen*, apparently, in three minutes. And now that he's here, now that I've met him and had my impression of him, I feel," said Mrs. Stringham, "that you've been magnificent."

"Of course I've been magnificent. When," asked Maud Manningham, "was I anything else? But Milly won't be, you know, if she marries Merton Densher."

"Oh it's always magnificent to marry the man one loves. But we're going fast!" Mrs. Stringham woefully smiled.

"The thing *is* to go fast if I see the case right. What had I after all but my instinct of that on coming back with you, night before last, to pick up Kate? I felt what I felt—I knew in my bones the man had returned."

"That's just where, as I say, you're magnificent. But wait," said Mrs. Stringham, "till you've seen him."

"I shall see him immediately"—Mrs. Lowder took it up with decision. "What *is* then," she asked, "your impression?"

Mrs. Stringham's impression seemed lost in her doubts. "How can he ever care for her?"

Her companion, in her companion's heavy manner, sat on it. "By being put in the way of it."

"For God's sake then," Mrs. Stringham wailed, "*put* him in the way! You have him, one feels, in your hand."

Maud Lowder's eyes at this rested on her friend's. "Is that your impression of him?"

"It's my impression, dearest, of you. You handle every one."

Mrs. Lowder's eyes still rested, and Susan Shepherd now felt, for a wonder, not less sincere by seeing that she pleased her. But there was a great limitation. "I don't handle Kate."

It suggested something that her visitor hadn't yet had from her—something the sense of which made Mrs. Stringham gasp. "Do you mean Kate cares for *him?*"

That fact the lady of Lancaster Gate had up to this moment, as we know, enshrouded, and her friend's quick question had produced a change in her face. She blinked—then looked at the question hard; after which, whether she had inadvertently betrayed herself or had only reached a decision and then been affected by the quality of Mrs. Stringham's surprise, she accepted all results. What took place in her for Susan Shepherd was not simply that she made the best of them, but that she suddenly saw more in them to her purpose than she could have imagined. A certain impatience in fact marked in her this transition: she had been keeping back, very hard, an important truth, and wouldn't have liked to hear that she hadn't concealed it cleverly. Susie nevertheless felt herself pass as not a little of a fool with her for not having thought of it. What Susie indeed, however, most thought of at present, in the quick, new light of it, was the wonder of Kate's dissimulation. She had time for that view while she waited for an answer to her cry. "Kate thinks she cares. But she's mistaken. And no one knows it." These things, distinct and responsible, were Mrs. Lowder's retort. Yet they weren't all of it. "*You* don't know it—that must be your line. Or rather your line must be that you deny it utterly."

"Deny that she cares for him?"

"Deny that she so much as thinks that she does. Positively and absolutely. Deny that you've so much as heard of it."

Susie faced this new duty. "To Milly, you mean—if she asks?"

"To Milly, naturally. No one else *will* ask."

"Well," said Mrs. Stringham after a moment, "Milly won't."

Mrs. Lowder wondered. "Are you sure?"

"Yes, the more I think of it. And luckily for *me*. I lie badly."

"*I* lie well, thank God," Mrs. Lowder almost snorted, "when, as sometimes will happen, there's nothing else so good. One must always do the best. But without lies then," she went on, "perhaps we can work it out." Her interest had risen; her friend saw her, as within some minutes, more enrolled and inflamed—presently felt in her what had made the difference. Mrs. Stringham, it was true, descried this at the time but dimly; she only made out at first that Maud had found a reason for helping her. The reason was that, strangely, she might help Maud too, for which she now desired to profess herself ready even to lying. What really perhaps most came out for her was that her hostess was a little disappointed at her doubt of the social solidity of this appliance; and that in turn was to become a steadier light. The truth about Kate's delusion, as her aunt presented it, the delusion about the state of her affections, which might be removed—this was apparently the ground on which they now might more intimately meet. Mrs. Stringham saw herself recruited for the removal of Kate's delusion—by arts, however, in truth, that she as yet quite failed to compass. Or was it perhaps to be only for the removal of Mr. Densher's?—success in which indeed might entail other successes. Before that job, unfortunately, her heart had already failed. She felt that she believed in her bones what Milly believed, and what would now make working for Milly such a dreadful upward tug. All this within her was confusedly present—a cloud of questions out of which Maud Manningham's large seated self loomed, however, as a mass more and more definite, taking in fact for the consultative relation something of the form of an oracle. From the oracle the sound did come—or at any rate the sense did, a sense all accordant with the insufflation she had just seen working. "Yes," the sense was, "I'll help you for Milly, because if that comes off I shall be helped, by its doing so, for Kate"—a view into which Mrs. Stringham could now sufficiently enter. She found herself of a sudden, strange to say, quite willing to operate to Kate's harm, or at least to Kate's good as Mrs. Lowder with a noble anxiety measured it. She found herself in short not caring what became of Kate—only convinced at bottom of the predominance of Kate's star. Kate wasn't in danger, Kate wasn't pathetic; Kate Croy, whatever happened, would take care of Kate Croy. She saw moreover by this time that her friend was traveling even beyond her own speed. Mrs. Lowder had already, in mind, drafted a rough plan of action, a plan vividly enough thrown off as she said: "You must stay on a few days, and you must immediately, both of you, meet him at dinner." In addition to which Maud claimed the merit of having by an instinct of pity, of prescient wisdom, done much, two nights before, to prepare that ground. "The poor child, when I was with her there while you were getting your shawl, quite gave herself away to me."

"Oh I remember how you afterwards put it to me. Though it was nothing more," Susie did herself the justice to observe, "than what I too had quite felt."

But Mrs. Lowder fronted her so on this that she wondered what she had said. "I suppose I ought to be edified at what you can so beautifully give up."

"Give up?" Mrs. Stringham echoed. "Why, I give up nothing—I cling."

Her hostess showed impatience, turning again with some stiffness to her great brass-bound cylinder-desk and giving a push to an object or two disposed there. "*I* give up then. You know how little such a person as Mr. Densher was to be my idea for her. You know what I've been thinking perfectly possible."

"Oh you've been great"—Susie was perfectly fair. "A duke, a duchess, a princess, a palace: you've made me believe in them too. But where we break down is that *she* doesn't believe in them. Luckily for her—as it seems to be turning out—she doesn't want them. So what's one to do? I assure you I've had many dreams. But I've only one dream now."

Mrs. Stringham's tone in these last words gave so fully her meaning that Mrs. Lowder could but show herself as taking it in. They sat a moment longer confronted on it. "Her having what she does want?"

"If it *will* do anything for her."

Mrs. Lowder seemed to think what it might do; but she spoke for the instant of something else. "It does provoke me a bit, you know—for of course I'm a brute. And I had thought of all sorts of things. Yet it doesn't prevent the fact that we must be decent."

"We must take her"—Mrs. Stringham carried that out—"as she is."

"And we must take Mr. Densher as *he* is." With which Mrs. Lowder gave a sombre laugh. "It's a pity he isn't better!"

"Well, if he were better," her friend rejoined, "you'd have liked him for your niece; and in that case Milly would interfere. I mean," Susie added, "interfere with *you.*"

"She interferes with me as it is—not that it matters now. But I saw Kate and her—really as soon as you came to me—set up side by side. I saw your girl—I don't mind telling you—helping my girl; and when I say that," Mrs. Lowder continued, "you'll probably put in for yourself that it was part of the reason of my welcome to you. So you see what I give up. I do give it up. But when I take that line," she further set forth, "I take it handsomely. So good-bye to it all. Good-day to Mrs. Densher! Heavens!" she growled.

Susie held herself a minute. "Even as Mrs. Densher my girl will be somebody."

"Yes, she won't be nobody. Besides," said Mrs. Lowder, "we're talking in the air."

Her companion sadly assented. "We're leaving everything out."

"It's nevertheless interesting." And Mrs. Lowder had another thought. "*He's* not quite nobody either." It brought her back to the question she had already put and which her friend hadn't at the time dealt with. "What in fact do you make of him?"

Susan Shepherd, at this, for reasons not clear even to herself, was moved a little to caution. So she remained general. "He's charming."

She had met Mrs. Lowder's eyes with that extreme pointedness in her own to which people resort when they are not quite candid—a circumstance that had its effect. "Yes; he's charming."

The effect of the words, however, was equally marked; they almost determined in Mrs. Stringham a return of amusement. "I thought you didn't like him!"

"I don't like him for Kate."

"But you don't like him for Milly either."

Mrs. Stringham rose as she spoke, and her friend also got up. "I like him, my dear, for myself."

"Then that's the best way of all."

"Well, it's one way. He's not good enough for my niece, and he's not good enough for you. One's an aunt, one's a wretch and one's a fool."

"Oh *I'm* not—not either," Susie declared.

But her companion kept on. "One lives for others. *You* do that. If I were living for myself I shouldn't at all mind him."

But Mrs. Stringham was sturdier. "Ah if I find him charming it's however I'm living."

Well, it broke Mrs. Lowder down. She hung fire but an instant, giving herself away with a laugh. "Of course he's all right in himself."

"That's all I contend," Susie said with more reserve; and the note in question—what Merton Densher was "in himself"—closed practically, with some inconsequence, this first of their councils.

— II —

It had at least made the difference for them, they could feel, of an informed state in respect to the great doctor, whom they were now to take as watching, waiting, studying, or at any rate as proposing to himself some such process before he should make up his mind. Mrs. Stringham understood him as considering the matter meanwhile in a spirit that, on this same occasion, at Lancaster Gate, she had come back to a rough notation of before retiring. She followed the course of his reckoning. If what they had talked of *could* happen—if Milly, that is, could have her thoughts taken off herself—it wouldn't do any harm and might conceivably do much good. If it couldn't happen—if, anxiously, though tactfully working, they themselves, conjoined, could do nothing to contribute to it—they would be in no worse a box than before. Only in this latter case the girl would have had her free range for the summer, for the autumn; she would have done her best in the sense enjoined on her, and, coming back at the end to her eminent man, would—besides having more to show him—find him more ready to go on with her. It was visible further to Susan Shepherd—as well as being ground for a second report to her old friend—that Milly did her part for a working view of the general case, inasmuch as she mentioned frankly and promptly that she meant to go and say good-bye to Sir Luke Strett and thank him. She even specified what she was to thank him for, his having been so easy about her behaviour.

"You see I didn't know that—for the liberty I took—I shouldn't afterwards get a stiff note from him."

So much Milly had said to her, and it had made her a trifle rash. "Oh you'll never get a stiff note from him in your life."

She felt her rashness, the next moment, at her young friend's question. "Why not, as well as any one else who has played him a trick?"

"Well, because he doesn't regard it as a trick. He could understand your action. It's all right, you see."

"Yes—I do see. It *is* all right. He's easier with me than with any one else, because that's the way to let me down. He's only making believe, and I'm not worth hauling up."

Rueful at having provoked again this ominous flare, poor Susie grasped at her only advantage. "Do you really accuse a man like Sir Luke Strett of trifling with you?"

She couldn't blind herself to the look her companion gave

her—a strange half-amused perception of what she made of it. "Well, so far as it's trifling with me to pity me so much."

"He doesn't pity you," Susie earnestly reasoned. "He just—the same as any one else—likes you."

"He has no business then to like me. He's not the same as any one else."

"Why not, if he wants to work for you?"

Milly gave her another look, but this time a wonderful smile. "Ah there you are!" Mrs. Stringham coloured, for there indeed she was again. But Milly let her off. "Work for me, all the same—work for me! It's of course what I want." Then as usual she embraced her friend. "I'm not going to be as nasty as this to *him*."

"I'm sure I hope not!"—and Mrs. Stringham laughed for the kiss. "I've no doubt, however, he'd take it from you! It's *you*, my dear, who are not the same as any one else."

Milly's assent to which, after an instant, gave her the last word. "No, so that people can take anything from me." And what Mrs. Stringham did indeed resignedly take after this was the absence on her part of an account of the visit then paid. It was the beginning in fact between them of an odd independence—an independence positively of action and custom—on the subject of Milly's future. They went their separate ways with the girl's intense assent; this being really nothing but what she had so wonderfully put in her plea for after Mrs. Stringham's first encounter with Sir Luke. She fairly favored the idea that Susie had or was to have other encounters—private pointed personal; she favored every idea, but most of all the idea that she herself was to go on as if nothing were the matter. Since she was to be worked for that would be her way; and though her companions learned from herself nothing of it this was in the event her way with her medical adviser. She put her visit to him on the simplest ground; she had come just to tell him how touched she had been by his good nature. That required little explaining, for, as Mrs. Stringham had said, he quite understood he could but reply that it was all right.

"I had a charming quarter of an hour with that clever lady. You've got good friends."

"So each one of them thinks of all the others. But so I also think," Milly went on, "of all of them together. You're excellent for each other. And it's in that way, I dare say, that you're best for me."

There came to her on this occasion one of the strangest of her impressions, which was at the same time one of the finest of her alarms—the glimmer of a vision that if she should go, as it were, too far, she might perhaps deprive their relation of facility if not of value. Going too far was failing to try at least to remain simple. He would be quite ready to hate her if she did, by heading him off at every point, embarrass his exercise of a kindness that, no doubt, rather constituted for him a high method. Susie wouldn't hate her, since Susie positively wanted to suffer for her; Susie had a noble idea that she might somehow so do her good. Such, however, was not the way in which the greatest of London doctors was to be expected to wish to do it. He wouldn't have time even should he wish; whereby, in a word, Milly felt herself intimately warned. Face to face there with her smooth strong director, she enjoyed at a given moment quite such another lift of feeling as she had known in her crucial talk with Susie. It came round to the same thing; him too she would help to help her if that could possibly be; but if it couldn't possibly be she would assist also to make this right. It wouldn't have taken many minutes more, on the basis in question, almost to reverse for her their characters of patient and physician. What *was* he in fact but patient, what was she but physician, from the moment she embraced once for all the necessity, adopted once for all the policy, of saving him alarms about her subtlety? She would leave the subtlety to him: he would enjoy his use of it, and she herself, no doubt, would in time enjoy his enjoyment. She went so far as to imagine that the inward success of these reflexions flushed her for the minute, to his eyes, with a certain bloom, a comparative appearance of health; and what verily next occurred was that he gave colour to the presumption. "Every little helps, no doubt!"—he noticed good-humouredly her harmless sally. "But, help or no help, you're looking, you know, remarkably well."

"Oh I thought I was," she answered; and it was as if already she saw his line. Only she wondered what he would have guessed. If he had guessed anything at all it would be rather remarkable of him. As for what there *was* to guess, he couldn't—if this was present to him—have arrived at it save by his own acuteness. That acuteness was therefore immense; and if it supplied the subtlety she thought of leaving him to, his portion would be none so bad. Neither, for that matter, would hers be—which she was even actually enjoying. She wondered if really then there mightn't be something for her. She hadn't been sure in coming to him that she was "better," and he hadn't used, he would be awfully careful not to use, that compromising term about her; in spite of all of which she would have been ready to say, for the amiable sympathy of it, "Yes, I *must* be," for he had this unaided sense of something that had happened to her. It was a sense unaided, because who could have told him of anything? Susie, she was certain, hadn't yet seen him again, and there were things it was impossible she could have told him the first time. Since such was his penetration, therefore, why shouldn't she gracefully, in recognition of it, accept the new circumstance, the one he was clearly wanting to congratulate her on, as a sufficient cause? If one nursed a cause tenderly enough it might produce an effect; and this, to begin with, would be a way of nursing. "You gave me the other day," she went on, "plenty to think over, and I've been doing that—thinking it over—quite as you'll have probably wished me. I think I must be pretty easy to treat," she smiled, "since you've already done me so much good."

The only obstacle to reciprocity with him was that he looked in advance so closely related to all one's possibilities that one missed the pleasure of really improving it. "Oh no, you're extremely difficult to treat. I've need with you, I assure you, of all my wit."

"Well, I mean I do come up." She hadn't meanwhile a bit believed in his answer, convinced as she was that if she *had* been difficult it would be the last thing he would have told her. "I'm doing," she said, "as I like."

"Then it's as *I* like. But you must really, though we're having such a decent month, get straight away." In pursuance of which, when she had replied with promptitude that her departure—for the Tyrol and then for Venice—was quite fixed for the fourteenth, he took her up with alacrity. "For Venice? That's perfect, for we shall meet there. I've a dream of it for October, when I'm hoping for three weeks off; three weeks during which, if I can get them clear, my niece, a young person who has quite the whip hand of

me, is to take me where she prefers. I heard from her only yesterday that she expects to prefer Venice."

"That's lovely then. I shall expect you there. And anything that,
in advance or in any way, I can do for you—!"

"Oh thank you. My niece, I seem to feel, does for me. But it will
be capital to find you there."

"I think it ought to make you feel," she said after a moment,
"that I *am* easy to treat."

But he shook his head again; he wouldn't have it. "You've not
come to that *yet.*"

"One has to be so bad for it?"

"Well, I don't think I've ever come to it—to 'ease' of treatment.
I doubt if it's possible. I've not, if it is, found any one bad enough.
The ease, you see, is for *you.*"

"I see—I see."

They had an odd friendly, but perhaps the least bit awkward
pause on it; after which Sir Luke asked: "And that clever lady—she
goes with you?"

"Mrs. Stringham? Oh dear, yes. She'll stay with me, I hope, to
the end."

He had a cheerful blankness. "To the end of what?"

"Well—of everything."

"Ah then," he laughed, "you're in luck. The end of everything
is far off. This, you know, I'm hoping," said Sir Luke, "is only the
beginning." And the next question he risked might have been a
part of his hope. "Just you and she together?"

"No, two other friends; two ladies of whom we've seen more
here than of any one and who are just the right people for us."

He thought a moment. "You'll be four women together then?"

"Ah," said Milly, "we're widows and orphans. But I think," she
added as if to say what she saw would reassure him, "that we shall
not be unattractive, as we move, to gentlemen. When you talk of
'life' I suppose you mean mainly gentlemen."

"When I talk of 'life,' " he made answer after a moment during
which he might have been appreciating her raciness—"when I
talk of life I think I mean more than anything else the beautiful
show of it, in its freshness, made by young persons of your age. So

go on as you are. I see more and more *how* you are. You can't," he went so far as to say for pleasantness, "better it."

She took it from him with a great show of peace. "One of our companions will be Miss Croy, who came with me here first. It's in *her* that life is splendid; and a part of that is even that she's devoted to me. But she's above all magnificent in herself. So that if you'd like," she freely threw out, "to see *her*—"

"Oh I shall like to see any one who's devoted to you, for clearly it will be jolly to be 'in' it. So that if she's to be at Venice I *shall* see her?"

"We must arrange it—I shan't fail. She moreover has a friend who may also be there"—Milly found herself going on to this. "He's likely to come, I believe, for he always follows her."

Sir Luke wondered. "You mean they're lovers?"

"*He* is," Milly smiled; "but not she. She doesn't care for him."

Sir Luke took an interest. "What's the matter with him?"

"Nothing but that she doesn't like him."

Sir Luke kept it up. "Is he all right?"

"Oh he's very nice. Indeed he's remarkably so."

"And he's to be in Venice?"

"So she tells me she fears. For if he is there he'll be constantly about with her."

"And she'll be constantly about with you?"

"As we're great friends—yes."

"Well then," said Sir Luke, "you won't be four women alone."

"Oh no; I quite recognize the chance of gentlemen. But he won't," Milly pursued in the same wondrous way, "have come, you see, for *me*."

"No—I see. But can't you help him?"

"Can't *you*?" Milly after a moment quaintly asked. Then for the joke of it she explained. "I'm putting you, you see, in relation with my entourage."

It might have been for the joke of it too, by this time, that her eminent friend fell in. "But if this gentleman *isn't* of your 'entourage'? I mean if he's of—what do you call her?—Miss Croy's. Unless indeed you also take an interest in him."

"Oh certainly I take an interest in him!"

"You think there may be then some chance for him?"

"I like him," said Milly, "enough to hope so."

"Then that's all right. But what, pray," Sir Luke next asked, "have I to do with him?"

"Nothing," said Milly, "except that if you're to be there, so may he be. And also that we shan't in that case be simply four dreary women."

He considered her as if at this point she a little tried his patience. "*You're* the least 'dreary' woman I've ever, ever seen. Ever, do you know? There's no reason why you shouldn't have a really splendid life."

"So every one tells me," she promptly returned.

"The conviction—strong already when I had seen you once—is strengthened in me by having seen your friend. There's no doubt about it. The world's before you."

"What did my friend tell you?" Milly asked.

"Nothing that wouldn't have given you pleasure. We talked about you—and freely. I don't deny that. But it shows me I don't require of you the impossible."

She was now on her feet. "I think I know what you require of me."

"Nothing, for you," he went on, "*is* impossible. So go on." He repeated it again—wanting her so to feel that to-day he saw it. "You're all right."

"Well," she smiled—"keep me so."

"Oh you'll get away from me."

"Keep me, keep me," she simply continued with her gentle eyes on him.

She had given him her hand for good-bye, and he thus for a moment did keep her. Something then, while he seemed to think if there were anything more, came back to him; though something of which there wasn't too much to be made. "Of course if there's anything I *can* do for your friend: I mean the gentleman you speak of—?" He gave out in short that he was ready.

"Oh Mr. Densher?" It was as if she had forgotten.

"Mr. Densher—is that his name?"

"Yes—but his case isn't so dreadful." She had within a minute got away from that.

"No doubt—if *you* take an interest." She had got away, but it was as if he made out in her eyes—though they also had rather got away—a reason for calling her back. "Still, if there's anything one can do—?"

She looked at him while she thought, while she smiled. "I'm afraid there's really nothing one can do."

— III —

Not yet so much as this morning had she felt herself sink into possession; gratefully glad that the warmth of the Southern summer was still in the high florid rooms, palatial chambers where hard cool pavements took reflexions in their lifelong polish, and where the sun on the stirred sea-water, flickering up through open windows, played over the painted "subjects" in the splendid ceilings—medallions of purple and brown, of brave old melancholy colour, medals as of old reddened gold, embossed and beribboned, all toned with time and all flourished and scalloped and gilded about, set in their great molded and figured concavity (a nest of white cherubs, friendly creatures of the air) and appreciated by the aid of that second tier of smaller lights, straight openings to the front, which did everything, even with the Baedekers and photographs of Milly's party dreadfully meeting the eye, to make of the place an apartment of state. This at last only, though she had enjoyed the palace for three weeks, seemed to count as effective occupation; perhaps because it was the first time she had been alone—really to call alone—since she had left London, it ministered to her first full and unembarrassed sense of what the great Eugenio had done for her. The great Eugenio, recommended by grand-dukes and Americans, had entered her service during the last hours of all—had crossed from Paris, after multiplied *pourparlers** with Mrs. Stringham, to whom she had allowed more than ever a free hand, on purpose to escort her to the Continent and encompass her there, and had dedicated to her, from

---

*Discussions (French).

the moment of their meeting, all the treasures of his experience. She had judged him in advance—polyglot and universal, very dear and very deep—as probably but a swindler finished to the finger-tips; for he was for ever carrying one well-kept Italian hand to his heart and plunging the other straight into her pocket, which, as she had instantly observed him to recognize, fitted it like a glove. The remarkable thing was that these elements of their common consciousness had rapidly gathered into an indestructible link, formed the ground of a happy relation; being by this time, strangely, grotesquely, delightfully, what most kept up confidence between them and what most expressed it.[19]

She had seen quickly enough what was happening—the usual thing again, yet once again. Eugenio had, in an interview of five minutes, understood her, had got hold, like all the world, of the idea not so much of the care with which she must be taken up as of the care with which she must be let down. All the world under-stood her, all the world had got hold; but for nobody yet, she felt, would the idea have been so close a tie or won from herself so patient a surrender. Gracefully, respectfully, consummately enough—always with hands in position and the look, in his thick neat white hair, smooth fat face and black professional, almost theatrical eyes, as of some famous tenor grown too old to make love, but with an art still to make money—did he on occasion con-vey to her that she was, of all the clients of his glorious career, the one in whom his interest was most personal and paternal. The others had come in the way of business, but for her his sentiment was special. Confidence rested thus on her completely believing that: there was nothing of which she felt more sure. It passed be-tween them every time they conversed; he was abysmal, but this intimacy lived on the surface. He had taken his place already for her among those who were to see her through, and meditation ranked him, in the constant perspective, for the final function, side by side with poor Susie—whom she was now pitying more than ever for having to be herself so sorry and to say so little about it. Eugenio had the general tact of a residuary legatee—which was a character that could be definitely worn; whereas she could see Susie, in the event of her death, in no character at all, Susie being insistently, exclusively concerned in her mere makeshift duration.

This principle, for that matter, Milly at present, with a renewed flare of fancy, felt she should herself have liked to believe in. Eugenio had really done for her more than he probably knew—he didn't after all know everything—in having, for the wind-up of the autumn, on a weak word from her, so admirably, so perfectly established her. Her weak word, as a general hint, had been: "At Venice, please, if possible, no dreadful, no vulgar hotel; but, if it can be at all managed—you know what I mean—some fine old rooms, wholly independent, for a series of months. Plenty of them too, and the more interesting the better: part of a palace, historic and picturesque, but strictly inodorous, where we shall be to ourselves, with a cook, don't you know?—with servants, frescoes, tapestries, antiquities, the thorough make-believe of a settlement."

The proof of how he better and better understood her was in all the lace; as to his masterly acquisition of which she had from the first asked no questions. She had shown him enough what she thought of it, and her forbearance pleased him; with the part of the transaction that mainly concerned her she would soon enough become acquainted, and his connexion with such values as she would then find noted could scarce help growing, as it were, still more residuary. Charming people, conscious Venice-lovers, evidently, had given up their house to her, and had fled to a distance, to other countries, to hide their blushes alike over what they had, however briefly, alienated, and over what they had, however durably, gained. They had preserved and consecrated, and she now—her part of it was shameless—appropriated and enjoyed. Palazzo Leporelli[20] held its history still in its great lap, even like a painted idol, a solemn puppet hung about with decorations. Hung about with pictures and relics, the rich Venetian past, the ineffaceable character, was here the presence revered and served: which brings us back to our truth of a moment ago—the fact that, more than ever, this October morning, awkward novice though she might be, Milly moved slowly to and fro as the priestess of the worship. Certainly it came from the sweet taste of solitude, caught again and cherished for the hour; always a need of her nature, moreover, when things spoke to her with penetration. It was mostly in stillness they spoke to her best; amid voices she lost the sense. Voices had surrounded her for weeks, and she had tried to listen, had cul-

tivated them and had answered back; these had been weeks in
which there were other things they might well prevent her from
hearing. More than the prospect had at first promised or threatened she had felt herself going on in a crowd and with a multiplied
escort; the four ladies pictured by her to Sir Luke Strett and a phalanx comparatively closed and detached had in fact proved a
rolling snowball, condemned from day to day to cover more
ground. Susan Shepherd had compared this portion of the girl's
excursion to the Empress Catherine's famous progress across the
steps of Russia; improvised settlements appeared at each turn of
the road, villagers waiting with addresses drawn up in the language
of London. Old friends in fine were in ambush, Mrs. Lowder's,
Kate Croy's, her own; when the addresses weren't in the language
of London they were in the more insistent idioms of American
centres. The current was swollen even by Susie's social connexions; so that there were days, at hotels, at Dolomite picnics, on
lake steamers, when she could almost repay to Aunt Maud and
Kate with interest the debt contracted by the London "success" to
which they had opened the door.

   Mrs. Lowder's success and Kate's, amid the shock of Milly's and
Mrs. Stringham's compatriots, failed but little, really, of the concert-
pitch; it had gone almost as fast as the boom, over the sea, of the
last great native novel. Those ladies were "so different"—different,
observably enough, from the ladies so appraising them; it being
throughout a case mainly of ladies, of a dozen at once sometimes,
in Milly's apartment, pointing, also at once, that moral and many
others. Milly's companions were acclaimed not only as perfectly
fascinating in themselves, the nicest people yet known to the ac-
claimers, but as obvious helping hands, socially speaking, for the
eccentric young woman, evident initiators and smoothers of her
path, possible subduers of her eccentricity. Short intervals, to her
own sense, stood now for great differences, and this renewed in-
halation of her native air had somehow left her to feel that she already, that she mainly, struck the compatriot as queer and
dissociated. She moved such a critic, it would appear, as to rather
an odd suspicion, a benevolence induced by a want of complete
trust: all of which showed her in the light of a person too plain and
too ill-clothed for a thorough good time, and yet too rich and too

befriended—an intuitive cunning within her managing this last—
for a thorough bad one. The compatriots, in short, by what she
made out, approved her friends for their expert wisdom with her;
in spite of which judicial sagacity it was the compatriots who
recorded themselves as the innocent parties. She saw things in
these days that she had never seen before, and she couldn't have
said why save on a principle too terrible to name; whereby she saw
that neither Lancaster Gate was what New York took it for, nor
New York what Lancaster Gate fondly fancied it in coquetting
with the plan of a series of American visits. The plan might have
been, humourously, on Mrs. Lowder's part, for the improvement
of her social position—and it had verily in that direction lights that
were perhaps but half a century too prompt; at all of which Kate
Croy assisted with the cool controlled facility that went so well, as
the others said, with her particular kind of good looks, the kind
that led you to expect the person enjoying them *would* dispose of
disputations, speculations, aspirations, in a few very neatly and
brightly uttered words, so simplified in sense, however, that they
sounded, even when guiltless, like rather aggravated slang. It
wasn't that Kate hadn't pretended too that *she* should like to go to
America; it was only that with this young woman Milly had constantly proceeded, and more than ever of late, on the theory of intimate confessions, private frank ironies that made up for their
public grimaces and amid which, face to face, they wearily put off
the mask.

These puttings-off of the mask had finally quite become the
form taken by their moments together, moments indeed not increasingly frequent and not prolonged, thanks to the consciousness of fatigue on Milly's side whenever, as she herself expressed
it, she got out of harness. They flourished their masks, the independent pair, as they might have flourished Spanish fans; they
smiled and sighed on removing them; but the gesture, the smiles,
the sighs, strangely enough, might have been suspected the greatest reality in the business. Strangely enough, we say, for the volume of effusion in general would have been found by either on
measurement to be scarce proportional to the paraphernalia of relief. It was when they called each other's attention to their ceasing
to pretend, it was then that what they were keeping back was most

in the air. There was a difference, no doubt, and mainly to Kate's advantage: Milly didn't quite see what her friend could keep back, was possessed of, in fine, that would be so subject to retention; whereas it was comparatively plain sailing for Kate that poor Milly had a treasure to hide. This was not the treasure of a shy, an abject affection—concealment, on that head, belonging to quite another phase of such states; it was much rather a principle of pride relatively bold and hard, a principle that played up like a fine steel spring at the lightest pressure of too near a football. Thus insuperably guarded was the truth about the girl's own conception of her validity; thus was a wondering pitying sister condemned wistfully to look at her from the far side of the moat she had dug round her tower. Certain aspects of the connexion of these young women show for us, such is the twilight that gathers about them, in the likeness of some dim scene in a Maeterlinck play; we have positively the image, in the delicate dusk, of the figures so associated and yet so opposed, so mutually watchful: that of the angular pale princess, ostrich-plumed, black-robed, hung about with amulets, reminders, relics, mainly seated, mainly still, and that of the upright restless slow-circling lady of her court who exchanges with her, across the black water streaked with evening gleams, fitful questions and answers. The upright lady, with thick dark braids down her back, drawing over the grass a more embroidered train, makes the whole circuit, and makes it again, and the broken talk, brief and sparingly allusive, seems more to cover than to free their sense. This is because, when it fairly comes to not having others to consider, they meet in an air that appears rather anxiously to wait for their words. Such an impression as that was in fact grave, and might be tragic; so that, plainly enough, systematically at last, they settled to a care of what they said.

There could be no gross phrasing to Milly, in particular, of the probability that if she wasn't so proud she might be pitied with more comfort—more to the person pitying; there could be no spoken proof, no sharper demonstration than the consistently considerate attitude, that this marvelous mixture of her weakness and of her strength, her peril, if such it were, and her option, made her, kept her, irresistibly interesting. Kate's predicament in the matter was, after all, very much Mrs. Stringham's own, and Susan Shepherd herself indeed, in our Maeterlinck picture, might well have hovered in the gloaming by the moat. It may be declared for Kate, at all events, that her sincerity about her friend, through this time, was deep, her compassionate imagination strong; and that these things gave her a virtue, a good conscience, a credibility for herself, so to speak, that were later to be precious to her. She grasped with her keen intelligence the logic of their common duplicity, went unassisted through the same ordeal as Milly's other hushed follower, easily saw that for the girl to be explicit was to betray divinations, gratitudes, glimpses of the felt contrast between her fortune and her fear—all of which would have contradicted her systematic bravado. That was it, Kate wonderingly saw: to recognize was to bring down the avalanche—the avalanche Milly lived so in watch for and that might be started by the lightest of breaths; though less possibly the breath of her own stifled plaint than that of the vain sympathy, the mere helpless gaping inference of others. With so many suppressions as these, therefore, between them, their withdrawal together to unmask had to fall back, as we have hinted, on a nominal motive—which was decently represented by a joy at the drop of chatter. Chatter had in truth all along attended their steps, but they took the despairing view of it on purpose to have ready, when face to face, some view or other of something. The relief of getting out of harness—that was the moral of their meetings; but the moral of this, in turn, was that they couldn't so much as ask each other why harness need be worn. Milly wore it as a general armor.

She was out of it at present, for some reason, as she hadn't been for weeks; she was always out of it, that is, when alone, and her companions had never yet so much as just now affected her as dispersed and suppressed. It was as if still again, still more tacitly and wonderfully, Eugenio had understood her, taking it from her without a word and just bravely and brilliantly in the name, for instance, of the beautiful day: "Yes, get me an hour alone; take them off—I don't care where; absorb, amuse, detain them; drown them, kill them if you will: so that I may just a little, all by myself, see where I am." She was conscious of the dire impatience of it, for she gave up Susie as well as the others to him—Susie who would have drowned her very self for her; gave her up to a mercenary

monster through whom she thus purchased respites. Strange were
the turns of life and the moods of weakness; strange the flickers of
fancy and the cheats of hope; yet lawful, all the same—weren't
they?—those experiments tried with the truth that consisted, at the
worst, but in practicing on one's self. She was now playing with the
thought that Eugenio might *inclusively* assist her: he had brought
home to her, and always by remarks that were really quite soundless, the conception, hitherto ungrasped, of some complete use of
her wealth itself, some use of it as a counter-move to fate. It had
passed between them as preposterous that with so much money
she should just stupidly and awkwardly *want*—any more want a
life, a career, a consciousness, than want a house, a carriage or a
cook. It was as if she had had from him a kind of expert professional measure of what he was in a position, at a stretch, to under-
take for her; the thoroughness of which, for that matter, she could
closely compare with a looseness on Sir Luke Strett's part that—at
least in Palazzo Leporelli when mornings were fine—showed as
almost amateurish. Sir Luke hadn't said to her "Pay enough
money and leave the rest to *me*"—which was distinctly what Eugenio did say. Sir Luke had appeared indeed to speak of purchase
and payment, but in reference to a different sort of cash. Those
were amounts not to be named nor reckoned, and such moreover
as she wasn't sure of having at her command. Eugenio—this was
the difference—could name, could reckon, and prices of *his* kind
were things she had never suffered to scare her. She had been willing, goodness knew, to pay enough for anything, for everything,
and here was simply a new view of the sufficient quantity. She
amused herself—for it came to that, since Eugenio was there to
sign the receipt—with possibilities of meeting the bill. She was
more prepared than ever to pay enough, and quite as much as ever
to pay too much. What else—if such were points at which your
most trusted servant failed—was the use of being, as the dear
Susies of earth called you, a princess in a palace?

   She made now, alone, the full circuit of the place, noble and
peaceful while the summer sea, stirring here and there a curtain
or an outer blind, breathed into its veiled spaces. She had a vision
of clinging to it; that perhaps Eugenio could manage. She was *in*
it, as in the ark of her deluge, and filled with such a tenderness for

it that why shouldn't this, in common mercy, be warrant enough? She would never, never leave it—she would engage to that; would ask nothing more than to sit tight in it and float on and on. The beauty and intensity, the real momentary relief of this conceit, reached their climax in the positive purpose to put the question to Eugenio on his return as she had not yet put it; though the design, it must be added, dropped a little when, coming back to the great saloon from which she had started on her pensive progress, she found Lord Mark, of whose arrival in Venice she had been un-aware, and who had now—while a servant was following her through empty rooms—been asked, in her absence, to wait. He had waited then, Lord Mark, he was waiting—oh unmistakably; never before had he so much struck her as the man to do that on occasion with patience, to do it indeed almost as with gratitude for the chance, though at the same time with a sort of notifying firmness. The odd thing, as she was afterwards to recall, was that her wonder for what had brought him was not immediate, but had come at the end of five minutes; and also, quite incoherently, that she felt almost as glad to see him, and almost as forgiving of his in-terruption of her solitude, as if he had already been in her thought or acting at her suggestion. He was somehow, at the best, the end of a respite; one might like him very much and yet feel that his presence tempered precious solitude more than any other known to one: in spite of all of which, as he was neither dear Susie, nor dear Kate, nor dear Aunt Maud, nor even, for the least, dear Eu-genio in person, the sight of him did no damage to her sense of the dispersal of her friends. She hadn't been so thoroughly alone with him since those moments of his showing her the great portrait at Matcham, the moments that had exactly made the high-water-mark of her security, the moments during which her tears themselves, those she had been ashamed of, were the sign of her consciously rounding her protective promontory, quitting the blue gulf of comparative ignorance and reaching her view of the trou-bled sea. His presence now referred itself to his presence then, re-minding her how kind he had been, altogether, at Matcham, and telling her, unexpectedly, at a time when she could particularly feel it, that, for such kindness and for the beauty of what they re-membered together, she hadn't lost him—quite the contrary. To

receive him handsomely, to receive him there, to see him interested and charmed, as well, clearly, as delighted to have found her
without some other person to spoil it—these things were so pleasant for the first minutes that they might have represented on her
part some happy foreknowledge.

She gave an account of her companions while he on his side
failed to press her about them, even though describing his appearance, so unheralded, as the result of an impulse obeyed on
the spot. He had been shivering at Carlsbad, belated there and
blue, when taken by it; so that, knowing where they all were, he
had simply caught the first train. He explained how he had known
where they were; he had heard—what more natural?—from their
friends, Milly's and his. He mentioned this betimes, but it was
with his mention, singularly, that the girl became conscious of
her inner question about his reason. She noticed his plural,
which added to Mrs. Lowder or added to Kate; but she presently
noticed also that it didn't affect her as explaining. Aunt Maud had
written to him, Kate apparently—and this was interesting—had
written to him; but their design presumably hadn't been that he
should come and sit there as if rather relieved, so far as *they* were
concerned, at postponements. He only said "Oh!" and again
"Oh!" when she sketched their probable morning for him, under
Eugenio's care and Mrs. Stringham's—sounding it quite as if any
suggestion that he should overtake them at the Rialto or the
Bridge of Sighs would leave him temporarily cold. This precisely
it was that, after a little, operated for Milly as an obscure but still
fairly direct check to confidence. He had known where they all
were from the others, but it was not for the others that, in his actual dispositions, he had come. That, strange to say, was a pity;
for, stranger still to say, she could have shown him more confidence if he himself had had less intention. His intention so
chilled her, from the moment she found herself divining it, that,
just for the pleasure of going on with him fairly, just for the pleasure of their remembrance together of Matcham and the
Bronzino, the climax of her fortune, she could have fallen to
pleading with him and to reasoning, to undeceiving him in time.
There had been, for ten minutes, with the directness of her welcome to him and the way this clearly pleased him, something of

the grace of amends made, even though he couldn't know it—amends for her not having been originally sure, for instance at that first dinner of Aunt Maud's, that he was adequately human. That first dinner of Aunt Maud's added itself to the hour at Matcham, added itself to other things, to consolidate, for her present benevolence, the ease of their relation, making it suddenly delightful that he had thus turned up. He exclaimed, as he looked about, on the charm of the place: "What a temple to taste and an expression of the pride of life, yet, with all that, what a jolly *home!*—so that, for his entertainment, she could offer to walk him about though she mentioned that she had just been, for her own purposes, in a general prowl, taking everything in more susceptibly than before. He embraced her offer without a scruple and seemed to rejoice that he was to find her susceptible.

— IV —

She couldn't have said what it was, in the conditions, that renewed the whole solemnity, but by the end of twenty minutes a kind of wistful hush had fallen upon them, as before something poignant in which her visitor also participated. That was nothing verily but the perfection of the charm—or nothing rather but their excluded disinherited state in the presence of it. The charm turned on them a face that was cold in its beauty, that was full of a poetry never to be theirs, that spoke with an ironic smile of a possible but forbidden life. It all rolled afresh over Milly: "Oh the impossible romance—!" The romance for her, yet once more, would be to sit there for ever, through all her time, as in a fortress; and the idea became an image of never going down, of remaining aloft in the divine dustless air, where she would hear but the splash of the water against stone. The great floor on which they moved was at an altitude, and this prompted the rueful fancy. "Ah not to go down—never, never to go down!" she strangely sighed to her friend.

"But why shouldn't you," he asked, "with that tremendous old staircase in your court? There ought of course always to be people at top and bottom, in Veronese* costumes, to watch you do it."

She shook her head both lightly and mournfully enough at his not understanding. "Not even for people in Veronese costumes. I mean that the positive beauty is that one needn't go down. I don't move in fact," she added—"now. I've not been out, you know. I stay up. That's how you happily found me."

Lord Mark wondered—he was, oh yes, adequately human. "You don't go about?"

She looked over the place, the story above the apartments in which she had received him, the sala corresponding to the sala below and fronting the great canal with its gothic arches. The casements between the arches were open, the ledge of the balcony broad, the sweep of the canal, so overhung, admirable, and the flutter toward them of the loose white curtain an invitation to she scarce could have said what. But there was no mystery after a moment; she had never felt so invited to anything as to make that, and that only, just where she was, her adventure. It would be—to this it kept coming back—the adventure of not stirring. "I go about just here."

"Do you mean," Lord Mark presently asked, "that you're really not well?"

They were at the window, pausing, lingering, with the fine old faded palaces opposite and the slow Adriatic tide beneath; but after a minute, and before she answered, she had closed her eyes to what she saw and unresistingly dropped her face into her arms, which rested on the coping. She had fallen to her knees on the cushion of the window-place, and she leaned there, in a long silence, with her forehead down. She knew that her silence was itself too straight an answer, but it was beyond her now to say that she saw her way. She would have made the question itself impossible to others—impossible for example to such a man as Merton Densher; and she could wonder even on the spot what it was a sign of in her feeling for Lord Mark that from his lips it almost tempted her to break down. This was doubtless really because she cared for

---

*Paolo Veronese (1528–1588), Venetian painter whose figures wore rich, colourful costumes.

him so little; to let herself go with him thus, suffer his touch to make her cup overflow, would be the relief—since it was actually, for her nerves, a question of relief—that would cost her least. If he had come to her moreover with the intention she believed, or even if this intention had but been determined in him by the spell of their situation, he mustn't be mistaken about her value—for what value did she now have? It throbbed within her as she knelt there that she had none at all; though, holding herself, not yet speaking, she tried, even in the act, to recover what might be possible of it. With that there came to her a light: wouldn't her value, for the man who should marry her, be precisely in the ravage of her disease? *She* mightn't last, but her money would. For a man in whom the vision of her money should be intense, in whom it should be most of the ground for "making up" to her, any prospective failure on her part to be long for this world might easily count as a positive attraction. Such a man, proposing to please, persuade, secure her, appropriate her for such a time, shorter or longer, as nature and the doctors should allow, would make the best of her, ill, damaged, disagreeable though she might be, for the sake of eventual benefits: she being clearly a person of the sort esteemed likely to do the handsome thing by a stricken and sorrowing husband.

She had said to herself betimes, in a general way, that whatever habits her youth might form, that of seeing an interested suitor in every bush should certainly never grow to be one of them—an attitude she had early judged as ignoble, as poisonous. She had had accordingly in fact as little to do with it as possible and she scarce knew why at the present moment she should have had to catch herself in the act of imputing an ugly motive. It didn't sit, the ugly motive, in Lord Mark's cool English eyes; the darker side of it at any rate showed, to her imagination, but briefly. Suspicion moreover, with this, simplified itself: there was a beautiful reason—indeed there were two—why her companion's motive shouldn't matter. One was that even should he desire her without a penny she wouldn't marry him for the world; the other was that she felt him, after all, perceptively, kindly, very pleasantly and humanly, concerned for her. They were also two things, his wishing to be well, to be very well, with her, and his beginning to feel her as threatened, haunted, blighted; but they were melting together for him, making him, by their combination, only the more sure that, as he probably called it to himself, he liked her. That was presently what remained with her—his really doing it; and with the natural and proper incident of being conciliated by her weakness. Would she really have had him—she could ask herself that—disconcerted or disgusted by it? If he could only be touched enough to do what she preferred, not to raise, not to press any question, he might render her a much better service than by merely enabling her to refuse him. Again, again it was strange, but he figured to her for the moment as the one safe sympathizer. It would have made her worse to talk to others, but she wasn't afraid with him of how he might wince and look pale. She would keep him, that is, her one easy relation—in the sense of easy for himself. Their actual outlook had meanwhile such charm, what surrounded them within and without did so much toward making appreciative stillness as natural as at the opera, that she could consider she hadn't made him hang on her lips when at last, instead of saying if she were well or ill, she repeated: "I go about here. I don't get tired of it. I never should—it suits me so. I adore the place," she went on, "and I don't want in the least to give it up."

"Neither should I if I had your luck. Still, with that luck, for one's *all*—! Should you positively like to live here?"

"I think I should like," said poor Milly after an instant, "to die here."

Which made him, precisely, laugh. That was what she wanted—when a person did care: it was the pleasant human way, without depths of darkness. "Oh it's not good enough for *that!* That requires picking. But can't you keep it? It is, you know, the sort of place to see you in; you carry out the note, fill it, people it, quite by yourself, and you might do much worse—I mean for your friends—than show yourself here a while, three or four months, every year. But it's not my notion for the rest of the time. One has quite other uses for you."

"What sort of a use for me is it," she smilingly inquired, "to kill me?"

"Do you mean we should kill you in England?"

"Well, I've seen you and I'm afraid. You're too much for me—

too many. England bristles with questions. This is more, as you say there, my form."

"Oho, oho!"—he laughed again as if to humour her. "Can't you then buy it—for a price? Depend upon it they'll treat for money. That is for money enough."

"I've exactly," she said, "been wondering if they won't. I think I shall try. But if I get it I shall cling to it." They were talking sincerely. "It will be my life—paid for as that. It will become my great gilded shell; so that those who wish to find me must come and hunt me up."

"Ah then you *will* be alive," said Lord Mark.

"Well, not quite extinct perhaps, but shrunken, wasted, wizened; rattling about here like the dried kernel of a nut."

"Oh," Lord Mark returned, "we, much as you mistrust us, can do better for you than that."

"In the sense that you'll feel it better for me really to have it over?"

He let her see now that she worried him, and after a look at her, of some duration, without his glasses—which always altered the expression of his eyes—he re-settled the nippers* on his nose and went back to the view. But the view, in turn, soon enough released him. "Do you remember something I said to you that day at Matcham—or at least fully meant to?"

"Oh yes, I remember everything at Matcham. It's another life."

"Certainly it will be—I mean the kind of thing: what I then wanted it to represent for you. Matcham, you know," he continued, "is symbolic. I think I tried to rub that into you a little."

She met him with the full memory of what he had tried—not an inch, not an ounce of which was lost to her. "What I meant is that it seems a hundred years ago."

"Oh for me it comes in better. Perhaps a part of what makes me remember it," he pursued, "is that I was quite aware of what might have been said about what I was doing. I wanted you to take it from me that I should perhaps be able to look after you—will, rather better. Rather better, of course, than certain other persons in particular."

---

*Here, "nippers" refers to the nosepiece of Lord Mark's eyeglasses.

"Precisely—than Mrs. Lowder, than Miss Croy, even than Mrs. Stringham."

"Oh Mrs. Stringham's all right!" Lord Mark promptly amended.

It amused her even with what she had else to think of; and she could show him at all events how little, in spite of the hundred years, she had lost what he alluded to. The way he was with her at this moment made in fact the other moment so vivid as almost to start again the tears it had started at the time. "You could do so much for me, yes. I perfectly understood you."

"I wanted you see," he despite this explained, "to *fix* your confidence. I mean, you know, in the right place."

"Well, Lord Mark, you did—it's just exactly now, my confidence, where you put it then. The only difference," said Milly, "is that I seem now to have no use for it. Besides," she then went on, "I do seem to feel you disposed to act in a way that would undermine it a little."

He took no more notice of these last words than if she hadn't said them, only watching her at present as with a gradual new light. "Are you *really* in any trouble?"

To this, on her side, she gave no heed. Making out his light was a little a light for herself. "Don't say, don't try to say, anything that's impossible. There are much better things you can do."

He looked straight at it and then straight over it. "It's too monstrous that one can't ask you as a friend what one wants so to know."

"What is it you want to know?" She spoke, as by a sudden turn, with a slight hardness. "Do you want to know if I'm badly ill?"

The sound of it in truth, though from no raising of her voice, invested the idea with a kind of terror, but a terror all for others. Lord Mark winced and flushed—clearly couldn't help it; but he kept his attitude together and spoke even with unwonted vivacity. "Do you imagine I can see you suffer and not say a word?"

"You won't see me suffer—don't be afraid. I shan't be a public nuisance. That's why I should have liked *this*: it's so beautiful in itself and yet it's out of the gangway. You won't know anything about anything," she added; and then as if to make with decision an end: "And you *don't*! No, not even you." He faced her through it with the remains of his expression, and she saw him as clearly—for *him*—bewildered; which made her wish to be sure not to have been unkind. She would be kind once for all; that would be the end. "I'm very badly ill."

"And you don't do anything?"

"I do everything. Everything's *this*," she smiled. "I'm doing it now. One can't do more than live."

"Oh live!" Lord Mark ejaculated.

"Well, it's immense for *me*." She finally spoke as if for amusement; now that she had uttered her truth, that he had learnt it from herself as no one had yet done, her emotion had, by the fact, dried up. There she was; but it was as if she would never speak again. "I shan't," she added, "have missed everything."

"Why should you have missed *anything*?" She felt, as he sounded this, to what, within the minute, he had made up his mind. "You're the person in the world for whom that's least necessary; for whom one would call it in fact most impossible; for whom 'missing' at all will surely require an extraordinary amount of misplaced good will. Since you believe in advice, for God's sake take *mine*. I know what you want."

Oh she knew he would know it. But she had brought it on herself—or almost. Yet she spoke with kindness. "I think I want not to be too much worried."

"You want to be adored." It came at last straight. "Nothing would worry you less. I mean as I shall do it. It *is* so"—he firmly kept it up. "You're not loved enough."

"Enough for what, Lord Mark?"

"Why to get the full good of it."

Well, she didn't after all mock at him. "I see what you mean. That full good of it which consists in finding one's self forced to love in return." She had grasped it, but she hesitated. "Your idea is that I might find myself forced to love *you*?"

"Oh 'forced'—!" He was so fine and so expert, so awake to anything the least ridiculous, and of a type with which the preaching of passion somehow so ill consorted—he was so much all these things that he had absolutely to take account of them himself. And he did so, in a single intonation, beautifully. Milly liked him again, liked him for such shades as that, liked him so that it was woeful to see him spoiling it, and still more woeful to have to rank him among those minor charms of existence that she gasped at moments to remember she must give up. "Is it inconceivable to you that you might try?"

"To be so favorably affected by you—?"

"To believe in me. To believe in me," Lord Mark repeated.

Again she hesitated. "To 'try' in return for your trying?"

"Oh I shouldn't have to!" he quickly declared. The prompt neat accent, however, his manner of disposing of her question, failed of real expression, as he himself the next moment intelligently, help-lessly, almost comically saw—a failure pointed moreover by the laugh into which Milly was immediately startled. As a suggestion to her of a healing and uplifting passion it *was* in truth deficient; it wouldn't do as the communication of a force that should sweep them both away. And the beauty of him was that he too, even in the act of persuasion, of self-persuasion, could understand that, and could thereby show but the better as fitting into the pleasant commerce of prosperity. The way she let him see that she looked at him was a thing to shut him out, of itself, from services of dan-ger, a thing that made a discrimination against him never yet made—made at least to any consciousness of his own. Born to float in a sustaining air, this would be his first encounter with a judgement formed in the sinister light of tragedy. The gathering dusk of *her* personal world presented itself to him, in her eyes, as an element in which it was vain for him to pretend he could find himself at home, since it was charged with depressions and with dooms, with the chill of the losing game. Almost without her needing to speak, and simply by the fact that there could be, in such a case, no decent substitute for a felt intensity, he had to take it from her that practically he was afraid—whether afraid to protest falsely enough, or only afraid of what might be eventually dis-agreeable in a compromised alliance, being a minor question. She believed she made out besides, wonderful girl, that he had never quite expected to have to protest about anything beyond his natu-ral convenience—more, in fine, than his disposition and habits, his education as well, his personal *moyens*,* in short, permitted.

---

*Means (French); his estate, wealth.

His predicament was therefore one he couldn't like, and also one she willingly would have spared him hadn't he brought it on himself. No man, she was quite aware, could enjoy thus having it from her that he wasn't good for what she would have called her reality. It wouldn't have taken much more to enable her positively to make out in him that he was virtually capable of hinting—had his innermost feeling spoken—at the propriety rather, in his interest, of some cutting down, some dressing up, of the offensive real. He would meet that halfway, but the real must also meet *him.* Milly's sense of it for herself, which was so conspicuously, so financially supported, couldn't, or wouldn't, so accommodate him, and the perception of that fairly showed in his face after a moment like the smart of a blow. It had marked the one minute during which he could again be touching to her. By the time he had tried once more, after all, to insist, he had quite ceased to be so.

By this time she had turned from their window to make a diversion, had walked him through other rooms, appealing again to the inner charm of the place, going even so far for that purpose as to point afresh her independent moral, to repeat that if one only had such a house for one's own and loved it and cherished it enough, it would pay one back in kind, would close one in from harm. He quite grasped for the quarter of an hour the perch she held out to him—grasped it with one hand, that is, while she felt him attached to his own clue with the other; he was by no means either so sore or so stupid, to do him all justice, as not to be able to behave more or less as if nothing had happened. It was one of his merits, to which she did justice too, that both his native and his acquired notion of behaviour rested on the general assumption that nothing—nothing to make a deadly difference for him—ever *could* happen. It was, socially, a working view like another, and it saw them easily enough through the greater part of the rest of their adventure. Downstairs again, however, with the limit of his stay in sight, the sign of his smarting, when all was said, reappeared for her—breaking out moreover, with an effect of strangeness, in another quite possibly sincere allusion to her state of health. He might for that matter have been seeing what he could do in the way of making it a grievance that she should snub him for a charity, on his own part, exquisitely roused. "It's true, you know, all the same, and I don't care a straw for your trying to freeze one up." He seemed to show her, poor man, bravely, how little he cared. "Everybody knows affection often makes things out when indifference doesn't notice. And that's why I know that *I* notice."

"Are you sure you've got it right?" the girl smiled. "I thought rather that affection was supposed to be blind."

"Blind to faults, not to beauties," Lord Mark promptly returned.

"And are my extremely private worries, my entirely domestic complications, which I'm ashamed to have given you a glimpse of—are they beauties?"

"Yes, for those who care for you—as every one does. Everything about you is a beauty. Besides which I don't believe," he declared, "in the seriousness of what you tell me. It's too absurd you should have *any* trouble about which something can't be done. If you can't get the right thing, who *can*, in all the world, I should like to know? You're the first young woman of your time. I mean what I say." He looked, to do him justice, quite as if he did; not ardent, but clear—simply so competent, in such a position, to compare, that his quiet assertion had the force not so much perhaps of a tribute as of a warrant. "We're all in love with you. I'll put it that way, dropping any claim of my own, if you can bear it better. I speak as one of the lot. You weren't born simply to torment us—you were born to make us happy. Therefore you must listen to us."

She shook her head with her slowness, but this time with all her mildness. "No, I mustn't listen to you—that's just what I mustn't do. The reason is, please, that it simply kills me. I must be as attached to you as you will, since you give that lovely account of yourselves. I give you in return the fullest possible belief of what it would be—" And she pulled up a little. "I give and give and give—there you are; stick to me as close as you like and see if I don't. Only I can't listen or receive or accept—I can't *agree*. I can't make a bargain. I can't really. You must believe that from me. It's all I've wanted to say to you, and why should it spoil anything?"

He let her question fall—though clearly, it might have seemed, because, for reasons or for none, there was so much that *was* spoiled. "You want somebody of your own." He came back, whether in good faith or in bad, to that; and it made her repeat her headshake. He kept it up as if his faith were of the best. "You want somebody, you want somebody."

She was to wonder afterwards if she hadn't been at this juncture on the point of saying something emphatic and vulgar—"Well, I don't at all events want *you!*" What somehow happened, nevertheless, the pity of it being greater than the irritation—the sadness, to her vivid sense, of his being so painfully astray, wandering in a desert in which there was nothing to nourish him—was that his error amounted to positive wrongdoing. She was moreover so acquainted with quite another sphere of usefulness for him that her having suffered him to insist almost convicted her of indelicacy. Why hadn't she stopped him off with her first impression of his purpose? She could do so now only by the allusion she had been wishing not to make. "Do you know I don't think you're doing very right?—and as a thing quite apart, I mean, from my listening to you. That's not right either—except that I'm *not* listening. You oughtn't to have come to Venice to see *me*—and in fact you've not come, and you mustn't behave as if you had. You've much older friends than I, and ever so much better. Really, if you've come at all, you can only have come—properly, and if I may say so honourably—for the best friend, as I believe her to be, that you have in the world."

When once she had said it he took it, oddly enough, as if he had been more or less expecting it. Still, he looked at her very hard, and they had a moment of this during which neither pronounced a name, each apparently determined that the other should. It was Milly's fine coercion, in the event, that was the stronger. "Miss Croy?" Lord Mark asked.

It might have been difficult to make out that she smiled. "Mrs. Lowder." He did make out something, and then fairly coloured for its attestation of his comparative simplicity. "I call *her* on the whole the best. I can't imagine a man's having a better."

Still with his eyes on her he turned it over. "Do you want me to marry Mrs. Lowder?"

At which it seemed to her that it was he who was almost vulgar! But she wouldn't in any way have that. "You know, Lord Mark, what I mean. One isn't in the least turning you out into the cold world. There's no cold world for you at all, I think," she went on;

"nothing but a very warm and watchful and expectant world that's waiting for you at any moment you choose to take it up."

He never budged, but they were standing on the polished concrete and he had within a few minutes possessed himself again of his hat. "Do you want me to marry Kate Croy?"

"Mrs. Lowder wants it—I do no wrong, I think, in saying that; and she understands moreover that you know she does."

Well, he showed how beautifully he could take it; and it wasn't obscure to her, on her side, that it was a comfort to deal with a gentleman. "It's ever so kind of you to see such opportunities for me. But what's the use of my tackling Miss Croy?"

Milly rejoiced on the spot to be so able to point out. "Because she's the handsomest and cleverest and most charming creature I ever saw, and because if I were a man I should simply adore her. In fact I do as it is." It was a luxury of response.

"Oh, my dear lady, plenty of people adore her. But that can't further the case of *all*."

"Ah," she went on, "I know about 'people.' If the case of one's bad, the case of another's good. I don't see what you have to fear from any one else," she said, "save through your being foolish, this way, about *me*."

So she said, but she was aware the next moment of what he was making of what she didn't see. "Is it your idea—since we're talking of these things in these ways—that the young lady you describe in such superlative terms is to be had for the asking?"

"Well, Lord Mark, try. She *is* a great person. But don't be humble." She was almost gay.

It was this apparently, at last, that was too much for him. "But don't you really *know*?"

As a challenge, practically, to the commonest intelligence she could pretend to, it made her of course wish to be fair. "I 'know,' yes, that a particular person's very much in love with her."

"Then you must know by the same token that she's very much in love with a particular person."

"Ah I beg your pardon!"—and Milly quite flushed at having so crude a blunder imputed to her. "You're wholly mistaken."

"It's not true?"

"It's not true."

His stare became a smile. "Are you very, very sure?"

"As sure as one can be"—and Milly's manner could match it—"when one has every assurance. I speak on the best authority."

He hesitated. "Mrs. Lowder's?"

"No. I don't call Mrs. Lowder's the best."

"Oh I thought you were just now saying," he laughed, "that everything about her's so good."

"Good for you"—she was perfectly clear. "For you," she went on, "let her authority be the best. She doesn't believe what you mention, and you must know yourself how little she makes of it. So you can take it from her. *I* take it—" But Milly, with the positive tremor of her emphasis, pulled up.

"You take it from Kate?"

"From Kate herself."

"That she's thinking of no one at all?"

"Of no one at all." Then, with her intensity, she went on. "She has given me her word for it."

"Oh!" said Lord Mark. To which he next added: "And what do you call her word?"

It made Milly, on her side, stare—though perhaps partly but with the instinct of gaining time for the consciousness that she was already a little further "in" than she had designed. "Why, Lord Mark, what should *you* call her word?"

"Ah I'm not obliged to say. I've not asked her. You apparently have."

Well, it threw her on her defence—a defence that she felt, however, especially as of Kate. "We're very intimate," she said in a moment; "so that, without prying into each other's affairs, she naturally tells me things."

Lord Mark smiled as at a lame conclusion. "You mean then she made you of her own movement the declaration you quote?"

Milly thought again, though with hindrance rather than help in her sense of the way their eyes now met—met as for their each seeing in the other more than either said. What she most felt that she herself saw was the strange disposition on her companion's part to disparage Kate's veracity. She could be only concerned to "stand up" for that.

"I mean what I say: that when she spoke of her having no private interest—"

"She took her oath to you?" Lord Mark interrupted.

Milly didn't quite see why he should so catechise her; but she met it again for Kate. "She left me in no doubt whatever of her being free."

At this Lord Mark did look at her, though he continued to smile. "And thereby in no doubt of *your* being too?" It was as if as soon as he had said it, however, he felt it as something of a mistake, and she couldn't herself have told by what queer glare at him she had instantly signified that. He at any rate gave her glare no time to act further; he fell back on the spot, and with a light enough movement, within his rights. "That's all very well, but why in the world, dear lady, should she be swearing to you?"

She had to take this "dear lady" as applying to herself; which disconcerted her when he might now so gracefully have used it for the aspersed Kate. Once more it came to her that she must claim her own part of the aspersion. "Because, as I've told you, we're such tremendous friends."

"Oh," said Lord Mark, who for the moment looked as if that might have stood rather for an absence of such rigors. He was going, however, as if he had in a manner, at the last, got more or less what he wanted. Milly felt, while he addressed his next few words to leave-taking, that she had given rather more than she intended or than she should be able, when once more getting herself into hand, theoretically to defend. Strange enough in fact that he had had from her, about herself—and, under the searching spell of the place, infinitely straight—what no one else had had: neither Kate, nor Aunt Maud, nor Merton Densher, nor Susan Shepherd. He had made her within a minute, in particular, she was aware, lose her presence of mind, and she now wished he would take himself off, so that she might either recover it or bear the loss better in solitude. If he paused, however, she almost at the same time saw, it was because of his watching the approach, from the end of the sala, of one of the gondoliers, who, whatever excursions were appointed for the party with the attendance of the others, always, as the most decorative, most sashed and starched, remained at the palace on the theory that she might whimsically want him—which she never, in her caged freedom, had yet done. Brown Pasquale, slipping in white shoes over the marble and suggesting to her perpetually charmed vision she could scarce say what, either a mild Hindoo, too noiseless almost for her nerves, or simply a bare-footed seaman on the deck of a ship—Pasquale offered to sight a small salver, which he obsequiously held out to her with its burden of a visiting-card. Lord Mark—and as if also for admiration of him—delayed his departure to let her receive it; on which she read it with the instant effect of another blow to her presence of mind. This precarious quantity was indeed now so gone that even for dealing with Pasquale she had to do her best to conceal its disappearance. The effort was made, none the less, by the time she had asked if the gentleman were below and had taken in the fact that he had come up. He had followed the gondolier and was waiting at the top of the staircase.

"I'll see him with pleasure." To which she added for her companion, while Pasquale went off: "Mr. Merton Densher."

"Oh!" said Lord Mark—in a manner that, making it resound through the great cool hall, might have carried it even to Densher's ear as a judgement of his identity heard and noted once before.

BOOK EIGHTH

– I –

Densher became aware, afresh, that he disliked his hotel—
and all the more promptly that he had had occasion of old
to make the same discrimination. The establishment,
choked at that season with the polyglot herd, cockneys of all
climes, mainly German, mainly American, mainly English, it appeared as the corresponding sensitive nerve was touched, sounded
loud and now sweet, sounded anything and everything but Italian,
but Venetian. The Venetian was all a dialect, he knew; yet it was
pure Attic beside some of the dialects at the bustling inn. It made,
"abroad," both for his pleasure and his pain that he had to feel at
almost any point how he had been through everything before. He
had been three or four times, in Venice, during other visits,
through this pleasant irritation of paddling away—away from the
concert of false notes in the vulgarized hall, away from the amiable
American families and overfed German porters. He had in each
case made terms for a lodging more private and not more costly,
and he recalled with tenderness these shabby but friendly asylums,
the windows of which he should easily know again in passing on
canal or through campo. The shabbiest now failed of an appeal to
him, but he found himself at the end of forty-eight hours forming
views in respect to a small independent *quartiere*,* far down the
Grand Canal, which he had once occupied for a month with a
sense of pomp and circumstance and yet also with a growth of initiation into the homelier Venetian mysteries. The humour of those
days came back to him for an hour, and what further befell in this
interval, to be brief, was that, emerging on a traghetto† in sight of
the recognized house, he made out on the green shutters of his
old, of his young windows the strips of white pasted paper that figure in Venice as an invitation to tenants. This was in the course of

---

*Apartment (Italian).
†Water taxi (Italian).

his very first walk apart, a walk replete with impressions to which
he responded with force. He had been almost without cessation,
since his arrival, at Palazzo Leporelli, where, as happened, a turn
of bad weather on the second day had kept the whole party con-
tinuously at home. The episode had passed for him like a series of
hours in a museum, though without the fatigue of that; and it had
also resembled something that he was still, with a stirred imagination, to find a name for. He might have been looking for the name
while he gave himself up, subsequently, to the ramble—he saw
that even after years he couldn't lose his way—crowned with his
stare across the water at the little white papers.

He was to dine at the palace in an hour or two, and he had
lunched there, at an early luncheon, that morning. He had then
been out with the three ladies, the three being Mrs. Lowder, Mrs.
Stringham and Kate, and had kept afloat with them, under a sufficient Venetian spell, until Aunt Maud had directed him to leave
them and return to Miss Theale. Of two circumstances connected
with this disposition of his person he was even now not unmind-
ful; the first being that the lady of Lancaster Gate had addressed
him with high publicity and as if expressing equally the sense of
her companions, who had not spoken, but who might have been
taken—yes, Susan Shepherd quite equally with Kate—for inscrutable parties to her plan. What he could as little contrive to
forget was that he had, before the two others, as it struck him—that
was to say especially before Kate—done exactly as he was bidden,
gathered himself up without a protest and retraced his way to the
palace. Present with him still was the question of whether he
looked a fool for it, of whether the awkwardness he felt as the gondola rocked with the business of his leaving it—they could but
make, in submission, for a landing-place that was none of the
best—had furnished his friends with such entertainment as was to
cause them, behind his back, to exchange intelligent smiles. He
had found Milly Theale twenty minutes later alone, and he had sat
with her till the others returned to tea. The strange part of this was
that it had been very easy, extraordinarily easy. He knew it for
strange only when he was away from her, because when he was
away from her he was in contact with particular things that made
it so. At the time, in her presence, it was as simple as sitting with

his sister might have been, and not, if the point were urged, very much more thrilling. He continued to see her as he had first seen her—that remained ineffaceably behind. Mrs. Lowder, Susan Shepherd, his own Kate, might, each in proportion, see her as a princess, as an angel, as a star, but for himself, luckily, she hadn't as yet complications to any point of discomfort: the princess, the angel, the star, were muffled over, ever so lightly and brightly, with the little American girl who had been kind to him in New York and to whom certainly—though without making too much of it for either of them—he was perfectly willing to be kind in return. She appreciated his coming in on purpose, but there was nothing in that—from the moment she was always at home—that they couldn't easily keep up. The only note the least bit high that had even yet sounded between them was this admission on her part that she found it best to remain within. She wouldn't let him call it keeping quiet, for she insisted that her palace—with all its romance and art and history—had set up round her a whirlwind of suggestion that never dropped for an hour. It wasn't therefore, within such walls, confinement, it was the freedom of all the centuries: in respect to which Densher granted good-humouredly that they were then blown together, she and he, as much as she liked, through space.

Kate had found on the present occasion a moment to say to him that he suggested a clever cousin calling on a cousin afflicted, and bored for his pains; and though he denied on the spot the "bored" he could so far see it as an impression he might make that he wondered if the same image wouldn't have occurred to Milly. As soon as Kate appeared again the difference came up—the oddity, as he then instantly felt it, of his having sunk so deep. It was sinking because it was all doing what Kate had conceived for him; it wasn't in the least doing—and that had been his notion of his life—anything he himself had conceived. The difference, accordingly, renewed, sharp, sore, was the irritant under which he had quitted the palace and under which he was to make the best of the business of again dining there. He said to himself that he must make the best of everything; that was in his mind, at the traghetto, even while, with his preoccupation about changing quarters, he studied, across the canal, the look of his former abode. It had done for the past, would it do for the present? would it play in any manner into the general necessity of which he was conscious? That necessity of making the best was the instinct—as he indeed himself knew—of a man somehow aware that if he let go at one place he should let go everywhere. If he took off his hand, the hand that at least helped to hold it together, the whole queer fabric that built him in would fall away in a minute and admit the light. It was really a matter of nerves; it was exactly because he was nervous that he *could* go straight; yet if that condition should increase he must surely go wild. He was walking in short on a high ridge, steep down on either side, where the proprieties—once he could face at all remaining there—reduced themselves to his keeping his head. It was Kate who had so perched him, and there came up for him at moments, as he found himself planting one foot exactly before another, a sensible sharpness of irony as to her management of him. It wasn't that she had put him in danger—to be in real danger with her would have had another quality. There glowed for him in fact a kind of rage at what he wasn't having; an exasperation, a resentment, begotten truly by the very impatience of desire, in respect to his postponed and relegated, his so extremely manipulated state. It was beautifully done of her, but what was the real meaning of it unless that he was perpetually bent to her will? His idea from the first, from the very first of his knowing her, had been to be, as the French called it, *bon prince** with her, mindful of the good humour and generosity, the contempt, in the matter of confidence, for small outlays and small savings, that belonged to the man who wasn't generally afraid. There were things enough, goodness knew—for it was the moral of his plight—that he couldn't afford; but what had had a charm for him if not the notion of living handsomely, to make up for it, in another way? of not at all events reading the romance of his existence in a cheap edition. All he had originally felt in her came back to him, was indeed actually as present as ever—how he had admired and envied what he called to himself her pure talent for life, as distinguished from his own, a poor weak thing of the occasion, amateurishly patched up; only it

---

*Good, decent (French).

irritated him the more that this was exactly what was now, ever so characteristically, standing out in her.

It was thanks to her pure talent for life, verily, that he was just where he was and that he was above all just *how* he was. The proof of a decent reaction in him against so much passivity was, with no great richness, that he at least knew—knew, that is, how he was, and how little he liked it as a thing accepted in mere helplessness. He was, for the moment, wistful—that above all described it; that was so large a part of the force that, as the autumn afternoon closed in, kept him, on his traghetto, positively throbbing with his question. His question connected itself, even while he stood, with his special smothered soreness, his sense almost of shame; and the soreness and the shame were less as he let himself, with the help of the conditions about him, regard it as serious. It was born, for that matter, partly of the conditions, those conditions that Kate had so almost insolently braved, had been willing, without a pang, to see him ridiculously—ridiculously so far as just complacently— exposed to. How little it *could* be complacently he was to feel with the last thoroughness before he had moved from his point of vantage. His question, as we have called it, was the interesting question of whether he had really no will left. How could he know—that was the point—without putting the matter to the test? It had been right to be *bon prince*, and the joy, something of the pride, of having lived, in spirit, handsomely, was even now compatible with the impulse to look into their account; but he held his breath a little as it came home to him with supreme sharpness that, whereas he had done absolutely everything that Kate had wanted, she had done nothing whatever that he had. So it was in fine that his idea of the test by which he must try that possibility kept referring itself, in the warm early dusk, the approach of the Southern night—"conditions" these, such as we just spoke of—to the glimmer, more and more ghostly as the light failed, of the little white papers on his old green shutters. By the time he looked at his watch he had been for a quarter of an hour at this post of observation and reflexion; but by the time he walked away again he had found his answer to the idea that had grown so importunate. Since a proof of his will was wanted it was indeed very exactly in wait for him—it lurked there on the other side of the Canal. A fer-

ryman at the little pier had from time to time accosted him; but it
was a part of the play of his nervousness to turn his back on that facility. He would go over, but he walked, very quickly, round and
round, crossing finally by the Rialto. The rooms, in the event,
were unoccupied; the ancient padrona was there with her smile all
a radiance but her recognition all a fable; the ancient rickety objects too, refined in their shabbiness, amiable in their decay, as to
which, on his side, demonstrations were tenderly veracious; so that
before he took his way again he had arranged to come in on the
morrow.

He was amusing about it that evening at dinner—in spite of an
odd first impulse, which at the palace quite melted away, to treat
it merely as a matter for his own satisfaction. This need, this propriety, he had taken for granted even up to the moment of suddenly perceiving, in the course of talk, that the incident would
minister to innocent gaiety. Such was quite its effect, with the aid
of his picture—an evocation of the quaint, of the humblest rococo, of a Venetian interior in the true old note. He made the
point for his hostess that her own high chambers, though they
were a thousand grand things, weren't really this; made it in fact
with such success that she presently declared it his plain duty to
invite her on some near day to tea. She had expressed as yet—he
could feel it as felt among them all—no such clear wish to go anywhere, not even to make an effort for a parish feast, or an autumn
sunset, nor to descend her staircase for Titan or Gianbellini. It was
constantly Densher's view that, as between himself and Kate,
things were understood without saying, so that he could catch in
her, as she but too freely could in him, innumerable signs of it, the
whole soft breath of consciousness meeting and promoting consciousness. This view was so far justified to-night as that Milly's
offer to him of her company was to his sense taken up by Kate in
spite of her doing nothing to show it. It fell in so perfectly with
what she had desired and foretold that she was—and this was what
most struck him—sufficiently gratified and blinded by it not to
know, from the false quality of his response, from his tone and his
very look, which for an instant instinctively sought her own, that
he had answered inevitably, almost shamelessly, in a mere time-
gaining sense. It gave him on the spot, her failure of perception,

almost a beginning of the advantage he had been planning for—
that is at least if she too were not darkly dishonest. She might, he
was not unaware, have made out, from some deep part of her, the
bearing, in respect to herself, of the little fact he had announced;
for she was after all capable of that, capable of guessing and yet of
simultaneously hiding her guess. It wound him up a turn or two
further, none the less, to impute to her now a weakness of vision
by which he could himself feel the stronger. Whatever apprehension of his motive in shifting his abode might have brushed her
with its wings, she at all events certainly didn't guess that he was
giving their friend a hollow promise. That was what she had herself imposed on him; there had been in the prospect from the first
a definite particular point at which hollowness, to call it by its least
compromising name, would have to begin. Therefore its hour had
now charmingly sounded.

Whatever in life he had recovered his old rooms for, he had not
recovered them to receive Milly Theale: which made no more difference in his expression of happy readiness than if he had been—
just what he was trying not to be—fully hardened and fully base.
So rapid in fact was the rhythm of his inward drama that the quick
vision of impossibility produced in him by his hostess's direct and
unexpected appeal had the effect, slightly sinister, of positively
scaring him. It gave him a measure of the intensity, the reality of
his now mature motive. It prompted in him certainly no quarrel
with these things, but it made them as vivid as if they already
flushed with success. It was before the flush of success that his
heart beat almost to dread. The dread was but the dread of the
happiness to be compassed; only that was in itself a symptom. That
a visit from Milly should, in this projection of necessities, strike
him as of the last incongruity, quite as a hateful idea, and above all
as spoiling, should one put it grossly, his game—the adoption of
such a view might of course have an identity with one of those numerous ways of being a fool that seemed so to abound for him. It
would remain none the less the way to which he should be in advance most reconciled. His mature motive, as to which he allowed
himself no grain of illusion, had thus in an hour taken imaginative
possession of the place: that precisely was how he saw it seated
there, already unpacked and settled, for Milly's innocence, for

Milly's beauty, no matter how short a time, to be housed with. There were things she would never recognize, never feel, never catch in the air; but this made no difference in the fact that her brushing against them would do nobody any good. The discrimination and the scruple were for *him*. So he felt all the parts of the case together, while Kate showed admirably as feeling none of them. Of course, however—when hadn't it to be his last word?— Kate was always sublime.

That came up in all connexions during the rest of these first days; came up in especial under pressure of the fact that each time our plighted pair snatched, in its passage, at the good fortune of half an hour together, they were doomed—though Densher felt it as all by *his* act—to spend a part of the rare occasion in wonder at their luck and in study of its queer character. This was the case after he might be supposed to have got, in a manner, used to it; it was the case after the girl—ready always, as we say, with the last word—had given him the benefit of her righting of every wrong appearance, a support familiar to him now in reference to other phases. It was still the case after he possibly might, with a little imagination, as she freely insisted, have made out, by the visible working of the crisis, what idea on Mrs. Lowder's part had determined it. Such as the idea was—and that it suited Kate's own book she openly professed—he had only to see how things were turning out to feel it strikingly justified. Densher's reply to all this vividness was that of course Aunt Maud's intervention hadn't been occult, even for *his* vividness, from the moment she had written him, with characteristic concentration, that if he should see his way to come to Venice for a fortnight she should engage he would find it no blunder. It took Aunt Maud really to do such things in such ways; just as it took him, he was ready to confess, to do such others as he must now strike them all—didn't he?—as committed to Mrs. Lowder's admonition had been of course a direct reference to what she had said to him at Lancaster Gate before his departure the night Milly had failed them through illness; only it had at least matched that remarkable outbreak in respect to the quantity of good nature it attributed to him. The young man's discussions of his situation—which were confined to Kate; he had none with Aunt Maud herself—suffered a little, it may be divined, by the sense that he couldn't put everything off, as he privately expressed it, on other people. His ears in solitude, were apt to burn with the reflexion that Mrs. Lowder had simply tested him, seen him as he was and made out what could be done with him. She had had but to whistle for him and he had come. If she had taken for granted his good nature she was as justified as Kate declared. This awkwardness of his conscience, both in respect to his general plasticity, the fruit of his feeling plasticity, within limits, to be a mode of life like another—certainly better than some, and particularly in respect to such confusion as might reign about what he had really come for—this inward ache was not wholly dispelled by the style, charming as that was, of Kate's poetic versions. Even the high wonder and delight of Kate couldn't set him right with himself when there was something quite distinct from these things that kept him wrong.

In default of being right with himself he had meanwhile, for one thing, the interest of seeing—and quite for the first time in his life—whether, on a given occasion, that might be quite so necessary to happiness as was commonly assumed and as he had up to this moment never doubted. He was engaged distinctly in an adventure—he who had never thought himself cut out for them, and it fairly helped him that he was able at moments to say to himself that he mustn't fall below it. At his hotel, alone, by night, or in the course of the few late strolls he was finding time to take through dusky labyrinthine alleys and empty *campi*,* overhung with mouldering palaces,[21] where he paused in disgust at his want of ease and where the sound of a rare footstep on the enclosed pavement was like that of a retarded dancer in a banquet-hall deserted—during these interludes he entertained cold views, even to the point, at moments, on the principle that the shortest follies are the best, of thinking of immediate departure as not only possible but as indicated. He had however only to cross again the threshold of Palazzo Leporelli to see all the elements of the business compose, as painters called it, differently. It began to strike him then that departure wouldn't curtail, but would signally coarsen his folly, and

---

*Public squares (Italian).

that above all, as he hadn't really "begun" anything, had only submitted, consented, but too generously indulged and condoned the
beginnings of others, he had no call to treat himself with superstitious rigor. The single thing that was clear in complications was
that, whatever happened, one was to behave as a gentleman—to
which was added indeed the perhaps slightly less shining truth that
complications might sometimes have their tedium beguiled by a
study of the question of how a gentleman would behave.[22] This
question, I hasten to add, was not in the last resort Densher's greatest worry. Three women were looking to him at once, and, though
such a predicament could never be, from the point of view of facility, quite the ideal, it yet had, thank goodness, its immediate
workable law. The law was not to be a brute—in return for amia-
bilities. He hadn't come all the way out from England to be a
brute. He hadn't thought of what it might give him to have a fortnight, however handicapped, with Kate in Venice, to be a brute.
He hadn't treated Mrs. Lowder as if in responding to her suggestion he had understood her—he hadn't done that either to be a
brute. And what he had prepared least of all for such an anti-
climax was the prompt and inevitable, the achieved surrender—*as*
a gentleman, oh that indubitably!—to the unexpected impression
made by poor pale exquisite Milly as the mistress of a grand old
palace and the dispenser of an hospitality more irresistible, thanks
to all the conditions, than any ever known to him.

This spectacle had for him an eloquence, an authority, a felicity—he scarce knew by what strange name to call it—for which he
said to himself that he had not consciously bargained. Her welcome, her frankness, sweetness, sadness, brightness, her disconcerting poetry, as he made shift at moments to call it, helped as it
was by the beauty of her whole setting and by the perception at the
same time, on the observer's part, that this element gained from
her, in a manner, for effect and harmony, as much as it gave—her
whole attitude had, to his imagination, meanings that hung about
it, waiting upon her, hovering, dropping and quavering forth
again, like vague faint snatches, mere ghosts of sound, of old-
fashioned melancholy music. It was positively well for him, he had
his times of reflecting, that he couldn't put it off on Kate and Mrs.
Lowder, as a gentleman so conspicuously wouldn't, that—well,

that he had been rather taken in by not having known in advance! There had been now five days of it all without his risking even to Kate alone any hint of what he ought to have known and of what in particular therefore had taken him in. The truth was doubtless that really, when it came to any free handling and naming of things, they were living together, the five of them, in an air in which an ugly effect of "blurting out" might easily be produced. He came back with his friend on each occasion to the blest miracle of renewed propinquity, which had a double virtue in that favoring air. He breathed on it as if he could scarcely believe it, yet the time had passed, in spite of this privilege, without his quite committing himself, for her ear, to any such comment on Milly's high style and state as would have corresponded with the amount of recognition it had produced in him. Behind everything for him was his renewed remembrance, which had fairly become a habit, that he had been the first to know her. This was what they had all insisted on, in her absence, that day at Mrs. Lowder's; and this was in especial what had made him feel its influence on his immediately paying her a second visit. Its influence had been all there, been in the high-hung, rumbling carriage with them, from the moment she took him to drive, covering them in together as if it had been a rug of softest silk. It had worked as a clear connexion with something lodged in the past, something already their own. He had more than once recalled how he had said to himself even at that moment, at some point in the drive, that he was not *there*, not just as he was in so doing it, through Kate and Kate's idea, but through Milly and Milly's own, and through himself and *his* own, unmistakably—as well as through the little facts, whatever they had amounted to, of his time in New York.

— II —

There was at last, with everything that made for it, an occasion when he got from Kate, on what she now spoke of as his eternal refrain, an answer of which he was to measure afterwards the precipitating effect. His eternal refrain was the way he came back to the riddle of Mrs. Lowder's view of her profit—a view so hard to reconcile with the chances she gave them to meet. Impatiently, at this, the girl denied the chances, wanting to know from him, with a fine irony that smote him rather straight, whether he felt their opportunities as anything so grand. He looked at her deep in the eyes when she had sounded this note; it was the least he could let her off with for having made him visibly flush. For some reason then, with it, the sharpness dropped out of her tone, which became sweet and sincere. " 'Meet,' my dear man," she expressively echoed; "does it strike you that we get, after all, so very much out of our meetings?"

"On the contrary—they're starvation diet. All I mean is—and it's all I've meant from the day I came—that we at least get more than Aunt Maud."

"Ah but you see," Kate replied, "you don't understand what Aunt Maud gets."

"Exactly so—and it's what I don't understand that keeps me so fascinated with the question. *She* gives me no light; she's prodigious. She takes everything as of a natural—!"

"She takes it as 'of a natural' that at this rate I shall be making my reflexions about you. There's every appearance for her," Kate went on, "that what she had made her mind up to as possible *is* possible; that what she had thought more likely than not to happen *is* happening. The very essence of her, as you surely by this time have made out for yourself, is that when she adopts a view she—well, to her own sense, really brings the thing about, fairly terrorizes with her view any other, any opposite view, and those, not less, who represent that. I've often thought success comes to her"—Kate continued to study the phenomenon—"by the spirit in her that dares and defies her idea not to prove the right one. One has seen it so again and again, in the face of everything, *become* the right one."

Densher had for this, as he listened, a smile of the largest response. "Ah my dear child, if you can explain I of course needn't not 'understand.' I'm condemned to that," he on his side presently explained, "only when understanding fails." He took a moment; then he pursued: "Does she think she terrorizes *us?*" To which he added while, without immediate speech, Kate but looked over the place: "Does she believe anything so stiff as that you've really changed about me?" He knew now that he was probing the girl deep—something told him so; but that was a reason the more. "Has she got it into her head that you dislike me?"

To this, of a sudden, Kate's answer was strong. "You could yourself easily put it there!"

He wondered. "By telling her so?"

"No," said Kate as with amusement at his simplicity; "I don't ask that of you."

"Oh my dear," Densher laughed, "when you ask, you know, so little—!"

There was a full irony in this, on his own part, that he saw her resist the impulse to take up. "I'm perfectly justified in what I've asked," she quietly returned. "It's doing beautifully for you." Their eyes again intimately met, and the effect was to make her proceed. "You're not a bit unhappy."

"Oh ain't I?" he brought out very roundly.

"It doesn't practically show—which is enough for Aunt Maud. You're wonderful, you're beautiful," Kate said; "and if you really want to know whether I believe you're doing it you may take from me perfectly that I see it coming." With which, by a quick transition, as if she had settled the case, she asked him the hour.

"Oh only twelve-ten"—he had looked at his watch. "We've taken but thirteen minutes; we've time yet."

"Then we must walk. We must go toward them."

Densher, from where they had been standing, measured the long reach of the Square. "They're still in their shop. They're safe for half an hour."

"That shows then, that shows!" said Kate.

This colloquy had taken place in the middle of Piazza San Marco, always, as a great social saloon, a smooth-floored, blue-roofed chamber of amenity, favorable to talk; or rather, to be exact, not in the middle, but at the point where our pair had paused by a common impulse after leaving the great mosque-like church. It rose now, domed and pinnacled, but a little way behind them, and they had in front the vast empty space, enclosed by its arcades, to which at that hour movement and traffic were mostly confined. Venice was at breakfast, the Venice of the visitor

and the possible acquaintance, and, except for the parties of importunate pigeons picking up the crumbs of perpetual feasts, their
prospect was clear and they could see their companions hadn't yet
been, and weren't for a while longer likely to be, disgorged by the
lace-shop, in one of the *loggie*,* where, shortly before, they had
left them for a look-in—the expression was artfully Densher's—at
Saint Mark's. Their morning had happened to take such a turn as
brought this chance to the surface; yet his allusion, just made to
Kate, hadn't been an overstatement of their general opportunity.
The worst that could be said of their general opportunity was that
it was essentially in presence—in presence of every one; every
one consisting at this juncture, in a peopled world, of Susan
Shepherd, Aunt Maud and Milly. But the proof how, even in presence, the opportunity could become special was furnished precisely by this view of the compatibility of their comfort with a
certain amount of lingering. The others had assented to their not
waiting in the shop; it was of course the least the others could do.
What had really helped them this morning was the fact that, on
his turning up, as he always called it, at the palace, Milly had not,
as before, been able to present herself. Custom and use had hitherto seemed fairly established; on his coming round, day after
day—eight days had been now so conveniently marked—their
friends, Milly's and his, conveniently dispersed and left him to sit
with her till luncheon. Such was the perfect operation of the
scheme on which he had been, as he phrased it to himself, had
out; so that certainly there was that amount of justification for
Kate's vision of success. He *had*, for Mrs. Lowder—he couldn't
help it while sitting there—the air, which was the thing to be desired, of no absorption in Kate sufficiently deep to be alarming.
He had failed their young hostess each morning as little as she
had failed him; it was only to-day that she hadn't been well
enough to see him.

That had made a mark, all round; the mark was in the way in
which, gathered in the room of state, with the place, from the
right time, all bright and cool and beflowered, as always, to re-

---

*Arcades (Italian).

ceive her descent, they—the rest of them—simply looked at each other. It was lurid—lurid, in all probability, for each of them privately—that they had uttered no common regrets. It was strange for our young man above all that, if the poor girl was indisposed to *that* degree, the hush of gravity, of apprehension, of significance of some sort, should be the most the case—that of the guests—could permit itself. The hush, for that matter, continued after the party of four had gone down to the gondola and taken their places in it. Milly had sent them word that she hoped they would go out and enjoy themselves, and this indeed had produced a second remarkable look, a look as of their knowing, one quite as well as the other, what such a message meant as provision for the alternative beguilement of Densher. She wished not to have spoiled his morning, and he had therefore, in civility, to take it as pleasantly patched up. Mrs. Stringham had helped the affair out, Mrs. Stringham who, when it came to that, knew their friend better than any of them. She knew her so well that she knew herself as acting in exquisite compliance with conditions comparatively obscure, approximately awful to them, by not thinking it necessary to stay at home. She had corrected that element of the perfunctory which was the slight fault, for all of them, of the occasion; she had invented a preference for Mrs. Lowder and herself; she had remembered the fond dreams of the visitation of lace that had hitherto always been brushed away by accidents, and it had come up as well for her that Kate had, the day before, spoken of the part played by fatality in her own failure of real acquaintance with the inside of Saint Mark's. Densher's sense of Susan Shepherd's conscious intervention had by this time a corner of his mind all to itself; something that had begun for them at Lancaster Gate was now a sentiment clothed in a shape; her action, ineffably discreet, had at all events a way of affecting him as for the most part subtly, even when not superficially, in his own interest. They were not, as a pair, as a "team," really united; there were too many persons, at least three, and too many things, between them; but meanwhile something was preparing that would draw them closer. He scarce knew what: probably nothing but his finding, at some hour when it would be a service to do so, that she had all the while understood him. He even had a presentiment of a juncture at which the understanding of every one else would fail and this deep little person's alone survive.

Such was to-day, in its freshness, the moral air, as we may say, that hung about our young friends; these had been the small accidents and quiet forces to which they owed the advantage we have seen them in some sort enjoying. It seemed in fact fairly to deepen for them as they stayed their course again; the splendid Square, which had so notoriously, in all the years, witnessed more of the joy of life than any equal area in Europe, furnished them, in their remoteness from earshot, with solitude and security. It was as if, being in possession, they could say what they liked; and it was also as if, in consequence of that, each had an apprehension of what the other wanted to say. It was most of all for them, moreover, as if this very quantity, seated on their lips in the bright historic air, where the only sign for their ears was the flutter of the doves, begot in the heart of each a fear. There might have been a betrayal of that in the way Densher broke the silence resting on her last words. "What did you mean just now that I can do to make Mrs. Lowder believe? For myself, stupidly, if you will, I don't see, from the moment I can't lie to her, what else there *is* but lying."

Well, she could tell him. "You can say something both handsome and sincere to her about Milly—whom you honestly like so much. That wouldn't be lying; and, coming from you, it would have an effect. You don't, you know, say much about her." And Kate put before him the fruit of observation. "You don't, you know, speak of her at all."

"And has Aunt Maud," Densher asked, "told you so?" Then as the girl, for answer, only seemed to bethink herself, "You must have extraordinary conversations!" he exclaimed.

Yes, she had bethought herself. "We have extraordinary conversations."

His look, while their eyes met, marked him as disposed to hear more about them; but there was something in her own, apparently, that defeated the opportunity. He questioned her in a moment on a different matter, which had been in his mind a week, yet in respect to which he had had no chance so good as this. "Do you happen to know then, as such wonderful things pass between you, what she makes of the incident, the other day, of Lord Mark's so very superficial visit?—his having spent here, as I gather, but the two or three hours necessary for seeing our friend and yet taken no time at all, since he went off by the same night's train, for seeing any one else. What can she make of his not having waited to see *you*, or to see herself—with all he owes her?"

"Oh of course," said Kate, "she understands. He came to make Milly his offer of marriage—he came for nothing but that. As Milly wholly declined it his business was for the time at an end. He couldn't quite on the spot turn round to make up to *us*."

Kate had looked surprised that, as a matter of taste on such an adventurer's part, Densher shouldn't see it. But Densher was lost in another thought. "Do you mean that when, turning up myself, I found him leaving her, that was what had been taking place between them?"

"Didn't you make it out, my dear?" Kate inquired.

"What sort of a blundering weathercock then *is* he?" the young man went on in his wonder.

"Oh don't make too little of him!" Kate smiled. "Do you pretend that Milly didn't tell you?"

"How great an ass he had made of himself?"

Kate continued to smile. "You *are* in love with her, you know."

He gave her another long look. "Why, since she has refused him, should my opinion of Lord Mark show it? I'm not obliged, however, to think well of him for such treatment of the other persons I've mentioned, and I feel I don't understand from you why Mrs. Lowder should."

"She doesn't—but she doesn't care," Kate explained. "You know perfectly the terms on which lots of London people live together even when they're supposed to live very well. He's not committed to us—he was having his try. Mayn't an unsatisfied man," she asked, "always have his try?"

"And come back afterwards, with confidence in a welcome, to the victim of his inconstancy?"

Kate consented, as for argument, to be thought of as a victim. "Oh but he has *had* his try at *me*. So it's all right."

"Through your also having, you mean, refused him?"

She balanced an instant during which Densher might have just wondered if pure historic truth were to suffer a slight strain. But she dropped on the right side. "I haven't let it come to that. I've been too discouraging. Aunt Maud," she went on—now as lucid as ever—"considers, no doubt, that she has a pledge from him in respect to me; a pledge that would have been broken if Milly had accepted him. As the case stands that makes no difference."

Densher laughed out. "It isn't *his* merit that he has failed."

"It's still his merit, my dear, that he's Lord Mark. He's just what he was, and what he knew he was. It's not for me either to reflect on him after I've so treated him."

"Oh," said Densher impatiently, "you've treated him beautifully."

"I'm glad," she smiled, "that you can still be jealous." But before he could take it up she had more to say. "I don't see why it need puzzle you that Milly's so marked line gratifies Aunt Maud more than anything else can displease her. What does she see but that Milly herself recognizes her situation with you as too precious to be spoiled? Such a recognition as that can't but seem to her to involve in some degree your own recognition. Out of which she therefore gets it that the more you have for Milly the less you have for me."

There were moments again—we know that from the first they had been numerous—when he felt with a strange mixed passion the mastery of her mere way of putting things. There was something in it that bent him at once to conviction and to reaction. And this effect, however it be named, now broke into his tone. "Oh if she began to know what I have for you—!"

It wasn't ambiguous, but Kate stood up to it. "Luckily for us we may really consider she doesn't. So successful have we been."

"Well," he presently said, "I take from you what you give me, and I suppose that, to be consistent—to stand on my feet where I do stand at all—I ought to thank you. Only, you know, what you give me seems to me, more than anything else, the larger and larger size of my job. It seems to me more than anything else what you expect of me. It never seems to me somehow what I may expect of *you*. There's so much you *don't* give me."

She appeared to wonder. "And pray what is it I don't—?"

"I give you proof," said Densher. "You give me none."

"What then do you call proof?" she after a moment ventured to ask.

"You doing something for me."

She considered with surprise. "Am I not doing *this* for you? Do you call this nothing?"

"Nothing at all."

"Ah I risk, my dear, everything for it."

They had strolled slowly further, but he was brought up short. "I thought you exactly contend that, with your aunt so bamboozled, you risk nothing!"

It was the first time since the launching of her wonderful idea that he had seen her at a loss. He judged the next instant moreover that she didn't like it—either the being so or the being seen, for she soon spoke with an impatience that showed her as wounded; an appearance that produced in himself, he no less quickly felt, a sharp pang of indulgence. "What then do you wish me to risk?"

The appeal from danger touched him, but all to make him, as he would have said, worse. "What I wish is to be loved. How can I feel at this rate that I *am?*" Oh she understood him, for all she might so bravely disguise it, and that made him feel straighter than if she hadn't. Deep, always, was his sense of life with her—deep as it had been from the moment of those signs of life that in the dusky London of two winters ago they had originally exchanged. He had never taken her for unguarded, ignorant, weak; and if he put to her a claim for some intenser faith between them this was because he believed it could reach her and she could meet it. "I can go on perhaps," he said, "with help. But I can't go on without."

She looked away from him now, and it showed him how she understood. "We ought to be there—I mean when they come out."

"They *won't* come out—not yet. And I don't care if they do." To which he straightway added, as if to deal with the charge of selfishness that his words, sounding for himself, struck him as enabling her to make: "Why not have done with it all and face the music as we are?" It broke from him in perfect sincerity. "Good God, if you'd only *take* me!"

It brought her eyes round to him again, and he could see how, after all, somewhere deep within, she felt his rebellion more sweet than bitter. Its effect on her spirit and her sense was visibly to hold her an instant. "We've gone too far," she none the less pulled herself together to reply. "Do you want to kill her?"

He had an hesitation that wasn't all candid. "Kill, you mean, Aunt Maud?"

"You know whom I mean. We've told too many lies."

Oh at this his head went up. "I, my dear, have told none!"

He had brought it out with a sharpness that did him good, but he had naturally, none the less, to take the look it made her give him. "Thank you very much."

Her expression, however, failed to check the words that had already risen to his lips. "Rather than lay myself open to the least appearance of it I'll go this very night."

"Then go," said Kate Croy.

He knew after a little, while they walked on again together, that what was in the air for him, and disconcertingly, was not the violence, but much rather the cold quietness, of the way this had come from her. They walked on together, and it was for a minute as if their difference had become of a sudden, in all truth, a split— as if the basis of his departure had been settled. Then, incoherently and still more suddenly, recklessly moreover, since they now might easily, from under the arcades, be observed, he passed his hand into her arm with a force that produced for them another pause. "I'll tell any lie you want, any your idea requires, if you'll only come to me."

"Come to you?"

"Come to me."

"How? Where?"

She spoke low, but there was somehow, for his uncertainty, a wonder in her being so equal to him. "To my rooms, which are perfectly possible, and in taking which, the other day, I had you, as you must have felt, in view. We can arrange it—with two grains of courage. People in our case always arrange it." She listened as for the good information, and there was support for him—since it was a question of his going step by step—in the way she took no refuge in showing herself shocked. He had in truth not expected of her that particular vulgarity, but the absence of it only added the thrill of a deeper reason to his sense of possibilities. For the knowledge of what she was he had absolutely to *see* her now, incapable of refuge, stand there for him in all the light of the day and of his admirable merciless meaning. Her mere listening in fact made him even understand himself as he hadn't yet done. Idea for idea, his own was thus already, and in the germ, beautiful. "There's nothing for me possible but to feel that I'm not a fool. It's all I have to say, but you must know what it means. *With* you I can do it—I'll go as far as you demand or as you will yourself. Without you—I'll be hanged! And I must be sure."

She listened so well that she was really listening after he had ceased to speak. He had kept his grasp of her, drawing her close, and though they had again, for the time, stopped walking, his talk—for others at a distance—might have been, in the matchless place, that of any impressed tourist to any slightly more detached companion. On possessing himself of her arm he had made her turn, so that they faced afresh to Saint Mark's, over the great presence of which his eyes moved while she twiddled her parasol. She now, however, made a motion that confronted them finally with the opposite end. Then only she spoke—"Please take your hand out of my arm." He understood at once: she had made out in the shade of the gallery the issue of the others from their place of purchase. So they went to them side by side, and it was all right. The others had seen them as well and waited for them, complacent enough, under one of the arches. They themselves too—he argued that Kate would argue—looked perfectly ready, decently patient, properly accommodating. They themselves suggested nothing worse—always by Kate's system—than a pair of the children of a supercivilized age making the best of an awkwardness. They didn't nevertheless hurry—that would overdo it; so he had time to feel, as it were, what he felt. He felt, ever so distinctly—it was with this he faced Mrs. Lowder—that he was already in a sense possessed of what he wanted. There was more to come—everything; he had by no means, with his companion, had it all out. Yet what he was possessed of was real—the fact that she hadn't thrown over his lucidity the horrid shadow of cheap reprobation. Of this he had had so sore a fear that its being dispelled was in itself of the nature of bliss. The danger had dropped—it was behind him there in the great sunny space. So far she was good for what he wanted.

— III —

S he was good enough, as it proved, for him to put to her that evening, and with further ground for it, the next sharpest question that had been on his lips in the morning—which his other preoccupation had then, to his consciousness, crowded out. His opportunity was again made, as befell, by his learning from Mrs. Stringham, on arriving, as usual, with the close of day, at the palace, that Milly must fail them again at dinner, but would to all appearance be able to come down later. He had found Susan Shepherd alone in the great saloon, where even more candles than their friend's large common allowance—she grew daily more splendid; they were all struck with it and chaffed her about it— lighted up the pervasive mystery of Style. He had thus five minutes with the good lady before Mrs. Lowder and Kate appeared—minutes illumined indeed to a longer reach than by the number of Milly's candles.

"*May* she come down—ought she if she isn't really up to it?"

He had asked that in the wonderment always stirred in him by glimpses—rare as were these—of the inner truth about the girl. There was of course a question of health—it was in the air, it was in the ground he trod, in the food he tasted, in the sounds he heard, it was everywhere. But it was everywhere with the effect of a request to him—to his very delicacy, to the common discretion of others as well as his own—that no allusion to it should be made. There had practically been none, that morning, on her explained non-appearance—the absence of it, as we know, quite monstrous and awkward; and this passage with Mrs. Stringham offered him his first license to open his eyes. He had gladly enough held them closed; all the more that his doing so performed for his own spirit a useful function. If he positively wanted not to be brought up with his nose against Milly's facts, what better proof could he have that his conduct was marked by straightness? It was perhaps pathetic for her, and for himself was perhaps even ridiculous; but he hadn't even the amount of curiosity that he would have had about an ordinary friend. He might have shaken himself at moments to try, for a sort of dry decency, to have it; but that too, it appeared, wouldn't come. In what therefore was the duplicity? He was at least sure about his feelings—it being so established that he had none at all. They were all for Kate, without a feather's weight to spare. He was acting for Kate—not, by the deviation of an inch, for her friend. He was accordingly not interested, for had he been interested he would have cared, and had he cared he would have wanted to know. Had he wanted to know he wouldn't have been purely passive, and it was his pure passivity that had to represent his dignity and his honour. His dignity and his honour, at the same time, let us add, fortunately fell short to-night of spoiling his little talk with Susan Shepherd. One glimpse—it was as if she had wished to give him that; and it was as if, for himself, on current terms, he could oblige her by accepting it. She not only permitted, she fairly invited him to open his eyes. "I'm so glad you're here." It was no answer to his question, but it had for the moment to serve. And the rest was fully to come.

He smiled at her and presently found himself, as a kind of consequence of communion with her, talking her own language. "It's a very wonderful experience."

"Well"—and her raised face shone up at him—"that's all I want you to feel about it. If I weren't afraid," she added, "there are things I should like to say to you."

"And what are you afraid of, please?" he encouragingly asked.

"Of other things that I may possibly spoil. Besides, I don't, you know, seem to have the chance. You're always, you know, *with* her."

He was strangely supported, it struck him, in his fixed smile; which was the more fixed as he felt in these last words an exact description of his course. It was an odd thing to have come to, but he *was* always with her. "Ah," he none the less smiled, "I'm not with her now."

"No—and I'm so glad, since I get this from it. She's ever so much better."

"Better? Then she *has* been worse?"

Mrs. Stringham waited. "She has been marvelous—that's what she has been. She *is* marvelous. But she's really better."

"Oh then if she's really better—!" But he checked himself, wanting only to be easy about it and above all not to appear engaged to the point of mystification. "We shall miss her the more at dinner."

Susan Shepherd, however, was all there for him. "She's keeping herself. You'll see. You'll not really need to miss anything. There's to be a little party."

"Ah I do see—by this aggravated grandeur."

"Well, it *is* lovely, isn't it? I want the whole thing. She's lodged for the first time as she ought, from her type, to be; and doing it—I mean bringing out all the glory of the place—makes her really happy. It's a Veronese picture,[23] as near as can be—with me as the inevitable dwarf, the small blackamoor, put into a corner of the foreground for effect. If I only had a hawk or a hound or something of that sort I should do the scene more honour. The old housekeeper, the woman in charge here, has a big red cockatoo that I might borrow and perch on my thumb for the evening." These explanations and sundry others Mrs. Stringham gave, though not all with the result of making him feel that the picture closed him in. What part was there for *him*, with his attitude that lacked the highest style, in a composition in which everything else would have it? "They won't, however, be at dinner, the few people she expects—they come round afterwards from their respective hotels; and Sir Luke Strett and his niece, the principal ones, will have arrived from London but an hour or two ago. It's for *him* she has wanted to do something—to let it begin at once. We shall see more of him, because she likes him; and I'm so glad—she'll be glad too—that *you're* to see him." The good lady, in connexion with it, was urgent, was almost unnaturally bright. "So I greatly hope—!" But her hope fairly lost itself in the wide light of her cheer.

He considered a little this appearance, while she let him, he thought, into still more knowledge than she uttered. "What is it you hope?"

"Well, that you'll stay on."

"Do you mean after dinner?" She meant, he seemed to feel, so much that he could scarce tell where it ended or began.

"Oh that, of course. Why we're to have music—beautiful instruments and songs; and not Tasso declaimed as in the guidebooks either. She has arranged it—or at least I have. That is Eugenio has. Besides, you're in the picture."

"Oh—I!" said Densher almost with the gravity of a real protest.

"You'll be the grand young man who surpasses the others and holds up his head and the wine-cup. What we hope," Mrs. Stringham pursued, "is that you'll be faithful to us—that you've not come for a mere foolish few days."

Densher's more private and particular shabby realities turned, without comfort, he was conscious, at this touch, in the artificial repose he had in his anxiety about them but half-managed to induce. The way smooth ladies, travelling for their pleasure and housed in Veronese pictures, talked to plain embarrassed workingmen, engaged in an unprecedented sacrifice of time and of the opportunity for modest acquisition! The things they took for granted and the general misery of explaining! He couldn't tell them how he had tried to work, how it was partly what he had moved into rooms for, only to find himself, almost for the first time in his life, stricken and sterile; because that would give them a false view of the source of his restlessness, if not of the degree of it. It would operate, indirectly perhaps, but infallibly, to add to that weight as of expected performance which these very moments with Mrs. Stringham caused more and more to settle on his heart. He had incurred it, the expectation of performance; the thing was done, and there was no use talking; again, again the cold breath of it was in the air. So there he was. And at best he floundered. "I'm afraid you won't understand when I say I've very tiresome things to consider. Botherations, necessities at home. The pinch, the pressure in London."

But she understood in perfection; she rose to the pinch and the pressure and showed how they had been her own very element. "Oh the daily talk and the daily wage, the golden guerdon or reward? No one knows better than I how they haunt one in the flight of the precious deceiving days. Aren't they just what I myself have given up? I've given up all to follow *her*. I wish you could feel as I do. And can't you," she asked, "write about Venice?"

He very nearly wished, for the minute, that he could feel as she did; and he smiled for her kindly. "Do *you* write about Venice?"

"No; but I would—oh wouldn't I?—if I hadn't so completely given up. She's, you know, my princess, and to one's princess—"

"One makes the whole sacrifice?"

"Precisely. There you are!"

It pressed on him with this that never had a man been in so many places at once. "I quite understand that she's yours. Only you see she's not mine." He felt he could somehow, for honesty, risk that, as he had the moral certainty she wouldn't repeat it and least of all to Mrs. Lowder, who would find in it a disturbing implication. This was part of what he liked in the good lady, that she didn't repeat, and also that she gave him a delicate sense of her shyly wishing him to know it. That was in itself a hint of possibilities between them, of a relation, beneficent and elastic for him, which wouldn't engage him further than he could see. Yet even as he afresh made this out he felt how strange it all was. She wanted, Susan Shepherd then, as appeared, the same thing Kate wanted, only wanted it, as still further appeared, in so different a way and from a motive so different, even though scarce less deep. Then Mrs. Lowder wanted, by so odd an evolution of her exuberance, exactly what each of the others did; and he was between them all, he was in the midst. Such perceptions made occasions—well, occasions for fairly wondering if it mightn't be best just to consent, luxuriously, to *be* the ass the whole thing involved. Trying not to be and yet keeping in it was of the two things the more asinine. He was glad there was no male witness; it was a circle of petticoats; he shouldn't have liked a man to see him.[24] He only had for a moment a sharp thought of Sir Luke Strett, the great master of the knife whom Kate in London had spoken of Milly as in commerce with, and whose renewed intervention at such a distance, just announced to him, required some accounting for. He had a vision of great London surgeons—if this one was a surgeon—as incisive all round; so that he should perhaps after all not wholly escape the ironic attention of his own sex. The most he might be able to do was not to care; while he was trying not to he could take that in. It was a train, however, that brought up the vision of Lord Mark as well. Lord Mark had caught him twice in the fact—the fact of his absurd posture; and that made a second male. But it was comparatively easy not to mind Lord Mark.

His companion had before this taken him up, and in a tone to confirm her discretion, on the matter of Milly's not being his princess. "Of course she's not. You must do something first."

Densher gave it his thought. "Wouldn't it be rather *she* who must?"

It had more than he intended the effect of bringing her to a stand. "I see. No doubt, if one takes it so." Her cheer was for the time in eclipse, and she looked over the place, avoiding his eyes, as in the wonder of what Milly could do. "And yet she has wanted to be kind."

It made him on the spot feel a brute. "Of course she has. No one could be more charming. She has treated me as if *I* were somebody. Call her my hostess as I've never had nor imagined a hostess, and I'm with you altogether. Of course," he added in the right spirit for her, "I do see that it's quite court life."

She promptly showed how this was almost all she wanted of him. "That's all I mean, if you understand it of such a court as never was: one of the courts of heaven, the court of a reigning seraph, a sort of a vice-queen of an angel. That will do perfectly."

"Oh well then I grant it. Only court life as a general thing, you know," he observed, "isn't supposed to pay."

"Yes, one has read; but this is beyond any book. That's just the beauty here; it's why she's the great and only princess. With her, at her court," said Mrs. Stringham, "it does pay." Then as if she had quite settled it for him: "You'll see for yourself."

He waited a moment, but said nothing to discourage her. "I think you were right just now. One must do something first."

"Well, you've done something."

"No—I don't see that. I can do more."

Oh well, she seemed to say, if he would have it so! "You can do everything, you know."

"Everything" was rather too much for him to take up gravely, and he modestly let it alone, speaking the next moment, to avert fatuity, of a different but a related matter. "Why has she sent for Sir Luke Strett if, as you tell me, she's so much better?"

"She hasn't sent. He has come of himself," Mrs. Stringham explained. "He has wanted to come."

"Isn't that rather worse then—if it means he mayn't be easy?"

"He was coming, from the first, for his holiday. She has known that these several weeks." After which Mrs. Stringham added: "You can *make* him easy."

"*I* can?" he candidly wondered. It was truly the circle of petticoats. "What have I to do with it for a man like that?"

"How do you know," said his friend, "what he's like? He's not like any one you've ever seen. He's a great beneficent being."

"Ah then he can do without me. I've no call, as an outsider, to meddle."

"Tell him, all the same," Mrs. Stringham urged, "what you think."

"What I think of Miss Theale?" Densher stared. It was, as they said, a large order. But he found the right note. "It's none of his business."

It did seem a moment for Mrs. Stringham too the right note. She fixed him at least with an expression still bright, but searching, that showed almost to excess what she saw in it; though what this might be he was not to make out till afterwards. "Say *that* to him then. Anything will do for him as a means of getting at you."

"And why should he get at me?"

"Give him a chance to. Let him talk to you. Then you'll see."

All of which, on Mrs. Stringham's part, sharpened his sense of immersion in an element rather more strangely than agreeably warm—a sense that was moreover, during the next two or three hours, to be fed to satiety by several other impressions. Milly came down after dinner, half a dozen friends—objects of interest mainly, it appeared, to the ladies of Lancaster Gate—having by that time arrived; and with this call on her attention, the further call of her musicians ushered by Eugenio, but personally and separately welcomed, and the supreme opportunity offered in the arrival of the great doctor, who came last of all, he felt her diffuse in wide warm waves the spell of a general, a beatific mildness. There

was a deeper depth of it, doubtless, for some than for others; what
he in particular knew of it was that he seemed to stand in it up to
his neck. He moved about in it and it made no splash; he floated,
he noiselessly swam in it, and they were all together, for that matter, like fishes in a crystal pool. The effect of the place, the beauty
of the scene, had probably much to do with it; the golden grace of
the high rooms, chambers of art in themselves, took care, as an influence, of the general manner, and made people bland without
making them solemn. They were only people, as Mrs. Stringham
had said, staying for the week or two at the inns, people who during the day had fingered their Baedekers, gaped at their frescoes
and differed, over fractions of francs, with their gondoliers. But
Milly, let loose among them in a wonderful white dress, brought
them somehow into relation with something that made them
more finely genial; so that if the Veronese picture of which he had
talked with Mrs. Stringham was not quite constituted, the comparative prose of the previous hours, the traces of insensibility
qualified by "beating down," were at last almost nobly disowned.
There was perhaps something for him in the accident of his seeing her for the first time in white, but she hadn't yet had occasion—circulating with a clearness intensified—to strike him as so
happily pervasive. She was different, younger, fairer, with the
colour of her braided hair more than ever a not altogether lucky
challenge to attention; yet he was loth wholly to explain it by her
having quitted this once, for some obscure yet doubtless charming
reason, her almost monastic, her hitherto inveterate black. Much
as the change did for the value of her presence, she had never yet,
when all was said, made it for *him*; and he was not to fail of the further amusement of judging her determined in the matter by Sir
Luke Strett's visit. If he could in this connexion have felt jealous
of Sir Luke Strett, whose strong face and type, less assimilated by
the scene perhaps than any others, he was anon to study from the
other side of the saloon, that would doubtless have been most
amusing of all. But he couldn't be invidious, even to profit by so
high a tide; he felt himself too much "in" it, as he might have said:
a moment's reflexion put him more in than any one. The way
Milly neglected him for other cares while Kate and Mrs. Lowder,
without so much as the attenuation of a joke, introduced him to

English ladies—that was itself a proof; for nothing really of so close a communion had up to this time passed between them as the single bright look and the three gay words (all ostensibly of the last lightness) with which her confessed consciousness brushed by him.

She was acquitting herself to-night as hostess, he could see, under some supreme idea, an inspiration which was half her nerves and half an inevitable harmony; but what he especially recognized was the character that had already several times broken out in her and that she so oddly appeared able, by choice or by instinctive affinity, to keep down or to display. She was the American girl as he had originally found her—found her at moments, it was true, in New York, more than at certain others; she was the American girl as, still more than then, he had seen her on the day of her meeting him in London and in Kate's company. It affected him as a large though queer social resource in her—such as a man, for instance, to his diminution, would never in the world be able to command; and he wouldn't have known whether to see it in an extension or a contraction of "personality," taking it as he did most directly for a confounding extension of surface. Clearly too it was the right thing this evening all round: that came out for him in a word from Kate as she approached him to wreak on him a second introduction. He had under cover of the music melted away from the lady toward whom she had first pushed him; and there was something in her to affect him as telling evasively a tale of their talk in the Piazza. To what did she want to coerce him as a form of penalty for what he had done to her there? It was thus in contact uppermost for him that he had done something; not only caused her perfect intelligence to act in his interest, but left her unable to get away, by any mere private effort, from his inattackable logic. With him thus in presence, and near him—and it had been as unmistakable through dinner—there was no getting away for her at all, there was less of it than ever: so she could only either deal with the question straight, either frankly yield or ineffectually struggle or insincerely argue, or else merely express herself by following up the advantage she did possess. It was part of that advantage for the hour—a brief fallacious makeweight to his pressure—that there were plenty of things left in which he must feel her will. They only told him, these indications, how much she was, in such close quarters, feeling his; and it was enough for him again that her very aspect, as great a variation in its way as Milly's own, gave him back the sense of his action. It had never yet in life been granted him to know, almost materially to taste, as he could do in these minutes, the state of what was vulgarly called conquest. He had lived long enough to have been on occasion "liked," but it had never begun to be allowed him to be liked to any such tune in any such quarter. It was a liking greater than Milly's—or it would be: he felt it in him to answer for that. So at all events he read the case while he noted that Kate was somehow—for Kate— wanting in luster. As a striking young presence she was practically superseded; of the mildness that Milly diffused she had assimilated all her share; she might fairly have been dressed to-night in the lit- tle black frock, superficially indistinguishable, that Milly had laid aside. This represented, he perceived, the opposite pole from such an effect as that of her wonderful entrance, under her aunt's eyes—he had never forgotten it—the day of their younger friend's failure at Lancaster Gate. She was, in her accepted effacement— it was actually her acceptance that made the beauty and repaired the damage—under her aunt's eyes now; but whose eyes were not effectually preoccupied? It struck him none the less certainly that almost the first thing she said to him showed an exquisite attempt to appear if not unconvinced at least self-possessed.

"Don't you think her good enough *now?*"

Almost heedless of the danger of overt freedoms, she eyed Milly from where they stood, noted her in renewed talk, over her further wishes, with the members of her little orchestra, who had ap- proached her with demonstrations of deference enlivened by na- tive humours—things quite in the line of old Venetian comedy. The girl's idea of music had been happy—a real solvent of shyness, yet not drastic; thanks to the intermissions, discretions, a general habit of mercy to gathered barbarians, that reflected the good manners of its interpreters, representatives though these might be but of the order in which taste was natural and melody rank. It was easy at all events to answer Kate. "Ah my dear, you know how good I think her!"

"But she's *too* nice," Kate returned with appreciation. "Everything suits her so—especially her pearls. They go so with her old lace. I'll trouble you really to look at them." Densher, though aware he had seen them before, had perhaps not "really" looked at them, and had thus not done justice to the embodied poetry—his mind, for Milly's aspects, kept coming back to that—which owed them part of its style. Kate's face, as she considered them, struck him: the long, priceless chain, wound twice round the neck, hung, heavy and pure, down the front of the wearer's breast—so far down that Milly's trick, evidently unconscious, of holding and vaguely fingering and entwining a part of it, conduced presumably to convenience. "She's a dove," Kate went on, "and one somehow doesn't think of doves as bejewelled. Yet they suit her down to the ground."

"Yes—down to the ground is the word." Densher saw now how they suited her, but was perhaps still more aware of something intense in his companion's feeling about them. Milly was indeed a dove; this was the figure, though it most applied to her spirit. Yet he knew in a moment that Kate was just now, for reasons hidden from him, exceptionally under the impression of that element of wealth in her which was a power, which was a great power, and which was dove-like only so far as one remembered that doves have wings and wondrous flights, have them as well as tender tints and soft sounds. It even came to him dimly that such wings could in a given case—*had*, truly, in the case with which he was concerned—spread themselves for protection. Hadn't they, for that matter, lately taken an inordinate reach, and weren't Kate and Mrs. Lowder, weren't Susan Shepherd and he, wasn't *he* in particular, nestling under them to a great increase of immediate ease? All this was a brighter blur in the general light, out of which he heard Kate presently going on.

"Pearls have such a magic that they suit every one."

"They would uncommonly suit you," he frankly returned.

"Oh yes, I see myself!"

As she saw herself, suddenly, he saw her—she would have been splendid; and with it he felt more what she was thinking of. Milly's royal ornament had—under pressure now not wholly occult—taken on the character of a symbol of differences, differences of which the vision was actually in Kate's face. It might have been in her face too that, well as she certainly would look in pearls, pearls were exactly what Merton Densher would never be able to give her. Wasn't *that* the great difference that Milly tonight symbolized? She unconsciously represented to Kate, and Kate took it in at every pore, that there was nobody with whom she had less in common than a remarkably handsome girl married to a man unable to make her on any such lines as that the least little present. Of these absurdities, however, it was not till afterwards that Densher thought. He could think now, to any purpose, only of what Mrs. Stringham had said to him before dinner. He could but come back to his friend's question of a minute ago. "She's certainly good enough, as you call it, in the sense that I'm assured she's better. Mrs. Stringham, an hour or two since, was in great feather to me about it. She evidently believes her better."

"Well, if they choose to call it so—!"

"And what do *you* call it—as against them?"

"I don't call it anything to any one but you. I'm not 'against' them!" Kate added as with just a fresh breath of impatience for all he had to be taught.

"That's what I'm talking about," he said. "What do you call it to me?"

It made her wait a little. "She isn't better. She's worse. But that has nothing to do with it."

"Nothing to do?" He wondered.

But she was clear. "Nothing to do with *us*. Except of course that we're doing our best for her. We're making her want to live." And Kate again watched her. "To-night she does want to live." She spoke with a kindness that had the strange property of striking him as inconsequent—so much, and doubtless so unjustly, had all her clearness been an implication of the hard. "It's wonderful. It's beautiful."

"It's beautiful indeed."

He hated somehow the helplessness of his own note; but she had given it no heed. "She's doing it for *him*"—and she nodded in the direction of Milly's medical visitor. "She wants to be for him at her best. But she can't deceive him."

Densher had been looking too; which made him say in a moment: "And do you think *you* can? I mean, if he's to be with us here, about your sentiments. If Aunt Maud's so thick with him—!"

Aunt Maud now occupied in fact a place at his side and was visibly doing her best to entertain him, though this failed to prevent such a direction of his own eyes—determined, in the way such things happen, precisely by the attention of the others—as Densher became aware of and as Kate promptly marked. "He's looking at *you*. He wants to speak to you."

"So Mrs. Stringham," the young man laughed, "advised me he would."

"Then let him. Be right with him. I don't need," Kate went on in answer to the previous question, "to deceive him. Aunt Maud, if it's necessary, will do that. I mean that, knowing nothing about me, he can see me only as he sees me. She sees me now so well. He has nothing to do with me."

"Except to reprobate you," Densher suggested.

"For not caring for *you*? Perfectly. As a brilliant young man driven by it into your relation with Milly—as all *that* I leave you to him."

"Well," said Densher sincerely enough, "I think I can thank you for leaving me to some one easier perhaps with me than yourself."

She had been looking about again meanwhile, the lady having changed her place, for the friend of Mrs. Lowder's to whom she had spoken of introducing him. "All the more reason why I should commit you then to Lady Wells."

"Oh but wait." It was not only that he distinguished Lady Wells from afar, that she inspired him with no eagerness, and that, somewhere at the back of his head, he was fairly aware of the question, in germ, of whether this was the kind of person he should be involved with when they were married. It was furthermore that the consciousness of something he had not got from Kate in the morning, and that logically much concerned him, had been made more keen by these very moments—to say nothing of the consciousness that, with their general smallness of opportunity, he must squeeze each stray instant hard. If Aunt Maud, over there with Sir Luke, noted him as a little "attentive," that might pass for a futile demonstration on the part of a gentleman who had to confess to having, not very gracefully, changed his mind. Besides, just now, he didn't care for Aunt Maud except in so far as he was immediately to show. "How can Mrs. Lowder think me disposed of with any finality, if I'm disposed of only to a girl who's dying? If you're right about that, about the state of the case, you're wrong about Mrs. Lowder's being squared. If Milly, as you say," he lucidly pursued, "can't deceive a great surgeon, or whatever, the great surgeon won't deceive other people—not those, that is, who are closely concerned. He won't at any rate deceive Mrs. Stringham, who's Milly's greatest friend; and it will be very odd if Mrs. Stringham deceives Aunt Maud, who's her own."

Kate showed him at this the cold glow of an idea that really was worth his having kept her for. "Why will it be odd? I marvel at your seeing your way so little."

Mere curiosity even, about his companion, had now for him its quick, its slightly quaking intensities. He had compared her once, we know, to a "new book," an uncut volume of the highest, the rarest quality; and his emotion (to justify that) was again and again like the thrill of turning the page. "Well, you know how deeply I marvel at the way *you* see it!"

"It doesn't in the least follow," Kate went on, "that anything in the nature of what you call deception on Mrs. Stringham's part will be what you call odd. Why shouldn't she hide the truth?"

"From Mrs. Lowder?" Densher stared. "Why should she?"

"To please you."

"And how in the world can it please me?"

Kate turned her head away as if really at last almost tired of his density. But she looked at him again as she spoke. "Well then to please Milly." And before he could question: "Don't you feel by this time that there's nothing Susan Shepherd won't do for you?"

He had verily after an instant to take it in, so sharply it corresponded with the good lady's recent reception of him. It was queerer than anything again, the way they all came together round him. But that was an old story, and Kate's multiplied lights led him on and on. It was with a reserve, however, that he confessed this. "She's ever so kind. Only her view of the right thing may not be the same as yours."

"How can it be anything different if it's the view of serving you?"

Densher for an instant, but only for an instant, hung fire. "Oh the difficulty is that I don't, upon my honour, even yet quite make out how yours does serve me."

"It helps you—put it then," said Kate very simply—"to serve *me*. It gains you time."

"Time for what?"

"For everything!" She spoke at first, once more, with impatience; then as usual she qualified. "For anything that may happen."

Densher had a smile, but he felt it himself as strained. "You're cryptic, love!"

It made her keep her eyes on him, and he could thus see that, by one of those incalculable motions in her without which she wouldn't have been a quarter so interesting, they half-filled with tears from some source he had too roughly touched. "I'm taking a trouble for you I never dreamed I should take for any human creature."

Oh it went home, making him flush for it; yet he soon enough felt his reply on his lips. "Well, isn't my whole insistence to you now that I can conjure trouble away?" And he let it, his insistence, come out again; it had so constantly had, all the week, but its step or two to make. "There *need* be none whatever between us. There need be nothing but our sense of each other."

It had only the effect at first that her eyes grew dry while she took up again one of the so numerous links in her close chain. "You can tell her anything you like, anything whatever."

"Mrs. Stringham? I *have* nothing to tell her."

"You can tell her about *us*. I mean," she wonderfully pursued, "that you do still like me."

It was indeed so wonderful that it amused him. "Only not that you still like me."

She let his amusement pass. "I'm absolutely certain she wouldn't repeat it."

"I see. To Aunt Maud."

"You don't quite see. Neither to Aunt Maud nor to any one else." Kate then, he saw, was always seeing Milly much more, after all, than he was; and she showed it again as she went on. "*There*, accordingly, is your time."

She did at last make him think, and it was fairly as if light broke,

though not quite all at once. "You must let me say I *do* see. Time
for something in particular that I understand you regard as possible. Time too that, I further understand, is time for you as well."

"Time indeed for me as well." And encouraged visibly by his
glow of concentration, she looked at him as through the air she
had painfully made clear. Yet she was still on her guard. "Don't
think, however, I'll do *all* the work for you. If you want things
named you must name them."

He had quite, within the minute, been turning names over; and
there was only one, which at last stared at him there dreadful, that
properly fitted. "Since she's to die I'm to marry her?"

It struck him even at the moment as fine in her that she met it
with no wincing nor mincing. She might for the grace of silence,
for favor to their conditions, have only answered him with her
eyes. But her lips bravely moved. "To marry her."

"So that when her death has taken place I shall in the natural
course have money?"

It was before him enough now, and he had nothing more to ask;
he had only to turn, on the spot, considerably cold with the
thought that all along—to his stupidity, his timidity—it had been,
it had been only, what she meant. Now that he was in possession
moreover she couldn't forbear, strangely enough, to pronounce
the words she hadn't pronounced: they broke through her controlled and colourless voice as if she should be ashamed, to the
very end, to have flinched. "You'll in the natural course have
money. We shall in the natural course be free."

"Oh, oh, oh!" Densher softly murmured.

"Yes, yes, yes." But she broke off. "Come to Lady Wells."

He never budged—there was too much else. "I'm to propose it
then—marriage—on the spot?"

There was no ironic sound he needed to give it; the more simply he spoke the more he seemed ironic. But she remained consummately proof. "Oh I can't go into that with you, and from the
moment you don't wash your hands of me I don't think you ought
to ask me. You must act as you like and as you can."

He thought again. "I'm far—as I sufficiently showed you this
morning—from washing my hands of you."

"Then," said Kate, "it's all right."

"All right?" His eagerness flamed. "You'll come?"

But he had had to see in a moment that it wasn't what she meant. "You'll have a free hand, a clear field, a chance—well, quite ideal."

"Your descriptions"—her "ideal" was such a touch!—"are prodigious. And what I don't make out is how, caring of me, you can like it."

"I don't like it, but I'm a person, thank goodness, who can do what I don't like."

It wasn't till afterwards that, going back to it, he was to read into this speech a kind of heroic ring, a note of character that belittled his own incapacity for action. Yet he saw indeed even at the time the greatness of knowing so well what one wanted. At the time too, moreover, he next reflected that he after all knew what *he* did. But something else on his lips was uppermost. "What I don't make out then is how you can even bear it."

"Well, when you know me better you'll find out how much I can bear." And she went on before he could take up, as it were, her too many implications. That it was left to him to know her, spiritually, "better" after his long sacrifice to knowledge—this for instance was a truth he hadn't been ready to receive so full in the face. She had mystified him enough, heaven knew, but that was rather by his own generosity than by hers. And what, with it, did she seem to suggest she might incur at his hands? In spite of these questions she was carrying him on. "All you'll have to do will be to stay."

"And proceed to my business under your eyes?"

"Oh dear no—we shall go."

"'Go?'" he wondered. "Go when, go where?"

"In a day or two—straight home. Aunt Maud wishes it now."

It gave him all he could take in to think of. "Then what becomes of Miss Theale?"

"What I tell you. She stays on, and you stay with her."

He stared. "All alone?"

She had a smile that was apparently for his tone. "You're old enough—with plenty of Mrs. Stringham."

Nothing might have been so odd for him now, could he have measured it, as his being able to feel, quite while he drew from her these successive cues, that he was essentially "seeing what she would say"—an instinct compatible for him therefore with that absence of a need to know her better to which she had a moment before done injustice. If it hadn't been appearing to him in gleams that she would somewhere break down, he probably couldn't have gone on. Still, as she wasn't breaking down there was nothing for him but to continue. "Is your going Mrs. Lowder's idea?"

"Very much indeed. Of course again you see what it does for us. And I don't," she added, "refer only to our going, but to Aunt Maud's view of the general propriety of it."

"I see again, as you say," Densher said after a moment. "It makes everything fit."

"Everything."

The word, for a little, held the air, and he might have seemed the while to be looking, by no means dimly now, at all it stood for. But he had in fact been looking at something else. "You leave her here then to die?"

"Ah she believes she won't die. Not if you stay. I mean," Kate explained, "Aunt Maud believes."

"And that's all that's necessary?"

Still indeed she didn't break down. "Didn't we long ago agree that what she believes is the principal thing for us?"

He recalled it, under her eyes, but it came as from long ago. "Oh yes. I can't deny it." Then he added: "So that if I stay—"

"It won't"—she was prompt—"be our fault."

"If Mrs. Lowder still, you mean, suspects us?"

"If she still suspects us. But she won't."

Kate gave it an emphasis that might have appeared to leave him nothing more; and he might in fact well have found nothing if he hadn't presently found: "But what if she doesn't accept me?"

It produced in her a look of weariness that made the patience of her tone the next moment touch him. "You can but try."

"Naturally I can but try. Only, you see, one has to try a little hard to propose to a dying girl."

"She isn't for you as if she's dying." It had determined in Kate the flash of *justesse** he could perhaps most, on consideration,

---

*Clear judgment (French).

have admired, since her retort touched the truth. There before him was the fact of how Milly to-night impressed him, and his companion, with her eyes in his own and pursuing his impression to the depths of them, literally now perched on the fact in triumph. She turned her head to where their friend was again in range, and it made him turn his, so that they watched a minute in concert. Milly, from the other side, happened at the moment to notice them, and she sent across toward them in response all the candor of her smile, the luster of her pearls, the value of her life, the essence of her wealth. It brought them together again with faces made fairly grave by the reality she put into their plan. Kate herself grew a little pale for it, and they had for a time only a silence. The music, however, gay and vociferous, had broken out afresh and protected more than interrupted them. When Densher at last spoke it was under cover.

"I might stay, you know, without trying."

"Oh to stay *is* to try."

"To have for herself, you mean, the appearance of it?"

"I don't see how you can have the appearance more."

Densher waited. "You think it then possible she may *offer* marriage?"

"I can't think—if you really want to know—what she may *not* offer!"

"In the manner of princesses, who do such things?"

"In any manner you like. So be prepared."

Well, he looked as if he almost were. "It will be for me then to accept. But that's the way it must come."

Kate's silence, so far, let it pass; but she presently said: "You'll, on your honour, stay then?"

His answer made her wait, but when it came it was distinct. "Without you, you mean?"

"Without us."

"And you yourselves go at latest—?"

"Not later than Thursday."

It made three days. "Well," he said, "I'll stay, on my honour, if you'll come to me. On *your* honour."

Again, as before, this made her momentarily rigid, with a rigor out of which, at a loss, she vaguely cast about her. Her rigor was more to him, nevertheless, than all her readiness; for her readiness was the woman herself, and this other thing a mask, a stop-gap and a "dodge." She cast about, however, as happened, and not for the instant in vain. Her eyes, turned over the room, caught at a pretext. "Lady Wells is tired of waiting: she's coming—see—to *us*."

Densher saw in fact, but there was a distance for their visitor to cross, and he still had time. "If you decline to understand me I wholly decline to understand you. I'll do nothing."

"Nothing?" It was as if she tried for the minute to plead.

"I'll do nothing. I'll go off before you. I'll go tomorrow."

He was to have afterwards the sense of her having then, as the phrase was—and for vulgar triumphs too—seen he meant it. She looked again at Lady Wells, who was nearer, but she quickly came back. "And if I do understand?"

"I'll do everything."

She found anew a pretext in her approaching friend: he was fairly playing with her pride. He had never, he then knew, tasted, in all his relation with her, of anything so sharp—too sharp for mere sweetness—as the vividness with which he saw himself master in the conflict. "Well, I understand."

"On your honour?"

"On my honour."

"You'll come?"

"I'll come."

BOOK NINTH

– I –

It was after they had gone that he truly felt the difference, which was most to be felt moreover in his faded old rooms. He had recovered from the first a part of his attachment to this scene of contemplation, within sight, as it was, of the Rialto bridge, on the hither side of that arch of associations and the left going up the Canal; he had seen it in a particular light, to which, more and more, his mind and his hands adjusted it; but the interest the place now wore for him had risen at a bound, becoming a force that, on the spot, completely engaged and absorbed him, and relief from which—if relief was the name—he could find only by getting away and out of reach. What had come to pass within his walls lingered there as an obsession importunate to all his senses; it lived again, as a cluster of pleasant memories, at every hour and in every object; it made everything but itself irrelevant and tasteless. It remained, in a word, a conscious watchful presence, active on its own side, for ever to be reckoned with, in fact of which the effort at detachment was scarcely less futile than frivolous. Kate had come to him; it was only once—and this not from any failure of their need, but from such impossibilities, for bravery alike and for subtlety, as there was at the last no blinking; yet she had come, that once, to stay, as people called it; and what survived of her, what reminded and insisted, was something he couldn't have banished if he had wished. Luckily he didn't wish, even though there might be for a man almost a shade of the awful in so unqualified a consequence of his act. It had simply *worked*, his idea, the idea he had made her accept; and all erect before him, really covering the ground as far as he could see, was the fact of the gained success that this represented. It was, otherwise, but the fact of the idea as directly applied, as converted from a luminous conception into an historic truth. He had known it before but as desired and urged, as convincingly insisted on for the help it would render; so that at present, *with* the help rendered, it seemed to acknowledge its of-

fice and to set up, for memory and faith, an insistence of its own.
He had in fine judged his friend's pledge in advance as an ines-
timable value, and what he must now know his case for was that of
a possession of the value to the full. Wasn't it perhaps even rather
the value that possessed *him*, kept him thinking of it and waiting
on it, turning round and round it and making sure of it again from
this side and that?

It played for him—certainly in this prime afterglow—the part of
a treasure kept at home in safety and sanctity, something he was
sure of finding in its place when, with each return, he worked his
heavy old key in the lock. The door had but to open for him to be
with it again and for it to be all there; so intensely there that, as we
say, no other act was possible to him than the renewed act, almost
the hallucination, of intimacy. Wherever he looked or sat or stood,
to whatever aspect he gave for the instant the advantage, it was in
view as nothing of the moment, nothing begotten of time or of
chance could be, or ever would; it was in view as, when the curtain has risen, the play on the stage is in view, night after night, for
the fiddlers. He remained thus, in his own theatre, in his single
person, perpetual orchestra to the ordered drama, the confirmed
"run"; playing low and slow, moreover, in the regular way, for the
situations of most importance. No other visitor was to come to
him; he met, he bumped occasionally, in the Piazza or in his
walks, against claimants to acquaintance, remembered or forgotten, at present mostly effusive, sometimes even inquisitive; but he
gave no address and encouraged no approach; he couldn't for his
life, he felt, have opened his door to a third person. Such a person
would have interrupted him, would have profaned his secret or
perhaps have guessed it; would at any rate have broken the spell of
what he conceived himself—in the absence of anything "to
show"—to be inwardly doing. He was giving himself up—that was
quite enough—to the general feeling of his renewed engagement
to fidelity. The force of the engagement, the quantity of the article
to be supplied, the special solidity of the contract, the way, above
all, as a service for which the price named by him had been magnificently paid, his equivalent office was to take effect—such items
might well fill his consciousness when there was nothing from outside to interfere. Never was a consciousness more rounded and fas-

tened down over what filled it; which is precisely what we have spoken of as, in its degree, the oppression of success, the somewhat chilled state—tending to the solitary—of supreme recognition. If it was slightly awful to feel so justified, this was by the loss of the warmth of the element of mystery. The lucid reigned instead of it, and it was into the lucid that he sat and stared. He shook himself out of it a dozen times a day, tried to break by his own act his constant still communion. It wasn't still communion she had meant to bequeath him; it was the very different business of that kind of fidelity of which the other name was careful action.

Nothing, he perfectly knew, was less like careful action than the immersion he enjoyed at home. The actual grand queerness was that to be faithful to Kate he had positively to take his eyes, his arms, his lips straight off her—he had to let her alone. He had to remember it was time to go to the palace—which in truth was a mercy, since the check was not less effectual than imperative. What it came to, fortunately, as yet, was that when he closed the door behind him for an absence he always shut her in. Shut her out—it came to that rather, when once he had got a little away; and before he reached the palace, much more after hearing at his heels the bang of the greater *portone*,* he felt free enough not to know his position as oppressively false. As Kate was *all* in his poor rooms, and not a ghost of her left for the grander, it was only on reflexion that the falseness came out; so long as he left it to the mercy of beneficent chance it offered him no face and made of him no claim that he couldn't meet without aggravation of his inward sense. This aggravation had been his original horror; yet what—in Milly's presence, each day—was horror doing with him but virtually letting him off? He shouldn't perhaps get off to the end; there was time enough still for the possibility of shame to pounce. Still, however, he did constantly a little more what he liked best, and that kept him for the time more safe. What he liked best was, in any case, to know *why* things were as he felt them; and he knew it pretty well, in this case, ten days after the retreat of his other friends. He then fairly perceived that—even putting their

---

*Entrance gate (Italian).

purity of motive at its highest—it was neither Kate nor he who made his strange relation to Milly, who made her own, so far as it might be, innocent; it was neither of them who practically purged it—if practically purged it was. Milly herself did everything—so far at least as he was concerned—Milly herself, and Milly's house, and Milly's hospitality, and Milly's manner, and Milly's character, and, perhaps still more than anything else, Milly's imagination, Mrs. Stringham and Sir Luke indeed a little aiding: whereby he knew the blessing of a fair pretext to ask himself what more he had to do. Something incalculable wrought for them—for him and Kate; something outside, beyond, above themselves, and doubtless ever so much better than they: which wasn't a reason, however—its being so much better—for them not to profit by it. Not to profit by it, so far as profit could be reckoned, would have been to go directly against it; and the spirit of generosity at present engendered in Densher could have felt no greater pang than by his having to go directly against Milly.

To go *with* her was the thing, so far as she could herself go; which, from the moment her tenure of her loved palace stretched on, was possible but by his remaining near her. This remaining was of course on the face of it the most "marked" of demonstrations—which was exactly why Kate had required it; it was so marked that on the very evening of the day it had taken effect Milly herself hadn't been able not to reach out to him, with an exquisite awkwardness, for some account of it. It was as if she had wanted from him some name that, now they were to be almost alone together, they could, for their further ease, know it and call it by—it being, after all, almost rudimentary that his presence, of which the absence of the others made quite a different thing, couldn't but have for himself some definite basis. She only wondered about the basis it would have for himself, and how he would describe it; that would quite do for her—it even would have done for her, he could see, had he produced some reason merely trivial, had he said he was waiting for money or clothes, for letters or for orders from Fleet Street, without which, as she might have heard, newspaper men never took a step. He hadn't in the event quite sunk to that; but he had none the less had there with her, that night, on Mrs. Stringham's leaving them alone—Mrs. Stringham

proved really prodigious—his acquaintance with a shade of awkwardness darker than any Milly could know. He had supposed
himself beforehand, on the question of what he was doing or pretending, in possession of some tone that would serve; but there
were three minutes of his feeling incapable of promptness quite in
the same degree in which a gentleman whose pocket has been
picked feels incapable of purchase. It even didn't help him, oddly,
that he was sure Kate would in some way have spoken for him—
or rather not so much in some way as in one very particular way.
He hadn't asked her, at the last, what she might, in the connexion,
have said; nothing would have induced him to put such a question
after she had been to see him: his lips were so sealed by that passage, his spirit in fact so hushed, in respect to any charge upon her
freedom. There was something he could only therefore read back
into the probabilities, and when he left the palace an hour afterwards it was with a sense of having breathed there, in the very air,
the truth he had been guessing.

Just this perception it was, however, that had made him for the
time ugly to himself in his awkwardness. It was horrible, with this
creature, to *be* awkward; it was odious to be seeking excuses for
the relation that involved it. Any relation that involved it was by
the very fact as much discredited as a dish would be at dinner if
one had to take medicine as a sauce. What Kate would have said
in one of the young women's last talks was that—if Milly absolutely must have the truth about it—Mr. Densher was staying
because she had really seen no way but to require it of him. If he
stayed he didn't follow her—or didn't appear to her aunt to be
doing so; and when she kept him from following her Mrs. Lowder
couldn't pretend, in scenes, the renewal of which at this time of
day was painful, that she after all didn't snub him as she might.
She did nothing in fact *but* snub him—wouldn't that have been
part of the story?—only Aunt Maud's suspicions were of the sort
that had repeatedly to be dealt with. He had been, by the same
token, reasonable enough—as he now, for that matter, well might;
he had consented to oblige them, aunt and niece, by giving the
plainest sign possible that he could exist away from London. To
exist away from London was to exist away from Kate Croy—which
was a gain, much appreciated, to the latter's comfort. There was a

minute, at this hour, out of Densher's three, during which he
knew the terror of Milly's uttering some such allusion to their
friend's explanation as he must meet with words that wouldn't destroy it. To destroy it was to destroy everything, to destroy probably
Kate herself, to destroy in particular by a breach of faith still uglier
than anything else the beauty of their own last passage. He had
given her his word of honour that if she would come to him he
would act absolutely in her sense, and he had done so with a full
enough vision of what her sense implied. What it implied for one
thing was that to-night in the great saloon, noble in its half-lighted
beauty, and straight in the white face of his young hostess, divine
in her trust, or at any rate inscrutable in her mercy—what it implied was that he should lie with his lips. The single thing, of all
things, that could save him from it would be Milly's letting him off
after having thus scared him. What made her mercy inscrutable
was that if she had already more than once saved him it was yet apparently without knowing how nearly he was lost.

These were transcendent motions, not the less blest for being
obscure; whereby yet once more he was to feel the pressure
lighten. He was kept on his feet in short by the felicity of her not
presenting him with Kate's version as a version to adopt. He
couldn't stand up to lie—he felt as if he should have to go down
on his knees. As it was he just sat there shaking a little for nervousness the leg he had crossed over the other. She was sorry for his
suffered snub, but he had nothing more to subscribe to, to perjure
himself about, than the three or four inanities he had, on his own
side, feebly prepared for the crisis. He scrambled a little higher
than the reference to money and clothes, letters and directions
from his manager; but he brought out the beauty of the chance for
him—there before him like a temptress painted by Titian—to do
a little quiet writing. He was vivid for a moment on the difficulty
of writing quietly in London; and he was precipitate, almost ex-
plosive, on his idea, long cherished, of a book.

The explosion lighted her face. "You'll do your book here?"

"I hope to begin it."

"It's something you haven't begun?"

"Well, only just."

"And since you came?"

She was so full of interest that he shouldn't perhaps after all be too easily let off. "I tried to think a few days ago that I had broken ground."

Scarcely anything, it was indeed clear, could have let him in deeper. "I'm afraid we've made an awful mess of your time."

"Of course you have. But what I'm hanging on for now is precisely to repair that ravage."

"Then you mustn't mind me, you know."

"You'll see," he tried to say with ease, "how little I shall mind anything."

"You'll want"—Milly had thrown herself into it—"the best part of your days."

He thought a moment: he did what he could to wreathe it in smiles. "Oh I shall make shift with the worst part. The best will be for *you*." And he wished Kate could hear him. It didn't help him moreover that he visibly, even pathetically, imaged to her by such touches his quest for comfort against discipline. He was to bury Kate's so signal snub, and also the hard law she had now laid on him, under a high intellectual effort. This at least was his crucifixion—that Milly was so interested. She was so interested that she presently asked him if he found his rooms propitious, while he felt that in just decently answering her he put on a brazen mask. He should need it quite particularly were she to express again her imagination of coming to tea with him—an extremity that he saw he was not to be spared. "We depend on you, Susie and I, you know, not to forget we're coming"—the extremity was but to face that remainder, yet it demanded all his tact. Facing their visit itself—to that, no matter what he might have to do, he would never consent, as we know, to be pushed; and this even though it might be exactly such a demonstration as would figure for him at the top of Kate's list of his proprieties. He could wonder freely enough, deep within, if Kate's view of that especial propriety had not been modified by a subsequent occurrence; but his deciding that it was quite likely not to have been had no effect on his own preference for tact. It pleased him to think of "tact" as his present prop in doubt; that glossed his predicament over, for it was of application among the sensitive and the kind. He wasn't inhuman, in fine, so long as it would serve. It had to serve now, accordingly, to help him not to sweeten Milly's hopes. He didn't want to be rude to them, but he still less wanted them to flower again in the particular connexion; so that, casting about him in his anxiety for a middle way to meet her, he put his foot, with unhappy effect, just in the wrong place. "Will it be safe for you to break into your custom of not leaving the house?"

" 'Safe'—?" She had for twenty seconds an exquisite pale glare. Oh but he didn't need it, by that time, to wince; he had winced for himself as soon as he had made his mistake. He had done what, so unforgettably, she had asked him in London not to do; he had touched, all alone with her here, the supersensitive nerve of which she had warned him. He had not, since the occasion in London, touched it again till now; but he saw himself freshly warned that it was able to bear still less. So for the moment he knew as little what to do as he had ever known it in his life. He couldn't emphasize that he thought of her as dying, yet he couldn't pretend he thought of her as indifferent to precautions. Meanwhile too she had narrowed his choice. "You suppose me so awfully bad?"

He turned, in his pain, within himself; but by the time the colour had mounted to the roots of his hair he had found what he wanted. "I'll believe whatever you tell me."

"Well then, I'm splendid."

"Oh I don't need you to tell me that."

"I mean I'm capable of life."

"I've never doubted it."

"I mean," she went on, "that I want so to live—!"

"Well?" he asked while she paused with the intensity of it.

"Well, that I know I *can*."

"Whatever you do?" He shrank from solemnity about it.

"Whatever I do. If I want to."

"If you want to do it?"

"If I want to live. I *can*," Milly repeated.

He had clumsily brought it on himself, but he hesitated with all the pity of it. "Ah then *that* I believe."

"I will, I will," she declared; yet with the weight of it somehow turned for him to mere light and sound.

He felt himself smiling through a mist. "You simply must!"

It brought her straight again to the fact. "Well then, if you say it, why mayn't we pay you our visit?"

"Will it help you to live?"

"Every little helps," she laughed, "and it's very little for me, in general, to stay at home. Only I shan't want to miss it—!"

"Yes?"—she had dropped again.

"Well, on the day you give us a chance."

It was amazing what so brief an exchange had at this point done with him. His great scruple suddenly broke, giving way to something inordinately strange, something of a nature to become clear to him only when he had left her. "You can come," he said, "when you like."

What had taken place for him, however—the drop, almost with violence, of everything but a sense of her own reality—apparently showed in his face or his manner, and even so vividly that she could take it for something else. "I see how you feel—that I'm an awful bore about it and that, sooner than have any such upset, you'll go. So it's no matter."

"No matter? Oh!"—he quite protested now.

"If it drives you away to escape us. We want you not to go."

It was beautiful how she spoke for Mrs. Stringham. Whatever it was, at any rate, he shook his head. "I won't go."

"Then *I* won't go!" she brightly declared.

"You mean you won't come to me?"

"No—never now. It's over. But it's all right. I mean, apart from that," she went on, "that I won't do anything I oughtn't or that I'm not forced to."

"Oh who can ever force you?" he asked with his hand-to-mouth way, at all times, of speaking for her encouragement. "You're the least coercible of creatures."

"Because, you think, I'm so free?"

"The freest person probably now in the world. You've got everything."

"Well," she smiled, "call it so. I don't complain."

On which again, in spite of himself, it let him in. "No I know you don't complain."

As soon as he had said it he had himself heard the pity in it. His telling her she had "everything" was extravagant kind humour,

whereas his knowing so tenderly that she didn't complain was terrible kind gravity. Milly felt, he could see, the difference; he might
as well have praised her outright for looking death in the face. This
was the way she just looked *him* again, and it was of no attenuation
that she took him up more gently than ever. "It isn't a merit—
when one sees one's way."

"To peace and plenty? Well, I dare say not."

"I mean to keeping what one has."

"Oh that's success. If what one has is good," Densher said at
random, "it's enough to try for."

"Well, it's my limit. I'm not trying for more." To which then she
added with a change: "And now about your book."

"My book—?" He had got in a moment so far from it.

"The one you're now to understand that nothing will induce either Susie or me to run the risk of spoiling."

He cast about, but he made up his mind. "I'm not doing a
book."

"Not what you said?" she asked in a wonder. "You're not writing?"

He already felt relieved. "I don't know, upon my honour, what
I'm doing."

It made her visibly grave; so that, disconcerted in another way,
he was afraid of what she would see in it. She saw in fact exactly
what he feared, but again his honour, as he called it, was saved
even while she didn't know she had threatened it. Taking his words
for a betrayal of the sense that he, on his side, *might* complain,
what she clearly wanted was to urge on him some such patience as
he should be perhaps able to arrive at with her indirect help. Still
more clearly, however, she wanted to be sure of how far she might
venture; and he could see her make out in a moment that she had
a sort of test.

"Then if it's not for your book—?"

"What *am* I staying for?"

"I mean with your London work—with all you have to do. Isn't
it rather empty for you?"

"Empty for me?" He remembered how Kate had held that she
might propose marriage, and he wondered if this were the way
she would naturally begin it. It would leave him, such an incident,

he already felt, at a loss, and the note of his finest anxiety might have been in the vagueness of his reply. "Oh well—!"

"I ask too many questions?" She settled it for herself before he could protest. "You stay because you've got to."

He grasped at it. "I stay because I've got to." And he couldn't have said when he had uttered it if it were loyal to Kate or disloyal. It gave her, in a manner, away; it showed the tip of the ear of her plan. Yet Milly took it, he perceived, but as a plain statement of his truth. He was waiting for what Kate would have told her of—the permission from Lancaster Gate to come any nearer. To remain friends with either niece or aunt he mustn't stir without it. All this Densher read in the girl's sense of the spirit of his reply; so that it made him feel he was lying, and he had to think of something to correct that. What he thought of was, in an instant, "Isn't it enough, whatever you may be one's other complications, to stay after all for *you?*"

"Oh you must judge."

He was by this time on his feet to take leave, and was also at last too restless. The speech in question at least wasn't disloyal to Kate; that was the very tone of their bargain. So was it, by being loyal, another kind of lie, the lie of the uncandid profession of a motive. He was staying so little "for" Milly that he was staying positively against her. He didn't, none the less, know, and at last, thank goodness, didn't care. The only thing he could say might make it either better or worse. "Well then, so long as I don't go, you must think of me all *as* judging!"

– II –

He didn't go home, on leaving her—he didn't want to; he walked instead, through his narrow ways and his *campi* with gothic arches, to a small and comparatively sequestered café where he had already more than once found refreshment and comparative repose, together with solutions that consisted mainly and pleasantly of further indecisions. It was a literal fact that those awaiting him there to-night, while he leaned back on his velvet bench with his head against a florid mirror and his eyes not looking further than the fumes of his tobacco, might have been regarded by him as a little less limp than usual. This wasn't because, before getting to his feet again, there was a step he had seen his way to; it was simply because the acceptance of his position took sharper effect from his sense of what he had just had to deal with. When half an hour before, at the palace, he had turned about to Milly on the question of the impossibility so inwardly felt, turned about on the spot and under her eyes, he had acted, by the sudden force of his seeing much further, seeing how little, how not at all, impossibilities mattered. It wasn't a case for pedantry; when people were at *her* pass everything was allowed. And her pass was now, as by the sharp click of a spring, just completely his own—to the extent, as he felt, of her deep dependence on him. Anything he should do or shouldn't would have close reference to her life, which was thus absolutely in his hands—and ought never to have reference to anything else. It was on the cards for him that he might kill her—that was the way he read the cards as he sat in his customary corner. The fear in this thought made him let everything go, kept him there actually, all motionless, for three hours on end. He renewed his consumption and smoked more cigarettes than he had ever done in the time. What had come out for him had come out, with this first intensity, as a terror; so that action itself, of any sort, the right as well as the wrong— if the difference even survived—had heard it in a vivid "Hush!" the injunction to keep from that moment intensely still. He thought in fact while his vigil lasted of several different ways for his doing so, and the hour might have served him as a lesson in going on tiptoe.

What he finally took home, when he ventured to leave the place, was the perceived truth that he might on any other system go straight to destruction. Destruction was represented for him by the idea of his really bringing to a point, on Milly's side, anything whatever. Nothing so "brought," he easily argued, but *must* be in one way or another a catastrophe. He was mixed up in her fate, or her fate, if that should be better, was mixed up in *him*, so that a single false motion might either way snap the coil. They helped him, it was true, these considerations, to a degree of eventual peace, for what they luminously amounted to was that he was to do nothing, and that fell in after all with the burden laid on him by Kate. He was only not to budge without the girl's leave—not, oddly enough at the last, to move without it, whether further or nearer, any more than without Kate's. It was to this his wisdom reduced itself—to the need again simply to be kind. That was the same as being still—as studying to create the minimum of vibration. He felt himself as he smoked shut up to a room on the wall of which something precious was too precariously hung. A false step would bring it down, and it must hang as long as possible. He was aware when he walked away again that even Fleet Street wouldn't at this juncture successfully touch him. His manager might wire that he was wanted, but he could easily be deaf to his manager. His money for the idle life might be none too much; happily, however, Venice was cheap, and it was moreover the queer fact that Milly in a manner supported him. The greatest of his expenses really was to walk to the palace to dinner. He didn't want, in short, to give that up, and he should probably be able, he felt, to stay his breath and his hand. He should be able to be still enough through everything.

He tried that for three weeks, with the sense after a little of not having failed. There had to be a delicate art in it, for he wasn't trying—quite the contrary—to be either distant or dull. That would not have been being "nice," which in its own form was the real law. That too might just have produced the vibration he desired to avert; so that he best kept everything in place by not hesitating or fearing, as it were, to let himself go—go in the direction, that is to say, of staying. It depended on where he went; which was what he meant by taking care. When one went on tiptoe one could turn off for retreat without betraying the maneuver. Perfect tact—the necessity for which he had from the first, as we know, happily recognized—was to keep all intercourse in the key of the absolutely settled. It was settled thus for instance that they were indissoluble good friends, and settled as well that her being the American girl was, just in time and for the relation they found themselves concerned in, a boon inappreciable. If, at least, as the days went on, she was to fall short of her prerogative of the great national, the great maidenly ease, if she didn't divinely and responsively desire and labour to record herself as possessed of it, this wouldn't have been for want of Densher's keeping her, with his idea, well up to it—wouldn't have been in fine for want of his encouragement and reminder. He didn't perhaps in so many words speak to her of the quantity itself as of the thing she was least to intermit; but he talked of it, freely, in what he flattered himself was an impersonal way, and this held it there before her—since he was careful also to talk pleasantly. It was at once their idea, when all was said, and the most marked of their conveniences. The type was so elastic that it could be stretched to almost anything; and yet, not stretched, it kept down, remained normal, remained properly within bounds. And he *had* meanwhile, thank goodness, without being too much disconcerted, the sense, for the girl's part of the business, of the queerest conscious compliance, of her doing very much what he wanted, even though without her quite seeing why. She fairly touched this once in saying: "Oh yes, you like us to be as we are because it's a kind of facilitation to you that we don't quite measure: I think one would have to be English to measure it!"—and that too, strangely enough, without prejudice to her good nature. She might have been conceived as doing—that is of being—what he liked in order perhaps only to judge where it would take them. They really as it went on *saw* each other at the game; she knowing he tried to keep her in tune with his conception, and he knowing she thus knew it. Add that he again knew she knew, and yet that nothing was spoiled by it, and we get a fair impression of the line they found most completely workable. The strangest fact of all for us must be that the success he himself thus promoted was precisely what figured to his gratitude as the something above and beyond him, above and beyond Kate, that made for daily decency. There would scarce have been felicity—certainly too little of the right lubricant—had not the national character so invoked been, not less inscrutably than entirely, in Milly's chords. It made up her unity and was the one thing he could unlimitedly take for granted.

He did so then, daily, for twenty days, without deepened fear of the undue vibration that was keeping him watchful. He knew in his nervousness that he was living at best from day to day and from hand to mouth; yet he had succeeded, he believed, in avoiding a mistake. All women had alternatives, and Milly's would doubtless be shaky too; but the national character was firm in her, whether as all of her, practically, by this time, or but as a part; the national character that, in a woman still so young, made of the air breathed a virtual non-conductor. It wasn't till a certain occasion when the twenty days had passed that, going to the palace at tea-time, he was met by the information that the signorina padrona* was not "receiving." The announcement met him, in the court, on the lips of one of the gondoliers, met him, he thought, with such a conscious eye as the knowledge of his freedoms of access, hitherto conspicuously shown, could scarce fail to beget. Densher had not been at Palazzo Leporelli among the mere receivable, but had taken his place once for all among the involved and included, so that on being so flagrantly braved he recognized after a moment the propriety of a further appeal. Neither of the two ladies, it appeared, received, and yet Pasquale was not prepared to say that either was *poco bene.*† He was yet not prepared to say that either was anything, and he would have been blank, Densher mentally noted, if the term could ever apply to members of a race in whom vacancy was but a nest of darknesses — not a vain surface, but a place of withdrawal in which something obscure, something always ominous, indistinguishably lived. He felt afresh indeed at this hour the force of the veto laid within the palace on any mention, any cognition, of the liabilities of its mistress. The state of her health was never confessed to there as a reason. How much it might deeply be taken for one was another matter; of which he grew fully aware on carrying his question further. This appeal was to his friend Eugenio, whom he immediately sent for, with whom, for three rich minutes, protected from the weather, he was confronted in the gallery that led from the water-steps to the court, and whom he always called, in meditation, his friend; seeing it was so elegantly presumable he would have put an end to him if he could. That produced a relation which required a name of its own, an intimacy of consciousness in truth for each — an intimacy of eye, of ear, of general sensibility, of everything but tongue. It had been, in other words, for the five weeks, far from occult to our young man that

---

*Young lady of the house (Italian); that is, Milly.
†Not well; indisposed (Italian).

Eugenio took a view of him not less finely formal than essentially vulgar, but which at the same time he couldn't himself raise an eyebrow to prevent. It was all in the air now again; it was as much between them as ever while Eugenio waited on him in the court.

The weather, from early morning, had turned to storm, the first sea-storm of the autumn, and Densher had almost invidiously brought him down the outer staircase—the massive ascent, the great feature of the court, to Milly's *piano nobile*.* This was to pay him—it was the one chance—for all imputations; the imputation in particular that, clever, *tanto bello*† and not rich, the young man from London was—by the obvious way—pressing Miss Theale's fortune hard. It was to pay him for the further ineffable intimation that a gentleman must take the young lady's most devoted servant (interested scarcely less in the high attraction) for a strangely casual appendage if he counted in such a connexion on impunity and prosperity. These interpretations were odious to Densher for the simple reason that they might have been so true of the attitude of an inferior man, and three things alone, accordingly, had kept him from righting himself. One of these was that his critic sought expression only in an impersonality, a positive inhumanity, of politeness; the second was that refinements of expression in a friend's servant were not a thing a visitor could take action on; and the third was the fact that the particular attribution of motive did him after all no wrong. It was his own fault if the vulgar view, the view that might have been taken of an inferior man, happened so incorrigibly to fit him. He apparently wasn't so different from inferior men as that came to. If therefore, in fine, Eugenio figured to him as "my friend" because he was conscious of his seeing so much of him, what he made him see on the same lines in the course of their present interview was ever so much more. Densher felt that he marked himself, no doubt, as insisting, by dissatisfaction with the gondolier's answer, on the pursuit taken for granted in him; and yet felt it only in the augmented, the exalted distance that was by this time established between them. Eugenio had of

---

*Main floor in a Renaissance building, usually one level about the ground floor and containing important reception rooms (Italian).
†Good-looking (Italian).

course reflected that a word to Miss Theale from such a pair of lips would cost him his place; but he could also bethink himself that, so long as the word never came—and it was, on the basis he had arranged, impossible—he enjoyed the imagination of mounting guard. He had never so mounted guard, Densher could see, as during these minutes in the damp *loggia* where the storm-gusts were strong; and there came in fact for our young man, as a result of his presence, a sudden sharp sense that everything had turned to the dismal. Something had happened—he didn't know what; and it wasn't Eugenio who would tell him. What Eugenio told him was that he thought the ladies—as if their liability had been equal—were a "leetle" fatigued, just a "leetle leetle," and without any cause named for it. It was one of the signs of what Densher felt in him that, by a profundity, a true deviltry of resource, he always met the latter's Italian with English and his English with Italian. He now, as usual, slightly smiled at him in the process—but ever so slightly this time, his manner also being attuned, our young man made out, to the thing, whatever it was, that constituted the rupture of peace.

This manner, while they stood a long minute facing each other over all they didn't say, played a part as well in the sudden jar to Densher's protected state. It was a Venice all of evil that had broken out for them alike, so that they were together in their anxiety, if they really could have met on it; a Venice of cold lashing rain from a low black sky, of wicked wind raging through narrow passes, of general arrest and interruption, with the people engaged in all the water-life huddled, stranded and wageless, bored and cynical, under archways and bridges. Our young man's mute exchange with his friend contained meanwhile such a depth of reference that, had the pressure been but slightly prolonged, they might have reached a point at which they were equally weak. Each had verily something in mind that would have made a hash of mutual suspicion and in presence of which, as possibility, they were more united than disjoined. But it was to have been a moment for Densher that nothing could ease off—not even the formal propriety with which his interlocutor finally attended him to the *portone* and bowed upon his retreat. Nothing had passed about his coming back, and the air had made itself felt as a nonconductor of messages. Densher knew of course, as he took his way again, that Eugenio's invitation to return was not what he missed; yet he knew at the same time that what had happened to him was part of his punishment. Out in the square beyond the *fondamenta** that gave access to the landgate of the palace, out where the wind was higher, he fairly, with the thought of it, pulled his umbrella closer down. It couldn't be, his consciousness, unseen enough by others—the base predicament of having, by a concatenation, just to *take* such things: such things as the fact that one very acute person in the world, whom he couldn't dispose of as an interested scoundrel, enjoyed an opinion of him that there was no attacking, no disproving, no (what was worst of all) even noticing. One had come to a queer pass when a servant's opinion so mattered. Eugenio's would have mattered even if, as founded on a low vision of appearances, it had been quite wrong. It was the more disagreeable accordingly that the vision of appearances was quite right, and yet was scarcely less low.

Such as it was, at any rate, Densher shook it off with the more impatience that he was independently restless. He had to walk in spite of weather, and he took his course, through crooked ways, to the Piazza, where he should have the shelter of the galleries. Here, in the high arcade, half Venice was crowded close, while, on the Molo, at the limit of the expanse, the old columns of the Saint Theodore and of the Lion were the frame of a door wide open to the storm. It was odd for him, as he moved, that it should have made such a difference—if the difference wasn't only that the palace had for the first time failed of a welcome. There was more, but it came from that; that gave the harsh note and broke the spell. The wet and the cold were now to reckon with, and it was to Densher precisely as if he had seen the obliteration, at a stroke, of the margin on a faith in which they were all living. The margin had been his name for it—for the thing that, though it had held out, could bear no shock. The shock, in some form, had come, and he wondered about it while, threading his way among loungers as vague as himself, he dropped his eyes sightlessly on the rubbish in

*Street flanking the canal (Italian).

shops. There were stretches of the gallery paved with squares of red marble, greasy now with the salt spray; and the whole place, in its huge elegance, the grace of its conception and the beauty of its detail, was more than ever like a great drawing-room, the drawing-room of Europe, profaned and bewildered by some reverse of fortune. He brushed shoulders with brown men whose hats askew, and the loose sleeves of whose pendent jackets, made them resemble melancholy maskers. The tables and chairs that overflowed from the cafés were gathered, still with a pretense of service, into the arcade, and here and there a spectacled German, with his coat-collar up, partook publicly of food and philosophy. These were impressions for Densher too, but he had made the whole circuit thrice before he stopped short, in front of Florian's with the force of his sharpest. His eye had caught a face within the café—he had spotted an acquaintance behind the glass. The person he had thus paused long enough to look at twice was seated, well within range, at a small table on which a tumbler, half-emptied and evidently neglected, still remained; and though he had on his knee, as he leaned back, a copy of a French newspaper—the heading of the *Figaro* was visible—he stared straight before him at the little opposite rococo wall. Densher had him for a minute in profile, had him for a time during which his identity produced, however quickly, all the effect of establishing connexions—connexions startling and direct; and then, as if it were the one thing more needed, seized the look, determined by a turn of the head, that might have been a prompt result of the sense of being noticed. This wider view showed him *all* Lord Mark—Lord Mark as encountered, several weeks before, the day of the first visit of each to Palazzo Leporelli. For it had been all Lord Mark that was going out, on that occasion, as he came in—he had felt it, in the hall, at the time; and he was accordingly the less at a loss to recognize in a few seconds, as renewed meeting brought it to the surface, the same potential quantity.

It was a matter, the whole passage—it could only be—but of a few seconds; for as he might neither stand there to stare nor on the other hand make any advance from it, he had presently resumed his walk, this time to another pace. It had been for all the world, during his pause, as if he had caught his answer to the riddle of the day. Lord Mark had simply faced him—as he had faced *him*, not placed by him, not at first—as one of the damp shuffling crowd. Recognition, though hanging fire, had then clearly come; yet no light of salutation had been struck from these certainties. Acquaintance between them was scant enough for neither to take it up. That neither had done so was not, however, what now mattered, but that the gentleman at Florian's should be in the place at all. He couldn't have been in it long; Densher, as inevitably a haunter of the great meeting-ground, would in that case have seen him before. He paid short visits; he was on the wing; the question for him even as he sat there was of his train or of his boat. He had come back for something—as a sequel to his earlier visit; and whatever he had come back for it had had time to be done. He might have arrived but last night or that morning; he had already made the difference. It was a great thing for Densher to get this answer. He held it close, he hugged it, quite leaned on it as he continued to circulate. It kept him going and going—it made him no less restless. But it explained—and that was much, for with explanations he might somehow deal. The vice in the air, otherwise, was too much like the breath of fate. The weather had changed, the rain was ugly, the wind wicked, the sea impossible *because* of Lord Mark. It was because of him, a *fortiori*, that the palace was closed. Densher went round again twice; he found the visitor each time as he had found him first. Once, that is, he was staring before him; the next time he was looking over his *Figaro*, which he had opened out. Densher didn't again stop, but left him apparently unconscious of his passage—on another repetition of which Lord Mark had disappeared. He had spent but the day; he would be off that night; he had now gone to his hotel for arrangements. These things were as plain to Densher as if he had had them in words. The obscure had cleared for him—if cleared it was; there was something he didn't see, the great thing; but he saw so round it and so close to it that this was almost as good. He had been looking at a man who had done what he had come for, and for whom, as done, it temporarily sufficed. The man had come again to see Milly, and Milly had received him. His visit would have taken place just before or just after luncheon, and it was the reason why he himself had found her door shut.

He said to himself that evening, he still said even on the morrow, that he only wanted a reason, and that with this perception of one he could now mind, as he called it, his business. His business, he had settled, as we know, was to keep thoroughly still; and he asked himself why it should prevent this that he could feel, in connexion with the crisis, so remarkably blameless. He gave the appearances before him all the benefit of being critical, so that if blame were to accrue he shouldn't feel he had dodged it. But it wasn't a bit he who, that day, had touched her, and if she was upset it wasn't a bit his act. The ability so to think about it amounted for Densher during several hours to a kind of exhilaration. The exhilaration was heightened fairly, besides, by the visible conditions — sharp, striking, ugly to him — of Lord Mark's return. His constant view of it, for all the next hours, of which there were many, was as a demonstration on the face of it sinister even to his own actual ignorance. He didn't need, for seeing it as evil, seeing it as, to a certainty, in a high degree "nasty," to know more about it than he had so easily and so wonderfully picked up. You couldn't drop on the poor girl that way without, by the fact, being brutal. Such a visit was a descent, an invasion, an aggression, constituting precisely one or other of the stupid shocks he himself had so decently sought to spare her. Densher had indeed drifted by the next morning to the reflexion — which he positively, with occasion, might have brought straight out — that the only delicate and honourable way of treating a person in such a state was to treat her as *he*, Merton Densher, did. With time, actually — for the impression but deepened — this sense of the contrast, to the advantage of Merton Densher, became a sense of relief, and that in turn a sense of escape. It was for all the world — and he drew a long breath on it — as if a special danger for him had passed. Lord Mark had, without in the least intending such a service, got it straight out of the way. It was *he*, the brute, who had stumbled into just the wrong inspiration and who had therefore produced, for the very person he had wished to hurt, an impunity that was comparative innocence, that was almost like purification. The person he had wished to hurt could only be the person so unaccountably hanging about. To keep still meanwhile was, for this person, more comprehensively,

to keep it all up; and to keep it all up was, if that seemed on consideration best, not, for the day or two, to go back to the palace.

The day or two passed—stretched to three days; and with the effect, extraordinarily, that Densher felt himself in the course of
them washed but the more clean. Some sign would come if his return should have the better effect; and he was at all events, in absence, without the particular scruple. It wouldn't have been meant
for him by either of the women that he was to come back but to
face Eugenio. That was impossible—the being again denied; for it
made him practically answerable, and answerable was what he
wasn't. There was no neglect either in absence, inasmuch as, from
the moment he didn't get in, the one message he could send up
would be some hope on the score of health. Since accordingly that
sort of expression was definitely forbidden him he had only to
wait—which he was actually helped to do by his feeling with the
lapse of each day more and more wound up to it. The days in
themselves were anything but sweet; the wind and the weather
lasted, the fireless cold hinted at worse; the broken charm of the
world about was broken into smaller pieces. He walked up and
down his rooms and listened to the wind—listened also to tinkles
of bells and watched for some servant of the palace. He might get
a note, but the note never came; there were hours when he stayed
at home not to miss it. When he wasn't at home he was in circulation again as he had been at the hour of his seeing Lord Mark.
He strolled about the Square with the herd of refugees; he raked
the approaches and the cafés on the chance the brute, as he now
regularly imaged him, *might* be still there. He could only be there,
he knew, to be received afresh; and that—one had but to think of
it—would be indeed stiff. He had gone, however—it was proved;
though Densher's care for the question either way only added to
what was most acrid in the taste of his present ordeal. It all came
round to what he was doing for Milly—spending days that neither
relief nor escape could purge of a smack of the abject. What was
it but abject for a man of his parts to be reduced to such pastimes?
What was it but sordid for him, shuffling about in the rain, to have
to peep into shops and to consider possible meetings? What was it
but odious to find himself wondering what, as between him and
another man, a possible meeting would produce? There recurred

moments when in spite of everything he felt no straighter than another man. And yet even on the third day, when still nothing had
come, he more than ever knew that he wouldn't have budged for
the world.

He thought of the two women, in their silence, at last—he at all
events thought of Milly—as probably, for her reasons, now intensely wishing him to go. The cold breath of her reasons was,
with everything else, in the air; but he didn't care for them any
more than for her wish itself, and he would stay in spite of her, stay
in spite of odium, stay in spite perhaps of some final experience
that would be, for the pain of it, all but unbearable. That would be
his one way, purified though he was, to mark his virtue beyond any
mistake. It would be accepting the disagreeable, and the disagreeable would be a proof; a proof of his not having stayed for the
thing—the agreeable, as it were—that Kate had named. The thing
Kate had named was not to have been the odium of staying in spite
of hints. It was part of the odium as actual too that Kate was, for
her comfort, just now well aloof. These were the first hours since
her flight in which his sense of what she had done for him on the
eve of that event was to incur a qualification. It was strange, it was
perhaps base, to be thinking such things so soon; but one of the intimations of his solitude was that she had provided for herself. She
was out of it all, by her act, as much as he was in it; and this difference grew, positively, as his own intensity increased. She had
said in their last sharp snatch of talk—sharp though thickly muffled, and with every word in it final and deep, unlike even the
deepest words they had ever yet spoken: "Letters? Never—*now*.
Think of it. Impossible." So that as he had sufficiently caught her
sense—into which he read, all the same, a strange inconsequence—they had practically wrapped their understanding in the
breach of their correspondence. He had moreover, on losing her,
done justice to her law of silence; for there was doubtless a finer
delicacy in his not writing to her than in his writing as he must
have written had he spoken of themselves. That would have been
a turbid strain, and her idea had been to be noble; which, in a degree, was a manner. Only it left her, for the pinch, comparatively
at ease. And it left *him*, in the conditions, peculiarly alone. He was
alone, that is, till, on the afternoon of his third day, in gathering

dusk and renewed rain, with his shabby rooms looking doubtless, in their confirmed dreariness, for the mere eyes of others, at their worst, the grinning padrona threw open the door and introduced Mrs. Stringham. That made at a bound a difference, especially when he saw that his visitor was weighted. It appeared part of her weight that she was in a wet waterproof, that she allowed her umbrella to be taken from her by the good woman without consciousness or care, and that her face, under her veil, richly rosy with the driving wind, was—and the veil too—as splashed as if the rain were her tears.

— III —

They came to it almost immediately; he was to wonder afterwards at the fewness of their steps. "She has turned her face to the wall."

"You mean she's worse?"

The poor lady stood there as she had stopped; Densher had, in instant flare of his eagerness, his curiosity, all responsive at sight of her, waved away, on the spot, the padrona, who had offered to relieve her of her mackintosh. She looked vaguely about through her wet veil, intensely alive now to the step she had taken and wishing it not to have been in the dark, but clearly, as yet, seeing nothing. "I don't know *how* she is—and it's why I've come to you."

"I'm glad enough you've come," he said, "and it's quite—you make me feel—as if I had been wretchedly waiting for you."

She showed him again her blurred eyes—she had caught at his word. "Have you been wretched?"

Now, however, on his lips, the word expired. It would have sounded for him like a complaint, and before something he already made out in his visitor he knew his own trouble as small. Hers, under her damp draperies, which shamed his lack of a fire, was great, and he felt she had brought it all with her. He answered that he had been patient and above all that he had been still. "As still as a mouse—you'll have seen it for yourself. Stiller, for three days together, than I've ever been in my life. It has seemed to me the only thing."

This qualification of it as a policy or a remedy was straightway for his friend, he saw, a light that her own light could answer. "It has been best. I've wondered for you. But it has been best," she said again.

"Yet it has done no good?"

"I don't know. I've been afraid you were gone." Then as he gave a headshake which, though slow, was deeply mature: "You *won't* go?"

"Is to 'go,'" he asked, "to be still?"

"Oh I mean if you'll stay for me."

"I'll do anything for you. Isn't it for you alone now I can?"

She thought of it, and he could see even more of the relief she was taking from him. His presence, his face, his voice, the old rooms themselves, so meagre yet so charged, where Kate had admirably been to him—these things counted for her, now she had them, as the help she had been wanting: so that she still only stood there taking them all in. With it however popped up characteristically a throb of her conscience. What she thus tasted was almost a personal joy. It told Densher of the three days she on her side had spent. "Well, anything you do for me—*is* for her too. Only, only—!"

"Only nothing now matters?"

She looked at him a minute as if he were the fact itself that he expressed. "Then you know?"

"Is she dying?" he asked for all answer.

Mrs. Stringham waited—her face seemed to sound him. Then her own reply was strange. "She hasn't so much as named you. We haven't spoken."

"Not for three days?"

"No more," she simply went on, "than if it were all over. Not even by the faintest allusion."

"Oh," said Densher with more light, "you mean you haven't spoken about *me?*"

"About what else? No more than if you were dead."

"Well," he answered after a moment, "I *am* dead."

"Then *I* am," said Susan Shepherd with a drop of her arms on her waterproof.

It was a tone that, for the minute, imposed itself in its dry despair; it represented, in the bleak place, which had no life of its own, none but the life Kate had left—the sense of which, for that matter, by mystic channels, might fairly be reaching the visitor—the very impotence of their extinction. And Densher had nothing to oppose it withal, nothing but again: "Is she dying?"

It made her, however, as if these were crudities, almost material pangs, only say as before: "Then you know?"

"Yes," he at last returned, "I know. But the marvel to me is that *you* do. I've no right in fact to imagine or to assume that you do."

"You may," said Susan Shepherd, "all the same. I know."

"Everything?"

Her eyes, through her veil, kept pressing him. "No—not everything. That's why I've come."

"That I shall really tell you?" With which, as she hesitated and it affected him, he brought out in a groan a doubting "Oh, oh!" It turned him from her to the place itself, which was a part of what was in him, was the abode, the worn shrine more than ever, of the fact in possession, the fact, now a thick association, for which he had hired it. *That* was not for telling, but Susan Shepherd was, none the less, so decidedly wonderful that the sense of it might really have begun, by an effect already operating, to be a part of her knowledge. He saw, and it stirred him, that she hadn't come to judge him; had come rather, so far as she might dare, to pity. This showed him her own abasement—that, at any rate, of grief; and made him feel with a rush of friendliness that he liked to be with her. The rush had quickened when she met his groan with an attenuation.

"We shall at all events—if that's anything—be together."

It was his own good impulse in herself. "It's what I've ventured to feel. It's much." She replied in effect, silently, that it was whatever he liked; on which, so far as he had been afraid for anything, he knew his fear had dropped. The comfort was huge, for it gave back to him something precious, over which, in the effort of recovery, his own hand had too imperfectly closed. Kate, he remembered, had said to him, with her sole and single boldness—and also on grounds he hadn't then measured—that Mrs. Stringham was a person who *wouldn't*, at a pinch, in a stretch of confidence, wince. It was but another of the cases in which Kate was always showing. "You don't think then very horridly of me?"

And her answer was the more valuable that it came without nervous effusion—quite as if she understood what he might conceivably have believed. She turned over in fact what she thought, and that was what helped him. "Oh you've been extraordinary!"

It made him aware the next moment of how they had been planted there. She took off her cloak with his aid, though when she had also, accepting a seat, removed her veil, he recognized in her personal ravage that the words she had just uttered to him were the one flower she had to throw. They were all her consolation for him, and the consolation even still depended on the event. She sat with him at any rate in the grey clearance, as sad as a winter dawn, made by their meeting. The image she again evoked for him loomed in it but the larger. "She has turned her face to the wall."

He saw with the last vividness, and it was as if, in their silences, they were simply so leaving what he saw. "She doesn't speak at all? I don't mean not of me."

"Of nothing—of no one." And she went on, Susan Shepherd, giving it out as she had had to take it. "She doesn't *want* to die. Think of her age. Think of her goodness. Think of her beauty. Think of all she is. Think of all she *has*. She lies there stiffening herself and clinging to it all. So I thank God—!" the poor lady wound up with a wan inconsequence.

He wondered. "You thank God—?"

"That she's so quiet."

He continued to wonder. "*Is* she so quiet?"

"She's more than quiet. She's grim. It's what she has never been. So you see—all these days. I can't tell you—but it's better so. It would kill me if she *were* to tell me."

"To tell you?" He was still at a loss.

"How she feels. How she clings. How she doesn't want it."

"How she doesn't want to die? Of course she doesn't want it." He had a long pause, and they might have been thinking together of what they could even now do to prevent it. This, however, was not what he brought out. Milly's "grimness" and the great hushed palace were present to him; present with the little woman before him as she must have been waiting there and listening. "Only, what harm have *you* done her?"

Mrs. Stringham looked about in her darkness. "I don't know. I come and talk of her here with you."

It made him again hesitate. "Does she utterly hate me?"

"I don't know. How *can* I? No one ever will."

"She'll never tell?"

"She'll never tell."

Once more he thought. "She must be magnificent."

"She *is* magnificent."

His friend, after all, helped him, and he turned it, so far as he could, all over. "Would she see me again?"

It made his companion stare. "Should you like to see her?"

"You mean as you describe her?" He felt her surprise, and it took him some time. "No."

"Ah then!" Mrs. Stringham sighed.

"But if she could bear it I'd do anything."

She had for the moment her vision of this, but it collapsed. "I don't see what you can do."

"I don't either. But *she* might."

Mrs. Stringham continued to think. "It's too late."

"Too late for her to see —?"

"Too late."

The very decision of her despair — it was after all so lucid — kindled in him a heat. "But the doctor, all the while —?"

"Tacchini? Oh he's kind. He comes. He's proud of having been approved and coached by a great London man. He hardly in fact goes away; so that I scarce know what becomes of his other patients. He thinks her, justly enough, a great personage; he treats her like royalty; he's waiting on events. But she has barely consented to see him, and, though she has told him, generously — for she *thinks* of me, dear creature — that he may come, that he may stay, for my sake, he spends most of his time only hovering at her door, prowling through the rooms, trying to entertain me, in that ghastly saloon, with the gossip of Venice, and meeting me, in doorways, in the sala, on the staircase, with an agreeable intolerable smile. We don't," said Susan Shepherd, "talk of her."

"By her request?"

"Absolutely. I don't do what she doesn't wish. We talk of the price of provisions."

"By her request too?"

"Absolutely. She named it to me as a subject when she said, the first time, that if it would be any comfort to me he might stay as much as we liked."

Densher took it all in. "But he isn't any comfort to you!"

"None whatever. That, however," she added, "isn't his fault. Nothing's any comfort."

"Certainly," Densher observed, "as I but too horribly feel, *I'm* not."

"No. But I didn't come for that."

"You came for *me*."

"Well then call it that." But she looked at him a moment with eyes filled full, and something came up in her the next instant from deeper still. "I came at bottom of course—"

"You came at bottom of course for our friend herself. But if it's, as you say, too late for me to do anything?"

She continued to look at him, and with an irritation, which he saw grow in her, from the truth itself. "So I did say. But, with you here"—and she turned her vision again strangely about her—"with you here, and with everything, I feel we mustn't abandon her."

"God forbid we should abandon her."

"Then you *won't?*" His tone had made her flush again.

"How do you mean I 'won't,' if she abandons *me?* What can I do if she won't see me?"

"But you said just now you wouldn't like it."

"I said I shouldn't like it in the light of what you tell me. I shouldn't like it only to see her as you make me. I should like it if I could help her. But even then," Densher pursued without faith, "she would have to want it first herself. And there," he continued to make out, "is the devil of it. She *won't* want it herself. She *can't!*"

He had got up in his impatience of it, and she watched him while he helplessly moved. "There's one thing you can do. There's only that, and even for that there are difficulties. But there *is* that." He stood before her with his hands in his pockets, and he had soon enough, from her eyes, seen what was coming. She paused as if waiting for his leave to utter it, and as he only let her wait they heard in the silence, on the Canal, the renewed downpour of rain. She had at last to speak, but, as if still with her fear, she only half-spoke. "I think you really know yourself what it is."

He did know what it was, and with it even, as she said— rather!—there were difficulties. He turned away on them, on everything, for a moment; he moved to the other window and looked at the sheeted channel, wider, like a river, where the houses opposite, blurred and belittled, stood at twice their distance. Mrs. Stringham said nothing, was as mute in fact, for the minute, as if she had "had" him, and he was the first again to speak. When he did so, however, it was not in straight answer to her last remark—he only started from that. He said, as he came back to her, "Let me, you know, *see*—one must understand," almost as if he had for the time accepted it. And what he wished to understand was where, on the essence of the question, was the voice of Sir Luke Strett. If they talked of not giving her up shouldn't *he* be the one least of all to do it? "Aren't we, at the worst, in the dark without him?"

"Oh," said Mrs. Stringham, "it's he who has kept me going. I wired the first night, and he answered like an angel. He'll come like one. Only he can't arrive, at the nearest, till Thursday afternoon."

"Well then that's something."

She considered. "Something—yes. She likes him."

"Rather! I can see it still, the face with which, when he was here in October—that night when she was in white, when she had people there and those musicians—she committed him to my care. It was beautiful for both of us—she put us in relation. She asked me, for the time, to take him about; I did so, and we quite hit it off. That proved," Densher said with a quick sad smile, "that she liked him."

"He liked *you*," Susan Shepherd presently risked.

"Ah I know nothing about that."

"You ought to then. He went with you to galleries and churches; you saved his time for him, showed him the choicest things, and you perhaps will remember telling me myself that if he hadn't been a great surgeon he might really have been a great judge. I mean of the beautiful."

"Well," the young man admitted, "that's what he is—in having judged *her*. He hasn't," he went on, "judged her for nothing. His interest in her—which we must make the most of—can only be supremely beneficent."

He still roamed, while he spoke, with his hands in his pockets, and she saw him, on this, as her eyes sufficiently betrayed, trying to keep his distance from the recognition he had a few moments before partly confessed to. "I'm glad," she dropped, "you like him!"

There was something for him in the sound of it. "Well, I do no more, dear lady, than you do yourself. Surely *you* like him. Surely, when he was here, we all liked him."

"Yes, but I seem to feel I know what he thinks. And I should think, with all the time you spent with him, you'd know it," she said, "yourself."

Densher stopped short, though at first without a word. "We never spoke of her. Neither of us mentioned her, even to sound her name, and nothing whatever in connexion with her passed between us."

Mrs. Stringham stared up at him, surprised at this picture. But she had plainly an idea that after an instant resisted it. "That was his professional propriety."

"Precisely. But it was also my sense of that virtue in him, and it was something more besides." And he spoke with sudden intensity. "I couldn't *talk* to him about her!"

"Oh!" said Susan Shepherd.

"I can't talk to any one about her."

"Except to *me*," his friend continued.

"Except to you." The ghost of her smile, a gleam of significance, had waited on her words, and it kept him, for honesty, looking at her. For honesty too—that is for his own words—he had quickly coloured: he was sinking so, at a stroke, the burden of his discourse with Kate. His visitor, for the minute, while their eyes met, might have been watching him hold it down. And he *had* to hold it down—the effort of which, precisely, made him red. He couldn't let it come up; at least not yet. She might make what she would of it. He attempted to repeat his statement, but he really modified it. "Sir Luke, at all events, had nothing to tell me, and I had nothing to tell him. Make-believe talk was impossible for us, and—"

"And *real*"—she had taken him right up with a huge emphasis—"was more impossible still." No doubt—he didn't deny it; and she had straightway drawn her conclusion. "Then that proves what I say—that there were immensities between you. Otherwise you'd have chattered."

"I dare say," Densher granted, "we were both thinking of her."

"You were neither of you thinking of any one else. That's why you kept together."

Well, that too, if she desired, he took from her; but he came straight back to what he had originally said. "I haven't a notion, all the same, of what he thinks." She faced him, visibly, with the question into which he had already observed that her special shade of earnestness was perpetually flowering, right and left—"Are you *very* sure?"—and he could only note her apparent difference from himself. "You, I judge, believe that he thinks she's gone."

She took it, but she bore up. "It doesn't matter what I believe."

"Well, we shall see"—and he felt almost basely superficial. More and more, for the last five minutes, had he known she had brought something with her, and never in respect to anything had he had such a wish to postpone. He would have liked to put everything off till Thursday; he was sorry it was now Tuesday; he wondered if he were afraid. Yet it wasn't of Sir Luke, who was coming; nor of Milly, who was dying; nor of Mrs. Stringham, who was sitting there. It wasn't, strange to say, of Kate either, for Kate's presence affected him suddenly as having swooned or trembled away. Susan Shepherd's, thus prolonged, had cast on it some influence under which it had ceased to act. She was as absent to his sensibility as she had constantly been, since her departure, absent, as an echo or a reference, from the palace; and it was the first time, among the objects now surrounding him, that his sensibility so noted her. He knew soon enough that it was of himself he was afraid, and that even, if he didn't take care, he should infallibly be more so. "Meanwhile," he added for his companion, "it has been everything for me to see you."

She slowly rose at the words, which might almost have conveyed to her the hint of his taking care. She stood there as if she had in fact seen him abruptly moved to dismiss her. But the abruptness would have been in this case so marked as fairly to offer ground for insistence to her imagination of his state. It would take her moreover, she clearly showed him she was thinking, but a minute or two to insist. Besides, she had already said it. "Will you do it if *he* asks you? I mean if Sir Luke himself puts it to you. And will you give him"—oh she was earnest now!—"the opportunity to put it to you?"

"The opportunity to put what?"

"That if you deny it to her, that may still do something."

Densher felt himself—as had already once befallen him in the quarter of an hour—turn red to the top of his forehead. Turning red had, however, for him, a sign of shame, been, so to speak, discounted: his consciousness of it at the present moment was rather as a sign of his fear. It showed him sharply enough of what he was afraid. "If I deny what to her?"

Hesitation, on the demand, revived in her, for hadn't he all along been letting her see that he knew? "Why, what Lord Mark told her."

"And what did Lord Mark tell her?"

Mrs. Stringham had a look of bewilderment—of seeing him as suddenly perverse. "I've been judging that you yourself know." And it was she who now blushed deep.

It quickened his pity for her, but he was beset too by other things. "Then *you* know—"

"Of his dreadful visit?" She stared. "Why it's what has done it."

"Yes—I understand that. But you also know—"

He had faltered again, but all she knew she now wanted to say. "I'm speaking," she said soothingly, "of what he told her. It's *that* that I've taken you as knowing."

"Oh!" he sounded in spite of himself.

It appeared to have for her, he saw the next moment, the quality of relief, as if he had supposed her thinking of something else. Thereupon, straightway, that lightened it. "Oh you thought I've known it for *true!*"

Her light had heightened her flush, and he saw that he had betrayed himself. Not, however, that it mattered, as he immediately saw still better. There it was now, all of it at last, and this at least there was no postponing. They were left with her idea—the one she was wishing to make him recognize. He had expressed ten minutes before his need to understand, and she was acting after all but on that. Only what he was to understand was no small matter; it might be larger even than as yet appeared.

He took again one of his turns, not meeting what she had last said; he mooned a minute, as he would have called it, at a window; and of course she could see that she had driven him to the wall. She did clearly, without delay, see it; on which her sense of having "caught" him became as promptly a scruple, which she spoke as if not to press. "What I mean is that he told her you've been all the while engaged to Miss Croy."

He gave a jerk round; it was almost—to hear it—the touch of a lash; and he said—idiotically, as he afterwards knew—the first thing that came into his head. "All *what* while?"

"Oh it's not I who say it." She spoke in gentleness. "I only repeat to you what he told her."

Densher, from whom an impatience had escaped, had already caught himself up. "Pardon my brutality. Of course I know what you're talking about. I saw him, toward the evening," he further explained, "in the Piazza; only just saw him—through the glass at Florian's—without any words. In fact I scarcely know him—there wouldn't have been occasion. It was but once, moreover—he must have gone that night. But I knew he wouldn't have come for nothing, and I turned it over—what he would have come for."

Oh so had Mrs. Stringham. "He came for exasperation."

Densher approved. "He came to let her know that he knows better than she for whom it was she had a couple of months before, in her fool's paradise, refused him."

"How you *do* know!"—and Mrs. Stringham almost smiled.

"I know that—but I don't know the good it does him."

"The good, he thinks, if he has patience—not too much—may be to come. He doesn't know what he has done to her. Only *we*, you see, do that."

He saw, but he wondered. "She kept from him—what she felt?"

"She was able—I'm sure of it—not to show anything. He dealt

her his blow, and she took it without a sign." Mrs. Stringham, it was plain, spoke by book, and it brought into play again her appreciation of what she related. "She's magnificent."

Densher again gravely assented. "Magnificent!"

"And *he*," she went on, "is an idiot of idiots."

"An idiot of idiots." For a moment, on it all, on the stupid doom in it, they looked at each other. "Yet he's thought so awfully clever."

"So awfully—it's Maud Lowder's own view. And he was nice, in London," said Mrs. Stringham, "to *me*. One could almost pity him—he has had such a good conscience."

"That's exactly the inevitable ass."

"Yes, but it wasn't—I could see from the only few things she first told me—that he meant *her* the least harm. He intended none whatever."

"That's always the ass at his worst," Densher returned. "He only of course meant harm to me."

"And good· to himself—he thought that would come. He had been unable to swallow," Mrs. Stringham pursued, "what had happened on his other visit. He had been then too sharply humiliated."

"Oh I saw that."

"Yes, and he also saw you. He saw you received, as it were, while he was turned away."

"Perfectly," Densher said—"I've filled it out. And also that he has known meanwhile for *what* I was then received. For a stay of all these weeks. He had had it to think of."

"Precisely—it was more than he could bear. But he has it," said Mrs. Stringham, "to think of still."

"Only, after all," asked Densher, who himself somehow, at this point, was having more to think of even than he had yet had—"only, after all, how has he happened to know? That is, to know enough."

"What do you call enough?" Mrs. Stringham inquired.

"He can only have acted—it would have been his sole safety—from full knowledge."

He had gone on without heeding her question; but, face to face as they were, something had none the less passed between them.

It was this that, after an instant, made her again interrogative. "What do you mean by full knowledge?"

Densher met it indirectly. "Where has he been since October?"

"I think he has been back to England. He came in fact, I've reason to believe, straight from there."

"Straight to do this job? All the way for his half-hour?"

"Well, to try again—with the help perhaps of a new fact. To make himself possibly right with her—a different attempt from the other. He had at any rate something to tell her, and he didn't know his opportunity would reduce itself to half an hour. Or perhaps indeed half an hour would be just what was most effective. It *has* been!" said Susan Shepherd.

Her companion took it in, understanding but too well; yet as she lighted the matter for him more, really, than his own courage had quite dared—putting the absent dots on several i's—he saw new questions swarm. They had been till now in a bunch, entangled and confused; and they fell apart, each showing for itself. The first he put to her was at any rate abrupt. "Have you heard of late from Mrs. Lowder."

"Oh yes, two or three times. She depends naturally upon news of Milly."

He hesitated. "And does she depend, naturally, upon news of *me?*"

His friend matched for an instant his deliberation.

"I've given her none that hasn't been decently good. This will have been the first."

"'This'?" Densher was thinking.

"Lord Mark's having been here, and her being as she is."

He thought a moment longer. "What has Mrs. Lowder written about him? Has she written that he has been with them?"

"She has mentioned him but once—it was in her letter before the last. Then she said something."

"And what did she say?"

Mrs. Stringham produced it with an effort. "Well it was in reference to Miss Croy. That she thought Kate was thinking of him. Or perhaps I should say rather that he was thinking of *her*—only it seemed this time to have struck Maud that he was seeing the way more open to him."

Densher listened with his eyes on the ground, but he presently raised them to speak, and there was that in his face which proved him aware of a queerness in his question. "Does she mean he has been encouraged to *propose* to her niece?"

"I don't know what she means."

"Of course not"—he recovered himself; "and I oughtn't to seem to trouble you to piece together what I can't piece myself. Only I 'guess,'" he added, "I *can* piece it."

She spoke a little timidly, but she risked it. "I dare say I can piece it too."

It was one of the things in her—and his conscious face took it from her as such—that from the moment of her coming in had seemed to mark for him, as to what concerned him, the long jump of her perception. They had parted four days earlier with many things, between them, deep down. But these things were now on their troubled surface, and it wasn't he who had brought them so quickly up. Women were wonderful—at least this one was. But so, not less, was Milly, was Aunt Maud; so, most of all, was his very Kate. Well, he already knew what he had been feeling about the circle of petticoats. They were all *such* petticoats! It was just the fineness of his tangle. The sense of that, in its turn, for us too, might have been not unconnected with his putting to his visitor a question that quite passed over her remark. "Has Miss Croy meanwhile written to our friend?"

"Oh," Mrs. Stringham amended, "*her* friend also. But not a single word that I know of."

He had taken it for certain she hadn't—the thing being after all but a shade more strange than his having himself, with Milly, never for six weeks mentioned the young lady in question. It was for that matter but a shade more strange than Milly's not having mentioned her. In spite of which, and however inconsequently, he blushed anew for Kate's silence. He got away from it in fact as quickly as possible, and the furthest he could get was by reverting for a minute to the man they had been judging. "How did he manage to get *at* her? She had only—with what had passed between them before—to say she couldn't see him."

"Oh she was disposed to kindness. She was easier," the good

lady explained with a slight embarrassment, "than at the other time."

"Easier?"

"She was off her guard. There was a difference."

"Yes. But exactly not *the* difference."

"Exactly not the difference of her having to be harsh. Perfectly. She could afford to be the opposite." With which, as he said nothing, she just impatiently completed her sense. "She had had *you* here for six weeks."

"Oh!" Densher softly groaned.

"Besides, I think he must have written her first—written I mean in a tone to smooth his way. That it would be a kindness to himself. Then on the spot—"

"On the spot," Densher broke in, "he unmasked? The horrid little beast!"

It made Susan Shepherd turn slightly pale, though quickening, as for hope, the intensity of her look at him. "Oh he went off without an alarm."

"And he must have gone off also without a hope."

"Ah that, certainly."

"Then it *was* mere base revenge. Hasn't he known her, into the bargain," the young man asked—"didn't he, weeks before, see her, judge her, feel her, as having for such a suit as his not more perhaps than a few months to live?"

Mrs. Stringham at first, for reply, but looked at him in silence; and it gave more force to what she then remarkably added. "He has doubtless been aware of what you speak of, just as you have yourself been aware."

"He has wanted her, you mean, just *because*—?"

"Just because," said Susan Shepherd.

"The hound!" Merton Densher brought out. He moved off, however, with a hot face, as soon as he had spoken, conscious again of an intention in his visitor's reserve. Dusk was now deeper, and after he had once more taken counsel of the dreariness without he turned to his companion. "Shall we have lights—a lamp or the candles?"

"Not for me."

"Nothing?"

"Not for me."

He waited at the window another moment and then faced his friend with a thought. "He *will* have proposed to Miss Croy. That's what has happened."

Her reserve continued, "It's you who must judge."

"Well, I do judge. Mrs. Lowder will have done so too—only *she*, poor lady, wrong. Miss Croy's refusal of him will have struck him"—Densher continued to make it out—"as a phenomenon requiring a reason."

"And you've been clear to him *as* the reason?"

"Not too clear—since I'm sticking here and since that has been a fact to make his descent on Miss Theale relevant. But clear enough. He has believed," said Densher bravely, "that I may have been a reason at Lancaster Gate, and yet at the same time have been up to something in Venice."

Mrs. Stringham took her courage from his own. "'Up to' something? Up to what?"

"God knows. To some 'game,' as they say. To some deviltry. To some duplicity."

"Which of course," Mrs. Stringham observed, "is a monstrous supposition." Her companion, after a stiff minute—sensibly long for each—fell away from her again, and then added to it another minute, which he spent once more looking out with his hands in his pockets. This was no answer, he perfectly knew, to what she had dropped, and it even seemed to state for his own ears that no answer was possible. She left him to himself, and he was glad she had declined, for their further colloquy, the advantage of lights. These would have been an advantage mainly to herself. Yet she got her benefit too even from the absence of them. It came out in her very tone when at last she addressed him—so differently, for confidence—in words she had already used. "If Sir Luke himself asks it of you as something you can do for *him*, will you deny to Milly herself what she has been so dreadfully to believe?"

Oh how he knew he hung back! But at last he said: "You're absolutely certain then that she does believe it?"

"Certain?" She appealed to their whole situation. "Judge!"

He took his time again to judge. "Do *you* believe it?"

He was conscious that his own appeal pressed her hard; it eased

him a little that her answer must be a pain to her discretion. She
answered none the less, and he was truly the harder pressed.
"What I believe will inevitably depend more or less on your action. You can perfectly settle it—if you care. I promise to believe
you down to the ground if, to save her life, you consent to a denial."

"But a denial, when it comes to that—confound the whole
thing, don't you see!—of exactly what?"

It was as if he were hoping she would narrow; but in fact she enlarged. "Of everything."

Everything had never even yet seemed to him so incalculably
much. "Oh!" he simply moaned into the gloom.[25]

— IV —

The near Thursday, coming nearer and bringing Sir Luke
Strett, brought also blessedly an abatement of other rigors.
The weather changed, the stubborn storm yielded, and the
autumn sunshine, baffled for many days, but now hot and almost
vindictive, came into its own again and, with an almost audible
pæan, a suffusion of bright sound that was one with the bright
colour, took large possession. Venice glowed and splashed and
called and chimed again; the air was like a clap of hands, and the
scattered pinks, yellows, blues, sea-greens, were like a hanging-out
of vivid stuffs, a laying-down of fine carpets. Densher rejoiced in
this on the occasion of his going to the station to meet the great
doctor. He went after consideration, which, as he was constantly
aware, was at present his imposed, his only, way of doing anything.
That was where the event had landed him—where no event in his
life had landed him before. He had thought, no doubt, from the
day he was born, much more than he had acted; except indeed
that he remembered thoughts—a few of them—which at the moment of their coming to him had thrilled him almost like adventures. But anything like his actual state he had not, as to the
prohibition of impulse, accident, range—the prohibition in other
words of freedom—hitherto known. The great oddity was that if he

had felt his arrival, so few weeks back, especially as an adventure, nothing could now less resemble one than the fact of his staying. It would be an adventure to break away, to depart, to go back, above all, to London, and tell Kate Croy he had done so; but there was something of the merely, the almost meanly, obliged and involved sort in his going on as he was. That was the effect in particular of Mrs. Stringham's visit, which had left him as with such a taste in his mouth of what he couldn't do. It had made this quantity clear to him, and yet had deprived him of the sense, the other sense, of what, for a refuge, he possibly *could*.

It was but a small make-believe of freedom, he knew, to go to the station for Sir Luke. Nothing equally free, at all events, had he yet turned over so long. What then was his odious position but that again and again he was afraid? He stiffened himself under this consciousness as if it had been a tax levied by a tyrant. He hadn't at any time proposed to himself to live long enough for fear to preponderate in his life. Such was simply the advantage it had actually got of him. He was afraid for instance that an advance to his distinguished friend might prove for him somehow a pledge or a committal. He was afraid of it as a current that would draw him too far; yet he thought with an equal aversion of being shabby, being poor, through fear. What finally prevailed with him was the reflexion that, whatever might happen, the great man had, after that occasion at the palace, their young woman's brief sacrifice to society—and the hour of Mrs. Stringham's appeal had brought it well to the surface—shown him marked benevolence. Mrs. Stringham's comments on the relation in which Milly had placed them made him—it was unmistakable—feel things he perhaps hadn't felt. It was in the spirit of seeking a chance to feel again adequately whatever it was he had missed—it was, no doubt, in that spirit, so far as it went a stroke for freedom, that Densher, arriving betimes, paced the platform before the train came in. Only, after it had come and he had presented himself at the door of Sir Luke's compartment with everything that followed—only, as the situation developed, the sense of an anti-climax to so many intensities deprived his apprehensions and hesitations even of the scant dignity they might claim. He could scarce have said if the visitor's manner less showed the remembrance that might have suggested expectation, or made shorter work of surprise in presence of the fact.

Sir Luke had clean forgotten—so Densher read—the rather remarkable young man he had formerly gone about with, though he picked him up again, on the spot, with one large quiet look. The young man felt himself so picked, and the thing immediately affected him as the proof of a splendid economy. Opposed to all the waste with which he was now connected the exhibition was of a nature quite nobly to admonish him. The eminent pilgrim, in the train, all the way, had used the hours as he needed, thinking not a moment in advance of what finally awaited him. An exquisite case awaited him—of which, in this queer way, the remarkable young man was an outlying part; but the single motion of his face, the motion into which Densher, from the platform, lightly stirred its stillness, was his first renewed cognition. If, however, he had suppressed the matter by leaving Victoria he would at once suppress now, in turn, whatever else suited. The perception of this became as a symbol of the whole pitch, so far as one might one's self be concerned, of his visit. One saw, our friend further meditated, everything that, in contact, he appeared to accept—if only, for much, not to trouble to sink it: what one missed was the inward use he made of it. Densher began wondering, at the great watersteps outside, what use he would make of the anomaly of their having there to separate. Eugenio had been on the platform, in the respectful rear, and the gondola from the palace, under his direction, bestirred itself, with its attaching mixture of alacrity and dignity, on their coming out of the station together. Densher didn't at all mind now that, he himself of necessity refusing a seat on the deep black cushions beside the guest of the palace, he had Milly's three emissaries for spectators; and this susceptibility, he also knew, it was something to have left behind. All he did was to smile down vaguely from the steps—they could see him, the donkeys, as shut out as they would. "I don't," he said with a sad headshake, "go there now."

"Oh!" Sir Luke Strett returned, and made no more of it; so that the thing was splendid, Densher fairly thought, as an inscrutability quite inevitable and unconscious. His friend appeared not even to make of it that he supposed it might be for respect to the crisis.

He didn't moreover afterwards make much more of anything—
after the classic craft, that is, obeying in the main Pasquale's inimitable stroke from the poop, had performed the maneuver by
which it presented, receding, a back, so to speak, rendered positively graceful by the high black hump of its *felze.** Densher
watched the gondola out of sight—he heard Pasquale's cry, borne
to him across the water, for the sharp firm swerve into a side-canal,
a short cut to the palace. he had no gondola of his own; it was his
habit never to take one; and he humbly—as in Venice it *is* humble—walked away, though not without having for some time
longer stood as if fixed where the guest of the palace had left him.
It was strange enough, but he found himself as never yet, and as
he couldn't have reckoned, in presence of the truth that was the
truest about Milly. He couldn't have reckoned on the force of the
difference instantly made—for it was all in the air as he heard
Pasquale's cry and saw the boat disappear—by the mere visibility,
on the spot, of the personage summoned to her aid. He hadn't
only never been near the facts of her condition—which counted
so as a blessing for him; he hadn't only, with all the world, hovered
outside an impenetrable ring fence, within which there reigned a
kind of expensive vagueness made up of smiles and silences and
beautiful fictions and priceless arrangements, all strained to breaking; but he had also, with every one else, as he now felt, actively
fostered suppressions which were in the direct interest of every
one's good manner, every one's pity, every one's really quite generous ideal. It was a conspiracy of silence, as the *cliché* went, to
which no one had made an exception, the great smudge of mortality across the picture, the shadow of pain and horror, finding in
no quarter a surface of spirit or of speech that consented to reflect
it. "The mere æsthetic instinct of mankind—!" our young man
had more than once, in the connexion, said to himself; letting the
rest of the proposition drop, but touching again thus sufficiently
on the outrage even to taste involved in one's having to *see*. So
then it had been—a general conscious fool's paradise, from which
the specified had been chased like a dangerous animal. What

---

*The gondola's small cabin (Italian); seen from behind.

therefore had at present befallen was that the specified, standing all the while at the gate, had now crossed the threshold as in Sir Luke Strett's person and quite on such a scale as to fill out the whole precinct. Densher's nerves, absolutely his heart-beats too, had measured the change before he on this occasion moved away.

The facts of physical suffering, of incurable pain, of the chance grimly narrowed, had been made, at a stroke, intense, and this was to be the way he was now to feel them. The clearance of the air, in short, making vision not only possible but inevitable, the one thing left to be thankful for was the breadth of Sir Luke's shoulders, which, should one be able to keep in line with them, might in some degree interpose. It was, however, far from plain to Densher for the first day or two that he was again to see his distinguished friend at all. That he couldn't, on any basis actually serving, return to the palace—this was as solid to him, every whit, as the other feature of his case, the fact of the publicity attaching to his proscription through his not having taken himself off. He had been seen often enough in the Leporelli gondola. As, accordingly, he was not on any presumption destined to meet Sir Luke about the town, where the latter would have neither time nor taste to lounge, nothing more would occur between them unless the great man should surprisingly wait upon him. His doing that, Densher further reflected, wouldn't even simply depend on Mrs. Stringham's having decided to—as they might say—turn him on. It would depend as well—for there would be practically some difference to her—on her actually attempting it; and it would depend above all on what Sir Luke would make of such an overture. Densher had for that matter his own view of the amount, to say nothing of the particular sort, of response it might expect from him. He had his own view of the ability of such a personage even to understand such an appeal. To what extent could he be prepared, and what importance in fine could he attach? Densher asked himself these questions, in truth, to put his own position at the worst. He should miss the great man completely unless the great man should come to see him, and the great man could only come to see him for a purpose unsupposable. Therefore he wouldn't come at all, and consequently there was nothing to hope.

It wasn't in the least that Densher invoked this violence to all probability; but it pressed on him that there were few possible diversions he could afford now to miss. Nothing in his predicament was so odd as that, incontestably afraid of himself, he was not afraid of Sir Luke. He had an impression, which he clung to, based on a previous taste of the visitor's company, that *he* would somehow let him off. The truth about Milly perched on his shoulders and sounded in his tread, became by the fact of his presence the name and the form, for the time, of everything in the place; but it didn't, for the difference, sit in his face, the face so squarely and easily turned to Densher at the earlier season. His presence on the first occasion, not as the result of a summons, but as a friendly whim of his own, had had quite another value; and though our young man could scarce regard that value as recoverable he yet reached out in imagination to a renewal of the old contact. He didn't propose, as he privately and forcibly phrased the matter, to be a hog; but there was something he after all did want for himself. It was something—this stuck to him—that Sir Luke would have had for him if it hadn't been impossible. These were his worst days, the two or three; those on which even the sense of the tension at the palace didn't much help him not to feel that his destiny made but light of him. He had never been, as he judged it, so down. In mean conditions, without books, without society, almost without money, he had nothing to do but to wait. His main support really was his original idea, which didn't leave him, of waiting for the deepest depth his predicament could sink him to. Fate would invent, if he but gave it time, some refinement of the horrible. It was just inventing meanwhile this suppression of Sir Luke. When the third day came without a sign he knew what to think. He had given Mrs. Stringham during her call on him no such answer as would have armed her faith, and the ultimatum she had described as ready for him when *he* should be ready was therefore—if on no other ground than her want of this power to answer for him—not to be presented. The presentation, heaven knew, was not what he desired.

That was not, either, we hasten to declare—as Densher then soon enough saw—the idea with which Sir Luke finally stood before him again. For stand before him again he finally did; just when our friend had gloomily embraced the belief that the limit of his power to absent himself from London obligations would have been reached. Four or five days, exclusive of journeys, represented the largest supposable sacrifice—to a head not crowned—on the part of one of the highest medical lights in the world; so that really when the personage in question, following up a tinkle of the bell, solidly rose in the doorway, it was to impose on Densher a vision that for the instant cut like a knife. It spoke, in fact, and in a single dreadful word, of the magnitude—he shrank from calling it anything else—of Milly's case. The great man had not gone then, and an immense surrender to her immense need was so expressed in it that some effect, some help, some hope, were flagrantly part of the expression. It was for Densher, with his reaction from disappointment, as if he were conscious of ten things at once—the foremost being that just conceivably, since Sir Luke *was* still there, she had been saved. Close upon its heels, however, and quite as sharply, came the sense that the crisis—plainly even now to be prolonged for him—was to have none of that sound simplicity. Not only had his visitor not dropped in to gossip about Milly, he hadn't dropped in to mention her at all; he had dropped in fairly to show that during the brief remainder of his stay, the end of which was now in sight, as little as possible of that was to be looked for. The demonstration, such as it was, was in the key of their previous acquaintance, and it was their previous acquaintance that had made him come. He was not to stop longer than the Saturday next at hand, but there were things of interest he should like to see again meanwhile. It was for these things of interest, for Venice and the opportunity of Venice, for a prowl or two, as he called it, and a turn about, that he had looked his young man up—producing on the latter's part, as soon as the case had, with the lapse of a further twenty-four hours, so defined itself, the most incongruous, yet most beneficent revulsion. Nothing could in fact have been more monstrous on the surface—and Densher was well aware of it—than the relief he found during this short period in the tacit drop of all reference to the palace, in neither hearing news nor asking for it. That was what had come out for him, on his visitor's entrance, even in the very seconds of suspense that were connecting the fact also directly and intensely with Milly's state. He had come to say he had saved her—he had come, as from Mrs.

Stringham, to say how she might *be* saved—he had come, in spite of Mrs. Stringham, to say she was lost: the distinct throbs of hope, of fear, simultaneous for all their distinctness, merged their identity in a bound of the heart just as immediate and which remained after they had passed. It simply did wonders for him—this was the truth—that Sir Luke was, as he would have said, quiet.

The result of it was the oddest consciousness as of a blest calm after a storm. He had been trying for weeks, as we know, to keep superlatively still, and trying it largely in solitude and silence; but he looked back on it now as on the heart of fever. The real, the right stillness was this particular form of society. They walked together and they talked, looked up pictures again and recovered impressions—Sir Luke knew just what he wanted; haunted a little the dealers in old wares; sat down at Florian's for rest and mild drinks; blessed above all the grand weather, a bath of warm air, a pageant of autumn light. Once or twice while they rested the great man closed his eyes—keeping them so for some minutes while his companion, the more easily watching his face for it, made private reflexions on the subject of lost sleep. He had been up at night with her—he in person, for hours; but this was all he showed of it and was apparently to remain his nearest approach to an allusion. The extraordinary thing was that Densher could take it in perfectly as evidence, could turn cold at the image looking out of it; and yet that he could at the same time not intermit a throb of his response to accepted liberation. The liberation was an experience that held its own, and he continued to know why, in spite of his deserts, in spite of his folly, in spite of everything, he had so fondly hoped for it. He had hoped for it, had sat in his room there waiting for it, because he had thus divined in it, should it come, some power to let him off. He was *being* let off; dealt with in the only way that didn't aggravate his responsibility. The beauty was also that this wasn't on system or on any basis of intimate knowledge; it was just by being a man of the world and by knowing life, by feeling the real, that Sir Luke did him good. There had been in all the case too many women. A man's sense of it, another man's, changed the air; and he wondered what man, had he chosen, would have been more to his purpose than this one. He was large and easy—that was the benediction; he knew what mattered and what didn't, he distin-

guished between the essence and the shell, the just grounds and
the unjust for fussing. One was thus—if one were concerned with
him or exposed to him at all—in his hands for whatever he should
do, and not much less affected by his mercy than one might have
been by his rigor. The grand thing—it did come to that—was the
way he carried off, as one might fairly call it, the business of making odd things natural. Nothing, if they hadn't taken it so, could
have exceeded the unexplained oddity, between them, of Densher's now complete detachment from the poor ladies at the
palace; nothing could have exceeded the no less marked anomaly
of the great man's own abstentions of speech. He made, as he had
done when they met at the station, nothing whatever of anything;
and the effect of it, Densher would have said, was a relation with
him quite resembling that of doctor and patient. One took the cue
from him as one might have taken a dose—except that the cue was
pleasant in the taking.

That was why one could leave it to his tacit discretion, why for
the three or four days Densher again and again did so leave it;
merely wondering a little, at the most, on the eve of Saturday, the
announced term of the episode. Waiting once more on this latter
occasion, the Saturday morning, for Sir Luke's reappearance at the
station, our friend had to recognize the drop of his own borrowed
ease, the result, naturally enough, of the prospect of losing a support. The difficulty was that, on such lines as had served them, the
support was Sir Luke's personal presence. Would he go without
leaving some substitute for that?—and without breaking, either,
his silence in respect to his errand? Densher was in still deeper ignorance than at the hour of his call, and what was truly prodigious
at so supreme a moment was that—as had immediately to appear—no gleam of light on what he had been living with for a
week found its way out of him. What he had been doing was proof
of a huge interest as well as of a huge fee; yet when the Leporelli
gondola again, and somewhat tardily, approached, his companion,
watching from the watersteps, studied his fine closed face as much
as ever in vain. It was like a lesson, from the highest authority, on
the subject of the relevant, so that its blankness affected Densher
of a sudden almost as a cruelty, feeling it quite awfully compatible,
as he did, with Milly's having ceased to exist. And the suspense

continued after they had passed together, as time was short, directly into the station, where Eugenio, in the field early, was mounting guard over the compartment he had secured. The strain, though probably lasting, at the carriage-door, but a couple of minutes, prolonged itself so for our poor gentleman's nerves that he involuntarily directed a long look at Eugenio, who met it, however, as only Eugenio could. Sir Luke's attention was given for the time to the right bestowal of his numerous effects, about which he was particular, and Densher fairly found himself, so far as silence could go, questioning the representative of the palace. It didn't humiliate him now; it didn't humiliate him even to feel that that personage exactly knew how little he satisfied him. Eugenio resembled to that extent Sir Luke—to the extent of the extraordinary things with which his facial habit was compatible. By the time, however, that Densher had taken from it all its possessor intended Sir Luke was free and with a hand out for farewell. He offered the hand at first without speech; only on meeting his eyes could our young man see that they had never yet so completely looked at him. It was never, with Sir Luke, that they looked harder at one time than at another; but they looked longer, and this, even a shade of it, might mean on his part everything. It meant, Densher for ten seconds believed, that Milly Theale was dead; so that the word at last spoken made him start.

"I shall come back."

"Then she's better?"

"I shall come back within the month," Sir Luke repeated without heeding the question. He had dropped Densher's hand, but he held him otherwise still. "I bring you a message from Miss Theale," he said as if they hadn't spoken of her. "I'm commissioned to ask you from her to go and see her."

Densher's rebound from his supposition had a violence that his stare betrayed. "*She* asks me?"

Sir Luke had got into the carriage, the door of which the guard had closed; but he spoke again as he stood at the window, bending a little but not leaning out. "She told me she'd like it, and I promised that, as I expected to find you here, I'd let you know."

Densher, on the platform, took it from him, but what he took brought the blood into his face quite as what he had had to take from Mrs. Stringham. And he was also bewildered. "Then she can receive—?"

"She can receive you."

"And you're coming back—?"

"Oh because I must. She's not to move. She's to stay. I come to her."

"I see, I see," said Densher, who indeed did see—saw the sense of his friend's words and saw beyond it as well. What Mrs. Stringham had announced, and what he had yet expected not to have to face, *had* then come. Sir Luke had kept it for the last, but there it was, and the colourless compact form it was now taking—the tone of one man of the world to another, who, after what had happened, would understand—was but the characteristic manner of his appeal. Densher was to understand remarkably much; and the great thing certainly was to show that he did. "I'm particularly obliged, I'll go to-day." He brought that out, but in his pause, while they continued to look at each other, the train had slowly creaked into motion. There was time but for one more word, and the young man chose it, out of twenty, with intense concentration. "Then she's better?"

Sir Luke's face was wonderful. "Yes, she's better." And he kept it at the window while the train receded, holding him with it still. It was to be his nearest approach to the utter reference they had hitherto so successfully avoided. If it stood for everything, never had a face had to stand for more. So Densher, held after the train had gone, sharply reflected; so he reflected, asking himself into what abyss it pushed him, even while conscious of retreating under the maintained observation of Eugenio.

BOOK TENTH

– I –

T"hen it has been—what do you say? a whole fortnight?—
without your making a sign?"

Kate put that to him distinctly, in the December dusk of
Lancaster Gate and on the matter of the time he had been back;
but he saw with it straightway that she was as admirably true as ever
to her instinct—which was a system as well—of not admitting the
possibility between them of small resentments, of trifles to trip up
their general trust. That by itself, the renewed beauty of it, would
at this fresh sight of her have stirred him to his depths if something
else, something no less vivid but quite separate, hadn't stirred him
still more. It was in seeing her that he felt what their interruption
had been, and that they met across it even as persons whose adventures, on either side, in time and space, of the nature of perils
and exiles, had had a peculiar strangeness. He wondered if he
were as different for her as she herself had immediately appeared:
which was but his way indeed of taking in, with his thrill, that—
even going by the mere first look—she had never been so handsome. That fact bloomed for him, in the firelight and lamplight
that glowed their welcome through the London fog, as the flower
of her difference; just as her difference itself—part of which was
her striking him as older in a degree for which no mere couple of
months could account—was the fruit of their intimate relation. If
she was different it was because they had chosen together that she
should be, and she might now, as a proof of their wisdom, their
success, of the reality of what had happened—of what in fact, for
the spirit of each, was still happening—been showing it to him for
pride. His having returned and yet kept, for numbered days, so
still, had been, he was quite aware, the first point he should have
to tackle; with which consciousness indeed he had made a clean
breast of it in finally addressing Mrs. Lowder a note that had led to
his present visit. He had written to Aunt Maud as the finer way;
and it would doubtless have been to be noted that he needed no

effort not to write to Kate. Venice was three weeks behind him—
he had come up slowly; but it was still as if even in London he
must conform to her law. That was exactly how he was able, with
his faith in her steadiness, to appeal to her feeling for the situation
and explain his stretched delicacy. He had come to tell her everything, so far as occasion would serve them; and if nothing was
more distinct than that his slow journey, his waits, his delay to re-
open communication had kept pace with this resolve, so the inconsequence was doubtless at bottom but one of the elements of
intensity. He was gathering everything up, everything he should
tell her. That took time, and the proof was that, as he felt on the
spot, he couldn't have brought it all with him before this afternoon. He *had* brought it, to the last syllable, and, out of the quantity it wouldn't be hard—as he in fact found—to produce, for
Kate's understanding, his first reason.

"A fortnight, yes—it was a fortnight Friday; but I've only been
keeping in, you see, with our wonderful system." He was so easily
justified as that this of itself plainly enough prevented her saying
she didn't see. Their wonderful system was accordingly still vivid
for her; and such a gage of its equal vividness for himself was precisely what she must have asked. He hadn't even to dot his i's beyond the remark that on the very face of it, she would remember,
their wonderful system attached no premium to rapidities of transition. "I couldn't quite—don't you know?—take my rebound with
a rush; and I suppose I've been instinctively hanging off to mini-
mise, for you as well as for myself, the appearances of rushing.
There's a sort of fitness. But I knew you'd understand." It was
presently as if she really understood so well that she almost appealed from his insistence—yet looking at him too, he was not unconscious, as if this mastery of fitnesses was a strong sign for her of
what she had done to him. He might have struck her as expert for
contingencies in the very degree of her having in Venice struck
him as expert. He smiled over his plea for a renewal with stages
and steps, a thing shaded, as they might say, and graduated;
though—finely as she must respond—she met the smile but as she
had met his entrance five minutes before. Her soft gravity at that
moment—which was yet not solemnity, but the look of a consciousness charged with life to the brim and wishing not to over-

flow—had not qualified her welcome; what had done this being much more the presence in the room, for a couple of minutes, of the footman who had introduced him and who had been interrupted in preparing the tea-table.

Mrs. Lowder's reply to Densher's note had been to appoint the tea-hour, five o'clock on Sunday, for his seeing them. Kate had thereafter wired him, without a signature, "Come on Sunday *before* tea—about a quarter of an hour, which will help us"; and he had arrived therefore scrupulously at twenty minutes to five. Kate was alone in the room and hadn't delayed to tell him that Aunt Maud, as she had happily gathered, was to be, for the interval— not long but precious—engaged with an old servant, retired and pensioned, who had been paying her a visit and who was within the hour to depart again for the suburbs. They were to have the scrap of time, after the withdrawal of the footman, to themselves, and there was a moment when, in spite of their wonderful system, in spite of the proscription of rushes and the propriety of shades, it proclaimed itself indeed precious. And all without prejudice—that was what kept it noble—to Kate's high sobriety and her beautiful self-command. If he had his discretion she had her perfect manner, which was *her* decorum. Mrs. Stringham, he had, to finish with the question of his delay, furthermore observed, Mrs. Stringham would have written to Mrs. Lowder of his having quitted the place; so that it wasn't as if he were hoping to cheat them. They'd know he was no longer there.

"Yes, we've known it."

"And you continue to hear?"

"From Mrs. Stringham? Certainly. By which I mean Aunt Maud does."

"Then you've recent news?"

Her face showed a wonder. "Up to within a day or two I believe. But haven't *you?*"

"No—I've heard nothing." And it was now that he felt how much he had to tell her. "I don't get letters. But I've been sure Mrs. Lowder does." With which he added: "Then of course you know." He waited as if she would show what she knew; but she only showed in silence the dawn of a surprise that she couldn't control. There was nothing but for him to ask what he wanted. "Is Miss Theale alive?"

Kate's look at this was large. "Don't you *know?*"

"How should I, my dear—in the absence of everything?" And he himself stared as for light. "She's dead?" Then as with her eyes on him she slowly shook her head he uttered a strange "Not yet?"

It came out in Kate's face that there were several questions on her lips, but the one she presently put was: "Is it very terrible?"

"The manner of her so consciously and helplessly dying?" He had to think a moment. "Well, yes—since you ask me: very terrible to *me*—so far as, before I came away, I had any sight of it. But I don't think," he went on, "that—though I'll try—I *can* quite tell you what it was, what it is, for me. That's why I probably just sounded to you," he explained, "as if I hoped it might be over."

She gave him her quietest attention, but he by this time saw that, so far as telling her all was concerned, she would be divided between the wish and the reluctance to hear it; between the curiosity that, not unnaturally, would consume her and the opposing scruple of a respect for misfortune. The more she studied him too—and he had never so felt her closely attached to his face—the more the choice of an attitude would become impossible to her. There would simply be a feeling uppermost, and the feeling wouldn't be eagerness. This perception grew in him fast, and he even, with his imagination, had for a moment the quick forecast of her possibly breaking out at him, should he go too far, with a wonderful: "What horrors are you telling me?" It would have the sound—wouldn't it be open to him fairly to bring that out himself?—of a repudiation, for pity and almost for shame, of everything that in Venice had passed between them. Not that she would confess to any return upon herself; not that she would let compunction or horror give her away; but it was in the air for him—yes—that she wouldn't want details, that she positively wouldn't take them, and that, if he would generously understand it from her, she would prefer to keep him down. Nothing, however, was more definite for him than that at the same time he must remain down but so far as it suited him. Something rose strong within him against his not being free with her. She had been free enough about it all, three months before, with *him*. That was what she was at present only in the sense of treating him handsomely. "I can be-lieve," she said with a perfect consideration, "how dreadful for you much of it must have been."

He didn't however take this up; there were things about which he wished first to be clear. "There's no other possibility, by what you now know? I mean for her life." And he had just to insist—she would say as little as she could. "She *is* dying?"

"She's dying."

It was strange to him, in the matter of Milly, that Lancaster Gate could make him any surer; yet what in the world, in the matter of Milly, wasn't strange? Nothing was so much so as his own behaviour—his present as well as his past. He could but do as he must. "Has Sir Luke Strett," he asked, "gone back to her?"

"I believe he's there now."

"Then," said Densher, "it's the end."

She took it in silence for whatever he deemed it to be; but she spoke otherwise after a minute. "You won't know, unless you've perhaps seen him yourself, that Aunt Maud has been to him."

"Oh!" Densher exclaimed, with nothing to add to it.

"For real news," Kate herself after an instant added.

"She hasn't thought Mrs. Stringham's real?"

"It's perhaps only I who haven't. It was on Aunt Maud's trying again three days ago to see him that she heard at his house of his having gone. He had started I believe some days before."

"And won't then by this time be back?"

Kate shook her head. "She sent yesterday to know."

"He won't leave her then"—Densher had turned it over—"while she lives. He'll stay to the end. He's magnificent."

"I think *she* is," said Kate.

It had made them again look at each other long; and what it drew from him rather oddly was: "Oh you don't know!"

"Well, she's after all my friend."

It was somehow, with her handsome demur, the answer he had least expected of her; and it fanned with its breath, for a brief in-stant, his old sense of her variety. "I see. You would have been sure of it. You *were* sure of it."

"Of course I was sure of it."

And a pause again, with this, fell upon them; which Densher, however, presently broke. "If you don't think Mrs. Stringham's news 'real' what do you think of Lord Mark's?"

She didn't think anything. "Lord Mark's?"

"You haven't seen him?"

"Not since he saw her."

"You've known then of his seeing her?"

"Certainly. From Mrs. Stringham."

"And have you known," Densher went on, "the rest?"

Kate wondered. "What rest?"

"Why everything. It was his visit that she couldn't stand—it was what then took place that simply killed her."

"Oh!" Kate seriously breathed. But she had turned pale, and he saw that, whatever her degree of ignorance of these connexions, it wasn't put on. "Mrs. Stringham hasn't said *that*."

He observed none the less that she didn't ask what had then taken place; and he went on with his contribution to her knowledge. "The way it affected her was that it made her give up. She has given up beyond all power to care again, and that's why she's dying."

"Oh!" Kate once more slowly sighed, but with a vagueness that made him pursue.

"One can see now that she was living by will—which was very much what you originally told me of her."

"I remember. That was it."

"Well then her will, at a given moment, broke down, and the collapse was determined by that fellow's dastardly stroke. He told her, the scoundrel, that you and I are secretly engaged."

Kate gave a quick glare. "But he doesn't know it!"

"That doesn't matter. *She* did by the time he had left her. Besides," Densher added, "he does know it. When," he continued, "did you last see him?"

But she was lost now in the picture before her. "*That* was what made her worse?"

He watched her take it in—it so added to her sombre beauty. Then he spoke as Mrs. Stringham had spoken. "She turned her face to the wall."

"Poor Milly!" said Kate.

Slight as it was, her beauty somehow gave it style; so that he continued consistently: "She learned it, you see, too soon—since of course one's idea had been that she might never even learn it at all. And she *had* felt sure—through everything we had done—of there not being between us, so far at least as you were concerned, anything she need regard as a warning."

She took another moment for thought. "It wasn't through anything *you* did—whatever that may have been—that she gained her certainty. It was by the conviction she got from me."

"Oh it's very handsome," Densher said, "for you to take your share!"

"Do you suppose," Kate asked, "that I think of denying it?"

Her look and her tone made him for the instant regret his comment, which indeed had been the first that rose to his lips as an effect absolutely of what they would have called between them her straightness. Her straightness, visibly, was all his own loyalty could ask. Still, that was comparatively beside the mark. "Of course I don't suppose anything but that we're together in our recognitions, our responsibilities—whatever we choose to call them. It isn't a question for us of apportioning shares or distinguishing invidiously among such impressions as it was our idea to give."

"It wasn't *your* idea to give impressions," said Kate.

He met this with a smile that he himself felt, in its strained character, as queer. "Don't go into that!"

It was perhaps not as going into it that she had another idea— an idea born, she showed, of the vision he had just evoked. "Wouldn't it have been possible then to deny the truth of the information? I mean of Lord Mark's."

Densher wondered. "Possible for whom?"

"Why for you."

"To tell her he lied?"

"To tell her he's mistaken."

Densher stared—he was stupefied; the "possible" thus glanced at by Kate being exactly the alternative he had had to face in Venice and to put utterly away from him. Nothing was stranger than such a difference in their view of it. "And to lie myself, you mean, to do it? We *are*, my dear child," he said, "I suppose, still engaged."

"Of course we're still engaged. But to save her life—!"

He took in for a little the way she talked of it. Of course, it was to be remembered, she had always simplified, and it brought back his sense of the degree in which, to her energy as compared with his own, many things were easy; the very sense that so often before had moved him to admiration. "Well, if you must know— and I want you to be clear about it—I didn't even seriously think of a denial to her face. The question of it—*as* possibly saving her—was put to me definitely enough; but to turn it over was only to dismiss it. Besides," he added, "it wouldn't have done any good."

"You mean she would have had no faith in your correction?" She had spoken with a promptitude that affected him of a sudden as almost glib; but he himself paused with the overweight of all he meant, and she meanwhile went on. "Did you try?"

"I hadn't even a chance."

Kate maintained her wonderful manner, the manner of at once having it all before her and yet keeping it all at its distance. "She wouldn't see you?"

"Not after your friend had been with her."

She hesitated. "Couldn't you write?"

It made him also think, but with a difference. "She had turned her face to the wall."

This again for a moment hushed her, and they were both too grave now for parenthetic pity. But her interest came out for at least the minimum of light. "She refused even to let you speak to her?"

"My dear girl," Densher returned, "she was miserably, prohibitively ill."

"Well, that was what she had been before."

"And it didn't prevent? No," Densher admitted, "it didn't; and I don't pretend that she's not magnificent."

"She's prodigious," said Kate Croy.

He looked at her a moment. "So are you, my dear. But that's how it is," he wound up; "and there we are."

His idea had been in advance that she would perhaps sound him much more deeply, asking him above all two or three specific things. He had fairly fancied her even wanting to know and trying to find out how far, as the odious phrase was, he and Milly had gone, and how near, by the same token, they had come. He had asked himself if he were prepared to hear her do that, and had had to take for answer that he was prepared of course for everything. Wasn't he prepared for her ascertaining if her two or three prophecies had found time to be made true? He had fairly believed himself ready to say whether or no the overture on Milly's part promised according to the boldest of them had taken place. But what was in fact blessedly coming to him was that so far as such things were concerned his readiness wouldn't be taxed. Kate's pressure on the question of what had taken place remained so admirably genial that even her present enquiry kept itself free of sharpness. "So then that after Lord Mark's interference you never again met?"

It was what he had been all the while coming to. "No; we met once — so far as it could be called a meeting. I had stayed — I didn't come away."

"That," said Kate, "was no more than decent."

"Precisely" — he felt himself wonderful; "and I wanted to be no less. She sent for me, I went to her, and that night I left Venice."

His companion waited. "Wouldn't *that* then have been your chance?"

"To refute Lord Mark's story? No, not even if before her there I had wanted to. What did it signify either? She was dying."

"Well," Kate in a manner persisted, "why not just *because* she was dying?" She had however all her discretion. "But of course I know that seeing her you could judge."

"Of course seeing her I could judge. And I did see her! If I had denied you moreover," Densher said with his eyes on her, "I'd have stuck to it."

She took for a moment the intention of his face. "You mean that to convince her you'd have insisted or somehow proved —?"

"I mean that to convince *you* I'd have insisted or somehow proved —!"

Kate looked for her moment at a loss. "To convince 'me'?"

"I wouldn't have made my denial, in such conditions, only to take it back afterwards."

With this quickly light came for her, and with it also her colour flamed. "Oh you'd have broken with me to make your denial a truth? You'd have 'chucked' me"—she embraced it perfectly—"to save your conscience?"

"I couldn't have done anything else," said Merton Densher. "So you see how right I was not to commit myself, and how little I could dream of it. If it ever again appears to you that I *might* have done so, remember what I say."

Kate again considered, but not with the effect at once to which he pointed. "You've fallen in love with her."

"Well then say so—with a dying woman. Why need you mind and what does it matter?"

It came from him, the question, straight out of the intensity of relation and the face-to-face necessity into which, from the first, from his entering the room, they had found themselves thrown; but it gave them their most extraordinary moment. "Wait till she *is* dead! Mrs. Stringham," Kate added, "is to telegraph." After which, in a tone still different, "For what then," she asked, "did Milly send for you?"

"It was what I tried to make out before I went. I must tell you moreover that I had no doubt of its really being to give me, as you say, a chance. She believed, I suppose, that I *might* deny; and what, to my own mind, was before me in going to her was the certainty that she'd put me to my test. She wanted from my own lips—so I saw it—the truth. But I was with her for twenty minutes, and she never asked me for it."

"She never wanted the truth"—Kate had a high headshake. "She wanted *you*. She would have taken from you what you could give her and been glad of it, even if she had known it false. You might have lied to her from pity, and she have seen you and felt you lie, and yet—since it was all for tenderness—she would have thanked you and blessed you and clung to you but the more. For that was your strength, my dear man—that she loves you with passion."[26]

"Oh my 'strength'!" Densher coldly murmured.

"Otherwise, since she had sent for you, what was it to ask of you?" And then—quite without irony—as he waited a moment to say: "Was it just once more to look at you?"

"She had nothing to ask of me—nothing, that is, but not to stay

any longer. She did to that extent want to see me. She had supposed at first—after he had been with her—that I had seen the
propriety of taking myself off. Then since I hadn't—seeing my propriety as I did in another way—she found, days later, that I was still
there. This," said Densher, "affected her."

"Of course it affected her."

Again she struck him, for all her dignity, as glib. "If it was somehow for *her* I was still staying, she wished that to end, she wished
me to know how little there was need of it. And as a manner of
farewell she wished herself to tell me so."

"And she did tell you so?"

"Face-to-face, yes. Personally, as she desired."

"And as *you* of course did."

"No, Kate," he returned with all their mutual consideration;
"not as I did. I hadn't desired it in the least."

"You only went to oblige her?"

"To oblige her. And of course also to oblige you."

"Oh for myself certainly I'm glad."

"'Glad'?"—he echoed vaguely the way it rang out.

"I mean you did quite the right thing. You did it especially in
having stayed. But that was all?" Kate went on. "That you mustn't
wait?"

"That was really all—and in perfect kindness."

"Ah kindness naturally: from the moment she asked of you such
a—well, such an effort. That you mustn't wait—that was the
point," Kate added—"to see her die."

"That was the point, my dear," Densher said.

"And it took twenty minutes to make it?"

He thought a little. "I didn't time it to a second. I paid her the
visit—just like another."

"Like another person?"

"Like another visit."

"Oh!" said Kate. Which had apparently the effect of slightly arresting his speech—an arrest she took advantage of to continue;
making with it indeed her nearest approach to an enquiry of the
kind against which he had braced himself. "Did she receive you—
in her condition—in her room?"

"Not she," said Merton Densher. "She received me just as

usual: in that glorious great *salone*,* in the dress she always wears, from her inveterate corner on her sofa." And his face for the moment conveyed the scene, just as hers equally embraced it. "Do you remember what you originally said to me of her?"

"Ah I've said so many things."

"That she wouldn't smell of drugs, that she wouldn't taste of medicine. Well, she didn't."

"So that it was really almost happy?"

It took him a long time to answer, occupied as he partly was in feeling how nobody but Kate could have invested such a question with the tone that was perfectly right. She meanwhile, however, patiently waited. "I don't think I can attempt to say now what it was. Some day—perhaps. For it would be worth it for us."

"Some day—certainly." She seemed to record the promise. Yet she spoke again abruptly. "She'll recover."

"Well," said Densher, "you'll see."

She had the air an instant of trying to. "Did she show anything of her feeling? I mean," Kate explained, "of her feeling of having been misled."

She didn't press hard, surely; but he had just mentioned that he would have rather to glide. "She showed nothing but her beauty and her strength."

"Then," his companion asked, "what's the use of her strength?"

He seemed to look about for a use he could name; but he had soon given it up. "She must die, my dear, in her own extraordinary way."

"Naturally. But I don't see then what proof you have that she was ever alienated."

"I have the proof that she refused for days and days to see me."

"But she was ill."

"That hadn't prevented her—as you yourself a moment ago said—during the previous time. If it had been only illness it would have made no difference with her."

"She would still have received you?"

"She would still have received me."

"Oh well," said Kate, "if you know—!"

"Of course I know. I know moreover as well from Mrs. Stringham."

"And what does Mrs. Stringham know?"

"Everything."

She looked at him longer. "Everything?"

"Everything."

"Because you've told her?"

"Because she has seen for herself. I've told her nothing. She's a person who does see."

Kate thought. "That's by her liking you too. She as well is prodigious. You see what interest in a man does. It does it all round. So you needn't be afraid."

"I'm not afraid," said Densher.

Kate moved from her place then, looking at the clock, which marked five. She gave her attention to the tea-table, where Aunt Maud's huge silver kettle, which had been exposed to its lamp and which she had not soon enough noticed, was hissing too hard. "Well, it's all most wonderful!" she exclaimed as she rather too profusely—a sign her friend noticed—ladled tea into the pot. He watched her a moment at this occupation, coming nearer the table while she put in the steaming water. "You'll have some?"

He hesitated. "Hadn't we better wait—?"

"For Aunt Maud?" She saw what he meant—the deprecation, by their old law, of betrayals of the intimate note. "Oh you needn't mind now. We've done it!"

"Humbugged her?"

"Squared her. You've pleased her."

Densher mechanically accepted his tea. He was thinking of something else, and his thought in a moment came out. "What a brute then I must be!"

"A brute—?"

"To have pleased so many people."

"Ah," said Kate with a gleam of gaiety, "you've done it to please *me*." But she was already, with her gleam, reverting a little. "What I don't understand is—won't you have any sugar?"

"Yes, please."

"What I don't understand," she went on when she had helped

him, "is what it was that had occurred to bring her round again. If she gave you up for days and days, what brought her back to you?"

She asked the question with her own cup in her hand, but it found him ready enough in spite of his sense of the ironic oddity of their going into it over the tea-table. "It was Sir Luke Strett who brought her back. His visit, his presence there did it."

"He brought her back then to life."

"Well, to what I saw."

"And by interceding for you?"

"I don't think he interceded. I don't indeed know what he did."

Kate wondered. "Didn't he tell you?"

"I didn't ask him. I met him again, but we practically didn't speak of her."

Kate stared. "Then how do you know?"

"I see. I feel. I was with him again as I had been before—"

"Oh and you pleased him too? That was it?"

"He understood," said Densher.

"But understood what?"

He waited a moment. "That I had meant awfully well."

"Ah, and made *her* understand? I see," she went on as he said nothing. "But how did he convince her?"

Densher put down his cup and turned away. "You must ask Sir Luke."

He stood looking at the fire and there was a time without sound. "The great thing," Kate then resumed, "is that she's satisfied. Which," she continued, looking across at him, "is what I've worked for."

"Satisfied to die in the flower of her youth?"

"Well, at peace with you."

"Oh 'peace'!" he murmured with his eyes on the fire.

"The peace of having loved."

He raised his eyes to her. "Is *that* peace?"

"Of having *been* loved," she went on. "That is. Of having," she wound up, "realized her passion. She wanted nothing more. She has had *all* she wanted."

Lucid and always grave, she gave this out with a beautiful authority that he could for the time meet with no words. He could only again look at her, though with the sense in so doing that he made her more than he intended take his silence for assent. Quite indeed as if she did so take it she quitted the table and came to the fire. "You may think it hideous that I should now, that I should *yet*"—she made a point of the word—"pretend to draw conclusions. But we've not failed."

"Oh!" he only again murmured.

She was once more close to him, close as she had been the day she came to him in Venice, the quickly returning memory of which intensified and enriched the fact. He could practically deny in such conditions nothing that she said, and what she said was, with it, visibly, a fruit of that knowledge. "We've succeeded." She spoke with her eyes deep in his own. "She won't have loved you for nothing." It made him wince, but she insisted. "And you won't have loved *me*."

— II —

He was to remain for several days under the deep impression of this inclusive passage, so luckily prolonged from moment to moment, but interrupted at its climax, as may be said, by the entrance of Aunt Maud, who found them standing together near the fire. The bearings of the colloquy, however, sharp as they were, were less sharp to his intelligence, strangely enough, than those of a talk with Mrs. Lowder alone for which she soon gave him—or for which perhaps rather Kate gave him—full occasion. What had happened on her at last joining them was to conduce, he could immediately see, to her desiring to have him to herself. Kate and he, no doubt, at the opening of the door, had fallen apart with a certain suddenness, so that she had turned her hard fine eyes from one to the other; but the effect of this lost itself, to his mind, the next minute, in the effect of his companion's rare alertness. She instantly spoke to her aunt of what had first been uppermost for herself, inviting her thereby intimately to join them, and doing it the more happily also, no doubt, because the fact she resentfully named gave her ample support. "Had you quite understood, my dear, that it's full three weeks—?" And she effaced herself as if to leave Mrs. Lowder to deal from her own point of view with this extravagance. Densher of course straightway noted that his cue for the protection of Kate was to make, no less, all of it he could; and their tracks, as he might have said, were fairly covered by the time their hostess had taken afresh, on his renewed admission, the measure of his scant eagerness. Kate had moved away as if no great showing were needed for her personal situation to be seen as delicate. She had been entertaining their visitor on her aunt's behalf—a visitor she had been at one time suspected of favoring too much and who had now come back to them as the stricken suitor of another person. It wasn't that the fate of the other person, her exquisite friend, didn't, in its tragic turn, also concern herself: it was only that her acceptance of Mr. Densher as a source of information could scarcely help having an awkwardness. She invented the awkwardness under Densher's eyes, and he marvelled on his side at the instant creation. It served her as the fine cloud that hangs about a goddess in an epic, and the young man was but vaguely to know at what point of the rest of his visit she had, for consideration, melted into it and out of sight.

He was taken up promptly with another matter—the truth of the remarkable difference, neither more nor less, that the events of Venice had introduced into his relation with Aunt Maud and that these weeks of their separation had caused quite richly to ripen for him. She had not sat down to her tea-table before he felt himself on terms with her that were absolutely new, nor could she press on him a second cup without her seeming herself, and quite wittingly, so to define and establish them. She regretted, but she quite understood, that what was taking place had obliged him to hang off; they had—after hearing of him from poor Susan as gone— been hoping for an early sight of him; they would have been interested, naturally, in his arriving straight from the scene. Yet she needed no reminder that the scene precisely—by which she meant the tragedy that had so detained and absorbed him, the memory, the shadow, the sorrow of it—was what marked him for unsociability. She thus presented him to himself, as it were, in the guise in which she had now adopted him, and it was the element of truth in the character that he found himself, for his own part, adopting. She treated him as blighted and ravaged, as frustrate and already bereft; and for him to feel that this opened for him a new chapter of frankness with her he scarce had also to perceive how it smoothed his approaches to Kate. It made the latter accessible as she hadn't yet begun to be; it set up for him at Lancaster Gate an association positively hostile to any other legend. It was quickly vivid to him that, were he minded, he could "work" this association: he had but to use the house freely for his prescribed attitude and he need hardly ever be out of it. Stranger than anything moreover was to be the way that by the end of a week he stood convicted to his own sense of a surrender to Mrs. Lowder's view. He had somehow met it at a point that had brought him on—brought him on a distance that he couldn't again retrace. He had private hours of wondering what had become of his sincerity; he had others of simply reflecting that he had it all in use. His only want of candor was Aunt Maud's wealth of sentiment. She was hugely sentimental, and the worst he did was to take it from her. He wasn't so himself—everything was too real; but it was none the less not false that he *had* been through a mill.

It was in particular not false for instance that when she had said to him, on the Sunday, almost cozily, from her sofa behind the tea, "I want you not to doubt, you poor dear, that I'm *with* you to the end!" his meeting her halfway had been the only course open to him. She was with him to the end—or she might be—in a way Kate wasn't; and even if it literally made her society meanwhile more soothing he must just brush away the question of why it shouldn't. Was he professing to her in any degree the possession of an aftersense that wasn't real? How in the world *could* he, when his aftersense, day by day, was his greatest reality? Such only was at bottom what there was between them, and two or three times over it made the hour pass. These were occasions—two and a scrap— on which he had come and gone without mention of Kate. Now that almost as never yet he had license to ask for her, the queer turn of their affair made it a false note. It was another queer turn that when he talked with Aunt Maud about Milly nothing else seemed to come up. He called upon her almost avowedly for that purpose, and it was the queerest turn of all that the state of his nerves should require it. He liked her better; he was really behaving, he had occasion to say to himself, as if he liked her best. The thing was absolutely that she met *him* halfway. Nothing could have been broader than her vision, than her loquacity, than her sympathy. It appeared to gratify, to satisfy her to see him as he was; that too had its effect. It was all of course the last thing that could have seemed on the cards, a change by which he was completely *free* with this lady; and it wouldn't indeed have come about if—for another monstrosity—he hadn't ceased to be free with Kate. Thus it was that on the third time in especial of being alone with her he found himself uttering to the elder woman what had been impossible of utterance to the younger. Mrs. Lowder gave him in fact, on the ground of what he must keep from her, but one uneasy moment. That was when, on the first Sunday, after Kate had suppressed herself, she referred to her regret that he mightn't have stayed to the end. He found his reason difficult to give her, but she came after all to his help.

"You simply couldn't stand it?"

"I simply couldn't stand it. Besides you see—!" But he paused.

"Besides what?" He had been going to say more—then he saw dangers; luckily however she had again assisted him. "Besides—oh I know!—men haven't, in many relations, the courage of women."

"They haven't the courage of women."

"Kate or I would have stayed," she declared—"if we hadn't come away for the special reason that you so frankly appreciated."

Densher had said nothing about his appreciation: hadn't his behaviour since the hour itself sufficiently shown it? But he presently said—he couldn't help going so far: "I don't doubt, certainly, that Miss Croy would have stayed." And he saw again into the bargain what a marvel was Susan Shepherd. She did nothing but protect him—she had done nothing but keep it up. In copious communication with the friend of her youth she had yet, it was plain, favored this lady with nothing that compromised him. Milly's act of renouncement she had described but as a change for the worse; she had mentioned Lord Mark's descent, as even without her it might be known, so that she mustn't appear to conceal it; but she had suppressed explanations and connexions, and indeed, for all he knew, blessed Puritan soul, had invented commendable fictions. Thus it was absolutely that he *was* at his ease. Thus it was that, shaking for ever, in the unrest that didn't drop, his crossed leg, he leaned back in deep yellow satin chairs and took such comfort as came. She asked, it was true, Aunt Maud, questions that Kate hadn't; but this was just the difference, that from her he positively liked them. He had taken with himself on leaving Venice the resolution to regard Milly as already dead to him—that being for his spirit the only thinkable way to pass the time of waiting. He had left her because it was what suited her, and it wasn't for him to go, as they said in America, behind this; which imposed on him but the sharper need to arrange himself with his interval. Suspense was the ugliest ache to him, and he would have nothing to do with it; the last thing he wished was to be unconscious of her—what he wished to ignore was her own consciousness, tortured, for all he knew, crucified by its pain. Knowingly to hang about in London while the pain went on— what would that do but make his days impossible? His scheme was accordingly to convince himself—and by some art about which he was vague—that the sense of waiting had passed. "What in fact," he restlessly reflected, "have I any further to do with it? Let me assume the thing actually over—as it at any moment may be—and I become good again for something at least to somebody. I'm good, as it is, for nothing to anybody, least of all to *her*." He consequently tried, so far as shutting his eyes and stalking grimly about was a trial; but his plan was carried out, it may well be guessed, neither with marked success nor with marked consistency. The days, whether lapsing or lingering, were a stiff reality; the suppression of anxiety was a thin idea; the taste of life itself was the taste of suspense. That he *was* waiting was in short at the bottom of everything; and it required no great sifting presently to feel that if he took so much more, as he called it, to Mrs. Lowder this was just for that reason.

She helped him to hold out, all the while that she was subtle enough—and he could see her divine it as what he wanted—not to insist on the actuality of their tension. His nearest approach to success was thus in being good for something to Aunt Maud, in default of any one better; her company eased his nerves even while they pretended together that they had seen their tragedy out. They spoke of the dying girl in the past tense; they said no worse of her than that she had *been* stupendous. On the other hand, however—

and this was what wasn't for Densher pure peace—they insisted
enough that stupendous was the word. It was the thing, this recognition, that kept him most quiet; he came to it with her repeatedly;
talking about it against time and, in particular, we have noted,
speaking of his supreme personal impression as he hadn't spoken
to Kate. It was almost as if she herself enjoyed the perfection of the
pathos; she sat there before the scene, as he couldn't help giving it
out to her, very much as a stout citizen's wife might have sat, during a play that made people cry, in the pit or the family-circle.
What most deeply stirred her was the way the poor girl must have
wanted to live.

"Ah yes indeed—she did, she did: why in pity shouldn't she,
with everything to fill her world? The mere *money* of her, the darling, if it isn't too disgusting at such a time to mention that—!"

Aunt Maud mentioned it—and Densher quite understood—
but as fairly giving poetry to the life Milly clung to: a view of the
"might have been" before which the good lady was hushed anew
to tears. She had had her own vision of these possibilities, and her
own social use for them, and since Milly's spirit had been after all
so at one with her about them, what was the cruelty of the event
but a cruelty, of a sort, to herself? That came out when he named,
as *the* horrible thing to know, the fact of their young friend's un-
approachable terror of the end, keep it down though she would;
coming out therefore often, since in so naming it he found the
strangest of reliefs. He allowed it all its vividness, as if on the principle of his not at least spiritually shirking. Milly had held with
passion to her dream of a future, and she was separated from it, not
shrieking indeed, but grimly, awfully silent, as one might imagine
some noble young victim of the scaffold, in the French Revolution, separated at the prison-door from some object clutched for
resistance. Densher, in a cold moment, so pictured the case for
Mrs. Lowder, but no moment cold enough had yet come to make
him so picture it to Kate. And it was the front so presented that had
been, in Milly, heroic; presented with the highest heroism, Aunt
Maud by this time knew, on the occasion of his taking leave of her.
He had let her know, absolutely for the girl's glory, how he had
been received on that occasion: with a positive effect—since she

was indeed so perfectly the princess that Mrs. Stringham always called her—of princely state.

Before the fire in the great room that was all arabesques and cherubs, all gaiety and gilt, and that was warm at that hour too with a wealth of autumn sun, the state in question had been maintained and the situation—well, Densher said for the convenience of exquisite London gossip, sublime. The gossip—for it came to as much at Lancaster Gate—wasn't the less exquisite for his use of the silver veil, nor on the other hand was the veil, so touched, too much drawn aside. He himself for that matter took in the scene again at moments as from the page of a book. He saw a young man far off and in a relation inconceivable, saw him hushed, passive, staying his breath, but half understanding, yet dimly conscious of something immense and holding himself painfully together not to lose it. The young man at these moments so seen was too distant and too strange for the right identity; and yet, outside, afterwards, it was his own face Densher had known. He had known then at the same time what the young man had been conscious of, and he was to measure after that, day by day, how little he had lost. At present there with Mrs. Lowder he knew he had gathered all—that passed between them mutely as in the intervals of their associated gaze they exchanged looks of intelligence. This was as far as association could go, but it was far enough when she knew the essence. The essence was that something had happened to him too beautiful and too sacred to describe. He had been, to his recovered sense, forgiven, dedicated, blessed; but this he couldn't coherently express. It would have required an explanation—fatal to Mrs. Lowder's faith in him—of the nature of Milly's wrong. So, as to the wonderful scene, they just stood at the door. They had the sense of the presence within—they felt the charged stillness; after which, their association deepened by it, they turned together away.

That itself indeed, for our restless friend, became by the end of a week the very principle of reaction: so that he woke up one morning with such a sense of having played a part as he needed self-respect to gainsay. He hadn't in the least stated at Lancaster Gate that, as a haunted man—a man haunted with a memory—he was harmless; but the degree to which Mrs. Lowder accepted, admired and explained his new aspect laid upon him practically the weight of a declaration. What he hadn't in the least stated her own manner was perpetually stating; it was as haunted and harmless that she was constantly putting him down. There offered itself however to his purpose such an element as plain honesty, and he had embraced, by the time he dressed, his proper corrective. They were on the edge of Christmas, but Christmas this year was, as in the London of so many other years, disconcertingly mild; the still air was soft, the thick light was grey, the great town looked empty, and in the Park, where the grass was green, where the sheep browsed, where the birds multitudinously twittered, the straight walks lent themselves to slowness and the dim vistas to privacy. He held it fast this morning till he had got out, his sacrifice to honour, and then went with it to the nearest post-office and fixed it fast in a telegram; thinking of it moreover as a sacrifice only because he had, for reasons, felt it as an effort. Its character of effort it would owe to Kate's expected resistance, not less probable than on the occasion of past appeals; which was precisely why he—perhaps innocently—made his telegram persuasive. It had, as a recall of tender hours, to be, for the young woman at the counter, a trifle cryptic; but there was a good deal of it in one way and another, representing as it did a rich impulse and costing him a couple of shillings. There was also a moment later on, that day, when, in the Park, as he measured watchfully one of their old alleys, he might have been supposed by a cynical critic to be reckoning his chance of getting his money back. He was waiting—but he had waited of old; Lancaster Gate as a danger was practically at hand—but she had risked that danger before. Besides it was smaller now, with the queer turn of their affair; in spite of which indeed he was graver as he lingered and looked out.

Kate came at last by the way he had thought least likely, came as if she had started from the Marble Arch; but her advent was response—that was the great matter; response marked in her face and agreeable to him, even after Aunt Maud's responses, as noting had been since his return to London. She had not, it was true, answered his wire, and he had begun to fear, as she was late, that with the instinct of what he might be again intending to press upon her she had decided—though not with ease—to deprive him of his chance. He would have of course, she knew, other chances,

but she perhaps saw the present as offering her special danger.
This, in fact, Densher could himself feel, was exactly why he had
so prepared it, and he had rejoiced, even while he waited, in all
that the conditions had to say to him of their simpler and better
time. The shortest day of the year though it might be, it was, in the
same place, by a whim of the weather, almost as much to their purpose as the days of sunny afternoons when they had taken their
first trysts. This and that tree, within sight, on the grass, stretched
bare boughs over the couple of chairs in which they had sat of old
and in which—for they really could sit down again—they might
recover the clearness of their prime. It was to all intents however
this very reference that showed itself in Kate's face as, with her
swift motion, she came toward him. It helped him, her swift motion, when it finally brought her nearer; helped him, for that matter, at first, if only by showing him afresh how terribly well she
looked. It had been all along, he certainly remembered, a phenomenon of no rarity that he had felt her, at particular moments,
handsomer than ever before; one of these for instance being still
present to him as her entrance, under her aunt's eyes, at Lancaster
Gate, the day of his dinner there after his return from America;
and another her aspect on the same spot two Sundays ago—the
light in which she struck the eyes he had brought back from
Venice. In the course of a minute or two now he got, as he had got
it the other times, his apprehension of the special stamp of the fortune of the moment.

Whatever it had been determined by as the different hours recurred to him, it took on at present a prompt connexion with an
effect produced for him in truth more than once during the past
week, only now much intensified. This effect he had already noted
and named: it was that of the attitude assumed by his friend in the
presence of the degree of response on his part to Mrs. Lowder's
welcome which she couldn't possibly have failed to notice. She
had noticed it, and she had beautifully shown him so; wearing in
its honour the finest shade of studied serenity, a shade almost of
gaiety over the workings of time. Everything of course was relative,
with the shadow they were living under; but her condonation of
the way in which he now, for confidence, distinguished Aunt
Maud had almost the note of cheer. She had so by her own air

consecrated the distinction, invidious in respect to herself though
it might be; and nothing, really, more than this demonstration,
could have given him had he still wanted it the measure of her superiority. It was doubtless for that matter this superiority alone that
on the winter noon gave smooth decision to her step and charming courage to her eyes—a courage that deepened in them when
he had presently got to what he did want. He had delayed after she
had joined him not much more than long enough for him to say
to her, drawing her hand into his arm and turning off where they
had turned of old, that he wouldn't pretend he hadn't lately had
moments of not quite believing he should ever again be so happy.
She answered, passing over the reasons, whatever they had been,
of his doubt, that her own belief was in high happiness for them if
they would only have patience; though nothing at the same time
could be dearer than his idea for their walk. It was only make-
believe of course, with what had taken place for them, that they
couldn't meet at home; she spoke of their opportunities as suffering at no point. He had at any rate soon let her know that he
wished the present one to suffer at none, and in a quiet spot, beneath a great wintry tree, he let his entreaty come sharp.

"We've played our dreadful game and we've lost. We owe it to
ourselves, we owe it to our feeling *for* ourselves and for each other,
not to wait another day. Our marriage will—fundamentally, somehow, don't you see?—right everything that's wrong, and I can't express to you my impatience. We've only to announce it—and it
takes off the weight."

"To 'announce' it?" Kate asked. She spoke as if not understanding, though she had listened to him without confusion.

"To accomplish it then—to-morrow if you will; *do* it and announce it as done. That's the least part of it—after it nothing will
matter. We shall be so right," he said, "that we shall be strong; we
shall only wonder at our past fear. It will seem an ugly madness. It
will seem a bad dream."

She looked at him without flinching—with the look she had
brought at his call; but he felt now the strange chill of her brightness. "My dear man, what has happened to you?"

"Well, that I can bear it no longer. *That's* simply what has happened. Something has snapped, has broken in me, and here I am. It's *as* I am that you must have me."

He saw her try for a time to appear to consider it; but he saw her also not consider it. Yet he saw her, felt her, further—he heard her, with her clear voice—try to be intensely kind with him. "I don't see, you know, what has changed." She had a large strange smile. "We've been going on together so well, and you suddenly desert me?"

It made him helplessly gaze. "You call it so 'well'? You've touches, upon my soul!—"

"I call it perfect—from my original point of view. I'm just where I was; and you must give me some better reason than you do, my dear, for *your* not being. It seems to me," she continued, "that we're only right as to what has been between us so long as we do wait. I don't think we wish to have behaved like fools." He took in while she talked her imperturbable consistency; which it was quietly, queerly hopeless to see her stand there and breathe into their mild remembering air. He had brought her there to be moved, and she was only immoveable—which was not moreover, either, because she didn't understand. She understood everything, and things he refused to; and she had reasons, deep down, the sense of which nearly sickened him. She had too again most of all her strange significant smile. "Of course if it's that you really *know* something—?" It was quite conceivable and possible to her, he could see, that he did. But he didn't even know what she meant, and he only looked at her in gloom. His gloom however didn't upset her. "You do, I believe, only you've a delicacy about saying it. Your delicacy to me, my dear, is a scruple too much. I should have no delicacy in hearing it, so that if you can *tell* me you know—"

"Well?" he asked as she still kept what depended on it.

"Why then I'll do what you want. We needn't, I grant you, in that case wait; and I can see what you mean by thinking it nicer of us not to. I don't even ask you," she continued, "for a proof. I'm content with your moral certainty."

By this time it had come over him—it had the force of a rush. The point she made was clear, as clear as that the blood, while he recognized it, mantled in his face. "I know nothing whatever."

"You've not an idea?"

"I've not an idea."

"I'd consent," she said—"I'd announce it to-morrow, to-day, I'd go home this moment and announce it to Aunt Maud, for an idea: I mean an idea straight *from* you, I mean as your own, given me in good faith. There, my dear!"—and she smiled again. "I call that really meeting you."

If it *was* then what she called it, it disposed of his appeal, and he could but stand there with his wasted passion—for it was in high passion that he had from the morning acted—in his face. She made it all out, bent upon her—the idea he didn't have, and the idea he had, and his failure of insistence when it brought up *that* challenge, and his sense of her personal presence, and his horror, almost, of her lucidity. They made in him a mixture that might have been rage, but that was turning quickly to mere cold thought, thought which led to something else and was like a new dim dawn. It affected her then, and she had one of the impulses, in all sincerity, that had before this, between them, saved their position. When she had come nearer to him, when, putting her hand upon him, she made him sink with her, as she leaned to him, into their old pair of chairs, she prevented irresistibly, she forestalled the waste of his passion. She had an advantage with his passion now.

— III —

He had said to her in the Park when challenged on it that nothing had "happened" to him as a cause for the demand he there made of her—happened he meant since the account he had given, after his return, of his recent experience. But in the course of a few days—they had brought him to Christmas morning—he was conscious enough, in preparing again to seek her out, of a difference on that score. Something *had* in this case happened to him, and, after his taking the night to think of it he felt that what it most, if not absolutely first, involved was his immediately again putting himself in relation with her. The fact itself had met him there—in his own small quarters—on Christmas

Eve, and had not then indeed at once affected him as implying that consequence. So far as he on the spot and for the next hours took its measure—a process that made his night mercilessly wakeful—the consequences possibly implied were numerous to distraction. His spirit dealt with them, in the darkness, as the slow hours passed; his intelligence and his imagination, his soul and his sense, had never on the whole been so intensely engaged. It was his difficulty for the moment that he was face to face with alternatives, and that it was scarce even a question of turning from one to the other. They were not in a perspective in which they might be compared and considered; they were, by a strange effect, as close as a pair of monsters of whom he might have felt on either cheek the hot breath and the huge eyes. He saw them at once and but by looking straight before him; he wouldn't for that matter, in his cold apprehension, have turned his head by an inch. So it was that his agitation was still—was not, for the slow hours, a matter of restless motion. He lay long, after the event, on the sofa where, extinguishing at a touch the white light of convenience that he hated, he had thrown himself without undressing. He stared at the buried day and wore out the time; with the arrival of the Christmas dawn moreover, late and grey, he felt himself somehow determined. The common wisdom had had its say to him—that safety in doubt was *not* action; and perhaps what most helped him was this very commonness. In his case there was nothing of *that*—in no case in his life had there ever been less: which association, from one thing to another, now worked for him as a choice. He acted, after his bath and his breakfast, in the sense of that marked element of the rare which he felt to be the sign of his crisis. And that is why, dressed with more state than usual and quite as if for church, he went out into the soft Christmas day.

Action, for him, on coming to the point, it appeared, carried with it a certain complexity. We should have known, walking by his side, that his final prime decision hadn't been to call at the door of Sir Luke Strett, and yet that this step, though subordinate, was none the less urgent. His prime decision was for another matter, to which impatience, once he was on the way, had now added itself; but he remained sufficiently aware that he must compromise with the perhaps excessive earliness. This, and the ferment set up

within him, were together a reason for not driving; to say nothing
of the absence of cabs in the dusky festal desert. Sir Luke's great
square was not near, but he walked the distance without seeing a
hansom. He had his interval thus to turn over his view—the view
to which what had happened the night before had not sharply reduced itself; but the complexity just mentioned was to be offered
within the next few minutes another item to assimilate. Before Sir
Luke's house, when he reached it, a brougham was drawn up—at
the sight of which his heart had a lift that brought him for the instant to a stand. This pause wasn't long, but it was long enough to
flash upon him a revelation in the light of which he caught his
breath. The carriage, so possibly at such an hour and on such a day
Sir Luke's own, had struck him as a sign that the great doctor was
back. This would prove something else, in turn, still more intensely, and it was in the act of the double apprehension that Densher felt himself turn pale. His mind rebounded for the moment
like a projectile that has suddenly been met by another: he stared
at the strange truth that what he wanted *more* than to see Kate
Croy was to see the witness who had just arrived from Venice. He
wanted positively to be in his presence and to hear his voice—
which was the spasm of his consciousness that produced the flash.
Fortunately for him, on the spot, there supervened something in
which the flash went out. He became aware within this minute
that the coachman on the box of the brougham had a face known
to him, whereas he had never seen before, to his knowledge, the
great doctor's carriage. The carriage, as he came nearer, was simply Mrs. Lowder's; the face on the box was just the face that, in
coming and going at Lancaster Gate, he would vaguely have noticed, outside, in attendance. With this the rest came: the lady of
Lancaster Gate had, on a prompting not wholly remote from his
own, presented herself for news; and news, in the house, she was
clearly getting, since her brougham had stayed. Sir Luke *was* then
back—only Mrs. Lowder was with him.

It was under the influence of this last reflexion that Densher
again delayed; and it was while he delayed that something else occurred to him. It was all round, visibly—given his own new contribution—a case of pressure; and in a case of pressure Kate, for
quicker knowledge, might have come out with her aunt. The pos-

sibility that in this event she might be sitting in the carriage—the thing most likely—had had the effect, before he could check it, of bringing him within range of the window. It wasn't there he had wished to see her; yet if she *was* there he couldn't pretend not to. What he had however the next moment made out was that if some one was there it wasn't Kate Croy. It was, with a sensible shock for him, the person who had last offered him a conscious face from behind the clear plate of a café in Venice. The great glass at Florian's was a medium less obscure, even with the window down, than the air of London Christmas; yet at present also, none the less, between the two men, an exchange of recognitions could occur. Densher felt his own look a gaping arrest—which, he disgustedly remembered, his back as quickly turned, appeared to repeat itself as his special privilege. He mounted the steps of the house and touched the bell with a keen consciousness of being habitually looked at by Kate's friend from positions of almost insolent vantage. He forgot for the time the moment when, in Venice, at the palace, the encouraged young man had in a manner assisted at the departure of the disconcerted, since Lord Mark was not looking disconcerted now any more than he had looked from his bench at his café. Densher was thinking that *he* seemed to show as vagrant while another was ensconced. He was thinking of the other as—in spite of the difference of situation—more ensconced than ever; he was thinking of him above all as the friend of the person with whom his recognition had, the minute previous, associated him. The man was seated in the very place in which, beside Mrs. Lowder's, he had looked to find Kate, and that was a sufficient identity. Meanwhile at any rate the door of the house had opened and Mrs. Lowder stood before him. It was something at least that *she* wasn't Kate. She was herself, on the spot, in all her affluence; with presence of mind both to decide at once that Lord Mark, in the brougham, didn't matter and to prevent Sir Luke's butler, by a firm word thrown over her shoulder, from standing there to listen to her passage with the gentleman who had rung. "*I'll* tell Mr. Densher; you needn't wait!" And the passage, promptly and richly, took place on the steps.

"He arrives, travelling straight, to-morrow early. I couldn't not come to learn."

"No more," said Densher simply, "could I. On my way," he added, "to Lancaster Gate."

"Sweet of you." She beamed on him dimly, and he saw her face was attuned. It made him, with what she had just before said, know all, and he took the thing in while he met the air of portentous, of almost functional, sympathy that had settled itself as her medium with him and that yet had now a fresh glow. "So you *have* your message?"

He knew so well what she meant, and so equally with it what he "*had* had" no less than what he hadn't, that, with but the smallest hesitation, he strained the point. "Yes—my message."

"Our dear dove then, as Kate calls her, has folded her wonderful wings."

"Yes—folded them."

It rather racked him, but he tried to receive it as she intended, and she evidently took his formal assent for self-control. "Unless it's more true," she accordingly added, "that she has spread them the wider."

He again but formally assented, though, strangely enough, the words fitted a figure deep in his own imagination. "Rather, yes—spread them the wider."

"For a flight, I trust, to some happiness greater—!"

"Exactly. Greater," Densher broke in; but now with a look, he feared, that did a little warn her off.

"You were certainly," she went on with more reserve, "entitled to direct news. Ours came late last night: I'm not sure otherwise, I shouldn't have gone to you. But you're coming," she asked, "to *me?*"

He had had a minute by this time to think further, and the window of the brougham was still within range. Her rich "me," reaching him moreover through the mild damp, had the effect of a thump on his chest. "Squared," Aunt Maud? She was indeed squared, and the extent of it just now perversely enough took away his breath. His look from where they stood embraced the aperture at which the person sitting in the carriage might have shown, and he saw his interlocutress, on her side, understand the question in it, which he moreover then uttered. "Shall you be alone?" It was, as an immediate instinctive parley with the image of his condition that now flourished in her, almost hypocritical. It sounded as if he wished to come and overflow to her, yet this was exactly what he didn't. The need to overflow had suddenly—since the night before—dried up in him, and he had never been aware of a deeper reserve.

But she had meanwhile largely responded. "Completely alone. I should otherwise never have dreamed; feeling, dear friend, but too much!" Failing on her lips what she felt came out for him in the offered hand with which she had the next moment consolingly pressed his own. "Dear friend, dear friend!"—she was deeply "with" him, and she wished to be still more so: which was what made her immediately continue. "Or wouldn't you this evening, for the sad Christmas it makes us, dine with me *tête-à-tête?*"

It put the thing off, the question of a talk with her—making the difference, to his relief, of several hours; but it also rather mystified him. This however didn't diminish his need of caution. "Shall you mind if I don't tell you at once?"

"Not in the least—leave it open: it shall be as you may feel, and you needn't even send me word. I only *will* mention that to-day, of all days, I shall otherwise sit there alone."

Now at least he could ask. "Without Miss Croy?"

"Without Miss Croy. Miss Croy," said Mrs. Lowder, "is spending her Christmas in the bosom of her more immediate family."

He was afraid, even while he spoke, of what his face might show. "You mean she has left you?"

Aunt Maud's own face for that matter met the enquiry with a consciousness in which he saw a reflexion of events. He was made sure by it, even at the moment and as he had never been before, that since he had known these two women no confessed nor commented tension, no crisis of the cruder sort would really have taken form between them: which was precisely a high proof of how Kate had steered her boat. The situation exposed in Mrs. Lowder's present expression lighted up by contrast that superficial smoothness; which afterwards, with his time to think of it, was to put before him again the art, the particular gift, in the girl, now so placed and classed, so intimately familiar for him, as her talent for life. The peace, within a day or two—since his seeing her last—had clearly been broken; differences, deep down, kept there by a diplomacy on Kate's part as deep, had been shaken to the surface by some exceptional jar; with which, in addition, he felt Lord Mark's odd attendance at such an hour and season vaguely associated. The talent for life indeed, it at the same time struck him, would probably have shown equally in the breach, or whatever had occurred; Aunt Maud having suffered, he judged, a strain rather than a stroke. Of these quick thoughts, at all events, that lady was already abreast. "She went yesterday morning—and not with my approval, I don't mind telling you—to her sister: Mrs. Condrip, if you know who I mean, who lives somewhere in Chelsea. My other niece and her affairs—that I should have to say such things to-day!—are a constant worry; so that Kate, in consequence—well, of events!—has simply been called in. My own idea, I'm bound to say, was that with *such* events she need have, in her situation, next to nothing to do."

"But she differed with you?"

"She differed with me. And when Kate differs with you—!"

"Oh I can imagine." He had reached the point in the scale of hypocrisy at which he could ask himself why a little more or less should signify. Besides, with the intention he had had he *must* know. Kate's move, if he didn't know, might simply disconcert him; and of being disconcerted his horror was by this time fairly superstitious. "I hope you don't allude to events at all calamitous."

"No—only horrid and vulgar."

"Oh!" said Merton Densher.

Mrs. Lowder's soreness, it was still not obscure, had discovered in free speech to him a momentary balm. "They've the misfortune to have, I suppose you know, a dreadful horrible father."

"Oh!" said Densher again.

"He's too bad almost to name, but he has come upon Marian, and Marian has shrieked for help."

Densher wondered at this with intensity; and his curiosity compromised for an instant with his discretion. "Come upon her—for money?"

"Oh for that of course always. But, at *this* blessed season, for refuge, for safety: for God knows what. He's *there*, the brute. And Kate's with them. And that," Mrs. Lowder wound up, going down the steps, "is her Christmas."

She had stopped again at the bottom while he thought of an answer. "Yours then is after all rather better."

"It's at least more decent." And her hand once more came out. "But why do I talk of *our* troubles? Come if you can."

He showed a faint smile. "Thanks. If I can."

"And now—I dare say—you'll go to church?"

She had asked it, with her good intention, rather in the air and by way of sketching for him, in the line of support, something a little more to the purpose than what she had been giving him. He felt it as finishing off their intensities of expression that he found himself to all appearance receiving her hint as happy. "Why yes— I think I will": after which, as the door of the brougham, at her approach, had opened from within, he was free to turn his back. He heard the door, behind him, sharply close again and the vehicle move off in another direction than his own.

He had in fact for the time no direction; in spite of which indeed he was at the end of ten minutes aware of having walked straight to the south. That, he afterwards recognized, was, very sufficiently, because there had formed itself in his mind, even while Aunt Maud finally talked, an instant recognition of his necessary course. Nothing was open to him but to follow Kate, nor was anything more marked than the influence of the step she had taken on the emotion itself that possessed him. Her complications, which had fairly, with everything else, an awful sound—what were they, a thousand times over, but his own? His present business was to see that they didn't escape an hour longer taking their proper place in his life. He accordingly would have held his course hadn't it suddenly come over him that he had just lied to Mrs. Lowder— a term it perversely eased him to keep using—even more than was necessary. To what church was he going, to what church, in such a state of his nerves, *could* he go?—he pulled up short again, as he had pulled up in sight of Mrs. Lowder's carriage, to ask it. And yet the desire queerly stirred in him not to have wasted his word. He was just then however by a happy chance in the Brompton Road, and he bethought himself with a sudden light that the Oratory*

---

*Brompton Oratory, a Roman Catholic church offering informal services; opened in 1884.

was at hand. He had but to turn the other way and he should find himself soon before it. At the door then, in a few minutes, his idea was really—as it struck him—consecrated: he was, pushing in, on the edge of a splendid service—the flocking crowd told of it— which glittered and resounded, from distant depths, in the blaze of altar-lights and the swell of organ and choir. It didn't match his own day, but it was much less of a discord than some other things actual and possible. The Oratory in short, to make him right, would do.

— IV —

The difference was thus that the dusk of afternoon—dusk thick from an early hour—had gathered when he knocked at Mrs. Condrip's door. He had gone from the church to his club, wishing not to present himself in Chelsea at luncheon-time and also remembering that he must attempt independently to make a meal. This, in the event, he but imperfectly achieved: he dropped into a chair in the great dim void of the club library, with nobody, up or down, to be seen, and there after a while, closing his eyes, recovered an hour of the sleep he had lost during the night. Before doing this indeed he had written—it was the first thing he did—a short note, which, in the Christmas desolation of the place, he had managed only with difficulty and doubt to commit to a messenger. He wished it carried by hand, and he was obliged, rather blindly, to trust the hand, as the messenger, for some reason, was unable to return with a gage of delivery. When at four o'clock he was face to face with Kate in Mrs. Condrip's small drawing-room he found to his relief that his notification had reached her. She was expectant and to that extent prepared; which simplified a little—if a little, at the present pass, counted. Her conditions were vaguely vivid to him from the moment of his coming in, and vivid partly by their difference, a difference sharp and suggestive, from those in which he had hitherto constantly seen her. He had seen her but in places comparatively great; in her aunt's pompous house, under the high trees of Kensington and the sto-

ried ceilings of Venice. He had seen her, in Venice, on a great occasion, as the centre itself of the splendid Piazza: he had seen her
there, on a still greater one, in his own poor rooms, which yet had
consorted with her, having state and ancientry even in their poorness; but Mrs. Condrip's interior, even by this best view of it and
though not flagrantly mean, showed itself as a setting almost
grotesquely inapt. Pale, grave and charming, she affected him at
once as a distinguished stranger—stranger to the little Chelsea
street—who was making the best of a queer episode and a place of
exile. The extraordinary thing was that at the end of three minutes
he felt himself less appointedly a stranger in it than she.

A part of the queerness—this was to come to him in glimpses—
sprang from the air as of a general large misfit imposed on the narrow room by the scale and mass of its furniture. The objects, the
ornaments were, for the sisters, clearly relics and survivals of what
would, in the case of Mrs. Condrip at least, have been called better days. The curtains that overdraped the windows, the sofas and
tables that stayed circulation, the chimney-ornaments that
reached to the ceiling and the florid chandelier that almost
dropped to the floor, were so many mementoes of earlier homes
and so many links with their unhappy mother. Whatever might
have been in itself the quality of these elements Densher could
feel the effect proceeding from them, as they lumpishly blocked
out the decline of the dim day, to be ugly almost to the point of the
sinister. They failed to accommodate or to compromise; they asserted their differences without tact and without taste. It was truly
having a sense of Kate's own quality thus promptly to see them in
reference to it. But that Densher had this sense was no new thing
to him, nor did he in strictness need, for the hour, to be reminded
of it. He only knew, by one of the tricks, his imagination so constantly played him, that he was, so far as her present tension went,
very specially sorry for her—which was not the view that had determined his start in the morning; yet also that he himself would
have taken it all, as he might say, less hard. *He* could have lived in
such a place; but it wasn't given to those of his complexion, so to
speak, to be exiled anywhere. It was by their comparative grossness
that they could somehow make shift. His natural, his inevitable,
his ultimate home—left, that is, to itself—wasn't at all unlikely to

be as queer and impossible as what was just round them, though doubtless in less ample masses. As he took in moreover how Kate wouldn't have been in the least the creature she was if what was just round them hadn't mismatched her, hadn't made for her a medium involving compunction in the spectator, so, by the same stroke, that became the very fact of her relation with her companions there, such a fact as filled him at once, oddly, both with assurance and with suspense. If he himself, on this brief vision, felt her as alien and as ever so unwittingly ironic, how must they not feel her and how above all must she not feel them?

Densher could ask himself that even after she had presently lighted the tall candles on the mantel-shelf. This was all their illumination but the fire, and she had proceeded to it with a quiet dryness that yet left play, visibly, to her implication between them, in their trouble and failing anything better, of the presumably genial Christmas hearth. So far as the genial went this had in strictness, given their conditions, to be all their geniality. He had told her in his note nothing but that he must promptly see her and that he hoped she might be able to make it possible; but he understood from the first look at her that his promptitude was already having for her its principal reference. "I was prevented this morning, in the few minutes," he explained, "asking Mrs. Lowder if she had let you know, though I rather gathered she had; and it's what I've been in fact since then assuming. It was because I was so struck at the moment with your having, as she did tell me, so suddenly come here."

"Yes, it was sudden enough." Very neat and fine in the contracted firelight, with her hands in her lap, Kate considered what he had said. He had spoken immediately of what had happened at Sir Luke Strett's door. "She has let me know nothing. But that doesn't matter—if it's what *you* mean."

"It's part of what I mean," Densher said; but what he went on with, after a pause during which she waited, was apparently not the rest of that. "She had had her telegram from Mrs. Stringham; late last night. But to me the poor lady hasn't wired. The event," he added, "will have taken place yesterday, and Sir Luke, starting immediately, one can see, and travelling straight, will get back tomorrow morning. So that Mrs. Stringham, I judge, is left to face in some solitude the situation bequeathed to her. But of course," he wound up, "Sir Luke couldn't stay."

Her look at him might have had in it a vague betrayal of the sense that he was gaining time. "Was your telegram from Sir Luke?"

"No—I've had no telegram."

She wondered. "But not a letter—?"

"Not from Mrs. Stringham—no." He failed again however to develop this—for which her forbearance from another question gave him occasion. From whom then had he heard? He might at last, confronted with her, really have been gaining time; and as if to show that she respected this impulse she made her enquiry different. "Should you like to go out to her—to Mrs. Stringham?"

About that at least he was clear. "Not at all. She's alone, but she's very capable and very courageous. Besides—!" He had been going on, but he dropped.

"Besides," she said, "there's Eugenio? Yes, of course one remembers Eugenio."

She had uttered the words as definitely to show them for not untender; and he showed equally every reason to assent. "One remembers him indeed, and with every ground for it. He'll be of the highest value to her—he's capable of anything. What I was going to say," he went on, "is that some of their people from America must quickly arrive."

On this, as happened, Kate was able at once to satisfy him. "Mr. Someone-or-other, the person principally in charge of Milly's affairs—her first trustee, I suppose—had just got there at Mrs. Stringham's last writing."

"Ah that then was after your aunt last spoke to me—I mean the last time before this morning. I'm relieved to hear it. So," he said, "they'll do."

"Oh they'll do." And it came from each still as if it wasn't what each was most thinking of. Kate presently got however a step nearer to that. "But if you had been wired to by nobody what then this morning had taken you to Sir Luke?"

"Oh something else—which I'll presently tell you. It's what made me instantly need to see you; it's what I've come to speak to you of. But in a minute. I feel too many things," he went on, "at seeing you in this place." He got up as he spoke; she herself remained perfectly still. His movement had been to the fire, and, leaning a little, with his back to it, to look down on her from where he stood, he confined himself to his point. "Is it anything very bad that has brought you?"

He had now in any case said enough to justify her wish for more; so that, passing this matter by, she pressed her own challenge. "Do you mean, if I may ask, that *she*, dying—?" Her face, wondering, pressed it more than her words.

"Certainly you may ask," he after a moment said. "What has come to me is what, as I say, I came expressly to tell you. I don't mind letting you know," he went on, "that my decision to do this took for me last night and this morning a great deal of thinking of. But here I am." And he indulged in a smile that couldn't, he was well aware, but strike her as mechanical.

She went straighter with him, she seemed to show, than he really went with her. "You didn't want to come?"

"It would have been simple, my dear"—and he continued to smile—"if it had been, one way or the other, only a question of 'wanting.' It took, I admit it, the idea of what I had best do, all sorts of difficult and portentous forms. It came up for me really—well, not at all for my happiness."

This word apparently puzzled her—she studied him in the light of it. "You look upset—you've certainly been tormented. You're not well."

"Oh—well enough!"

But she continued without heeding. "You hate what you're doing."

"My dear girl, you simplify"—and he was now serious enough. "It isn't so simple even as that."

She had the air of thinking what it then might be. "I of course can't, with no clue, know what it is." She remained none the less patient and still. "If at such a moment she could write you one's inevitably quite at sea. One doesn't, with the best will in the world, understand." And then as Densher had a pause which might have stood for all the involved explanation that, to his discouragement, loomed before him: "You *haven't* decided what to do."

She had said it very gently, almost sweetly, and he didn't instantly say otherwise. But he said so after a look at her. "Oh yes— I have. Only with this sight of you here and what I seem to see in it for you—!" And his eyes, as at suggestions that pressed, turned from one part of the room to another.

"Horrible place, isn't it?" said Kate.

It brought him straight back to his inquiry. "Is it for anything awful you've had to come?"

"Oh that will take as long to tell you as anything *you* may have. Don't mind," she continued, "the 'sight of me here,' nor whatever—which is more than I yet know myself—may be 'in it' for me. And kindly consider too that, after all, if you're in trouble I can a little wish to help you. Perhaps I can absolutely even do it."

"My dear child, it's just because of the sense of your wish—! I suppose I'm in trouble—I suppose that's it. He said this with so odd a suddenness of simplicity that she could only stare for it— which he as promptly saw. So he turned off as he could his vagueness. "And yet I oughtn't to be." Which sounded indeed vaguer still.

She waited a moment. "Is it, as you say for my own business, anything very awful?"

"Well," he slowly replied, "you'll tell me if you find it so. I mean if you find my idea—"

He was so slow that she took him up. "Awful?" A sound of impatience—the form of a laugh—at last escaped her. "I can't find it anything at all till I know what you're talking about."

It brought him then more to the point, though it did so at first but by making him, on the hearthrug before her, with his hands in his pockets, turn awhile to and fro. There rose in him even with this movement a recall of another time—the hour in Venice, the hour of gloom and storm, when Susan Shepherd had sat in his quarters there very much as Kate was sitting now, and he had wondered, in pain even as now, what he might say and mightn't. Yet the present occasion after all was somehow the easier. He tried at any rate to attach that feeling to it while he stopped before his companion. "The communication I speak of can't possibly belong—so far as its date is concerned—to these last days. The postmark, which is legible, does; but it isn't thinkable, for anything else, that she wrote—!" He dropped, looking at her as if she'd understand.

It was easy to understand. "On her deathbed?" But Kate took an instant's thought. "Aren't we agreed that there was never any one in the world like her?"

"Yes." And looking over her head he spoke clearly enough. "There was never any one in the world like her."

Kate, from her chair, always without a movement, raised her eyes to the unconscious reach of his own. Then when the latter again dropped to her she added a question. "And won't it further depend a little on what the communication is?"

"A little perhaps—but not much. It's a communication," said Densher.

"Do you mean a letter?"

"Yes, a letter. Addressed to me in her hand—in hers unmistakably."

Kate thought. "Do you know her hand very well?"

"Oh perfectly."

It was as if his tone for this prompted—with a slight strangeness—her next demand. "Have you had many letters from her?"

"No. Only three notes." He spoke looking straight at her. "And very, very short ones."

"Ah," said Kate, "the number doesn't matter. Three lines would be enough if you're sure to remember."

"I'm sure I remember. Besides," Densher continued, "I've seen her hand in other ways. I seem to recall how you once, before she went to Venice, showed me one of her notes precisely *for* that. And then she once copied me something."

"Oh," said Kate almost with a smile, "I don't ask you for the detail of your reasons. One good one's enough." To which however she added as if precisely not to speak with impatience or with anything like irony: "And the writing has its usual look?"

Densher answered as if even to better that description of it. "It's beautiful."

"Yes—it *was* beautiful. Well," Kate, to defer to him still, further remarked, "it's not news to us now that she was stupendous. Anything's possible."

"Yes, anything's possible"—he appeared oddly to catch at it.

"That's what I say to myself. It's what I've been believing you," he a trifle vaguely explained, "still more certain to feel."

She waited for him to say more, but he only, with his hands in his pockets, turned again away, going this time to the single window of the room, where in the absence of lamplight the blind hadn't been drawn. He looked out into the lamplit fog, lost himself in the small sordid London street—for sordid, with his other association, he felt it—as he had lost himself, with Mrs. Stringham's eyes on him, in the vista of the Grand Canal. It was present then to his recording consciousness that when he had last been driven to such an attitude the very depth of his resistance to the opportunity to give Kate away was what had so driven him. His waiting companion had on that occasion waited for him to say he *would*; and what he had meantime glowered forth at was the inanity of such a hope. Kate's attention, on her side, during these minutes, rested on the back and shoulders he thus familiarly presented—rested as with a view of their expression, a reference to things unimparted, links still missing and that she must ever miss, try to make them out as she would. The result of her tension was that she again took him up. "You received—what you spoke of— last night?"

It made him turn round. "Coming in from Fleet Street—earlier by an hour than usual—I found it with some other letters on my table. But my eyes went straight to it, in an extraordinary way, from the door. I recognized it, knew what it was, without touching it."

"One can understand." She listened with respect. His tone however was so singular that she presently added: "You speak as if all this while you *hadn't* touched it."

"Oh yes, I've touched it. I feel as if, ever since, I'd been touching nothing else. I quite firmly," he pursued as if to be plainer, "took hold of it."

"Then where is it?"

"Oh I have it here."

"And you've brought it to show me?"

"I've brought it to show you."

So he said with a distinctness that had, among his other oddities, almost a sound of cheer, yet making no movement that matched his words. She could accordingly but offer again her expectant face, while his own, to her impatience, seemed perversely to fill with another thought. "But now that you've done so you feel you don't want to."

"I want to immensely," he said. "Only you tell me nothing."

She smiled at him, with this, finally, as if he were an unreasonable child. "It seems to me I tell you quite as much as you tell me. You haven't yet even told me how it is that such explanations as you require don't come from your document itself." Then as he answered nothing she had a flash. "You mean you haven't read it?"

"I haven't read it."

She stared. "Then how am I to help you with it?"

Again leaving her while she never budged he paced five strides, and again he was before her. "By telling me *this*. It's something, you know, that you wouldn't tell me the other day."

She was vague. "The other day?"

"The first time after my return—the Sunday I came to you. What's he doing," Densher went on, "at that hour of the morning with her? What does his having been with her there mean?"

"Of whom are you talking?"

"Of that man—Lord Mark of course. What does it represent?"

"Oh with Aunt Maud?"

"Yes, my dear—and with you. It comes more or less to the same thing; and it's what you didn't tell me the other day when I put you the question."

Kate tried to remember the other day. "You asked me nothing about any hour."

"I asked you when it was you last saw him—previous, I mean, to his second descent at Venice. You wouldn't say, and as we were talking of a matter comparatively more important I let it pass. But the fact remains, you know, my dear, that you haven't told me."

Two things in this speech appeared to have reached Kate more distinctly than the others. "I 'wouldn't say'?—and you 'let it pass'?" She looked just coldly blank. "You really speak as if I were keeping something back."

"Well, you see," Densher persisted, "you're not even telling me now. All I want to know," he nevertheless explained, "is whether there was a connexion between that proceeding on his part, which was practically—oh beyond all doubt!—the shock precipitating for her what has now happened, and anything that had occurred with him previously for yourself. How in the world did he know we're engaged?"

– V –

Kate slowly rose; it was, since she had lighted the candles and sat down, the first movement she had made. "Are you trying to fix it on me that I must have told him?"

She spoke not so much in resentment as in pale dismay—which he showed he immediately took in. "My dear child, I'm not trying to 'fix' anything; but I'm extremely tormented and I seem not to understand. What has the brute to do with us anyway?"

"What has he indeed?" Kate asked.

She shook her head as if in recovery, within the minute, of some mild allowance for his unreason. There was in it—and for his reason really—one of those half-inconsequent sweetnesses by which she had often before made, over some point of difference, her own terms with him. Practically she was making them now, and essentially he was knowing it; yet inevitably, all the same, he was accepting it. She stood there close to him, with something in her patience that suggested her having supposed, when he spoke more appealingly, that he was going to kiss her. He hadn't been, it appeared; but his continued appeal was none the less the quieter. "What's he doing, from ten o'clock on Christmas morning, with Mrs. Lowder?"

Kate looked surprised. "Didn't she tell you he's staying there?"

"At Lancaster Gate?" Densher's surprise met it. " 'Staying'?— since when?"

"Since day before yesterday. He was there before I came away." And then she explained—confessing it in fact anomalous. "It's an accident—like Aunt Maud's having herself remained in town for Christmas, but it isn't after all so monstrous. We stayed—and, with my having come here, she's sorry now—because we neither of us, waiting from day to day for the news you brought, seemed to want to be with a lot of people."

"You stayed for thinking of—Venice?"

"Of course we did. For what else? And even a little," Kate wonderfully added—"it's true at least of Aunt Maud—for thinking of you."

He appreciated. "I see. Nice of you every way. But whom," he inquired, "has Lord Mark stayed for thinking of?"

"His being in London, I believe, is a very commonplace matter. He has some rooms which he has had suddenly some rather advantageous chance to let—such as, with his confessed, his decidedly proclaimed want of money, he hasn't had it in him, in spite of everything, not to jump at."

Densher's attention was entire. "In spite of everything? In spite of what?"

"Well, I don't know. In spite, say, of his being scarcely supposed to do that sort of thing."

"To try to get money?"

"To try at any rate in little thrifty ways. Apparently however he has had for some reason to do what he can. He turned at a couple of days' notice out of his place, making it over to his tenant; and Aunt Maud, who's deeply in his confidence about all such matters, said: 'Come then to Lancaster Gate—to sleep at least—till, like all the world, you go to the country.' He was to have gone to the country—I think to Matcham—yesterday afternoon: Aunt Maud, that is, told me he was."

Kate had been somehow, for her companion, through this statement, beautifully, quite soothingly, suggestive. "Told you, you mean, so that you needn't leave the house?"

"Yes—so far as she had taken it into her head that his being there was part of my reason."

"And *was* it part of your reason?"

"A little if you like. Yet there's plenty here—as I knew there would be—without it. So that," she said candidly, "doesn't matter. I'm glad I am here: even if for all the good I do—!" She implied however that that didn't matter either. "He didn't, as you tell me, get off then to Matcham; though he may possibly if it *is* possible, be going this afternoon. But what strikes me as most probable— and it's really, I'm bound to say, quite amiable of him—is that he has declined to leave Aunt Maud, as I've been so ready to do, to

spend her Christmas alone. If moreover he has given up Matcham
for her it's a *procéde** that won't please her less. It's small wonder
therefore that she insists, on a dull day, in driving him about. I
don't pretend to know," she wound up, "what may happen between them; but that's all I see in it."

"You see in everything, and you always did," Densher returned,
"something that, while I'm with you at least, I always take from
you as the truth itself."

She looked at him as if consciously and even carefully extract-
ing the sting of his reservation; then she spoke with a quiet gravity
that seemed to show how fine she found it. "Thank you." It had for
him, like everything else, its effect. They were still closely face to
face, and, yielding to the impulse to which he hadn't yielded just
before, he laid his hands on her shoulders, held her hard a minute
and shook her a little, far from untenderly, as if in expression of
more mingled things, all difficult, than he could speak. Then
bending his head he applied his lips to her cheek. He fell, after
this, away for an instant, resuming his unrest, while she kept the
position in which, all passive and as a statue, she had taken his
demonstration. It didn't prevent her, however, from offering him,
as if what she had had was enough for the moment, a further indulgence. She made a quiet lucid connexion and as she made it
sat down again. "I've been trying to place exactly, as to its date,
something that did happen to me while you were in Venice. I
mean a talk with him. He spoke to me—spoke out."

"Ah there you are!" said Densher who had wheeled round.

"Well, if I'm 'there,' as you so gracefully call it, by having refused to meet him as he wanted—as he pressed—I plead guilty to
being so. Would you have liked me," she went on, "to give him an
answer that would have kept him from going?"

It made him a little awkwardly think. "Did you know he was
going?"

"Never for a moment; but I'm afraid that—even if it doesn't fit
your strange suppositions—I should have given him just the same
answer if I had known. If it's a matter I haven't, since your return,

thrust upon you, that's simply because it's not a matter in the memory of which I find a particular joy. I hope that if I've satisfied you about it," she continued, "it's not too much to ask of you to let it rest."

"Certainly," said Densher kindly, "I'll let it rest." But the next moment he pursued: "He saw something. He guessed."

"If you mean," she presently returned, "that he was unfortunately the one person we hadn't deceived, I can't contradict you."

"No — of course not. But *why*," Densher still risked, "was he unfortunately the one person — ? He's not really a bit intelligent."

"Intelligent enough apparently to have seen a mystery, a riddle, in anything so unnatural as — all things considered and when it came to the point — my attitude. So he gouged out his conviction, and on his conviction he acted."

Densher seemed for a little to look at Lord Mark's conviction as if it were a blot on the face of nature. "Do you mean because you had appeared to him to have encouraged him?"

"Of course I had been decent to him. Otherwise where *were* we?"

" 'Where' — ?"

"You and I. What I appeared to him, however, hadn't mattered. What mattered was how I appeared to Aunt Maud. Besides, you must remember that he has had all along his impression of *you*. You can't help it," she said, "but you're after all — well, yourself."

"As much myself as you please. But when I took myself to Venice and kept myself there — what," Densher asked, "did he make of that?"

"Your being in Venice and liking to be — which is never on any one's part a monstrosity — was explicable for him in other ways. He was quite capable moreover of seeing it as dissimulation."

"In spite of Mrs. Lowder?"

"No," said Kate, "not in spite of Mrs. Lowder now. Aunt Maud, before what you call his second descent, hadn't convinced him — all the more that my refusal of him didn't help. But he came back convinced." And then as her companion still showed a face at a loss: "I mean after he had seen Milly, spoken to her and left her. Milly convinced him."

"Milly?" Densher again but vaguely echoed.

"That you were sincere. That it was *her* you loved." It came to him from her in such a way that he instantly, once more, turned, found himself yet again at his window. "Aunt Maud, on his return here," she meanwhile continued, "had it from him. And that's why you're now so well with Aunt Maud."

He only for a minute looked out in silence—after which he came away. "And why *you* are." It was almost, in its extremely affirmative effect between them, the note of recrimination; or it would have been perhaps rather if it hadn't been so much more the note of truth. It was sharp because it was true, but its truth appeared to impose it as an argument so conclusive as to permit on neither side a sequel. That made, while they faced each other over it without speech, the gravity of everything. It was as if there were almost danger, which the wrong word might start. Densher accordingly at last acted to better purpose: he drew, standing there before her, a pocket-book from the breast of his waistcoat and he drew from the pocket-book a folded letter to which her eyes attached themselves. He restored then the receptacle to its place and, with a movement not the less odd for being visibly instinctive and unconscious, carried the hand containing his letter behind him. What he thus finally spoke of was a different matter. "Did I understand from Mrs. Lowder that your father's in the house?"

If it never had taken her long in such excursions to meet him it was not to take her so now. "In the house, yes. But we needn't fear his interruption"—she spoke as if he had thought of that. "He's in bed."

"Do you mean with illness?"

She sadly shook her head. "Father's never ill. He's a marvel. He's only—endless."

Densher thought. "Can I in any way help you with him?"

"Yes." She perfectly, wearily, almost serenely, had it all. "By our making your visit as little of an affair as possible for him—and for Marian too."

"I see. They hate so your seeing me. Yet I couldn't—could I?—not have come."

"No, you couldn't not have come."

"But I can only, on the other hand, go as soon as possible?"

Quickly it almost upset her. "Ah don't, to-day, put ugly words into my mouth. I've enough of my trouble without it."

"I know—I know!" He spoke in instant pleading. "It's all only that I'm as troubled *for* you. When did he come?"

"Three days ago—after he hadn't been near her for more than a year, after he had apparently, and not regrettably, ceased to remember her existence; and in a state which made it impossible not to take him in."

Densher hesitated. "Do you mean in such want—?"

"No, not of food, of necessary things—not even, so far as his appearance went, of money. He looked as wonderful as ever. But he was—well, in terror."

"In terror of what?"

"I don't know. Of somebody—of something. He wants, he says, to be quiet. But his quietness is awful."

She suffered, but he couldn't not question. "What does he do?"

It made Kate herself hesitate. "He cries."

Again for a moment he hung fire, but he risked it. "What *has* he done?"

It made her slowly rise, and they were once more fully face to face. Her eyes held his own and she was paler than she had been. "If you love me—now—don't ask me about father."

He waited again a moment. "I love you. It's because I love you that I'm here. It's because I love you that I've brought you this." And he drew from behind him the letter that had remained in his hand.

But her eyes only—though he held it out—met the offer. "Why you've not broken the seal!"

"If I had broken the seal—exactly—I should know what's within. It's for *you* to break the seal that I bring it."

She looked—still not touching the thing—inordinately grave. "To break the seal of something to you from *her*?"

"Ah precisely because it's from her. I'll abide by whatever you think of it."

"I don't understand," said Kate. "What do you yourself think?" And then as he didn't answer: "It seems to me I think you know. You have your instinct. You don't need to read. It's the proof."

Densher faced her words as if they had been an accusation, an accusation for which he was prepared and which there was but one way to face. "I have indeed my instinct. It came to me, while

I worried it out, last night. It came to me as an effect of the hour."
He held up his letter and seemed now to insist more than to confess. "This thing had been timed."

"For Christmas Eve?"

"For Christmas Eve."

Kate had suddenly a strange smile. "The season of gifts!" After
which, as he said nothing, she went on: "And had been written,
you mean, while she could write, and kept to *be* so timed?"

Only meeting her eyes while he thought, he again didn't reply.
"What do *you* mean by the proof?"

"Why of the beauty with which you've been loved. But I won't,"
she said, "break your seal."

"You positively decline?"

"Positively. Never." To which she added oddly: "I know without."

He had another pause. "And what is it you know?"

"That she announces to you she has made you rich."

His pause this time was longer. "Left me her fortune?"

"Not all of it, no doubt, for it's immense. But money to a large
amount. I don't care," Kate went on, "to know how much." And
her strange smile recurred. "I trust her."

"Did she tell you?" Densher asked.

"Never!" Kate visibly flushed at the thought. "That wouldn't, on
my part, have been playing fair with her. And I did," she added,
"play fair."

Densher, who had believed her—he couldn't help it—continued, holding his letter, to face her. He was much quieter now, as
if his torment had somehow passed. "You played fair with me,
Kate; and that's why—since we talk of proofs—I want to give *you*
one. I've wanted to let you see—and in preference even to myself—something I feel as sacred."

She frowned a little. "I don't understand."

"I've asked myself for a tribute, for a sacrifice by which I can peculiarly recognize—"

"Peculiarly recognize what?" she demanded as he dropped.

"The admirable nature of your own sacrifice. You were capable
in Venice of an act of splendid generosity."

"And the privilege you offer me with that document is my reward?"

He made a movement. "It's all I can do as a symbol of my attitude."

She looked at him long. "Your attitude, my dear, is that you're afraid of yourself. You've had to take yourself in hand. You've had to do yourself violence."

"So it is then you meet me?"

She bent her eyes hard a moment to the letter, from which her hand still stayed itself. "You absolutely *desire* me to take it?"

"I absolutely desire you to take it."

"To do what I like with it?"

"Short of course of making known its terms. It must remain— pardon my making the point—between you and me."

She had a last hesitation, but she presently broke it. "Trust me." Taking from him the sacred script she held it a little while her eyes again rested on those fine characters of Milly's that they had shortly before discussed. "To hold it," she brought out, "is to know."

"Oh I *know!*" said Merton Densher.

"Well then if we both do—!" She had already turned to the fire, nearer to which she had moved, and with a quick gesture had jerked the thing into the flame. He started—but only half—as to undo her action: his arrest was as prompt as the latter had been decisive. He only watched, with her, the paper burn; after which their eyes again met. "You'll have it all," Kate said, "from New York."

— VI —

It was after he had in fact, two months later, heard from New York that she paid him a visit one morning at his own quarters—coming not as she had come in Venice, under his extreme solicitation, but as a need recognized in the first instance by herself, even though also as the prompt result of a missive delivered to her. This had consisted of a note from Densher accompanying a letter, "just to hand," addressed him by an eminent American legal firm, a firm of whose high character he had become conscious while in New York as of a thing in the air itself, and whose head and front, the principal executor of Milly Theale's copious will, had been duly identified at Lancaster Gate as the gentleman hurrying out, by the straight southern course, before the girl's death, to the support of Mrs. Stringham. Densher's act on receipt of the document in question—an act as to which and to the bearings of which his resolve had had time to mature—constituted in strictness, singularly enough, the first reference to Milly, or to what Milly might or might not have done, that had passed between our pair since they had stood together watching the destruction, in the little vulgar grate at Chelsea, of the undisclosed work of her hand. They had at the time, and in due deference now, on his part, to Kate's mention of her responsibility for his call, immediately separated, and when they met again the subject was made present to them—at all events till some flare of new light—only by the intensity with which it mutely expressed its absence. They were not moreover in these weeks to meet often, in spite of the fact that this had, during January and a part of February, actually become for them a comparatively easy matter. Kate's stay at Mrs. Condrip's prolonged itself under allowances from her aunt which would have been a mystery to Densher had he not been admitted, at Lancaster Gate, really in spite of himself, to the esoteric view of them. "It's her idea," Mrs. Lowder had there said to him as if she really despised ideas—which she didn't; "and I've taken up with my own, which is to give her her head till she has had enough of it. She *has* had enough of it, she had that soon enough; but as she's as proud as the deuce she'll come back when she has found some reason—having nothing in common with her disgust—of which she can make a show. She calls it her holiday to which, once a year or so, as she says, the very maids in the scullery have a right. So we're taking it on that basis. But we shall not soon, I think, take another of the same sort. Besides, she's quite decent; she comes often—whenever I make her a sign; and she has been good, on the whole, this year or two, so that, to be decent myself, I don't complain. She has really been, poor dear, very much what one hoped;

though I needn't, you know," Aunt Maud wound up, "tell *you*, after all, you clever creature, what that was."

It had been partly in truth to keep down the opportunity for this that Densher's appearances under the good lady's roof markedly, after Christmas, interspaced themselves. The phase of his situation that on his return from Venice had made them for a short time almost frequent was at present quite obscured, and with it the impulse that had then acted. Another phase had taken its place, which he would have been painfully at a loss as yet to name or otherwise set on its feet, but of which the steadily rising tide left Mrs. Lowder, for his desire, quite high and dry. There had been a moment when it seemed possible that Mrs. Stringham, returning to America under convoy, would pause in London on her way and be housed with her old friend; in which case he was prepared for some apparent zeal of attendance. But this danger passed—he had felt it a danger, and the person in the world whom he would just now have most valued seeing on his own terms sailed away westward from Genoa. He thereby only wrote to her, having broken, in this respect, after Milly's death, the silence as to the sense of which, before that event, their agreement had been so deep. She had answered him from Venice twice, and had had time to answer him twice again from New York. The last letter of her four had come by the same post as the document he sent on to Kate, but he hadn't gone into the question of also enclosing that. His correspondence with Milly's companion was somehow already presenting itself to him as a feature—as a factor, he would have said in his newspaper—of the time whatever it might be, long or short, in store for him; but one of his acutest current thoughts was apt to be devoted to his not having yet mentioned it to Kate. She had put him no question, no "Don't you ever hear?"—so that he hadn't been brought to the point. This he described to himself as a mercy, for he liked his secret. It was as a secret that, in the same personal privacy, he described his transatlantic commerce, scarce even wincing while he recognized it as the one connexion in which he wasn't straight. He had in fact for this connexion a vivid mental image—he saw it as a small emergent rock in the waste of waters, the bottomless grey expanse of straightness. The fact that he had on several recent occasions taken with Kate an out-of-the-way walk that was each time to define itself as more remarkable for what they didn't say than for what they did—this fact failed somehow to mitigate for him a strange consciousness of exposure. There was something deep within him that he had absolutely shown to no one—to the companion of these walks in particular not a bit more than he could help; but he was none the less haunted, under its shadow, with a dire apprehension of publicity. It was as if he had invoked that ugliness in some stupid good faith; and it was queer enough that on his emergent rock, clinging to it and to Susan Shepherd, he should figure himself as hidden from view. That represented no doubt his belief in her power, or in her delicate disposition to protect him. Only Kate at all events knew— what Kate did know, and she was also the last person interested to tell it; in spite of which it was as if his *act*, so deeply associated with her and never to be recalled nor recovered, was abroad on the winds of the world. His honesty, as he viewed it with Kate, was the very element of that menace: to the degree that he saw at moments, as to their final impulse or their final remedy, the need to bury in the dark blindness of each other's arms the knowledge of each other that they couldn't undo.

Save indeed that the sense in which it was in these days a question of arms was limited, this might have been the intimate expedient to which they were actually resorting. It had its value, in conditions that made everything count, that thrice over, in Battersea Park—where Mrs. Lowder now never drove—he had adopted the usual means, in sequestered alleys, of holding her close to his side. She could make absences, on her present footing, without having too inordinately to account for them at home— which was exactly what gave them for the first time an appreciable margin. He supposed she could always say in Chelsea—though he didn't press it—that she had been across the town, in decency, for a look at her aunt; whereas there had always been reasons at Lancaster Gate for her not being able to plead the look at her other relatives. It was therefore between them a freedom of a purity as yet untasted; which for that matter also they made in various ways no little show of cherishing as such. They made the show indeed in every way but the way of a large use—an inconsequence that they almost equally gave time to helping each other to regard as natu-

ral. He put it to his companion that the kind of favor he now enjoyed at Lancaster Gate, the wonderful warmth of his reception
there, cut in a manner the ground from under their feet. He was
too horribly trusted—they had succeeded too well. He couldn't in
short make appointments with her without abusing Aunt Maud,
and he couldn't on the other hand haunt that lady without tying
his hands. Kate saw what he meant just as he saw what she did
when she admitted that she was herself, to a degree scarce less embarrassing, in the enjoyment of Aunt Maud's confidence. It was
special at present—she was handsomely used; she confessed accordingly to a scruple about misapplying her license. Mrs. Lowder
then finally had found—and all unconsciously now—the way to
baffle them. It wasn't however that they didn't meet a little, none
the less, in the southern quarter, to point for their common benefit the moral of their defeat. They crossed the river; they wandered
in neighborhoods sordid and safe; the winter was mild, so that,
mounting to the top of trams, they could rumble together to
Clapham or to Greenwich. If at the same time their minutes had
never been so counted it struck Densher that by a singular law
their tone—he scarce knew what to call it—had never been so
bland. Not to talk of what they *might* have talked of drove them to
other ground; it was as if they used a perverse insistence to make
up what they ignored. They concealed their pursuit of the irrelevant by the charm of their manner; they took precautions for the
courtesy they had formerly left to come of itself; often, when he
had quitted her, he stopped short, walking off, with the aftersense
of their change. He would have described their change—had he
so far faced it as to describe it—by their being so damned civil.
That had even, with the intimate, the familiar at the point to
which they had brought them, a touch almost of the droll. What
danger had there ever been of their becoming rude—after each
had long since made the other so tremendously tender? Such were
the things he asked himself when he wondered what in particular
he most feared.

Yet all the while too the tension had its charm—such being the
interest of a creature who could bring one back to her by such different roads. It was her talent for life again; which found in her a
difference for the differing time. She didn't give their tradition up;

she but made of it something new. Frankly moreover she had never been more agreeable nor in a way—to put it prosaically— better company: he felt almost as if he were knowing her on that defined basis—which he even hesitated whether to measure as reduced or as extended; as if at all events he were admiring her as she was probably admired by people she met "out." He hadn't in fine reckoned that she would still have something fresh for him; yet this was what she had—that on the top of a tram in the Borough he felt as if he were next her at dinner. What a person she would be if they *had* been rich—with what a genius for the so-called great life, what a presence for the so-called great house, what a grace for the so-called great positions! He might regret at once, while he was about it, that they weren't princes or billionaires. She had treated him on their Christmas to a softness that had struck him at the time as of the quality of fine velvet, meant to fold thick, but stretched a little thin; at present, however, she gave him the impression of a contact multitudinous as only the superficial can be. She had throughout never a word for what went on at home. She came out of that and she returned to it, but her nearest reference was the look with which, each time, she bade him good-bye. The look was her repeated prohibition: "It's what I *have* to see and to know—so don't touch it. That but wakes up the old evil, which I keep still, in my way, by sitting by it. I go now—leave me alone!—to sit by it again. The way to pity me—if that's what you want—is to believe in me. If we could really *do* anything it would be another matter."

He watched her, when she went her way, with the vision of what she thus a little stiffly carried. It was confused and obscure, but how, with her head high, it made her hold herself! He really in his own person might at these moments have been swaying a little aloft as one of the objects in her poised basket. It was doubtless thanks to some such consciousness as this that he felt the lapse of the weeks, before the day of Kate's mounting of his stair, almost swingingly rapid. They contained for him the contradiction that, whereas periods of waiting are supposed in general to keep the time slow, it was the wait, actually, that made the pace trouble him. The secret of that anomaly, to be plain, was that he was aware of how, while the days melted, something rare went with them.

This something was only a thought, but a thought precisely of such freshness and such delicacy as made the precious, of whatever sort, most subject to the hunger of time. The thought was all his own, and his intimate companion was the last person he might have shared it with. He kept it back like a favorite pang; left it behind him, so to say, when he went out, but came home again the sooner for the certainty of finding it there. Then he took it out of its sacred corner and its soft wrappings; he undid them one by one, handling them, handling *it*, as a father, baffled and tender, might handle a maimed child. But so it was before him—in his dread of who else might see it. Then he took to himself at such hours, in other words, that he should never, never know what had been in Milly's letter. The intention announced in it he should but too probably know; only that would have been, but for the depths of his spirit, the least part of it. The part of it missed for ever was the turn she would have given her act. This turn had possibilities that, somehow, by wondering about them, his imagination had extraordinarily filled out and refined. It had made of them a revelation the loss of which was like the sight of a priceless pearl cast before his eyes—his pledge given not to save it—into the fathomless sea, or rather even it was like the sacrifice of something sentient and throbbing, something that, for the spiritual ear, might have been audible as a faint far wail. This was the sound he cherished when alone in the stillness of his rooms. He sought and guarded the stillness, so that it might prevail there till the inevitable sounds of life, once more, comparatively coarse and harsh, should smother and deaden it—doubtless by the same process with which they would officiously heal the ache in his soul that was somehow one with it. It moreover deepened the sacred hush that he couldn't complain. He had given poor Kate her freedom.

The great and obvious thing, as soon as she stood there on the occasion we have already named, was that she was now in high possession of it. This would have marked immediately the difference—had there been nothing else to do it—between their actual terms and their other terms, the character of their last encounter in Venice. That had been *his* idea, whereas her present step was her own; the few marks they had in common were, from the first moment, to his conscious vision, almost pathetically plain. She was as grave now as before; she looked around her, to hide it, as before; she pretended, as before, in an air in which her words at the moment itself fell flat, to an interest in the place and a curiosity about his "things"; there was a recall in the way in which, after she had failed a little to push up her veil symmetrically and he had said she had better take it off altogether, she had acceded to his suggestion before the glass. It was just these things that were vain; and what was real was that his fancy figured her after the first few minutes as literally now providing the element of reassurance which had previously been his care. It was she, supremely, who had the presence of mind. She made indeed for that matter very prompt use of it. "You see I've not hesitated this time to break your seal."

She had laid on the table from the moment of her coming in the long envelope, substantially filled, which he had sent her enclosed in another of still ampler make. He had however not looked at it—his belief being that he wished never again to do so; besides which it had happened to rest with its addressed side up. So he "saw" nothing, and it was only into her eyes that her remark made him look, declining any approach to the object indicated. "It's not 'my' seal, my dear; and my intention—which my note tried to express—was all to treat it to you as not mine."

"Do you mean that it's to that extent mine then?"

"Well, let us call it if we like, theirs—that of the good people in New York, the authors of our communication. If the seal is broken well and good; but we *might*, you know," he presently added, "have sent it back to them intact and inviolate. Only accompanied," he smiled with his heart in his mouth, "by an absolutely kind letter."

Kate took it with the mere brave blink with which a patient of courage signifies to the exploring medical hand that the tender place is touched. He saw on the spot that she was prepared, and with this signal sign that she was too intelligent not to be, came a flicker of possibilities. She was—merely to put it at that—intelligent enough for anything. "Is it what you're proposing we *should* do?"

"Ah it's too late to do it—well, ideally. Now, with that sign that we *know*—!"

"But you don't know," she said very gently.

"I refer," he went on without noticing it, "to what would have been the handsome way. Its being dispatched again, with no cognisance taken but one's assurance of the highest consideration, and the proof of this in the state of the envelope—*that* would have been really satisfying."

She thought an instant. "The state of the envelope proving refusal, you mean, not to be based on the insufficiency of the sum?"

Densher smiled again as for the play, however whimsical, of her humour. "Well yes—something of that sort."

"So that if cognisance *has* been taken—so far as I'm concerned—it spoils the beauty?"

"It makes the difference that I'm disappointed in the hope—which I confess I entertained—that you'd bring the thing back to me as you had received it."

"You didn't express that hope in your letter."

"I didn't want to. I wanted to leave it to yourself. I wanted—oh yes, if that's what you wish to ask me—to see what you'd do."

"You wanted to measure the possibilities of my departure from delicacy?"

He continued steady now; a kind of ease—from the presence, as in the air, of something he couldn't yet have named—had come to him. "Well, I wanted—in so good a case—to test you."

She was struck—it showed in her face—by his expression. "It *is* a good case. I doubt whether a better," she said with her eyes on him, "has ever been known."

"The better the case then the better the test!"

"How do you know," she asked in reply to this, "what I'm capable of?"

"I don't, my dear! Only with the seal unbroken I should have known sooner."

"I see"—she took it in. "But I myself shouldn't have known at all. And you wouldn't have known, either, what I do know."

"Let me tell you at once," he returned, "that if you've been moved to correct my ignorance I very particularly request you not to."

She just hesitated. "Are you afraid of the effect of the corrections? Can you only do it by doing it blindly?"

He waited a moment. "What is it that you speak of my doing?"

"Why the only thing in the world that I take you as thinking of. Not accepting—what she has done. Isn't there some regular name in such cases? Not taking up the bequest."

"There's something you forget in it," he said after a moment. "My asking you to join with me in doing so."

Her wonder but made her softer, yet at the same time didn't make her less firm. "How can I 'join' in a matter with which I've nothing to do?"

"How? By a single word."

"And what word?"

"Your consent to my giving up."

"My consent has no meaning when I can't prevent you."

"You can perfectly prevent me. Understand that well," he said.

She seemed to face a threat in it. "You mean you won't give up if I *don't* consent?"

"Yes. I do nothing."

"That, as I understand, is accepting."

Densher paused. "I do nothing formal."

"You won't, I suppose you mean, touch the money."

"I won't touch the money."

It had a sound—though he had been coming to it—that made for gravity. "Who then in such an event *will?*"

"Any one who wants or who can."

Again a little she said nothing: she might say too much. But by the time she spoke he had covered ground. "How can I touch it but *through* you?"

"You can't. Any more," he added, "then I can renounce it except through you."

"Oh ever so much less! There's nothing," she explained, "in my power."

"I'm in your power," Merton Densher said.

"In what way?"

"In the way I show—and the way I've always shown. When have I shown," he asked as with a sudden cold impatience, "anything else? You surely must feel—so that you needn't wish to appear to spare me in it—how you 'have' me."

"It's very good of you, my dear," she nervously laughed, "to put me so thoroughly up to it!"

"I put you up to nothing. I didn't even put you up to the chance that, as I said a few moments ago, I saw for you in forwarding that thing. Your liberty is therefore in every way complete."

It had come to the point really that they showed each other pale faces, and that all the unspoken between them looked out of their eyes in a dim terror of their further conflict. Something even rose between them in one of their short silences—something that was like an appeal from each to the other not to be too true. Their necessity was somehow before them, but which of them must meet it first? "Thank you!" Kate said for his word about her freedom, but taking for the minute no further action on it. It was blest at least that all ironies failed them, and during another slow moment their very sense of it cleared the air.

There was an effect of this in the way he soon went on. "You must intensely feel that it's the thing for which we worked together."

She took up the remark, however, no more than if it were commonplace; she was already again occupied with a point of her own. "Is it absolutely true—for if it is, you know, it's tremendously interesting—that you haven't so much as a curiosity about what she has done for you?"

"Would you like," he asked, "my formal oath on it?"

"No—but I don't understand. It seems to me in your place—!"

"Ah," he couldn't help breaking in, "what do you know of my place? Pardon me," he at once added; "my preference is the one I express."

She had in an instant nevertheless a curious thought. "But won't the facts be published."

"'Published'?"—he winced

"I mean won't you see them in the papers?"

"Ah never! I shall know how to escape that."

It seemed to settle the subject, but she had the next minute another insistence. "Your desire is to escape everything?"

"Everything."

"And do you need no more definite sense of what it is you ask me to help you to renounce?"

"My sense is sufficient without being definite. I'm willing to believe that the amount of money's not small."

"Ah there you are!" she exclaimed.

"If she was to leave me a remembrance," he quietly pursued, "it would inevitably not be meagre."

Kate waited as for how to say it. "It's worthy of her. It's what she was herself—if you remember what we once said *that* was."

He hesitated—as if there had been many things. But he remembered one of them. "Stupendous?"

"Stupendous." A faint smile for it—ever so small—had flickered in her face, but had vanished before the omen of tears, a little less uncertain, had shown themselves in his own. His eyes filled—but that made her continue. She continued gently. "I think that what it really is must be that you're afraid. I mean," she explained, "that you're afraid of *all* the truth. If you're in love with her without it, what indeed can you be more? And you're afraid—it's wonderful!—to be in love with her."

"I never was in love with her," said Densher.

She took it, but after a little she met it. "I believe that now—for the time she lived. I believe it at least for the time you were there. But your change came—as it might well—the day you last saw her; she died for you then that you might understand her. From that hour you *did*." With which Kate slowly rose. "And I do now. She did it *for* us." Densher rose to face her, and she went on with her thought. "I used to call her, in my stupidity—for want of anything better—a dove. Well she stretched out her wings, and it was to *that* they reached. They cover us."

"They cover us," Densher said.

"That's what I give you," Kate gravely wound up. "That's what I've done for you."

His look at her had a slow strangeness that had dried on the moment, his tears. "Do I understand then—?"

"That I do consent?" She gravely shook her head. "No—for I see. You'll marry me without the money; you won't marry me with it. If I don't consent *you* don't."

"You lose me?" He showed, though naming it frankly, a sort of awe of her high grasp. "Well, you lose nothing else. I make over to you every penny."

Prompt was his own clearness, but she had no smile this time to spare. "Precisely—so that I must choose."

"You must choose."

Strange it was for him then that she stood in his own rooms doing it, while, with an intensity now beyond any that had ever made his breath come slow, he waited for her act. "There's but one thing that can save you from my choice."

"From your choice of my surrender to you?"

"Yes"—and she gave a nod at the long envelope on the table—"your surrender of that."

"What is it then?"

"Your word of honour that you're not in love with her memory."

"Oh—her memory!"

"Ah"—she made a high gesture—"don't speak of it as if you couldn't be. *I* could in your place; and you're one for whom it will do. Her memory's your love. You *want* no other."

He heard her out in stillness, watching her face but not moving. Then he only said: "I'll marry you, mind you, in an hour."

"As we were?"

"As we were."

But she turned to the door, and her headshake was now the end. "We shall never be again as we were!"

THE END

Endnotes

1. (p. 3) *Long had I turned it over . . . seeing the theme as formidable*: Henry James is writing the preface in 1909, years after he first sketched out his ideas for the story in his notebooks (1894), and after the actual writing of the novel (1901–1902). In *The Ambassadors*, he worked from a lengthy and very detailed outline that he had submitted to his publishers; this outline survives, and is now in the Widener Library at Harvard University. James prepared a similar but shorter and less detailed outline for *Wings* at some point and submitted it to his publishers, but it has been lost.

2. (p. 4) *the poet essentially can't be concerned with the act of dying. . . . it is still by the act of living that [the sick] appeal to him, and appeal the more as the conditions plot against them and prescribe the battle*: This is as clear a statement as one finds in the novel summing up James's negative attitude toward the death scene of the nineteenth-century novelistic tradition. Characters in James's novels are not depicted on a death bed, surrounded by mourning relatives and gasping out final words. Death is more of a disappearance. Characters die offstage and out of sight, and the focus is on the impact of the death on the living.

3. (p. 13) *There is no economy of treatment without an adopted, a related point of view*: James's conception of the well-made novel stressed the importance of the point of view from which the story is told or narrated, an idea that has been influential in modern literary criticism. See R. P. Blackmur, "Introduction," in James's *The Art of the Novel: Critical Prefaces*, pp. vii–xxxix (see "For Further Reading").

4. (p. 33) *He put the question with a charming air of sudden spiritual heat. . . . "what's called in the business world, I believe, an 'asset'"*: James seems to have originally projected a larger role for Lionel Croy in the story, but Croy disappears after book first. Croy's comments on the business world, as well as subsequent references by Lord Mark, display a hostility to all things commercial that was probably close to what James himself felt. James never had much direct experience with or knowledge of industry and commerce, but he was keenly aware of the business details of publishing. He did not like the tendencies that were evident even in his own time for publishers to push the popular "blockbuster" over serious fiction. Some of these issues

are explored in James's short story "The Figure in the Carpet" (1896); see Peter Rawlings, ed., *Henry James' Shorter Masterpieces*, vol. 2, pp. 46–88.

5. (p. 53) *the present winter's end*: James does not tell us exactly when the novel takes place. We infer that it is set at the end of the Victorian era—around the turn of the century. The 1997 Iain Softley movie version of *The Wings of the Dove* assigns a later date (1910), perhaps to bring the setting closer to World War I and heighten the sense of foreboding that hovers over the action.

6. (p. 55) *all the high dim things she lumped together as of the mind*: James does not tell us in detail what education Kate Croy has received. We learn that she has attended schools on the Continent and has become attracted to all things foreign. In post-Victorian England, women were not yet "in business" or in "the professions." While young Victorian women of any social standing usually received enough education to become governesses if they were not able to marry, the general intent was to have one's daughters exposed to art, music, and modern languages with a view to finding a desirable partner in marriage. Kate Croy felt shortchanged in the life of the mind and was attracted to Densher in part because he filled this need. His eclectic knowledge, along with his schooling on the continent, impressed her deeply.

7. (p. 72) *he asked himself what was to be expected of a person who could treat one like that*: This passage and the several long paragraphs that follow are good examples of how James enters into the minds of his protagonists and reveals to us what they are thinking. Nothing much is actually happening here. Densher is waiting and is pacing the room. But his mind wanders as he ponders his situation. James summarizes and paraphrases Densher's thoughts, a literary device that critics refer to as "the first person attached" point of view. James does this more with Densher, who is a reflective and intellectual type, and with Milly Theale, whose consciousness is more important to us than her frail body, than he does with Kate Croy. We get to know Kate more by what she says and does or by a look or gesture, a shake of the head, than by James telling us what she is thinking. Kate is a less cerebral and a more forceful person than Densher, so the device of exploring her thoughts is less necessary.

8. (p. 100) *we shall really ourselves scarce otherwise come closer to her than by feeling their impression and sharing, if need be, their confusion*: James's use of this expression and his reference a few sentences later to "our young woman" illustrate the way in which he departs occasionally from the use of the unseen omniscient author and appears

to inject himself into the narrative. He "shares" the confusion of the characters and "feels" their impressions.

9. (p. 105) *I hasten to add*: Although James's narrator uses the personal pronoun "I" here, he never becomes an actual character in the story. Joseph Conrad in his short story *The Nigger of the "Narcissus"* (1897) employs a similar device. The omniscient narrator knows all; he is, in fact, on board the *Narcissus* when it capsizes. But the narrator never actually appears in the story. His apparently invisible presence on-board becomes known to us only when he tells us at the end of the story that he was so frightened he will never again go to sea.

10. (p. 138) *of Thackerayan character*: Kate presumably reminds Mrs. Stringham a little of Becky Sharp, the captivating but unscrupulous heroine of William Makepeace Thackeray's *Vanity Fair* (1848).

11. (p. 150) *but it was clear Mrs. Condrip was . . . in quite another geography*: This is a good illustration of Milly's increasing sophistication and awareness of the complexities she is encountering in London. Book fourth in its entirety is an example of the growth of Milly's consciousness. She understands that she is in a "labyrinth," that she teeters on the edge of an "abyss." She revels in it, however, even though she is frightened, because this is what she understands as being more fully aware and more truly alive. She is not interested in tourism but in people and in the complexity of social circumstance.

12. (p. 169) *"but mine's several shades greener"*: This scene is one of a number of memorable passages in the very rich and complex fifth book. Milly is here trying to make light of the emotional experience she has just undergone in viewing the Bronzino portrait that resembles her. She has had intimations of mortality; she feels that she will be, like the lady in the portrait, "dead, dead, dead." Critics and literary scholars have seen Milly's reaction as a critical turning point, a sign that she can no longer keep up a brave front.

13. (p. 177) *"I shan't trouble you again"*: Milly makes a critical decision here. She adores Kate, values her friendship, and enjoys her company. But she is bothered by the fact that Kate has avoided mentioning Densher, which, to Milly, seems to suggest a degree of dissembling on Kate's part. So Milly decides to set some limits on her friendship with Kate, not to trust her fully. This small choice propels Milly toward the isolation she will ultimately face in her struggle with her illness. Only Susan Stringham and hired servants will be with her in the end.

14. (p. 185) *"you ought of course . . . to get out of London"*: Why does Sir Luke advise Milly to get out of London? Is it merely because London is hot and uncomfortable in August? Sir Luke is perhaps too subtle for that. Presumably he feels Milly's privacy might be jeopardized if word

got around London that she was seeing him. She could feel freer somewhere else. Besides, he might have felt she had already "done" London and might want to experience something new.

15. (p. 192) *Gibbon and Froude and Saint-Simon:* Edward Gibbon (1737–1794) wrote *The History of the Decline and Fall of the Roman Empire;* James Froude (1818–1894) was a historian and disciple of Carlyle; Claude Henri de Saint-Simon (1760–1825) was a French social reformer and founder of "positivist" philosophy.

16. (p. 210) *"Oh you may very well loathe me yet!":* It is impossible to tell, in this extraordinary passage, whether Kate has already conceived her scheme to link Densher and Milly. Kate does not know for sure that Milly is ill, though she surely suspects it. Milly is acute enough to be frightened by this creature who paces "like a panther," but the die is cast. Milly, despite her unease, is sure that along this route lies life, and she will not shrink from it. In the lines that follow, Kate, perhaps misreading Milly's mild reply, uses the dove image for the first time in the book.

17. (p. 242) *"I'll tell you another time":* Here, presumably, is a clear sign that Kate suspects the seriousness of Milly's illness, and is laying the groundwork for her plan. Densher is not quite ready to be brought in on the scheme.

18. (p. 289) *"You don't need to see":* This dialogue strikingly illustrates how James's narrative technique of letting us know Densher's thoughts contrasts with the way he portrays Kate by her gestures and her spoken words. The technique reinforces the portrayal of Kate as decisive, utterly sure of herself, a brilliant psychologist, and ruthless, and of Densher as full of doubts, sensitive but weak, and so in love with Kate that she can "lead him by the nose." She has been so completely caught up in the social "game" as to have become morally obtuse. But she does not kid herself; she knows what she is doing. Densher's vacillations and moral evasions are perhaps even less attractive than Kate's cynicism.

19. (p. 314) *and what most expressed it:* The action now shifts to Venice, where Milly has rented an expensive palazzo. It is now October. Eugenio, an Italian with a sharp eye for making money off tourists, has been hired to manage Milly's household. Though he spends Milly's money freely, he is an efficient manager and organizer and has a very good relationship with Milly and Mrs. Stringham. Milly sees him as taking charge of all practical matters and assisting Susan when Milly's health worsens. That it costs a great deal of money to keep the somewhat dilapidated old villa in good repair and to staff it with an array of servants is, of course, of no concern to Milly.

20. (p. 315) *Palazzo Leporelli:* The fictional palazzo is modeled on the

actual Palazzo Barbaro, built in the fifteenth century and owned by friends of Henry James. In 1887 Henry James stayed there with his friends the Daniel Curtises and wrote the short story "A London Life."

21. (p. 347) *dusky labyrinthine alleys and empty* campi, *overhung with mouldering palaces:* This image conveys James's sense of the decadence that affects European civilization. The physical decay—empty public squares, crumbling palaces, deserted banquet halls—parallels the moral corruption of a London society dominated by money grubbing, of the grasping servants led by Eugenio at the Palazzo Leporelli, and of the trio of Kate, Mrs. Lowder, and Densher maneuvering to fleece Milly.

22. (p. 348) *complications might sometimes have their tedium beguiled by a study of the question of how a gentleman would behave:* Densher's self-exculpatory reasoning puts him in an unfavorable light here. He is justifying himself on the ground that he didn't start the whole scheme and that he will always be a "gentleman." He realizes that being a gentleman is not always easy to define and that being as passive as he has been is not a great thing. He wants to assert himself, but he is not sure how. He can't run; he is in too deep. When he does assert himself, it is in a most unfortunate way. He compels Kate to come to his apartment to consummate their relationship, a crude trade of sex for his full cooperation that cheapens his relationship with her.

23. (p. 362) *"It's a Veronese picture":* Scholars have concluded that James is here referring to the Venetian painter Paolo Veronese's *Marriage at Cana* (1562–1563), which depicts a banquet scene of great richness and prodigality.

24. (p. 364) *he shouldn't have liked a man to see him:* This exchange with Mrs. Stringham is one of Densher's least appealing moments. He suddenly feels ashamed of being a sensitive man, and, under the guise of honesty, displays a degree of male chauvinism that is even worse than Lord Mark's. His perfidy seems to be gender-neutral. For a discussion of Densher's dilemma from the perspective of gender relations and the complexities of gender issues in *The Wings of The Dove*, see Julie Olin-Ammentorp, "'A Circle of Petticoats': The Feminization of Merton Densher," *Henry James Review* 14 (1993).

25. (p. 420) *"Oh!" he simply moaned into the gloom:* This agonizing tête-à-tête between Densher and Mrs. Stringham shows James at his masterly best in posing the central moral questions of the novel: From what depths of hatred does Lord Mark act? Is he beyond mere cynical exploitation of the situation? Does Densher perceive, to his horror, that *he* was doing essentially what Lord Mark was trying to do? Should Densher lie to Milly—as Mrs. Stringham, in essence, urges—

to give her some happiness as death approaches? Did Kate, in fact, reveal to Lord Mark her relationship with Densher as a way to stave him (Lord Mark) off and/or to confound her aunt? That Densher can only moan into the gloom at least shows him more favorably than than he has appeared to this point. He begins to appreciate more fully what he has done; his "conversion" has begun.

26. (p. 440) *"She never wanted the truth. . . . She wanted* you. *. . . For that was your strength, my dear man—that she loves you with passion"*: Kate poses a key question: Is she correct in thinking Milly would have been comforted by Densher's lying to her even though she knew it was a lie? And is Densher more concerned with his own honor than with Milly's feelings?

Comments & Questions

In this section, we aim to provide the reader with an array of perspectives on the text, as well as questions that challenge those perspectives. The commentary has been culled from sources as diverse as reviews contemporaneous with the work, letters written by the author, literary criticism of later generations, and appreciations written throughout the work's history. Following the commentary, a series of questions seeks to filter Henry James's The Wings of the Dove *through a variety of points of view and bring about a richer understanding of this enduring work.*

Comments

WILLIAM JAMES

I have read *The Wings of the Dove* (for which all thanks!) but what shall I say of a book constructed on a method which so belies everything that *I* acknowledge as law? You've reversed every traditional canon of story-telling (especially the fundamental one of *telling* the story, which you carefully avoid) and have created a new *genre littéraire* which I can't help thinking perverse, but in which you nevertheless *succeed*.

—from a letter to Henry James (Fall 1902)

J. P. MOWBRAY

In trying to form anything like a comprehensive estimate of Mr. James's mature work, the effeminacy of it has to be counted with. One cannot call it virile, and—with the best examples still with us—hardly Saxon.

—from *Critic* (November 1902)

SATURDAY

[*The Wings of the Dove*] consists of 576 closely printed pages. We were curious to know the average number of dashes, commas and

semi-colons on a page; and we found the calculation entirely beyond our powers. Suffice it to say it is enormous; and most of these
interruptions serve no purpose save that of making the reading
more difficult. The effect is irritating: what might have been clean
prose is broken, finicked, piffled away. Yet we see plainly enough
that such lame writing is essential to the effect Mr. James wished
to get. He wanted to make us feel all those artificial, subtle, trifling
or meaningless changes of mood; and the more he makes us feel
them the more artificial, trifling, meaningless we find them, and
the less inclined we are to read on. We even suggest that the
achievement of such a prose has become with Mr. James somewhat of an end in itself. The incessant 'perhaps' -es, and 'consciousness of something deeper still,' and 'clearly, as yet, seeing
nothing'—these not only give that effect of blurred vision and lack
of definite intention, but weave into a word-tissue which Mr.
James seems to like and which we heartily dislike. It is a word-
tissue that hides the author's thought—that gives one a sense of his
reserve, aloofness. There is no energy, passion, color, and because
there is no motion, there is no rhythm in this prose. The prose becomes as trivial as the trivial moods aroused by trivial
middle-class things it is meant to express; and not from Mr. Henry
James nor another do we require 576 pages of such prose fine-spun
out with such an object.

After all, this kind of writing, crabbed, finicking, tedious in its
struggle to be exact about nothing, marks a strong reaction against
the kind that prevailed until twenty years ago or even later.

—January 1903

JOSEPH CONRAD

One is never set at rest by Mr. Henry James's novels. His books end
as an episode in life ends. You remain with the sense of the life still
going on; and even the subtle presence of the dead is felt in that
silence that comes upon the artist-creation when the last word has
been read. It is eminently satisfying, but it is not final. Mr. Henry
James, great artist and faithful historian, never attempts the impossible.

—from *North American Review* (January 1905)

GEORGE MOORE

I've read nothing of Henry James's that didn't suggest a scholar; so there shall be none of the old taunts—why does he not write complicated stories? Why does he always avoid decisive action? In his stories a woman never leaves the house with her lover, nor does a man ever kill another man or himself. Why is nothing ever accomplished? In real life murder, adultery, and suicide are of common occurrence; but Mr. James's people live in a calm, sad, and very polite twilight of volition. Suicide or adultery has happened before the story begins, suicide or adultery happens some years after the characters have left the stage, but in front of the reader nothing happens. . . . Is there really much to say about people who live in stately houses and eat and drink their fill every day of the year? The lady, it is true, may have a lover, but the pen finds scanty pasturage of the fact; and in James's novels the lady only considers the question on the last page, and the gentleman looks at her questioningly.

—from *Confessions of a Young Man* (1916)

VIRGINIA WOOLF

How consciously Henry James set himself to look for the weak place in our amour of insensibility it is not necessary to decide. Let us turn to another story, *The Friends of Friends*, and judge whether he succeeded. This is the story of a man and woman who have been trying for years to meet but only accomplish their meeting on the night of the woman's death. After her death the meetings are continued, and when this is divined by the woman he is engaged to marry she refuses to go on with the marriage. The relationship is altered. Another person, she says, has come between them. 'You see her—you see her; you see her every night!' It is what we have come to call a typically Henry James situation. It is the same theme that was treated with enormous elaboration in *The Wings of the Dove*. Only there, when Milly has come between Kate and Densher and altered their relationship for ever, she has ceased to exist; here the anonymous lady goes on with her work after death. And yet—does it make very much difference? Henry James has only to take the smallest steps and he is over the border. His characters with their extreme fineness of perception are already halfway out of the body. There is nothing violent in their release. They seem rather to have achieved at last what they have long been attempting—communication without obstacle. But Henry James, after all, kept his ghosts for his ghost stories. Obstacles are essential to *The Wings of the Dove*.

—from *Times Literary Supplement* (December 22, 1921)

W. SOMERSET MAUGHAM
Henry James had turned his back on one of the great events in the world's history, the rise of the United States, in order to report tittle-tattle at tea parties in English country houses.

—from *Cakes and Ale: or, The Skeleton in the Cupboard* (1930)

Questions

1. What does the prose style of *The Wings of the Dove* accomplish that a more direct style does not? What can it not accomplish that a more direct style can? How would you formulate a description of James's late style? He himself in an offhand moment described it as "sub-aqueous."

2. Of James's late fiction George Moore asks, "Why does he always avoid decisive action? . . . Why is nothing ever accomplished? . . . Mr. James's people live in a calm, sad, and very polite twilight of volition. . . . Is there really much to say about people who live in stately houses and eat and drink their fill every day of the year?" Has George Moore got it right? Is he being fair? And what do you think about Somerset Maugham's observation that what James does is "report tittle-tattle at tea parties in English country houses"?

3. Some readers of *The Wings of the Dove* have found in the novel a sense of doom, a sense of a civilization in a decline and about to crash. Do you see this in the book? How is this sense or atmosphere created?

4. In spite of the somewhat rarified milieu of the novel, do the characters seem to you to be motivated by the same ambitions, emotions, fears, and desires as, say, a group of average Americans? Or a group of movie stars, factory workers, or Appalachian Amish—in spite of the differences in circumstances? In other words, are James's characters fully human?

5. What would you say is an accurate characterization of Merton Densher? He thinks too much? He's weak? He has flaws but is essentially a good man? He begins ill and ends well? He is despicable? Instead of doing what he did, what should he have done?

For Further Reading

Bibliography and Reference

Edel, Leon, and Dan H. Laurence. *A Bibliography of Henry James*. 1957. Third edition, revised with the assistance of James Rambeau. Oxford: Clarendon Press, 1982.

Foley, Richard Nicholas. *Criticism in American Periodicals of the Works of Henry James from 1866 to 1916*. Washington, DC: Catholic University of America Press, 1944.

Freedman, Jonathan, ed. *The Cambridge Companion to Henry James*. Cambridge and New York: Cambridge University Press, 1998.

James, Henry. *The Notebooks of Henry James*. Edited by F. O. Matthiessen and Kenneth B. Murdock. New York: Oxford University Press, 1947.

Putt, S. Gorley. *Henry James: A Reader's Guide*. Ithaca, NY: Cornell University Press, 1966.

Stafford, William T. *A Name, Title, and Place Index to the Critical Writings of Henry James*. Englewood, CO: Microcard Editions, 1975.

Taylor, Linda J. *Henry James, 1866–1916: A Reference Guide*. Boston, G. K. Hall, 1982.

Biography

Dupee, Frederick W. *Henry James*. Garden City, NY: Doubleday, 1956.

Edel, Leon. *Henry James: A Life*. New York: Harper and Row, 1985. A condensed and revised version of Edel's original five-volume biography *Henry James* (1953–1972).

———. *Henry James: The Master: 1901–1916*. Philadelphia: Lippincott, 1972. This final volume of Edel's five-volume biography covers the last period of James's life.

———, and Gordon N. Ray. *Henry James and H. G. Wells: A Record of Their Friendship, Their Debate on the Art of Fiction, and Their Quarrel*. Urbana: University of Illinois Press, 1958.

Horne, Philip. *Henry James and Revision: The New York Edition*. Oxford: Clarendon Press and New York: Oxford University Press, 1990.

Matthiessen, F. O. *The James Family*. New York: Alfred A. Knopf, 1947.

Monteiro, George. *Henry James and John Hay: The Record of a Friendship*. Providence, RI: Brown University Press, 1965.

Moore, Harry T. *Henry James*. New York: Viking Press, 1974.

Letters

Edel, Leon, ed. *Henry James: Selected Letters*. Cambridge, MA: Belknap Press of Harvard University Press, 1987.

Horne, Philip, ed. *Henry James: A Life in Letters*. New York: Viking Press, 1999.

Lubbock, Percy, ed. *The Letters of Henry James*. New York: Scribner, 1920.

Powers, Lyall H., ed. *Henry James and Edith Wharton: Letters, 1900–1915*. New York: Scribner's, 1990.

Literary Criticism and Commentary

Allen, Elizabeth. *A Woman's Place in the Novels of Henry James*. New York: St. Martin's Press, 1984.

Anderson, Quentin. *The American Henry James*. New Brunswick, NJ: Rutgers University Press, 1957.

Auchard, John. *Silence in Henry James: The Heritage of Symbolism and Decadence*. University Park: Pennsylvania State University Press, 1986.

Banta, Martha. *Henry James and the Occult: The Great Extension*. Bloomington: Indiana University Press, 1972.

Bloom, Harold, ed. *Henry James*. New York: Chelsea House, 1987.

Bowden, Edwin T. *The Themes of Henry James: A System of Observation Through the Visual Arts*. New Haven, CT: Yale University Press, 1956.

Bradbury, Nicola. *Henry James: The Later Novels*. Oxford: Clarendon Press, 1979.

Bradley, John R., ed. *Henry James and Homo-Erotic Desire*. Introduction by Sheldon M. Novick. New York: St. Martin's Press, 1999.

Cameron, Sharon. *Thinking in Henry James*. Chicago: University of Chicago Press, 1989.

Crews, Frederick C. *The Tragedy of Manners: Moral Drama in the Later Novels of Henry James.* New Haven, CT: Yale University Press, 1957.

Freedman, Jonathan. *Professions of Taste: Henry James, British Aestheticism and Commodity Culture.* Stanford, CA: Stanford University Press, 1990.

———, ed. *The Cambridge Companion to Henry James.* New York, Cambridge University Press, 1998.

Gard, Roger, ed. *Henry James: The Critical Heritage.* London and New York: Routledge and Kegan Paul, 1968.

Hocks, Richard A. *Henry James: A Study of the Short Fiction.* Boston: Twayne Publishers, 1990.

Hocks, Richard A. *Henry James and Pragmatist Thought: A Study in the Relationship Between the Philosophy of William James and the Literary Art of Henry James.* Chapel Hill: University of North Carolina Press, 1974.

Holland, Laurence B. *The Expense of Vision: Essays on the Craft of Henry James.* Princeton, NJ: Princeton University Press, 1964.

James, Henry. *The Art of the Novel: Critical Prefaces.* With an introduction by Richard P. Blackmur. New York: Scribner's, 1937.

———. *Henry James' Shorter Masterpieces, Volume 2.* Edited by Peter Rawlings. Brighton, Sussex: Harvester Press, and Totowa, NJ: Barnes and Noble Books, 1984.

———. *The Portable Henry James.* Edited and with an introduction by John Auchard. New York: Penguin Books, 2004.

Krook, Dorothea. *The Ordeal of Consciousness in Henry James.* Cambridge and New York: Cambridge University Press, 1962.

McWhirter, David. *Desire and Love in Henry James: A Study of the Late Novels.* Cambridge and New York: Cambridge University Press, 1989.

Matthiessen, F. O. *Henry James: The Major Phase.* London and New York: Oxford University Press, 1944.

Pippin, Robert B. *Henry James and Modern Moral Life.* Cambridge and New York: Cambridge University Press, 2000.

Rowe, John Carlos. *Henry Adams and Henry James: The Emergence of a Modern Consciousness.* Ithaca, NY: Cornell University Press, 1976.

Seltzer, Mark. *Henry James and the Art of Power.* Ithaca, NY: Cornell University Press, 1984.

Sicker, Philip. *Love and the Quest for Identity in the Fiction of Henry James.* Princeton, NJ: Princeton University Press, 1980.

Stevens, Hugh. *Henry James and Sexuality*. Cambridge and New York: Cambridge University Press, 1998.

Williams, Merle A. *Henry James and the Philosophical Novel: Being and Seeing*. Cambridge and New York: Cambridge University Press, 1993.

Theater, Fictional Portray, and Film

Bradley, John R., ed. *Henry James on Stage and Screen*. New York: Palgrave, 2000.

Griffin, Susan M., ed. *Henry James Goes to the Movies*. Lexington: University Press of Kentucky, 2002.

James, Henry. *The Complete Plays of Henry James*. Edited by Leon Edel. Philadelphia: J. B. Lippincott, 1949.

Kossmann, Rudolph R. *Henry James: Dramatist*. Groningen, Netherlands: Wolters-Noordhoff, 1969.

Lodge, David. *Author, Author*. New York: Viking, 2004. A novel based on James's life in the 1880s and 1890s.

Toibin, Colm. *The Master*. New York: Scribner, 2004. A fictionalized account of James's life.

Timeless works. New scholarship. Extraordinary value.

Look for the following titles, available now and forthcoming from
BARNES & NOBLE CLASSICS.

Visit your local bookstore for these fine titles.
Or to order online go to: WWW.BN.COM/CLASSICS

BARNES & NOBLE CLASSICS

(continued)

Title	Author	ISBN	Price
The Last of the Mohicans	James Fenimore Cooper	1-59308-065-4	$4.95
Les Misérables	Victor Hugo	1-59308-066-2	$9.95
Little Women	Louisa May Alcott	1-59308-108-1	$6.95
Main Street	Sinclair Lewis	1-59308-036-0	$5.95
The Metamorphosis and Other Stories	Franz Kafka	1-59308-029-8	$6.95
Middlemarch	George Eliot	1-59308-023-9	$8.95
Moby-Dick	Herman Melville	1-59308-018-2	$9.95
My Ántonia	Willa Cather	1-59308-024-7	$4.95
Narrative of the Life of Frederick Douglass, an American Slave	Frederick Douglass	1-59308-041-7	$4.95
Notes From Underground, The Double and Other Stories	Fyodor Dostoevsky	1-59308-037-9	$4.95
O Pioneers!	Willa Cather	1-59308-019-0	$4.95
The Odyssey	Homer	1-59308-009-3	$5.95
Oliver Twist	Charles Dickens	1-59308-030-1	$4.95
The Origin of Species	Charles Darwin	1-59308-077-8	$7.95
Persuasion	Jane Austen	1-59308-048-4	$4.95
The Picture of Dorian Gray	Oscar Wilde	1-59308-025-5	$4.95
The Portrait of a Lady	Henry James	1-59308-096-4	$7.95
Portrait of the Artist as a Young Man and Dubliners	James Joyce	1-59308-031-X	$7.95
Pride and Prejudice	Jane Austen	1-59308-020-4	$4.95
The Prince and Other Writings	Niccolò Machiavelli	1-59308-060-3	$5.95
The Red Badge of Courage and Selected Short Fiction	Stephen Crane	1-59308-010-7	$3.95
Robinson Crusoe	Daniel Defoe	1-59308-011-5	$4.95
The Scarlet Letter	Nathaniel Hawthorne	1-59308-012-3	$3.95
Selected Stories of O. Henry	O. Henry	1-59308-042-5	$5.95
Sense and Sensibility	Jane Austen	1-59308-049-2	$4.95
Sons and Lovers	D. H. Lawrence	1-59308-013-1	$7.95
The Souls of Black Folk	W. E. B. Du Bois	1-59308-014-X	$5.95
The Strange Case of Dr. Jekyll and Mr. Hyde and Other Stories	Robert Louis Stevenson	1-59308-054-9	$3.95
A Tale of Two Cities	Charles Dickens	1-59308-055-7	$4.95
The Three Musketeers	Alexandre Dumas	1-59308-079-4	$6.95
The Time Machine and The Invisible Man	H. G. Wells	1-59308-032-8	$4.95
Uncle Tom's Cabin	Harriet Beecher Stowe	1-59308-038-7	$5.95
The Varieties of Religious Experience	William James	1-59308-072-7	$7.95
Walden and Civil Disobedience	Henry David Thoreau	1-59308-026-3	$4.95
The War of the Worlds	H. G. Wells	1-59308-085-9	$3.95

JB

BARNES & NOBLE CLASSICS

If you are an educator and would like to receive an
Examination or Desk Copy of a Barnes & Noble Classic edition,
please refer to Academic Resources on our website at
WWW.BN.COM/CLASSICS
or contact us at
B&NCLASSICS@BN.COM.

FINES
5¢ PER DAY
FOR
OVERDUE BOOKS

All prices are subject to change.